THOMAS CLAYTON

Thomas Clayton

Randy J. Harvey, PhD

iUniverse LLC
Bloomington

Thomas Clayton

iUniverse books may be ordered through booksellers or by contacting:

iUniverse LLC
1663 Liberty Drive
Bloomington, IN 47403
www.iuniverse.com
1-800-Authors (1-800-288-4677)

ISBN: 978-1-4759-6923-8 (sc)
ISBN: 978-1-4759-6924-5 (hc)
ISBN: 978-1-4759-6925-2 (e)

Library of Congress Control Number: 2012924182

Printed in the United States of America

iUniverse rev. date: 1/15/2013

Dedication

For my wife, Shelly; my children, Jessica, Andrew, Brianna, and Kiel; and their children, though the grandkids will have to grow a bit before they read this story. And for the storytellers in the Harvey clan who have gone before me and told me the tales that no doubt served as a foundation for this yarn—men who never let the truth get in the way of a good story.

Special thanks to Toastmasters International, who helped me find my voice and gave me the opportunity to use it around the world.

Most of all, this book is dedicated to my dad, "Fatdad," or so I called him while growing up. This manuscript began with a few dozen handwritten pages that my dad started before he died, and I finished the tale with his memory sitting on my shoulder. My folks, Jay Leonard Harvey and Mary Lou (Travis) Harvey, were great people, solid Americans who loved their only son and their extended family.

Contents

1. The Bastard Boats 1
2. Turnbuckle 10
3. Pipe, Fast Food, and Fig Newtons 19
4. The First Date 41
5. Fussin' and Fightin' 61
6. Football 76
7. Picking the Team 87
8. Mama's Love 96
9. The Fix Is In 107
10. Cheerleader Tryouts and Trouble 121
11. Children's Services Ain't 134
12. The Fight Is On 147
13. Sleepin' with the Old Man, Learnin' 'bout Life 158
14. Justice, Always Justice 172
15. Doc's Dead; the Dog's Not 181
16. Combine Calculations 197
17. Chubb's Warning 204
18. Doc's Documents Tell the Tales 219
19. Time for the Mouse to Roar 227
20. Coach's Target 241

21. Korean Cowboy 257
22. Set Up for Victory 264
23. Police Work and the Damn Dog 271
24. Blackmail Money Pays Unwanted Dividends 282
25. The Storm Begins; Boats Sinks 301
26. The Combine Slips a Few Gears 321
27. The Play for T. C. 332
28. Judge Watkins's Sentence 352
29. The Fix Isn't 364
30. Police Politics 378
31. Mechanics of Killin' a Judge 391
32. Boats's Secret 404
33. Vegas 415
34. Handicapped Parking Penalty 427
35. Hospital Homicide 444
36. Letch and the Party Shack 455
37. Call for the Cavalry 461
38. Cancel the Insurance 465
39. Gone Fishing 477
40. A Letter from Mama 484
41. It's a Wrap 489
42. The Cycle of Life 491

Chapter 1

The Bastard Boats

I stood watching the coach and players on the football practice field and pushed up my Stetson with one finger in an effort to let the fading breeze blow some sweat off my forehead. It had been over a hundred for the last ten days, and the humidity level was nearly the same.

The players drew me back to when I had arrived here as a boy. I remembered the color rising in Boats's face—probably because I'd just told him to go fuck himself—as he sternly informed me that I'd be going out for all sports. "I was all-conference my junior year and all-state my senior year," he told me. "Doubt if you can do that well—or even half that, considerin' who your worthless pa was—but you had damn sure better be good enough to letter." Ma talked constantly about Boats while I was growing up. From what she said, I knew that he had hurt her in some way, though she didn't say how. She never got a chance to explain it, though, because Pa ran off the road in Florida, killing himself, Ma, and Sis.

Boats was Pa's half brother, and from the first minute I walked into Boats's house, I instantly hated the bastard. I learned later that Pa had felt the same way. Before Pa married Ma, Boats had been dating her, and they broke up. Boats told the town that Ma had married Pa to get his money but that the joke was on her because his half brother didn't have any. Pa was working for Nichols

Casing, the largest oil casing company in the Southwest. It once belonged to Boats's dad, my stepgrandfather. The day after Ma and Pa married, Pa went back to work and there was a big argument and blowup. Boats fired my pa. Ma and Pa packed and left the next day.

This was all on top of the fact that Pa was only a truck driver with grease under his fingernails. He was a simple roughneck in the oil fields, working for his stepdad's company, as if he weren't related at all. Pa's working-class status added fuel to Boats's highbrow hatred for him. Boats never spoke to my parents again, some fourteen years. He was a complete stranger to me the day we met. I knew him only by the pictures my ma and pa had of him.

Ma and Pa hadn't made it back by ten o'clock, so I had gone to bed. I woke to the smell of stale cigarettes and musty bourbon. Boats stood backlit in my bedroom door, his white suit and Stetson throwing a red-yellow aura hiding his face, 'cept for the glowing ash of his unfiltered Marlboro cigarette. He was short, turning his head to the side and blowing smoke into the hallway. "Git up, boy. We gotta talk." As I was sitting in my underwear and T-shirt on the flowered love seat my ma had just covered, Boats told me that my folks and Sis were dead. His voice was emotionless and his speech slurred. He was drunk. He was restraining any emotion. Then he commented, "Your fucking pa killed 'em all when he drove off the road."

Boats sent a snarly cur of a man into my bedroom to collect my things. In the limo, they sat silently on the drive to the airport, and I tried to suppress my sobs.

A day later Boats and I were back in Tishomingo. My family's bodies were shipped back and buried in the local cemetery. My first fight with the bastard Boats was at their funeral and only the beginning of a hate/hate relationship.

I realized that Boats must be a very important man, judging from the number of people at the funeral. A lady named Shirley, who was introduced as Boats's private secretary, took me in tow. When people came by, she stopped and introduced them to me: senators, congressmen, the governor, and over five hundred other people I couldn't recall.

After the services were held at the Baptist church, the bodies of Ma and Sis were put into two different hearses. I didn't see Pa's coffin at the church. Shirley led me to the third black car, behind the ones hauling Ma and Sis, where I would ride to the cemetery. I asked her where my pa was, and she pointed to a hearse in the lot, just ahead of the two for Ma and Sis. When we arrived at the cemetery, the hearse carrying Pa went straight ahead and turned into a gate about a block from the entrance we went through. By the time Shirley got me up to the gravesite, my ma's and sister's coffins had been carried into the white-iron-fenced courtyard and lay suspended on rails beneath the gaze of a marble statue of Gabriel. She led me over and sat me down beside the bastard Boats.

I sat looking around, wondering where Pa's coffin was. It took more than fifteen minutes for all the people to get gathered around. It finally dawned on me that only two graves had been dug. Turning to Boats, I said, "Where's my pa?"

Boats continued jabbering with a tall, lanky man covered by a Stetson a size too big. The hat pressed on his ears, making him look like a six-foot elf. He looked annoyed.

Reaching out, I took hold of Boats's arm and jerked it. Boats turned and barked, "Can't you see I'm talkin' to someone? Use some manners, boy."

"Where's my pa?"

"I will talk to you later, back at the house," he replied.

"I want to know where my pa is right now."

"Not now, boy," he said. "We'll talk this evenin'."

The Baptist preacher's voice interrupted. "Let us bow our heads in prayer." He dropped both of his chins to his barrel chest, supported by a bloated gut. His belly lopped over his silver belt buckle and hid the silver tips of his cowboy boots from his downward gaze. The preacher's voice was deep and gravelly as he asked Jesus to join us.

I stood up and shouted, "Hold on, Preacher!" Turning to Boats, I insisted, "Before this goes any further, are you going to tell me what's goin' on here?"

Boats reached up and grabbed me by the back of the neck. "Shut up and sit down."

The anger had been building in me for the previous two days and erupted in a furious torrent. I threw my right arm up, striking Boats's forearm and ripping his hand off my neck. I spun on him and screamed, "Take your goddamn hand off me, you mealymouthed son of a bitch! I'm not sittin' here listenin' to some hypocrite preacher pray over Ma and Sis while my pa ain't here!"

Boats straight-armed me, knocking me back into the folding chair, which rocked back and would have tumbled over had I not grabbed at Shirley's dress to steady myself, tearing it in the process.

Boats shouted at me through clenched teeth, "Now sit there and shut up, or I swear I'll break your goddamned little neck!"

I tried to free myself from the chair, but Boats had pinned me in place with his left arm, his elbow stuck in my sternum and his hand holding the curled edge of the steel folding chair. He looked at the preacher and said, "Please continue."

A few minutes later, Boats relaxed his grip and I bolted, surprising both him and Shirley. I cut around the end of the coffins and, leaning over them, shouted at Boats, "Go ahead! Put on your show, but I'm not stayin'!"

As Boats rose from his seat, I ran like a tailback through would-be tacklers, parting the surprised crowd and angling in the direction of the first hearse, the one carrying Pa.

I caught sight of the hearse and a mound of dirt, where two men in sweat-soaked clothes methodically dropped spades of dirt into the hole. The men stopped their work and stood silent as I slid to a stop in front of them. The hole was partially filled.

"Is my pa in that hole?"

"'Pends on who you is, boy," the older man said as he wiped sweat from his brow on a dirty sleeve. "Is you Tommy Gurley?"

"Yes."

"Then this is yer pa."

"Have they already finished the service?"

"We's just doin' what we's told, boy."

"You mean what Boats told you."

"No, we'uns work for the undertaker. He told us to bury your pa."

"Well, you stop right now, ya hear?" I said. "Till I can go get a preacher to say words over my pa."

"We cain't do that, son. We's just followin' orders."

"Orders or not, you see that shovel over there?" I pointed to a spade lying on the ground.

"We sees it."

I walked over and lifted the shovel above my head. "If you don't stop right now, I'm goin' to knock the hell out of you with this shovel."

The men looked at me with tears running down my face and then at each other. Then they dropped their shovels, walked back to their truck, rolled up the windows, locked the doors, and drove off.

I stood there watching the dust rise behind the truck as it disappeared through the cemetery gate. As I turned, I realized that the driver still sat in the hearse that had brought my daddy to this spot. I walked over and opened the passenger door, focusing my fury on the man holding a cigarette between his thumb and first finger, and I smelled the alcohol from the open bottle of Jack Daniel's tucked between his legs. "Who told them to throw dirt on my pa without a preacher?" I demanded.

"Those was our instructions."

"Whose instructions? Boats's?"

"Nope. The undertaker's."

"Nothin' else is to be done until I get a preacher. You understand?"

"Understood. I'll tell the undertaker."

"You do that."

Turning around, I could see that the people were leaving Ma's and Sis's gravesites. I hurried back, looking for the preacher.

I caught hold of him as he was trying to get into his car. "Preacher, I want you to come over and say some words over my pa."

The minister's face reddened, and he fumbled for words. "I—I'm sorry, son, but I have another engagement I need to get on to."

"You mean you won't say a prayer over my pa?"

"I'm sure you can find a minister of God of your dad's faith to give him final rites."

"What you mean 'final rites'?"

"Well, after all, boy, I understand your pa was a Catholic."

"You pray to the same God, don't you?" I asked.

"Son, you don't understand."

"I understand you won't say a prayer over my pa. What the hell kind of goddamn heathen are you, anyway?"

My voice and hand started to raise as I started to really let him have it, when Boats's hand fell on my shoulder.

"There you are, boy. Over your mad yet?" Boats smiled at me as he cast a furtive look at the preacher. "What's the problem, Minister?" Boats said to the preacher, his smile widening.

"The boy here wanted me to say a prayer over his dad's gravesite."

"Well, you can do that for him, can't you, Walt?"

"If you wish, Mr. Nichols, but you know he was a papist."

"I know it isn't as if he was a Christian or anythin', but even the papists need a send-off."

I swung around, with Boats still keeping a tight grip on my shoulder. "You keep away from my pa. Neither one of you bastards go anywhere near him."

"Don't get your spurs up, son," Boats said. "Just tryin' to help. I wouldn't go down there anyway." Turning, he called Shirley over and handed me off. "Take this boy and keep 'im out of trouble."

I stood straight with my fists clenched, feet spread, eyes locked on Boats—oblivious to Shirley's arm draped across my shoulder.

"It's a damn good thing I ain't a man right now or I'd kill you where you stand and that bastard preacher too."

Boats laughed and turned to talk to a gathered group vying for his attention. Shirley wrapped me up and led me away to the car. I heard Boats apologizing to the preacher and the gathered onlookers.

When we got back to the house, Boats's driver, Pike, met us. I recognized him as the cur dog that had gathered my belongings in Florida. He was grizzled. His face was marked with deep scars, obviously a brawler. His gray, close-cropped hair displayed his age, which was contradicted by the youth in his clear blue eyes. His eyes missed nothing. Shirley put a hand on my back and pushed me toward Pike. I started to protest, but Pike's right hand caught my wrist. The instant pain from his calloused grip compelled me along. He led me to a small room in the bunkhouse out behind the big house. "Boats said you'd be better off down here."

"Damn straight," I said. "I couldn't stand to be in the same house with that bastard Boats."

Pike smirked at me and whispered, "Watch yer mouth, boy. Not many people call Boats a bastard and walk away. Yer bein' kinfolk will only buy you so much rope, and if'n he don't kick yer ass for it, I just might for sport."

It was 1965; I was three months short of being fifteen when they buried my family. I was five-nine, a hundred and forty-five pounds of barbed wire, browned by the Florida and Oklahoma sun, pissed off, and spoiling for a fight. Living in a corner of the bunkhouse like an angry cur, I took up my role as a gopher for Boats and any other adult around the place who took to barking orders at me. That first summer, I hauled, fetched, and carried whatever the crews needed. Getting wrenches and pipe chains; fixing flats; shoveling mud, dirt, and grease—I did any dirty job that needed to be done. For ten to fourteen hours a day, including Saturdays and Sundays, I worked in the shipyard, cleaning up the yard and using the steam cleaner to clean the tanks and other equipment. Slowly I got over the aches and pains. Often working without a shirt, I blackened like an olive in the hundred-degree heat. One evening in August, the foreman told me, "Boats wants you up to the house."

Walking toward the house, I spotted Boats sitting in a cane chair on the front porch. I placed my right foot on the steps and rested my elbow on my knee, and I stopped and looked up at Boats. "You want to see me. Here I am."

"Been wantin' to talk to you, but button your shirt first. Buck tells me you're a helluva good worker, which surprises me."

"What do you want, Boats?" I sneered from under furrowed brows as I finished buttoning my shirt.

"School starts in two weeks. Understand you're gonna be a sophomore. That right?"

"Yeah."

"Two things I want, boy. You will get a B-plus average or above. We never had a dummy Nichols in the family, and we ain't startin' now."

"I'm only half Nichols, and that's too damn much."

That's when Boats told me I would be going out for all sports, and I told him, "You can go fuck yourself, Boats."

"Probably won't be doing that anytime soon, son, but you'd better watch that mouth of yours, and your tone. You want anything, boy?"

"Yeah, I want some money. I need school clothes."

"Just like your pa, a damned leech. You get paid. Take it out of your own wages."

"I ain't gettin' paid," I said.

"Nobody works for me without being paid—even you. I told Shirley to put you on the payroll."

"I don't give a damn what you told Shirley. I ain't been paid a red cent."

Boats turned and hollered through the screen door, "Shirley, get your fat ass out here!"

The screen door creaked and slammed against the clapboard siding, and Shirley stood there barefoot, barelegged, and holding her bathrobe together with both hands." You want me, honey?"

"Thought I told you to put the kid here on the payroll."

"I did, the first day he got here."

"Not according to him."

"Well, the checks are all down at the office," she answered. "He's never been in to pick 'em up."

"Ever think about getting off your dead ass and takin' 'em out to him? Go get some clothes on and bring me a bourbon and branch."

Turning to me, he said, "Pick 'em up at the office tomorrow. Also, football practice starts Monday. Be there."

The only thing I recall from my sophomore year was being a tackling dummy with the rest of the scrubs for the varsity to pound on. The coach used us for defense, and day after day we took a beating from the varsity. One thing about being light, I learned how to throw a block and tackle without meeting them head on. The first couple of times I tried that, I almost got killed. Coach Blackman told me after a month that if I'd gain about thirty to forty pounds, I'd be one hell of a football player. He assigned me to do weight training and isometrics. By the time school let out, I had managed to get junior varsity letters in boxing, football, basketball, and baseball.

Three days after school was over, I was working off a catwalk when Boats came by. The closer he came, the more apparent it was that he'd been drinking. He brushed against the pipe that I was carrying, and it left a streak of grease across his white suit.

Boats looked at the black grease on his suit and barked, "Hey, dumb shit, watch what you're doin'! This is a five-hundred-dollar suit."

I ignored him and continued up the catwalk to drop the pipe into place.

Buck Hagan, the straw boss, told me to go get two made-up turnbuckles for the one-inch cable. I climbed the catwalk and grabbed two of the greasy steel turnbuckles I had made up earlier in the day. They were about three pounds each and had a hook at one end and an eyelet at the other to secure the cable. The hook could be dropped over the edge, and tension could be removed from the cable by turning the fly—a small metal frame with right-hand threads on one end and left-hand threads on the other. When it was turned, the tension was taken from the line. I held the hook ends in my hand and swung them in rhythm with my stride.

As I passed Boats, I heard him cussing in a drunken stupor under his breath. Buck yelled down to him, "The kid's one hell of a worker, Mr. Nichols!"

Coming back with the turnbuckles, I heard Boats yell back to Buck, "He wouldn't have to be much to be better than his deadbeat dad! A no more worthless, lazy, shiftless, wormy son of a bitch ever lived."

I was two feet above Boats on the catwalk when he finished. I didn't give it a thought—before I realized what I'd done, the two turnbuckles caught Boats behind the left ear and shoulder, launching him forward, off the boardwalk, and into the trench pond filled with water, sour mud, sludge grease, and piss. Most men didn't go to the outhouse to relieve themselves when the trench was so handy. Boats bellowed like a stuck pig and scrambled up the wall of the trench pond, cussing and spitting in an effort to find traction. Buck ran to the edge of the catwalk and yelled for me to get my ass up to the platform.

The other men suppressed their laughter as Boats screamed, "I'm gonna beat the shit out of that little prick!"

Buck didn't tell me till a year later what happened after I ran for cover. That night, when the men returned to the ranch in the Crummy, a broken-down, ol' rusted bucket of bolts, half bus and half pickup, used to haul men home at shift's end, I got the word. I hadn't been back but a couple hours when Buck came into the bunkhouse and told me, "Pack your things, boy. You're comin' to live with me."

Chapter 2

Turnbuckle

My entire wardrobe didn't fill a single gunnysack. As Buck and I drove out, I saw Boats standing on the porch, held up by a pillar and mouthing something, sloshing his bourbon and branch across the porch as he flailed his arm.

Buck and I had always gotten along. He was in his late thirties and was a pleasant, soft-spoken man with iron in his soul. He took the time to explain things to me with each new task he gave me. He also explained why he did things a certain way, so I learned both the how and the why of work. Buck explained the purpose of each tool and made sure that I learned to care for them and keep each in its designated place. In less than a year, I was able to anticipate most of the tools and equipment needed by the crew before they asked for them. I developed a meticulous respect and care for tools.

After school and practice each night, Boats had a man pick me up and take me to the nearest rig, where I worked till ten or eleven. A man would then drop me off at Buck's house. The work didn't hurt me, and it continued to build my body and tempered my bitterness toward Boats, like reheated steel. I hadn't forgotten Boats's words about Pa, nor would I for the rest of my life. I wasn't through with him. On weekends, I worked in the loading yard with Buck, loading steel pipe, tanks, and cable. I rode in the truck next to Buck as he drove equipment through the streets of Tishomingo, and I learned my way around the county.

One Saturday night we drove through Tishomingo, and I sat silently watching Buck out of the corner of my eye. I admired the soft-spoken man. He was different from Pa, but beneath that gentle face was a hardness and confidence that I admired. Buck didn't yell and scream like other foremen, but his men never questioned his direction or challenged his knowledge. He had a quiet confidence you could trust.

"Want a Coke, T. C.?" he asked.

"Not right now. Thanks."

"I'm a Coke-aholic. I used to be a champion beer drinker. But one day Rosie gave me an ultimatum—I could switch to something besides beer or something besides her. It wasn't a difficult choice."

Buck was married with a son and a daughter, and he adored all of them. He put pictures of them everywhere in the cheap motels we stayed in when traveling with equipment. He never went out at night drinking and carousing like the rest of the crew. Instead he listened to the radio and read biographies, books on history, and the Bible. He was a strange sort of roughneck that always kept something to read close at hand. When teased about being a bookworm, he said life's too short to waste the extra minutes you get drinking beer when you could be learning something useful. He told me to keep a book with me at all times, 'cause you never know when you would have downtime, and you shouldn't waste the minutes God gives you. He kept a couple of books and a pocket-size New Testament in the glove compartment of his truck, just in case I forgot one of my own.

The truck slowed, and Buck turned into a Stop and Go market, went inside, and soon came out with a six-pack of Coke and a brown paper sack containing a carton of cigarettes and two packs of Fig Newtons. He cranked up the truck, and we lumbered down the street. A Coke in one hand and an unfiltered Lucky Strike in the other, he honked and waved at nearly every vehicle that passed. It seemed like he knew everyone, and it was clear that they liked him. The town vanished, and we made our way into the countryside.

Out of the silence, Buck cocked his head and grinned. "Why did you hit him with the turnbuckle, son?"

The question startled me. That was nearly a year ago. "What?"

"I said, why did you hit him?"

"For something he said about my pa," I answered.

"You made two mistakes, son. You want to know what they were?"

"Yes, sir."

"Don't 'sir' me. You know my name. The first mistake you made was when you hit him with that turnbuckle. The second was when you just stood there when he hit that sludge pit. If you start something, always be prepared to finish it, boy. Once you've decided to slug someone, whether on impulse or having thought it through, carry through on it. Never let 'em git up to hurt you. You jump on 'em like fleas on a dog, and you make sure they don't get up. You never get anyplace in this world goin' 'bout things half-assed. Right or wrong, boy, you can't back up once you start on something. Understand?"

"Yeah, but—"

"There's no *buts* in this world, son. Nothin' is black or white, clear or clouded. You start somethin', you finish it. You knock a man down, you make sure he stays down and doesn't git up to hurt you. You start a task, you follow through on it. Right or wrong, don't back off. Don't back up. Okay?"

Then Buck burst into laughter. "You didn't see the look on Boats's face, with sludge and moss hanging from his mouth, spittin' piss and a-cussin' sludge balls. It was worth the price of admission. We'd been peein' in that trough for a month. He definitely had to buy a new five-hundred-dollar suit. Bet he had sludge in the crack of his ass for a week. Seein' that foaming, piss-soaked mud on his face made my day."

By the time we turned into the driveway of Buck's pretty brick house, set back off the road, we were laughing and taking turns drinking the second Coke that Buck had opened, and Fig Newton crumbs stuck to the grease on our shirts and trousers. Around the place, I had noticed that Buck was never very far from an open Coke bottle. Every night it was the same routine—as we hit the edge of the front yard, a boy and a girl came screaming out of the house, "Daddy! Daddy!" They hollered like a pack of hounds.

Right behind them was a pretty lady who leaned against the door with a smile and green eyes fixed on Buck. He shut off the engine as we rolled to a stop in front of the garage. The woman called to him, "Buck, you keep those children off you until you take those clothes off and have a shower. I haven't been able to get that oil out of Sister's dress since the last time you was home." She was smiling as she said it, and the mock anger faded like Buck's blue jeans.

The kids jumped beside the truck like turkey vultures anticipating a fresh meal. Stepping to the ground, Buck looked down at the children. "Kids, you heard your mama. No roughhousin' till I get cleaned up, okay?"

The kids tamed their enthusiasm, though it clearly churned just beneath the surface, awaiting the slightest provocation from Buck. A mere wink could release their onslaught. The events repeated themselves every night as if they had never occurred before.

The first time he brought me home, he turned to me with a smile and said, "I don't usually get home this early. You know how late these jobs can get to be. Most of the time I put in ninety hours a week. Get your things out of the back of the truck, and I'll show you where you can sleep."

As I pulled my grip from the back of the truck, Buck came walking around the front, the kids each holding to a hand and wrapped around a leg, their feet perched atop his work boots. Rosie shook her head, absent the heart to deny her children the simple pleasure of a moment with Dad, despite the grease.

"Buck, what did I tell you? I can hardly get your clothes halfway clean."

"Aw, honey, it won't hurt 'em. Come on out and give Buck a kiss."

She must have been convinced because she came outside and kissed him, standing between the children with her arms 'round his neck and her apron pressed to his greasy body. Her apron stuck to his clothes as she pulled back to look at me with her arms still stuck to his neck.

"You're home early, honey. What happened?"

"I'll tell you later, baby. I want you to meet Tommy. I've mentioned him to you before. He's gonna be bunkin' with us for a while. For now, he can sleep on the back porch. We can fix up the spare bedroom for him tomorrow."

As a fifteen-year-old, it was the first time I had recognized a truly beautiful woman. And she was even prettier up close: big, green eyes beneath the sandy, reddish-brown hair that shined in the early evening sun; five-two; about a hundred and two pounds; a hint of freckles dancing across her nose; and a smile that captured my heart.

"Get off, kids. I want you to meet T. C.," Buck said. "T. C., my kids. This red-haired devil is Andrew, and this sweetie here is Sissy. 'Course, her real name is Lyla May, but nobody in the family calls her that."

"I haven't fed your chickens yet, honey," Buck's wife said. "I was going to after supper. You go take care of them, and don't take all night about it. I'll go throw on some more supper." With that, she turned and disappeared into the house.

Buck led me to the back of the house, opened up the door, and said, "Throw your stuff in here, T. C., and we'll go take care of my birds."

We walked around the corner of an outbuilding, and there were about a hundred chickens, each with one leg tied by a cord to a separate box. There were reds, grays, clarets—just about every color in the rainbow. Buck opened up a door, and we went inside. There were pens with roosters in them and a bench up against the wall with a rug tacked on top of it. Buck said, "You ever feed any chickens before?"

"No. Never have. Haven't even been close to one. Don't know a thing about 'em."

"Well, while I'm takin' care of these in here, I'll show you how to take care of those outside." He opened up a big wooden box against the wall. "Come here."

I walked over, and inside the box were partitions separating different kinds of grain.

"Hand me one of those five gallon buckets." He took a scoop and started taking grain out of each section. "I'll show you how to mix this later on when we have time. Right now, we'd better get done or my baby will be out here after us."

We walked outside, and Buck took a large handful of grain and threw it to one of the roosters tied to a box. He showed me the amount to throw to each of them. When I ran out of feed, I went back and found another bucket sitting there, so I finished up and walked back to the shed. When I opened the door, Buck was standing there rubbing a big rooster's back.

"What you doin', Buck?"

"Gettin' these in condition to fight. My brother Chuck and I fight these roosters when we have time, which isn't very often. Chuck gets to fight them more often than I do, so I keep some in shape all the time, just in case one of us has a weekend off. There's a fight someplace every weekend. It's legal in Oklahoma, you know."

"I don't know anything about 'em," I replied.

"Well, you'll learn if you stay around here," he said with a laugh. He threw a rooster in a pen and took another one out of the rows of boxes nailed up on the wall. He ran the rooster up and down on the bench with the rug on it, held him by the tail, and flew him up and down. All this time, the rooster was clucking and making strange noises.

Buck had a contented smile on his face and seemed more relaxed than I had ever seen him before. "You know, boy, I can work thirty hours at a time, come in here 'round these birds, and it seems to take the tiredness right out of me. It's a good thing we men don't have the attitude of these birds, or the human race would be at war all the time."

Sissy knocked on the door and said, "Daddy, Mom says supper's on and for you two to come in before it's cold."

Buck put the rooster in another one of the pens. "Come on, son. Let's put on the feed bag."

We walked in through the back porch, kicked our boots off, and then went through the kitchen and into a bathroom. Buck turned on the water and started washing. He grabbed a block of pumice soap off the back of the sink and shoved it at me. "C'mon, boy. Get in here beside me and get that dirt off."

I took the pumice, ran the short-bristled brush across it twice, and then worked it over my fingers and palms to get the grease out. As we dried and walked into the kitchen, sharing a towel, Andrew and Lyla May were already at the table, and Rosie stood admiring the spread and her newly washed husband. They shared a look that I caught but couldn't quite grasp.

Rosie blushed. She reached for the chair and said, "Tommy, you take the chair next to Andy."

The chair squeaked as I pulled it across the wood plank floor. As Buck and I sat down and waited for Rosie to put the roasting ears and mashed potatoes on the table, Buck smiled at each of his kids and winked at me. When Rosie finally sat down, Buck said, "Tommy, would you like to say grace?"

"I don't know how. We never—"

"That's all right, T. C., but a man has to pay reverence to his maker. We'll discuss it one of these days. Thank you, Jesus, for this fine food, fine family, my good wife, and for bringing us Tommy. Amen."

We had pork chops, mashed potatoes, brown gravy, corn on the cob, and full stomachs. We finished it off with apple spice cake with cream-cheese frosting. Rosie was amazing. She kept pressing me to eat more, and I kept eating just to keep her happy. I don't know where it went, but it was better than bunkhouse grub.

"Let him get used to us, baby," Buck said to Rosie. "Nobody could keep eating the way you're feedin' him and stay as skinny as he is. Let him get used to us." These events were played out night after night in the Hagan house, and I never tired of it over the entire time I lived with them.

After supper, Buck told me, "Let's finish up out in the cock house. Honey, we won't be long."

Buck immediately pulled out another rooster and began exercising him on the carpet-topped workbench. "Tommy, you sit over there. We'd better talk. Tom, Boats was going to haul your ass down to the sheriff's and have you locked up for a few days to teach you a lesson. I talked him out of it. One reason, you're a good kid; another, I'd have to train someone on the crew to replace you. For another, I kind of figured Boats had it coming. And finally, I need someone to help me 'round the place. Boats is going to pay me a hundred dollars a month to take care of you, and we can use the money. You're out of school for the summer, aren't you?"

I sat rolling my fingers around the inside of my ball cap, carefully avoiding Buck's gaze. I knew it was hard for Buck to talk to me about this stuff, and it wasn't all that easy for me to listen.

"Yes, sir," I said as I finally raised my eyes to meet Buck's.

"Don't call me sir. It's Buck. Another thing, I knew your pa and ma. I liked them both, and your pa was one hell of a man, so I don't blame you for clocking that son of a bitch Boats. But don't make a habit of it. I won't be able to save your butt again. Try to keep that temper under control. You can never do anything when your emotions rule your life."

I shifted my back into the corner of the barn and raised my left leg and knee onto a box so that I was halfway facing Buck. "I can't guarantee I won't clock the son of a bitch again given half a reason," I said and grinned at Buck.

"I'm sure we'll get along fine, Tom." A broad smile spread across Buck's face as he focused on the bird he was running back and forth on the counter. "Oh, by the way, Boats told me yesterday that he has a job coming up down in Texas pretty quick before the summer's over and that, if I want it, I can have the foreman's job. I don't want to leave the family, and I'm just waiting for my baby to make up her mind on whether or not she'll move with me. If she won't go, I won't either. It would mean a foreman's job, a big raise in pay, but I ain't leavin' my family."

I stood and said, "Wow, that sounds great. What would you do about this place?"

"Price Pierce, who lives next door, would take care of the place. My brother would come down and get the birds to keep until we get back. The reason I'm telling you this is that if we go, you would have to come with us. Boats doesn't want you around for a while."

"Well, I sure as hell ain't interested in spendin' time with the bastard Boats myself." We stepped out into the cool evening air and headed for the house.

The next morning, as Buck and I drove to work, he told me that Rosie had decided to move to Texas with him for the summer. For the next month, we worked hard finishing up the work in Tishomingo so that the new man taking Buck's place wouldn't have to try and figure out what had been done and what needed to be done.

At the end of June, we packed our belongings in one of the trucks. Buck and I drove the truck, and Rosie and the kids followed in the car.

Buck had already arranged for the oil company we were contracted with to rent us a house. It took us two days to get to Leland, Texas, a small, nearly invisible town northeast of El Paso. We spent the first two days lining up two casing crews. The night before we started work, Buck, Rosie, and I sat on the porch, watching the bats pick bugs out of the sky. Buck said, "How much you weigh now, Tom?"

"I don't know," I said. "I haven't paid much attention."

"Well, you've grown a bit since you came, haven't you? Aren't you about a hundred and fifty now?"

"Yeah, I think so."

Rosie reached over and wrapped her arm around my waist, as if measuring, and then took the measure of my shoulders. "Well, Buck, he's growin' faster than I can buy clothes for him."

I held up my right arm to flex a bicep for Rosie to squeeze. "Solid iron, Rosie," I said, laughing.

"Good," Buck said, apparently missing the humor. "I need someone I can depend on to haul pipe. We have to use two men, a driver and a hauler. If you think you can handle it, I'd like to have you do it, 'cause you know what happens when the casing isn't there."

"Honey, isn't that pretty heavy work for a young man like Tom?" Rosie asked.

"Yeah, baby, it is. But you know these oil workers. If you don't have someone keep an eye on them, you don't ever get anything done. Besides, after we get going and get the job laid out, it will only take three to four hours a day to make the deliveries. Then Tom can do it after school."

I stood and struck a bodybuilder pose in front of Rosie and Buck, who were seated on the porch. "Guys, I can handle it."

Rosie continued, oblivious to my input. "Buck, you surely don't expect this boy to do that heavy work after school starts, do you?"

"*Man,* Rosie. I'm a man, not a boy. Please!" I said.

Buck went on as if I weren't there. "I have to, honey. That's the agreement I made with Boats when he agreed to let Tom come down here with us."

"I really don't know why you work for that man. He don't have a bit of compassion in him." Rosie turned on the step and folded her arms. I'm surprised she didn't pick up a sliver, she spun so quick.

"Baby, you know what the Bible says. 'Judge not, lest you be judged.'"

"Bible? I ain't judging him, Buck. I'm just callin' a mangy dog a mangy dog. I think that's too heavy of a workload for Tommy."

I put my work boot on the step at their feet. "I can do it, Rosie," I interrupted.

Buck was undeterred and focused on Rosie. "'Sides, baby, he's the only one I can depend on. I can't get a driver who likes to booze it up or something else. I have to depend on him. We'll have four to six jobs going at one time, and I don't have time to be worrying about pipe."

Rosie wasn't letting go of it. "Didn't you say that pipes are heavy?"

"They weigh about two hundred to two hundred fifty pounds per section. He will be sore for a couple of weeks until he gets broke in, but with two men handling the pipe, it won't be too bad. I did it when I was sixteen, so T. C. should be able to handle it."

Rosie had retreated to the top step and leaned back against a post. She was softening. "I know, honey, but Tommy says he has to go out for football, too."

Buck turned to me as he finished his discourse with Rosie. "I know that, but I got to do it that way. Boats was clear about it. It's okay with you, isn't it, T. C.?"

"I'll do my best," I said, glad to be part of the conversation once again.

"That's all I ask."

Chapter 3

Pipe, Fast Food, and Fig Newtons

The next two weeks, we were swamped. We wrestled pipe from six in the morning till midnight every day. The first two days, I couldn't straighten up or raise my arms above my shoulders. I didn't see Buck except for at breakfast. He was always either coming or going, or I was. We had six wells that had been started on the same day. Buck would call in the footage of pipe needed for the well, and it was my job and Pete's to get it to them. I had worked with Pete up at Tishomingo. He liked his beer, but he showed up, hungover or not. I asked Buck at breakfast one morning after working with Pete if it was proper for Pete to always have a six-pack of beer in a cooler in the cab of the truck.

Buck laughed and grabbed a biscuit out of the bowl, crumbled it, and slapped a dipper of gravy on it. "Son, most men need a crutch to get through the day. I've known Pete for over ten years, and I've never seen him drunk on the job. He's a hell of a worker, a good driver, and someone you can depend on to get there every day. The only thing he doesn't handle well is the time. He can never get anywhere on time. The last job we had, we were always two to three days late 'cause he couldn't get us pipe on time." Buck poured some cold buttermilk into his glass and shook salt and pepper into it. The spoon clinked the glass as he stirred. "So let him drink his beer. You just keep him on time and keep that pipe coming. You're doin' a hell of a job."

The days and nights ran together, and things got easier after the first two weeks. I was still so tired that I could hardly move when I got home. I just grabbed a sandwich and hit the bed. It didn't matter what time I came in, Rosie was always up to fix me something. I kept telling her it wasn't necessary.

"You are one of my menfolk, Tom. My mama always told me my job was to care for my menfolk, so you keep quiet. Go take a quick shower, and your food will be ready when you're done."

Some nights, we would sit and talk for an hour or so. It seemed like I always slept better on those nights. Between working, eating, and sleeping, my appetite was enormous. I could never seem to get enough to eat to get full. During the day, Pete was always stopping at a store to get him a six-pack, and I would get me a couple of fast-food sandwiches, Fig Newtons, fruit, and anything edible that caught my eye. Then I'd wash it down with a quart of milk.

Pete kept kidding me about girls. During the afternoon runs, he would make sure and drive past the park to look at the sunbathers. One afternoon, he whistled at a pair of girls in shorts who had their tops dropped to expose the tops of their breasts to the sun. The girls scrambled to cover themselves, and Pete punched me on the shoulder. "There you go, boy! Hot pussy and sharp titties!" Pete revved the engine and blew the air horn.

"Aren't you married, Pete?" I asked.

"Nope, and ain't never gonna be neither, boy! I fall in love with every woman I take out. Now if I could find one like Rosie, I might be married, but there is no loyalty among 'em anymore. I was born to be a bachelor. I'm dating a woman now, but I'm pretty sure she's steppin' out on me, being as we're working so many long hours. She's a nice enough gal, but you can't hope to meet a true-type woman in the bars I go to. She takes care of my needs good enough and isn't too bad a cook, but she's like me—a long way from perfect."

Pete downshifted as we made the wide turn toward the lower fields. "You don't seem to expect much," I said.

Pete worked his way through the gears as we gained speed, and he double clutched the old Dodge as the gears ground. "I can tell I'm going to have to get me another one pretty quick. She's beginnin' to get that gleam of marriage in her eye, and I'm beginnin' to get sly comments 'bout how compatible we are, how she has always wanted a home. I can't understand it. You start out, it's strictly sex. And then pretty soon, they want to move in with you, start fixin' you meals, takin' care of all your needs, and then the marriage talk starts. Betty—that's the woman I'm with now—she's great in bed, best I've ever had. But marriage is out of the question. I'm forty-two years old, and I'm not about to change."

I looked out the side window at the fields in the distance. "Don't you want a family?"

"I want to be able to go and come when I want to, and if I see a chick I want to fuck and leave, then I don't want to have to explain it to anyone." Pete looked at me with a grin. "Ain't you dipped your wick yet, son?"

"Ain't I dipped what?" I knew what he was talking about, but it wasn't a conversation I wanted to have with Pete. My nonexistent sex life was none of his concern.

"How old are you, T. C.?"

"Fifteen. Be sixteen next month."

"Ever kissed a girl?"

"No."

"Why not? You're a hell of a nice-looking kid."

"Don't know. Haven't had an opportunity. Guess it's 'cause I'm so small."

"Small, hell. You must've grow'd a couple inches this summer alone. You've gained at least forty pounds since I met you last year." We pulled to a stop at the fields. Thank God, that conversation was over.

That night when I got home, I picked up a new pair of Levi's that Rosie had bought for me. My jeans wore out so fast. I hadn't been paying that much attention; I just wore them. I had been wearing twenty-nines with a thirty-inch leg when the summer started. These I held in my hand had a thirty-two-inch waist and thirty-two-inch length. They fit tight, and the length was short to keep the hem out of the muck. I had grown, no doubt about it.

Rosie was setting my supper on the table when I walked back into the kitchen. "You know, I was just looking at my pants. I hadn't realized I had grown so much."

"I know. You and Buck are so much alike in one way. You spend so much time workin' and worryin' about work, I believe you would either go naked or wear the same clothes day after day if I didn't put out clean ones for you every night."

"How much do I owe you for the clothes? I haven't talked to Buck about my pay. Funny, Rosie—here I've been workin' all summer, and I haven't even asked if I was being paid. I just used the money you and Buck leave on the dresser on top of my clothes."

"I have been takin' your clothes out of your checks, being as you've never said anything about it. Buck and I just assumed as long as you had spendin' money or if'n you needed some or more than we had been leavin' out, you would say something. Just a minute."

She left the kitchen and went into their bedroom. I heard a dresser drawer being pulled out. She came back with a little green book, and without a word she laid it in front of me on the maple kitchen table.

I reached out and spread it open. It was filled with deposits from the time I had started living with Buck and Rosie. "I didn't realize Boats had been payin' me for the last year," I said. I leaned back in the kitchen chair and slid my butt across the Naugahyde to get comfortable.

Buck grinned at me and pushed a piece of apple pie in his mouth, spitting a few crumbs as he started to talk. "You can say a lot about the man, T. C., but he isn't cheap. He pays his men really well, better than any other casing crew in the country. That's the reason he can always hire good men. He gave me this book. When we left up there, I just transferred it down here. They use the same kind of deposit book, so it was easy. All the girl did was mark through your old number and write in a new one."

I picked up the book and waved it in front of my face. "You mean that I have over nine thousand dollars saved up?"

"Well, you have more than that," Rosie said. "I've been kind of lazy lately. I still have yours and Buck's last two checks. I've got to take them to the bank tomorrow. You know, Tom, you bring home over a thousand dollars after take out every month. It isn't what you make that counts, it's what you save. You saved a lot 'cause you don't spend much. There's something else we have to discuss."

What could that possibly be? I thought. *I'm already wealthy.* "What's that?"

Rosie stood to Buck's side and let her right arm fall around his neck as she stood on one foot, leaning into him. "I called the high school, and you have a choice. This area has grown so fast that both high schools are overcrowded. They're in the process of buildin' a junior high, but that won't be finished for another year. So, being a junior, you'll have to attend one of them, and the first day of school is on the twenty-fourth of August. So you'll have to decide which school you want to attend."

I picked up the plates and walked to the sink, scraping the scarce leftovers into the pail under it. "Do you know which is the biggest and which one has the best football team?" I asked her.

"Don't have any idea."

I turned the water on and rinsed the dish, swiping the sponge across it twice for good measure. "Would you do me a favor and find out? I know that since I'll be a junior I may have a shot at gettin' on the varsity. I want to go to the smallest one. Boats is always braggin' about what a great football player he was. Well, I'm going to show him. I'm going to be the best damn football player he's ever seen. I better start gettin' in shape too."

Buck spit his coffee out on the table. "Get in shape! Good God, Tommy, haven't you looked in the mirror lately? I'll bet half the men in the United States wish they were in as good a shape as you're in. It's a good thing you're not swell-headed. Before you go to bed tonight, you'd better look in the mirror."

Rosie stepped away from Buck and started picking up the kids' plates and clearing the table. "I'll find out about the schools for you tomorrow, and then you can decide what you want to do."

I headed for bed, exhausted. "'Night, Tom."

Rosie was smiling as Buck turned his head to watch me leave.

"Good night, Rosie," I said.

Before I turned in, I undressed in front of the mirror. To tell the truth, I hadn't expected what I saw. My arms had filled out; they were three times the size they had been a few months earlier. I had crisp ripples down my stomach, where a firm six-pack stood out. My legs bulged as the sharp cut of muscle jumped to attention when I flexed my leg. I easily weighed a hundred and eighty pounds, and as I moved my face to the mirror, I realized that hair had appeared on my face and a mustache had presented itself, which I had previously attributed to grease from the steel pipes I had been lifting all summer. My body had snuck up on me. I had been oblivious to the building of this body. I vaguely remembered seeing a body like this in a magazine with a different head on its shoulders. I looked good, and I felt great when I crawled into bed that night.

The next morning when I showed up to work, Pete wasn't there. I waited for about an hour and then called around trying to find Buck. After the third call, I got him out at Fletcher field.

"What's the problem, Tom?"

"Pete didn't show up this morning."

"Oh, hell. I meant to tell Rosie this morning. Betty called last night. Pete had his appendix taken out. I meant to tell one of the men to come over and take his place. You at Warden's Pipe?"

"Yeah."

"Well, it will be a couple of hours until I can get someone out there. Just take it easy, and I'll get them there as quick as I can."

I walked out of the office and was greeted by the irritating odor of sage, which filled the field next to the warehouse. The foreman, Jesus, asked if I had found out anything about Pete. "He had his appendix out last night. They're sendin' another guy over."

"You're kidding. I didn't think people his age were bothered with that."

"Guess so," I said. "It was probably soaked in Old Milwaukee beer." I paused a minute and then said, "Say, Jesus, you got a minute?"

"Sure. What's up?" Jesus sat on a three-legged chair that was leaning up against the building. I looked at him from where I stood on the ground below the loading dock.

"Well, I have to start to school pretty quick, and I'm livin' in that new addition at Leland. They say I can either attend the high school at the west end of El Paso or the one on the other side of town. I'm into sports—not too good yet, but I don't want to get into a school where I won't get a chance to play. I know I'll probably have to be on JV, but I'd like to make the team."

Jesus leaned toward me and dropped his elbows on his knees, clasping his hands in front of him. "Well, the west end school has been a football powerhouse in the state for the last twenty years. I graduated from there in '49, second-string halfback. I got to play in two downs the year we won the state championship. My name is on the state champion roster in the trophy case up there."

I leaned my hand against the dock and listened to him. "That's pretty awesome. I can't imagine playing in a state championship."

Jesus kept talking as if daydreaming. "The other school is about half the size of Sam Houston High. It's called Le High. They've had the same coach for the last twenty-five years. He turns out a real decent club about every four or five years. They play double-A ball, where Sam Houston is triple A. If it's the fundamentals you want and you want to play, I would attend Le High."

"Thanks, Jesus." I started to walk toward the school, but Jesus kept talking and pulled me back.

"I've only seen them play twice. The last time was in '64. Half as many kids go out for football, but they're really well coached. I've met the coach several times, and he's a really nice fellow. You'd most likely get along with him fine if you want to learn. Say, how long before your driver gets here?"

"Couple of hours, from what Buck said."

Jesus stood up and walked toward the office. "I have to go pick up some supplies on the other side of the school. You can ride along if you'd like to look it over."

"Sure we'll we be back in time?" I asked.

"Only take about fifteen minutes, and that's driving slow."

"Fine. I'd like to."

Jesus picked up his pace, hurrying to the office. "I'll tell the girl in the office and be right back."

He emerged a few minutes later, and we headed for the school. The front of the school was an old brick two-story with some kind of new addition on the back.

Jesus used the Jake brake to slow the old Peterbilt, sending black smoke roiling from the twin stacks. The truck hissed to a stop as the brake set. "Get out and look around. The football field is about a block over that way. I'll only be about twenty-five minutes. I'll drive by, and if you're not here, I'll come over to the field."

I started toward the school and waved over my shoulder. "Thanks," I said. A black man appeared at the door to the school with a collection of keys hanging from his belt.

"Is the school open?" I asked as he pushed the door open, backing me up on the concrete porch.

"Not for enrollment. It starts next Wednesday."

"No, I just wanted to look around. I have to enroll either here or at Sam Houston, and I'm trying to decide which one." I shielded my eyes from the sun's reflection in the door glass.

He smiled at me. "Where you live? Leland addition?"

"Yeah. How'd you know?" I reached out to hold the door so he could pull back and relax his grip.

"Oh, we've had this problem for the last four years. That's the only area around that isn't in any school district. Kind of slipped through the cracks." He invited me with a swing of his hand to step into the building and out of the hot sun.

"You a teacher here?" I asked.

"Sorry, should have introduced myself. I'm Sawyer. Terrance Sawyer. I'm the assistant principal here at Le High."

"I'm Tom Gurley—T. C. to my friends." I reached out and shook his hand. His grip was pretty solid.

"Well, T. C., I'm glad to meet you. What grade—senior?"

"Only a junior."

"You look older, but when you get to be my age, you young people fool us."

I realized that I was looking him in the eye; we were the same height. "Say, Mr. Sawyer, I'm thinkin' about going out for football. The coach wouldn't be around, would he?" I shifted my weight back and forth and was unable to decide what to do with my hands.

"Sure. I was on my way over to the field. Walk along with me, and I'll introduce you." Mr. Sawyer pushed the door open and walked briskly toward the field, stopping long enough to make sure I was following. "Where did you attend school before?"

"Originally, I'm from Florida. Last year I went to Tishomingo and lived with my uncle."

"Know where it's at. Was born about forty minutes from there. There's Coach Baker over there. I talked to him earlier. He will most likely be glad to see you." As we approached the coach, Mr. Sawyer said, "Hey, Jerry."

"Hi, Terrance. Need something?" Jerry Baker was six five with not an ounce of fat and had thinning hair hidden by a ball cap. His neck was bright red from being in the sun and living in the Deep South before finding his way to Texas. There wasn't a lick of nonsense about anything he did, and his visual inspection made me feel like I had left my clothes at the truck.

"Want to get that athletic inventory."

Baker broke his stare and turned to Sawyer. "Sure, it's in the file here." He stepped away and returned with the folder of disheveled papers.

"Jerry, I want you to meet Tom Gurley—goes by T. C."

Baker reached out, grabbed my hand, and gave it a tug to determine if I had any balance. "Glad to know you, T. C." When I didn't falter, he pumped my hand twice and then turned it over, whistling as he stared at my palm. "Man, I haven't seen calluses like that in years." He turned my hand over to examine the back. "What do you do, T. C.?"

"Work a pipe truck for six casing crews."

Baker whistled and chortled. "Say no more, son. I've been there."

Sawyer interjected, "T. C. here lives in Leland addition. He's trying to decide which school he wants to attend. He says he'd like to play football, so he wanted to meet you. I'll let you boys visit, and I'll get on back to the office."

"Terrance, I also have the budget for you. It's in the top right-hand drawer of my desk. Got your key?"

Sawyer nodded. "See ya later. Nice meeting you, T. C. Hope to see you this fall."

"Thanks, Mr. Sawyer. You might." He turned and started toward a building behind the grandstands.

"Played football before, T. C.?"

"One year, sir."

"What position?"

"Defensive back and left half."

"Varsity?"

"No. J. V. Scrub."

"How much you weigh?"

"About one seventy."

"You look heavier. How tall?"

"Last time I measured, sometime last year, about five foot eight."

"You're a lot taller than that, near six foot one, I'd say. What year?"

"Junior."

"Fooled me on that."

"That's what Mr. Sawyer said."

"How's your speed?"

I shifted my weight. "Last year I was the fastest man on the squad at Tishomingo High."

"Okay. Keith Hartman still coaching up there?"

"Yes, sir."

"I assume you know the basics of tackling and blocking pretty good, then."

"Well, sir, if you mean being run over by everybody on the team, I knew that well enough. I've had an awful lot of blockin' and tacklin' practice."

Baker grinned. "If you decide to go to our school, football practice will start a week from next Monday, two practices a day: ten in the morning and five thirty at night for two hours each. If you decide to go here, I'll be looking for you. Been nice talking to you."

I hadn't had time to get back to the curb when Jesus pulled up in the Peterbilt, black smoke still bellowing from its pipes. "What do you think of the school?" he asked.

I climbed into the cab. "Well, how big is it, anyway? I couldn't tell from walking through it."

"Don't really know but somewhere around four hundred. Can't be much over that and still be a 2A school. My son attends here."

"Does he play football?"

"Manny plays every sport, just about," Jesus laughed. "He just likes to play—mostly with his girlfriend though."

A man was standing by our truck when we pulled back into the yard. He was a sinister-looking, short, sly man carrying an unusual knife that curled in a sheath from his belt. I was about ten feet from the truck when he said, "You Tom?"

"Yeah. Ready to load?"

"Buck said to take a load of ten inch out to the Blackwell site number three. They ran out last night."

We loaded the truck and had started through the gate when the office girl waved us down and said, "Buck called, and he's broke down out near Holyshake number nine. Wants you to pick him up."

As we pulled out, I asked the driver, "By the way, what's your name?"

"They call me Snake. Real name's Orville Robertson, so you can see why I needed a nickname."

"That's an interesting nickname. How long you been working for Nichols Casing?" I noticed that Snake spoke with a lisp, making it sound like he was hissing.

"'Bout fourteen years. I got hired on by Boats after I got out of the Army Rangers in Korea. His driver, Pike, was buddies with the senior master sergeant in my unit. The army is where I picked up the nickname Snake."

"Is that where you got the knife too?" He pulled it out of its sheath and handed it to me. It looked like a single lion's claw with a hole in the handle for his finger. The blade was sharp on both sides and about four or five inches long.

"Yeah, it went with me everywhere in Asia. I've just gotten used to carrying it. I notice Buck calls you Tom and all the others call you T. C. Which you prefer?"

"T. C. or Tom, either one suits me just fine." I handed the knife back to Snake, and he slipped it back in place without looking.

Buck was standing by his pickup when we arrived. A tow truck pulled in at the same time. "Damn transmission went out," Buck said. He talked to the driver of the tow truck for a couple of minutes and then hopped into our truck. "Tom, how you been? Hello, Snake. Ben pick you?"

"Yeah. Ben lost his license last week on that drunk driving charge."

"Yeah, forgot all about that." We talked for a minute, and then I said, "Say, Buck, I talked to the coach at Le High. Football practice starts next Monday two times a day, at ten and five thirty. What you want me to do—forget it or what?"

"No, Boats wants you going out for athletics. We'll figure it out. You don't have a driver's license yet, do you?"

"No, but I know how to drive."

"Yeah, I knew that, but when are you sixteen?"

"Monday, next week."

"Well, you'd better stop at the Department of Public Safety office and get you a driver's manual. That way, next Monday you can go down and get your license. I'll talk to Boats about a car or truck for you."

"Rather have a pickup if it's all right with you, Buck."

"Fine with me. Let me out here in front. What time you be through tonight?"

"About ten, I hope."

Snake dropped me in front of the house at about a quarter to eleven.

The lights were all on in the front room. Rosie called out, "We're in the kitchen, Tom."

She was sitting on Buck's lap when I walked in. They were both smiling.

"Looks like you had a rough day, boy," Buck said.

"Had two flats and two job sites out of pipe before we could get to them. We need a new set of tires on that pile of junk."

"I know. I talked to Boats about that this afternoon, all this worn-out equipment. He agreed to let me get the new trucks. Caught him at the right moment, I guess. 'Course, he just got the contract on the Bidwell field up in Johnston County. That should be a big one. Since 1938, the first well they brought in was over thirty thousand barrels a day. And they say we got a gas and oil problem."

Buck was at the table, ready to eat. I got the pitcher of milk from the fridge and sat down. "That guy Snake is kinda scary, with the knife and all."

Buck cocked his head and reached for the greens. "Yeah, he's just a bit off, but you would be too if you had done the things he has in the war."

"What do ya mean?"

Rosie brought the pork chops to the table stacked on a wooden platter that popped with grease. "Well, I understand from talking to Pike that Snake got his name from crawling down enemy tunnels on search-and-destroy missions. He would go down the hole with his knife and kill whatever or whoever he found. Apparently, he is an expert with that knife."

Buck stuck a fork in a sizzling chop and dropped it on his plate next to the mashed potatoes he had piled and buried in butter. "Couple years ago, a Mexican in a bar came after him with a knife when we were all out for dinner and drinks. Snake sliced him up real bad without getting a scratch. Every time Snake cut him, he would make this sound through his teeth, imitating a rattler. It was spooky. He was deathly calm and fearless. Scared the shit out of me. Normally he's an easy-going guy, but flip the switch and he can be a pretty mean son of a bitch. I wouldn't tangle with him. So don't you piss him off."

I dropped back in my chair, taking in everything Buck had said. "Don't worry about that. I won't," I said. "He just seems kinda twisted."

Rosie interrupted and slid a bowl of gravy on the table. "Tom, the coach from school called about six. Said he talked to the coach at Tishomingo. He gave you a good recommendation for effort. Coach Baker said the coach up there said, 'Too bad he's so small. He sure is fast.' He asked if you grow'd much this year, and Coach Baker told him, ''Bout three inches and forty pounds.' He said that kids that grow that quick don't usually have much strength. Buck walked in then, so I let Buck talk to him about your strength."

Buck laughed. "Yeah, I told him he didn't have to worry 'bout your strength. Told him I didn't know many grow'd men could keep up with you throwing two-hundred-fifty-pound pipe around all day. Oh, yeah. Boats told me to tell you to go down and get a pickup after you get your driver's license and have them call him for a purchase order."

Buck continued, "By the way, Tom, you'll have to make some runs to the fields before practice."

"Buck, he can't do all that and practice too," Rosie said, playing the protector again.

"Has to, honey. I'm gonna see if I can find someone that can work split hours. I can't keep Snake on there too long. He's my best mud man, and I'm having trouble keeping up without him."

"Jesus, the foreman at Warden's Pipe Yard, asked me if his son might get a job with us," I offered.

"Talk to him in the morning. If the kid can handle it, take him on. I don't have time for talking to a bunch of people right now. Most of the Mexicans are excellent workers."

Rosie said, "You go and grab a quick shower. Your food will be ready in about ten minutes."

As I was leaving, I heard Rosie telling Buck, "You're puttin' too much on that boy. He is only fifteen years old."

When I got back from my shower, Buck and I dug in. We laughed and talked till almost one in the morning. I was still sleepy when I crawled into Snake's truck at six the next morning. Buck came out with me and said, "Snake, if Tom can hire another man this mornin', you come on over to Holyshake number nine. I'm havin' trouble."

"Sure thing, Boss."

Jesus was standing on the loading dock when we pulled in. "Mornin', Snake, T.C.. You look sleepy T.C."

"Went to bed late."

"Can't stand too much of that on this job."

"I know," I said. "I'm tired already, and the whole day's ahead of us."

"Which load you want first?" We walked to the pallet of pipe and began pulling it onto the truck parked next to the dock.

"Give us the ten for Tempest," I said. "They should be the lowest. Besides, they're the farthest out. Maybe I can catch a quick ten."

"Now you're learnin', son," Snake hissed.

I turned to Jesus, who had just walked out on the dock. "Say, you said your son was looking for a job. Can he drive? I mean, does he have a chauffeur's license?"

"Sure does."

"Could you get him down here this mornin' by the time we get back from Tempest? Snake has to get back to the field, and Buck says if he can handle it, to hire him."

"You bet. He will be here when you get back."

We pulled back into the yard just after nine and saw a young Mexican talking to Jesus.

"T. C., this is Manuel, my oldest boy."

He was about five foot eleven and 180 pounds, well muscled. He turned and stuck out his hand. "Glad to know you, T. C. Call me Manny."

"You got it, Manny."

I turned to his dad and said, "Jesus, we want to take the pipe for Holyshake next."

As we loaded the truck, I told Manny, "We start our men off at seven-eighty. If everything works out, you get a dollar raise after a month and then another one after six months. You get all hospitalization and dental as well."

"Sounds fine to me."

"The hours will be kinda funny 'cause, come Monday after next, I have to start football practice."

"What school?"

"Le High."

"That's my school," he said. "I'm a junior. I've been looking for a part-time job during school, but I really need the job. It doesn't matter that I can only work until school, does it?"

"Heck, no! It might work out better than you think. I have to go to school too, and I still have to deliver pipe evenings after school and practice. So maybe we can both work part time."

"Hey, man, that could work great. I had thought about going out for football again this year. Last year I worked in a drive-in, cooking nights, but they sold out and the man who bought it had a big family like mine, so his kids do all the work."

"You on varsity?"

"Yeah, played right halfback and fullback. Coach was talking about making me a quarterback this year. He was sorry when I told him I was going to have to work to help out the family."

"Well, being as I'm going to have to work split shifts, I'll talk to Buck. Maybe we can both play football."

When we pulled into the yard for our last load of the night, the guard asked, "One of you Tom Gurley?"

"Yeah, I am."

"Buck called and said to have you call the house when you came in."

I walked into the office. The door was open, but two of the panels had been replaced with sheet steel because someone had kicked the wooden ones out. The room was stale and smelled of grease and cigarettes. The floor was covered in sawdust to pick up the grease tracked in from the supply yard. The old oak rolltop desk was worn, and the plies of wood were broken along the front corner. The carbon-black phone had a shoulder rest attachment stuck to the hand piece so you could use both hands and talk at the same time. I dropped into the chair and was surprised when it shot back. Apparently, the tension spring holding the chair erect was broken. The phone rang twice before Buck picked it up. "Tom, that you?" he said.

"Yeah, what's up?"

"Rosie's mother died—heart attack, I guess. Anyway, we have to get up to Kansas. We should be gone about a week."

"I'm 'bout broke, Buck. Could you have Rosie leave some money on my dresser?"

"Let the work go for tonight and come on in. I have to talk to you."

"Sure. Be there as quick as I can."

Manny was talking to the guard when I walked out of the shed. "Manny, let's pack it in. Rosie's mother died, and they want me at the house."

"Sure. What about work tomorrow?"

"Should be the same as today."

"You not going to the funeral?" he asked.

"No, I don't think so. Buck wants to talk to me about something."

The lights were all turned on as we pulled into the driveway. I asked Manny to come in, but he refused, death being a private matter to his family.

When I entered the house, I saw two suitcases sitting in the living room. Rosie and Buck were talking in one of the back rooms. Rosie was sitting on the edge of the bed, and Buck was kneeling in front of her. Tears rolling down her face had wet the front of Buck's shirt.

Buck saw me when I walked to the door. "I'll be right out, Tom."

I walked into the kitchen, pulled a cake from the fridge, and sat down at the table. About ten minutes later Buck walked in, took a slice of Rosie's spice cake, and sat down next to me. "Snake will be runnin' the job while I'm gone. You know your job, so you shouldn't have any problems."

"Manny's outside. I didn't know what to tell him."

"Same as usual."

"Let me go tell him," I said.

"Come right back."

Manny sat slumped, dozing in the truck as I approached. "Manny, it's like I thought. Pick me up six in the mornin'."

"Tell 'em I'm sorry 'bout Rosie's mama," he said. "Later, man."

The truck lumbered off as Manny skillfully worked the gears.

Rosie and Buck were sitting at the table when I came back in.

"I don't know what to say, Rosie."

"The thought is appreciated, Tommy. There's nothing anyone can do. I better finish packing."

"Are you guys leaving tonight?" I asked.

"We have to," Rosie said. "Dad is up there alone, so we want to get there as fast as possible. I put two hundred dollars on your dresser, and your bank book is in the top right-hand drawer in case you need any more."

"That should be more than enough. Thanks, Rosie."

"You're welcome." She went back to the bedroom, and I could hear her packing.

Buck turned to me at the table and said, "Tomorrow is Wednesday, and you start football next Monday. You and Manny better work the weekend. Get ahead as far as you can. I'll get back as soon as possible, but you never can tell 'bout these things. Your birthday is Monday, ain't it?"

I leaned onto the table and dropped my elbows comfortably. "Yeah, sweet sixteen, waiting to be kissed. Ain't that what they say?"

Buck grinned. "Somethin' like that. By the way, you plannin' on gettin' your license?" He stood and walked to the coffeepot, filling his blackened coffee cup.

"First thing Monday mornin'." I turned to catch his gaze as he leaned back against the wall.

"Well, you be careful. I don't want you drivin' the pipe truck 'cept on the job and in the pipe yard. You still let Manny have it on the road. Understand?" He took a long drink of his coffee.

I turned my chair and said, "Sure, Buck, but I have to start sometime."

He saw the mail on the counter and leafed through it nonchalantly. "Well, better take it slow. After you get your license, stop over at Cable's Ford and see Junior Hopkins. Boats bought you a pickup. Rosie and I had 'em install an AM/FM stereo with a tape player in it. That's our birthday present. Just take it easy, Tom," he said as he turned back to me. "We don't want you getting hurt. You never have been a wild kid, or I wouldn't dream of letting you have the truck without me being here. Just take it easy for me, okay?"

My face must have lit up because Buck was grinning when he looked at me. "Sure will," I said. We could hear Rosie getting the kids up.

Buck started for the bedrooms. "Guess I'd better get in there and help her. I left the phone number of her dad's place lying next to your money. If anything comes up, you call me." I followed him into the bedrooms to lend a hand.

I helped them take the suitcase out to Rosie's white T-bird, walked back in, and took Lyla out of Rosie's arms. She was still sound asleep when I buckled her in the back behind Rosie's seat. I waved as they backed out of the drive and disappeared around the corner in the dark.

Manny woke me the next morning; he liked to kick the door down. I ran to the door. He was standing there with a big grin on his face, looking at me barefoot and in boxer shorts. "What you gonna do, amigo? Loaf around all day with the boss out of town?"

"C'mon in, Manny. Let me get dressed. Must have forgot to set the alarm." I jumped into my clothes, and we took off for the yard.

"What time is it?" Manny asked.

"'Bout six, somewhere. Let's grab a fast load, and then when we get back, I want to stop at the DPS office and see if I can get my license."

"You don't have a license, hombre?"

"Wasn't old 'nough."

"You're kidding!"

"Nope."

"How old are you? I thought you was my age, seventeen."

"Turned sixteen today."

"Man, you could've fooled me. You seem a lot older. What you gonna use to take the driver's test?"

"Hadn't thought about it."

"Well, you have to have a car."

"I've got a new pickup at Cable's Ford, but I'll have to have you go with me and drive it out there to the office."

"Be glad to, man."

We pulled up to Cable's at about eight o'clock. As we started into the showroom, Manny said, "Man, look at that short-box pickup over there. Ain't that a honey?"

A salesman caught up to us at the door. "What can I do for you boys today?" he asked.

"I have a new pickup here," I replied. "Is Junior Hopkins 'round?"

"That's him over there, the middle-aged man in the blue suit."

Junior looked up as we approached. It was clear that he loved donuts because, as he turned, he had one in his hand, powdered sugar down his shirt, and twenty years of donuts drooping over his belt buckle. When we walked up, he grinned with a spot of donut jelly on his chin. "Help you fellas?"

"I'm Tom Gurley," I said.

"Oh, yeah. Buck said you would be in today. Where's he?"

"Rosie's mama died. He had to go to Kansas."

"Sorry to hear it. Might as well get the paperwork done 'fore we take a look at your truck. The company sent a purchase order. Boats picked it out hisself last week. Just need to git you to sign for receipt of the vehicle to make it all proper." He pulled out a folder and started pointing out places for me to sign.

"What kinda truck did they get for me?"

"You should've walked right by it on the way in. It's the silver short-box with the special paint job, right outside the showroom. I had the lot boy spiff it up for yers. Boats wanted it to sparkle when ya saw it."

"Hey, it's that dolled-up truck I pointed out to you when we came in," Manny said. "Man, that's a beauty!"

We walked out to the truck. It had a short, wide box; big chrome wheels; and silver paint with a metallic blue-and-maroon stripe running down the side. A big chrome roll bar sat above the cab with three lights across the top.

Junior stuck a paper in the rear window. "That's your temporary license, till your plates come in 'round a week from now. Stop by and we'll put 'em on for ya. If anything goes wrong with it, just keep a list and bring it on in when you want 'em fixed. Boats said, by God, we'd better take good care of ya." Hopkins dropped the keys in my open hand. "It's all yours, boy. Enjoy!"

As I sat in my new truck, I struggled to understand how the bastard Boats, who didn't give a shit about me, had seen fit to buy me a new truck. It didn't add up, but I sure as hell wasn't going to contradict him, lest he sober up and demand it back.

I handed the keys to Manny. He grinned as he jumped into the cab and said, "I've dreamed of owning one of these ever since I've been old enough to drive. Boy, what a honey. It even has AM/FM and an eight track in it."

At the DPS office, taking the written test and then the driver's test took about an hour and a half. The old guy running the tests was a crusty old fart, and I didn't think I had passed judging by the way he grunted and sputtered. As he crawled out of the pickup, he said, "Good job, young man. I'll overlook the mediocre parallel parking. You'll get better with time. Give my best to yer uncle Boats. My wife has worked for 'im for years keepin' his Texas accounts."

When I walked out waving my license, I saw that Manny had the hood up on the truck. "Something wrong?" I asked.

"No, amigo, just wanted to look at what kind of a mill you had in there. That's a 454 cube in there."

"It ain't a standard engine?"

"You kiddin' me? That's the biggest engine Ford makes. It'll haul ass 'fore you know your foot's on the pedal."

We went back to Warden's Pipe to finish up. Manny said, "T. C., Mom told me to bring you home for supper tonight."

"Thanks, Manny, but I'd better get on home. I'm too filthy to go to someone's house for anything."

"Hey, amigo, you want to get me in Dutch with my ma? She'll skin me if she doesn't see your face right behind mine. That's what Dad and I were talking about this morning for so long. I told him about you being alone, and there's no way you're getting out of dinner at my place tonight."

As we walked toward the truck, I tossed Manny the keys. "You know where we're going," I said. "You drive."

When we reached the edge of town, Manny made two quick turns, and we found ourselves pulling into the A&W drive-in. A pretty, dark-eyed girl with long black hair came over and leaned against the truck, looking in through the driver's window. As I leaned forward to look at her, a smile spread across her face. "Manny, where'd you get the truck?"

"Belongs to my buddy T. C. You know, I told ya 'bout him."

"Hi, T. C.," she said. "Heard a lot about you."

"All bad or all good?" I asked.

"Good, of course," she said with a grin.

"Watch him close. He'll lie about other things," I quipped.

"You workin' tomorrow night, babe?"

"No. Why?"

"Thought we might take in the party over at the old quarry. All the crew is going. Starting football practice Monday."

She said, "I thought you weren't going to be able to play this year."

"T. C. and I have a plan. Tell you 'bout it later. We have to get home for supper." Then, turning to me, he said, "Hey, you want to go to the party with us?"

"Thanks, Manny, but I don't want to horn in on your date."

"No problem—got an idea. Tess, is that little blonde still workin' here?"

"She's inside."

"Why not go get her, and we'll see if we can get T. C. here fixed up on a date."

"Hey, Manny, I'm not fit to meet a girl right now. 'Sides, I don't know nothin' 'bout girls."

"Can't think of a better time to learn, amigo," he said.

Tess reappeared with a blonde, about five foot tall and bouncing across the sidewalk, her long blonde hair and breasts keeping time with her step. She was wearing short shorts that didn't require a sixteen-year-old boy to have an imagination. A short jacket hung on her shoulders, and her short-cut tank top revealed a well-developed girl that made it hard for a guy to look at her face. They walked up to the truck, and it was a while before I realized Tess was talking.

"Marylyn, you know Manny. This is his friend, T. C."

"Hi, fellas!" She smiled at me, and my tongue swelled in my mouth to the point that I couldn't talk. I leaned across Manny and stuck my hand out the window. "Glad to meet you, Marylyn," I managed.

"Like I told you, Mar, Manny and I are going out to the quarry tomorrow night for the party and thought you might go along as T. C.'s date."

I got out of the pickup and walked around to the other side. "If you don't want to go, I'll understand," I said. "I told Manny I wasn't cleaned up enough to meet a girl."

"Doesn't bother me none as long as it's honest dirt. I'd love to go. Pick me up here at whatever time you want to leave."

"I'll call you tomorrow when we know what time we'll be gettin' off," Manny said as we backed out. "'Night."

Fifteen minutes later, we pulled into the driveway in front of an old two-story house. Dogs and kids were running everywhere. A goose meandered aimlessly across the yard, squawking and hissing when a kid or dog got too close.

Jesus and a very large lady sat on the porch. Jesus got up and waved us in as we got out of the truck. "Come in, boys. Marie has your supper sittin' on the stove."

Manny hugged a couple of the kids who had quit playing and were surrounding us. "T. C., I would introduce you to all the wild animals, but you'll get to know them in time anyway. They're brothers, sisters, or cousins."

I counted about fifteen kids standing and at least five dogs. When we got to the porch, the lady pried herself from the wicker chair. "T. C., this is my wife, Marie," Jesus said.

"Glad to know you, ma'am."

"You are welcome in our home," she said. "I hope you will be comfortable. Manuel, take T. C. out to the washroom, and you boys get cleaned up for supper."

On the back of the kitchen was a big washroom with three sinks, a washer and dryer, and a big, oversized water heater.

"Dad made that water heater and installed it himself. Ma's a stickler for hot water and cleanliness, and with all my brothers and sisters, we need a lot of hot water."

As I was washing, I heard whispering behind my back. I had taken my shirt off, and as I turned, I heard a little girl say, "See, I told you he was an Anglo." The kids and the dogs were gathered in the doorway, watching us wash.

Manny turned and told them, "You kids go out and play. We'll be out in a minute."

Marie hollered, "Hurry up, boys! Supper'll be stone cold 'fore you eat it. Food's on the table, Manuel."

When we walked through the kitchen, I could see Jesus sitting at the head of a table that had to be fourteen feet long. There were benches on either side and big armchairs at the ends. All the food was placed at the opposite end of the table from Jesus.

"Sit down and dig in, T. C.," Manny said, pushing me from behind.

We sat down on the ends of the benches across from each other. I could see Manny grinning through the steam rising off platters of Marie's food. He handed me a big bowl of red beans when Marie's voice called from the kitchen, "Manny, you forgettin' something, ain't you?"

"Sorry, Ma." Manny crossed himself and bowed his head. "Bless us, O Lord, and these thy gifts, which we're about to receive from thy bounty. Through Christ our Lord, amen."

I glanced up at Marie standing in the kitchen doorway as I raised my head. She was smiling.

Fried meat, red beans, fried potatoes, ripe red tomatoes, corn on the cob, and dark gravy—I figured life didn't get better than this, at least until Marie appeared with a three-layer chocolate cake. She cut me a quarter and dropped it on a saucer that became invisible beneath it.

"I couldn't begin to eat all that, Marie," I said.

"Well, you get started, and we'll see. Never seen a boy couldn't make his way 'round a piece of my chocolate cake."

The last three bites were pure torture, but they were helped along by cream frosting and a cold glass of milk poured from a stainless steel pitcher on the table.

"You boys go out to the front porch and sit with Papa. We'll do up the dishes and join you." A girl about eighteen or nineteen walked into the kitchen as we were leaving.

"Valerie, this is Tom. Tom, my older sister, Valerie."

She nodded, bowed her head, and went on into the kitchen. "Don't give her any mind, T. C. Her and her boyfriend just had a fight, and she isn't feeling too good right now."

We sat on the porch talking for about an hour, and the sun was already surrendering control to the moon. I thanked Jesus and Marie for the food and took my leave.

Chapter 4

The First Date

The next morning, Manny was standing by the truck, all grins from ear to ear. "What's so funny?" I asked.

"Had Dad stop by Tess's place on the way in. We're supposed to meet the girls at the drive-in tonight at seven. Marylyn told Tess she thinks you're one helluva good-lookin' fella."

"You're joking, or she's blind as hell."

"Nope. She told Tess you were about the best-lookin' guy she'd seen in a long time. Didn't know you were so great, did you?"

"Come on. Let's get to work before you have me in a beauty pageant. If we're going to get off early, we've got a helluva lot of pipe to get out."

We stopped working at five that afternoon. I was getting nervous and more and more excited as the day went along. It would be my first date, and I didn't even know how to act.

As Manny was going to meet his dad, he said, "T.C., will you pick me up?"

"Sure. 'Bout six thirty?"

"Be fine, hombre."

"What you going to wear?"

"Pair of Levi's and a sport shirt."

I went home and went through ever' piece of clothing I owned—twice. When I went through the closet, I discovered ten shirts in the back I hadn't ever seen. Rosie had bought me some nice shirts, but I hadn't even noticed them before. I picked out a blue-green short-sleeved shirt, grabbed a pair of briefs and a T-shirt, and headed for the tub. After I toweled off, I wrapped the towel around my waist and went into Buck and Rosie's bathroom. I opened the medicine cabinet above the sink and found what I was looking for. I took the razor, lathered up my face, and shaved for the first time. All I had was fuzz, but I wanted to look my best. Buck had a half-used bottle of Old Spice, so I splashed some on my face. It burned like hell, but I would smell good for Marylyn.

I pulled up to Manny's at 6:28, not that I was anxious or anything. Jesus and Manny came walking out to the truck. "T. C., you and Manny behave yourselves tonight. No drinking or smoking, okay?"

"Sure, Mr. Cantu," I said. "I don't do either one."

Manny looked at me as we pulled out of the driveway. "Man, you have got to be kidding."

"About what?"

"No drinkin' or smokin'."

"No, I'm not."

"Guess I'm goin' to have to educate you, hombre."

"Not on that, you won't."

"What kind of party you think we're goin' to?" Manny asked.

"I don't know. Why?" I still didn't get what he was talking about.

"Man, it's a kegger!"

"What's that?"

"Come on, T. C. You've never seen a keg of beer?"

"No, I mean it. What's a kegger?"

"Guess you ain't kiddin', hombre. There's the girls. Man, they're sharp."

Tess had on a deep red blouse, no bra, and a pair of jeans that fit so tight there wasn't a wrinkle in sight. Marylyn had on the same kind of jeans and a pink blouse. As I stepped down out of the truck, I looked right down Marylyn's blouse and saw that her bra was missing as well.

She noticed my stare and smiled up at me. "Like 'em?"

"Oh, yeah," I said.

"I was hopin' you would." I opened the driver's door, and as I helped her up into the truck, my hand brushed her left breast. She slid across the seat, stopping behind the gear shift. She caught my hand and squeezed it as I slid in and reached for the floor shift. Manny opened the door, and Tess slid up against Marylyn. Manny struggled to close the door, squeezing himself in and punching the door lock. He directed me as we went laughing and joking out in the country.

As I pulled to a stop sign, Manny said, "Hey, girls, guess you know we have a virgin in the truck." Then he laughed.

It didn't seem funny to me—at all. I remember clearly when my pa caught me playing with myself once when I was thirteen. He wasn't mad or anything. He sat down right then and explained everything to me. He told me that for a young man, masturbating was like any other bodily function. You wouldn't go a week without taking a dump, and a young man needs to relieve himself. One thing Pa said to me after our long talk was, "Son, never go to bed with a woman if you couldn't bring her home and introduce her to your ma. It's somethin' you share with someone you love and respect. Otherwise, don't do it." He told me, "Save sex for the one you want to marry." I hadn't ever worried about being a virgin until now, and now I was just embarrassed.

Tess asked, "Oh? Where?"

"T. C. over there," said Manny, pointing at me.

"You puttin' us on, Manny?" Tess said.

"Nope," Manny answered for me. "Ain't that right, T. C.?" I turned to face the trio that was staring at me.

"If you mean I've never been to a kegger before, that's right."

"You know 'zactly what I mean, ol' buddy. I was talkin' 'bout girls."

"Well, we all have to start sometime."

Marylyn had been holding my hand during the entire conversation. She released it and slid her left hand onto my leg just above the knee. I suddenly pressed the accelerator and my other foot slipped off the clutch. The truck jumped like a jackrabbit scared from its hole as the four-barrel carb on the 454 bellowed and fell silent. We sat there in the middle of the four-way intersection with the engine stalled and all four of us laughing.

"Whoa, hot shot! You'll give us all whiplash," Manny laughed. "Thought you was a good driver, amigo."

"Well, my driver's license was a charitable contribution from my uncle Boats, who musta bribed the DPS. But like the inspector said, I'll 'get better with time.'" I fired the truck up and left about ten feet of black rubber on the road as I turned hard left and floored it. As I hunted for second gear, the sound of grinding metal subsided when I remembered to push in the clutch.

Marylyn continued to rub the inside of my thigh and occasionally crossed my groin on her way to the inside of my other thigh. It was tough to concentrate on the road. My pecker was uncomfortably hard and inconveniently bent in an unnatural position. Marylyn must have noticed because she made several passes over it, which only increased the discomfort I felt.

When we pulled into the quarry, there were about thirty cars parked all around. Couples and groups were standing around laughing and talking. The biggest group was over at the base of a rock wall. I could see that they all had paper cups in their hands, and they were filling them from a pair of kegs in the back of a pickup with racks that had "Steven's Hardware" in gold lettering across the side.

We piled out of the pickup, and I turned quickly to disguise the erection I had suffered during the ride there. Marylyn almost caught me as she grabbed my hand and pulled me to catch up with Tess and Manny, who were halfway to the kegs.

"C'mon, T. C. I'll introduce you to some of the kids you'll be going to school with." Marylyn wrapped herself around my bicep and said, "You still in school?"

"Yeah. Aren't you?"

"Yeah, I'm a junior at Le High."

"That's where I'm going."

"What grade?" she asked.

"Junior."

"I figured you'd be a senior."

"What made you think that?"

"You just seem older's all."

As we walked up, five fellows were standing with a group of farm girls a little apart from the rest of the group. A dark-skinned Mexican, my height but with long black hair, saw us approaching and yelled something at Manny in Tex-Mex that I didn't understand. The one who didn't have a girl with him said, "Hey, Manny! When you start hangin' with gringos?"

"Any damn time I want to, Sanchez."

"S'pose you got him a date with my girl too?"

"Didn't know she was your girl," Manny replied. "Heard she dumped your sorry ass last month."

"Once they mine, they always mine," Sanchez shot back. "What's the matta? Can't the gringo talk?"

Manny took my arm. "Come on, T. C. Let's grab a beer."

As we headed for the kegs, Sanchez called to Marylyn, "You come over here, girl."

Manny kept hold of my arm and led Marylyn and me on toward the beer. "Don't pay attention to that idiot, T. C. He's a loser if there ever was one. Did you go out with him, Marylyn?"

"I did for a while, till I figured out he likes to hurt people. If he don't get his way, he can get real mean."

"We going to have trouble with him, Manny?" I asked.

"Not as long as I'm around, we won't. He'd rather wrestle an ape than monkey around with me. When I was in fifth grade and he was in sixth, he and his buddies tried to steal Valerie's and my lunches. We kicked the shit out of all three of 'em. Then a couple of years ago, when I was on the freshman team, he picked a fight with me behind the locker room. I worked him over, and since then he has stayed out of my way—'cept for now. Don't worry. If he steps outta line, I'll handle him."

"Nobody has to fight for me, Manny," I said.

"You ever been in a fight, T. C.?"

"Sure, when I was a kid. Always got the crap kicked out of me 'cause I was so small."

"Hey, let's not look for trouble, boys. We're here to have fun," Tess said.

Manny filled four Styrofoam cups with beer and handed them out. After the first sip, I decided I didn't like beer. It was bitter and burned the back of my mouth. "You like this stuff, Manny?"

"Sure, amigo. This and a couple of sticks of Mary Jane and you feel like a king. 'Sides, if you have a girl that's willin', you can make love all night. Ain't that right, Tess?"

"Cut it out, Manny. You'll give T. C. the wrong idea 'bout me." She grabbed him by the neck.

"What idea, girl? You a woman, I'm a man—you just do what comes natural."

I turned to Marylyn and said, "You sure are being quiet."

"I been watching Sanchez, and he keeps makin' gestures at me."

"Well, don't pay any attention to him. There won't be any problem unless you want there to be."

"I don't."

We stood around talking. Each of my three friends drank about six cups of beer. They were laughing and telling jokes. We found a spot between the rocks close to the water, and a bunch of kids were skinny dipping. Hell, the girls were buck naked, and so were the guys. I thought, *We aren't in Kansas anymore, Toto.* I had never seen a naked woman before in my life, except my sister and she was a little girl. There was nothing little about these girls. I guess I knew girls had hair in their private parts, but I could see it for real now. Someone had turned on a radio, and several couples were dancing on a big rock shelf. Some were making out, and their hands were all over each other. I was way out of my league.

Marylyn was sitting real close to me and had her arm wrapped around mine, holding my hand. "You're a very strange boy," she said.

"Why's that?" I diverted my eyes from the naked girls coming out of the water.

"You haven't tried to kiss me or feel anything. Something wrong with me?"

"No, you're one of the prettiest girls I've ever seen." I felt my face flush with embarrassment at being caught looking at the naked girls and with the growing belief that my innocence and ignorance were on display.

"Manny was right, wasn't he?"

"About what?" I pretended not to know where this conversation was going.

"You've never been with a girl before, have you?"

"No, I've never been out with a girl before."

"Turn toward me."

I followed her directions, and she wrapped her arms around my neck and brought her mouth up to mine. I couldn't believe the sensations. Her perfume possessed me before her lips. Both were soft and warm pressing against my lips. My skin tingled. She held her lips against mine for the longest time, and I realized I was holding my breath. I broke away, gasping for air.

Marylyn laughed. "Silly, you're supposed to breathe through your nose."

"Let's try it again," I said. I put my arms around her and brought my lips to hers.

She pulled back and said, "Relax your lips. Just let them be natural. You'll enjoy it more." *Relax?* How in hell could I relax? Every muscle in my body was at attention, and the animal in me had escaped from its cage and was running lose, refusing to go back in. I was about to explode.

Manny and Tess had gone to dance, and by the time they got back, we were in the middle of our second kiss.

"Look at that, Tess. He's not as slow as I figured. Hey, you two, come up for air." As we parted, they handed us more beer. Manny sat down next to me, pulled two cigarettes from his pocket, and handed one to me.

"Don't smoke, Manny. You know that."

"Hey, man, these are joy toys."

Marylyn reached over and took one. "I'll show you how, T. C." She leaned across me, and Manny lit it.

The smell was acrid, like burning trash. "Try it," Marylyn said as she held it to my mouth.

"I don't think so. I don't smoke."

"Just once. Here, let me show you. Watch. Take a deep puff. Then inhale and hold your breath for as long as you can, and then slowly exhale." She pushed the reefer into my mouth.

I drew a deep breath and then exploded into a coughing fit. I was choking and couldn't catch my breath. No sooner did I regain the ability to breathe than my head started spinning. Everything got hazy; my eyes wouldn't focus. Between the tears filling my eyes and my lack of balance, I thought I was on a ship in rough seas. The three of them looked like they were fading in and out of a cloud bank.

Manny said, "You okay, amigo?"

"Dizzy."

"Other than that, how you feel?"

"Great. Feel warm all over."

"Try it again, amigo. Only this time, don't take so much smoke in your mouth."

The second puff was a lot easier. I still coughed, but the glow was beginning to spread all over. I continued to draw on the joint for twenty minutes as we passed it around. Finally, when I stood up, I felt like I was walking on a cloud. Marylyn never let go of my arm. Things were coming into and going out of focus, and I was euphoric. One minute things were clear, and the next I disappeared into a cloud.

"Sit back down, T. C." Marylyn guided me to the ground. "Let's finish the toke, and then we can go dance."

After the fourth round, anything that anyone said to me was funny. I would take a puff and then lean over and kiss Marylyn. We would exhale in each other's mouths. By the time we finished, I was the happiest human being around. We sat there necking and talking.

"Manny says you're a good football player."

"Oh, sure," I said. "I'm a star."

"No kidding? Are you going out for the team?"

"Yeah. Start practice Monday mornin'."

"I'm going out for the cheerleading squad again this year. Won't make it, though."

"Why not?"

"I've been tryin' to get on it since the seventh grade, but the instructor never picks me."

"Ever ask her why?"

"No."

"Well, this year, if they don't pick you, I would walk right up and ask, 'Are other girls prettier or smarter than me?'"

"No," Marylyn said.

"I'm not very old and I'm not very smart, but this I do know—you never get anything by wishin' for it. Either work for it or fight for it. That's the only way you get it."

Marylyn said something else, but I couldn't hear. I had started laughing.

"What you laughin' at?"

"I don't know. Everything's funny. Every time someone says somethin', I can't help laughin' at it." Five minutes later, all four of us were giggling and laughing regardless of what was said.

"Come on, T. C. Let's go dance," Marylyn said. We walked up to the rock ledge where people were dancing to the Righteous Brothers' "You've Lost That Lovin' Feelin'." I'd never danced before. Like all boys, I had tried out the moves I'd seen on TV in the privacy of my room, but I had never actually danced with a girl. Everything was so hazy anyway that I moved right out and we started in.

Marylyn was really good so I just tried to copy her. Every time we would get close, she would smile up at me.

When a commercial came on the radio, she moved in and said, "You're pretty good. Where'd you learn to dance like that?"

"Just practiced in my room."

"Without a partner?"

"Yep."

"My girlfriend and I have been doing that ever since I was ten."

"You're sure a lot better than me."

"Had a lot more practice."

Just then, Linda Ronstadt came on, singing a slow song. Marylyn came into my arms, stuck her head under my chin, and wrapped her arms around my waist, pushing a hand into each of my back pockets. It wasn't really dancing, but we swayed together, moving slowly in a tight circle. It was so nice and relaxing as the song wound to an end. Marylyn turned her face up to mine and pulled our lips together. Her tongue slipped into my mouth and explored. It was hot, and I felt that heat radiate through my body.

My arm was almost jerked out of my body as I was spun around. I felt a flash of pain on the left side of my face, and I saw the knife just as it started back toward me. Sanchez held it in his right hand. A group of girls screamed as I spun toward him.

Just as he lunged at me, Manny struck him in the back of the head with a rock, and he dropped to his hands and knees. He was trying to get up when Manny kicked him on the side of the head, and he was down for good.

Marylyn pulled the handkerchief from my back pocket that she had been fingering earlier and pressed it to my face. It burned like hell. My group led me to my truck, and Manny asked for the keys. I fumbled for them in my pocket and dropped them in the dirt, but Manny picked them up and then pushed us all into the pickup. My face was on fire, but every time I tried to touch it, Marylyn would push my hand away.

"Manny, you have another handkerchief?" she pleaded.

"I have Kleenex," Tess replied. Manny handed her a second handkerchief. He turned the key, and the 454 roared to life. He stuck his foot in it, and all four barrels came up like thundering cannons on a battlefield. We were driving so damn fast that the telephone poles clicked by like pickets in a fence. The next thing I knew, we were near a large white building, and I saw the neon

"Emergency Room" sign glowing above my head. We went in, and there was a fuss as the nurse peeled back the blood-drenched handkerchiefs that Marylyn held to my face. The nurse took me into a large room with beds separated by curtains and laid me down. I heard her tell someone to "get a doctor in here, stat."

The nurse took a packet from a chest next to the bed and started washing and swabbing my face. The minute that stuff hit my face, volcanic pain erupted. Fire and blood drenched one bandage after another.

"I know it burns and stings," she said, "but I have to get it clean. That's a very nasty cut. How'd it happen?"

"We were playing tag football, and he ran into the mirror on a pickup. It broke and cut him," Manny explained. I hadn't noticed, but Manny had walked up while she was cleaning my face.

"Looks like a knife or razor to me," the nurse said to Manny while looking over the rim of her glasses. "It's too straight to be a piece of glass."

"Well, that's what did it."

A young man about twenty-six years old and wearing whites walked in. "Get me a suture kit, nurse, with ought two catgut if you can find it," he barked. "Nasty cut. You know it's going to leave a scar. I'll try to make it as small as I can, but there is going to be a scar." As he picked up a syringe, he said, "This will sting a bit for just a minute or two."

Behind Manny in the corridor, I saw the nurse talking to two uniformed police officers.

Manny turned, saw them, and stood up. As he walked out to them, I heard him say, "Hello, Dave. What you doin' out here?" I listened intently, propped up on the hospital bed with the curtains drawn on either side. Straight ahead, I could see Manny and the cops talking. Manny leaned back with one foot pressed against the wall behind him. He was talking with his hands, pointing and gesturing.

"Had a call about that kid Gurley in there being cut up," one of the officers said.

"Look, Dave. I told 'em how he got cut."

"Manny, this is Officer Perez, my partner."

"Glad to know you," Manny said.

"We have to talk to the doctor, and then we want to talk to you." They came into the cubicle where the doc was working me over. "We got a couple of questions, Doc."

"Just a minute," the doctor said. "I've got a couple more stitches. Would you mind waiting just outside? This isn't a passageway through here."

"Sure, Doc."

"Now, Tom, this will be very sore tomorrow and Sunday," the doctor said to me. "I'm going to give you a tube of salve and some pain pills. Take the pills as needed for pain. Put the salve on in the morning and evening. Another thing—don't pick at it. The less infection we get, the smaller the scar. You can take the bandage off Sunday night. You work?"

I nodded.

"If you're going to be around a lot of dust, grease, or dirt, keep it covered up. The more you can keep it uncovered, the better off you'll be, but don't get dirt in it. Nurse, put a butterfly bandage on there, not too tight, though. The more help those stitches have, the better. Tom, you come back and see me next Thursday. Here's my card. It has my office address on it. About five."

"Say, Doc, I'm going out for football. Will it be all right?"

"Sure, but no contact until I give you the word. You're built like a football player. Looks like you're in great shape." As the nurse started putting the bandages on, the doc headed out and the police officers stopped him.

"What do you think, Doc?" one asked.

"About what?"

"The kid in there. Was he cut with a knife?"

"I don't know. His friend says he cut it by running into a mirror on a pickup. It could be; I don't know. Seems to be an awful nice kid, so I think I'll take his friend's word for it."

"May we have your name and address, Doc?"

"Certainly, here's my card. However, I intend to enter it as an accident on the medical record."

"Thank you, Dr. Martin."

Manny walked into the cubicle as the doctor was walking away, and the cops were right behind him.

Officer Perez asked, "Your name's Tom Gurley, and is the address given here a correct address?"

I looked at Manny, who said, "Yeah, that's his address. I filled out the forms."

"All right, Gurley, you want to tell me what happened?"

"It's like Manny told you. We were playing tag football, and I ran into the mirror on the side of a pickup."

"Your pickup?"

"No, somebody else's."

"Where at?"

"I don't know. I haven't been here for that long. Some park on the west side of town."

"What park, Manny?" Dave asked.

"Detweiler, on Grand and Park."

"Funny, we drove past there about an hour ago and there wasn't anybody there. Sure this didn't happen out at the quarry at a keg party?"

"Don't know anything about it, Dave," Manny lied.

"Another funny thing, Manny—your pal Sanchez is in the other receiving room. Got a knot on the back of his head the size of a baseball. Said he dove on a rock out at the quarry."

"Maybe he did. Don't know. He's always been kinda stupid."

"If the knot was on his forehead, I might believe it, but on the back of the head? He also looks like he's been kicked in the face. Got laces imprinted on the side of his face."

"Well, that would be an improvement to his looks, ya ask me. Like I said, Dave, I don't know nothin' about it."

"Okay, Manny, you guys can go on home. We will probably want to talk to you later."

"You didn't get his address, Dave," Perez said.

"I date his sister. Know exactly where he lives."

The girls were sitting in the waiting room when we entered. Marylyn ran over and hugged me. Blood was all over her pretty pink blouse. Her hands and arms were clean, and I could see where she had tried to wash the blood off her blouse and jeans. "Tommy, I'm so sorry this happened. It's all my fault."

"Why yours?"

"I knew Sanchez would be out there. I never should have gone."

"It's not your fault. It's mine. Let's just forget it. Let me take one of these pain pills, and let's get out of here."

As we were driving down the street, Manny said, "You hungry, T. C.?"

"No, but I'm sure thirsty. Wherever you want to go is fine with me."

"Sure you don't want to go home?"

"Heck, no. That pain pill did the trick. I feel great."

"Marylyn, you want to go home and change clothes?" Manny asked.

"Sure would like to. I'm a mess."

"Sure are a pretty mess, though," I said. She was sitting there with both hands folded up in her lap. She still looked like she wanted to cry. I leaned down and kissed her on the cheek. "Come on, Shorty, give me a smile." The corners of her mouth trembled. I said it again. "Come on, Shorty, give me a smile."

She glanced up at me, and her blue eyes filled with water. "Oh, Tommy, I feel so lousy."

"Hey, come on. Don't spoil it. I have the first date of my life with a very pretty girl, and she cries. Come on, Short Stuff, cut it out. Give me one of those super smackers of yours. As my ol' pappy used to say, 'Kiss me, lady. I'm thirsty.'"

She giggled, raised up, and kissed me. "You know you're a nut. That didn't make no sense at all."

"I know, but I must be good, lookin' at the price us nuts is bringin' today."

We pulled into a four-plex parking lot. "Let me out, and I'll go change," Marylyn said.

"Need any help?" I offered.

"No, but you can come in if you want to. Mom's at work." She took a key out of her pocket as we approached the door and handed it to me. It was a two-bedroom apartment with a small kitchen, living room, and bath.

"Take a chair. I'll be right out."

"Have anything in your fridge to drink?"

"Should be. Take a look." She headed for the bedroom door on the right. I heard a door open and a drawer slam as I opened the refrigerator. There were a couple of Cokes, some Tab, and a 7-Up. I pulled out a Coke. "Where's the opener?"

"In the drawer on the right side of the sink."

I pulled the drawer and found the opener, popped the top off the bottle, and heard someone moving behind me. I turned, and there was Marylyn, finishing with the buttons on her blouse. I felt myself blush as her breasts disappeared under her blouse.

"I'm not a very modest person, T. C.," she said.

"Who is these days?"

"No, I don't mean it in that way. I've only known you for a little over a day. I want to go out with you again, but after tonight, I don't have much chance, do I?"

"Look, Marylyn—"

"Call me Mar. I only let people I really like call me that, and T. C., I really like you. You're different from anybody I ever been with."

"You mean dumber than a bag of rocks, don't you?"

"No, nice. You are the nicest boy I have been out with."

"Fine, if I call you Mar, you call me T. C. or Tommy, whichever you prefer."

She finished buttoning her blouse, raised up on her tiptoes, put her arms around my neck, and gave me a slow, warm, lingering kiss. We stood there looking at each other. "You know, Mar, Manny was right. You are the first girl I've dated or kissed."

"I knew that. Most girls can tell."

"I would like to ask you a question, being so dumb about these things."

"You're not dumb, just inexperienced. What you wanna know?"

"That's the word, *inexperienced*. When you kiss a girl, what do you do with your hands?"

She just laughed, the first real laugh I'd heard from her. "Just anything the lady will let you do, Tom. Just anything she will allow." She grabbed my hand. "Let's go before they start gettin' the wrong idea."

Manny and Tess were in a tight clinch when we opened the door of the truck. When the dome light came on, Manny's hands were under Tess's blouse. Both turned red as Manny's hands reappeared.

"We thought you guys were spendin' the night in there," Manny said. "We were just makin' use of our time."

"Yeah, noticed that," I said. "I wouldn't be here now, but Mar ran me off."

"Liar," Mar said as she stuck her finger in my ribs.

"Hey, T. C., give me a drink of that Coke," Manny said. "That smoke made me thirsty."

"Sure. Let's go over to the drive-in and get some more."

"Might as well. We spend enough time waiting on people there; we should let somebody wait on us," Tess said as she straightened her blouse.

Manny had no sooner pulled into the drive-in than the truck was surrounded by people who had been at the quarry.

"Hey, Manny, how's the boy?" a rather plump and round-faced Mexican asked.

"Fine, Chico," Manny answered.

"What happened at the hospital?"

"Couple cops showed up askin' questions, 'bout an hour ago. T. C., come out here. I want you to meet some fellas. Chico, meet T. C."

I stuck out my hand, and he grabbed it thumbs up.

"That's Harry, Malin, Chris, and the big Mexican bandito over there is Pedro Gonzales. Get to know him real well. He plays tackle for the team."

"Hey, guys." I knew it would take me a while to keep track of all of these faces. The good news was that they were all friendly. Harry reminded me of somebody, but I couldn't quite place him.

Chico asked, "You goin' to play ball at Le High?"

"Hope to, if I can make the team."

"If you are any good at all, you will. We won't have much talent this year."

"I don't believe that," I said. I knew that Manny was a horse, and the guys I was talking to were large enough to pull a hay wagon.

"Chico plays outside linebacker and tight end. Harry there is the coach's son, offensive guard." Clearly, that's where I recognized Harry from. He looked a lot like Coach Baker, except Harry had a smile; Coach didn't.

"Chris plays offense and defense, don't you?" Manny slapped Chris on the back, and it was solid. Chris was huge. He looked like a pyramid turned upside down, broad at the shoulders, narrow at the waist, and thighs like oak trees. When he spoke, his voice was deep, a slow-talking baritone.

"I will this year. Didn't play enough last year to break a sweat. Goin' to be out there Monday mornin'?" Chris asked.

"If you're going to play, you'd better be," Harry chimed in. "That ol' man of mine made me sit out two games last year 'cause I missed two practices with the flu. He's a stickler for making practice."

Malin was thick, tall, and soft-spoken, the oldest son of the Methodist minister in town. He didn't drink or smoke, but the story was that he was a wild one with the ladies. He was a tight end and didn't speak much at all. He said his dad did enough talking for the entire town.

"T. C., what happened out there?" Harry asked. "You never did say. None of us knew anything was goin' on till we heard the women scream." Harry pressed for an answer.

"I don't really know myself. First thing I knew, the guy called Sanchez cut me with a knife. I looked up just in time to see Manny there clock him with a rock."

We piled out of the truck and went into Pepi's restaurant while the girls stayed back in the truck talking.

When all the guys had piled into a couple of booths and a nearby table, Harry continued the inquiry. "I was going to ask why, but seeing who you're out with, I know the why." Harry grinned. "I didn't think they were that tight, but Sanchez went fuckin' nuts." Harry was so gleeful that he looked like he was about to pee his pants.

"They weren't as far as she was concerned," Chico said. "She was the first gringo girl he went out with. To him, she's a status symbol. You'd better keep a lookout for Sanchez, amigo."

I pointed to my face. "I already found that out." When I tried to laugh my face erupted in pain.

"You know Sanchez is on the football team, don't you?" Chico grinned and dropped his hand into a basket of fries that just seemed to appear from the back.

"No, Manny never mentioned it." I started to realize that Sanchez was going to be a regular pain in my ass.

Malin finally spoke up. "Well, he is. Plays first string, left half-back and full-back. He's short but stocky and weighs about one eighty. Heavier than you think."

"Can't help it," I said. "I have to play football, so he will have to get used to me." I reached for some fries and then thought better of it when the salt from the fries came in contact with my cut.

"I doubt that," Harry said. "I've been going to school with him since fifth grade. He is one of the hardest-headed, meanest bastards I've ever met. Ain't that right, Pedro?"

"Who's a bastard?" Pedro asked as he came to the table with three more baskets of fries.

"Sanchez. I said he's a hardheaded, mean bastard."

"Boy, you got that right. Like a pit bull, he don't give up. Speak of the devil, look who's here." Pedro stepped back and pointed to the door. I looked up just in time to see Sanchez come through the crowd. I noticed Manny slip in beside me.

Sanchez stuck a finger in Manny's chest, pushing him back into the side of the booth. "Understand you're the son of a bitch who hit me with a rock."

"Sure am. Too damned bad I didn't kill you, you mangy bushwhackin' cocksucker. Not even man enough to take somebody on face to face." Manny slapped his hand away.

"Don't worry about it, Manny. You will get yours."

"If I do, it will be just like you, you queer motherfucker, to do it from behind. You ain't got the balls to take me on by yourself. See you brought your gang with ya."

"Yeah. Want you to meet Helio. Comes from Hawaii. Played first-string quarterback for the state team over there, and I talked him into coming to Le High. Told him he wouldn't have any competition for quarterback. As for you, gringo," Sanchez said as he turned and stepped toward me, "I'll take care of you when your brother there doesn't have any rocks."

"Whenever you're ready, dipshit," I said. "Next time, though, grow a pair of balls and don't be such a fucking coward. Come at me face to face, you backstabbing prick!"

"I'll show you a coward!" Sanchez yelled. His hand slipped into his pocket and was halfway out when Pedro laid his hand on Sanchez's shoulder.

"You don't want to do that, amigo. The last time you started trouble in here, they almost closed Dad down. I told you then and I'm telling you now, no more." Pedro was convincing. His left hand covered Sanchez's entire right shoulder, and his right hand had Sanchez by the wrist in a grip that kept the blood from flowing to his hand.

Sanchez spun toward Pedro, pushed his hand back into his pocket, and pushed Pedro in the chest with his other hand. Pedro didn't budge but released his hold on Sanchez. Sanchez just glared at me. "Understand you're goin' out for football. I really hope so." With a wave of a single finger on his right hand, Sanchez was gone. His buddies followed him like a gaggle of geese in single file out the door and around to the other side of my truck.

Marylyn was sitting there with her arm out the window, and he laid his hand on her arm. She jerked it away as I headed toward the truck. I heard him tell her, "You'll get yours, bitch."

I started after him, but someone had me by the shoulder. I turned to see Pedro's huge paw gripping me. He squeezed, and I realized that escape was impossible—trying wouldn't be very smart either. I couldn't have done anything anyway.

The guys and gals went inside and gathered at two tables. Joking, laughing, and telling lies masked as stories, it was the first time I had been included in anything in my life, and I enjoyed it. Everyone there accepted me at face value, and I was included in the practical jokes too. It felt great.

About twelve, Manny said, "We better go. We still have two days of hard hauling before Monday."

"Manny, the hell you do!" Chico popped off. "We know what you want to do—go off somewhere and neck."

"Neck, hell," Harry bellowed. "Manny's a greater lover than that. He don't neck; he makes romance."

"Kiss my Mexican ass, Harry," Manny said with a grin. "You're just jealous."

"See there, romance. That's all that Latin lover dreams of." The jeers, whoops, and laughter followed us to the truck. Manny drove for about twenty minutes and then pulled into a long, tree-lined gravel road. He drove down it for about a mile and pulled off onto a small side road, killed the engine, and slid out of the driver's seat, pulling Tess behind him. They walked around to our side of the truck, reached in, and pulled a blanket from behind the seat.

"Back in a little while, amigo."

"Sure. We'll be here," I said.

Mar said, "How you feelin', Tom? Your face hurt?"

"No, I took another pain killer back at the drive-in. Feels fine."

"I can't see your face, sittin' here beside you this way. That bandage hides it."

"Turn around and put your feet up on the seat." I reached out and pulled her feet across my lap.

"That will be even worse," she said. But she didn't resist.

As soon as she turned, I put my hands under her arms and lifted her up on my lap. "That better?"

"Much."

Her face was level with mine. I kept my arm around her waist as I kissed her.

She turned and pressed against me, and then she leaned back and looked into my eyes. "Tom, I wish this was my first date like it is yours."

"Man, I don't. That would be horrible. Imagine neither one of us knowing what to do. Be kind of clumsy, wouldn't it?"

"You know what I mean."

"Think I do, but it doesn't matter now. We like each other, and I want to go with you, Shorty."

"Do you, Tom?"

"Sure. How about we take in a show tomorrow? Then we'll see what we can do on Sunday."

"I have to go to church on Sunday morning. That's one thing my mother insists on."

"That's fine. I have to haul pipe till about two anyway."

She reached up, circled my neck, pulled me to her, and kissed me. She drew back and then pressed her lips to my cheek. "I've gone with you for a day and feel like you have been part of me my whole life."

"I hope we can be good friends," I said clumsily.

"I think it will be more than that, Tommy."

"Mar, the most important thing is loyalty and friendship. Before anything else can happen, these are first."

"You are strange."

"Why?"

"We've been together for over six hours now, and you're sittin' here talkin' 'bout friendship instead of me having to fight you off."

"Why would I want to make you fight me off? Like you said, I can put my hands any place you let me. I've never had sex with anyone, and I have a very funny personal code: respect, love, tenderness. I saw what those things meant to my ma and pa, and ain't nothing like it. Mar, I had wonderful parents, and my pa taught me to save sex for the one I want to marry."

"I don't remember much about my dad 'cept Mama told me he was a military advisor and got killed in Vietnam in '61," Marylyn said. "Mom raised me. When I got to be fourteen, she and I went down to the church, and she had the minister talk to me. The next day when I came home from school, she handed me this packet of pills. She told me, 'I know what it's like being a young girl. I am not givin' you permission to go out and go to bed with every boy you date. I want you to finish school, Mar, and get a good education. Please don't wind up like me, a waitress and part-time bartender. It's an honest living but not what I want for you.'"

"You ever use any of them?" I said with an obvious interest.

"I don't think I want to answer that, Tom. I'm not being dishonest, but I want you to get to know me a lot better. Then if you want to ask me, I'll tell you."

"Hello in the truck. We're coming in." Manny and Tess were approaching with the blanket over their shoulders. Manny tucked the blanket back behind the seat.

"Turn on the light, honey," Tess said. "I need to fix my hair." Manny switched the light on, and Tess began to comb her hair and put fresh lipstick on. She straightened her blouse and belt. There was no doubt about what they had been doing.

"That's a nice shade of lipstick on you, Manny," I remarked as we pulled back out on to the highway. We dropped Mar off first and then Tess. When we were back on the road, Manny asked, "You want to spend the night at my place, amigo?"

"Heck, uh, I'll go on home. Bein' as your dad won't be going into town in the mornin', want to drop me off and then come get me in the morning?"

"Ain't you worried about lettin' me keep your truck overnight?"

"Why—you plannin' on wreckin' it?"

"No, I just assumed—"

"Don't," I interrupted. "I know you'll take care of it just as well as I would, probably better. So drop me off. I need another pain pill."

I took another pill, set the alarm, and crashed into bed. Sure had been a long day.

Chapter 5

Fussin' and Fightin'

Manny woke me up the next morning pounding on my window. I yelled, "I'm up! Come to the back door."

"Man, I thought something had happened to you," he said. "I been beatin' on that door and window for ten minutes."

"Guess it must have been all those pills I took last night. Come on in. My head is bustin'. Let me take another pill, and we can stop and get something to eat. Funny, I'm sick, but I'm hungry. Ever been that way?"

"Nope. Your face looks a bit swollen behind the bandage. Let's take a look."

He pulled the bandage off. "No, it looks okay. Just a bit of swelling around the eye."

"I forgot that salve the doc gave me in the jockey box of the truck. Would you get it for me while I get dressed?" I walked into the bathroom and, without thinking, splashed water on my face. It felt like hot coals hitting my face, the fire clawing up and down my face like a hysterical cat. I had a cut running from the corner of my eye almost to the corner of my mouth, and the puckers around the stitches were swollen, red, and inflamed. I was up to counting eighteen stitches when Manny walked in. I put the salve on and found some gauze in

Rosie's medicine cabinet to make a bandage, along with some tape. Manny made up the bandage and taped it to my face.

We stopped at Pepi's restaurant and had breakfast before going on to work. About three, as we were loading our fourth truck for the day, I told Manny, "Let's stop at the A&W on the way out and grab a bite."

"What about the truck?"

"Park it in the street."

"We might get a ticket," Manny complained.

"So what? Boats can afford it."

"You kind of go for Marylyn, don't you?"

"She's nice," I said.

"Don't get too serious about her."

"I'm not serious. She's just a nice-looking girl and fun to be with."

"Okay, T. C., but take it slow," Manny said.

"You know somethin' I should know?"

"Just hearsay—she's been around."

"What do you mean, 'she's been around'?"

"You know, T. C."

"If I knew, I wouldn't be askin'."

"Look, buddy, let's just forget it. I should keep my Hispanic mouth shut."

"No, you said it," I said. "I want to know what you know."

"Look, T. C., all I know is what I heard from Sanchez and locker room talk last year at the high school."

"So?"

I could tell Manny was embarrassed by my attitude. He wouldn't look at me and his voice was edgy; I could tell he wished he had never started it. "Manny, I had a buddy once in the fifth grade. He was supposed to be tough, a liar, and a thief and had been in trouble all his life. Supposedly he was white trash. After I got to know him, I discovered that he never stole or lied, he had nothing, and nobody believed in him. He was a good friend. My folks and I thought a lot of him. I'll bet Mar is the same way if given a chance."

"Fine, T. C. I'm sorry I said anything."

"My pa taught me to take everyone at face value," I explained. "They treat me right, and I'll treat them right."

When we got to the A&W, there were only two cars in the parking lot, so we pulled into the far end of the lot and took up a couple of spaces with the truck. Manny blew the horn, and Tess came out of the dining area.

"Hey, what you guys doing here?"

"The two best-lookin' guys in town came out to see the two best-lookin' girls," Manny said. "Where's Marylyn?"

"She was in the restroom when I came out. You guys want something to eat?"

"Couple of burgers and a shake, double order of fries and onion rings," Manny said.

"Only make mine a cheddar cheeseburger with bacon, and tell Mar I'd like to see her," I said.

"I don't have to tell her. Here she comes."

I had thought she was pretty before, but as she walked toward us in the red and black vest with a white blouse and hot pants, everything about her looked perfect. She worked her way around the truck, and when her eyes caught mine, her face erupted in a coy smile. She hopped up on the truck's running board. I reached out, caught her by the arm, and held on to her.

"How's the face, Tommy?" she asked.

"Feels sore, but it will be okay. Is our date still on for tonight?"

"Sure is. What time?"

I turned to Manny. "What time you think we can finish that load out to Blackwell?"

"Should be home by six thirty, don't you think?"

"Hope so. How about eight?" I asked Marylyn. "I'll pick you up at your place. Only, don't be mad if I'm a little late."

"I won't be. I better get back to work. A car just pulled into my station. See you later." She squeezed my hand as she bounced down off the running board. She looked over her shoulder and smiled as she hurried off to the knucklehead honking his horn at her station.

Tess, in the meantime, was on her way out with our order. We paid her and turned the truck around to drive out. Just then, an old, beat-up pickup pulled up to turn in, and Sanchez leaned across the driver and yelled, "See you Monday, gringo! If you have the guts to show up."

Manny flipped him off, and we pulled out into the street. "You're going to have a lot of trouble with that asshole, T. C."

"Can't be helped. It won't come from me. Let's get busy. Got a lot of work to do and a hot date tonight."

We finished up two loads and pulled back into the yard at six. My head and face hurt like hell, so I took a couple of Doc's magic pills.

"Where you and Marylyn going tonight?" Manny asked.

"Thought we'd take in a show. Why—you want to tag along with Tess?"

"Yeah, Papa always lets me use the station wagon on Saturday nights."

"What you going to do?"

"We always go out to Mama Z's at Central Highlands."

"What is it, a beer joint?"

"Yeah, but she has a big platform for dancing out back, and all the kids go there to dance."

"I'm not old enough to get in," I said.

"Most of the kids there ain't either, but being as the dance floor is outside, you don't have to worry about it. The band plays for donations. They pass the hat a couple of times a night, and everyone's happy."

"I'll talk to Mar. If she wants to go, we may do that."

"We goin' to work tomorrow?" he asked.

"I think we should. We're way ahead, but the further we can get out, then the less we'll have to do after football starts."

"Fine. See you later."

When I pulled up to the house, my head was killing me. I went in and lay down on the sofa. I was asleep in a minute. I woke up slowly and thought the pounding was still in my head, but then I realized that it was somebody at the door. Mar was standing there, and I could see a car at the curb. "What time is it, Mar?" I looked down at my watch. It was a quarter to eight.

"Mom had to go to work early, so I had her drop me by early. You don't mind, do you?"

"Heck, no. Come on in."

"You come out and meet my mother."

"I'm not cleaned up. I was taking a nap."

"Don't matter. She doesn't like me comin' over here to your house. She don't trust young men."

We walked out to a 1955 Ford Country Squire station wagon, green with wood sides. It was freshly washed and waxed, and the whitewall tires glistened in the waning sunlight. Behind the wheel was a beautiful blonde in her forties, clearly Mar's mom, though their age difference wasn't that prominent. She wasn't wearing a lick of makeup, but she was beautiful, with her pearl-white arm resting on the door and a bright white smile. "Tom, I want you to meet my mom, Pauline. Mom, this is Tommy."

"I'm glad to meet you, Tom."

"I'm glad to meet you, Mrs. ..." I turned to Mar.

She laughed. "It's Birchley, Mrs. Birchley."

"Mrs. Birchley," I stumbled.

"Call me Pauline, Tom, and I'm glad to meet you. Sorry about what happened last night."

"Can't be helped now. I'll get over it."

"I have to be off to work. You kids have fun and behave yourselves."

Mar leaned in and kissed Pauline on the cheek. "We will, Mom. You drive careful."

"Nice to have met you, Pauline," I said.

"You too, Tom." And with that she drove off.

"Sure glad you decided to come over, Mar. I would never have woke up otherwise."

"I had to get away from our place."

"Any special reason?" I asked.

"Sanchez said he was coming over."

"You invite him?"

"No, he just thinks he's somethin' special and doesn't like a girl to dump him."

"Oh, let me take a fast shower. Turn on the radio and make yourself at home. I'll hurry."

"No rush."

I went into the bedroom, taking off my shirt and T-shirt as I went, and then turned and went back into the living room. Mar had opened up the cabinet stereo and was leaned over, moving the dials. The squeak and squawk of the stations as she turned the dial hid my approach. She was dressed in white pants and a deep dark-blue blouse.

I reached out and touched her, and she jumped straight up and whirled around. "You startled me!"

"Sorry. I wanted to ask you—Manny wanted us to come out to Mama Z's. Did you want to do that or go to a show?"

"Whatever you want to do is fine with me. I love to dance."

"Fine, then I'll wear a pair of Levi's. I was going to dress up for the occasion."

"No need for me, Tom." She stood there looking at me with a half-smile on her face. "How old are you?"

"Sixteen."

"That's what Tess told me. I'm seventeen."

"Yeah, I know. Does it make a difference?"

"Not to me. You look older. You have a better build than most grown men. I've never seen anyone muscled up like you are."

"It's just from working."

While we were talking, she stepped close to me and ran her fingers up the ripples on my stomach and across my shoulders, and her hands came together behind my neck. I leaned down and kissed her. Her mouth opened, and she drew my tongue into her mouth. I could feel a strange sensation running through my body: half shiver and half electricity. My arms tightened around her.

She pulled back a ways. "You're hurting me, Tommy."

"Sorry. I didn't realize how tight I was holding you."

She stopped my apology by putting her finger on my lips. "I think you better take your shower and get ready."

When I came out of the shower, I pulled a pair of white Levi's from the closet, dug in the back of my closet, and found a dark blue cowboy shirt nearly the color of Mar's blouse, with mother-of-pearl snap buttons. That Rosie had an eye for clothes. I was standing in front of the mirror when I noticed that the bandage had slipped off my face. I went back into the bathroom to get the material to put on a new one. My shirt wasn't buttoned, and I hadn't buttoned my Levi's all the way yet, which exposed my white boxer shorts.

"You dressed yet?" Mar asked.

"Yeah, come on in." I was watching the bedroom door when she walked in. The smile on her lips slowly disappeared, and her face dissolved in sadness.

"That's a horrible-looking cut, Tom."

I turned and looked in the mirror. Some of the redness was gone, but it was swollen more than it had been that morning. "It looks better than it did."

She saw the bandage and scissors and came into the room. "Here, sit down near the head of the bed." She placed the bandage on the nightstand next to her and started cutting a piece of gauze.

"You have to put some of that salve on first," I said. "Here, you'll get it all over your hands. Let me do it." I started to rise, but she placed her hand on my chest.

"Not so fast there, cowboy."

Her touch was soft and feathery when she applied the salve. I kept watching her face. I could tell she was being extra careful by her changing expressions. The closer I got to her, the more beautiful she was. Her complexion was perfect. I didn't think blondes tanned very well, but hers was even. The small amount of lipstick she had on only accented the beauty of her face. She finished putting on the last piece of tape, said "There," and bent down and kissed me.

I reached up and took hold of her arms. She had started to step back, and her foot hit mine. She stumbled, and I pulled at the same time. She fell into me and onto the bed.

She was laughing when I bent down and kissed her. Her arms came around me, and we were lying there on the bed as close to each other as we could possibly get. The warmth I had felt before was nothing like the heat rising in me now. Mar was molded up against me. I could feel every inch of her pressed against me. I could feel her breasts against my bare chest and the warmth of her legs wrapped around my leg. Her lips were there, and her tongue filled my mouth. Every movement just accentuated the warmth and excitement I felt.

A low moan rose from somewhere inside Mar. My left hand slid inside her blouse and cupped her left breast. The sweat trickled from my armpit, and my face was beaded with sweat. My heart was racing and pounding in my chest. Her right hand slid off my hip and slid across the bulge in my open Levi's. I pulled back from her and looked down at her half-closed eyes, and I saw that her forehead, like mine, was covered with beads of sweat that also collected on her upper lip.

She caught the back of my neck in her hand and pulled me to her lips. I was slowly submerging into passion again. My father's words echoed in the back of my brain. *Sex is a wonderful thing, son. Be sure you never do it just because you can. Respect and understanding for the person you are with makes love so much better. Only animals mate uncontrollably. Man uses his brain. I should say, some men do, not all. Just be sure that no one will be hurt by what you're doing.*

Mar was pressed against me. Her mouth was real warm, and she was using more and more strength, pulling me in toward her.

I pulled my head back, smiled at her, and said, "I think we'd better get out of here, babe, before we get into something we shouldn't."

Her eyes came fully open, and she raised and sat on the side of the bed. "I think you're right."

The closet door was open, and I stepped inside to grab my shirt and straighten my pecker out so that my erection could be hidden behind the zipper. I left the shirt untucked so that my interest in Mar wasn't so obvious. I pulled out my cowboy boots and pulled them on gingerly so as not to increase my discomfort—bending was a problem.

Mar saw my hat and asked, "Is that yours?"

"Yeah, why?"

"Most guys wear them 'round here. Put it on so I can see how it looks."

I installed it properly on my head with just the right cant and the buffalo strips hanging off the back. I looked down at Mar. "What ya think, Missy? Want to ride the range with me?"

"Boy, howdy, that looks great on you," she said. "Wear it!"

I grabbed her hand, pulled her up off the bed, and kissed her. "You betcha. Let's hit the road, darlin'."

She said, "You gotta tuck that shirt in, mister," and she spun me around so I was looking away from her. She grabbed my shirttail and punched it into the back of my pants, and then she began working her way to the front. Before she got to my manhood, I grabbed her hands and said, "I can finish." She looked at me funny and then looked down at the front of my pants. A wicked smile appeared on her face. "Looks like your six-gun's loaded, pardner." I could feel myself turning bright red, and for once I was speechless. I reached for her hand and said, "Let's git."

On the way out of town, I asked her if she wanted a Coke or anything.

"Sure, let's stop at the A&W on the way."

We pulled into the drive-in, and a young black-haired girl took our order. Mar climbed down out of the truck and met her at the front. While they were talking, I noticed a frown on her face, and she glanced at me several times. She finished talking and climbed back into the truck. As we pulled back onto the street, Mar asked, "So you really want to go out to Mama Z's?"

"Sure. Told Manny I'd be there. Besides, I have his check. Why don't you just say what's really on your mind?"

"Why don't we drop it off and go someplace else?"

"Any special reason?"

"Sanchez."

"He don't bother me if he don't bother you," I said.

"It's not that. He came by the drive-in right after I left work. I usually sit around and gab with the girls after work, but being as we was going out, I left. Guess I missed him by five minutes."

"So?"

"He wanted to know where I was. Pam thought I was still going with him, so she told him she thought I was going to a movie. I went home to get ready for our date. Sanchez said that if I came in to tell me to meet him at Mama Z's if I knew what was good for me. Manny and Tess came by about thirty minutes ago, and Pam told them what Sanchez had said. They took off to go looking for us."

"Mar, I'm not tough, but I'm not runnin' from scum like Sanchez."

"I know that. I just think it's better to avoid him if possible."

"It probably would be, but I ain't changing my plans on account of Sanchez. Where is this place, anyway?" Mar scooted closer to me and wrapped herself around my right arm.

"Straight out of town on this road. It's on the right about a mile out of town." I started to speed up when Mar told me, "Keep it slow. They watch this road real close for speeders."

Just then a car sped up behind me and flashed its lights. When I looked in the rearview mirror, the car wasn't there. It had already pulled into the oncoming lane to pass me. As it pulled alongside, I recognized Tess waving out of the passenger window, signaling for us to pull over. I pulled the pickup over to the curb and shut down the 454. Manny pulled the wagon in front of me, jumped out, and headed for the truck. We met at the front fender.

"Thought that was your truck, but I saw the cowboy hat and didn't know if it was you or not." Manny chuckled.

"Mar was partial to it."

"Don't blame her," he said. "Looks great. Guess I'll take mine out and wear it. You know about Sanchez?"

"Yup."

"Are you positive you want to run into him again?"

"Look, I appreciate the way everyone wants to look out for me. It's great to know I have that type of friends, amigo, but like I told Mar, I won't walk around him."

"Fine. At least I can make it even. He's with three of his fellows."

"Thanks."

"Follow me out to Mama Z's and park behind me so we can make a getaway if necessary."

"Fine."

We could hear the music from the dance floor as we pulled into the parking lot. Mar and I started from the truck when Manny hollered, "Be sure and lock your truck, amigo. That radio and eight track won't last a minute if you leave it open." We walked back and locked the truck.

As we turned the corner, we saw about two hundred people standing and sitting around on the grass. Manny and Tess headed toward a group of about fifteen or so people to the left of the dance floor. It was built about two feet off the ground, made out of lumber with a short two-by-four rail four feet high around the outside.

The bandstand was built about four feet higher on the back end of the floor. Several of the guys there were the ones I had met at the drive-in the previous night.

"Hey, Manny, T. C. We were wondering if you were gonna show," Pedro said with a serious expression.

"Why's that, Pedro? We're always here less'n it rains," Manny said, grinning.

"Just some things I heard."

"Sanchez."

"Yeah, his Mexican bandits."

"Think he'll bother T. C. tonight?" Manny asked.

"He'll have to. He's been shootin' his mouth off all day at the drive-in, and he's been drinkin' heavy all afternoon. He's itchin' for a fight. What you want me to do?"

"All I want to do is make it a fair fight if it comes to that. He's too damn big for his boots, anyway."

"Chris, Chico, Harry, you want part of this?" Pedro asked.

"Hell, yeah," they answered.

I looked at my new friends. "Guys, I appreciate what you're saying, but I don't want anyone to get hurt on my account. I'll leave before I let that happen."

Chris barked in a half-pissed-off tone, "Look, T. C., this bastard has been a prick to all of us at one time or another. If you're gonna have a run-in with him, it's best you have somebody with you. He don't have a fair bone in his body. So watch out for him. I'm not kidding. Don't cut him a break 'cause he won't give you one."

I turned to Mar. "Come on, Shorty. Let's dance." We headed for the dance floor. Manny and Tess were right behind us.

For the next three hours, we danced and drank Coke, laughing and joking and really enjoying ourselves. I noticed that whenever either Mar or I went someplace, there was always one or two of the crowd with us, even in the bathroom.

I asked Manny, "Hey, this is kind of silly, ain't it?"

"Nope," he replied.

So we just kept on having fun. Mar stayed real close to me most of the time, except for the bathroom and a couple of times when the girls got together, laughing and joking.

I saw Sanchez for the first time when Mar and I were waltzing. He was looking through the railing up at us. I could tell he was pretty drunk, and he had two of his buddies with him.

Manny and Tess were waiting for us when we got back. Manny said, "This place will close in an hour and a half. The kids want to go down to Rock Creek Park and have a weenie roast, being as this is the next-to-last night before football practice. Curfew starts Monday."

"Sounds like fun," I said.

"Good. We need a donation for the food." Manny held out his empty wallet and turned it upside down.

"Oh, heck," I said. "I have your check here. I plum forgot about it. How much you need?"

"About five bucks."

"Here, take ten for you and me."

"I don't want your money, amigo."

"So what? Pay me back Monday."

"Will do."

The music started up again, and Mar and I started toward the dance floor. Mar started up the steps when someone grabbed me by the shoulder. Without thinking, I whirled and ducked at the same time. Sanchez had already started his swing when I ducked. He was too far gone on his swing, and it landed flush on the crown of my head and cowboy hat. I heard the bones in his hand break despite the loud music and noise. I fell backward, landing my ass on the corner of a step, which I later saw had left a crease in my ass and a bruise that looked like a zebra stripe. I sprang back up.

Sanchez let out a small, shrill scream and grabbed his hand, backing away. Two of Sanchez's banditos jumped in to grab me.

I caught the first of them with a left hook on his right cheekbone and felt the grinding crunch of bone beneath my fist. He spun backward into Harry's grasp. Harry smashed his nose, laid him out cold.

The other grabbed me but was instantly jerked backward. Chico dropped his right paw on top of his head like a mallet, and the kid wilted. It appeared to be over.

I looked around, and the guys were all there. They had arrived like the cavalry, preempting the ambush.

Manny jumped to the top step and said, "You guys want to continue this or let Sanchez and T. C. finish it?"

Sanchez stood there holding his hand. "I can't fight. My hand's broke."

"What about it, T. C.?"

"Let him go. I can't fight a guy with one hand."

Manny said, "I sure as hell could. He deserves an ass whoopin'."

I turned to Mar and said, "Let's dance," and we walked out onto the dance floor.

Mar picked up my hat, straightened it out, and placed it properly on my head.

I looked at her and saw tears running down her cheeks. "What's wrong now, girl?"

"Oh, Tommy, I'm so sorry."

"Let's don't get started on that again. We came here to dance. Nothin's gonna spoil our night. You don't have anything to do with this."

"If you weren't with me, it wouldn't have happened."

"Are you tellin' me you didn't want to hang out with me tonight?"

"No, I'm not sayin' that. I want to be with you more than anything in the world."

"Then let's forget it and dance."

When we got back from the dance floor, over half the group was gone.

"Come on, T. C.! Let's go," Manny shouted.

We all loaded up and headed for Rock Creek. On the way out there, Mar sat real close and held on to my arm, leaning up several times to kiss me on the cheek. She started to bring up the subject of Sanchez, and I cut her off.

After the party, we had no sooner pulled up in front of Mar's house than her mother pulled up right behind us.

"Out kinda late, aren't you, Marylyn?" her mother said as she walked up to the side of the truck.

"We've been out to Rock Creek on a picnic," Mar explained.

"Don't be too long."

"I won't, Mama."

We walked up to the door, and I took her in my arms and kissed her good night. "See you tomorrow evening?" I asked.

"Sure. What time?"

"Whenever I get off work, probably 'round seven."

"Fine. I'll be home. Good night." Her smile continued to draw me to her, but I had to go.

As I entered the house, the phone was ringing. I looked at the clock as I picked up the phone. It was five thirty in the morning.

"Hello?"

"Tom, where you been?" Buck asked.

"Went to a dance and picnic with Manny."

"Until five damn thirty in the freakin' morning?"

"I met a girl," I said.

"Oh! It had to happen. Nice?"

"I think she is."

"Talked to Snake last night. He said you've really been workin'. Also something about you being hurt."

"Was gonna tell you about that. I got into a scrape with a guy."

"Which one?"

"The girl and I dated Friday night, and last night the girl's ex-boyfriend and I got into it."

"How old is this girl?"

"Seventeen."

"Rosie's been out of her mind ever since I talked to Snake last night."

"Everything's fine, Buck. I got cut on the face."

"How? A fistfight?"

"No, he cut me with a knife."

"Just how bad is it?"

"It took quite a few stitches to sew me up. The doc says it'll leave a small scar, but it's not real bad. With this bandage on my face, it looks a lot worse than it really is."

"Just a minute, Tom." I could hear him talking to someone in the background. When Rosie came on the line, I explained everything again to her. I finished up by asking when they would be back.

"We're closin' up Dad's house, and he's comin' back with us. We plan on bein' there late Wednesday. Now you take care of yourself, Tommy, and you stay away from that girl."

"I can't do that, Rosie."

"Well, she can't be too nice a girl to run 'round with someone who goes 'round cutting people with a knife."

"Wait till you meet her 'fore you decide somethin' like that. You'll like her as much as me."

"All right, but please be careful till we're home."

"I will, Rosie. See you Wednesday."

"Wait a minute. Buck wants to talk to you."

"Tom?"

"Yeah."

"Snake's putting a couple of other men on the truck in the morning. That way all you and Manny have to do is a couple of runs every evening to keep up. Take care, and we will see you Wednesday."

After hanging up the phone, I looked up Manny's number and called him. The phone had only rung once when it was answered. "Cantu residence."

"Mrs. Cantu, this is T. C."

"You want to talk to Manuel?"

"No. Can you just give him a message for me?"

"Certainly," she said.

"Can you tell him we're goin' to take the day off tomorrow and have him call me about noon? Please, and I'm sorry for calling so early in the morning."

"It's no problem, T. C. We always up on Sundays for early mass. Bye."

After hanging up, I headed for bed, but I had hardly found my pillow when the ringing of the phone sat me up in bed. I stumbled to the phone. "Yeah?"

"T. C., Mama said you wanted me to call you."

"Yeah, at noon."

"Well, it's nearly one," Manny said.

"Oh. Just wanted to tell you that I talked to Buck, and we have the day off. He also said he'd have a crew work days so we would only have to make a couple of runs after school. Also, you want me to pick you up for school tomorrow?"

"Yeah, that would be great. What you doing the rest of the day?"

"Mar and I are just hanging out. She wants to visit some old school friends."

"Okay, see ya in the morning."

Chapter 6

Football

Jerry Baker had been coach of the Le High Cougars for twenty-five years. He pulled out a chair, turned it around, and sat down with his arms folded over the back. He slowly turned his attention to four assistant coaches sitting at the table. It was eight o'clock, and football practice started in two hours. He looked at Doug Farrington, a hulk of a man with a chew in his lip. He had been at Le High for ten years as defensive coach. Vic Cobb, the offensive and defensive line coach, was a little All-American pulling guard from Linfield College up in Oregon. He was only five nine but carried two hundred and ten pounds and could run the forty-yard dash at age fifty in somewhere around 4.8 seconds. The only thing faster was his temper and lack of tolerance for slow learners. During his first year of teaching, in 1960, he was suspended for two days for smacking a senior boy on the ass with a hockey stick on the first day of school for making a wise-ass remark in his PE class. Vic's brother, Burton, was the running back coach. Where Vic was quick, Burt was slow and methodical. He taught his running backs by repetition. Leroy Clemmons, defensive backs and ends coach, looked like Moses, with a big beard, and had the patience of Job. Clemmons was the problem solver and a deacon at the Presbyterian church. As a group, they enjoyed one another's company and wanted a state championship.

Pedro sat on the grass just outside the coaches' locker room, which was in the partial basement beneath the stadium. The windows in the coaching room opened just above the cut grass. By sitting behind the holly near the window, which was cracked to let in as much fresh air as could be found in August in Texas, we could find out what the coaches said. Pedro got the short straw, so there he sat, eavesdropping on the coaches' meeting. He would share all the details with the guys at Pepi's that night so they would know ahead of time who would be on the team and what the coaches were planning the next day.

"Well, gentlemen," Baker said in a clinical manner, "looks like it's going to be a halfway decent season. With most of our linemen returning, the only thing we lost from last year was our quarterback and fullback. I figure Manny Cantu for quarterback, Sanchez or Gonzales fullback."

"Not this year," Cobb said. "Sanchez got in a fight Saturday night and broke his right hand."

"Damn, he was our fastest man. Without some speed, our offense is dead. Vic, how are we set up on the line?"

"We have all but two of our starters. We lost the left tackle; however, Pedro Salinas filled in more than adequately last year for the last three games. Left end—I'm just going to have to see what's available, but the preacher's kid is looking pretty good to me right now."

"Doug, we should be pretty well set on defense, ain't we?" Jerry asked.

"Yeah, except for middle linebacker, Sanchez. Don't know if he'll continue to play both ways."

"Anyone you can think of to fill in for him?"

"Not that I know of. It's going to be tough finding someone fast and tough like he is. He's meaner than a pissed off rattlesnake, just what we need at middle linebacker."

"We had a kid stop by last week—T. C. something-or-other." Baker was nonchalant about the conversation, although his eyes sparkled a bit as he recounted his conversation with Hartman. "I talked to his coach from last year. You remember Keith Hartman, Burt. He's up at Tishomingo and said this kid was greased lightning but small. Well, apparently he's grow'd and filled out since then. I want you, Burt and Leroy, to pay attention to this kid if he shows up. If he is half as fast as Hartman says, he'll be a nice addition. Kid must work hard. His hands are as calloused as any roughneck in Texas."

"Manny told me yesterday that he had decided to go to school here," Cobb barked.

The door opened and an elderly man came in. "Jerry, you going to issue suits today like last year, or later?"

"We'll wait till next Monday, Henry. Last year we lost over twenty kids the first week, and it took three months to get the suits back. Remember?"

"Sure do."

"Henry Plummet, you know everyone here except Leroy Clemmons. Leroy, meet Henry. He's been the athletic storekeeper here since this school opened. Whatever you need, just get a hold of Henry."

They spent the next hour going over the known kids that would show up. At 9:45 Jerry said, "Okay, let's go look at our athletes."

The collection of us sitting in a booth at Pepi's stared open-mouthed as Pedro sat down when he finished his report on the coaches' meeting. He had an amazing knack for mimicking each of the coaches, down to the details of how they stood, waved their hands, pointed their fingers, and spit their tobacco. It was spooky. We all applauded.

On the next day, as I walked onto the football field for the first time as a sixteen-year-old, I saw groups of young men standing near the foot of the stands. Then, *they* walked out of the upper office. Coach Baker climbed a small tower set up beside the stands. He turned on the loudspeaker, and it squawked to life. Pedro walked up to our group and leaned over my shoulder. "Coach thinks you are a fast hombre," he said. "He's got plans for you." Later at Pepi's, I got all the details and the rundown on each coach.

"Okay," Coach Baker began. "Fellas, gather around here at the foot of the tower. All of you sit down. I want to explain your function. I am Coach Baker, the head coach. On my left are Doug Farrington and Leroy Clemmons; on the right, Vic and Burton Cobb. We start, gentlemen, with the premise that these coaches are here for one reason." Coach Baker was monotone. His face was expressionless as he leaned over the railing, peering down on his plebes. "Our goal is to teach you how to play football, as well as how to do the exercises and work it takes to play football. We will not accept anything but your best. If you are not prepared to give it to us, and to give us your undivided attention along with 100 percent of your effort, we don't want you." Baker's gestures were stilted, stiff, and slow, yet a line of white spittle collected at the right corner of his mouth.

"There is one thing to remember: this school's team has been state champions twice, and it can happen again. The only difference between a winner and a loser, gentlemen, is effort and dedication. Each of you here can contribute to making this the best football team in the state. It is up to you. All we can do as coaches is prepare you." Nobody dared break from Coach's gaze. While it wasn't an inspiring speech, showing any inattentiveness would have been perilous.

"Your execution and playing have to be done by you. Now then, this first week will be taken up with physical training. If you are not in good physical shape, then, gentlemen, you are going to suffer. The way to avoid injury in this game is to be in perfect shape." As I listened, I realized I was in for a lot of pain. I hadn't been working out, running, or preparing for football practice.

"We as coaches intend to produce that within you. On Friday night, five nights from now, I expect each one of you backs and ends to be able to run a mile in full football equipment in under six minutes. Linemen will have eight minutes. Those who can't will run this mile every night after ball practice until they do. Understood?"

I groaned along with all the rest of the team.

Coach Baker peered down from his tower, his glasses dropping to the tip of his nose. His voice deepened, and he spoke from somewhere deep within. He was shouting without raising his voice; it was extremely intimidating. "Gentlemen, this is a team game. From now until this season is over, you think, walk, talk, and act as a team. The failure of one man on the team can let everyone down and doom this team to failure. So when I ask you a question as a group, I expect an answer as a group, not murmurs or answers here and there. I want to hear a roar of voices answering me. Understood?"

"Yes, sir!" the boys shouted in broken unison.

"Come on, gentlemen! You are not pussies. You going to be Cougars or not?"

"Yes, sir!"

"That's better, gentlemen. Now, did everyone bring their own shoes as instructed?"

"Yes, sir!"

Coach Baker lifted his clipboard and signaled the assembled coaches by pointing it to the corners of the field and lifting his head to express one thought: *Get going.* Then Coach turned his attention to all of us.

"You will have five minutes to get ready. When you are ready to start, the coaches will give you a blank form. You will take this form home tonight, have your parents or guardian sign it, and bring it back tomorrow. Failure to bring it back will stop you from playing football until it is signed."

Coach walked to the corner of the elevated tower closest to the upperclassmen gathered where I was. "Okay, now men, get ready," he said. "Put on your shoes and get your registration papers. When finished, come out on the field. You seniors and juniors make sure the lowerclassmen get their asses to the right spot.

"At the north end of the field you will see two flags, a yellow one on one side of the goalpost and a red one on the other side. The men going out for the backfield, gather under the red flag with Coach Burt; ends and split receivers under the yellow flag with Coach Cummings. On the south end of the field, there is a green flag and a blue flag. Offensive linemen under the green flag with Coach Vic, and defensive linemen under the blue flag with Coach Nichols. If this is your first year and you haven't decided, gather under the yellow sign at the north end. We will get it straightened out later in the week. No walking. Let's go!"

Manny and I picked up our forms and started toward the north end of the field. As we were jogging, Manny punched me in the ribs and nodded to a group of guys in front of us. "There's Sanchez."

"I saw him."

"Wonder what he's doing here. He can't play with a broken hand."

"Pedro told me last night the doc said he would be able to play in about a month," I said. "Mar and I stopped at Pepi's yesterday."

"That should make for an interesting season."

As we approached the group under the red flag, Sanchez came out to meet us. "Understand you're goin' out for the backfield, Gurley."

"That's right."

"Well, don't get too secure. If you hadn't broke my hand, you wouldn't be good enough to carry my water."

"Look, Sanchez, I came to play football. I know you're a problem, but let's keep it out of practice."

"No way, punk," he replied. "Sooner or later you're going to answer to me."

Coach Burt called out, "All right, gentlemen, whenever you're ready, we're waiting." About fifteen kids were already standing under the red flag. "In case any of you gentlemen didn't catch my name, it's Cobb, like *corn cob* but with two *B*'s. And yes, I'm rough as a cob and can irritate the hell out of you. I will enjoy it; you won't. How many of you men have played backfield before?" Six hands went up. "Sanchez, how 'bout that hand?"

"I talked to Coach Baker a few minutes ago, and the doc said the cast comes off in three weeks. He said that if I keep moving my fingers, it should be in good shape."

"Fine. We will need you," Coach Burt said. "The only thing you have to do then is get in shape. Now, gentlemen, for the next two hours we are going to run wind sprints. If you will look down the field there to the forty-yard line, I will be there with a stopwatch. You will start here at the goal line. I will blow a whistle to start you one at a time. On your first three trials, I want you to start and go as fast as you can. Now line up and give me your last names."

I was fifth in line. I caught a couple of names. A thick, heavyset kid right in front of me said, "Mueller," then it was me, and then Manny.

"Okay, men, line up again in the order you gave me your names. Spread out in a straight line. I want you to start jogging in place. When I say, 'Faster,' run in place just to get you loosened up."

I jogged in time with the rest, wishing I'd run more that summer. After about five minutes, I was wringing wet with sweat. I glanced behind me and saw that Manny wasn't even sweating.

We went faster, then slowed, and then sped up for about ten minutes.

"Hold it," the coach finally said. "Catch your breath now, gentlemen. When you get to the line, I want everything you got. I don't want to see any of you walking on the playing field. You run or you jog whenever you are on the field."

Coach Burt jogged down to the forty-yard line, clipboard in hand. His whistle bounced around on his chest till he found his spot and turned to face the hopefuls. He punched the whistle into his mouth, grabbed the stopwatch, and blew a quick burst on the whistle. The first kid flew down to the forty, where Coach Burt punched the stopwatch and wrote the time down on the clipboard. Another whistle burst, and the next kid did the same.

I watched each kid who went before me. None seemed very fast until Mueller, who was in front of me, was on the line. He was about my height, outweighed me by twenty pounds, and was blond with bright blue eyes. Mueller got into a three-point stance, and when the whistle blew, he was off. He started low to the ground and seemed to gain speed with each stride. When Mueller crossed the line, Coach Burt shouted, "Nice speed, Mueller!"

I got down in a three-point stance. When the whistle blew, I also pushed off as hard as I could, keeping my hands and arms as close to my sides as possible, like I had learned last year. I ran as hard as I could. It seemed like forever before I hit the forty-yard stripe.

"Nice run, Gurley," Coach Burt said.

I glanced at the coach and then jogged to the end of the line. Manny came flying by as I neared the goalpost. He had a grin on his face and was really digging. We ran through the line three times, as hard as we could.

"Take a break, gentlemen," Coach Burt said, "till I can get things correlated, then we will run some double sprints."

My breath was coming in spurts. Manny and I just lay on the grass, taking large gasps of air.

"On your feet, gentlemen. When I call off your names, line up in pairs." Cobb called off four names, then "Mueller! Gurley! Cantu! Sanchez!"

I walked up to the line next to Mueller and stuck out my hand. "T. C. Gurley."

"Eric Mueller."

"You play football last year?"

"Yeah, second year at San Antonio, where my dad had a furniture store."

"What position?" I asked.

"Fullback, second string."

"Did you letter?"

"Yeah, I just barely got enough playing time. I wanted to go to El Paso High, but my dad wouldn't let me."

"Why not?" I was interested in this guy who had twenty pounds on me and looked fast.

"He owns a furniture store about eight blocks from here. Dad figures it might bring him some business if I play this close to the store." Mueller didn't seem to be too happy about the decision. He was all business.

"It doesn't really matter as long as you get to play," I said.

"Yes, it does. I want to go to college, and if you play for a bigger school, you get more exposure for a scholarship." Mueller was clearly motivated; his dad's store didn't sound too lucrative.

"I hadn't given that much thought," I said. "I've mostly been focused on getting a spot on the team."

Coach Burt interrupted our conversation by quizzing each of us on the position we were interested in playing and then lining us up in order from tallest to shortest.

Mueller continued, "It's the only thing I've thought about. I have to go to college, and I'm going to need that scholarship."

Coach Burt was talking to the lowerclassmen, who had their paperwork all screwed up and were snaring him in endless questions.

I turned to Mueller and asked, "What grade you in?"

"Senior, so this is my last chance."

"You'll most likely make it."

"Not unless this team gets into the playoffs, I won't."

"It's a long season. Anything can happen. We could make the playoffs."

Sanchez spoke up from behind. "What do you mean *we*, Gurley? You gonna just pack water for us starters."

Manny barked, "Knock it off, Sanchez."

"What are you, his babysitter?" Sanchez said.

"No, and I'm not yours either," Manny retorted. "Leave your prejudices off the field."

"Sanchez, Manny, and Mueller, shut up and pay attention," Coach called. "Get in line. I'm not working you near hard enough if you got time to talk. Let's get some times down on paper." Cobb was half-mad after being irritated by the rookies.

The two backs in front of us took off. Mueller and I lined up, both in a three-point stance. When the whistle blew, we both jumped at the same time. Mueller fell behind in the first ten steps, but I kept watching out of the corner of my eye. He was just starting to catch up when I crossed the forty. We turned and jogged back to the rear of the line.

"You're pretty fast, T. C.," he said.

"Not any more than you. I just got away faster. You almost caught me at the forty."

"I can't seem to start fast, like the coach said last year, but my acceleration is good."

"You going out for fullback again this year?"

"If I can make it."

"How much you weigh?"

"About 205."

"You'll make it with your speed and weight," I said.

"Man, I hope so."

After we ran the double sprints two more times, Coach Burt told us to gather at the crow's nest. Another five minutes passed, and then all the squads gathered around. Coach Baker said, "Nice workout, gentlemen. Take two laps around the track, and we will see you back at five thirty this afternoon. Get at it!"

We all headed for the track. Manny and I were around the middle of the pack. We had completed three quarters of the first lap when someone tripped me from behind. I started to fall on my face, but someone caught one arm and someone else grabbed my other arm to keep me from hitting the ground. I looked to each side, and there were Manny and Mueller. Sanchez was running on ahead, laughing.

We finished out the laps and stopped over at the grandstand to pick up our shoes and bags. While we were changing, several guys showed up around us. Mueller was sitting about five feet away. I called to him, "Eric, come on over here. You know these guys?"

"Seen them around some this summer."

"Manny, you met Eric. Introduce him around."

"Chico, Pedro, Malin, Harry, this is Eric Mueller. Those two black-looking fellows over there are Kevin and Delucian Blackman. Twins, this is Eric. And over here with the bandage on his face is the great T. C., the one responsible for Sanchez's broken hand—a bit hardheaded, you might say."

"Cut it out, Manny," I said.

Malin said, "We going over to Pepi's for a while, T. C. You and Manny coming?"

"Sure, for a little while," I said. "Then Manny and I have to go load some pipe to haul. That will only take an hour or so."

Malin looked at Pedro. "Reason I asked is that Harry and I can't stand to ride with these two spics over here, Poncho Villa and Capitan Pedro."

Pedro said, "You gringos have no sense of adventure."

Then Chico grabbed Malin from behind and Pedro picked up his feet, and they turned him upside down. Malin started talking real nice. "Come on, fellas. You know I was only kidding."

"Did it sound like he was only kidding to you, Pedro?" Chico asked with a grin.

"I don't know, Chico—maybe. But he called us spics. My granddaddy turned over in his grave."

"Mine too, Pedro. I heard him calling to me avenge his honor."

"What you think we ought to do?"

"We could use him for a tackling dummy," Pedro said. "Or we could drag him behind your beautiful car like a tin can."

Malin said, "Beautiful car? That piece of junk looks like cold dog puke."

Chico's voice raised to a shrill scream. "Pedro, did you hear that—my beautiful car being talked about like that? This calls for very serious action. You agree?"

"Most certainly. Severe penalties are called for."

Harry, in the meantime, had slipped up behind Pedro and knelt on all fours. Chico and Pedro suspended Malin upside down. Seeing Harry in place, Malin reached over and grabbed at Pedro's privates, causing him to step backward. Pedro tried to stop, but with Harry knelt down and rolling into the back of Pedro's legs, he couldn't. He went over backward, pulling Malin and Chico with him, till they all fell in a heap. Harry and Malin were the first two up and immediately ran up the bleachers behind Manny and me.

"Let's go, T. C.," Manny laughed, "'fore they start the Mexican Revolution all over again."

We headed for the truck. There was a garish orange-and-purple '56 or '57 Dodge sitting alongside my truck. The tail fins sticking up were painted a hideous yellow.

Chico came up. "See, T. C.? Isn't that the most beautiful sight you ever saw?"

Manny spoke first. "Come on now, Chico. Don't ask this man to lie to you. That's a sin."

"But Manny, it's beautiful," Chico protested.

"You are the only guy in this world whose taste runs to shit and calls it sunshine," Manny said.

Chico called to Pedro, "Let's get out of here, amigo, and leave these heathens. They have no taste for the finer things in life."

"Eric, we're going over to Pepi's for a Coke," I said. "Want to come along?" Malin and Harry hopped into the bed of the truck.

"I think I'd like that. Thanks," Eric replied.

Manny pushed the pickup door open and slid to the center. Eric hopped into the passenger seat. We started to pull out when Sanchez and two of his buddies roared out around us and into the street.

Eric leaned forward. "Maybe I shouldn't ask, T. C., but what's up with you and Sanchez?"

Manny spoke up, "He's got a hard-on for T. C. over a girl."

"Just wondered. Had a couple of guys tell me when I first moved here last spring that he wasn't someone to monkey with."

"T. C. isn't either," Manny said. "Did you see Sanchez's broken hand? T. C. did that with his forehead."

"With his forehead?"

"Yeah. T. C. hit him right in the fist with his forehead. I've only known T. C. for a month and thought he was a bit hardheaded. Now I know he is."

"That how you got the bandage on your face?" Eric asked me.

"No, that was another one of Sanchez's little deals," I said. "I'll tell you that story one of these days."

Chapter 7

Picking the Team

Coach Baker and the assistants poured themselves coffee and pulled out chairs around the conference table in the athletic office. "Well, fellas, after our first practice, what do you think our outlook will be? Vic?" Harry sat outside the open window, taking notes for the guys. He lost the draw this time. He knew that if his dad caught him, he wouldn't just be off the team; he'd get kicked out of his home too.

"From what I saw," Coach Vic said, "I think our line will be better than last year. Several of these kids have really grown. Pedro and Chico have each put on about twenty pounds, and the Wartham kid, who played center last year, gives me a solid core on the left side. I saw a couple more, after I beat the shit out of 'em, that I believe will fit right in. Our interior line should all be over two hundred pounds and fast enough."

Vic was nearly gleeful. "We got a couple fairly fast pulling guards. That's if'n they don't all quit like they did last year. I'm a bit worried, Jerry, that this one-mile run will kill 'em off 'fore I can teach 'em anything."

"Burt, we have any speed and size in the backfield?" Coach Baker asked.

"There are about six or seven with good size and speed—Manny, you know, and Sanchez."

Harry was scribbling so he could give us all the details when we gathered for the update at Pepi's.

Burt said, "Sanchez told me his hand will be ready in three weeks. There are two new kids, Mueller and Gurley. Both run the forty in under 4.6, and they have good size. Mueller, if he can take a hit, should be a helluva fullback. If not, Leroy might want to look him over. With his size and speed, he would make a damn good middle linebacker."

"What about that kid T. C.?" Coach Baker asked.

"That's the Gurley kid. He's easily the fastest one on the squad."

"Leroy?"

Leroy set his coffee aside and pulled out his clipboard. "I like everything I saw today. We have three lettermen back, and there are four new kids. I can't believe the size these kids are getting to be: Mueller's six foot one and 245 pounds. Gurley is six foot and weighed in at 191. Cantu is pushing 195, and his arm is pretty damn good."

Coach Baker started to say something, but Leroy kept talking. "They may be the biggest backs in the league except for Stateline. There is an Indian boy, Nathan Breedlove, about six one, just shy of a hundred and eighty pounds. He's quicker than a Cherokee rabbit—turns like one too—and sure runs his cuts on the pass patterns like a fox is chasing him. If his hands are any good, he should be a natural wide receiver."

Baker stood up with a coffee cup in his hand, walked over in front of the blackboard, and stood looking at his three coaches. "I have something I want to say, but first I want your promise that it will go no further than this room." He watched each coach as they nodded at him with questioning looks on their faces. "Friday night, gentlemen, I received a call. I am one of two men being considered for the head coaching job at one of the Southwest Conference schools. I can't tell you which one—I gave my word—but I was told that if I had another winning season, I should have the job nailed down. If I get it, you know what that means. I will take all of you with me, if you wish to go. The assistant's pay starts at thirty-two five, plus benefits. So you can see what's on the line.

"I want this football team to be in the best condition of any team in Texas. I want you to get on these kids and stay on 'em. Let's tear them down and build them back up. Our first game is in three weeks. If what you're telling me is right, and we work their butts off and ours too, we should be in the playoffs in

November. Let's not waste any time on kids who don't want to play football. Starting with the workout this afternoon, I want to double their workload in the two and a half hours. Also, I was going to wait till Friday before our first mile run, but I'm going to change that. Starting tonight, instead of two laps at the end of the workouts, I want five. Those who don't complete it, without a good, valid reason, weed them out. Let's get rid of the loafers and crybabies on this first day. Okay, men? Fine. I'll see you this afternoon. Remember, not a word of this to anyone, your wives included. Damn, I want that job!"

Harry jumped up as Burton Cobb walked over to close the window. He froze as Burton poured his coffee out the window and then slammed it shut and locked it. Harry barely escaped without being discovered. He would relate everything to the guys that night, except the part about his dad planning to take another job. The guys didn't need to know absolutely everything. He had great notes on everything else.

The team was already into their exercises when Manny and I arrived. We had changed shoes in the truck, so we ran out and lined up. We spent the next twenty minutes doing sit-ups, push-ups, knee bends, and sideslips, with no pause in between. Coach Baker called a halt. "Take five."

Coach Burt came over to Manny and me. "I didn't miss your arrival, boys. You were late. How come, T. C.?"

"We have a job hauling pipe, Coach, and we were late getting back."

"Coach Baker has a rule," Cobb said, "one lap for every five minutes late. Three lates and you're off the team. If you have to work and could be late more than that, then you need to talk to the coach. Right now, get out there and run your lap."

Manny and I took off around the track. The jeers and taunts from the team followed us around the track. "Hey, look! Manny runs like a sand crab." "Hurry up, ladies! You're late for practice." "Seen better legs on a high chair." "Looks like a windmill."

Manny and I had no sooner flopped down when Coach had us back on our feet doing wind sprints. For a solid two hours they ran us, worked us, and then ran us some more.

Coach Baker stopped the workout and told us on the bullhorn, "Starting tonight, after every workout you will run five laps. Next week, you will run ten, and within ten days you will be doing fifteen. If for some reason you cannot complete these runs, you will be excused for the first time, but if you fail to complete the run two times in a row, you will be dropped from the football team. The only excuse will have to come from a doctor, and then it will be accepted only for a period of one week. I do not wish to see any man on that track loafing. Everything you do, do it to the best of your ability. In that way you will never be a loser. Another thing—next Monday, a week from today, we will hold our mile trial run, and any back or end here who cannot run the mile in seven minutes or less will not—I repeat, will not—make the team. You linemen who can't run a ten-minute mile will not make the team. Now, out on the track and run your five laps."

Manny, Mueller, Chico, Pedro, and I all started in the same pack. On the third lap, Mueller, Manny, and I were coming up behind the stragglers. I was running in a straight line behind Mueller and Manny when I heard someone behind me say, "Move over, you bastard, and let a runner get by."

I moved out of the inner lane and let Sanchez take it. He laughed as he went by. He got about fifteen paces in front and stayed there. By this time, we had caught up to the back of the pack. We moved up on the outer side of the track and started passing the slower ones.

Mueller moved over next to me. He gasped between strides, "If you're going to best Sanchez out of the left halfback spot, I wouldn't let him finish first."

"What lap we on?"

"Fourth coming up."

I looked forward and saw that Sanchez had pulled to about fifty feet ahead. I lengthened my stride and, glancing over, saw that Mueller was staying with me. By the time we reached the lap pole, I had gained about twenty-five feet on Sanchez. My breath was beginning to become labored, and sweat was getting into my eyes, blurring my vision. I started thinking of Marylyn to take my mind off of the pain that I was beginning to feel in my chest and that the sweat in the cut on my cheek was causing.

Slowly but surely, Mueller and I were closing in on Sanchez. We were right on his heels as we passed the lap pole again.

Mueller grunted, "Let's go. He's slowing down."

Sanchez glanced over his shoulder and saw us right behind him. He tried to speed up, but he was beginning to stagger and weave, his stride no longer even or straight.

We moved up to the outside and passed him. He tried to say something, but his breath was coming in such gasps that we couldn't understand him.

As we turned the corner, my legs were completely mush. They felt like I was packing fifty pounds of red gumbo mud from the oil fields. I looked over at Mueller, who looked as fresh as when we had started. He gave me a wink and then slowed his pace. We crossed the finish line together and immediately flopped on the grass.

It was only a couple of seconds before someone shook my shoulder. "Come on, Gurley, on your feet. Start walking. You'll cramp up laying there."

I opened my eyes and saw that Coach Burt was leaning over me. As I rose, I saw Eric and Manny standing behind him. They crossed over to me and put their arms over my shoulders, and the three of us started walking out across the field. Eric said, "Hey, Manny, did you see the look on Sanchez's face when he came in?"

"Did you beat him?" I asked Manny.

"No, we crossed in a dead heat. But, boy, was he pissed. You know he has won every five-mile run for the last two years, even holds the track record in the mile for double-A schools."

"Well, you can't win all the time."

"You do," Manny said. "He hasn't beat you yet."

My temperature and breath slowly started to settle down. "How come you didn't finish out the race first?" I asked Eric. "You let me win."

"I've been runnin' all summer, and I wasn't the one who wanted to beat Sanchez; you were. It didn't cost me nothin'."

Coach Baker approached us. "Nice run, gentlemen. Rest until the rest of the squad finishes."

We walked over to sit on the bleachers and watch as some of the squad finished their last two laps. Manny pointed. "My God. Look at how many didn't finish."

We started counting and determined that eighteen had dropped out. The ones who had quit were gathered in a knot, and Coach Farrington was talking to them. Several of the boys walking away had their heads lowered, and we could tell they had been put off the squad.

Coach Baker came on the bullhorn and said, "Gather round over here."

As we passed Coach Burt, we heard one of the boys tell him, "Look, Coach"—he held up his foot, which had a huge blister on it—"these are new shoes. I can run ten miles. I just never had a chance to break these in. Can't I try again?"

We walked on over and joined the group at the base of the tower.

"This is just your first day of practice. Most of you came through like champions. That is what we are until someone shows us that they are better than we are. Right?"

"Right!"

"Starting right now, I want all of you to think of nothing but football, 'cause when school starts, you can think of studies and, maybe once in a while, your girl."

A laugh went up at that one.

"So let's see you back here tomorrow, ready to go again at ten. Before you crawl into bed tonight, do twenty push-ups and twenty sit-ups. Do that every night. Increase it if you want to, but do them and you will sleep a lot better. See you in the morning." He shut off the bullhorn and started climbing down.

The boys huddled quickly and picked numbers between one and fifty. I chose thirty-five. The person who missed by the most got assigned to eavesdrop. Harry was the last spy, so he picked the number forty-nine. Manny picked five, and everyone else fell between them. Manny hustled to get into position behind the holly before the coaches got started. He had his notepad and began to take detailed notes. He would report with Harry at that night's meeting at Pepi's.

All of the coaches headed to the office. "You're right about Gurley and Mueller, Burt," Coach Baker said.

"Did you see that exchange between Gurley and Sanchez on the track?" Coach Burt asked.

"I saw something being said but didn't pay much attention."

"They tell me that the bandage on Gurley's face was courtesy of Sanchez and a knife," Coach Vic offered.

"Who told you that?" asked Coach Baker.

"Chico and the Blackman twins. Seems that they were out at the quarry when it happened."

"Drinking or what?"

"Over a girl, is what they say."

"That Birchley girl?" Coach Baker asked. "She went with Sanchez last year, didn't she?"

"God, I don't know," Vic said. "I can't even keep up with my own love life, and I'm married."

They laughed as they went into the office.

Manny slipped out of position and ran to the lot to catch up with me. He filled me in on all of the details of the coaches' meeting in advance of telling the rest of the guys. We all met at Pepi's at nine o'clock to hear Harry's and Manny's reports. Needless to say we were all happy with the news. Harry didn't say anything about Coach seeking another job. I didn't find out till much later.

The practices and the work between practices made Tuesday pass fast. I was tired when I rose on Wednesday morning.

Manny was on the deck in the loading yard when I pulled in. "Hey, old partner, you look tired this morning. You and Marylyn out late last night?"

"No. Went over to A&W for a root beer float and hung out for an hour or so. Then I took her home."

"Snake left a message for us. They want a load of six inch over at Blackwell number three as fast as we can get it there."

The truck wouldn't start when we tried it. Jesus came out and tried jumping the battery and checking the points. I finally told him, "Better call a garage and see if they can get a mechanic out here. You have a CB in your car?"

"No, but we have one in the office, a base station. Use it."

"Better get a hold of Snake and tell him we can't deliver the pipe," I said.

We walked into the office, and Jesus picked up the mic to try to locate Snake. Manny and I fell into the dilapidated leather sofa pushed back against the wall. After the third try, Snake came on. I recognized him by his lisp.

"Snake, T. C. here," I said. "Our truck broke down, and we can't get that six-inch pipe out to Blackwell number three. We're calling the garage. Should be fixed this afternoon."

"Hope so," he said. "There's six men standing out there waiting for it."

"Could the other truck handle it?"

"I can try and reach them. Where you going to be?"

"We have football practice at ten, so we won't be back here at the yard until about one."

"Fine. What time is Buck due in?"

"Don't know. He just said Wednesday."

"Okay, see you later."

Jesus said to me, "The mechanic from the shop said he would be over in about an hour."

I turned to Manny. "Let's run over and get some coffee and donuts or something. I'm starvin'."

"Fine."

There was only one car in the parking lot when we pulled in at Pepi's. Manny and I got out and walked in. The cool rush of air-conditioned air welcomed us. Marylyn, Tess, and two other girls were sitting in a booth. Marylyn's face lit up in a big smile, and she stuck up her hand in a little wave. Tess and one of the other girls turned to see who she was waving at.

Tess asked, "What're you guys doing here?"

"Cotton-pickin' truck broke down," Manny told her. "Could we get some coffee?"

"What else you want, T. C.?" Marylyn said with a grin.

"I'm lookin' at it."

"No, I mean something to eat."

Tess, Manny, and the two girls burst out laughing.

Marylyn's face got red as a beet. The flush started at the vee in her blouse and went all the way to her hairline. One of the girls I didn't know said, "Well, look at Little Miss Modesty. I haven't seen a blush like that since I was in the eighth grade and saw my first cock."

Mar's face got even redder. Everyone looked at her and laughed.

I slid into the booth, turned her head toward me, and kissed her.

Mar pulled back, smiled at me, and put her left hand in mine.

Tess said, "T. C., the girl on your left is Nida, and across the table is Pam. Both go to Le High."

Manny started to sit down next to Tess when she said, "Let me out, Manny, and I'll get your coffee. Want anything else?"

I said, "I'll have a couple of donuts."

"Don't have no donuts. Either pie or a honey bun."

"I'll take the honey bun with butter."

"What about you, lover?" Tess winked at Manny.

"Just coffee and you, baby."

At nine thirty, we jumped in the truck and headed for practice. I loved the way Marylyn said good-bye. Her kisses were warm and intoxicating.

At ten, we were standing under the rusting tower that had been a fixture at Le High for as long as Coach had been here. He grunted as he climbed the ladder and then deigned to peer on us mere mortals from the lofty heights. "Boys, after we get through with our exercises and wind sprints, we are going to start issuing pads and uniforms this afternoon. We're going to start tackling and blocking practice."

Due to the issuing of uniforms, Manny and I were late getting back to the yard. Jesus met us as we pulled in. "Buck called. Said he was home and for you to come home as soon as you could." I ran back to the truck and punched it, fishtailing and throwing gravel against the tin building. I kept forgetting that the 454 under the hood liked to play.

CHAPTER 8

Mama's Love

Marylyn closed the door, turned off the light in the front room, and walked the short hall to her bedroom. Then she stopped and walked back to the hall mirror. Her cheeks were red. She leaned in, her breath fogging a spot on the glass beneath her nose. *Sanchez never made me happy,* she thought. *Tommy is so sweet and tender. I think my life couldn't get any better right now.* She smiled and continued down the hall, peeling her clothes off and letting them drop wherever. She felt a shadow in the door and turned with a start.

Her mom was in the open door. "How you doing, honey?"

Her face told the story. Marylyn knew a conversation was coming from the look on her mama's face. She backed away from the dresser and lowered herself onto the corner of her bed. "Fine, Mama. How was work tonight?"

Pauline leaned against the door jamb. She looked tired—it was a tiredness beyond having worked a long shift. She looked worn. Her voice was haggard, and she had to clear her throat twice before she could speak. "Same collection of would-be cowboys and drunk farmers as every other Saturday night. I bet my butt is black and blue. Don't know what possesses a drunk to feel that every woman's butt has a bull's-eye on it for them to slap."

She turned and looked down at her bottom, rubbing it with her right hand. The hall light exposed her thin frame through the sheer linen frock she wore.

She walked over to the bed, dropped down beside her daughter, and slipped her arm around Marylyn's shoulders. Marylyn leaned her head into the crevice between her mother's shoulder and neck.

Marylyn whispered, "Mama, you're a very pretty woman. They're just bein' hopeful."

"Well, they ain't got any hope far as I'm concerned. Men are lost children. They see a pretty woman, and they act like they're in third grade again. Baby, you're awful good-lookin' yourself. That's why I wanted to talk to you. I heard something that scared me."

"What you got to be scared of?" Marylyn asked.

Pauline turned her head toward Marylyn's. Her left arm came up, and she pulled her daughter to her, hugging her close. "Did Tom get into a fight the other night?" she asked.

"Yes." *Where is this coming from?* Marylyn thought. *How did she hear about that?*

"Do you think you should go with such a violent young man?"

Marylyn sat up straight and looked her mother in the eyes. "It isn't like that, Mama. It wasn't his fault. It's mine."

Pauline turned on the bed, bringing her knee up on the bed, grabbing it with both her hands, and pulling it up under her chin. "How can it be your fault, baby? The first time you go out with him, he gets into a knife fight." Marylyn started to interrupt. "Wait a minute. Then, on your second date, he gets into a fistfight and breaks a guy's arm?"

Marylyn reached out and put her hands on her mother's intertwined hands. "Oh, Mama, I'm trying to tell you that he didn't start it either time. Sanchez did."

"That's the Mexican boy you went with last year, isn't it?"

"He's the one."

"Why would he start a fight? I thought you broke it off with him a couple months ago."

"I did. He wanted what I wouldn't give him, like your drunken cowboys, but he doesn't want me to go with anyone else. I swear, Mama. My Tom didn't start either one of those fights. He is so sweet and tender with me. He wouldn't hurt anyone on purpose."

"But breaking a man's arm, honey—that would take an awful mean person."

"That didn't happen, Mama! Who told you that?"

"One of the guys who was out there and saw the fight," Pauline said. "He said Tom knocked him down and then stomped on his arm." Pauline's keen eyes were staring at her daughter's face, looking for any discrepancies between her words and her expressions. Pauline always knew when Marylyn was lying.

"That's not true, Mama," Marylyn said. "Tom and I had started up on the dance floor, and Sanchez grabbed Tom and spun him around. Tommy ducked, and Sanchez hit him on the top of the head, breaking his hand. I swear to God, that's all that happened. Tommy had the chance to take advantage of Sanchez's broken hand but chose to walk away. Tom has never hit him yet, and that's the God's honest truth."

Of course, Pauline dissected every word. "What do you mean *yet*? You think he is going to keep after Sanchez?"

"No, Mama, he's not pursuing Sanchez. I think Sanchez ain't going to leave Tommy alone. I think Tommy is the nicest, gentlest boy I have ever gone out with." Marylyn pushed herself up on the bed and crossed her legs, leaning across them to look her mama in the eyes.

"You think a lot of him, don't you?" Pauline's face softened, and Marylyn could see her concern.

"Yes, I do. I can't explain it, but just bein' around him makes me feel warm and safe. It's just a peaceful, nice feeling. You know what I mean?"

"I think I do, honey, but you haven't known him for that long. And you might be reading something that isn't there."

She wasn't arguing with her daughter. She slid up on the bed and crossed her legs, forming a mirror image of Marylyn, their foreheads inches apart.

"I don't believe so," Marylyn said. "He is such a gentle person. He is just so nice to me."

Pauline's face lightened, and a smile struggled to emerge. "That is one thing in his favor—he has to be the nicest-looking boy you have ever gone with. No long hair, very clean-cut, and even with that bandage on his face, he is very nice-looking." She was truly smiling.

Marylyn leaned in and pressed her forehead against Pauline's. "I think so too, Mama," she said.

Pauline wrapped her arms around Marylyn, interlacing her fingers behind her daughter's neck. "Just don't get tied up too tight, honey," she said. "Don't forget your promise to me that you will graduate. Still promise, baby?"

Marylyn whispered, "You know I will, Mama. It's just that I really like him, and I want to go with him."

Pauline dropped her hands and moved to the edge of the bed. "I never have picked your friends, baby, and it would be a little late to start now. I don't know this boy, but I do like him better than Sanchez. But then you always did know what I thought of Sanchez."

Marylyn turned and threw her legs over the edge of the bed, pressing her feet to the oak hardwood floors. The wood was cool on the soles of her feet. "I just wish I would have listened to you about him. If anything stops Tommy from going with me, it will be the trouble that Sanchez causes."

Pauline stopped in the doorway and turned to look at her. She smiled and tilted her head, letting her long blonde hair fall forward. "Just be yourself, honey," she said, "and he will see what I already know. You're a lovely person."

Marylyn lifted the covers and pushed her feet deep into the cold hollow of the sheets, pulling the coverlet up under her chin as she dropped back onto her pillow. "Thanks, Mama. Going to church with me in the morning?"

"What do you mean *morning*? Let's forget church and sleep in. I'm awful tired."

"That sounds good to me. Good night, Mama."

"Good night, honey." Pauline walked back to Marylyn's bed, leaned in, and kissed her on the forehead. Then she disappeared through the door and down the hallway to her room.

Pauline took her nightgown from the dresser, took off her frock, and hung it up. She put her panties and bra in the laundry hamper and turned the water on for a shower before bed. Her thoughts went back to her talk with Mar.

I should have told her about Joe, she thought. *I would have, but I just don't know how she will react to him.* Joe, whom she had been secretly seeing for three months, was beginning to put pressure on her. She loved spending time at his small ranch about thirty miles outside of town, where he had beautiful quarter horses. Joe was pretty well off, and Pauline reasoned that she and Marylyn could have a wonderful life on the ranch, which was paid off. Joe made good money from selling about a hundred horses at a quarter horse auction each fall. He was a good man, but there was something below the surface. Pauline couldn't quite understand what was going on with him, but she really enjoyed the place and the way he treated her.

She stepped into the shower. The water was refreshing as its warmth spread over her head, wet her long hair, and rushed down her body, spreading its warm euphoria into every crevice. Her muscles started at last to relax. The heat opened the door to her mind and yesterday afternoon.

The drive to the ranch had been beautiful, as the sun through the leaves danced on the hood of the pickup. She could smell the hay that had been cut for baling and laid neatly in rows, waiting for the bailer to process it into food for winter. At ten in the morning, the dew had just recently escaped the earth. Pauline enjoyed working with Joe and taking care of several of his mares and their foals in the stables. She wore a pair of rubber boots to slog through the muck and held Joe's hand as they walked through the tall grass, moving the brood mares to a new pasture.

They walked back to the house at about two o'clock. Joe's arm lay easily across her shoulder as they walked up to the house. She was comfortable in his kitchen. She enjoyed cooking and was excited to make him a meal. Joe walked in with a couple of drinks, Crown and Coke. As Pauline chopped the vegetables, he set his drink down and then hoisted himself up onto the counter to watch her.

He reached out for her hand and pulled her to him, and she looked up into his eyes as she stood between his knees. The kiss was long, accepting, comfortable. She wrapped her arms around his waist and pulled herself into his body. His hands caressed her back, and it was so comfortable. The moment was broken by billowing smoke from the stove top.

Breaking free from Joe, Pauline grabbed the skillet, stuck it under cold water, and was nearly overcome by the smoke, steam, popping grease, and excitement. She stepped out onto the back porch, trying to clear her eyes and catch her breath. Joe came out behind her, laughing. "I guess it's too much to expect a lady to be beautiful and a good cook, too," he said.

She turned to him with tears running down her face from the smoke and emotion of the moment. He was standing there with a big smile on his face. "I'm sorry," she said. "I wanted to cook you a good meal."

"What for? It's as much my fault as yours. I'm the one who distracted you. 'Sides, I'm not very hungry anyway. Let's have another drink, and then I'll get cleaned up and take you out to dinner in town. No sense worrying about a few burnt taters." Joe took her hand and led her back into the house.

He got a fan and set it in the doorway to clear the smoke out of the kitchen.

Pauline sat wiping her tears in the living room when Joe appeared with another drink. He handed it to her and said, "I'll take a fast shower. You have to be at work by eight, don't you?"

"By six. I have to bathe and change out of these pants."

As the shower started up, Pauline wandered into the kitchen. The smoke was gone, but the burnt smell lingered. She picked up the dishes and put the ingredients back into the fridge. The skillet was still in the sink, so she dug around in the cabinet, pulled out a Brillo pad, and started scrubbing the crusty black char out of the pan.

After a few minutes, Joe appeared in the kitchen. Pauline glanced over her shoulder to see him standing there bare chested, wearing only a pair of Levi's that were partially unbuttoned. He was definitely sexy. She recognized that amorous glint in his eyes. It was inviting. She dropped the Brillo pad, placed the pan in the warm water, and turned toward him. He stepped closer and put his arms around her waist. With very little pressure, he pulled her tight up against him.

"Joe, my hands are wet and soapy," she said. She tried to step back without touching him.

He had hold and wasn't letting go. He pulled her in; her lower body was pulled even tighter, and she could feel a bulge in his blue jeans. She started to speak. "Joe, let me loo—"

He cut her off with a kiss. His hands slipped from her waist and cupped her hips in his hands, drawing her closer still. His lips were warm and tender. He gently molded his lips to hers.

As she stood there in the shower, with Mar sleeping in the other room, it was all cascading back and her body was aroused again, here and now, simply by recalling the events of the day before.

She wanted to pull away, to stop, but she wanted more to continue. Completely lost in indecision, she could feel the heat from his body and smell Irish Spring soap, freshly washed skin, Old English aftershave, and coconut hair conditioner. Her senses were on high alert, sensitive to arousal. They awakened memories of passion and excitement, and she found that her arms had already circled his neck and that her body was pressed against his. She was physically aroused, fully awake to the passion Joe had triggered.

Joe's hands slid up her side under her blouse and found their way to her breasts, gently squeezing and releasing them through her bra. And presently, as she stood in the shower, her soapy fingers slid across her breasts as she recalled that moment.

Joe was the first man Pauline had dated in three years. After they had dated a half dozen or so times, he had kissed her only twice. She was surprised that, this time, she was so attracted to him, responding to his touch. His hand slipped under her bra, and his fingers rolled across her nipples.

The urges she had been suppressing had overcome her. He was a good-looking, gentle man. She opened her eyes and leaned back away from him.

He was looking her right in the eyes and whispered a single word, "Please."

Such a little boy—how could she refuse? She nodded and raised her hands to his face, holding it and kissing him softly on the mouth. He reached for her hand and began to lead her to the bedroom. She reached back with her other hand and grabbed the dish towel to dry her hands.

She sat on the edge of the bed and dried her hands with the dish towel before tossing it at the wall. She unbuttoned her blouse, rolling it off the back of her shoulders. She pushed down the straps on her bra and turned it around to undo the clasp that had been behind her back, revealing her breasts to him.

She lifted her leg, and Joe tugged one boot off and then the other. As she lay back on the bed, Joe grabbed the cuff of her Levi's and pulled. The pants resisted at first and then, as she adjusted her hips, they slid off, pulling her panties down on her hips and revealing the crest of her pubic hair.

Joe was intensely focused. As she lay there on her back, looking up at him with her panties askew and her feet still in white gym socks, Joe stepped between her dangling feet and kneeled to pull off one sock and then the other. She pushed her flowered cotton panties down over her knees, lifted one knee, and kicked them to the side with one foot. Joe slid down on the bed next to her as she rolled to her side to face him.

She moved her hand to the first button that was done on his Levi's. She struggled to free it from its loop, finally bringing her other hand up to help. She worked her way down to each button and soon realized that Joe had no underwear on. His erect penis peeked from its hiding spot, and she slipped her right hand around it as if to tug it from hiding.

The memories were flooding through her mind. She was pressed against the wall of the shower as her own hands caressed her breasts and reached for her vagina. She was on fire, reliving the events as the water cascaded across her body, just like the heat of Joe's body yesterday. She was caught up in the memory, reliving every second.

Joe pushed his pants down and rolled to his back to kick his jeans off. Pauline didn't let go, holding his erect organ and looking into his eyes. He turned to her again, kissing her breasts and taking each in his mouth repeatedly. She stroked his organ gently up and down, and he picked a spot on her neck and devoured it.

She moaned and slipped her left arm under his side, through that opening just above his hip, and pulled him on top of her. She cradled him by raising her knees and then wrapping her legs around his back just above his buttocks. With her legs, she pushed his penis down toward her wet opening. He was larger than Mar's father; Pauline didn't know if he would fit. No man had been there since she had lost Mar's dad. But then she opened. The pain and pleasure pulsed through her.

Joe entered and pushed as she slid her hand to the base of his penis and cupped his testicles. His weight settled on her, and she felt the spasms and explosive release as she pulled her hand from between their flesh. She felt his thrust and pushed against him, driving him hard and deep.

He rocked, groaned, and pulled her hips up off the bed. He got up on his knees and pulled her to him, thrusting harder and harder. She was wet and grunting in unison with him. She could feel her vagina contracting on his penis as he drove it harder into her. A spasm would finish, and another would start. She continued to moan as her body went from one crest to the next, each one higher, harder, and stronger.

He reached for a pillow, pulled it under her hips, and continued. He was holding back the explosion with all the force he could manage, and then it broke. He released his river, grunting and pushing and pushing and then collapsing on top of her.

Finally, Pauline took a breath. The blood rushed to her head, and she could feel the contractions pushing his wilting erection out of her. She rolled him to his back and lay on top of him, kissing his face and neck as his penis fell flaccid.

They lay there, kissing and caressing as heads cleared and fought off the desire to doze. Joe's penis began to catch a second wind as she cupped his balls and tugged his wet organ, encouraging it to wake up and play.

As it came to life anew, she pumped it up and then straddled him, guiding his weapon to her waiting sheath. Joe steadied her hips as she began to rock, like a sixteen-year-old equestrian learning to post in an English saddle. Her contractions came in waves. Joe slid his hands to her breasts and pulled, increasing her downward thrust. They were one, moving in rhythm to a perfect tempo of slapping flesh.

She felt him swell in that pre-ejaculation moment, and as he came, he pinched her nipples.

It wasn't pain that she felt. It was indescribable. There were no words to capture the sheer ecstasy. For the first time in her life, she nearly fainted. Her body fell limp to his chest, and he caught her, lowering her gently and then holding her. She was overcome in ecstasy.

Not knowing what to do, he hugged her and continued to move rhythmically inside of her till his failing penis fell out on its own.

She rolled onto her side, lying next to him. He sweetly pushed the hair out of her face and rubbed his hands across her breasts and down to the vee between her legs. She opened her eyes slowly and blinked in the afternoon sun peeking through the window. He kissed her. The room around was laid out in forties furnishings. The bed had a strand of rope inlaid in the headboard. The sheets were flannel and soft to the touch.

"You're something else, baby." Joe's demeanor was odd. His expression was one that she had never seen before. It was dark, foreboding, and half-threatening.

"What do you mean?" Pauline felt an unexplainable bolt of fear run through her.

"I've never had anything that good in my life."

"If that is supposed to be a compliment, I don't like it!" she snapped. She felt cheap in that moment. What had been so delightful had turned to dust in a flash. She found herself sitting in a musty room, having given in to animal emotions. She wanted out of that room. She was scared and anxious, but she couldn't understand why. She swung her legs over the side of the bed and frantically gathered her clothes.

Joe reached out and took her by the arm. "Hey, baby, I didn't mean anything by what I said."

"Never mind, Joe. Just let it go," she snapped. *Why am I so pissed off?* she thought. She had wanted this to happen, to make love to him, and now she was angry without any reason. What was it that she saw in his face that she hadn't ever seen before? Or had she? Something was there, but she couldn't identify it. Now, in a simple question, some veil had been pulled back, and something behind his eyes scared her.

"But I never—" he started.

"*Let it go, Joe.* I'm just touchy I guess. I haven't done this in three years." That was true. She was lying about being touchy, though. She was scared.

She slipped into her clothes and raced into the bathroom. When she came out, Joe was sitting there with his clothes on, just pulling on his boots. As they walked out to his pickup, he said, "I guess this means you've decided to move in with me."

Pauline was surprised and shocked, still trying to grasp the fear that had settled in her soul. "No, it doesn't mean that," she said. "You just caught me in a weak moment. I told you that with my daughter—I would never do that to her." Mar was a welcome excuse. Pauline couldn't find her footing here with her mind in turmoil. She couldn't balance Joe's tenderness with the darkness she had perceived.

"What if I asked you to marry me?" he said.

"I would have to discuss it with my daughter," she replied. *Unless I know what you're hiding,* she thought, *it ain't going to happen.*

"Well, would you consider it?"

"Joe, we don't really know anything about each other. Our likes and dislikes … It's something I would have to think about for a long time. I'm sorry for what happened today. I'm not that type of person at all." She was starting to feel the shame of letting herself go for sheer pleasure.

"That is not the reason I would ask you to marry me." Joe looked righteously indignant that she would assume he was in it for the sex.

"It may or may not be, but I would rather just forget it for the time being." *Now I've hurt his feelings. How much more guilt can I pile on myself?*

The drive into town was long and silent. Finally, Joe pulled up in front of Pauline's apartment and got out to open the door for her, but she was already out the door and flying toward her front door as he rounded the front of the truck. He called to her, "Can I meet you later after work?"

"Not tonight. Give me some time to think, Joe." She fumbled for her house key and shoved it into the lock. She could hear him still talking.

"I'll see you later at the club," he said. He got back into the truck and drove off. Her back was to the door, and her heart was pounding. *What is going on with me?* she thought. *No time to think about it—got to get to work.*

The night at work was pure hell. The bar was jam packed. Don Williams, the country-and-western singer, was performing, and it was standing room only. Tables for four had eight. It seemed that everybody from El Paso had come to town to hear him. Pauline didn't stop moving from eight o'clock until she got off at two thirty. Not only that, but Joe had taken the barstool right next to the waitress station and kept trying to talk to her every time she came near. After about two hours, she finally told him, "I don't have time to talk to you, Joe. Please leave me alone." She knew she had been a lot harder on him than she should have been. She could tell his feelings were hurt.

He got up and started to walk off, but he turned and said, "I'll call you tomorrow." In that moment as he looked at her, she saw it again—that veil of darkness just behind his eyes.

At home later, the water was starting to cool. Joe's darkness had dampened any arousal she had initially felt from the warm water coming from the showerhead. She knew she would have to break it off with Joe if she couldn't figure out what was going on with him. She turned the shower handle and pushed the curtain back, grabbing a towel to dry her hair. When she finally got to bed around three thirty, she was still thinking about her conversation with Marylyn, the young man named Tom, and her troubles with Joe.

Chapter 9

The Fix Is In

I swung by Manny's and picked him up. When we arrived for practice, the coaches handed out our playbooks, white three-ring, one-inch binders with our names on the front. The sheets smelled of mimeograph fluid and were still moist. They must have just finished printing them.

The team sat on the bleachers at the stadium. Coach Baker took on an air of serious resolve. "Now, I don't believe I have to tell you this, but I will anyway. These playbooks are the property of Le High. Some of the other schools in our league would love to have them. If you lose the book, it will cost you twenty-five bucks. Get the plays down in your mind until they are second nature. When you have them memorized, give the books back. I don't want them floating around. Now let's get our workouts and exercises underway."

The coaches lined us up in eleven-man squads to start running plays. Manny was put in one, and I was in another. Mueller, Pedro, Chico, Malin, and Harry were in the same squad. The quarterback on my squad was the kid called Helio, who had been with Sanchez the other night at Z's.

Each squad was shown a play in the book, and then we would run that play over and over. On the second series of plays, the ball was supposed to be handed off to me. When we started to run the series on the count of two, I darted off and reached for the ball, but it fell from my fingers to the ground.

The next time, it happened the same way. I got my hands on the ball, but Helio pulled it right out of my hands, turning me sideways and tripping me up. The ball dropped. Then Helio stood there looking at me. "What's wrong with you, Gurley? Can't hang on to the ball?"

Coach Burt walked over and asked the same. "Don't matter how fast you are if you ain't got the ball in your hands when you cross the goal line. Okay! Now again."

Coach Burt stood there in the backfield, watching the play. Helio handed it off perfectly under Cobb's watchful eye and ran the play. Coach Vic, the line coach, came over, saw one of the linemen out of position, and moved him. Then he said, "Okay, run it again." The two Cobbs stood behind us, watching their respective responsibilities for errors in execution.

I started running at the snap of the ball. As I grabbed the ball, Helio stuck out his leg and tripped me. I plunged forward, face first, into the ground. My face mask was plugged with dirt and grass, and the dust blinded me momentarily.

Coach Burt stood there looking down at me. "Are you always so damn clumsy, Gurley? Run it one more time!" The coach stood in the backfield again, watching the next series of plays. Everything went smoothly. Helio tried to knock the wind out of me by slamming the ball into my stomach, but I aggressively grabbed it from him to keep him from yanking it out of my grasp. Helio was clearly trying to show me up. We ran through the rest of the plays without another mishap.

After about forty-five minutes, we changed lines and quarterbacks. During the break, Manny asked me, "What happened over there?"

"Helio tried to make me look bad," I answered. "He made bad handoffs and even tripped me once. Unfortunately, I think he did a pretty good job."

"Okay, then, let's show them what you can do."

Manny and I worked like greased gears together. There were no bobbles or false starts, no dropped balls, and no missed plays. We ran several plays. We even tried several pass plays, which worked to perfection.

At seven thirty, Manny and I knocked off and headed to the yard to finish up. Buck's car was there in the driveway when we pulled in. When I entered the house, Buck was talking on the phone. He stuck up his hand in greeting, and Rosie came hurrying out of the kitchen, grabbed me, and hugged me. "Wash up, Tommy," she said. "Your supper is waiting."

I went into the bathroom to clean up. As I took off my shirt and dropped it into the hamper, an old man walked up to the bathroom door.

"Tom, I'm Roscoe Walgrin, Rosie's dad. Guess you're going to have to share your room with me for a while."

We shook hands. He was about my height and had big blue eyes and a shock of pure white hair. His grin was easy and natural. I liked him immediately.

"Just call me Rocky," he said. "Everybody does."

"I better get cleaned up, Rocky."

"Yeah, you do that, son."

As I entered the kitchen, Buck rose and stuck out his hand. When I reached to shake it, he pulled me in and gave me a big hug before he stepped back and looked at me. I had washed my face and left the bandage off.

"Pretty bad cut there, Tom."

"Doc says it won't be bad."

I glanced over at Rosie; she had tears on her cheeks. "Had any more trouble with the guy who did it?" Rocky asked.

"Had a couple more run-ins with him."

"Such as?" Buck asked intently.

"I broke his hand with my head."

Rosie spoke up. "Sit down and eat, Tommy. Tell us about it, and don't leave anything out."

I started in where I met Mar and what had transpired since then. Of course, I left out the marijuana and beer, though I think they figured there was beer involved. When I finished, I sat there looking at them.

Buck asked, "What you plannin' on doin' about it?"

"I don't know. I know I am goin' to have to fight him. I don't want to, but if I have to I will."

"I know that, son, but it scares the hell out of me," Buck said. "From what you say about him, there's not a fair bone in his body. He proved that with a knife."

Rocky spoke up. "I've never seen any man that runs with a pack like you say he has that would fight fair. For one thing, he needs the rest of them to keep his courage up, besides to help him out if he gets into trouble. You ever been in a fight, young man?"

"Not since I was in the sixth grade and I got my ass kicked," I answered.

"I'm not talkin' about kid fights, son."

Rosie said, "If you are going to have to fight this boy, why not switch and go to school at El Paso?"

"I'm not runnin', Rosie."

Buck answered, "She's not talkin' 'bout runnin'," Buck interjected. "She's just tryin' to avoid trouble for you."

"I know that, but I still would be goin' with Mar and that's what's buggin' him—not school."

Rosie asked, "Is she that important?"

"She is to me. Got any more coffee?"

She brought the coffeepot over and filled all three cups.

Buck said, "All right, Tom. If that's how it is, you're goin' to have to learn how to fight."

Rosie put the coffeepot on the table and lowered herself onto Buck's lap. "What are you going to do, honey?"

"Teach him how to fight," Buck said as he slid his arms around Rosie's lovely waist.

"I don't like that. You know what I think about fightin', Buck Hagan."

"Look, honey, I can't have him going into this not knowin' anything."

"I know, but isn't there any other way to resolve it?" Rosie asked.

"Not that I know of. I could have a couple of the roughnecks out at the field handle it."

"Buck, you don't mean it." Rosie's frown clearly tipped Buck off to the correct answer to that question.

"No, honey, I don't mean it, but it would serve him right. You want to learn how to fight, Tom?"

"If I have to. I'm not backin' down."

"Okay, then, tomorrow we will start."

"I don't know when. Between football practice and haulin' pipe, I don't have time to turn around."

"I know. I can't hardly spare the time myself, but I'll figure out something. You'd better hit the sack."

I told Rosie good night, and as I was leaving, I heard Buck tell Rocky, "Do me a favor in the morning."

The minute I hit the bed, I was asleep. I halfway felt Rocky climb into the bed later.

Rocky shook me awake. "Breakfast in ten minutes, Tom." He was already up and dressed.

They were all sitting at the table when I walked in. Rosie handed me a cup of coffee before she sat down and started eating breakfast.

"Tom, I have things figured out," Buck said. "It will be tiring on you, but from now on after football practice, I'll meet you at the yard. I talked to Jesus, and he gave me a corner of one of the sheds. Meet me there.

"Fine. I'll be there."

As I started out the door, I heard Andy and Sissy hollering and whooping as they came near. Both of them ran up and grabbed and hugged me. Then they both stepped back and looked at the bandage on my face.

Sissy asked, "Does it hurt, Tommy?"

"No, honey, it don't hurt anymore."

"Did it hurt much?" Andy asked.

"For a while it hurt a lot. I've got to go to work now. See you later."

Sissy pulled on my hand. I bent over, and she whispered in my ear, "I'm glad you weren't hurt bad, Tommy."

I kissed and hugged her, and then I waved as I went off to work.

The minute we were dressed and went out on the field, Coach Baker spit his chaw on the ground and said in his uniquely monotone voice, "All right, gentlemen, today is when we start separating the men from the boys. If I call off your name, pick up a black shirt from Coach Farrington. You will be on defense." Several of the people he called I knew slightly. None of the group I ran with was called.

I walked over to Coach Burt, whose soft and welcoming demeanor belied his intellect and perception of reality. "May I talk to you a minute, Coach?"

"Yeah, Gurley, what is it?"

"I can't be here for practice tonight."

"Why's that?"

"Doctor's appointment to get these stitches out," I answered.

"He say anything about you playing football?

"No, just to be careful."

"He say anything about physical contact?"

"No, just to be careful."

"Okay, go in and see Henry, and ask him if we have one of those extra padded helmets and hurry back." I could tell he was genuinely interested in my welfare, which was the opposite of Coach Vic's attitude about playing through the pain and dying on the field of battle if you have to.

It took me about five minutes to find Henry in the equipment room, and by the time I got back out, they had already gone through their exercises and were running plays.

When I ran up, Coach Burt said, "Gurley, replace Breedlove at left half. Tell him to switch to right half, and have Martin come out."

When I arrived in the huddle, I noticed for the first time that Helio was the quarterback. On the second play, they called my number—slant off left, tackle on two. On two, I took two steps forward and reached for the ball, and Helio pulled it back. Try as I might, I couldn't get hold of it. The ball hit the ground. Coach Baker spit, swore, and hollered, "Watch the damn ball, Gurley! Don't try to run till you get it in your hands!"

We ran three more plays and then my number was called again, and Helio did the same thing.

Coach Baker exploded, spittin' and cussin' like a crazy man who had smashed his thumb with a hammer. "Get Martin back in there! Gurley's got hands of stone!"

When I came out, Coach Burt said, "Go over to that team, Gurley, and take left half." Coach Burt kept his eyes on Helio the entire time he was talking to me. He was pissed and perplexed, and he raised his hand to his chin, stroking his five-day beard. "Helio don't work too well with you, does he?" he asked.

I didn't answer. I just ran over and joined the other team.

Manny said, "Hello, gringo," when I joined the huddle.

We ran plays for over an hour, and things went like they were supposed to. Coach Baker called a rest.

Coach Burt yelled to me, "Gurley, come over here!"

I jumped up and ran over to him.

"I been watchin' you," he said, "and you ain't dropped a ball for the last hour, even running plays you just learned. So I figure must be something 'sides your hands. Are you and Helio having problems?"

"We don't like each other, if that's what you mean," I answered.

"You know dang well what I mean," Burton said as he peered at me over his bifocals. "That the reason you dropped the ball, trying to make him look bad?"

"No. It wasn't *me* trying to make *him* look bad!"

"Is that all you have to say?" he asked.

"That's it, Coach."

"Then you're saying it's something that he's doing?"

"You said it, Coach, not me."

"Fine, Gurley. Go on back and rest."

On the next session, Manny and I were transferred over to the first team, and we finished out practice.

Rosie's T-bird was sitting next to the shed on the left of the yard when we pulled in. We pulled up and parked, and Rocky walked out of the shed. "Howdy, Tom."

"Rocky, meet Manny," I said. The two of them stepped forward and shook hands.

"Glad to meet you, son. Come on in. I've got things all set up."

I had told Manny all about our talk the night before. Across the vacant warehouse, in a corner, Rocky had set up a punching bag and a sandbag. They hung from the sheet-metal siding about ten feet above the concrete floor. A couple of old kitchen chairs had been dragged in and pushed against the wall. A makeshift ring had been set up with four oil drums arranged in a square about thirty feet on the diagonal. Also, a cotton clothes line had been suspended from the barrels to represent the ropes around the boxing ring. The smell of steel pipe and grease was strong in the amplified heat of an all-steel building.

To keep us hydrated, Rocky had a couple of jugs of water sitting on the old table he had brought in. He must have gotten it from the same place he got the dining room chairs.

Manny walked over to the punching bag and started slamming away on it. He really made it dance. When he stopped, Rocky asked him, "You box before, son?"

"Used to belong to the Police Athletic League. They taught me."

"That's good. You can teach Tom here how to punch a bag."

I stepped up to the bag and tapped it a couple of times, and the third time I tried to hit it, I missed. "More to it than it looks like," I said.

Manny said, "Not really. It's just a matter of timing and coordination. Here, watch." He showed me how to turn my hands each time I hit the bag so that it bounced away in a straight line each time. "Now start off slow. The speed will come later."

I had been hitting the bag for about ten minutes when Buck walked in. "I see you started without me. How you been?"

"Fine, Buck," I said.

"Who showed you how to pound the bag?"

"Manny."

"You box, Manny?" Buck asked.

"Yeah, used to. Still work out with my brothers and cousins."

"Thank God. Sure will help out." Buck turned and smiled at Rocky.

Rocky looked at me with a serious expression. "Now, Tom, I want you to work on the two bags. You have plenty of muscles; it's just learning how to use them."

Rocky showed me how to hit the sandbag so I wouldn't hurt my hands, and then he brought out a big pair of boxing gloves for me.

Buck said, "Now I'm going to try to hit you. You block it with the glove or your arms."

We sparred for about five minutes in the makeshift boxing ring. When we stopped, Buck said, "You're faster than I thought. You block real well. Now I'm going to start correcting you." He proceeded to show me how to block and counter.

Rocky interrupted us. "Buck, it's two thirty."

"Thanks, Rocky. That will have to do for today, Tom. You boys had better get some of that pipe loaded for Blackwell. See you later."

We walked out to the trucks. Manny and I hauled a load of pipe and came back into the yard. "I've got that doctor's appointment at five," I said. "Want me to drop you off at the field?"

"No, Dad's letting me use the car tonight. Tess and Marylyn are going out for cheerleader. I'm takin' Tess. You takin' Marylyn?"

"Don't know. She hasn't said anything to me about it."

"See you in the mornin' then."

When I reached the house, I took a bath and then drove to the doctor's office, getting there right at five. After waiting for ten minutes and filling out some insurance papers, I was ushered into a small room. A nurse came in and took the bandage off my face. The doctor entered and looked at the cut. "Did a pretty nice job, if I do say so myself. I think we can take these stitches out. Nurse, get me a pair of scissors. Have any problems, Tom?"

"None, Doctor."

As he clipped the stitches and pulled them out, my face stung. "You have any numbness?"

"Not that I noticed."

"Good. Keep this covered over the weekend," he said. "You can take it off around Sunday."

"Thanks, Doctor."

"Come back and see me in a couple of weeks. See the receptionist on the way out."

My watch said it was 5:30 when I climbed into my truck. It took me ten minutes to reach Mar's.

Pauline answered the door after the first ring. "Come on in, Tom. Marylyn is taking a bath. I'll tell her you're here. Can I get you a Coke or coffee or anything?"

"Either would be fine. Thank you." Wow—Pauline was beautiful for her age. She and Mar could be sisters, as they say.

Pauline came out of the kitchen carrying two cups of coffee. As she handed me a cup, she asked, "Not workin' today?"

"Had to go to the doctor and have the stitches removed, ma'am." I noticed that she was observing me closely.

"Tom, you have to understand, I love my daughter and don't want her hurt. Have you ever been in trouble, Tom?"

"How do you mean, ma'am?" I knew exactly what she meant but wanted to buy myself some time. I slid back on the brown tufted sofa, pressing my back deep in the corner to give myself plenty of room to answer.

"With the police?"

"No, ma'am. I know there've been problems since I started going with Mar, but it isn't my doing." Did she think I was a hood? I took a sip of the coffee and realized that it was pretty good. I was too used to drinking that swill at the pipe yard.

"You sayin' that you never started any of this that has happened 'tween you and Sanchez?"

"Yes, ma'am, that is what I'm sayin'. I don't like to fight. In fact, I don't really know how." *If she knew I was taking lessons,* I thought, *she might be a bit upset. Best to keep that a secret.*

"Couldn't you have avoided it?" She sat on a recliner, but she was leaning in toward me. I felt her eyes probing every part of my face, looking for any sign of dishonesty.

"For my part, yes, ma'am, I would have. But he jumped me both times, and I didn't have a chance."

"Marylyn tells me you have never hit him. Is that right?" She never took her eyes off me. I was getting the third degree—no rubber hose or bright lights, but Pauline didn't need them. She was probing for an answer and wasn't going to let up till she had it.

"Yes, ma'am. Look, ma'am, I wouldn't do anything to hurt Mar. She's the first girl I've ever dated, and I would like to keep going with her." She still didn't soften her appearance. Her face and eyes were still focused. I was trapped on the sofa, and I was going to answer.

She pressed her point, "If you had a choice, when you were out with Marylyn, would you fight?"

"No, ma'am. I wouldn't fight at any time unless it's forced on me. But a man has to defend himself and the people he cares about."

"I know that. It's just that I am going to ask you to do everything in your power to avoid it when you are with Marylyn."

"I will do my best, ma'am." With that, Pauline actually relaxed and pushed herself back in the recliner.

She stroked the arm of the recliner. "This was Mar's dad's favorite chair. Evenings, he would sit here and read the paper while Mar played with dolls on the floor. Sundays, he would take a nap here after church."

"Mother, who you talkin' to?" Marylyn walked into the room. She wore a light pink housecoat and had a towel wrapped around her head. The hair framing her face was damp and curled. Her face broke into a wide smile when she saw me. At last, I was rescued from the chief inquisitor.

"Hi, Tommy. What you doin' here?"

"Manny told me you and Tess were going to the high school to try out for the cheerleaders. Thought I'd take you, if you don't mind."

"I'd love it. I told Tess not to say anything. Have to talk to that girl. Hey, ain't you supposed to be practicin' football?"

"Doctor's appointment. Got my stitches out." Mar walked over to the sofa and sat next to me under the watchful eye of Pauline.

"Is it bad?" Mar asked as she stroked my cheek.

"What?"

Marylyn looked at my cut. "The scar—is it going to look bad?" Her face reflected her concern.

"Don't know. Didn't get to look at it after he took the stitches out. Doc says it's going to be fine."

"Sure, but it isn't his face." Mar lifted her legs across my lap, and her mother pulled herself out of the recliner and went to the kitchen to refill her coffee cup. "More coffee, Tom?" Pauline asked from the kitchen.

"No, thanks, Mrs. Birchley."

"Call me Pauline."

"Okay, Pauline. I'm fine with the coffee I have."

I turned to Mar and kissed her lips while Pauline's back was turned. "I came over to take you out for dinner before tryouts, if you'd like to."

"Mother and I were fixin' to go out for pizza." There was no question in her statement—it was more of an imperative for me to go along.

"Fine. I'd love to take you."

"You don't have to do that, Tom," Pauline said. "You and Marylyn go ahead."

"We can't do that, Pauline. You will have to go with us. I won't take no for an answer." I thought this might be a good time to show Pauline how normal I really was.

"All right, but you'd better get ready, Marylyn. I have to be to work by eight." Mar gave me a quick peck on the cheek and ran down the hall toward her room. Her bathrobe caught a breeze, exposing the upper part of her legs, and I realized again how attractive she was to me.

"Be just a minute," she called as she disappeared into her room.

"Your dad works in the oil field, Tom?" Pauline was back in the recliner, and the interrogation had resumed.

"No. Buck, I guess, is my foster dad. My parents are dead. They were killed in a car wreck along with my sister."

"I'm sorry. I didn't know." Pauline was definitely moved with sadness. She turned her gaze to the worn carpet at her feet.

"That's okay. The wreck was almost two years ago in Florida."

"How did you wind up down here?" She raised her eyes to engage me again, only this time it was concern instead of interrogation.

"My uncle owns the company we work for. He's a bachelor who doesn't really want a family. I like living with Buck and Rosie." I felt myself smiling at the thought of Buck and Rosie being my parents. They took me in, of course, but I was starting to feel like we were family.

Mar walked in wearing a pleated skirt and blouse and had her hair pulled back in a ponytail. If it hadn't been for her body, she would have looked like a twelve-year-old, which made me think thoughts no teenager should think about a twelve-year-old.

"Boy, you look nice," I said. I hoped I wasn't slobbering when I said it.

"Thank you, kind sir."

"First time I've seen you in a skirt," I added. I realized that I liked Mar in skirts. Her legs were awesome.

"Well, I am a girl, you know." She cocked her head at me and grinned in a way that spelled trouble.

"Somehow, I had that idea. Shall we go?" I was convinced that Pauline could read my mind and that if this conversation continued, she would throw me out of the house.

I opened the passenger door of the truck, and Mar jumped in, followed by Pauline. I offered Pauline my hand, ever the thoughtful gentleman. As we started down the street, I told them that I had to swing by my place. I hadn't thought ahead but was pretty sure I didn't have enough money. Andy and Sissy were playing in the front yard when I pulled in. Both of them came running over to the truck when I stopped. When I stepped out, they each grabbed a leg. I reached down and picked each one up. When they saw Marylyn and Pauline, they quieted right down. "This is Andrew and Lyla. We call her Sissy," I said. "Kids, this is my girl and her mom."

Sissy smiled and said, "Hello."

Andrew just sat there and looked at them. Mar and Pauline both said hello and smiled at them.

"Would you like to come in?" I asked.

Mar said, "No, we'll wait out here for you."

I started for the house with the kids. Sissy said, "Leave me here so I can talk to the pretty ladies." I grinned and sat her on the driver's seat.

Andy and I went into the house. Rocky was sitting there watching the news on TV. "Howdy, son," he said with enthusiasm.

"Hello, Rocky. Where's Rosie?"

"I'm in the kitchen, Tom." She was standing by the stove when I walked in. "You going to be home for supper?"

"No, I'm taking Mar and her mother out to dinner. I need some money."

"Get my purse out of our bedroom. What time you pickin' them up?"

"They're outside in the truck," I said.

"Tommy, where are your manners? You should have invited them in."

"I did."

"Take what you need out of my purse. I'm going out to invite them in." She undid her apron, threw it on the counter next to the stove, and started out to the truck before I reached the bedroom door. Her purse was sitting on the dresser. I took fifty and went out. Rosie was on Pauline's side of the truck talking when I walked up. I heard her saying, "Supper is about ready. You are more than welcome to join us."

Pauline said, "I'd love to, Mrs. Hagan, but I have to be to work at eight. Some other time, if we may." Sissy was sitting in Mar's lap, jabbering away.

"Come on, squirt," I said. "We have to go." I started to pick her up.

She said, "Just a minute," stood up on the seat, and gave Mar a kiss on the cheek. "Okay, I'm ready now." I put her on the ground and slipped into the truck.

Mar leaned over and said, "She told me you were her boyfriend but that she didn't care if I went with you because I was prettier and older than she is."

"She's a real nice kid. Rosie makes them mind," I said.

Pauline said, "She seems like one of the people I grew up with up in Kansas."

"Funny you should say that. They came from Kansas. Buck met her while workin' in an oil field. Then they were married within two weeks after they met."

"I could tell. Every time she mentioned her husband, her face lit up. I had that with Marylyn's daddy. It's nice."

"You know, Mama, that's the first time I've heard you mention Daddy in over a year," Marylyn said.

"I know, honey. It just brings back memories when I meet someone happily married."

"Which pizza parlor do you ladies want to go to?" I asked.

"Let's go over to Sandy's, Mama. We haven't been there in a long time."

Pauline was real quiet through dinner. It was almost seven thirty when we finished.

"Why don't you kids drop me off at the club?" she said. "I can take a taxi home after work. That way you won't be late for tryouts." Pauline had just stepped out of the truck and was talking to Mar when a man pulled up in a pickup, stepped out, and walked up behind her. She was telling Mar, "Wish you luck, honey," when the man put his arm around her waist. She jumped and pulled away. "Oh, hello, Joe."

"Hi, baby doll. This your daughter?"

Marylyn stared at the slender-looking cowboy in blue jeans and a pearl-button cowboy shirt. He was a bit older than her mom but handsome nevertheless. I noticed that Pauline was clearly nervous about Joe being there. She was flustered. I actually halfway enjoyed seeing the inquisitor a bit embarrassed.

Joe slipped beside Pauline and leaned up against the open door of my truck to shake hands with Mar and me.

"Yes. Marylyn, Tom, this is Joe."

I leaned across Mar to shake Joe's hand.

"She looks a lot like you, baby, just younger. You tell her about us?" Pauline looked panicked to me. She clearly wanted to get Joe away from Mar and me to talk with him.

"You kids go ahead. I'll see you later," Pauline said nervously, and then she turned and started into the club, Joe walking after her.

Mar turned to me. "Wonder what he meant by 'about us'?"

"I don't know, but he sure seems serious about your mama and your mama seems a bit nervous around him."

"You think they're talkin 'about marriage?"

"No way of knowing unless your mama tells you, baby." I reached out and slid my hand down the inside of Mar's left leg on my way to grabbing the gear shift.

"Let's go, Tommy, or I'll be late," she said.

I fired up the 454, and we headed for the high school.

Chapter 10

Cheerleader Tryouts and Trouble

Manny and I sat in the bleachers in the gym. The girls who were trying out for cheerleader positions were put into groups by the instructor. For the next two hours, they ran through different routines and yells, moving from one end of the gym to the other. The instructor kept transferring girls from one group to another. It appeared that she was sorting the good, the bad, and the ugly into groups. When the tryouts ended, she called the girls to center court.

"You girls may take a break now. I will post your names in about ten minutes on the bulletin board. Thank you all for coming. If you don't make the varsity cheerleader squad, you are invited back to try out for the junior varsity."

Tess and Mar bounded up the bleachers toward us. Manny and I had been sitting up in the bleachers watching, counting the number of moves that resulted in a panty shot. I'm sure we looked guilty, but the girls didn't figure out why.

They sat down with us.

Tess asked, "What you think, Mar?"

"Who knows. Remember last year?"

"Sure do. They didn't even think we were good enough for the JV."

"Well, both of us thought you were the best on the floor, didn't we, Manny?" I said.

Manny agreed. "There wasn't any competition."

"Well," Mar said to Tess, "at least they know how to make us girls feel good."

"Look, Mar, she's leaving the gym. I bet she's puttin' up the list. Let's go check."

We all got up and started toward the exit into the hallway and the bulletin board. One of the girls we had met at Pepi's walked past us, having just scanned the list. I raced past her and read the list.

Tess said to the girl, "Hey, did Pam make it?"

I hurried back as Tess was finishing the question and answered for the unsuspecting girl, "No, but you and Marylyn did."

"Hey, great!" Manny said. "Let's go have a party!"

The girls were jumping up and down and ran down the hallway to read the board themselves. Some girls were shouting; others were crying. It was chaos.

As we were standing there at the bulletin board, the door opened, and two policemen walked in. They were the same two that had talked to me at the hospital. They stopped and talked to the instructor for a minute and then came toward us.

Manny said, "Hello, Dave, Officer Perez. How you doin'?"

I nodded at the officers.

"Fine, Manny. Hello, Gurley. See you're still wearing your bandage."

"Healin' up fine, officer," I said.

"Glad to hear it." He turned to Mar. "You Marylyn Birchley?"

"Yes."

"Would you come with me, please? Your mother was hurt and is at the hospital."

Mar had been standing there holding my hand. When Dave said the word *hospital,* Mar squeezed my hand tight.

"What happened to her?"

"We don't know, Miss. She told someone where she works that you were here."

"Can I take her, Dave?" I asked.

"No. We were ordered to pick her up and bring her in."

"Well, can I go with her?"

"No, but we're taking her over to Memorial Hospital. You can meet us there. Take her out to the car, Perez. I'll be right there." Marylyn looked over her shoulder at me as Perez led her away.

"Marylyn, I'll be right behind you in the truck!" I shouted as she was led away.

"Can Tess ride with her?" Manny asked Dave.

"'Fraid not. Does she have any relatives in this area?" Dave looked at Tess. "You know of any?"

"Nope, sure don't."

I directed my attention to Officer Dave. "What you need relatives for? Is Marylyn in trouble?"

"Look, I've got to go, but you be sure and come on down to the hospital. Her mother has been shot, and I don't think she'll make it."

"Can't you tell us any more?" I couldn't believe he wasn't telling us everything.

"Can't do it, Gurley. Got to go."

Tess turned to me. "What are we going to do?"

"Is there a phone anyplace 'round here we could use?" I asked.

Tess was exasperated. "No, all the offices are locked up. There's one two blocks down the street at the Texaco station on the right side of the street."

The cheerleading instructor walked up. "What did the police want with Marylyn?" She was looking at me.

"Her mother's been shot. She's in the hospital, and we need to make some calls," I said.

"Why didn't you say so?" The instructor pulled a ring of keys out of her pocket and opened the office.

The phone had rung only once when Rocky answered.

"Rocky, this is Tom. Is Rosie there?"

"You don't sound good, Tom."

"Yeah, Rocky, let me speak to Rosie, please. I'll explain everything later."

After a short pause, Rosie picked up. "Yes, Tommy? What is it?"

"Mar's mother was shot. She's at Memorial Hospital. The police just took Mar there. She doesn't have any family close. Would you please come down? I don't know what to do."

"Honey, Buck's in the shower right now. We will be there as soon as possible."

"Thanks, Rosie."

"You at the hospital now?"

"No, we're still at the school."

"You go ahead. We should be there the same time as you. Don't drive too fast."

Rosie's T-Bird pulled into the emergency room driveway right in front of me.

Buck asked me as we climbed out, "What happened?"

"I don't know." We walked through the door as I was answering. "There's the officers. Let's ask them."

Buck approached Dave and Officer Perez. "Where's Mar?"

"She's in that room with the detectives," replied Dave.

"Dave, these are my friends Buck and Rosie Hagan."

"How's her mother?" Rosie asked.

"She was dead on arrival, ma'am."

"Does Marylyn know yet?" Rosie asked.

"I don't know, ma'am, if the detectives have told her yet. They're getting a statement, I believe."

"I'm going in there."

"Ma'am, you can't do that," Dave protested.

"Oh, the hell I can't! That young girl is sitting in there with two detectives and don't even know her mama's dead!" With that, Rosie pushed right around Dave and Perez and opened the door, with me right behind her.

Two men were sitting there. Marylyn's face showed that she had been crying. When she saw us, she jumped up and came running to me. She grabbed me in a desperate hug and buried her face in my chest.

Rosie walked over and said something to the two men. They shook their heads, got up, and walked out.

I stood there holding Mar. She was sobbing so hard that her whole body shook.

Rosie came up and put her arm around Mar's waist. "Honey, we have to talk to you."

Marylyn turned her head with her cheek still pressed against my chest. "Mama's dead, isn't she?"

"Yes, honey, she is."

Her arms got even tighter around me, and then she spoke again. "I knew she was before I even got here. The detectives told me that the man we met tonight did it."

"Do they know why?"

"He said they were still piecing it together. You know he shot himself too?"

"Who did?"

"Joe, that man we met. What am I going to do?"

"For right now, you're comin' home with us. That your jacket there?" Rosie asked. "Tommy, you go ahead and take her home." I led Mar out into the waiting room. Everyone was standing there looking at us as we walked out.

Tess came running over. Mar took one look at her and burst out crying even harder. Tess put her arms around her, tears running down her face as well. She kept repeating over and over, "Mar, I'm so sorry. Lord, but I'm sorry."

As I looked around the room, I realized that everyone had tears in their eyes. I looked at Buck, and his face was pained as he looked back at me. God, I hurt inside.

Rosie talked to Dave and then walked over to Buck. Buck walked up to me and said, "Let's take her home, son."

Marylyn pulled out of Tess's embrace. Looking up at me, she said, "Can I see my mama, Tommy?"

I looked over at the detectives, who were shaking their heads. "Not tonight, baby. I don't think your mama would want you to see her the way she is right now."

"But I have to see her. I can't leave her alone, Tommy."

"She isn't alone, baby. Please come on home with me. We will see her tomorrow."

"Are you sure?"

"We'll try, honey. Please, let's go." As we walked out, she had hold of me so tight, and the tears were still running down her face. Her blouse was wet down the front, and my shirt stuck to my chest, drenched through by her tears and mine. As we got into the truck, Mar was sitting half on me and half on the seat with her arms around my neck and her face buried in my chest. She had such a grip on me that steering was difficult. I had to reach through the steering wheel to start the truck and put it in gear.

"Tommy, I'm scared," were the first words she said in the truck.

"Why, honey?"

"I don't have anyone left. The only relative I have is my grandmother in Kansas, and she's in a rest home. What am I going to do?"

"Baby, please don't worry about it now. We will think of something."

"It hurts."

"I know it does, sweetheart. But I won't let anything happen to you."

We walked into the house. Rocky was sitting there watching TV. He got up, came over, and took Mar's hand. As he did, Mar looked up at him. For the rest of my life, I will never forget the love and compassion in Rocky's eyes and face. Mar released my hand and let Rocky lead her over to the kitchen table. He pulled a chair out for her and then scooted it in for her. He sat in the chair right next to her and again took her hand in his. "Rosie called from the hospital and told me what happened. Marylyn, you don't know me. I'm just a foolish old man who has outlived his usefulness, but there is one thing to think of at a time like this. The good Lord puts us all on the face of this earth for a reason. None of us ever get the satisfaction of knowing what that reason is. One of the reasons your mama was put here was to bear you. Another was to raise you in a loving home. Another was to teach you right and wrong. The most important of all was to teach you love and tenderness. We will never know why the good Lord called your mama home. All we know is that God knows best."

"But, Rocky, why did she have to die that way?"

"Honey, people die every day. I buried a lady last week who had been my entire life for forty-two years. She had a heart attack and was gone in two minutes. But for the last ten years, she had lived in pain, horrible pain. She had crippling arthritis. I was thankful the good Lord took her the way he did. Honey, never dwell on how your mama died. Just remember the way she lived, the way you knew her—kind, loving, gentle, and understanding."

"You never met my mama," she said.

"No, that was my loss. Tommy there told me about how sweet you are. Your mother had to be the source of that. She had to be a nice person to have raised someone like you."

"Thank you."

Buck and Rosie walked in and sat down at the table. Rosie asked, "How you feeling, honey?"

"I can't think of anything. Everything seems crazy. My mind is going in circles. Is that normal?"

Rocky said, "Honey, no one knows what normal is in circumstances like this. All of us are different. The Lord made some of us out of glass, some of steel, some gold, some silence, and then a few of them he made out of diamonds, one of the hardest things known to man. It's things like this that determine what you are to be."

"I'm so tired," Mar said.

Rosie got up and put her hand on Mar's shoulder. "Honey, come with me."

Mar came over to me, hugged me, and kissed me. Her lips were salty, wet, and cool from her tears. Then she followed Rosie out of the room.

"Buck, what can I do for her?" I asked.

"Don't know right now, Tommy. There is no need to make a decision right now. Let's let things settle down. We'll talk tomorrow. You going to bed?"

"Where's Mar sleeping?"

"With Rosie. It's all settled. Go to bed."

A hand on the side of my face woke me up. As my eyes opened, Mar's nose brushed mine. She was kneeling beside the bed. Her eyes were red rimmed, her lips trembled, and her body shook. She had on one of Rosie's nightgowns, and her tiny body was lost in it. She looked like a little girl playing dress-up. I raised the covers, and she slid into the bed next to me. She was shivering.

As I moved to make room for her, I felt Rocky at my back, and he woke up. Seeing Mar, he patted her shoulder through the family quilt that was pulled up under her chin where my head lay on hers. My arms were wrapped around her, trying to give her all the warmth my body could muster.

Mar rolled toward me, wrapped her arm over my chest, and brought her hand under my neck to rest her head on my breast. She seemed to be listening for my heart. I could feel her warm, soft breath through my T-shirt. Her voice was quiet when she said, "What am I going to do, Tommy? I don't have anyone left."

I pulled her close with my arm around her, rubbing her back. "You do, baby. You know what you mean to me. We won't let anything happen to you.

At a time like this, honey, is when you find out just how many friends you do have."

"Where will I live? What will I do?" Her voice had a note of terror in it.

I leaned back and looked down at her face. Her eyes were flashing back and forth. It made me think of a dog I had once seen caught in a trap when I was eight years old. I put my hand on the side of her face. "Look at me, Mar. Mar, look at me."

Her eyes slowly focused on me.

"You know I love you. Please, baby, relax. I'll take care of you."

The tears slowly started rolling out of her eyes. Then she began to sob. Pulling herself tight against me, she sobbed so hard that her body shook the bed. I felt Rocky slide out of bed. I glanced over and saw him slip his pants on and quietly walk out of the room.

I lay there stroking her hair, holding her close, letting her cry. After several minutes she slowly quieted down. I felt her body gradually begin to warm. I tried to keep my mind on other things, but the way she was lying pressed against me, her leg wrapped over mine, was starting to affect me. I glanced down, and her bare breasts were out of her nightgown and crushed up against my chest. I slowly tried to pull away, but every time I tried to move, she moved with me, keeping closely pressed against me. Her sobbing had subsided. "You feeling better, baby?"

She didn't speak but slowly nodded her head underneath my chin.

My mind was in chaos—a riot was occurring, and a fire was raging in my groin. I would have to do something quick. I looked up, and Rosie stood in the doorway.

Rosie pointed to Mar and then pointed to herself. I slowly shook my head. Rosie nodded hers and turned and left.

We lay there for several minutes. Her breath was slow and even. I slowly pulled back. Her eyes were closed, and she was sleeping. I waited another minute and then carefully eased out of bed and got dressed.

Buck, Rocky, and Rosie were sitting at the kitchen table drinking coffee when I entered. Rosie asked, "She sleepin'?" as she rose and poured me a cup of coffee.

"Yeah," I said. "Buck, how we going to help her?"

"Don't know, son, but we will do something. We were just discussin' it.

Rosie said she told her last night that she doesn't have any relatives." Buck dropped down in his recliner.

"Nothing 'cept a grandmother in a rest home in Kansas." I looked at Buck for help. I was leaning forward on the couch, elbows on my knees and hands wrapped in a clump under my chin, and I was rocking.

"How old is she?" Rocky asked from the other end of the couch.

"She's seventeen a few months ago. She'll be eighteen 'fore school's out."

"Well, unless we can come up with someplace for her to live, juvenile authority will take and put her in a foster home. At least until she's eighteen," Rocky said more as a question than a statement.

"I don't think she could stand that." I was worried I would lose her, that the state would ship her off someplace and I wouldn't see her.

"She might have a friend she could live with," Buck said, hopeful but not expectant.

"I don't know, Buck. Tess is the only one we've run around with. She knows a lot of people, but whether they would let Mar live with them is something else."

"You can bet on one thing, son, we will do everything we can to take care of her," Rocky said.

"Could she come live with us? I would pay for her living expenses. Rosie?" I knew the answer before I asked, but I had to ask. I was looking at Rosie, who had just walked in and sat on the arm of Buck's recliner.

Rosie responded, "If we can't do anything else. I just don't think it would be too good of an idea." Rosie looked at Buck and Rocky.

"I know you don't know her. She's a stranger, but she is an awfully nice girl."

"That's not the reason, Tommy. I can tell from watching you when you're around her what you think of her. I just don't believe having you both in the same house would work."

"I don't know what you mean." I knew exactly what she meant, but I couldn't give up. I needed Mar.

Buck looked at me. "If you stop and think a minute, you'll know what my baby here is talking about."

"Buck, I've lived with you for over a year. You and Rosie mean just about as much to me as my own mom and dad. I would never do anything to hurt either of you." Buck started to speak, but I cut him off. "Let me finish. If it comes to it, I will take Mar and leave. She is not going to a foster home!" I watched them closely to gauge their reaction. Rosie nodded, and Buck spoke.

"Son, let's not borrow trouble. That little girl in there is going to have a real tough time for the next couple of days. Let's get her through them and then see what happens."

I was adamant. "Fine. I just wanted you to know my feelings on the subject."

"Well, they are pretty clear, son." Buck was half smiling as he looked at Rosie and winked.

"What should I do about work?" I asked as an afterthought.

"I've called Snake. He's sendin' someone out to the yard to help Manny."

"What do we do now?" I looked to Buck for guidance.

"Nothin'. Later this mornin' we'll have to take Marylyn to a mortuary and arrange the funeral. We also should get hold of the police and find out what happened. She will want to know."

Rocky got up and walked into the kitchen. He returned with three coffee cups held by the handles in one hand and a pot of coffee in the other. "Have some coffee, folks. Helps the thinking."

Buck took the coffee from Rocky and then turned to Rosie. "Sweetie, I have to go out to the job for a little while. She's going to need some clothes and personal things. You can help her do that. If anything comes up, you can get me on the CB."

Turning to me, he said, "Let's run out to Blackwell. I've got to run to the yard, and then I'll be right back to pick you up." Buck took his coffee out the front door, we heard his truck fire up, and he was gone. We all moved into the kitchen to scrounge for something to eat. As Rosie grabbed food from the fridge, Sissy and Andy came running into the kitchen. Sissy climbed up on my lap. "Tommy, that pretty lady is in your bed."

"I know she is, sweetheart."

"How come? Don't she have a home?"

"Not right now, sweetie. She doesn't feel good."

"She sick?"

"In a way, baby."

"Mommy can get her well, can't she?"

"She's going to try."

"I hope so. It don't feel good to be sick."

Rosie intervened, "Sissy, you and Andy go get dressed. Be real quiet so you don't wake the pretty lady."

Buck pulled back in and walked through the door. Rosie gave him a kiss and asked, "What you want on your sandwich, honey?"

"Nothin'. Tommy and I will stop on the way over to the job site. You want to join us, Rocky?"

"No, thanks. I'll look after the kids. You go ahead."

On the way, we pulled into a restaurant. After ordering our breakfast and coffee, Buck asked, "You pretty serious about this girl, ain't you?"

"I sure am."

"Look, I know what the first girl means to every man. I'll never forget mine. You always have a soft spot for them. But you're only sixteen. You have a lot of livin' to do yet."

"Maybe, maybe not. I'm an old sixteen, Buck. Death has a way of bringing you around. How old were you when you went out on your own?"

"I went into the army at eighteen."

The waitress delivered two glasses of ice water and a couple of menus, and then she disappeared into the kitchen.

"You know about me. If it hadn't been for you and Rosie, I would be on my own right now. There is no way I would have stayed with that bastard Boats. You know that."

"I know. What I'm trying to say is, don't do anything foolish."

The waitress arrived again. "Know what you boys want for breakfast?"

Buck ordered the usual. "Bacon, eggs, biscuits, and gravy. Eggs over easy, bacon crisp, and black coffee."

"Make that two, please. Extra bacon and three eggs, please." I realized that I hadn't eaten since last night. I returned to the conversation.

"Like what?" I looked at Buck.

"Like runnin' off. I've told you before, you never get any place by runnin'. If you do, you will run the rest of your life. All I am asking is, before you do anything, talk to me. Will you do that?" Buck was leaning forward and looking right into my eyes.

"You should know me better than that. I wouldn't do anything to hurt you or Rosie."

The waitress was back. "Forgot to ask you boys if you wanted the hash browns as well?"

"Yeah, we can handle that," Buck said with a grin.

After we ate, we got into the truck and drove on out to the field. Buck checked the progress, and then we started on over to Blackwell, talking about the work we had accomplished since we had arrived.

"When you think the job will be done?" I asked.

"The way things have been going, we should finish up in April or May next year."

"Then what?"

"Well, I've told you about Boats getting the Bidwell field up at Tishomingo. By the way, on the way back from Kansas, we stopped at Tishomingo. Boats wanted to know all about you."

"He can go suck eggs for all I care."

"I know your feelings, Tom, but in a lot of ways he's a good man. And believe it or not, he really does care about you, though I know you don't believe it."

"I don't think he cares about anything but money and power. His likes don't include people."

"Anyway, he told me to tell you that he took the money from the sale of your folks' house and bought you eight oil leases in the Bidwell field."

"He don't have any right to do that, does he?" I said with some disgust.

"Yes, he does. He's your guardian, and I assume he cleared it with Judge Watkins."

"Who's Judge Watkins?"

"Judge in Johnston County."

"Knowing Boats the way I do, I bet he owns him." I just couldn't think of a single good thing to say about the bastard Boats.

"Wouldn't go quite that far, but I imagine the judge does listen."

"No doubt."

"Say, while we're talkin' about family, Officer Perez called earlier and told me that Pauline's body isn't going to be released from the morgue for a couple days. I'm really concerned about telling …"

The CB let out a loud squawk, and then a voice came on. "Breaker, breaker, calling Nichols 1. Nichols 1, come back."

"This is Nichols 1. Go ahead," Buck said.

"Buck, Rosie. Can you come back to the house right away? Over."

"Sure. What's up? Over."

"It will be self-evident when you get here. Please hurry. Over."

"Okay, baby, on my way. Over and out." Buck pulled off on the gravel shoulder, turned the wheel sharply, and punched the gas. The tires threw a boatload of gravel into the nearby wheat field as we spun a cookie and headed for home, well above the speed limit.

Chapter 11

Children's Services Ain't

It took us about thirty minutes to get there.

There was a gray sedan sitting in the driveway with a seal on the side that said "The State of Texas, Department of Family and Protective Services." We jumped out and hurried into the house. Rosie, Rocky, Mar, and a lady about thirty years old were sitting at the table in the kitchen. This woman looked like, and laughed like, the Wicked Witch of the West from *The Wizard of Oz*, absent the green skin. I halfway expected a flying monkey to leap from her briefcase. I hated her the moment I met her.

"This is my husband, Buck, and our foster son, Tom," Rosie said. "This is Ms. Bertha Keech. She is from juvenile services in El Paso."

"Nice to know you, Ms. Keech," Buck said.

I just nodded to the witch and said nothing.

"What's the problem?" Buck asked.

"Marylyn here was brought to our attention this morning. It is our understanding that she has no relations and, therefore, being a juvenile, she falls under our jurisdiction. I have come out to pick her up."

"Does it have to be done this mornin'?" Buck asked.

I made my way to the counter and watched Keech from a vantage point that allowed me to block her way if she made a move for Marylyn.

"We have found in these cases that the sooner we put them into a controlled atmosphere, the easier it is for all concerned."

Buck pulled up a chair directly across the table from Keech. "Whose concern—yours or the child's?"

"Both the child's and the department's," Keech said with a nasal tone of condescension.

Buck met her eyes and said, "She is not going anywhere, Ms. Keech. We have still not made arrangements for her mama's funeral. We will assume responsibility for her for the next few days."

Keech raised herself up in her chair and dropped her arms on the table emphatically. "We can't let you do that. According to the law, we have to assume control. No exceptions!"

Buck moved his chair closer, leaned in toward Keech, and spoke in slow, measured tones through clenched teeth. "What do you mean *control?* Where you planning to take her?"

Keech was snippy and curt. "We don't think that is any of your business, Mr. Hagan."

Buck pressed her. "Maybe not. Maybe what you think or don't think is unimportant, but we are her friends and her welfare is our concern."

Keech went on the attack, pushing her untouched cup of coffee to the side. "I don't know how you can say that, Mr. Hagan. You never met her until last night, according to her. She has been dating your foster son, and I don't believe it's in her best interest, in the state of mind she is in, to be staying in the same house as he is. Look, Mr. Hagan, I am the law here. There is no use discussing this further. I am going to take Marylyn with me."

Buck was steamed. "No, ma'am, you are not!"

"Why, what do you mean?" Keech was stunned that someone was talking back to her. Buck wasn't a little child who could be bullied by Keech; he was a roughneck—a roughneck foreman, at that—and scrapping with hardhearted sons a bitches was his stock in trade.

"Let me 'splain it to you, Keech," Buck continued. "Without a court order, you are not taking anyone out of my home."

Keech was livid. "We will see about that. Where is your phone?"

Buck stood. "I'm afraid you will have to go somewhere else to use the phone, Ms. Keech. I will be using mine to call our attorney."

"Then you are going to fight us on this?" Keech said indignantly.

"Damn straight! Now, if you wish to be reasonable, we will be too. You tell me what you're plannin' on doin', and we might go along with you." Buck's voice softened, but his resolve didn't.

"Well, first we would take her to juvenile hall, arrange a hearing before a judge, and then see if we could place her in a foster home."

Buck smiled. "Why not leave her here and do that? At least she would be around someone who cares about her."

Keech became indignant at the suggestion. "*We* care about her, Mr. Hagan. That's what I'm doing out here."

"Ms. Keech," Rosie interjected, "we understand your position—it's your job. But we believe, after what Marylyn has been through, she would be better off in a family situation."

"You would be right, Mrs. Hagan, except for one thing."

"What's that?" Rosie asked.

"I would not be doing my job if we allowed her to live in the same house as her boyfriend. It's just not proper."

"Ms. Keech, may I ask a question?" I said, stepping up to the table where they were all seated.

"Certainly, Tom. It is Tom, isn't it?"

"Yes, ma'am. What if I moved out for the next few days?"

"That would not be a good solution at all."

"Why not?" I asked.

"Because you would still be around, coming and going, and we would not like that."

Buck pressed her. "What do your likes and dislikes got to do with it?"

"I mean the regulations and laws we go by. Like I told you before, the quicker Marylyn is put into a controlled atmosphere, the better for her." Keech was cracking; her resolve was weakened.

"I don't buy that," Buck said gruffly.

"You don't have to buy it, Mr. Hagan. If you do not allow me to take Marylyn with me, I will see if I can't have you arrested for interfering with an officer of judicial process." Keech was struggling to intimidate Buck, without effect.

"Are you an officer of the law?"

"In a way. I am an officer of the court." Keech was on uncertain ground.

"What is your classification?" Buck continued.

"I am a judicial administrator."

"A judicial administrator, not an officer. So since you are not a law officer, you are not takin' Marylyn anyplace until I talk to my attorney."

Keech said, "All right. You go call your attorney. I will wait for just that long, and then I am going to take Marylyn."

Buck and I walked into the living room. He got his phone and address book out and looked up the number, picked up the phone, and dialed. "This is Buck Hagan from Nichols Casing. Is Mr. Conway there?" He listened for a minute. "Mary, this is an emergency. I must speak to him. It is very urgent. Yes, ma'am. Hello, Jim. Buck here. I've got a problem. Yes, here it is ..."

He ran through the whole thing. When he finished, he stood listening. "Fine, Jim, you do that, but be sure he calls right away because she is sitting here right now, waiting to take her."

After he hung up, he turned to me and said, "He doesn't handle these types of cases, but he taped what I told him and is calling one of his partners at home. He's supposed to call us right back."

We sat there waiting in silence for the phone to ring. When it did, we both jumped. "Buck Hagan here. Yes, sir. How long will it take? I think so. She just seems to be interested in her job, not the welfare of Marylyn. Yes, I will tell her. Think you can? Fine. Yes, I'll try. Good-bye."

We walked back into the kitchen. "Ms. Keech, we got our attorney. He is right now talkin' to Judge Leiper. He told me that under no circumstances should I let you take Marylyn from this house."

"Then I will go get a court order and bring back two police officers to enforce it." Keech stood to leave when Buck invited her to sit again.

"That shouldn't be necessary, Ms. Keech. The judge is supposed to call you here within the next ten minutes." Buck was confident, which put Keech ill at ease.

"Why should he call here?" Keech barked, though she was packing considerably fewer teeth than she had when she arrived.

"Because our attorney is getting an injunction till we can have a court hearing to stop your interference." Buck smiled.

"Interference? What interference? We are just concerned with this child's welfare, and living with a young man is not in her best interest. I am just doing my job!"

"Tom, have you and Marylyn done anything wrong?" Buck asked, turning to me.

"No, Buck, we haven't. Ask Mar. Have we, Mar?"

Mar turned to Keech with fire in her eyes. "No, but if we had, it wouldn't be anyone's business but ours."

"See what I mean? I fear for her morals if you allow her to stay here," Keech proclaimed with finality, the evidence having been provided, in her view.

"I don't think, Ms. Keech, that it's up to you to judge their morals," Buck said. "We prefer to leave those kinds of judgments to the Almighty, not a mere mortal such as yourself." Buck turned to Rosie, who was nodding her agreement.

"You just don't know the morals of teenagers of today," Keech proclaimed.

"I know Tommy," Rosie said. "A more honest, hard-working, moral person I've never known. I have never heard a swear word from him in over the year's time he has lived with us. I also know this about him: he would not go with a girl unless she was a fine moral person," Rosie opined. Keech had raised Rosie's ire, an uncommon occurrence in this house but one that was clearly avoided at all costs. Keech was dangerously close to having Rosie rip her head off and spit down her neck.

"That's what I mean. You just don't know teenagers of today. The people they live with are the last to really know them." Keech was halfway talking to herself.

Rosie started to say something when the phone rang. Buck walked into the other room and picked it up. "Ms. Keech, you are wanted on the telephone," he called.

"Hello? Yes, sir, Your Honor. I was going to pick her up under the Guardians of Minors Statute, commonly referred to as the Waif Statute."

"Ms. Keech, do I appear to you to be new to Texas law?" The judge was loud, sounding nearly as irritated as I was, but he was kinder about it. Keech was holding the phone away from her ear. The wicked witch was clearly teetering on her broom.

"No, sir. I mean, yes, sir. I mean, you don't appear to be new to the law, Your Honor. But yes, sir, there are other people, but I don't think she should be allowed to stay here. It's her boyfriend's house. Yes, sir, there are other people here."

I could visualize the judge throwing that bucket of cold water on this witch. She was melting before my eyes as the stern tenor of the judge came over the phone.

"Yes, in their thirties. Yes, sir, they are employed. If you say so, yes, sir. When will the hearing be? Thank you, Your Honor."

To say that Keech was pissed off would be an understatement. She spoke to us through clenched teeth as she hung up the phone and turned to Buck. "Marylyn's hearing has been set for next Thursday at 10:00 a.m. You just make sure nothing happens between this young man and her."

"Thank you, Ms. Keech." Buck took her gently but firmly by the arm and led her to the door.

"That Keech is a witch!" Rosie said. "Could you imagine being married to a rule book like that?"

I grinned at Buck as he walked back into the kitchen. I walked to Mar's chair, and she got up, put her arm around my waist, and lay her head on my chest. "Is everything all right?"

"Boats's attorney got everything straightened out for the time being. You have a hearing next Thursday. That gives us a week. We should be able to do somethin' by then. Excuse me, honey. I have to talk to Buck." I nodded to Buck, and we walked into the living room.

"What is it?" he asked.

"We didn't get to finish our discussion this morning before Keech interrupted us. I was trying to talk to you about arrangements for the funeral. Officer Perez called while you were gone to the yard this morning. The cops won't release Pauline's body until day after tomorrow. I can't take Marylyn down to the morgue to see her mother after what Perez told me about Pauline's head wound."

"Then you better think of something to tell her because she has already asked Rosie twice about taking her to see her mom."

"Pop always told me the truth was the best."

"In this case, I think you're right."

"I think I'll take her for a drive so we can talk," I said.

Mar sat close to me, and I kept glancing sideways at her. Her face was calm and peaceful, but every once in a while a tear would roll out on her cheek. She would reach up with her right hand and wipe it away. I pulled off the road and turned onto the dirt road leading down to the river. I grabbed the blanket from behind the seat and walked Mar down the narrow dirt trail to the riverbank, where we spread the blanket out and sat listening to the water roll over the rocks. The sound of the water was soothing.

Mar's head lay against my shoulder and neck, with my arm supporting her. "You know, Mama and I used to go for long drives when I was a little girl. We'd always stop someplace and buy a fudge sundae. I would always get it all over my face. Then when I was done eatin', she would stop beside the road and wash my face with a handkerchief, using spit for moisture. Sounds gross, but I never thought of it that way. I think I enjoyed that more than the sundae. She always made a game out of it, tellin' me some big story she made up about a pretty young blonde girl with large brown eyes and a big nose. I'm really going to miss her."

I pulled her to my chest. "I know you are, sweetheart."

Mar was talking so softly that I could barely hear her over the water slipping by. "You know, in our girl talk at school, all the girls complained about their moms. It's funny. I could talk to mine about anything."

Mar turned and stretched her legs over mine, and she pulled herself onto my lap. We sat, pulling the blanket up around us, like an old Indian with two heads, the blanket around us forming a tepee.

Mar was reminiscing. "Mom never seemed to get mad at me, not since I was about seven years old. If I did somethin' she didn't think was right, she would call me in or come into my room and ask me about it."

I squeezed Mar and said, "I know all about your mom's interrogation sessions."

Mar continued dreamily, "If I did do somethin' that she really disapproved of, she would tell me, 'Honey, I think you had better sit down and think that over.' You know, I would usually go to her after I had thought about it. In some instances, after we had talked about it and I told her my thoughts, she would agree that I was right and she was wrong."

Mar wasn't that heavy, but my legs were asleep. I didn't want to stop her, so I pulled her across my lap so that we were sitting facing each other. Mar continued, "When I told the girls at school about the way she was, they didn't believe me. They even asked Tess about it. They couldn't believe my mom was that understanding. Did you have a good mother, Tom?"

"I think so, but I believe that most moms are special in their children's eyes. Yours was just a little more special than most."

"That was beautiful, Tom. Thank you for that."

"For what?"

"For just being the nice person you are."

"You're welcome, from the bottom of my heart. I guess you know by now, Mar, that in the few short days we've known each other, you have grown to be very important to me." I took her hands, which were wrapped around my neck, pulled them to my lap, and gave them a slight squeeze.

She glanced up at me and gave me a small smile. "Yes, I could tell, and I think you know the feeling is mutual. We'd better go back. I want to go see my mama." With that, Mar stood up and reached for my hand to pull me up. I stood, but both my legs were asleep and I was unsteady. When I got the blood flowing again, I took hold of her.

"Baby, that's why I wanted you to come on the drive and down to the river with me. They won't let you see your mama until Saturday."

"That's two whole days," she cried. "How come they won't let me see her?"

"Well, it's not that you can't see her, Mar; it's just that they won't release her body from the police laboratory until then."

"But they know how Mama died and who killed her. That should be enough."

"Evidently, it isn't enough for them. Anyway, that's what they told me."

"I don't believe they can keep me from seein' Mom. I want to see her, and I will!"

"I'm not sayin' that they said you could never see her. It's just a suggestion that you wait until she has been turned over to a mortuary. Honey, take my word for it. I saw my parents after their car wreck. They had them in the morgue, and I had to make a legal identification. It was awful." I couldn't prevent the tears from running down my face. I hadn't thought of that moment for two years, and now the images of Sis, Mom, and Dad renewed the feeling of loss and released my tears. My heart broke for Mar at this moment. "I won't go into it, but please, baby, wait till Saturday."

"I'd like to see her, Tom."

"I know that, but I know that your mama wouldn't want you to see her that way. You decide about the funeral, Mar?"

"In a way, it's strange. About a month ago, Mama and I discussed this very thing. She told me she would like to be cremated and have her ashes put with my father up in Kansas. We had been driving in the country and pulled to the roadside."

We walked back to the truck and headed back into town. At the first stoplight, a car pulled up alongside and honked its horn. I glanced over and saw that it was Tess leaning out the window. She hollered, "Stop at Pepi's!" I nodded, and we pulled out to follow her into town.

Tess was standing, waiting, as we pulled in. When we climbed out, she came up to Mar and hugged her. We went in and sat at a booth. Manny, Chico, Mueller, and the rest of the guys were there. Mar and Tess were surrounded by their girlfriends from school, who kept coming up to Mar and giving her condolences. We stayed for an hour, and then Tess, Manny, Mar, and I walked out to the truck. Finally, the four of us were alone.

Tess asked, "You know what you're going to do, Mar?"

"No. Some lady from juvenile tried to take me in this mornin'."

"Why would they do that?"

"'Cause I'm underage and don't have any relatives. After Mama's funeral, they are going to put me in a foster home."

"Are you going to let them?" Manny asked.

"Don't know. I don't think so."

I had been sitting there listening, thinking, but not really paying attention. "You don't think what, Mar?"

"That I will let them put me in a foster home."

"I told you this mornin' we wouldn't let that happen."

"Maybe you can't stop them."

"Then we can leave, can't we?" I said.

Tess asked, "Would you like to come live with me, Mar?"

"Would your mother let me?"

"I'm sure she would. She has always liked you, and she never minds having you around. I'll go call her."

She went back into the restaurant for about five minutes. She came back out with a big smile on her face and said, "Mom said we would be honored to have you come live with us."

"Do you think they would let me, Tom?"

"There is one thing I've learned from watching my uncle," I said. "If you are willin' to fight, you can usually win."

"When we get through, let's go home and get a hold of that lawyer and see what we can do."

On the way home, I asked Mar, "You sure you want to live with Tess?"

"She's been my best friend for the last two years. She's the sister I've never had."

When we pulled up at home, there was a white four-door Ford sitting in the driveway. In the house, the same two detectives who had been at the hospital after Pauline was shot sat with coffee on the sofa. When we walked in, they stood up.

Buck said, "Marylyn, Tom, this is Salvatore Gomez and Patrick Delvaney. They would like to talk to you, Marylyn. Would you like us to leave you alone?"

The one named Patrick said, "That's not necessary."

Marylyn took my hand, and we sat on the love seat. One of the detectives moved to the easy chair so he could be in front of us.

Mar asked them, "Did you find out what happened?"

"Yes, we finally got everything pieced together. You said last night that you didn't know your mom had been dating this man."

"She had never mentioned him to me, but that was not unusual for Mama. She tried to keep her social life separate from me. The last time she dated was three years ago."

"We now know what caused what happened last night." Detective Delvaney explained everything they knew. The facts were pretty straightforward—Joe Moore shot Pauline.

According to the detective, Joe Moore and Pauline were lovers. Last night, they walked into the club together. Since Pauline was early, she and Moore sat down at a table. Nobody knew what was said, except for what the bartender heard when he took them their drinks. Pauline seemed to be trying to break it off with Moore. They sat and talked for at least thirty minutes, and Moore kept getting madder and madder. When the owner walked over and told Pauline she would have to get to work, he heard her tell Moore, 'I have told you my feelings, Joe. I do not want to get tied up right now. I would like to be your friend, but I can't—no, I won't—go out with you again.'"

Because of gaps in the manager's recollection, the detectives were uncertain about what happened next, but Moore had apparently leaned over to Pauline and talked about something that had happened the afternoon before. "Your mother told him that it had nothing to do with whatever had happened; it was just that she had a daughter to raise."

Delvaney continued. "Moore shouted at Pauline, 'You're just like that slut I was married to! Play with a man's affections and love him; then drop him for someone else. Who is he?' Moore was apparently jealous. He disappeared for a couple of hours and then returned. A friend of Pauline's, George Becker, came to the bar looking for her. Apparently, Becker and his wife are long-time friends of Pauline and her late husband from back in Kansas, but Becker now lives in Alaska and was in town for an oil deal. When Pauline walked into the bar from the kitchen, she saw Becker and they hugged each other. She agreed to meet Becker after work to catch up. Moore and the bartender both heard the conversation, and apparently Moore thought there was something between Pauline and Becker and became enraged.

"Joe was drinking straight shots of tequila. He gulped down his drink, got up, and started for the door. Moore grabbed Pauline as she walked by. Two people at the bar heard him tell her, 'So that's the son of a bitch you're leaving me for.' She told him, 'I didn't even know he was in town. If you wish to believe that, go ahead. Just leave me alone. I would rather have you for a friend, but if not, so be it. You're hurting my arm. Turn me loose.' Moore was not convinced, though, and said, 'I'll hurt more than that. You and that slut I was married to are just alike. All you want to do is hurt people.' The bartender came out and made him turn loose of her and leave."

The detective explained that Moore had stayed gone for two hours. He also said that Moore had made a phone call from the pay phone in the entrance of the club. "We know he went out to his ranch and came back. We also know he made a call from his ranch to an attorney in El Paso. We have not been able to contact the attorney to find out what for. That leaves an hour we can't account for. According to witness testimony, Moore walked back into the club at eleven fifteen, and the club was real busy.

"Nobody noticed him walk in until they heard your mother scream, 'No, Joe! No!' After he shot your mother, he turned the gun on himself."

Mar sat in shock, processing all that Delvaney had relayed to all of us gathered in the living room.

Detective Gomez then started to explain his part of the investigation, telling us that Moore had previously been married to a woman until about five years ago. They had a son. It seems that his wife stepped out on him all the time. Anyway, she left their son in the backseat of her car while she was in a motel with another man. The temperature was over a hundred and ten, and the baby died from heat exhaustion. When Joe found out, he went berserk and went after his wife with a gun. He chased her down Grande Road here in town—her in one car, him in another.

"The police stopped him before he could kill her," Gomez said. "He wound up in a mental institution for two years. From looking at the pictures of his former wife and your mother, we noticed that their faces and figures are similar."

"We can only assume that when your mother rejected him, he reverted to the emotional state he had been in previously. Do you have any questions?"

"Not now," Mar said. "Maybe later."

"We will be glad to answer them if we can, Miss Birchley," Detective Delvaney said. "Now, we would like your permission to search your apartment."

"What for?"

"We would like to check on some things that have turned up. We are just trying to tie up the loose ends. We can get a search warrant if we have to. You haven't been back to your apartment, have you?"

"No, I need to go over, though, and get some clothes to wear."

"If we have your permission, we can be through in thirty minutes. We have a guard at your apartment until such time as we can search it."

"You have my permission," Mar said. "Do you want me to go with you?"

"No, ma'am, that won't be necessary," said Delvaney. "We will need a key to get in, though."

"Just a moment and I'll get it."

After she left the room, Detective Gomez said, "She's quite a little lady, isn't she?"

I answered, "*I* think so. Is there any way we can get her mother's body released? I'm about out of excuses to keep her away from the morgue."

"That's no place to view a loved one," Gomez said. "We will see if we can get it turned loose this afternoon. Who do you want it released to?"

I turned to Buck. "We contacted Tubbs Mortuary," he said. "They are supposed to talk to the coroner."

"We will do what we can."

Mar walked in and handed Gomez the key. After they left, Buck asked me, "Did you notify the coach about not being there today?"

"Good gosh, no! I completely forgot about it. What time is it?"

"Four forty-five."

"Honey, I'd better go or I'm going to get thrown off the team," I said.

"If you don't mind, I'd like to go along with you," Mar said in a manner that implied she couldn't be refused.

CHAPTER 12

The Fight Is On

I left Mar in the bleachers and went into the locker room to change. As I was finishing up and putting on my shoes, Manny walked in.

"Is that Marylyn up there?" he asked.

"Yes. Why?"

"Sanchez was talking to her. I wasn't sure it was her or I would have intervened."

I jumped up, grabbed my helmet, and ran out. As I topped the stairs going up to the bleachers, I saw Sanchez in front of Mar with both hands on her shoulders. I could tell she was trying to rise, but Sanchez was leaning over real close to her face, saying something. He had on his uniform.

I was about ten feet away, running toward him, when he must have heard my cleats on the concrete. He turned his head, saw me, and straightened up just in time for me to hit him with my shoulder pads. We landed about five feet away. Sanchez was lying with his shoulders hanging off of the bleachers bench. I had landed straddling him and was looking right into his face. My balled-up fist caught him on the right side of his face. As I started to swing my left, I realized that I was still holding my helmet. I tossed it aside in a sweeping motion and followed through, punching Sanchez with my left.

I was ready to throw another punch when someone hit me from behind.

As I fell to the side, I saw Helio with a helmet in his hand. I was trying to straighten up when Sanchez hit me on the head with his cast. My ear was on fire, along with the back of my head where Helio's helmet had left its mark.

Sanchez grabbed me with his left hand, holding on to my sweatshirt. I swung my left again, catching Sanchez flat on the nose. He let out a squall, released my shirt, and covered his face with his hands.

Helio kicked me in the back with his cleats, scraping my skin and catching a spike in my rib pads, causing me to stumble and fall to the bleachers.

I heard someone else arrive. I turned in time to see Manny tackle Helio; they landed about three feet from me. Manny was a flurry of punches, using Helio's face like the speed bag at his dad's warehouse.

In the next moment, the coaches were there, pulling us apart.

Coach Clemmons shouted, "All right, Gurley, why did you start the fight?"

"I'll not discuss it out here, Coach," I replied.

"You won't what?" Clemmons was indignant that I was talking back to him.

"I said I will not discuss it out here, Coach."

Just then, Coach Baker walked up and spit at my feet. The Copenhagen smell was pungent. "Bring them down to the office. Come on. Let's go." Seven of us assembled in Coach Baker's office—all three coaches, Manny, Helio, Sanchez, and me. We were crammed in like a dozen fat people in a small elevator.

Baker threw his feet up on his cluttered desk and said, "Okay, Gurley, why did you start the fight?"

"I didn't like Sanchez handling my girl," I said. I was still breathing hard after the tussle.

"That right, Sanchez?" Baker turned to look at him.

"Just talking to her, Coach."

"Did you have your hands on her?" Baker dropped his head, and his glasses slid to the end of his nose. He peered over them, daring Sanchez to lie to him.

"Just her shoulders," he said.

"You like other guys handling your girlfriend, Sanchez?"

"No, sir," Sanchez answered.

"Then I guess you understand why Gurley is a bit offended at your conduct." Baker didn't wait for an response. "I understand you two boys have had trouble over her before. That right, Gurley?"

"Not of my making, Coach."

"Sanchez, I understand you're the one who cut his face up with a knife."

"Not me, Coach," Sanchez lied. "He told the cops he cut it on a broken mirror on a pickup."

"That right, Gurley?"

"That's what I told them," I said.

"Is it the truth?"

"Look, Coach, how I got cut has nothing to do with today. I told you why I jumped Sanchez."

Coach dropped his feet to the floor and slammed his fist on the desk. He spit in the garbage can next to his desk. "All right, now I'm going to tell you fellas something, and you are damn sure going to pay attention! You hear me?"

"Yes, Coach," we said in unison.

"For fighting, you can be expelled from school and fuck up the plans for our entire team. I'm going to let today pass, but if I see one more instance of any type of hostility, I will personally kick your asses off the team and make sure you are also kicked out of school. That understood?" Coach was so worked up that he spit pieces of Copenhagen all over the top of his desk as he shouted.

We all nodded.

"Also, while we have you four in here—Sanchez, we saw you trip Gurley here the other day. If it hadn't been for Manny and Mueller, he could have fallen and hurt himself. Also, Helio, the tricks you were playing with the ball and tripping Gurley were childish. Gentlemen, don't think that because we are old we don't have eyes. This shit is stopping *today*. I will not have personalities here at practice. I told you the first day—we are a team. We play as a team. If you can't keep your personal life on the outside, then throw in your suits and we will use someone who can! Understood?"

"Yes, sir," came from all around.

"Sanchez, you and Helio go out for practice. Coaches, let's get practice started." As Sanchez, Helio, and the other coaches left, Baker turned to me and Manny.

"I can't blame you after what has happened, but I meant what I said. Understand?"

We both said, "Yes, sir. Thank you."

"You're welcome. Another thing, Gurley—if you and Manny there would use the fire and spirit you used in that fight out there, you would be all-state. Now get the hell out there and practice."

Coach Vic told Baker, "Sanchez told me the doctor told him he could play football if we would let him."

"You know, when I was in high school, I played five games with a cast," Coach Baker said. "Put him on defense."

When we lined up for scrimmage, I looked across at the defense and saw Sanchez looking at me, grinning.

The first two times they called my number, Sanchez really stuck it to me. Both times I went straight toward him. In running the next few plays, I got to thinking about last year and how I had learned to avoid blocks by spinning. The next time they called my number, I went into the pack at the snap of the ball. I saw Sanchez coming and spun on my left foot. Sanchez's shoulder and arms hit my thighs, but my spinning prevented him from grabbing me. I gained nine yards.

Manny grinned in the huddle. "That's using your head, T. C."

From then on, we settled down in the running plays. I gained yardage on every play after that. When we finished practice, I took a shower and walked out.

Tess had joined Mar, and Mueller and Manny walked up. "Marylyn, Tess, this is Eric Mueller, a good friend of ours."

Mar and Tess both greeted him.

Eric said, "You guys want to stop at Pepi's? I'm buying."

"That's great. I'm thirsty," Manny said.

I turned to Mar, the question in my eyes.

"I'd like to."

"You want to ride with us, Eric?" I asked.

"Love to."

We climbed into the truck, with Eric sitting in the middle and Tess sitting on Manny's lap.

As we took off, Manny said, "You know, Tess, you been eatin' too many tacos or somethin'. You gettin' heavy."

"Well, I like them. You know, of course, you're no prize catch yourself, and another thing—"

"Hold it! Hold it," Manny interjected. "I was just kidding. Holy cow, can't a man make a joke?"

Eric said, "Never about a lady's age or weight, Manny."

"See?" Tess said. "He knows how to treat a lady."

"What lady?"

Tess planted two quick elbows in Manny's chest and a slap upside his head.

"Okay, I give up," Manny whined.

When we pulled into Pepi's, the whole gang was there. The big booth was crowded, so we pulled some chairs up around the outside.

Pedro hollered, "All right, quiet down! I want to talk to our fighters over here." The group got quiet.

Pedro looked at Manny. "As I was drying off, I heard the coaches talking."

"About what?" Manny asked.

"They were agreeing on the starting lineup 'if things keep progressing,' as Coach Baker put it."

Malin and Harry piped up at the same time. "Come on, Pedro. Tell us."

"Well, before I left, I looked at the blackboard to confirm it. It said, 'Quarterback: Manny. Left half: T. C. Full back: Mueller. Right half: Breedlove.' Then they had the offensive line listed, but I knew we were starting."

"Who is this Breedlove?" Manny asked. "He hasn't practiced with the backs."

"He's been practicing with the receivers. I heard Coach Baker tell Coach Burton to transfer him tomorrow to the number one team."

Mar leaned over and told me she would like to go. We said good-bye and left.

When we were outside, she asked, "Can we stop by the apartment and get me some clothes?" As we pulled up to her place, the two detectives were just leaving. They had a paper sack filled with something. They nodded, got in their car, and drove off.

"Wonder what they took," Marylyn said.

"Don't have the least idea. Want me to come in with you?"

"No, I'd like to go in alone."

I sat listening to a Johnny Cash tape. Mar must have been in there for thirty minutes before she came out carrying a suitcase. She dropped it into the back and then climbed in the truck. "Let's go," she said. "Would you mind driving me over to Tess's house?"

"Sure, honey. Just give me directions."

After a ten-minute drive, we were in an old neighborhood with old trees hanging over the sidewalks and out into the streets. The houses were large. It had been a well-to-do neighborhood in the forties; now it was blue collar. I pulled up to a large two-story house. It had a wraparound porch supported by round columns that had been painted so many times that a chip revealed ancient colors from previous decades. The door was oak with an etched picture of a majestic elk standing on a hill in front of mountains. The doorbell played a series of chimes reminiscent of church bells, and the door promptly opened to reveal Tess's mama—a large woman, jolly and eager to hug any human being. "Want to come in?" she said to me as Mar entered, being accustomed to Tess's mom.

"If you want me to," I said to Mar, looking for her approval.

"Yes, I do," she said.

Once in the foyer, this large lady, short but heavyset, wrapped each of us up in a huge and prolonged hug to show us we were welcome. It was easy to tell that she was Tess's mama. She opened her arms and embraced Mar repeatedly, telling her how sorry she was about her mom.

"Mama Santos," Mar said, "this is Tommy."

"Welcome to our home, Tommy. Come—come on in." Mama Santos pulled us into the parlor, a room that was clearly seldom used. It was furnished with Italian furnishings, which seemed odd considering the Santoses' Hispanic heritage.

"This is beautiful furniture, Mrs. Santos," I said.

"Yeah, Tess's papa picked it up at an estate sale in Galveston. Too fancy for me, but he thought it showed our culture. Tess isn't home yet. That girl's most likely out with Manny. He's a nice boy, but when they get together, they never pay any attention to time. Please, sit down. All I do is talk anymore. I have no manners whatever. Can I offer you something to drink?"

"No, thanks. We just come from Pepi's."

"That place—all you kids do is hang out there. Guess it's better than running the streets." She sat down in front of Marylyn and took her hands in hers. "I'll have a bedroom all cleaned up for you, honey. You can move in anytime you want to, and we'll finish getting it ready as we need to."

"Thank you, Mama. But I'm not sure I can move in with you."

"Why not, child?"

"I guess it will be up to the court."

"Why should you be in a court? You haven't done anything."

"It's not that, Mama," Marylyn said. "It's just I don't have any relations, and I guess that makes me a ward of the state."

"You talking about welfare, child?"

"I don't know. There was a Ms. Keech over at Tom's place this morning. She had come to pick me up."

"You talking 'bout Bertha Keech from Juvenile?"

I spoke up. "That's the one, Mrs. Santos."

"Call me Mama, Tommy. Everyone does. Well, I can fix that. Just a minute." She walked over to a small desk in the corner, where she reached up in a little cubicle, took out a small book, and opened it up. She picked up the phone and dialed.

"Hello, Bertha. Mama here. Yes, fine. And you? That's good. What? Oh, yes. The reason I'm calling—you know the girl Marylyn Birchley? Yes, that's the one. What? Yes, I know her well. Yes, real pretty girl. What? Certainly—know her real well. Been in my home many times over the last two years. That's the reason I'm calling. She's going to live with Tess and me. Bertha, I don't want any excuses. You just fix it up. Yes, thank you. I would love to, whenever you have the time. Yes. All right, good-bye."

She turned, smiled, walked back over, and sat down. "That takes care of your problem."

"You mean she agreed just like that?" I asked in disbelief.

"Well, certainly. I have had a lot of dealings with Bertha over the years. I have raised twenty-three foster children in this house."

Mar said, "I didn't know that."

"Oh, yes. Nine of my own and twenty-three foster. It's been a beautiful life."

"Thank you so much, Mama. Now, what I came over for—I was wondering if I could store some of my and my mother's things here. Some of them are very special to me, and I just can't bear to part with them."

"I hadn't thought about it, but of course you would have things of your own. And of course, you can keep them here."

"Thank you, Mama. Tom and I have to be going. We'll see you real soon."

"Fine, honey. When is the funeral going to be?"

"We'll have to let you know, Mama. Thank you again."

"Think nothing of it, child. Tom, you be sure and stop by again," she said.

"Thank you, Mama."

It was completely dark when we entered the house. The light in the kitchen was the only light on in the house. We found Buck and Rosie sitting at the table, sipping coffee. Rosie asked, "You kids want something to eat?"

"No, thanks, not for me," I said. "Mar, you hungry?"

"None for me. Rosie, may I see you a moment?"

"Sure, honey." They walked into the other room. They were gone for about ten minutes, and then Rosie came back alone.

"Where's Mar?" I asked.

"She needs a little time for herself. What you kids been doing?"

I related to Rosie our conversation with Mama Santos and her call to Keech. "I tell you, Mama Santos is a force. Keech didn't have a chance!"

Turning to Buck, I said, "Mar was asking me this afternoon about her legal rights. She wanted to know if she could sell some of the stuff of theirs. Like she said, there's a lot of things she can't keep."

"The best thing to do is take her down to an attorney. First thing tomorrow, we'll get an appointment."

Mar came in and stood next to my chair, putting her hand on the back of my neck.

"I was just asking Buck about those things you wanted to get rid of, babe."

"While I was at home, I took Mama's jewelry box. And in taking some things out of the drawer, I found an insurance policy. I was wondering if you would look at it, Buck."

"Sure, honey," he said. "Where is it?"

"Just a minute. I'll get it." She went into the bedroom and came out with a sheaf of papers in a brown envelope. She handed it to Buck.

He pulled them out and laid them on the table. He looked in the envelope and turned it upside down, and two small, brown books fell out on the table. He picked them up and opened them. He looked at Mar. "Did you know about these savings accounts?"

"I knew Mama had a college savings account set up for me. I didn't know about the other. A couple of years ago, she had me sign some papers when she started using that bank."

"You are going to have to see a lawyer tomorrow. I think I'm right that both of these accounts are in yours and your mama's name, so they should automatically revert to your name." He picked up the insurance papers and looked at them. "We have no way of knowing if these policies are in force, but if they are, your mama had a fifteen-thousand-dollar life insurance policy. Wait a minute." He read for a minute. "If I'm right, this one is double indemnity accident."

"What does that mean?"

Buck explained, "That means the policy doubles if she is accidentally killed."

"Would the way she died be considered an accident?"

"I'm pretty sure it would. You can check with the attorney tomorrow."

Buck continued holding the pass books Mar had laid on the table. "From looking at your pass books and these policies, I can tell your mother was sure thinking about your future, honey."

"She always told me she wanted to be sure I had enough money for school."

"It looks like she made sure of that. Counting your savings and the policies, you have almost fifty thousand dollars. I'll have Rocky double check my figures, but that's what it looks like to me." Buck smiled at Mar and pushed the documents back across the table.

"That's an awful lot of money," Rocky said.

"It sure is." Buck turned to Rosie. "We better hit the sack. I've got to be on the job awful early in the mornin'."

Mar said, "Buck, you sleep in your own bed. I'll sleep on the sofa."

"You will not," he replied.

"Please, Buck. I don't feel right. Let me sleep in here, please."

Rosie said, "Come on, Buck."

They left us alone. Mar had been standing there with her arm around my neck and shoulders. She swung around and sat down in my lap. I put my arms around her, pulled her in close, and kissed her.

She leaned back, looking at me. "Your bandage is loose." She reached up and slowly pulled it off. "The scar is sure red."

"The doctor says it will go away in a couple of months."

"It sure looks bad. I just wish I hadn't caused it."

"Marylyn, if you ever say something like that to me again, I am going to be very mad at you."

"But Tommy—"

"Baby, I don't want no *buts*. I mean it. There is no way this was your fault. When you first met Sanchez, I'll bet you thought he was nice. If you had known he was the type of person he is, you would have never dated him. Honey, when it comes to some things, we all have a screw loose. Look, I don't want to discuss him anymore."

We sat there close for several minutes, Mar sitting on my lap, her arms around me, her face pressed against mine. Soon, the closeness and warmth of her sitting there started to arouse my senses. I gently pushed her away from me. "Time we went to bed, Shorty."

"I hate to. It's so nice just sittin' here. The dark scares me, Tommy."

"You never said you were afraid of the dark before."

"I wasn't, and in a way I'm not now. It's just that I'm uncomfortable—irritated or something. Seems like everything moves in on me.... My mind doesn't stop racin'."

"I'm sorry, honey. Wish there was somethin' I could do."

"You being here is a lot of help. Most likely I'll settle down." She got up and took my hand, pulling to help me up. We walked out of the kitchen, turning off the light, and into the living room. The house was dark and quiet except for the nightlight that Rosie kept turned on in the bathroom for the kids. We stood there embracing, pressed close together, kissing. Marylyn's kisses kept getting warmer and wilder. She seemed to be trying to get inside me. Every time I tried to pull away, she would tighten her embrace and kiss me harder.

Finally, after a long kiss, she leaned back, looked up at me, and whispered, "I love you, Tommy."

"I know, honey. I love you too."

She slowly pulled away from me. "Good night."

Quietly entering the bedroom, I undressed and slipped into bed.

Rocky asked, "How's she makin' it, son?"

I rolled onto my back. "Not too good. She's confused."

"Death has a way of doing that to a person. When you get to be my age, it's a constant companion. Sometimes it's a gentle companion; other times it's harsh. Death is always harsh to the young because it's unexpected. It has a way of makin' all people equal, the mighty and the lowly. Rich, poor, pauper, and peon, we all have to meet our maker. You believe in God, son?"

I was surprised by Rocky's question. "You mean God like they taught me in church when I was a real young? Like they teach in the Bible?"

"Exactly like that."

"No. I'm only sixteen, but I don't believe in God as they teach it. Can't see a just God taking my little sister, mom, and dad. It ain't fair. Do you believe in God?"

"Very definitely I do. It has to be."

"How can you? Life is too cruel for me to believe in the love and compassion junk they hold out to people in church. When my folks died, the pastor of our Baptist church stood there tellin' me it was God's will, that I had to get on my knees and pray for my soul so that when I died I could join them. That's bullshit, and you know it."

"Not really, Tom. If it wasn't for God, this would be a terrible world. Man's basic nature is mean and nasty. The Bible teaches that belief in God is all that separates us from the animals. You haven't lived long enough to see God's mercy."

"I respect your beliefs, Rocky, and some parts of it I believe, just not all of it. There has to be a supreme being. I know I don't believe that we crawled out from under a rock or out of the sea. But I also don't go for all their love and compassion crap. My belief is that you love those who love and respect you, but I don't believe in loving those who hate you. And that stuff about turning the other cheek? I don't buy it. Do you?"

"That's what the Book says, and I have to tell you I have never been wrong when I followed the Book."

"I know what it says. I attended Sunday school for as long as I can remember. Ma and Pa took me every week. They never hurt a soul that I know of, and look what happened to them. Look at Mar's mother. No, Rocky, if someone slaps my cheek, I'll turn the other cheek, but if he is stupid enough to slap me again, I'll tear his damn head off and piss down his throat."

Rocky laughed. "Can't say I blame you there, son. I've done that a few times in my life. We'd better get some sleep. It's late. 'Night, son."

"'Night, Rocky."

CHAPTER 13

– Sleepin' with the Old Man, Learnin' 'bout Life –

I woke up the next morning when Rocky slid out of bed. The clock said 5:30. I rolled over and watched Rocky standing there, looking out of the window. "Gonna be a nice day?" I asked.

"Looks like it. Just can't get used to this Texas sky. Don't think I've seen three green lawns in this whole damn state."

"What's Kansas like?" I asked as I pulled on my Levi's.

"Mostly rolling hills, but at least in towns we watered the grass."

"Think you're homesick." Rocky looked so frail standing at the window in his boxers and T-shirt.

"Yeah, guess I am, son. Funny, most people who have lost their partners say that the evenings are when they miss them most. Not me. It's in the still of a beautiful morning like this. To roll over in bed and kiss the warm, loving lips of your partner, to stand and watch a golden sunrise and plan your day, to know that come hell or high water, right or wrong, your partner will be there beside you to back you up. Listen to me, will you? Sound like a senile old fart, don't I?"

"Not to me, you don't. Just someone that up till recently had a good life."

"That I did, son. That I did. Come on. Get your lazy ass out of that bed, and let's get some coffee." Rocky pulled on his pants, threw on a shirt, and headed for the kitchen. I headed for the bathroom.

Everyone was sitting at the table when I came out of the bathroom. Andy was sitting on Mar's lap, eating cereal. I leaned over and kissed Mar's cheek. "What did you do, honey—get you another boyfriend?" I asked.

"You got to admit he's good-looking," she replied.

"Can't fault you there."

Rosie handed me a cup of coffee, and I turned to Buck. "Manny and I will get that load of pipe out first thing this morning." Then I turned to Mar. "Buck will give you the phone number of that attorney. See if you can get an appointment around two this afternoon." I kissed her and Andy good-bye.

Manny and I pulled into the yard at 12:45 after football practice. Buck's pickup was sitting next to the south shed, and Buck was standing in the door.

"What you doing, Buck?"

"Waiting for our workout."

"Forgot about it."

"Can't do that," he said. "Got to teach you how to protect yourself, even if it kills both of us."

For the next hour, I punched bags and sparred with Buck and Manny.

"I'll help you with the load," Buck told Manny when we were finished. "Tommy has to go with Marylyn to the attorney."

The lawyer's office was on the fourth floor of the Brandon Building, a modest brick building in a lovely business neighborhood that had been taken over by industry. It stood out among the industrial service buildings like a diamond in a mud puddle. We entered the reception area, and the girl told us that we were expected and led us into the office. The youngest one of three men sitting there got up and came forward to meet us. He stuck out his hand, though on close inspection I saw that he wasn't young at all. He was thin and athletic, while the two other attorneys sat like overfed toads on a lily pad. "Miss Birchley, I'm Jim Conway," the thin one said. He turned to me and said, "And you are Tom Gurley."

Jim pointed to the other two attorneys. "These are my partners—my brother, Justin Conway, and the senior partner, Robert Stuck." Stuck seemed like a person to be wary of. He didn't seem to have the ability to give a straight answer to any question he was asked, often answering a question with a question. "Please sit here," Jim continued. "We are sorry about your mother, Marylyn."

"Thank you."

"Now, the Department of Family and Protective Services contacted us this morning," Jim said, starting the discussion. "From them, we understand that they have worked out your problems. You are going to live with your friend's mother?"

"Yes, that's right," Marylyn said.

"Understand you have some papers you want us to look at?" Jim asked.

"Yes, I have a couple of insurance policies. I want to find out if they are in force and, if so, to make a claim on them."

Jim took them and handed them to Justin. "Why not make a call on these and see what you can find out?"

"Now, Marylyn, we also have some good news for you. Mr. Stuck, tell her."

"Marylyn, last Saturday afternoon I got a call from a Mr. Joseph Moore," he began.

"That's the man who shot my mother."

"Yes, ma'am, it is. Anyway, I was working late on a case. As I said, he called and wanted to come right over and see me. He came in and told me what he wanted. I told him we would do what he wished and have it ready for him on Tuesday. That wouldn't do for him; he wanted it done right then. Being as my legal secretary was here, we went ahead and set it up."

"I don't understand, Mr. Stuck. Did what?"

"I'm getting to it. Mr. Moore wanted a will made out in favor of your mother."

"You mean the man who killed my mother and himself left his estate to my mother?"

"Yes, ma'am, he did."

"I won't accept it," Marylyn said.

"Why not, Miss Birchley?" Jim asked.

"It just don't seem right, is all."

"The only thing I can say is, it's legal, and if he hadn't willed it to you, your legal right would have been to sue his estate anyway."

"I wouldn't have done that. Nothing he had could ever replace my mama."

Marylyn was squeezing my hand so hard that she was cutting off my circulation and my hand was tingling.

"No, ma'am. We know that. However, there is one thing you should know. Mr. Moore owned one of the largest and nicest horse ranches in the United States. He sold horses all over. His registered quarter horses are very valued animals. He owned ten thousand deeded acres. The important part of that are the oil and gas rights. We have been dickering with several oil and gas companies."

I looked around the room. The tabletop was thick, black granite, and the walls appeared to be raised cherry panels. Original oil paintings hung on the wall, and I began wondering how these attorneys made their money.

"If there is oil there, Mr. Stuck, why hasn't it been drilled before?" I asked. Things didn't add up.

"There are several reasons it has not been done." Stuck shifted in his black leather chair and leaned onto the table for support.

"Would you mind telling me what they are?" I said, trying not to sound suspicious.

"First, this place was left to Joe by his dad. He was in Vietnam when his dad died. At that time, they did not have the technology to drill like they do today. Next, it wasn't worth the time to drill as deep as they would have to go. Foreign oil was cheaper for them. Also about this time, Joe got married. He had a lot of problems with this marriage. He did not want to sell oil leases and have more money to divide up if his marriage ended in divorce. As you know, it did, and Joe ended up in a mental institution. We handled all of his legal matters while he was in treatment."

"What about his wife?" Marylyn asked.

"After what happened between Joe and his wife, she was real happy to get a divorce. It became final well over a year ago."

"Didn't he have any other relatives?"

"In the will, he left two nephews ten thousand dollars each. All other properties were willed to your mother. You knew Joe, of course." Stuck was looking at Marylyn.

"No, sir, I didn't. Tom and I both met him for the first time the night he murdered my mother. I'm sorry, Mr. Stuck, but I don't think I want to accept this. Tommy, what do you think?"

"I wouldn't make a decision on it right now if you feel that you don't want to accept it," I said. "However, if I were you, I would take it."

"Why, Tommy? He killed my mother!"

I turned my black leather swivel chair to face her. "I know that. Money cannot replace a human being, Mar, but there is no reason that you should have to worry about money, especially being that Moore is the one that caused it."

"I agree with Tom here, Miss Birchley," Stuck chimed in. "No one will think less of you for accepting it."

Justin entered. "Excuse me, Bob. Miss Birchley, these policies are in force, and the claim paperwork has already been set in motion for collection."

Justin walked to the chair next to Mar's, sat, and laid the documents out on the stone table in front of her. He methodically asked her a series of questions, beginning with, "Your mother was at work at the time of her death, was she not?"

"Yes, she was," Mar replied.

"You are a minor?"

"Seventeen."

"When will you be eighteen?"

"Fourth of May, next year."

"That's about seven months from now. We will have to have an executor appointed till you are eighteen." Justin made a note on his yellow pad.

"What's an executor?" Marylyn asked.

"Usually, it's a family member or good friend who is appointed to take care of your interests. If you have none of these, then either a lawyer or a bank will be appointed."

"Do you have any preferences for the job, Miss Birchley?"

Mar turned to me. "Do you think Rocky would do it?"

"He most likely would. But you'd better ask him."

Mar turned to Justin. "I'll have to let you know on that later, Mr. Conway."

Jim said, "There is one thing to remember, Miss Birchley. You are talking about a big estate right now—I would say in excess of a million dollars or more. You will have to have someone who is business minded. If the man you are thinking of doesn't work out, we would be proud to handle your account. That is, of course, if you intend to retain our firm. There will be several matters that have to be settled right away."

Mar turned to me again. "What should I do?"

"For right now, we'll go home and discuss it with Rocky. There's no decision that has to be made now. Mr. Stuck, could you set up another appointment tomorrow afternoon at the same time? We'll let you know then." We stood and walked to the massive double doors leading from the conference room into the hallway and then on into the foyer.

"Certainly, Mr. Gurley. Would you wait just a moment?" He pressed the intercom. "Linda, would you bring the Nichols file off my desk to Jim Conway's office?"

I was surprised that the attorney would have a file for me.

A young lady walked in carrying a manila folder and handed it to Stuck. He pulled out several bunches of papers stapled together. "Tom, Boats sent these documents to have you sign. There are eight oil lease agreements on tracts of land known as the Bidwell plat. You know about it?"

"Yes, I have been informed. However, being a minor, I don't see what my signatures are required for."

"I don't know either, Tom. Being as Boats is your guardian, he is authorized to invest your money as he sees fit. In our business dealings with Mr. Nichols, we have found it best to do as he asks, though."

"I know. Boats can be a pain," I said. He showed me the places to sign, and I did. "Is this all, Mr. Stuck?"

"That's it. Oh, yes, Ms. Birchley, when you come in tomorrow, if you wish for us to represent you, could you find out … Never mind. You are entitled to ten thousand dollars in workers compensation. We will find out the coverage and then let you know tomorrow. Thank you for coming in."

After football practice and delivering a load of pipe, I walked into the house at ten o'clock. When I entered, Rosie and Mar set my supper on the table. Mar leaned over and kissed me. "Tired?"

"Nope. Feel pretty good." I halfway imagined what it would be like coming home to Mar for dinner each night. It was a nice dream. "Where's Rocky?"

"In the bathroom. He hasn't been feeling too good," Rosie said, looking a bit worried.

I remembered that he had been missing his wife that morning when we got up, and I turned to Rosie.

"He's not sick, Rosie. He's bored and lonesome."

"You know, Buck, I'd bet that's what it is," Rosie said.

"Well, sweetie, I've tried to get him to go out with me to the oil fields, but he's just not interested."

"Did you talk to them?" I asked Mar.

"No, I waited for you. I can't think of half the things they were talking about."

Rosie had fixed her famous meatloaf for dinner, and I was on my second slice, along with a pile of mashed potatoes and gravy. Rocky finally walked in, got a cup of coffee, and sat down. "How's it goin', son?"

"Just fine, Rocky. Marylyn has a favor to ask of you. You'll even be paid for it."

"She knows I'll do anything I can for her. As for gettin' paid, what are you two tryin' to do, hurt my feelin's?"

Mar went over and put her hand on his shoulder. "You know I wouldn't hurt your feelings for all the money in the world."

"Just kiddin', honey.'

"No, I need someone to be an executor for me," she said. "I have had so much thrown at me in the last two days, I'm lost."

Buck said, "I think you better explain, son."

I told them about all that had transpired that afternoon. When I finished, Buck said, "Strangest thing I've heard of in a long time. What you think, Rocky?"

Rocky turned to Marylyn. "I think that in the mornin', Marylyn and I should drive out and take a look at this ranch. Then I think I had better go see a different set of lawyers from the ones the kids saw. Also, Marylyn, did your mother leave a will?" Rocky was perking up. He was sharp, and his mind was clicking.

"Yes, it's in the bank deposit box with her jewelry and other papers."

"Was your name on her bank book and deposit box?"

"Yes, but I've never wrote a check."

"That doesn't matter as long as you can. We can find out in the morning how much is in the account. Tom, those lawyers actually told you that this Moore's estate was worth a million?"

Rocky grabbed the bowl of mashed potatoes and dropped three dollops on his plate, sliced two pieces of meatloaf and dropped them on his plate, and then covered it all with gravy. Things were looking up for Rocky, starting with his appetite.

"That's what they said, isn't it, Mar?"

"They said in *excess* of a million," Marylyn said.

Rocky was shaking his head. "In excess of a million? That scares me." Rocky was noticeably troubled.

"Why is that, Dad?" Rosie asked.

"Anytime you start talkin' about that kind of money, people's hands start itchin'. It bothers me."

"Isn't there some way to set it up so that it can't be touched?" Buck asked.

"That's a lawyer's business to set things up in such a way that they can spend time. Doctors and lawyers are the only people I know of who can charge you anything they want to with no results. Time, to them, is money—big money."

I interjected, "Mar isn't sure she wants to take the estate." Rocky turned to look at Mar.

"Why is that, honey?"

"It just doesn't feel right, takin' from someone who killed my mother."

"I would think you would be more entitled to it than someone else," Rocky said as he dropped butter on the gravy covering his potatoes.

"It seems like blood money to me. Doesn't it to you, Rosie?"

"In a way. However, I believe you are more entitled than someone with blood ties."

"Would you take it, then?"

"I sure would. For one reason, it will secure your future; for another, it will keep people like Ms. Keech off your back."

Rocky shoved a fork full of meatloaf in his mouth. I shuddered at the sound of Keech's name.

"How will that help?"

Buck answered, "They don't usually make a person a ward of the state when they have as much money as you will. From what I understand, they appoint a guardian and conservator to provide for your care. They won't need to spend tax dollars when you can afford to care for yourself."

"Then all of you think I should accept it?"

"There is no question about that, honey," Rosie answered. "It's just how to set it up for your best advantage." Rosie put an apple pie on the table and then went back to the refrigerator to get the vanilla ice cream.

Rocky said, "Give me a couple of days, and then we'll talk it over." With that, he dove into his plate, and Rosie dished out pie and ice cream for the rest of us.

The rest of the week went fast with the work in the pipe yard, football practice, boxing, and planning for the funeral. When Sunday came, I was plum worn out. Mar and Rocky had agreed to take a trip to the ranch and check it out. They were up and gone the same time they were every morning. That day, Rocky took her and Tess to the mortuary to settle accounts. The funeral had been on Friday afternoon. All of Mar's and my friends were there, as were people Pauline had worked with. Rocky had arranged for Pauline's ashes to be shipped to Kansas and buried beside her husband.

Jim told us that probating the will could take up to a year or more; however, since his firm had prepared the will, he arranged to appoint an executor that would manage the ranch until all was resolved. The executor would assign Rocky to manage the operation of the ranch, subject to his approval on all transactions, until the probate was concluded. Jim was setting up an appointment with Rocky and the executor to lay out the expectations. The bottom line was that Mar could move to the ranch with Rocky and us as soon as Jim settled a bit of paperwork. It really wasn't clear how Jim was swinging this, but he was confident and we weren't going to argue.

Early on Sunday, Buck and I took our pickups and moved Mar's things over to Mama Santos's. In the afternoon, the family drove out to Mar's ranch. It wasn't more than ten miles out of town, and the drive was lovely. Alongside the long drive to the main house, the pastures were surrounded with white wooden fences. The fields were green compared to most of Texas; there was obviously an irrigation system in place. Our suspicions were confirmed when we saw a tractor hitched to a pipe trailer that was stacked with irrigation pipe.

I had never been to Kentucky for the Derby or anything else, but this ranch is what I imagined Kentucky would be like. Andy and Sissy were enthralled by the horses. Mar, Rocky, and I drove around the ranch while Buck, Rosie, and the kids explored the house. The yard around the main house was filled with southern magnolias. Out in the pastures, clumps of chalk maple trees provided shade for the horses.

Rocky must have been doing a lot of homework in his previous trips to the ranch. He had a small black ledger with him, and when we would stop to look at the horses in any of the forty different pastures that were sectioned off, he would look in the book and give us a rundown on the mares in each one. I had noticed a cluster of black oak nearly fifty feet tall, about a quarter of a mile behind the house, so Rocky decided we should head that way. As we approached, we saw a long building among the trees, along with three pickups and a car. Two men walked out when we drove up.

I unloaded, and Rocky introduced me. Frank Tobin was about five ten, a hundred and sixty pounds, well-built, and wearing typical cowboy gear. Roy Childs was a replica, only taller. After the introductions, Rocky asked, "Any trouble, Frank?"

"None, Rock. We moved a couple of the mares after they got to fighting. I meant to tell you, we'll be gone for several days next week. Three of us have to go out back to bring in the mares and colts that have been running out. I'll leave Keno here to take care of the place. Also, I'd recommend that we destroy Redbird's colt."

"That the one with the turned-in forelegs?" Rocky asked.

Frank nodded. "I told Joe when he bred that mare that he was breeding too close. He was kind of stubborn on some things."

"Is that what causes it?"

"Seems to be. Both of the parents are from different branches of the Three Bar family. Joe just liked the stud's look when he was a yearling and paid fifteen thousand for him. Most of his colts have those tendencies—weakness in the forelegs—when they are bred to Three Bar stock."

Mar asked, "Can you get the original cost back?"

"You should do better than that, ma'am—Joe turned down twenty-five for him at two years—less'n the buyer is spooked by these Three Bar colts he sired."

"Do you know the person who made the offer?"

"Yes, ma'am. Cliff Barnes from Colorado."

Rocky said, "Give him a call and ask thirty. See what he says."

On the way back to the main house, Rocky asked, "Start to school tomorrow, don't you?"

I answered, "Yep, first thing in the morning."

"Remember, Marylyn," Rocky said, "we have to be in court in the afternoon.

We're filing for executor and the will for probate. Jim Conway told me he received an inquiry from one of the nephews about the will."

"Does he think there will be any problem with him?"

"He hasn't any idea. Like he said and like I told you the other night, when you get involved with this amount of money, anything can happen and usually does."

"I don't want any trouble, Rocky."

At the house, Rosie stepped out on the covered porch and called out, "We fixed a snack. Let's eat."

I walked toward the house and realized that it was like the ones I had seen in pictures of the ranch houses in Australia's sheep country. It had a pyramid-type roof and an expansive wraparound porch. It was built up off the ground so that the air could circulate underneath, and the double doors at the front and back of the house, along with the tall windows around the house, could be opened to allow maximum circulation. It was a working house, designed for lots of people and social gatherings. I walked up the long flight of stairs to the front porch and saw the family sitting around tables, eating roast beef sandwiches and barbecue potato chips.

As we were eating, Rocky asked, "What do you think, Rosie?"

"It would work out real nice, Dad."

Rocky turned to Marylyn and Tom. "We could see no reason for continuing to rent a house and having Marylyn staying at another home. If the application to the court is approved tomorrow, making me the executor and guardian of Marylyn, we intend to move the entire family out here to the ranch."

"Won't that create a problem, her and me living at the same place?" I asked. "I thought Keech made it plain that she didn't trust Mar and me living together."

"A problem for who?" Rocky asked. "Her guardian will be living in the same house. I talked to Jim Conway, and he thinks it's a good idea." Rocky was smiling.

Buck said, "You know the old saying, Tom. Possession is nine-tenths of the law."

"You want to live out here, Mar?"

"I just want to be with you, Tommy. I don't care where. Don't you?"

"You know my feelings, honey."

Rocky said, "All right, then. It's settled. If everything goes right in court, we will plan on moving next weekend."

Rocky told me, "I'll ride back into town with Buck and Rosie. Take Marylyn by and let her pick up her mother's car."

"Marylyn," he continued, turning to her, "you are going to have to spend the night over at Mama Santos's. When we go into court, I want to be able to say you're living with Mama Santos."

"Any particular reason?" I asked.

"Sure is. Just in case Ms. Keech or anyone else is there, I want everything looking right."

We all agreed to the plan. Mar and I finished our sandwiches and headed for town.

I dropped Mar off at her house to get her mom's car and then followed her to Tess's house to help her get her things put away. It was hard to say good night, but we agreed that when things worked out, we would be together.

I pulled up to the house around eleven thirty. As I stepped into the kitchen, Rosie, Rocky, and Buck were eating pie and ice cream.

"Glad you made it home," Buck said with a laugh. "Thought I would have to send a rescue crew out to get you. Sit down here. We're talkin' 'bout some things you need to know. Rocky gave me the oil maps and seismologist reports for the ranch. If they're anywhere near right, that place is loaded."

Rocky chimed in. "From what I read, I thought it was. I knew there was a reason that your uncle's lawyers were eager to handle the deal."

"The only other readings I've seen that were better than these were some of the Brownsville and Bidwell plats that Boats showed me when we were up in Tishomingo." Buck was glowing with excitement.

Rosie asked, "They that good, honey?"

"That little girl in love with Tommy is a very rich young lady. Wouldn't you say, Rocky?"

"Couldn't happen to a nicer kid either. Just hope Moore's nephew lets things alone."

"Tell me about that," Buck said. "He starting to cause trouble?" Buck was leaning in to grab the coffeepot to refill his cup.

"Just that one of Moore's nephews retained a lawyer. They wish to meet with us before the court hearing tomorrow morning."

"You tell Marylyn about the meeting, Dad?" Rosie asked.

"No. From what you've told me, she would probably chuck the whole thing. I told them that she would not want to fight with Moore's nephew for the money. That is just beyond her nature."

"You're probably right," Rosie said. "She does have a very strict sense of moral values. From what she has told me, if either one of those boys took her to court, she would turn it over to them without a fight."

Buck said, "Whatever we do, Rocky, we must not let that happen. She has lost everything, and we ain't lettin' these turds take another damn thing from her."

Rosie swatted Buck's shoulder. "Buck Hagan, you watch that language. The kids may be listening."

Rocky looked at Buck. "You met Bob Stuck. I don't trust him very far. He has too many angles to suit me. However, he came up with a couple of ideas that we intend to throw at them."

"Think they'll work?

"Boats always said Stuck was a sharp knife that could cut either way—just make sure you pay him enough to keep him on your side. Clearly, Stuck is sharp. Boats said, in fact, 'He's one of the few men I've met who could crawl through a barrel of broken razor blades backward and not get a mark on him.'"

"That's high praise from the bastard Boats," I said, thinking of Boats's malevolence.

"You don't trust him much, do you?" Rocky said with a smirk.

I said, "I don't trust neither of them, Boats or Stuck."

"Well, I was talking about Stuck, but no, I don't trust him and I've let him know it, too. Over the years I've found the way to work with them. Always be out front and let them know you're lookin' over their shoulder on every move." I had learned in the few short months of living with Rocky that he was short on words but got to the point.

"What did he come up with?" Buck asked as he stood and carried his plate to the sink.

"The one nephew giving us the trouble has been in trouble all his life. Been in the state pen twice—once for armed robbery, the other time for rape."

Rocky leaned back in his chair and pushed his hands against the edge of the table. "Stuck seems to think he's just out to try and steal whatever he can. Anyway, he thinks that showing him that we know about his background and also that if he pursues any litigation whatever, we intend to file a countersuit against Moore's estate for at least three million, we'll make our point."

Rosie walked over from the sink where she had been washing the dishes and sat down by Rocky, drying her hands on a dish towel she had brought with her. "She couldn't get even a part of that, could she, Dad?"

"There's a lot of precedents for such a suit, honey," Rocky answered. "Deprivation of her mother's civil rights, companionship, income from her mother, and several others Stuck talked about. He's positive the suit is winnable, though he couldn't file it because he prepared the will. We would have to hire another attorney. But he thinks we would win, and win big."

"That is, if Marylyn would let you," I said.

"Tomorrow, after I'm appointed her guardian, I can do anything that I feel is in her best interest. She wouldn't have to know a thing about any of them. One thing for sure, I intend to protect her interests and flush these scumbags back down the toilet they crawled out of."

"How about the other brother?" Rosie asked. "Aren't there two of them?"

"Yeah, there are two. When this came up, Stuck contacted him. He's a stockbroker in Denver, and he told Stuck he had no interest in any claims. According to Stuck, he's loaded. He's the one who informed us that his brother had a criminal record. Stuck has already sent him a release form to sign, and he faxed it back. Anyway, we'll find out in the morning."

Rosie, Rocky, and Buck stayed up talking, but I was done. I couldn't keep my eyes open. I crawled into bed after a quick shower and didn't wake till Rocky was shaking me in the morning.

Chapter 14

Justice, Always Justice

Rocky, Robert Stuck, and Jim Conway entered Royal Carroll's law office exactly at 10:00. The receptionist told them that Mr. Carroll was waiting for them and ushered them into his office.

Two men were seated there talking. Bob introduced Rocky, saying, "You know Jim, and this is Royal Carroll."

Royal shook Rocky's hand and introduced the other man to them as Harold Moore, Joe's brother. After they had been seated, Royal said, "Gentlemen, the reason we called this meeting is that Mr. Moore thinks—as I do—that we would stand a good chance of overturning Joe's will. We believe that he was coerced into making out that will. We all know that Mr. Moore was of an unstable mind. We can prove that the lady in question spent the afternoon in Mr. Moore's bedroom. And less than two hours later, he had you make out this will."

"How can you prove such a thing?" Rocky asked.

Royal pulled out a sheet of paper and handed it to Stuck. Bob read it and handed it to Rocky, who quickly read through it. The statement, signed by Roy Childs, stated that while doing some yard work, he had seen Joe and Pauline naked in the bedroom. His statement about what they were doing was very graphic.

Rocky handed the paper back to Royal. "That being the case, Royal, why did you call this meeting? If I had hard evidence like that, I would have taken it to court."

"Well, we thought the young lady had been hurt enough. There is no reason to embarrass her any more than we have to."

"That's a bunch of horseshit, and you know it," Rocky said. "Just tell us what you want."

"I have been appointed as coexecutor of Joe Moore's estate. This afternoon when you go into court, we will ask for a closed hearing on the case. That way, none of this will come out in public. You will sign a release against the estate. In return, we will pay Ms. Birchley one hundred thousand dollars for indemnity and damages."

"And you expect us to go for that?" Stuck asked.

"I don't believe you have any choice."

"It's funny," Stuck said, "but that is exactly half the deal we were going to offer you."

"Then I guess we have nothing further to discuss, do we?"

"Oh, I believe we do. For one thing, we know everything there is to know about Harold there, alias Harold Compton, Harold Walgenback, plus a few others. I'm sure that Mr. Moore's brother told you that Harold has a warrant out in Denver, Colorado, for stealing two thousand in cash off of him. It won't be served as long as he stays out of Denver. Also, there are two warrants out for a Harold Compton, alias Walgenback, in Salt Lake City for armed robbery. "

Moore jumped up. "What you trying to pull? I've never been in Salt Lake in my life."

Royal said, "Sit down, Harold. It's just a bluff."

"It's no such thing," Stuck countered. "Harold here was committed to the Utah State Pen in 1960 for five to twenty for armed robbery—paroled in '66. Also, he was convicted in '54 for rape and released in '59."

Royal turned and looked at Moore. "Is this information correct?"

"I don't—"

"Don't lie to me," Royal said. "I believe every word he said. Get the hell out of my office. Bob, I'm sorry to have wasted your time."

"No problem, Royal, but just a minute, Mr. Moore. Royal, to forestall any problems in the future, we will still offer Mr. Moore half the amount you mentioned to release all claims against the estate. Fifty thousand dollars is more than sufficient. However, to stop any litigation, we will pay it. I would advise your former client there to accept it."

Royal sat for a moment. "Sit down, Moore," he said. "What about those warrants in Utah?" he asked Stuck.

"Nothing in the law says we have to notify the police immediately. Here is what we will do. When we finish the court hearing this afternoon, I will bring you a cashier's check for the money. However, right now, I want an iron-clad release signed by Mr. Moore to take into court with me."

Royal turned to Moore. "I believe that, if I were you, I would accept this offer and then get out of town quick."

"It's not enough money," Moore complained. "That place and the houses are worth at least ten times that."

"What it's worth is immaterial. You can't use it in jail, can you?"

"No, but I can have it when I come out. You're taking advantage of me because I'm in a little trouble."

"I don't call two warrants for armed robbery a little trouble, Mr. Moore, but it's up to you. Make up your mind."

"When can I have the money?"

Stuck said, "It will be delivered to you as soon after the court hearing as I can get here, most likely by four or four thirty."

"Well, I'll take it, but I think you people had this planned before we ever came in here."

Royal turned to Moore. "If you say another goddamned word, Mr. Moore, I will personally pick up the phone and call the cops. Bob, when you get that check, make it out to Mr. Moore. I want nothing to do with this transaction."

"What about your fee?" Stuck asked.

"I don't do business with people who lie to me." He picked up the intercom. "Betty, bring your pad in a minute, would you please?" When she came in, he dictated a release, pausing to ask Bob a couple of questions in the process. Between them, they completed it.

In less than ten minutes, the secretary returned and laid the form on Royal's desk. Moore signed it; Royal and Jim Conway signed as witnesses. Royal then stood up and said, "Mr. Moore, I want you to leave my office. Your check will be given to the secretary. In the future, you will stay away from my office. Also, first thing in the morning, I will notify the police that you are in town. Judge yourself accordingly. Now get out."

After he left, Royal said, "Sometimes I wonder why I became a lawyer. How in the world did you get all that information on him in such a short time, Bob?"

"His uncle and brother had told me all about him over the years. We sent money to him for Joe while he was in the pen."

"We appreciate it, Royal," Rocky said. "We better get some lunch before court. Thanks again."

Royal gave Rocky a hard handshake, saying, "Sorry about this, sir. It's been nice meeting you."

"Same here, Royal. Thank you."

Rocky met Marylyn and me in the hallway outside Judge Stillwell's courtroom. Marylyn left for the bathroom, and Rocky brought me up to speed on his earlier meeting with the lawyers and Joe's nephew. He was giving me the blow by blow when Marylyn came back.

"Sweetie, would you mind waiting in the back of the courtroom for a couple minutes while Rocky finishes filling me in on what happened today with the attorneys?" I said.

Mar smiled, kissed me, and went into the courtroom. Rocky finished telling me the details and showed me the release that Joe's nephew had signed.

"It's done," Rocky said. "I think I found the only honest attorney in Texas too."

We walked into the courtroom, and Rocky and Mar went up to the third row. I sat in the shadows of the last row. The courtroom was imposing, probably sixty years old and filled with carved oak. The solid bench seats were uncomfortable, and the polish had worn off several years ago, no doubt because of an uncomfortable audience.

The bailiff called the court into session. After the attorneys made their appearances, the judge asked for a copy of the petition. Judge Stillwell took the sheaf of paper handed to him by the court clerk. "These been entered in the ledger?"

"Yes, Your Honor," Stuck said as he stood. "They have the case number entered in the lower right corner."

"I see them." He sat there reading them. "These seem to be in order, Mr. Stuck. Is Mr. Roscoe Walgrin in the courtroom?"

"Yes, sir, Your Honor. Right here." Rocky stood to face the judge, holding his Stetson in front of him at his waist.

"Do you understand the functions you are being appointed for, Mr. Walgrin?"

"Yes, sir, most of it anyway."

"Any questions you have can be answered by either this court or your attorney, Mr. Stuck. Have you ever been in trouble with the law, Mr. Walgrin?"

"No, sir, Your Honor."

"I notice the only references you give are up in Kansas."

"Yes, sir. I lived in the same town for sixty-two years."

"The court will check them out. In the meantime, I can see no reason not to appoint you on an interim basis. Is the person receiving the estate in the courtroom?"

"Yes, Your Honor," Stuck replied. "She is sitting in the third row with Mr. Walgrin. But before we get to that, Your Honor, we also applied for guardianship of Marylyn J. Birchley to be considered."

"Yes, the court received those documents this morning. However, we understand that the Department of Family and Protective Services has something to say on this matter. Ms. Keech, is that the reason you are here?"

"Yes, Your Honor."

Rocky saw that, in the front row, Ms. Keech had risen.

"You may address the court, Ms. Keech."

"Thank you, Your Honor. Your Honor, the Department of Family and Protective Services is opposed to granting guardianship to Mr. Walgrin."

"For what reason, Ms. Keech?"

"We do not believe the stability is there for her, Your Honor. For one thing, she hasn't known these people very long. The only reason these people take an interest in her is that she dates Mr. Walgrin's foster grandchild. Now I understand she has inherited quite a sum of money. I believe that also enters the picture. We—and by *we* I mean the Department, Your Honor—do not believe she should be allowed to live in the same house as her boyfriend. I tried the other day to remove her from their clutches, but Mr. Hagan interfered."

"Your Honor," Stuck said as he stood up, "we object to her use of the word *clutches*."

"There is no jury here to impress, Mr. Stuck. Let Ms. Keech finish."

"Thank you, Your Honor."

"Mr. Walgrin," the judge said, "you and Ms. Birchley please come forward to the table there on the left."

Marylyn reached over and took Rocky's hand. Holding hands, the two walked up to the table and seated themselves.

"Ms. Keech, please come forward and sit at the table on your right." When she complied, the judge said, "Continue, Ms. Keech."

"We believe, Your Honor, that it would be in the young lady's interest to either be declared a ward of the court or have some prominent person appointed as her guardian."

"Is this the young lady in question?"

Mr. Stuck rose. "It is, Your Honor."

"Ms. Keech, has your department checked out this family?" The judge shifted forward and leaned across his desk with his hands folded to hear her answer.

"Yes, we have, Your Honor."

"What does the report show?"

"We can find nothing derogatory about them, Your Honor. Buck Hagan, Mr. Walgrin's son-in-law, had a drinking problem some years back."

"Nothing recently, Ms. Keech?"

"No, Your Honor."

"You check them out completely?"

"Yes, Your Honor."

"Then give this court a complete rundown so I can make a decision."

Keech began reading her report. "Mr. Walgrin has an excellent reputation in his former hometown, excellent credit references, is well liked. Said to be honest and hardworking. The report shows that he owns a large wheat ranch in Kansas, plus a townhouse. Buck Hagan and his wife, Rosie, have two children. They are clean and seem to be well behaved. Mr. Hagan makes a good living and pays his bills."

"To your knowledge," the judge asked, "have any of the persons in question been in trouble with the law?" The judge was impatient, and his tolerance seemed to be waning.

"Not to our knowledge, Your Honor. However, although we can't prove it, Thomas Gurley, Marylyn's boyfriend, the foster child of Buck and Rosie, has been in trouble twice since he came here two months ago."

"In what way, Ms. Keech? Has he been arrested?"

"His face was cut up by a Mexican boy, and then a week later he broke this Mexican boy's hand. This doesn't say much, Your Honor, for his moral caliber, does it?"

The judge was focused. "Was the boy who did the cutting arrested?"

"No, Your Honor. The report to the police said that Gurley's face was cut on a broken mirror on a pickup when playing football."

"What about the broken hand?"

"We understand that the Mexican boy tried to hit him, and he ducked. The Mexican hit him on the head and broke his hand."

"That would seem normal to me, Ms. Keech. If someone tried to hit me, I would duck, too. I fail to see any criminal conduct in ducking. Do you?"

"I shared these instances, Your Honor, to show the moral character of the boy. It shows a violence that we don't think Marylyn should be associated with. Also, Your Honor, we don't believe it is in her best moral interest to live in the same house as her boyfriend."

"Well, now the real squirrel has run out of the log. It's about time, Ms. Keech. Let's get it out in the open, Ms. Keech. You are worried about sex between these two young people, aren't you?"

"Put that way, yes, Your Honor, we are."

"Marylyn, how old are you?" The judge turned his gaze to her.

"Seventeen, Your Honor."

"How old is Tom, my dear?"

"Sixteen, Your Honor."

"Have you and Tom had sex, Marylyn?" The judge was looking intently at her so he could perceive any equivocation in her answer.

"No, Your Honor, I swear we haven't."

"Has he ever tried?" the judge pressed.

"No, Your Honor."

"Are you in love with him, Ms. Birchley?"

"Yes, Your Honor."

"How long have you known him?"

"About a month, Your Honor."

"That puts a different light on this entire proceeding."

Marylyn was bold. "May I ask why, Your Honor?"

"I don't believe you know enough about this family to justify placing your entire future in their hands."

Marylyn spoke up. "Well, it isn't my entire future, Your Honor. As I understand it, I will be of legal age in seven months, when I reach eighteen. Isn't that correct?"

"That's the law, young lady."

"I'm sure that Rocky, Tommy, and I would not object to any type of supervision this court wishes to order for us. Your Honor, at no time in my life have I ever been in trouble. I am still a virgin, Your Honor. I am a straight-A student in school. My mother taught me to be self-sufficient. My mother left me well fixed, even without Mr. Moore's estate. I believe that I have enough experience in my young life to spot a phony. You have never seen a more loving and honest person than any one of them. It is nice to know there are families like this left in the world. They have shown me love, compassion, understanding, and help when I needed it. I can truly say, Your Honor, that they would have done the same thing for me even without Tommy in the picture. If the function of this court is to guard my welfare, then, sir, without a doubt, in the entire state of Texas, you couldn't find anyone who will guard my welfare more than Rocky, Buck, Rosie, or Tommy."

"Thank you, Marylyn," the judge said. "Are you living with them now?"

"No, Your Honor. Rocky made me move into Mama Santos's house."

Ms. Keech added, "But only since last night, Your Honor."

"Mr. Walgrin, do you plan on having her stay there?"

"No, Your Honor. If I am awarded guardianship over Marylyn, we plan on moving out to her ranch next week. The reason for that is that I believe she should have her own room. Staying with us, she had to sleep with Rosie, and I don't think that was best for her."

"At the ranch, would she have her own room?"

"Yes, sir, two if she wants them. It has a seven-bedroom house."

"Can you guarantee the court that there will be no hanky-panky between them?"

"No, sir, I can't do that. I have no way of controlling a person's emotions. This I will guarantee, Your Honor: if at any time I think or assume there is any danger to Marylyn's moral fiber, I will notify this court immediately."

"Thank you, Mr. Walgrin. After listening to all facets of the testimony, I am going to award guardianship to you. Just keep it a sacred trust, Mr. Walgrin, and the court will be satisfied."

"Your Honor?" Ms. Keech interjected.

"Yes, Ms. Keech?"

"It is my duty to inform the court and Mr. Walgrin that we will keep a close watch on Marylyn, and if we see anything out of line, we will be right back in court."

"This court and, I'm sure, Mr. Walgrin understand the function of the Department of Family and Protective Services. However, Ms. Keech, I must warn you: if you interfere in any way with Mr. Walgrin's responsibilities or duties to Marylyn, he also has recourse to the court. It is a two-edged sword, Ms. Keech. Do I make myself clear?"

"Yes, Your Honor."

That night, the group sitting around the kitchen table was happy. I had stopped at Mama Santos's and packed up Mar's things.

The rest of the week flew by. We went to our first game at Deming, New Mexico, and it was run to perfection. The final score was thirty-six to eight. I rushed for 115 yards. Mueller got 105, Breedlove had 83, and Manny passed and ran for 160 yards. We moved to the ranch over Saturday and Sunday. It was great being back together again.

Chapter 15

Doc's Dead; the Dog's Not

Lee Bob Whetzel stood on the steps of the county jail. It had been a long night. He found it difficult to stay awake as he drove his cruiser home. He had just climbed into bed with his wife, Joy, when the phone rang. "Lee Bob, it's Junior at the jail."

"Why the hell you callin' this time of night?"

"Joe Bill and Zeke just called in. They found Doc Leftan."

"Is that any damn reason to call me? Tell them to take the son of a bitch home to his dog and let him sober him up."

"You don't understand, Sheriff. He's been killed."

"Can't be. Who in the hell would want to murder that old bastard?"

"I don't know, but Joe Bill wants to know if you want to call the state investigator team."

"Hell, no. He knows what I think of them shitheads. Tell him I'm on my way."

Joy sat up in bed. "What you cussin' fer, and where you goin'?"

"Doc Leftan got himself kilt."

Joy became livid. "Well, sweet Jesus, can't those idiots of yours handle it? I've tried to get you in bed for over a week now."

"I'm sorry, babe. I've got to go—it's murder."

"It sure as hell is. If you think I'm going to keep on going without sex till you get ready, buddy boy, you have another think coming."

"Damn it, Joy, I'm trying to tell you that someone murdered the doc."

"No one would kill that old fart. The child-molesting cocksucker had enough dirt on everyone in this county that no one would dare mess with him."

"I wish you would watch your language."

"You mean like you?"

"Oh, hell, go to sleep. I'll grope you when I get home."

"Don't bother," Joy retorted. "I got a vibrator in the drawer that'll last longer than you and is more reliable. Couple of D batteries and I don't need your limp dick at all. 'Sides, it never fails to hit the right spot."

The sheriff slammed the front door and threw his coat against the passenger window as he slid into his cruiser. He flipped on his lights and keyed up the radio. "Tishomingo one to Tishomingo four, come in." He had to call three times before Joe Bill answered. "Where you located? Over."

"Out behind Doc's place, north of the golf course. He is half-in and half-out of Brighton Creek. Over."

"Well, don't touch him. You call for Adolph yet? Over."

"Not yet. Over."

"Well, get on the damn horn and get him the hell out there. Who the shit you think has all the photography equipment?" Lee Bob hit his siren and headed east out of town. For fourteen years, he had been sheriff of this county. He kept asking himself, *How in the hell did I wind up with every damn numbnuts in the county for a deputy?* He already knew the answer—every one of them was related to someone who had power in the county. Hell, they couldn't make a living otherwise. Two of them had come off state aid when they got the job as it was. As he topped the hill, he saw the squad car lights. He took off on the road down to the house. His tires rumbled on the wooden bridge, and he saw his man with a flashlight.

Joe Bill opened his car door when the sheriff stopped. The lower two buttons of Joe Bill's shirt were unbuttoned, and his T-shirt was showing. No one made a shirt that could contain that sixty-inch belly teetering above a thirty-four-inch waist. "How'd he die, Joe Bill?"

"Someone strangled him. I think they completely tore his house up. His black bag is missing."

"Is Zeke down with the body? Did you move it?"

"We had to move it to tell if he was dead or not." While they were talking, they walked down to where the body lay. It was alongside the water, its upper half wet.

Zeke was walking along the bank looking for any sign of what had happened. In contrast to Joe Bill, Zeke was a stick. He ate like a summer hog but didn't gain a pound. Lee Bob always said he must have a tapeworm the size of a boa constrictor.

Lee Bob knelt down and felt Doc's face. In the flashlight glare, he could see that Doc was wet from the waist up. The knees on both pant legs had mud on them, and the toes of his shoes showed little gobs of mud. Lee Bob asked, "How was he layin'?"

"Face down in the water, Sheriff," Joe Bill said.

"Then why in the goddamn hell did you move him?"

"I told you—to see if he was dead."

"Tell me, Joe Bill, how may live people you know lay face down in the water and don't move? Hell, how come you were out here anyway?"

"Judge Watkins asked us to look for him. You know how he likes to play dominoes. He said Doc hadn't been around for a couple of days."

"Yeah, I know. Well, at least here comes Adolph. Do you think it would be too much trouble to place the body back the way it was when you found it? And please make it as close to the way he was as you can."

"Come on, Zeke," Joe Bill said. "Help me move him. Was it his right or left arm above his head? Oh, yeah, his right. There, Sheriff. That's the way he was. Oh, yeah, there's some footprints." He stood there as Adolph snapped pictures. On the third picture, he saw something in the water reflecting the flash. "Hold it, Adolph. Shoot another picture from that same angle. Watch out there in the water when he takes the picture. Okay, shoot!"

When the light hit the water, he saw the flash again. "You boys see what I saw?"

"What's that, Sheriff?"

"That flash out there in the water."

"Well, yeah, I saw it a few minutes ago when my flashlight hit it."

"Then, for God's sake, get your asses out there and find it. Adolph, when you get through down here, come on up to the house." Lee Bob walked up the hill to the house. As he stepped up on the wooden planks of the porch, he heard something. He listened, and he heard it again—a whining and scratching on the door. As he laid his hand on the doorknob, the whining changed to a growl. He gently pulled the door open a couple of inches and tried to shine his light into the crack. The dog hit the door and had him by the arm before he could move. He felt the teeth tear into his arm, shredding it like a cabbage as the dog swung his head from side to side.

The sheriff's scream stopped the three deputies at the creek bank. "My God, Joe Bill," Zeke said. "Didn't you tell the sheriff about the dog?" They had just reached the top of the hill when the shot startled them to a standstill.

The sheriff stood on the porch holding his arm as they finally reached the house. "Did you goddamned idiots put that dog in the house?" he asked.

"Sheriff, you know that dog was the meanest thing in the county."

"Did any one of you have half a notion to tell me the bastard was in the house?"

"Well, I forgot, Sheriff," Zeke said from under the brim of his hat. He was afraid to look the sheriff in the face.

"How in the hell did you get the son of a bitch in the house?"

"Zeke drove out to the back of the house, and I parked in front," Joe Bill said. "The dog stayed with me. Zeke slipped in through the back door and opened up the front door. The dog saw him, and he slipped into the kitchen and slammed the door while I closed the front."

"Why did you go to all that trouble if you didn't know if Doc was here?"

"'Cause when we pulled over the bridge, we heard the dog barking and I put my spotlight down there, and I saw the body."

"So you saw Doc laying face down in the water and spent ten to twenty minutes catching the dog, and then you went down to check on Doc with his head submerged and you still thought he might be alive? My God, Zeke, have you ever had a logical thought in your life? And of course you didn't think it was important to tell me about that 180-pound rottweiler laying in wait for me in Doc's house. Now you're standing there with your thumb in your ass while I bleed to death on the porch. One of you shitheads get me a first-aid kit."

"I'll get it." Zeke ran off the porch and came right back with the kit.

"Give it to Adolph and you guys get back down there and find that object in the water."

"We would be able to find it a lot better in the morning," Joe Bill whimpered.

"Goddamn it! They forecasted rain, and the lightning has been going on for the last ten minutes. You know how that creek rises when it rains. Now dammit, get that item, or so help me God, I'll drown both your sorry asses next to Doc."

"Sheriff, with that lightning coming, it ain't safe in the water," the other deputy said.

"Junior, you and Zeke have a choice. You can get your asses out there and find that sparkly thing in the water and risk being killed by lightning, or I will shoot you right now and save the county from havin' to pay your stupid asses."

The deputies turned and disappeared into the dark without another word.

Lee Bob and Adolph stepped into the house and turned on the lights. The sheriff's arm was torn almost all the way around, and blood was running off his hand onto the floor.

Adolph took the kit. "Let's go into the bathroom, Sheriff." He led the way, stepping across the rottweiler with half its torso blown away. Adolph had Lee Bob put his arm in the bathtub and run water over it. Lee Bob groaned and commenced cussing as the water hit his open flesh.

When the bleeding slowed down, Adolph looked at the wound. "You're going to have to have this sewn up, Sheriff. See that blood squirting? That mutt opened an artery there."

"Give me one of those towels." Lee Bob wrapped it around his arm. "You stay here. The coroner is supposed to be on his way out. Keep those idiots out there lookin'. If they do find it, don't let them touch anything. Make them search the creek bank. Just keep them busy."

"I'll do it, Sheriff. Now go to the hospital and get that sewn up."

"Your car keys in your cruiser?"

"Yeah, take it and go."

The sheriff sat in the squad car, called central, and told the dispatcher to get a hold of the hospital and get a doctor there right away. By the time he reached the main highway, Junior came back on the horn.

"What do you want, Junior? Over."

"The hospital wants to know the type of emergency. They're still on the phone. Over."

"You tell those shitheads I've got my arm about half ripped off and I need a doctor. Also, tell them I'm on a case. But for God sakes, don't tell them what case. Over."

"They say they heard most of it, and they will get a doctor there as quick as they can. Over."

Lee Bob thought as he drove through town with his lights and siren on, *Man, is the shit going to hit the fan on this one.* Doc had been a fixture in Tishomingo County for the last sixty years. He had delivered over half the people who now lived there. He hadn't practiced for the last twenty years, ever since the medical board lifted his license for drug addiction. Doc had made his living since then selling dope. Lee Bob had nailed him about ten years ago. Doc's car had been loaded with a bale of grass in the trunk, three large boxes of amphetamines, black mollies, speed—a lot of them he didn't even know. He never would forget the half smile on Doc's face when he confronted him. "Told you I would get you," he said.

"Who's got who, Lee Bob?"

"What's that supposed to mean?"

"All I can tell you is, before this goes any further, you had better go over to the store and call Judge Watkins. I ain't going no place."

"Bullshit, Doc. You're going to jail."

"You're going to make more of an ass out of yourself than you already are if you don't listen to me. Look, I'll walk over there with you, but you'd better call the judge."

"Why? What for?"

"Because, Mr. Sheriff, if I go to jail, then about a third of Johnston County goes with me, you included."

"What the hell you talkin' about?"

"Okay, big shot, do you remember those two runaway girls you picked up the second year you were in office? Well, I have photos and tape recordings of the whole thing. You ought to be in porn movies, Sheriff. You would make a fortune."

Lee Bob pulled into the hospital parking lot, got out, and went to the main desk. The towel around his arm was completely soaked; blood was dripping to the floor.

The night nurse led him into the emergency room, removed the towel, and started swabbing off the wound. She saw the spurts, pushed his shirt sleeve up, and placed a finger on the inner side of his elbow. The blood slowed and then stopped. They sat there and waited for the doctor.

Sitting there, he started thinking of Doc again. Doc and he had gone over to the phone and called the judge. He explained the situation before giving the judge a chance to talk. He ended up with, "Should I bring him in?"

"Lee Bob, didn't he tell you what he has on you?"

"Sure, but I don't believe it any of it."

"Well, Sheriff, if I were you, I would believe it. I have seen the pictures, and they're beauties. Did you know those girls were only fourteen years old? But of course you did. You brought them in. Look, Lee Bob, just turn old Doc loose and come on over to my office. I have something to show you."

Lee Bob replied, "I can't do that, Judge. I'm bringing him in."

"Just a minute, Lee Bob. Someone here wants to speak to you."

"Hello, Lee Bob. Adam Halsey. Judge Watkins is giving you sound advice. I can tell you right now that Doc will never be prosecuted by my office. Lee Bob, you still there?"

"Yeah, but I don't like it one bit."

"Frankly, Sheriff, we don't give a damn about your likes or dislikes. You are a member of Doc's club just like we are. Now, you turn that old son of a bitch loose and get your ass in here." The phone went dead in his ear, and then the dial tone came back on.

The doctor walked in. "Hello, Lee Bob. What the hell bit your arm?"

"A dog got a hold of it."

"I'd say he did. Got the artery, I see. Nurse, get me a shot of procaine. Will hurt a bit, Lee Bob."

He sat there feeling his arm get numb, thinking back to the other Doc. He had walked into the judge's office after taking samples of everything in Doc's car. The judge's legal secretary, Ethel Cheves, said, "Go on in, Lee Bob. He's not busy." Ethel was a voluptuous woman, not thin but properly proportioned enough for the sheriff to be interested. She was dating some farmhand, though, from what the sheriff had heard, and besides, he didn't want to mess with the judge's staff.

The judge, with thinning white hair, held a Churchill cigar in one hand and a brandy snifter in the other. As long as the sheriff had known the judge, he had kept that decanter of brandy on the back shelf for those occasions when the boys dropped by. Adam Halsey was the district attorney of the county. He had gotten heavy over time, and his wallet had grown thick from what the sheriff believed were payoffs. Ben Willis, the deputy district attorney, also held a cigar. The three sat around the judge's conference table playing pinochle. The minute that Lee Bob walked in, the judge walked to his desk and drew out a brown manila envelope. Without a word, he handed it to the sheriff and went back to playing cards.

Lee Bob sat in a cloth wingback chair in front of the judge's desk, usually reserved for attorneys. The three card players were watching as he opened the envelope. One of the photos fell out and landed face up on the floor. Reaching down to pick it up, Lee Bob found that he was looking at himself, naked, with two young girls in the same state of dress. One of the girls was standing on the bunk in a cell and kissing him, while sitting between her legs on the bunk and giving him a blow job was the other one.

The judge said, "Pretty good photography, isn't it, Lee Bob?"

Lee Bob stood there looking at about twenty prints, every one taken from a different angle. "Yes," he said, "but Adolph always did like photography. Okay, Judge, where do we go from here?"

Adam spoke up. "Nowhere, Lee Bob. Just keep your hands off Doc."

"You mean he has something on all of us?"

"Hell, he has something on half the population of Johnston County. Now that you're a member of the club, you'll learn. Haven't you ever wondered about the conversations that stopped in the middle when you would walk up?"

"I just assumed it was something they didn't want me to hear. Hell, everyone does that when the law shows up."

"Most of them won't anymore."

"Look, Judge, how in hell am I going to do my job if there's certain people I can't touch?" Lee Bob asked.

"There are no certain people, Lee Bob," Adam said. "They know that if they get caught breaking the law, they pay. The only one you can't touch is Doc."

"Judge, this is like a house of cards," Lee Bob warned. "Any kind of vibration, and everything comes tumbling down."

Dr. Zitlack said, "There you are, Lee Bob."

The sheriff was snapped out of his memories, brought back to the present.

"What—what did you say?" His eyes refocused, and he realized that he was in the emergency room.

"I said you're all done. Here are some pain pills. Come into the office day after tomorrow and let me look at it. You know you're the second dog-bite victim I've treated tonight? The other one was a little less serious. Jordan Stevonich had leg and arm bites just about as bad as yours."

"He say where he got them?"

"Said he was coming back from fishing in Nichols Pond and walked through the back of the golf course, and then a dog jumped him."

"Thanks, Doc," Lee Bob said. "See ya later."

"Don't forget to get that dog and have him tested for rabies," the doctor said.

"I'll do that, Doc. Thanks again."

Lee Bob got into his car and started back to the murder scene. He got on the horn. "Junior?"

"Yeah, Sheriff?"

"Who's over in the Ada area tonight? Over."

"Hector Inman. Over."

"Tell him to go over to Stenovich's place and bring him in. Over."

"What charge, Chief? Over."

"No charge. Bring him in for questioning. And if you ever call me chief again, I'm gonna slap the shit out of you. I've told you that before. Now damn you, you'd better remember. Out!"

The coroner's station wagon was sitting there when he pulled up. Someone had sent him back to the jail to get the floodlights. With those, Lee Bob could see his four deputies looking up and down the creek bank. Several people were standing on the hill across the creek from Doc's house. They had pulled Doc out of the creek and put him on a stretcher.

"Howdy, Digger," the sheriff said to his friend Fred Barnes, the county coroner and owner of the county mortuary and crematorium. He was a thin waif of a man, partial to vodka and orange juice. He had a dusting of a mustache that he had been trying, without success, to grow since high school. That was thirty-eight years ago. He had a dark sense of humor, too, that blazed brilliant in the company of law enforcement officers discussing the status of unlucky humans who had become corpses.

"How you tonight, Sheriff?"

"Tired, and the night isn't half-over."

"Yeah, these things can make for long hours, all right."

"Can you tell me anything?" Lee Bob asked.

"I'm pretty sure he died from drowning."

"Hell, Fred, you couldn't drown a red fire ant in that creek."

"You can if someone holds your head under it. See these abrasions on the back of his neck? Somebody wanted to make sure Doc met God tonight."

"No question in your mind about it being murder then?"

"Not really. I'm pretty sure he has skin under his fingernails on the right hand as well."

"When can I get that information?" Lee Bob asked.

"We should have it by the afternoon. I'll call you."

"Yeah, do that, Fred."

The sheriff called Joe Bill. "You find out what that was in the water?"

"It was a watch."

"Where is it?"

"I gave it to Adolph," Joe Bill answered.

"Where is he—up in the house?"

"Yeah, and there's someone else up there in the house with him."

"So?"

"It's Purvis Jarvis."

"What in hell is he doing here?"

"Said he was on his way to Tulsa when he heard a radio transmission."

"Anybody but Adolph talk to him?"

"No, sir."

"You sure?"

"Yes, sir."

"Good," the sheriff said. "Keep it that way. Keep on searchin'."

"What are we looking for?"

"How in the hell would I know, Joe Bill? Maybe the killer wrote his name on a piece of paper and hung it on a bush." He wondered as he walked up to the house how in God's name he managed to solve as many cases as he did.

Purvis and Adolph were standing in the middle of the room when he walked in. "Purvis, how are you and what the hell are you doing at my crime scene?" Lee Bob asked. "This ain't no place for the captain of the state police in this region."

No love was lost between Purvis and Lee Bob. Purvis had worked for the previous sheriff, whom Lee Bob had replaced, but Lee Bob didn't have a place for Purvis as a deputy.

"Just fine, Lee Bob. Could tell I was in Johnston County when I heard your radio transmission."

"How's that?"

"You can say more swear words in a minute than anybody I know uses in a week."

"It's my goddamn radio as long as I'm sheriff, and I ain't changin' the fuckin' way I talk."

"Don't any of the little ol' ladies with scanners ever call you?"

"Once in a while. I tell them that if'n they don't like it, turn the goddamn scanner the hell off. But I know you didn't stop to talk about my disk jockey voice. What can I do for you?"

"Just wondered if you wanted me to bring my crew in to help out with Doc's murder," Purvis said.

"Things so slow you have to drum up business?"

"Nope. Being as I was here, thought I would offer."

"Thanks, but not right now. We just started."

"Well, if we can help, give us a call."

"Thanks, Purvis. We will in another fucking lifetime."

As he left, the sheriff turned to Adolph. "Understand they found a watch."

"Yeah, the watch band is broken. We also found some blood and a piece of cloth from a pair of Levi's."

"Bet it was on top of the hill on the other side of the golf course edge," the sheriff said.

"How would you know that?" Adolph asked. "That's exactly where we found it."

"How about the house here? Anything?"

"No, but I want to show you something." He led the way into the bedroom. Next to the closet was a box set down inside the floor. The floorboards were stacked neatly in a pile against the wall. The lid to the box was thrown back, and the box was empty.

"You sure the box was empty when you found it?"

"I swear, Sheriff. I sure as hell don't want that stuff. It could get a man killed."

Lee Bob grinned at Adolph. "I think it did, Adolph. I think it did. Did you try to take the box out?"

"Sure did. It's nailed in, and the floor joists are built in such a way to keep it there."

"Smart old bastard, wasn't he?"

"I always thought he was a little crazy."

"Like a fox he was crazy. I never did ask you, Adolph—what did he have on you to make you take those pictures of me and the teenyboppers?"

"I can't tell you."

"Well, there's one thing I know."

"What's that?"

"If all that stuff gets into the wrong hands, we're all dead."

"Some of us more than others."

Lee Bob sat on the bed and looked up at the mirrors on the ceiling.

"Well, at least all it will cost me is reelection. The statute of limitations has run out on my little fiasco."

"I wouldn't be too sure, Sheriff. Doc always kept his files updated. If you have done anything in the last seven years, you can bet your life that Doc knew it and that it went into the file." Adolph was peering into the black hole in the floor from which Doc's secrets had been stolen.

"Did you know that Purvis used to work for me?" Lee Bob asked.

"No, I didn't know that." Adolph's ears perked up. That would explain a lot of the friction between the two.

"Yeah, for about two months. He was a carryover from Spender, the previous sheriff. When I was elected, he applied to the state police and they accepted him. As a patrolman, he solved a couple of murders for them, so they appointed him to the special squad. Now, ten years later, he's a captain and running it."

"Must be pretty sharp." Adolph sat in the only chair in Doc's bedroom.

"Purvis got smart with me one time in one of those classes they run—you know those profile classes we have to attend to comply with our county ordinances."

"Yeah, I know. What did he get smart about?"

"I can't recall what it was over, but I had asked a question. He said that if I had been paying attention, I wouldn't have had to ask."

Adolph grinned in anticipation. "What did you tell him?"

"I told him that there was three things I couldn't stand and, being as he was such a good detective, he could figure out which one he fit. 'What three things is that?' he asked. I told him, 'Hot beer, wet toilet paper, and a pimple on my ass.' Then I walked out. That was two years ago, and I haven't been back."

"Hasn't the commissioner said anything to you?"

"Hell, no," Lee Bob answered. "He's another one of Doc's boys."

"I can't believe that. Doc had a file on the commissioner too?" Adolph said.

"I don't know what it was, but every time he saw Doc, he got white as a sheet and scurried for cover. I thought he was having a heart attack one time."

"I'd never have thought he was capable of impropriety in a thousand years. Hell, Lee Bob, his wife petrifies the crap right out of him. He didn't take a shit without permission from her."

"She would petrify the hell out of you, too, if you were married to her. She must weigh three hundred pounds, and she has a bellow like a locomotive. She could stop a charging bull with that steely eyed stare of hers."

"Guess you're right there." Adolph was laughing when the sheriff came back to topic.

"You sure you checked everything in here?"

"Sure did, and also dusted for prints. Got some, not many."

"Well, send 'em off in the mornin'. We might get lucky."

"Be the first time as far as Doc's concerned," Adolph remarked.

"You got that right. Let's pack it in and send all the boys home. Leave Joe Bill here. I'll have him relieved in the morning."

"You going home?" Adolph asked.

"No, I'm going down to the office to question the guy that left that cloth and blood you told me about."

"Who is it?"

"Stenovich."

"From Ada?"

"Yeah."

"Think he did it?"

"Maybe. See you."

"'Night, Sheriff."

Lee Bob punched the accelerator, flew across the wooden plank bridge from Doc's house, hit the state highway, and pulled up to the jail in seventeen minutes.

Stenovich was sitting in the chair in front of Lee Bob's desk when the sheriff arrived. His right cowboy boot was laying across his left leg, and the toe was bouncing to a beat that wasn't playing anywhere. He was nearly shaking as the sheriff sat still, watching him.

"How you tonight, Jordan?" Lee Bob watched him to see if he was hiding something.

"Fine, Sheriff. What did I do wrong?"

"Nothing that I know of. Understand you went fishin' yesterday."

"Went out to Nichols Pond, but I have permission to fish there."

"I know that, Jordan. On your way home last night, did you see anything out of the ordinary?"

"No, a dog attacked me."

"Doc's dog?"

"Yeah. I was a little tired, so I sat down on the hill by the fourth tee. First thing I knew, that dog was all over me. You ought to put him down, Sheriff."

"I already have. Did you see anyone?"

"No, not that I can recall."

"Isn't the fourth tee just a hundred yards or so from Doc's house? You have a clear view of Doc's place from there, as I recall. You ever go to Doc's house?"

"Hell, no, Sheriff. I didn't go to Doc's house. That damn dog will kill anyone who gets close to his house."

"How about a car? You see a car out there last night?"

"Didn't see one, but I heard it. It was a Chrysler product," Stevonich said.

"If you didn't see it, how do you know it was a Chrysler?"

"I was a mechanic for a number of years—first in the army and then in El Paso before the wife and I moved here. You can tell a lot 'bout a car by listenin' to it."

"What time was this?"

"Right about dusk."

"That would be about seven thirty?"

"Somewhere 'round there." Stenovich was staring at the linoleum tiles. The sheriff didn't keep anything on the walls of this room.

"Don't you wear a watch, Jordan?"

"Can't. Have too much toxicity in my body. Everything turns green on me."

"Jordan, I want you to spend a lot of time for the next couple of days thinking about last night. Now, if you do think of something—I don't care how small it seems to you—write it down. Whatever you do, don't try to remember it. Write it down. Will you do that for me?"

"Okay, Sheriff."

"One other thing, Jordan. Did you stay at the Nichols bunkhouse last night or at home with your wife?"

"I always stay with my wife. I just hang at the bunkhouse, you know, when I'm workin' at the ranch."

"Jordan, you let me know if you think of anything, ya hear?"

"Sure. Be glad to help if I can. May I ask what this is all about?"

"Ol' Doc got hisself murdered last night," Lee Bob answered.

"Oh, my God! Think it was the murderer's car I heard?"

"Could have been. I need your help, so try to recall everything you can. You can go now." Jordan slid the plastic and steel chair back, squeaking on the unwaxed floors.

Lee Bob called Hector. "Take Jordan home. Stop over at the Chalet and buy him breakfast. Put it on the county tab."

"Will do, Sheriff."

Lee Bob pulled out his chair and flopped down. He looked at his watch and was surprised to see that it was a quarter to seven. Pulling over the phone, he dialed the judge's number. Alice picked up after the first ring, and she recognized Lee Bob's voice. "He's in the bathroom, Lee Bob. Sure too bad about Doc, isn't it? Such a harmless old man."

"No one is harmless, Alice—just degrees of dangerous is all."

"What in the world do you mean by that? He brought me into the world. He was a real nice man before he lost Jewell," Alice said in a wispy voice. "Here's the judge."

"Lee Bob," the judge said. "Been a long night."

"Sure has. See you heard about Doc."

"Couldn't keep from it. The whole damn town has called since six this morning."

"You in your office?" Lee Bob asked. "I'll be right down." He stepped off the stoop and went to meet the judge.

CHAPTER 16

Combine Calculations

The five men sitting in the bank boardroom were the five richest, most powerful, and most influential men in the county, known collectively as the Combine. John Ross was the president of Tishomingo County Bank, sixty years old, and a crook. He was plump and dressed the part of the banker in the game of Monopoly. John had a tendency to talk fast when he was nervous. He was one of Doc's boys, enjoying marijuana and sex with prostitutes. Doc had a full file on John, which included John's felonious dealings in stealing property from clients by trading on secret information about their accounts.

Elmer Boats Nichols owned Nichols Casing and Oil Company. Boats was the richest of the Combine members; he didn't talk a lot but was by far the smartest of the pack. He was a bachelor for the most part, though he kept his secretary, Shirley, close to meet his male needs and wait on him. She was well compensated. Boats had Pike keep tabs on all the other Combine members.

Leon Ritchie, of Ritchie Land and Cattle Company, was a devious bastard with a sick sexual addiction that included his fully grown stepdaughters. Leon was a land and cattle baron. He owned more actual property than any of the other Combine members and raised cattle on multiple feedlots. He had built his empire by squeezing out the small farmers, especially those who had oil on their land, a fact that he carefully concealed from them.

Pike had done his homework. He hated Coy most of all because of his predilection to men and boys. Bigotry was among Pike's not-so-endearing qualities. It was common knowledge among the Combine that Coy Purcell, who owned Purcell Distributing Company, was not just an improper businessman; he was a closet drag queen. He liked his young men strong, taut, and beautiful. He traded on his goods and fuel business to cheat and defraud his customers, driving them into bankruptcy so the Combine could steal their property for little or nothing. Pike's report to Boats, dripping with disdain, said, "Coy makes frequent trips to Dallas to hook up with other men for weekends of frolic and fucking."

Clyde C. Watkins, a circuit court judge for Johnston County, had been on the bench for forty years. Past retirement age, he kept his post to provide cover for the Combine. He had been married to the same wife for forty years and was a principled crook who preferred not to soil his hands with active crime—he left that to the rest of the Combine. He had vast land holdings and millions in gas and oil leases acquired for him by his buddy Boats.

John kicked off the meeting. "All right, Coy, you called the meeting. You have the floor." The boys of the Combine sat in the same chairs they had sat in during every meeting of the Combine for the last thirty-five years. The bank's boardroom was finished in cherry panels for the bottom forty inches of the walls. Above that, the walls were plastered and bore copies of masterpiece paintings from American artists Charles Marion Russell and Frederic Remington, as well as Albert Bierstadt, who wasn't an American but was included because John loved his landscapes.

"All right," Coy began. "You all know we have been after Parmenter Manufacturing Company to put a plant here in Johnston County. It took us three years of hard work to get them to even look."

"Shit, Coy, don't take all day. I've got a court case in an hour," Judge Watkins quipped.

"Keep your shorts on, Judge. Anyway, you know the president of the company took land tests all over the county. Well, yesterday afternoon he called me. They have decided to build a $35 million plant here. Isn't that great?"

John Ross spoke up. "Yes, it is great, but there must be a hang-up or you would have told us on the phone."

"There is one little hitch. They want Spender's place." After that pronouncement, Coy tilted his oak chair back till it creaked from the strain.

Leon said, "I have tried for twenty years to get that hundred and eighty acres. As long as Charlie Spender's daughter is alive and living on the place, forget it. That husband of hers is an asshole. She gets everything she wants."

Judge Watkins asked, "Don't you have the mortgage on the place, John?"

"Only for fifteen thousand. That's only for his stock and inventory in the store. The ranch land is free and clear."

Coy said, "Look, there has to be some way we can put pressure on him. I heard one thing that might help us. I heard the other day his wife has cancer."

John asked, "You think it's true?"

"It could be," Coy said. "Leon, doesn't your son-in-law handle his insurance?"

"He has in the past. I can find out. Coy, don't you deliver his gas?"

"Yeah, but what the hell has that got to do with it?"

Leon asked, "How big are his tanks?"

"I don't know, about thirty-five hundred, I suppose," Coy answered. "Why?"

"How much money would it cost him to put in ten thousand–gallon tanks?" Leon continued.

"Several thousand, I imagine. I still don't get it," Coy said.

"Boats, you know what I'm getting at?" Leon asked.

"Sure, Leon. What are we trying to do here?"

"We are trying to get him in trouble," Leon answered. "Well, besides wife trouble, what's the worst trouble a man can get into?"

Coy was so confused that he stood up and started pacing beneath the Fredric Remington print called *The Apaches*.

"Hell, I don't know. What?" Coy nearly shouted in exasperation.

"Money, dammit! Money!" Boats said.

"Leon is telling us, let's see if we can't put him in a money bind."

Judge Watkins stood. "Well, you gentlemen figure it out. I've got a court hearing."

"You agree to go along with what we figure out?" Leon asked.

"Certainly, up to a point."

"Before you leave, Judge," said Coy, "what you got on Doc's murder?"

"Not a thing. I'm leaving it up to Lee Bob. He can handle it. It's as much to his advantage as ours."

"Aren't you worried?" Coy asked.

"What for? You'll find out that there are some things you cannot change. Good day, gentlemen."

John Ross told Leon, "Go call your son-in-law. See if it's true that his wife has cancer." While Leon was on the phone, John told the other two, "You should all recall Allan Suggs. He wouldn't sell me his drive-in, and it only took us three months to get him out. Boats, your company does quite a bit of business at Spender's, doesn't it?"

"We run about a thousand a month. I'll have that shut down this afternoon. Coy, start shorting him on gas delivery. He doesn't check your delivery truck, does he?"

"Never has. When he needs it, we deliver."

"Is he on a pay-as-you-go basis?"

"No, we've been reading his pumps every Monday morning, and he pays for what he has sold," Coy answered.

"Then call him this afternoon and inform him that you can no longer operate in this fashion," Boats said.

"Any idea what kind of excuse I can use?" Coy asked.

"Sure, tell him I'm putting the squeeze on you due to the high interest rate."

"I don't understand why you want me to short him on deliveries," Coy said.

Boats said, "Coy, if your old man hadn't left you his business, I swear you would be on state aid. Listen close—if you can short him a hundred to three hundred on every delivery, he will assume, or you can tell him, that he must have a leak in his tanks."

John also contributed, saying, "When you talk to him this afternoon, you tell him that the way business has been, he is a marginal account, and due to expenses, you don't know how long you can continue to deliver gas in such a small amount. Got it?"

"Now I understand," Coy said. "Sure, I'll take care of it."

Leon hung up the phone. "It's confirmed, John. Althea does have cancer."

"Did Paul know the type and prognosis?" John asked.

"He said Larry told him when he paid his car insurance last week that it is a slow-acting blood type. He's taking her to Odell twice a week for chemotherapy."

"Did you find out how he pays his medical insurance?"

"Funny you should ask," Leon said. "Larry had just finished talking to him. His fire and liability are due, and he should be in this afternoon to pay it. Paul also mentioned that he pays his medical quarterly, and it is also due."

"I want you to take Paul to lunch today, Leon. When Larry comes in to pay for those two insurance policies, have Paul take his checks but make damn sure Paul doesn't give him a receipt for either payment. Have him lose those checks. That should do it for now. If any of you think of anything to help us out, let me know. Let's break it up. I've got several things hanging over the fire."

Coy and Leon rose and left the office. Boats just sat there at the head of the table, looking at John.

"Problem, Boats?" John was looking smug.

"None that I know of, but you knew about the manufacturing plant before Coy opened his mouth, didn't you?"

"That's the reason I don't play poker with you guys, Boats. Never could fool you, could I?" John said with a smile.

"Not very often," Boats agreed. "How much of the financing are we going to get on the plant?" Boats's steely eyes were riveted on John because he believed the bastard would lie. But he didn't. Boats had already listened to a recorded call between John and Parmenter's president, unbeknownst to John. Boats stood and walked to the liquor cabinet, filled his highball glass with ice, and pulled out a bottle of Kentucky bourbon. He poured two ounces in his glass, added four ounces of tap water, and swished the contents in a counterclockwise motion.

"Most of it," John answered. "We have been talking interest for the last two months. "We finally settled on 10.75 percent."

"What kind of clause?" Boats was like a hound on a scent. He sipped the bourbon and branch.

"Know me like a book, don't you?" John laughed nervously.

"You forget I run the gambling show in Johnston County, John. I can make book on your behavior. Remember, I'm the one who set you up with this bank to start with. It was you who married the bank president's daughter to seal the deal."

"Got to admit it got me ahead."

Boats pressed, "How did you set up the clause?"

"They have agreed to 2 percent," John answered.

"In other words, if interest goes up 3 percent, you can raise our rates 2 percent." Boats was staring coldly at John as he continued the counterclockwise swishing of his bourbon and branch.

"Correct. That's it in a nutshell. How much you going to want of it?" John asked.

"My company will take ten million," Boats answered.

"Kind of greedy, aren't you?"

"Not really. I was thinking fifteen, but I bought into Bidwell kind of heavy."

"Yes, I know," John said. "But that only leaves fourteen million for the rest of us."

"It only leaves nine million. The judge wants five."

"No way, Boats," John protested. "We've always taken equal shares. The other boys won't buy it."

"They have no choice. The judge and I are the only ones who will not benefit from this plant. The only thing we'll receive is the interest on the loan. You will make it work for the rest, or I may have to release information I have on the demise of your father-in-law, the former president of this fine bank."

"When are you going to stop threatening me with my father-in-law?" John asked. "And how do you figure we'll benefit more than you?"

"John, when your father-in-law walks through that door alive, I won't have anything on you," Boats said. "As for the money, I'm far from stupid. Your bank will handle all the transactions for the company—not only for the construction but also for the plant payroll, with over two hundred employees. You're not telling me you won't make money."

"What about Coy and Leon?" John asked. "They will scream to high heaven."

"Let them scream. Coy has the only grocery and gas distribution in the county, plus he handles all the local shipping. Leon has those sixty-odd tract houses he jumped in and built two years ago. It's taken time, but he will finally get his plant. So let's not argue. The judge and I will take fifteen, and you boys may split the difference."

"I'll talk to them, but they ain't going to like it," John said.

"They don't get it, John, and you know it. They are both pussies, and you know that too. Now stop yanking my dick and get it done."

"We still have to get the Spender property, and it has to be ours by next spring."

"There is one thing I thought of," Boats said. "Larry started up that pawn shop. It's small, but he does quite a bit of business. What would happen if Lee Bob caught him buying stolen property?"

"We should be able to set that up real easy, don't you think?"

"Maybe. Sometimes Lee Bob can be a real asshole 'bout stuff like that." Boats put his empty glass on the table and started to leave.

"Lee Bob will come around when Adam or the judge talk to him," John said. "Leave it to me." He stubbed out his cigar and called Leon and Coy to lay out the deal on Parmenter.

CHAPTER 17

Chubb's Warning

Adolph returned to the office and put the special tool box on the sheriff's gun cabinet.

"Well," said Lee Bob, "did you get those bugs in place at Spender's store and pawn shop?"

"Sure did, Sheriff. They should be fully operative now if you want to try them out."

The two walked to the back of the office. Lee Bob stuck a key in the door, opened it, and flipped the switch to his left, lighting the surveillance room. "Who you going to put on listening detail?" Adolph asked, praying he could dodge the assignment.

"I'm thinking you or Zeke are the only fellas who can keep your mouths shut, and since I've got other work for you, it'll have to be Zeke. Get his ass over here tonight. I want this up and running right away."

Larry Chubb finished packaging the groceries and thanked the customer. Turning to his wife, he said, "You ready to leave, Al?"

"Whenever you are," Althea answered. "Tired of sitting in the house." Larry, Althea, and one other clerk were the only people there, if you don't count Zeke, who was listening through the bugs at the sheriff's office.

"Sorry about the hours I've been putting in, sweetie." Larry hugged his wife.

"I understand. Saves on wages, what with my medical bills and all." Althea looked especially weak that night.

Larry told the clerk he would be back in a couple of hours. When he and Althea got to the car, he opened the door for her, and as she bent down to get in, he kissed her on the cheek.

Zeke switched to the car bug. He couldn't pick up any conversation in the parking lot, but the bug in the car's radio transmitted to the sheriff's office whether the radio was on or not.

Althea smiled at Larry as she seated herself. "Thank you, love."

"Honey, I'm sorry these treatments make you so sick," Larry said, reaching to pat Althea's knee.

"Price you pay to stay alive, I guess." Althea smiled at her husband.

"Have you thought about smoking pot like old Doc suggested?" Larry asked.

"It sounds stupid to me. How can pot help fight cancer?"

"I don't know. Doc swears it will work," Larry said.

Althea touched her hand to her chest and then brought it up to cover her mouth. The coughing binges were wretched. "One thing is certain," she said. "I've never been sicker in my life."

"Why not try it? It might help." Larry pleaded.

"Where would we get it?"

"I bought some off Doc over a week ago," Larry said. "I've even rolled up a few for you to try." He pulled out onto the highway and headed home.

"What can I lose? Give me one and I'll try it. How do you smoke them?"

"Doc says take a deep drag and then hold it as long as you can. I'll get you set up when we get home."

Larry and Althea smoked two joints at the house. An hour later, on the way back to the store, Althea told Larry, "I don't feel half as bad as I used to after a treatment. Let me have another one."

"Later, sweetie. When I get off work, we'll smoke another joint."

Zeke picked up the phone. "Hey, Sheriff. Got some good stuff for you." Twenty minutes later, the sheriff was in the surveillance room and listening carefully. "Sounds like we got a dealer on our hands. May have to pay the Chubbs a visit and arrest them for dealing pot."

Larry closed the store at ten and hurried home. Althea was lying on the sofa when he walked in. At first, he assumed she was sleeping, but on closer examination he discovered that she was stoned.

She tried to rise. "Oh, Larry, I feel great."

"You mean you didn't get sick?"

"Just a little bit, but after a few of those cigarettes, I feel great."

"That's good, honey."

"Not only that, but I feel sexy. How do you feel?"

"Like a rampaging bull in rut. That's the description, all right. Let me take a fast shower, and I'll be right out."

The alarm woke Larry at six. He shaved and then poured himself a cup of coffee from the pot brewed automatically by his clock radio. Coffee cup in hand, he walked from the house up to the store. Unlocking the door, he entered the cooler to get the money bag from its hiding place. He cleared the register, wrote yesterday's sales into the books, took the keys out, and unlocked the gas pumps. Two children came in to buy candy bars while waiting for their bus.

A car pulled in, and the driver walked in. "Morning, Larry."

"Hi, Paul. Nice morning."

"Stopped by to pick up those checks. With Althea the way she is, you can't afford to let them lapse."

"Forgot all about them," Larry said. "Just a moment and I'll make them out."

When Larry had finished writing two checks, he handed them to Paul. "Thanks, Larry. I'll get them mailed in."

"See you, Paul."

A gray-haired stranger came through the door. "You the manager?" he asked.

"Yes. May I help you?"

"I need money, and I understand you run a hock shop?"

"Just a small one," Larry said. "What you got?"

"Smith and Wesson .38 pistol and a .308 deer rifle."

"You have a bill of sale on them?"

"Not anymore," the man said. "I've had them for years."

"Haven't seen you around here before," Larry said.

"I've been in your store here several times. Been here about three months."

"Well, bring them in and let me look at them."

The man went out to his car and then came back in, laying the pistol and the rifle on the counter.

"How much you need?" Larry asked.

"I'd like a hundred."

"You have any identification?"

The man laid down a driver's license and two credit cards.

Larry filled out the cards, got the man's signature, and handed him five twenty-dollar bills.

During the rest of the morning, several people came in, his clerk showed up, and they spent the morning stocking shelves.

Three people pawned a few items, including an almost new twenty-one-inch RCA TV set.

Althea came in at ten to twelve. "Larry, can you take off and go to lunch with me?"

"Sure, honey. We're not very busy."

On their way downtown, Althea said, "Honey, some man called me this morning. It was a very strange call."

"What was it about?" Larry quizzed her.

"He wouldn't tell me who he was, but he said that we are in for a lot of trouble. I started to ask him a question, and he told me, 'Mrs. Chubb, please shut up and listen. I am at work and might have to hang up at any time. You tell Larry to meet me at the houses on the wildlife refuge at five thirty this afternoon.'"

She paused. "I asked what it was all about, and he said, 'Please be quiet. I can't explain it on the phone. If you and Larry don't want to lose everything you own and have Larry wind up in jail, tell him to be there at five thirty.'"

"What trouble could we be in, Al?" Larry said. "Business has been great. We're ahead on all of our payments. And me going to jail? He's crazy."

"You going to meet him?" she asked.

"Do you think I should?"

Larry downshifted and pulled into the Chalet parking lot. They sat there to finish their conversation.

"It frightens me, sweetheart. I knew the voice; I just can't place it."

"Well, should I go?" Larry asked, looking in his wife's frightened face.

"No, I don't want you to. If he keeps bothering us, we'll call Lee Bob."

"Less we have to do with Lee Bob, the better I like it," Larry said. "He has got to be the most foul-mouthed public official anywhere."

"He has done a good job," Althea offered.

"Only when he wants to. I just can't trust him, Al. I've told you that before."

"I know, but it is only rumor."

Larry just shook his head. He pulled around to the drive-through and ordered takeout.

"Al, the longer I think about it," Larry said after a while, "the more I think I should go meet that man."

"Honey, I wish you wouldn't. Somehow I feel it will cause a lot of trouble, besides being dangerous."

"I can take a gun." He accelerated into traffic.

"It doesn't make sense. Evidently you feel the same as I do or you wouldn't take a gun. Please, honey, don't go."

"All right, but I would like to find out what he's talking about."

"Well, if he wants you to know, he can find some other way to do it."

They finished lunch, and Larry returned to the store to finish out the day. Five thirty came and went, and Larry didn't go to the refuge.

At seven, the sheriff walked into the surveillance room and sat down to listen to the conversations that had been recorded that day. When he heard Althea and Larry talking about the five thirty meeting, he shouted for Zeke.

Zeke stuck his head in the door and said, "What you need, Sheriff?"

"What the fuck you been doing in here all day? Did you hear the Chubbs talking about meeting a mole at the refuge?" Lee Bob was staring at Zeke, waiting for an answer.

"I remember something about a meeting, Sheriff, but Joe Bill came in and needed to get into the evidence locker, so I missed part of that conversation."

"You ignorant son of a bitch. Next time, throw the fucking keys at Joe Bill and stick to this tape. It's eight fucking thirty now, and we missed an opportunity to identify the mole, who may have Doc's papers. I swear, if those papers get out because of your dumb ass, I'm going to see it dropped in a shit hole somewhere. Get Adolph on the horn and have him meet me at Chubb's house."

When Larry got home, Althea was in the bathroom kneeling in front of the commode. He heard her retching before he reached the doorway. He went over to the sink and wet a washcloth, came back, and wiped off her forehead and neck. She reached up, took the washcloth, and washed her face. "Why didn't you call me, Al?" he asked.

"I didn't have time. Lord, I'm sick. Help me to bed."

Larry reached down and picked her up.

"I can walk," she said.

Paying no attention, he carried her into the bedroom and gently placed her on the bed. He was sitting on the edge of the bed when the phone rang.

Larry went to the kitchen to answer it. "Hello?"

"Larry, why didn't you show up?"

"Who is this?"

"I can't identify myself until you meet with me."

"Then we will never meet," Larry said. "I have no way of knowing what kind of game you're playing, but we don't want any part of it."

"You have to meet me, or they are going to ruin you."

"Ruin me how?"

"Larry, you have to believe me," the stranger pleaded. "I have some tapes I want you to hear."

"About what?"

"I've said all I'm going to. I'm sure they suspect me already."

"You keep saying *they*?"

"Bye, Larry. I'll call again." Then there was a dial tone.

Larry slammed the phone down.

"Same guy, honey?" Althea called from the bedroom.

"Persistent bastard, anyway," Larry said almost to himself.

"Don't swear, honey," Althea said. "You know how I feel."

"Sorry, babe. It slipped. How you feel?"

"Give me one of those cigarettes."

"I'll have to roll you one, honey. Just a minute."

A few moments later, Larry sat and watched his wife inhaling. She finished the joint and stubbed it out. She was asleep almost instantly. He gently disengaged her hand from his arm, went into the kitchen to make himself a sandwich, poured a glass of milk, and sat, thinking.

The grocery store, the gas station, and the house they lived in had been a gift from former sheriff Spender, Althea's daddy. From the time Spender handed Larry the deed until his death five years ago, they had never had a cross word between them.

Larry had been in such deep thought that he hardly heard the doorbell ring. It rang twice before he came to attention. Before he thought about what he was doing, he opened the door and found Lee Bob. "Evening, Larry."

"Lee Bob, what you doing here?"

"I need you to come over to the store and open it up."

"Any particular reason?" Larry asked.

"Understand you loaned money on some guns this morning. That right?"

"I loaned a hundred on them."

"Well, I have to take a look at them."

"Look, Lee Bob, those guns will be there in the morning. Althea has been real sick. She's sleeping right now. I don't want to wake her up, and I sure can't let her wake up without me being here."

"Sorry about Althea, Larry, but I have a job to do, so I have to see those guns."

Larry saw movement farther out in the yard. Reaching back inside with his left hand, he hit the porch light. Joe Bill and Adolph were standing at the foot of the porch steps. "What is this, Lee Bob?" he asked.

"It ain't nothing, Larry. Now come on over and open the store."

"Not tonight, Sheriff. You come back in the morning." He tried to step back inside and close the door.

Lee Bob grabbed his arm and yanked him out onto the front porch. Joe Bill and Adolph rushed up on the porch and each grabbed an arm. Lee Bob reached in and closed the door.

"Put him in the car and bring him along," Lee Bob ordered. He climbed in his car while they placed Larry in the back of their squad car. They followed Lee Bob down the driveway.

They pulled into the store parking lot behind Lee Bob. He stood there waiting for them to get Larry out. "Okay, Larry, open the door," he said.

"Afraid not, Lee Bob, not without a search warrant."

Reaching into his shirt pocket, Lee Bob pulled out a folded-up sheet of paper. He unfolded it and handed it to Larry.

Stepping under the light, Larry saw that it was a warrant to search Spender's Grocery and all properties of Larry and Althea Chubb. Without a word, Larry opened the front door, turned on the light, and waited.

Lee Bob told him, "Go back and unlock your loan room."

Larry walked back and undid the lock on a sliding wire door, turned the light on, and watched.

Lee Bob stood beside him and handed Adolph a typewritten note. "Check it out."

Adolph handed Joe Bill a copy of the list. He immediately went to the gun locker. Larry watched him take a gun out and put it back. The third gun he took out he put on the counter. Altogether he put seven guns on the counter.

Adolph walked up. "He has four of them on the list, Sheriff."

Joe Bill called out, "There's seven of them here, chief."

"Got the registration cards on these items?" Lee Bob asked Larry.

"What is this about?"

"Just get the cards, Larry."

He got out the small metal box and walked over to where the guns were lying. There were five pistols and two rifles. He recognized the two he had taken in that morning, but three of the pistols he didn't recognize. He found the cards on one pistol and the two rifles. He thumbed through the cards several times before he realized that he had never seen those guns before.

"We don't have all night," the sheriff said. "Give me the cards."

"I've never saw these guns before in my life, Lee Bob."

"You mean you loaned on them and never made out a card on them?"

"No, I mean I never saw these particular guns before."

"What are you trying to say—someone put them here?" Lee Bob pulled a handkerchief from his pocket and wiped his forehead.

"Well, it may sound funny, but it's the truth." Larry kept flipping through the box in hopes of finding an explanation.

"Larry, why in the fuck can't you crooks come up with something more original than 'It ain't mine'?" Then, turning to Adolph, he said, "What about the TV sets and stereos?"

"Five of them are on the list. Several of the musical instruments and some of the jewelry fit also."

"Joe Bill, read him his rights."

"What in the hell are you talking about *my rights?*" Larry was frantic. He couldn't believe this was happening.

"You are under arrest for receiving stolen property. Take him down and book him."

"What about Althea? She's asleep. You can't put me in jail. There's nobody to take care of her."

"What the hell makes you think you're so fucking special?"

"You know what I mean! Dammit, Sheriff, I'm not going anyplace. I live in this community."

"Yes, you are. You're going to jail."

"But what about Althea?"

"I'll tell her when she calls or when I search the house."

"What the hell for?"

"Don't be so damn dumb, Larry. Why not tell me the whole thing now and I'll wait till tomorrow to search your house?"

"What in goddamn hell you talking about, Lee Bob?"

"I got to admit, you're pretty good, but I have suspected you for years."

"Suspected me of what, for God's sake?"

"Receiving stolen property and selling it, and dealing in dope."

"You're crazier than a peach-orchard boar in fly season, Lee Bob."

"Yeah, but I'm not the one under arrest, am I, Larry?"

"You're not kidding, are you?"

"What the hell does it take to get through that fucking thick skull of yours? You're in a lot of trouble, Larry!"

"Can I make a phone call?" he asked.

"Sure. You're entitled to one—not to your wife, though. We don't want to give her a chance to get rid of the dope. Joe Bill, drag his ass to jail and don't let him call anybody for at least an hour."

Then it hit him. *Oh, my God, the pot.* He had left it sitting on the kitchen table. "I want to call Odie and have her come over and stay with Althea," he said.

"Better wait until we search your place," Lee Bob answered. "If we find what I think we will, she will be with you."

"Lee Bob, if you or any one of your animals even think or mention such a thing again, I'll kill you."

"I've been threatened before."

"I'll tell you what you see—a little 135-pound peckerwood who most likely couldn't whip a pat of butter. But, I swear, you lay one hand on her, and you and whoever else has anything to do with it is dead."

"Make your phone call," Lee Bob said.

Larry called Odie and briefly told her what was happening. She said she would go right over—and call a lawyer.

"Joe Bill, you take him in and book him. Leave the charges open till I get there."

Larry was sobbing as Joe Bill dragged him off.

When Althea opened the door, Lee Bob and Adolph were standing there. She immediately asked if something had happened to Larry. "What is it, Lee Bob? Where's Larry? He isn't here. Has something happened to him? Has he been in an accident?"

"Slow down, Althea. Nothing has happened to him. I had him taken down to the courthouse."

"For what?"

"Can I come in?" the sheriff asked.

"Not till I know why you have Larry."

"Get out of the way, Althea. We have a search warrant and intend to search your house."

Lee Bob and Adolph pushed their way in, shoving Althea aside. Lee Bob told Adolph, "You take the kitchen and that end of the house. I'll search back here."

"Tell me what you're looking for, and I'll help you find it," Althea said.

"Stolen property and dope."

"You lost your mind?"

"Hey, Sheriff, come in here," Adolph called.

"Althea, you sit down on that sofa and don't move," Lee Bob ordered.

He walked into the kitchen. "What is it?"

"Look on the table there."

"Go get your camera. I want a picture of this. I'll look around while you're gone." After he left, Lee Bob reached into his inner pocket to get the packet of pills he had taken out of the property room at the jail. He arranged the boxes and waited for Adolph. It didn't look quite right, so he opened up a few and spread them around on the tabletop. He also took four boxes and put them in Althea's linen closet.

"Sheriff, you want me to let Odie in?" Adolph asked.

"Yeah, but get on in here."

When Adolph came into the kitchen, he asked, "Where in the world did you find all that stuff, Sheriff?"

"In the linen closet. I left some in there so you can get a photo of that, too."

When he finished, he looked up and saw that Althea and Odie were standing there.

Althea asked, "What is all that stuff?"

"Little miss innocent, aren't you?" Lee Bob said.

Odie said, "It's dope, honey."

"Where did it come from?" Althea asked, frantic.

"Ain't she something, Adolph?" The sheriff laughed mercilessly.

Adolph looked at the sheriff. "Known her since she was a girl. Never thought I would be doing this to her."

"Doing what? To who? Odie, do you know what's going on?" Althea still didn't understand.

Odie looked at the two lawmen and said, "I'm beginning to get a strange smell, and it ain't roses."

"I don't understand. Where is Larry?" Althea struggled to throw off the marijuana fog, without success.

"Get your pictures, Adolph," Lee Bob said. "Pick up the evidence, mark it, and put it in that plastic bag. Don't forget the boxes in the closet. Althea, get dressed. You're under arrest."

"You can't do that, Lee Bob," Odie said.

"Well, you are the second person tonight to tell me that. The other person is in jail, where Althea will be pretty quick."

"Can I talk to you alone?" Odie asked.

"Sure." They walked into the living room.

"Lee Bob, you know what you're doing?"

"Just doing my job, Odie."

"For criminy sake, Lee Bob, don't you know that Althea is dying of blood cancer?"

"You sure?"

"Hell, yes, I'm sure. She takes treatment twice a week. She has one tomorrow. You know, I don't have the least idea why I'm telling you this."

"I'm glad you did. Thanks, Odie."

"Don't thank me. I did it for Althea. I have always thought you was the most foul-mouthed son of a bitch I've ever met."

"Everyone has a right to their own opinion. Hey, Adolph, you ready to go?"

"Althea isn't dressed yet."

"Changed my mind. We'll leave her here."

"Whatever you say, Sheriff."

He waited while Adolph walked in to the living room. "Take Odie with us," he said.

"What for, Sheriff?"

"Prostitution."

Odie said, "You can't make that stick."

"No, I might not, but I am sure as hell going to try. Bring her along, Adolph."

Odie tried to get away, but Adolph grabbed her, dragged her out, and threw her into the car.

Zeke heard Althea stumbling from the bedroom and calling for Odie. Nobody answered, and Zeke heard her walk through the house and open the doors. He assumed she was looking outside and realizing that Odie was gone. Zeke heard the disoriented Althea calling for Odie again and then for Larry. Then he heard her in the bedroom dialing the phone and asking for her attorney. Zeke quickly flipped to the phone tap.

"Althea, there is nothing we can do until in the morning. I'll call the judge at nine tomorrow morning and have bail set. So don't worry. I'll have him out by noon."

At nine the next morning, Seth Wilburton called Judge Watkins. "Morning, Judge," Seth said. Zeke ran the tape and immediately called the sheriff on the radio, telling him to come in for special traffic reports, a code they had agreed to use for any important "traffic" in this case.

"Good morning, Seth," the judge replied. "How's the missus?"

"Just fine. I'll tell her you asked."

"Do that, son. Always glad to see her. She's so pretty. Know why you called, Seth, and would consider it a favor if you would turn this case down."

Seth stuttered on the phone. He couldn't believe the turn in this conversation. "But Judge, I told Althea last night that I'd have him out on bail by noon."

"Not this time, son. I have to go out of town for a couple of days' fishing. Call me Friday."

"What will I tell Althea?" Seth asked.

"Wait till late this afternoon, and then tell her I'm out of town and you couldn't reach me. Tell her you can't get bail set until I get back. Also, tell her you're real busy and you're not sure you can take the case, but you'll try and work it in, that you'll call her on Friday. Then you go out of town Thursday night."

"You want to tell me why, Judge? This doesn't seem appropriate."

"Sure. Because you owe me a couple of favors, and another reason is that you practice in my court. It's appropriate because I'm telling you it's what I want. Need any more reasons?"

"I think I understand."

"I thought you would. Remember me to your lady," the judge said.

At eleven, a call went through to Althea from Odie. Althea was sprawled out on the couch in the living room, where she had passed out after the sheriff had left last night. Ol' Lee Bob never frisked her, and she had two joints in her bathrobe, which she promptly smoked after he left. She couldn't tell how long the phone had been ringing, but when she picked it up she recognized Odie's voice. She had to make Odie repeat everything a couple of times, but she understood that Odie wanted her to send $177 in bail money.

"For Larry's bail?" Althea was confused.

"No, honey. That's my bail," Odie said.

"What are you in jail for?" Althea couldn't shake the marijuana haze so she could understand everything.

"Didn't you wonder why I wasn't at your place last night?"

"Yeah, I wondered. Thought you had changed your mind and gone home. I'll call a clerk at the store and have them—"

Odie interrupted, "Althea, there's no one at the store."

Althea's head was clearing slowly, the events coming into focus. "I've been so worried about Larry that I forgot all about the store. Just a minute, Odie. There's someone at the door."

Zeke heard the phone drop to the counter and Althea's footfalls to the door.

When she came back to the phone, Althea said, "Odie, it's the clerk. Wants to know about the store. I'll send her down with the money."

Althea took the keys and went over to the store. She was happy to do anything to keep her from sitting around thinking. She had no sooner opened the store than the phone rang.

"Spender's Grocery," she said.

"Althea, don't talk, just listen. I told you and Larry yesterday that something was going to happen."

"Listen, mister. Why do you keep callin' me? Who is this?" Althea demanded.

"Listen. There will be a box delivered to you sometime this afternoon. Be careful with it, and whatever you do, keep everyone from knowing you have it. It can get you killed real fast. Also, Seth is working with the judge. He will not get Larry out. Call Conrad Peale in Odell. Do it now."

Althea stood there with the phone in her hand. She couldn't get it figured out. Over the years, she had seen things like this happen to other people. For some reason, someone was out to get them, but she couldn't imagine why. A more honest person than Larry she had never known. Several times she knew of, Larry could have lied and gotten out of trouble. He never did.

She picked up the phone and dialed long distance information. She got the number for Conrad Peale and proceeded to make the call. A lady answered and then put her on hold.

"Hello, may I help you?"

Althea identified herself and then explained her and Larry's situation. "Can you handle it?"

"I can have him out this afternoon," Conrad said. "However, I will need a retainer of five hundred dollars."

"I have a treatment this afternoon. I'll drop the money off then."

Odie and the clerk came into the store about that time. "Odie, can you drive me over to Odell?" Althea asked.

"Sure, Althea. When you want to leave?"

"Right now."

They stopped at the bank on the way out of town. Althea met with the attorney, and as she started into the treatment room, she recalled the phone call about the box. On the way back to Tishomingo, she was so sick that she couldn't sit up. Odie had to stop twice to let her throw up. Arriving at the store, Althea had Odie stop to see if the box had come.

Odie came out. "There is a box, but it's too heavy for me to carry."

"Back the car up to the door and have our clerk help you put it in the trunk," Althea said.

Chapter 18

Doc's Documents Tell the Tales

Althea sat on the sofa, listening to the slow strains of Chet Atkins. Dusk was slowly moving in. She wondered why it was that sadness and the blues always seemed to creep in on people when they had problems. She was so deep in thought that she didn't realize that Larry had entered until he asked, "You sick?"

As she tried to rise, he knelt in front of her and took her in his arms.

"You all right, Larry?"

"I'm fine, honey. Just worried about you."

"How did you get out?" Althea asked. "No one called about bail money."

"Judge Watkins wasn't here, so the attorney you hired went to district court in Reagan. After he explained the charges and our position in this area, the judge over there released me on my own recognizance. I thought you had hired Seth, though. He stopped at the jail this morning and said the judge was out of town but that he would try and get me out when he returned."

"He sold us out, Larry."

"Why do you say that? He has always done our legal work."

"I got a phone call. That's the reason I called Mr. Peale, or you would still be in jail."

"For some reason, Al, someone is out to cause us trouble," Larry said, perplexed by it all.

"But why? Oh, I had a call from that man again. He sent us a box. It's in the trunk of the car."

Althea followed Larry to the car, and they both peered at it sitting in the trunk. It must have weighed sixty-five to seventy pounds. It was wrapped in brown paper with tape all over it. On one side was written, "Open this side."

Larry pulled it from the trunk and carried it to the kitchen, where he slit the tape and paper. The box was packed with manila envelopes. On top of the folders was a tape and a typewritten note. Picking it up, he started to read.

Althea reached in and pulled out one of the manila folders. Opening it, she said, "Oh, my God. Larry, look at this. It's horrible."

He looked down at the picture she was holding. There was Coy Purcell dressed like a woman with two other men who were completely naked. One man had Coy's dress hiked over Coy's back and was having anal sex with him at the same time that Coy was giving oral sex to the third man seated on a table.

Althea started looking at other pictures. She turned one of the pictures over and saw names, dates, and places written there. She reached for another folder.

"Hold it, Althea. Listen to this," Larry said. He started to read.

> Dear Larry and Althea,
>
> Inside this box you will find photostatic copies of Doc's records. They contain all the information he acquired over the years. Doc was the major source of all the dope in this area. These are copies and therefore are not admissible in court. Before you go through these files, I suggest that you listen to the tape. I recorded this in the boardroom at Tishomingo National Bank. It will tell you the reason for your arrest and let you know of future things planned for you. Good luck.

Larry took the tape and threaded it into the tape player. They sat there and listened to all that had been said that morning.

When it was over, Althea said, "Well, that answers all of it, doesn't it?"

Larry was smirking. "You know," he said, "you and I have worked hard all our lives. For several years now, we have wanted to take a vacation. I think we should."

"We can't do that, hon. We don't have the money, and I have to take treatments. We have to keep running the store, so how can we go on vacation? You're not talking about blackmail?" Althea was worried.

"Blackmail, no. Retribution, yes. You have told me several times that later in life you'd like to sell out here and move to Florida."

"Yes, but you know, baby, I'm not going to survive for too long," Althea said. "I would like to spend it around my friends." She took Larry's arm imploringly.

"I would like to spend more time with you, too. With no more money than we have, there is no way."

"Honey, with our insurance, we won't be out much money on my sickness. I pray every night that you will be able to continue after I die." Althea was tearing up. Larry reached around and pulled her to his chest as they stood in the kitchen.

"Did you hear that on the tape about our insurance?" Larry asked. He knew that Althea wasn't understanding much of what he was trying to tell her.

"I heard it, but I didn't understand."

"Paul didn't send our checks in on our insurance, so they will cancel it. Being as I have no receipt for the checks, it's his word against mine." There was a distinct rage growing in Larry's voice.

"You know, I can't understand people doing things like that for money." Althea was starting to cry as the magnitude of events pierced the fog in her brain.

"It's not only money, honey. They want the power money brings. Would you care if I sold our farm?" Larry pulled his head back and looked down into Althea's wet eyes.

"Honey, you do whatever you want to. Just promise me that you won't go back to jail. I couldn't take another two days like these have been. I love you, sweetheart, very, very, much." Althea pulled herself back to Larry's chest and tucked her head under his chin.

"I know, baby. You will never realize how great these years have been for me. I have never loved anyone other than you. You are the only lady I have ever been to bed with. I do love you very much. That is the reason we're going to be able to do anything we want."

"Please be careful," Althea said as she squeezed Larry's waist and rocked side to side.

"I'm not gonna break any laws, but before this is over, I intend to make those men pay for what they've done to us."

"You gotta do somethin'," Althea consented. "These have been the worst days of our lives."

Larry picked up the kitchen phone and turned to Althea. "I know, sweetie. Do you know Odie's phone number? I want her to work the store."

"What are you going to do?"

"I have some things to buy and a lot to do." Larry seemed determined, as if he had resolved it all in his mind.

"Do you want to look at any more of those folders, babe?" Althea asked.

"No, I have a pretty good idea that everything I need will be in there." Larry spun the dial on the phone and listened as it rang through to Odie.

For the next four days, with the equipment he bought, he completely reproduced the contents of the box. On Monday morning, he called John Ross.

"Hello, Larry. Sorry to hear about your troubles," John said. "What can I do to help you?"

"I was wondering if I could see you this morning."

"Well, I am kind of busy. Could you give me a hint what it's about?"

"Certainly, John. With the trouble I'm having and Althea's sickness, I've been thinking about selling the farm. You told me if I ever decided to sell to let you know."

"Why don't you come on down and we'll discuss it."

The minute he arrived, he was ushered into John's office, a magnificent monument to John Ross's ego. While the waiting room chairs were worn and had fading fabric, John's office had cordovan leather chairs with polished brass tacks, and above and behind his desk was a Frederic Remington painting of a buffalo meeting its end at the point of an Apache lance. They shook hands, and Larry was seated. Larry set his briefcase beside the chair and leaned it into the chair so it wouldn't fall over. The deep, plush carpet was new, and he breathed in the toxic aroma of carpet glue. Sitting there looking at John, he felt a surge of power for the first time in his life.

"Now, Larry, when would you like to sell your place?" John wasted no time getting to the point.

"Oh, I'm not going to sell the whole place, John, just the farm." Larry smiled.

"What about the store?" John asked in surprise.

"I intend to give that to Odie."

"Odie Miller? Whatever for?" John flopped back in his swivel chair, and it thumped against the credenza behind his desk.

"Well, I figured you and Boats owed her that much."

"What do you mean?" John asked. "I don't know about Boats, but I don't owe her a cent. I know that she and Althea are good friends, and I don't know what she has told you. But I wouldn't be interested in your place if the store isn't included." John was so flummoxed that he was spitting as he talked.

Larry pressed forward. "What would you pay for it, John?"

"Well, looking at property values, the store, and all, I would go $175,000."

Larry smiled. "That's lower than what Coy offered for it last year."

"Well, circumstances change. What kind of money were you thinking about?" John leaned forward onto his desk, thinking he had Larry where he wanted him.

"I was thinking three and a half million."

"You crazy?" John shoved himself back from his desk, hitting the credenza with such force that papers on it fell to the floor.

"Not as crazy as you're going to be if I don't get it." Now Larry leaned onto the desk.

"Are you threatening me?"

"You bet your sorry ass I am." Larry was looking the fat bastard right in the eyes, and his steely stare made it clear to John that he meant business.

"Chubb, Althea's sickness and your trouble have affected your mind." John was trying to regain his composure, but it wasn't working.

"You know, John, you're right. It has completely changed my outlook on life." A smile crossed Larry's face, but the fire in his eyes was still burning through John Ross's soul.

"Let me call Dr. Zitlack."

Larry sat back in his chair. "That's a good idea, John, but for you, not me."

"I'm really worried about you. You have always been real level-headed."

"I always thought so too, but that was before you and your friends decided to fuck me out of everything I own. Then I got a bit pissed off!"

"I'm calling Lee Bob. You're beginning to sound dangerous." He started to pick up the phone.

"Before you do that, John, I believe you had better look at this folder." He reached down and picked up his briefcase, opened it, took out the folder, and slid it across the marble top of John's desk. He watched as John thumbed through the pictures and read the letters and information included.

"You want to tell me where you got this?" John's demeanor sank into disbelief.

Larry picked up his right leg and dropped his boot on his left knee, pulling on the boot heel before looking up at a defeated John Ross. "You know where it came from just as well as I do."

"Lee Bob will be glad to find out who killed Old Doc." John's voice was shaking.

"I'm afraid you will have to pin that on someone else, John. Althea and I were in Odell with five doctors until well past eleven." Larry chuckled as he said it.

"You could have hired someone."

Larry went back to pulling on his boot heel. "I could have, but having never been a violent man, I never thought of it."

"You know, of course, this is blackmail." John's voice told Larry everything he needed to know. John was a pussy when he didn't have the upper hand on folks so he could bully them.

"In a way, John, I guess it is. But I would prefer to call it justice—and just payment for your villainy."

"I will have to talk to some people."

"I figured you might. I have protected myself. If anything happens to me, Purvis Jarvis—I believe you know him—will receive these records. It is now eleven o'clock. I will be home until five this afternoon. If I find you are not interested, I will make sure Mr. Jarvis receives them." Larry dropped his foot to the floor and was leaning in, preparing to stand and leave.

"I'm not sure—"

Larry interrupted. "No excuses. By five. And John, I want it fixed up in such a way that I don't have to pay taxes on it. Just think about how many lawsuits you could get into if the way you and your cronies worked your swindling got out. It's cheap. Besides that, if some of those pictures got out, several fathers in this area would gladly kill you."

"Pictures can be manufactured and faked."

Larry stood, holding his briefcase, and stepped away from the chair. "You're right, of course," he said. "However, I would like to tell you with very extreme pleasure ..."

John started to get up but then thought better of it and sat back down. "What's that?"

"You are undoubtedly the sorriest excuse for a man I ever saw. Good-bye, John. Five o'clock. Don't forget!"

He left the bank and drove over to the jail.

Lee Bob was sitting behind his desk when Larry walked in. He closed the door and sat down in front of the sheriff's desk.

"What do you want, Chubb?"

"Why, I just wanted to talk at you, Lee Bob, about law and order."

"Look, you sawed-off piece of shit, I'm in no mood for your bullshit. Get the fuck out of my office."

With a sudden movement, Larry came up out of his chair. In his hand he held a snub-nosed .38. Lee Bob was halfway out of his chair when Larry smashed him in the left temple with the butt of the revolver, causing Lee Bob to slump back into his chair. Larry worked quickly, pulling Lee Bob's handcuffs from the back of his leather belt, cuffing his hands behind his back and through the rails of the oak office chair. Larry reached into his briefcase and pulled out a nearly spent roll of duct tape and fastened two strips across Lee Bob's mouth. When Lee Bob woke, his mouth was taped shut and his hands were locked behind his back.

Clearly, the sheriff was foggy.

Larry sat on the edge of the sheriff's desk, the .38 pointed at his nose. He had pushed Lee Bob's chair back just far enough to allow Larry to have his feet propped up on its arms.

"You came awake faster than I thought you would, Lee Bob. Guess I should have hit you harder."

Lee Bob tried to say something through the tape.

"Another curse word, Lee Bob? Shame on you." With that Larry kicked him in the groin and laughed when Lee Bob's obvious agony jackknifed him forward, caused his body to quiver, and forced an involuntary moan.

Larry waited for several minutes until Lee Bob had partly pulled himself together. "Now Sheriff, I just wanted you to feel some of the pain and suffering my wife and I have went through for the past few days. I am going to take the tape off your mouth. If you make a sound, I'll shoot you square between the eyes. So please, do me a favor—make a noise."

Lee Bob shook his head and glared at Larry.

"It's nice to see the hate in your eyes, Lee Bob. I'm sure, if you look closely in mine, you will see the same thing."

He cocked the pistol, leaned forward, put it on the bridge of Lee Bob's nose, and pressed it snugly between his eyes before he pulled the tape off. "You know, Sheriff, I know why you put my wife and me through the hell you did. To be perfectly honest, I don't know why I haven't blowed your brains out already."

"Larry, look, man. I was just doing my job."

"You mean framing people is your job?"

"I didn't frame you, I swear it."

"Like you said the other night, Lee Bob, at least you could come up with something more original than that."

"What do you want?"

"I just wanted to see you squirm like my wife and I have." Reaching behind him, he picked up the manila folder he had laid on the desk. "I never realized until the other day how rotten this county really is." He opened the folder and took out several of the photos inside. "If these pictures got out, several husbands in this town would blow your brains out. If you so much as say hello to me in the future, Sheriff, or my wife, you will live to regret it." He stood, put the gun back in his briefcase, and started out the door.

"Chubb! You can't leave me handcuffed this way!"

"I just found out, Lee Bob, that I can do any damn thing I want to. And you know? It feels real good."

Chapter 19

Time for the Mouse to Roar

Paul Craig heard someone ask for him in the outer office. He rose from his chair and walked out into the hall, where he was confronted by Larry Chubb.

"Hello, Larry. How are you?"

"A lot finer than you're going to be in a few minutes. Let's go in your office and talk."

Seating himself behind his desk, Paul asked, "What can I do for you?"

"It's what I can do for you that counts," Larry said with a confident tone.

Paul was put off by Larry's demeanor. "What do you mean by that?"

"I know about the checks."

Paul was frozen by the words. "About what checks?" He had always been so secure there in his insurance office. It was his domain. He could forget his wife and father-in-law, who made his life hell. This was the first time he had ever felt scared.

"The checks you turned over to Leon."

"I don't know what you're talking about." *How could he know?* Paul thought. *Leon and I were the only ones present when it was discussed. Wrong word.* His brain was going a mile a second. They hadn't discussed it. Leon had come into his office and told him what he was going to do.

"What would happen if I went to the insurance commissioner's office with the accusation that you took my money and deliberately kept the checks?"

Paul's mind snapped to a passage in the insurance book: "It shall be a felony upon conviction of not less than five years or more than fifteen years, with a fine of not less than five hundred dollars and not more than ten thousand." He decided to bluff it out. "Again, Larry, I don't know what you are talking about."

"Paul, you and I are a lot alike." Larry's voice softened, appealing to Paul. "We have done our work and tried to be decent people, so I am going to show you something. But first—I know you will think it's none of my business—do you love your wife?" Larry looked carefully for Paul's reaction, to see if his eyes revealed the truth.

"What has that got to do with this? You're not making any sense." Paul was clearly surprised by the question.

"You and I both know that everyone in this town has laughed and joked about the way your wife and Leon treat you. You would have to be completely stupid not to know that your wife sleeps with people that Leon does business with to sweeten the deal or blackmail them, whichever tactic works best." Again, Larry stared at Paul's face for any hint of a reaction.

Paul was unsure in his response. "My family life is none of your business."

Larry slid his chair closer to Paul's desk, the chair gliding on the polished linoleum. "I never like to hurt anyone's feelings. I know that Leon put you in the middle of this deal." Paul started to deny it. "Wait a minute. Let me finish," Larry said. "Over the years, we have done a lot of business. I have got to know you real well. You remind me so much of myself before I met and married Althea, and if you love your wife, I don't want to destroy it for you." Larry's confident voice displayed a note of tenderness. Paul seemed confused, unsure, looking for some hint of how to respond.

Paul fumbled for words. "Larry, you're talking way over my head," Paul said. "You come in here and accuse me of some crooked deal on some checks. Then you bring my father-in-law into it and then start asking me about my personal life. I don't think it's any of your business." His voice trailed off, unconvincing in his opposition.

"You have sold me insurance for several years now. I have always liked you. We all know that Leon gave you the money to buy this insurance agency.

I will be violating a confidence to tell you this, but I know what most of your married life has been like."

"How could you know that?" Paul was shocked. He was pushing his chair back from the desk, attempting to distance himself from the hard facts coming at him.

"Odie told Althea, and Althea told me."

Paul thought, *She worked for us for four years.* She had heard and knew of the terrible arguments they had gotten into. He thought back to the day that Christine Ritchie Craig had fired Odie. She said she had caught her listening to them arguing. It was usually the same thing. Christine had her own bedroom, and if he was lucky, she would let him sleep with her once a month, and then it had to be done quickly, like she was ashamed. He had put up with it because Christine and Leon had made it clear that they would take his insurance agency and ruin him. He had watched Christine through high school as she manipulated guys into doing whatever she wanted. In college, he had seen her and Leon destroy a former suitor by accusing him of being homosexual and publishing doctored pictures of him that, Paul later learned, involved drugging the kid and getting a male prostitute to stage various acts with his unconscious body. Leon blackmailed the kid's father in a business deal.

He had no excuse for falling in love with her. He had nothing when they married, so he didn't consider the possibility of being the target of one of her manipulations. While they were engaged, Leon had set him up in the insurance business. That, above all, was his world, and he didn't want to lose it.

He brought his thoughts back to Larry, who was sitting there watching him. "All right, Larry. It's something that over half of the people who know us are aware of. No, I don't love her. I stay with her because of business reasons."

"Then if I tell you something about her and her stepfather, it won't hurt you."

"No, there is nothing you could tell me about them that would hurt me. That ended a long time ago. I would give anything to be free of them. That is, if I can keep my business. Another thing, Larry, you were right about the checks. I will have them in the mail this afternoon. One thing I want you to know is that I am sorry about it."

"I know. Before I met Althea as a young man, I did a lot of stuff that I'm not proud of. I don't quite know how to go about this because what I am going to tell you and show you is something that doesn't happen very often."

"What doesn't happen very often?"

"Paul, there are times you find out things that you don't want to believe. At these times, I believe a man should be by himself." He pulled Leon's folder from his briefcase and laid it on Paul's desk. "I pray that I am doing the right thing and that this doesn't destroy your life. Whatever happens, I hope you won't hold it against me."

Paul sat there looking at the folder as Larry left the office. He called his secretary into his office and told her to make out a check for the Chubbs' account and mail it to the home office. After she left, he picked up the folder and slowly raised the cover. There were several typewritten notes, and he started reading them. The first one was dated August 17, 1958. It laid out how Leon and John had swindled a Mr. and Mrs. Clarence Tinsay out of six hundred acres of land in the southern part of the county. The oil and gas lease on the property brought them several hundred thousand dollars and was still producing. There were pictures of Christine as a teenager fucking Tinsay. Paul read through several pages, picking each one individually. Each sheet contained a different transaction, all shady or unlawful in some way.

He started to pick up another sheet of paper when he saw the edge of a photograph sticking out from under the paper. He slowly pulled it out. There was Christine and her stepfather lying naked on a bed. They were in the act of lovemaking. The rage completely engulfed him. He picked up one picture after another, each with the date and time printed on the back. The dates went back to well before he and Christine were married. One date caught his eye. It was taken the day he and Christine had returned from Las Vegas. He recalled that Leon had arrived soon after they had gotten home. He had told Paul that there had been a lot of problems with the agency he had bought them a week before the wedding and that Paul had better go down and get it straightened out. That night, Christine had turned him down for the first time. According to the dates, she and her stepfather had gone to bed three times during the week after they returned from their honeymoon. Christine had moved into a bedroom of her own and almost completely shut off their sex life.

He sat there for over two hours going through the folder, reading the letters, and returning time after time to the photographs. He had heard fellows talk about sexual acts he had only dreamed of. Once, he had tried to have sex with Christine from behind, and she slapped his face, called him an animal, and refused him sex for two months. Yet according to these pictures, she engaged in every sort of debauchery in his own bed with her own stepfather.

There were pictures of Christine naked at an orgy with men and women he didn't recognize out at Leon's line shack. She was a whore, and he was a joke to his own wife and a fool to his father-in-law. Everyone in the county but him was fucking his wife. Part of him wanted to feel sorry for Christine, having that bastard stepfather of hers groping her, but that didn't explain the manipulation and blackmail. It didn't explain the orgies with townspeople and strangers at Leon's shack. He realized that, despite any excuse she could give him, she was a despicable human being.

Then he saw it—a form that looked like a medical report, filled out by Doc Leftan. Seven and one-half months after they were married, Christine had an abortion. The report said, "Male fetus, second trimester." Doc had handwritten a note: "Christine says it's Paul's baby. Could be, blood type matches Paul." *She killed my son,* Paul thought. *The worthless bitch killed my boy.*

The anger exploded in him and turned to cold rage. He wondered how it would feel to take a gun, tie up his father-in-law and wife, cut their clothes off, castrate him, and then blow his brains out.

He fantasized about the terror and revenge he would relish by stabbing her in the heart after she watched her stepfather die. He planned it over and over. Then he thought, *I can't do it.* For one thing, he didn't want to go to prison for killing garbage like them. He took the folder and walked out. He told his secretary, "I will be gone for the rest of the day."

"Will there be any place I can reach you?"

"No, I'm going to be busy. Anything comes up, put it on hold till I get back." He spoke through clenched teeth.

He entered the house, the folder under his arm. Walking into the living room, he saw Christine coming out of the bathroom.

She turned toward him. "What are you doing home?"

"I need something."

"Well, get it. Someone is coming over later, and I have to get dressed." She was standing there in a lace robe her stepfather had bought her. He could see the black brassiere and panties she had taken to wearing lately.

She saw him looking at her and pulled the robe together at the top. "Well, get whatever it is and go." She turned and went back into the bathroom.

Walking toward his bedroom, he heard the shower start up. He put the folder in his top dresser drawer, sat down on the edge of the bed, and took off his shoes. Slowly, he undressed. When he was naked, he pulled the covers back from the pillows, pulled them out, lay down, and propped his head up. He heard the shower shut off and Christine humming as she finished up in the bathroom. He lay there, his door open, his penis erect and pulsing with blood, waiting for her to come down the hall. His cock was standing above his navel, its head deep purple and throbbing.

She paused at his door. "Is that supposed to turn me on?"

He said, "Whatever."

She took a couple of steps into her bedroom. "You get your damn clothes on and get out of here."

"Not this time, Christine."

"Not this time, Christine?" she said in a mocking voice. "Do you remember the last time you tried this? You had sore balls for a month. If you don't want them kicked again, get your ass off that bed and get out of here."

She had walked toward the bed while she was talking. She was within arm's reach when she stopped. He quickly reached out and grabbed her arm. He pulled her toward him, rising to a sitting position while dragging her down to the bed. Cursing, she tried to scratch him with her other hand. He grabbed her other arm, rolled her over, and straddled her body. He had both her arms pulled above her head and was looking down into her face, his cock lying hard between her breasts.

"You know what will happen when I tell Daddy about this?"

"Guess what, bitch! I don't care about your daddy no more." He pulled both her arms together and clasped them with one hand, leaned back, and with his open palm slapped her twice across the face. Her mouth came open to either say something or scream, but he never gave her a chance. He slapped her as hard as he could.

A loud moan came out of her mouth, and a small spot of blood appeared in the corner of her mouth. She struggled to get her hands loose. Raising her lower body, she tried to throw him off.

He sat there watching her. When she had quit moving, he again slapped her as hard as he could.

"Don't, Paul. Please don't hit me again."

He watched as her tongue licked at the blood in the corner of her mouth. He slid off of her and stood up. "Get up, you slut."

She slowly raised herself to a sitting position on the bed. "Why are you doing this?"

"I figure after all these years I'm entitled to one good piece of ass before I throw you out into the middle of the street."

"Daddy will kill you for this."

He reached out and undid the belt on her robe, grabbed the front of it, and slapped her back to the bed.

She started to scream, but he grabbed her by the throat, cutting off her air. Again he slapped her. The right side of her face was beginning to get puffy.

Looking down on her, he could see the terror starting in her eyes. They darted back and forth and rolled in their sockets. They reminded him of the Viet Cong solider his squad had caught and shot in 'Nam. The pleasure he was beginning to feel was almost as good as a climax in sex.

"Please, Paul, do what you want."

"The first thing I want is for you to take Daddy's robe off." He reached down and pulled her off the bed. She couldn't stand steadily as she unbuttoned the robe and let it drop. The black lace panties fit like a bikini, with several layers of fine lace around them.

"Some more of Daddy's presents?" She stood looking at him. Raising his hand, he said, "I asked you a question, bitch."

"He gave them to me for my birthday."

"That was over five months ago, and these are new. Try again, bitch!" He grabbed her short hair and turned her face sideways toward him using his left hand, and then he slapped her again.

She slumped against his hand holding her hair and slid down to the edge of the bed. "Please, Paul, don't hit me anymore. I'll do whatever you want me to."

"Take off your bra."

She pulled the straps under her arms, slid it around her body, and undid the three snaps.

"Get up."

She slowly rose.

He crawled over and lay in the middle of the bed, watching her all the time.

He noticed her eyes quickly glance at the door. "Try it, baby. Try to get away, and what I have given you is just a sample."

"I don't understand why you're doing this."

"I want you to get on the bed and suck my cock like you do for Daddy."

Her head jerked up, and her eyes opened up wide. "When did you find out?"

"It doesn't matter. You have about one second to get started or I am going to half kill you."

She slowly crawled onto the bed, lay down, and wrapped her fingers around his cock, pulling it to her lips.

He grabbed a handful of her hair. "Suck, damn you."

The warm wetness of her mouth took in his cock, sliding past her lips. She licked the tip of his cock and drew it into her mouth again, sliding up and down, pausing briefly to lick the tip.

The explosion was unexpected—across the bridge of her nose into her right eye. She jerked back, and his semen continued to shoot across his stomach.

"Why in hell did you do that?" he asked.

"'Cause I don't like it in my mouth."

"Well, from now on, lady, it isn't what you like around here that matters. Get me a towel and a washcloth, and don't try anything stupid."

He had thought that after he got his revenge, he would throw her out. But lying on the bed, he figured, *Why not give them back some of the misery they've given me?*

Christine came back and started to hand him the washcloth and towel. She held them out to him.

"You do it. You made the mess."

After she had washed him off, he told her, "All right, do it again."

She took his flaccid dick into her mouth and played with it in her mouth, rolling it with her tongue. She licked the base of his cock and his balls, sucking them into her mouth until the blood flowed into his penis again. Her head bobbed on his throbbing cock for the next several minutes until he came again, holding her head down on his ejaculating prick.

At four o'clock, he was standing at the back door when he heard his father-in-law's truck stop and the door slam.

Leon came through the back door. He stopped, surprised, when he saw Paul. "What are you doing here?"

Paul said, "I live here," as he moved toward him.

"Where's Chrissie?"

Paul lunged at Leon and threw a punch as hard as he could right above his belt buckle. The unexpected blow dropped Leon to his knees. As he tried to rise, Paul's foot caught him upside the head. Paul dragged him out to the driveway and left him lying there like roadkill. Paul peered out the window periodically to see if the ol' opossum had come alive yet. Finally, Leon used the curb to help him sit upright. The punch to his midsection had hurt his stomach muscles so badly that he couldn't straighten up easily, and the kick to the head left him with a splitting headache and ringing ears. Paul watched him move toward the back door. Leon tried to turn the handle, but it was locked. He rapped to be let in. Paul could see that Leon's eyes were still hazy when he opened the door.

"Why are you still here, Leon? Didn't you get the message that you are *persona non grata?*"

"What? I don't understand." Leon's mind was fuzzy and the entire situation surreal.

"Maybe you will understand this." Paul walked back through the house and drug Christine to the door. Leon had stepped into the house. His stepdaughter stood naked in front of him, and Paul had a handful of her hair.

"What the hell are you doing, Paul, you insane son of a bitch?"

Paul pushed the fumbling Leon back through the still open door and yanked Christine into the doorway, and when she turned to face him, he kicked her in the stomach. She fell back into her stepfather, and they both fell down the steps to the cobblestone driveway.

"You insane bastards killed my son, tortured me for years, and made a fool of me, and if I ever see either of you around my house again, it won't stop with a beating—I will kill you!" Paul closed and locked the door. He watched Leon and Christine hobble to Leon's truck. Paul walked back into his bedroom and slept till eight o'clock the next morning.

He had never felt better in his life. When the bank opened at ten that morning, he strolled down and deposited yesterday's money. Seeing Delbert at his desk, Paul walked over.

Looking up, Delbert said, "Good morning, Paul."

"Del, how are you?"

"Getting by. What can I do for you?"

"I've decided to buy that old printer's building," Paul said.

"Thought you had made up your mind against it."

"No, my father-in-law decided against it. I think it's a good investment. Mrs. Snell does still want to sell?"

"Most certainly. Real anxious."

"Good. Make out the papers on it, and I will be back at three this afternoon to sign."

"Fine, Paul. Would you excuse me just a moment? Don't go away. I'll be right back." With a harried look, he took off for John Ross's office. Sure enough, in a couple of minutes, here they came, Delbert almost running to keep up with John. "Morning, Paul," John said. Not waiting for him to answer, he added, "What's this about you wanting to buy the Snell Building? Thought Leon told me he had decided it was too much of a risk for you to take right now."

As Paul started to speak, John held up his hand. "Hold it. I went to a lot of trouble to get Mrs. Snell to give you back your earnest money. You know, Craig, it's not good business practice to keep changing your mind."

Paul had always heard that John used people's last names to show that he was irritated with them. John stood there glaring at him. Several of the businesspeople making their deposits had turned and were listening and watching. Paul grinned and said loudly enough so everyone could hear, "Well, I'll tell you, Ross, why don't you keep your big goddamned nose out of my business? That goes for my father-in-law too. I never authorized the earnest money to be issued to Mrs. Snell, and furthermore, if you don't want my business, say so. I'm sure the bank in Cottonwood will be glad to accept it."

Delbert stood there with his mouth half-open, as did the others.

John couldn't speak he was so mad. He stood there stuttering.

"Ross, I will be in here at three o'clock to sign those papers. If you decide you don't wish to handle the transaction, then have my accounts closed—not only personal but business also. Good day."

He had never felt so good in his life, except last night when he had drifted off to sleep. On rising that morning, he had taken the folder with him to the office and put it in his safe. Later in the week, he would rent a safety deposit box over in Cottonwood. He hadn't been back in his office ten minutes when the phone rang. Without picking up the phone, he knew it was Leon.

"Hello, Craig's Insurance."

"Paul, you must be going crazy, doing what you have the last two days."

"Shut up and pay attention, 'cause I am going to tell you this one time and one time only. I know you talked to Christine, so let's skip all the bullshit. You know I have Doc's file and know about every sick goddamn thing you two have done since I married your sorry excuse of a stepdaughter. As I told you last night, keep away from me. If you don't, I swear I'll kill you. You are going to ensure that I get an uncontested divorce from Christine. She is going to walk away with nothing, and everything is going to be transferred into my name. In case Christine didn't give you all the details, Leon, I have the complete file on you and her, and I'm protected. So unless you want the people you have screwed to receive a copy of how it was done, you will take heed. Don't get any ideas about finding them because they are in a very safe place with instructions that if anything happens to me, they are to be sent to the FBI in Dallas. How does it feel to be fucked? Oh, yes, one other thing. I want you to send ten thousand in cash over to the office—down payment on Snell's property. Have it here by two this afternoon or else." Paul slammed the phone down.

Lee Bob walked gingerly into Adam's office. Pulling a chair up to the desk, he asked, "You know what happened to me yesterday afternoon?"

"Heard you spent it playing with handcuffs."

"Very funny. This case is gettin' out of fuckin' hand. Did you know two case files of Doc's showed up?"

"Who's got them?"

"Larry Chubb and Paul Craig," Lee Bob said.

"Hell, neither one of them has guts enough to kill Doc."

"I didn't think so either until Larry clocked me upside the head with a fuckin' gun. Then this morning Paul told John Ross in no uncertain terms to go to hell."

"Could they have done it together?" Adam asked.

"Hell, no. All they have are copies, but if they get into the wrong hands, we're ruined. Have you talked to John?"

Adam shook his head. "No, I had just walked into the office when you came in. Why?"

"I don't know. He wanted to talk to you. Said if I saw you to tell you."

Adam dialed John's number. "John, Adam here. Lee Bob said you wanted to get a hold of me. Do you know how he is coming along on the investigation?"

"I don't have the least idea," John said. "The judge told me to leave it alone. So I have. So what the hell does he do but go out of town. Well, Adam, I'll tell you, I've had two guys in this town that have been worms all their lives stand up to my face and tell me to go to hell. So you tell that idiot Lee Bob that he'd better get Doc's killer and get those records, or so help me God, I'll kill that dumb son of a bitch myself. Good-bye."

Adam dropped the phone in the cradle and turned to Lee Bob. "You know what's got Ross so mad?"

Lee Bob leaned the oak office chair up against the wall, threw his boots up on Adam's desk, and crossed them. "Understand that Chubb and Craig stood up to him this morning and yesterday and told him to go get fuckin' hosed."

Adam said, "Why don't you just make yourself comfortable. I knew about Chubb, but Craig—hell, he wouldn't say shit if he had a mouthful."

"He beat the hell out of Leon last night." Lee Bob chuckled as he said it.

"Are you sure?" Adam asked in disbelief. He stood, walked over to the door, and shouted to his assistant, "Ginger, get us some hot coffee and buns, and don't lollygag!"

"Hell, yes, I'm sure. Leon tried to get me to arrest him for assault."

"What happened?"

Lee Bob shrugged. "I told Leon I would talk to him today."

"Well, did you talk to him?"

Lee Bob dropped his feet to the floor, and the chair slammed on the linoleum. "Hell, no. He called me about eleven o'clock and told me to forget it."

Ginger pushed open the door after rapping twice and came in with donuts and two mugs of black coffee. Neither man said anything until she closed the door behind her.

"Man, it sure don't sound like Leon. He is usually a mean, sadistic bastard." Adam was stroking his chin as he reached for the raspberry-filled treasure.

Lee Bob swallowed the fresh coffee and said, "I'm pretty sure Paul got a hold of Doc's file on Leon and that convinced Leon to drop it."

"Damn, Lee Bob, how you doing on that case? If we don't get something done on it, those files will be scattered to hell and gone." Adam was talking around the jelly filling in his mouth, spitting donut glaze down onto his tie and jacket.

"What did Doc have on you, Adam?" Lee Bob said with a smile as he leaned in to get the custard-cream-filled donut.

"Go to hell, Lee Bob. I haven't received the arrest and booking card on Chubb yet, and there ain't no way in hell I'm giving you blackmail material on me."

"You aren't going to get Chubb's arrest record either, and I can't believe you have so little trust in me."

"Good God, you telling me Chubb has Doc's file on you?"

"Doc's file on me? Hell, he's got Doc's fuckin' file on everybody, son. Where do you think Paul got his copy?"

"By God, we are going to stop Chubb come hell or high water." Adam started pacing in front of his single-pane windows.

Lee Bob stopped just short of another bite of his donut. "How?"

"Kill him—kill the bastard or tear him up enough to scare him to death." Adam pounded his fist in his hand and kept pacing.

Lee Bob put his donut down, wiped his chin with a napkin, and stared at Adam.

Adam continued, "Do you think he keeps Doc's files in his house?"

"I doubt it. He told me that if anything happens to him, everything will be sent to Purvis Jarvis." Lee Bob reached for the half-eaten custard-filled donut.

"Man, if Jarvis ever got his hands on those records, Tishomingo would be short about a hundred of its leading citizens." Adam was noticeably worried.

"Yeah, including you, me, the judge—even including a state senator and most likely a US congressman." Lee Bob stuck his forefinger in his mouth to make sure the donut made it to his stomach.

"You mean ol' Doc had something on Mattock?"

"Hell, yes. Old Mattock got rich on these state parks around here, rumor has it."

"Well, I'll be damned. Wish I'd have known that."

"Why?"

"No reason. It's just that that oily tongued old fart gets under my skin, that's all. What about Doc's murder? You doing anything on it?"

"Well, I know the murderer had a very expensive watch. Also, he has AB negative blood."

"How do you know that?" Adam, always the prosecutor, was looking for details.

"Well, you knew we found that Rolex watch, but under Doc's fingernails on the right hand we found skin and blood. We have contacted the watch distributor to find out which places sell the watch in a two-hundred-mile radius. Oh, we'll get him all right. You know, most evil people die in bed of old age."

Adam wasn't amused. "Well, I want you to do something about Chubb quick."

"I will, when the judge gets back. But not until I talk to him. It means as much to me and you as him. The judge and Boats run this county, and they ain't gonna agree to no killing, period!"

"I still think something should be done."

"Somethin's being done. Chubb and his wife are both under surveillance. So until the judge gets back to town, we will wait."

"I don't like it, Sheriff. What if he gives some more of those files out?"

"We have our eye on him. We'll wait till the judge and Boats are back."

Chapter 20

Coach's Target

All four of us sat in Pepi's. I stretched my legs under the table, my arms over my head, and then dropped an arm around Mar. It was late Saturday afternoon, and the football season was eight weeks old. Le High was undefeated. The previous night's game ended with a score of forty-two to seven. At the start of the season, we had been unranked, but before the previous night's game, we had moved up to third in the state. We had played three nonleague and five league games. The following week, we were due to play Stateline High, state champions last year. They had returned most of their players from that team and had rolled over every team they had met.

The papers and radio had started a buildup over a week earlier. According to them, it was a perfect matchup. Le High used a power veer. Except for the first game, every man in the backfield had averaged over a hundred yards per game. Stateline used what the reporters called the run, gun, and shoot offense. At least half of their offense was passes to their ends or backs. Both teams had been averaging over four hundred yards per game. Even though the game was being played here at Le High, Stateline was still predicted to be a one-touchdown favorite.

For the previous two weeks, on every workout we had, the defensive team had worked on the run and shoot. We also put in a couple of new offensive sets. Although Manny was an excellent passer, we had used it sparingly. In between the workouts, we practiced the new plays until we were running them letter perfect.

Sitting in the booth, Manny asked me, "Man, I know they're worried about Stateline, but I have never seen such intensity as the coaches have had for the last week. Have you?"

"I've got to admit they've been pushing us awful hard. Sometimes I get the feeling that it's not only football."

"You know, I hadn't thought anything of it until you said that, but the other day Cobb and Clemmons had Helio, the ends, and me in the office going over these new sets on offense. They were trying to draw the routes on the blackboard and had to erase it two or three times to get it all in. Anyway, Clemmons told Cobb, 'Next year in our new job we'll have the equipment.' Cobb just looked at him. Clemmons got a strange look on his face and turned away."

Tess turned to Marylyn and asked, "Where were you this afternoon?"

"Rocky and I went down to the lawyer's office. Something to do with oil and gas leases on the ranch."

"Did you sell the leases?"

"Not yet. I want to talk to Tommy about them."

"Guess you're going to be a very rich person," Tess said. "Better be careful, or you will wind up in El Paso high society."

"Not me. I prefer us poor folk," Marylyn said.

Pedro walked up and asked Manny if he could talk to him a minute. Manny got up from the booth, and they walked off to the corner stools. I sat there, half-listening to Tess and Mar talking about the evening gowns they had gotten for the queen's ball that would be held after the homecoming game on Friday night. While listening, I was also watching Manny and Pedro. When Pedro was talking, Manny turned and looked my way several times. Finally, Manny saw me watching him. He waved his hand at me to join them. When I walked up, Manny asked, "You read the paper today?"

"Very seldom pick one up. Why?"

Pedro said, "They have a big spread in sports on our team. Quite a write-up on you, Manny, and Mueller, but mostly you."

"Why me? I'm just one of the team."

"Not according to the buildup Coach Baker has given you. According to him, you're the greatest high school running back he has ever seen."

"Now, why do you think he would do that? Every time I turn around, him and Cobb are all over me."

"Pedro and I were just talking about that, and we think we know. We think Coach Baker wants them to key on you next Friday night."

"Why would he want to do that?"

"Well, if he can get them to concentrating on you, they can spring either Mueller or Breedlove. Also, those new sets the coaches have put in would really go if they can get the secondary concentrating on you."

I was focusing on them when I heard the voice behind me.

"What do you know, Helio? Here's two of the football stars of Le High."

I turned and saw that Sanchez had his hand in his pocket playing with his knife, and Helio was just behind and to his left. "Hello, Sanchez. Helio," I said.

"Saw you in here and thought we better come in and take a closer look at you," Sanchez said. "Wasn't sure the paper was talking about the Gurley I knew." Helio was leaning on the booth divider.

"Must be me, Sanchez. There aren't any others on the team." I smiled at him and took a sip of my Coke.

"You know, Gurley, that's what I like about you the most—your modesty." Sanchez smiled at Helio and looked around the room.

I opened my hands and lifted them up in the air. "Well, you know the saying, Sanchez: when you got it, flaunt it."

"Just wanted you to know, Gurley, the rest of the team don't like it." Sanchez pushed back from the divider.

"Don't like what?"

Sanchez threw the paper on the table. "You hogging all the paper space. There's more people out there than you, you know."

Pedro stepped forward aggressively toward Sanchez. "That's hogwash, and you know it, Sanchez. He didn't have anything to do with the article."

"That's funny, 'cause I just heard Coach Baker talking to them on the phone. He said he hadn't talked to anyone from the paper, and boy, was he mad."

"What's that to me?" I asked.

"Hell, it don't take anyone with brains to figure out that you got to know who talked to the paper."

"You know, Sanchez, you must have worked awful hard to get as stupid as you are," I said.

Pedro jumped up and got between us.

"That's all right, Pedro," said Sanchez. "I don't want no trouble. Just wanted to see this hotshot. Come on, Helio. Let's leave these two stars."

As they walked off, Manny said, "You know, T. C., you're gonna have to fight him one of these days."

"Maybe, but until then it won't worry me very much."

On the way out to the ranch, Mar asked me what Manny had wanted, and I told her all that had gone on. Then we discussed the meeting at the law office. I asked, "What did Rocky think?"

"For one thing, he is not satisfied with the drilling requirements. He wants a stipulation that they will drill within two years."

"Sounds reasonable to me."

Marylyn added, "The oil company says no one gets that kind of an agreement, but Rocky told him that we intended to or else we might drill it ourselves."

"Rocky is a tough old bird," I laughed.

"Well, he kept at 'em, but they were saying something about it takin' two to three million dollars to sink a well and pushing Rock to see if we could afford that. He just went right at 'em again, sayin' he wasn't worried about the money as much as the make of the men he was working with."

"Sounds like Rocky was getting pretty feisty." I smiled and patted her leg.

"Well, that's not the best part. Rocky turned to Jim Conway and said, 'Okay, Jim, that's it. We have wasted enough time. Contact Mr. Nichols and tell him we will accept his deal.' He stood up and started to leave. That ol' oilman was so nervous and flustered. He said, 'You mean you won't negotiate on these points?'

"Rocky told 'im that we had been negotiatin' for six weeks and he was through with 'em. Then the oil guys started beggin' for a couple weeks to see if they could put the deal together. Rocky dropped the hammer and said he'd give 'em till noon next Tuesday."

"Dang, ol' Rocky has a tough side I ain't seen before." I was laughing at Marylyn's storytelling.

Marylyn said, "That's about it."

"Honey, you mentioned Nichols. Would that be my uncle?" I asked.

"I didn't ask Rocky. It might be." We pulled into the yard, and I parked the pickup under the magnolia tree. I turned to face her, leaning my back against the corner of the seat and the driver's side door. She lifted her left knee up on the seat to face me.

"All I can say is I hope not."

Mar reached out and put her right hand on the inside of my left leg, rubbing it softly. "Why not? He took you in and seems to care for you."

"Boats Nichols never cared for anyone except himself," I said. "He proved that to me when he took me in and then proceeded to run both my parents down every chance he got." I reached down and took Mar's hand. She was getting my attention in a way that I wanted but didn't need at the moment. My uncle was horning in on my life.

"If it wasn't for him, though, I never would have met you." Mar started rubbing my leg with her other hand.

"I hadn't thought of it, but you're right. Him letting me live with Buck and Rosie was the greatest thing he could have done." I turned and opened the door, stepped to the dirt, and pulled Mar gently out my door. She looked up at me, and I put my arm over her shoulder as we walked toward the new foals' corral.

She said in a soft voice, "Most people I have met have some good in them."

"Well, in Boats's case, you would have to drill a deep hole to find it."

We stood at the corral, watching the foals romp, jump, and frolic. "You know, Buck was telling me the other night that those oil leases Boats bought for you will make you a lot of money," she said.

"I know. He's told me the same thing, but somehow it doesn't mean very much to me. Does it to you?"

She turned into me and wrapped her arms around my chest inside my jacket. "Yes, it does. If things hadn't turned out the way they did, do you realize I could have wound up in juvenile court or a foster home with no say whatever about my life?"

"Yeah, but it didn't, Mar." I pushed her back to look at her face.

"But for only one reason, Tommy, and the reason is money." Mar sounded like she was starting to get upset.

"You don't know that for sure."

Mar stepped back from me and leaned against the wooden whitewashed fence, half-sitting on the second rail and looking up at me. "Yes, I do. Mr. Stuck, the attorney, has told me so. Haven't you seen the way the teachers treat me?"

"Hadn't noticed." I did notice, however, that she was over there and I was standing here with my hands in my pocket, turning to the side to hide the evidence of the effects of her stroking the inside of my leg.

Mar was oblivious to my plight and continued. "Well, Stuck's daughter teaches history, and I know she told the other teachers that I'm rich because they are way too polite and nice to me."

I walked over and sat on the second rail next to her, our feet out, pressing us up against the fence to hold us in place. "Could be because of what happened to your mother."

"Not a chance. Oh, well, it's not important. I'll take the way they treat me and the grades I've been getting." She chuckled at the thought.

I reached over and put my left hand on the inside of her thigh. "You know, Mar, that sounds snobbish."

"Could be, but I like my life Tommy. I'm sorry about my mother, and I miss her something fierce. Apart from that, my life is good and getting better."

Rosie walked out onto the porch and raised her hand above her eyes to shield them from the sun. She was looking at us from the porch. "Have you noticed lately that Buck and Rosie have been keeping closer tabs on us?" I asked.

"I think they're afraid we're getting a little too serious. The other night when Rosie and I were doing the wash, we had a girl-to-girl talk. She reminds me an awful lot of my mother."

"Funny you should say that, because Buck and Rosie are real close to being the way I recall my mama and papa. Buck has been hinting and prying a bit about my relationship with you."

I reached down, took Mar's hand, and pulled her up from the fence. We started walking toward the house.

Mar asked, "Are we going back into town tonight?"

"Not unless you want to. I told Frank I'd help him and Buck move some horses in the morning."

"Can I help?"

"You know the saying, lady: you own the joint, so why not. 'Course, you know it's going to be awful cold."

"I don't care," she said. "Just being around the horses makes me happy."

We got to the porch, and my boots clomped on the wooden boards. I stepped through the door, and there on the left, in Rosie's old overstuffed chair, sat Boats, cup of coffee in one hand and a sheaf of papers in the other.

Boats sat the coffee and papers down, stood up, came over, and stuck out his hand. I just stood there and looked at him. He said, "I know you're still sore at me for what I said about your dad, and I want to apologize for it. I am sorry for my words and actions, Tom. Please believe me. That was the whiskey talking, and it was mean."

I reached out and shook his hand.

Buck got up from the sofa and came over. "I'm glad to see you two get back together again. Family should stick together."

Boats looked at Buck and me. "Is there someplace Tom and I could talk?"

"Sure. Use the kitchen," said Buck.

We walked into the kitchen and to the table.

Boats dragged one of the new maple dining chairs across the linoleum and sat at the head of the table. "Son, you have really grow'd since I saw you last. You're what now, sixteen?"

"Yeah, be seventeen in a few months. But you didn't come down here to talk about my growth." I walked over to the coffeepot and filled a mug, and then I turned to look at Boats.

"No, I didn't. Guess you know you are the only family I have left."

I held the mug in front of me and stared at him. "Never got to know you that well."

"Guess you're right. That's my fault, not yours. That's the reason I came down to see you. Would you move back up to Tishomingo with me? There won't be any more talk about your dad or mom. She hurt me real bad when she married your father." He was staring into his coffee cup.

"I don't know why, Boats. She loved him very much and was real happy, from what she told and showed me."

"I know. She wrote me several letters every year. But being bullheaded, I never did answer them."

"She told me an awful lot about you, and I can't recall her ever saying a bad word about you," I said. "That's the reason I couldn't understand why you talked about her and Pa the way you did."

Boats hung his head a bit and looked at the coffee in his cup. "Just meanness, Tom. I've had things my own way too long. She was the only one that didn't believe that if I said it was wrong, it was wrong. Then when you showed up looking a lot like her with the same kind of spirit, I wanted to knock it out of you."

I took a draw on my coffee, saw Rosie's coffee cake on the counter, and pulled a piece off the plate. "It didn't work that way."

"I found that out, son. People have to live their own lives."

"I have to live mine."

"Any reason you can't live it with me?"

I realized I was dropping crumbs on Rosie's floor, turned to the cupboard, and searched for a saucer. "Not right now, Boats. When we finish up the job down here next spring, then maybe we can work it out."

I could feel his eyes on my back. "How about if I transfer Buck back up to take over the Bidwell job?"

"I would try to stay here." I walked to the end of the table, put my saucer of coffee cake and my coffee cup on the table, and sat looking at Boats across the table.

"That pretty young woman you came in with?" Boats asked, smiling.

"Yes." Now I was looking in my coffee cup.

"You're not ready for that kind of a commitment, Tom."

"Because of my age?"

"That's one of the main reasons. You will be in love three or four times before you're ready to settle down. At your age, I fell in love with every girl I went out with. I still fall in love with every woman I go to bed with."

I looked Boats in the eyes. "That's one of the reasons I don't like you."

"What's that?" He met my stare.

"You don't have too many morals, do you?"

Boats dropped his gaze to his coffee cup again. "What's morals got to do with it? You will find as you grow older that you take what you can get."

I had both hands wrapped around my mug, the hot coffee warming my hands. "I hope not. Marylyn and I have something special, and I want to keep it."

"Sure thing, son. Just don't get serious. I've got a lot of plans for you." Boats got up, walked to the cupboard for a saucer, and took a slice of the coffee cake. He then turned to face me, holding the saucer and cake in front of him.

"I've got plans for myself, Boats. And to be perfectly honest with you, mine are more important than yours." I turned in my chair to face him.

He swallowed a bite of cake. "You know that everything I own is going to belong to you one of these days."

I pushed my chair back from the table and sat sideways in it, facing him directly. "No, I didn't, but it really doesn't mean that much, does it?"

"What are you talkin' about, boy? Money is everything in this world." Boats's mouth was open and his hands spread, saucer in one, coffee cake in the other.

"Maybe to you it is. It isn't to me. Personal feelings mean more to me than money."

Boats was a bit irritated. He walked back to his chair and sat down again, setting his cake to his right. "What kind of damn communist crap they been teaching you down here?"

"No one has been teaching me anything. I can look at Buck and Rosie, listen to Rocky talk about his wife, see what my ma and pa had, and know I want the same thing." I turned my chair and body back to face him across the table.

"What in the hell are you talking about, boy?" Boats was leaning back in the kitchen chair.

"Love, Boats. Love. The feelings between two human beings who love each other and build a life together." I was resting my elbows on the table, hands clenched under my chin.

"With my money, you can have all the love you want."

"If you feel that way, I can see why you never married."

"The reason I never married is that I never met a woman that wasn't after my money. Anyway, I can get what I want without marriage."

"No, you can't. You can get sex, the same as two animals going at it."

Boats's face flushed red. His ire was up; apparently, I had struck a nerve. "Who in the hell do you think you are to question me about my life or call me an animal? I am a very successful man."

"Sure you are, if you want to count money. But stop and think—who do you have that really cares about you as a person? Who do you have that, when the chips are all gone, will still be standing there backing you up? Do you have someone you can trust like that?"

"Who needs it, boy? I have my work and my company."

"I need it. I wouldn't trade all the money in the world for what Marylyn and I have. She is the reason I can't—or won't—move back up to Tish right now."

"So what will be changed in the spring that allows you to come to Tish?" Boats seemed calm again.

"Marylyn will be eighteen and out of guardianship. She will be able to go anyplace she wants to. We've talked it over, and she's going to move up there with us."

"What would you say if I told you that you didn't have any other choice?"

"You know what I'd say? Sooner or later, you are going to learn that I make my own decisions."

"You're damn bullheaded, but so am I. I'm not going to try to force you, son."

"Good, 'cause I wasn't going anyway." I stood and went back for another piece of coffee cake.

"There's a couple more reasons I came down."

"Figured there was. You never been the social butterfly."

"No, Tom, the most important reason was you. Do you realize that this is more talking than we did in the year you lived with me?" I turned and faced Boats, my mouth full of coffee cake.

"I tried."

Boats dropped his head. "I know you did, son. Like I told you, it was my fault."

"What was the other reason you come down—money?"

"For one thing, I have been trying to get the oil leases on this property."

"I know. I heard about it today. What's the other reason?"

"I wanted to meet this young lady. But the most important reason was I had to make out a will and, being as you're sixteen, I wanted to talk to you about who to name executor."

"You'd know more about that than me. I thought you and Judge Watkins were good friends."

"Business associates, son, not friends."

"No, there's no one up there I would want to name. What about Buck?"

"Hell, Tom, he's only a working man. You couldn't give him control of our company."

I walked to the table and sat down again, realized my coffee mug was empty, and got up to fill it. "I could, Boats, because I trust him."

"You don't understand, boy. Do you have any idea how much money I'm talking about?" Boats was watching me walk across the kitchen with my freshly filled mug of coffee.

"It doesn't matter. Whether it was a dime or ten million, Buck wouldn't steal a penny of it."

Boats guffawed. "Hell, boy, it's a helluva lot more money than that."

Boats's tone irritated me. "You asked me, and I told you. It doesn't matter anyway. You're too mean to die, and I'll be eighteen in a year or so."

"Well, nobody knows when the man upstairs is gonna punch your ticket, and it's those few months I'm thinkin' about. I haven't worked all these years to have someone else wind up with my company."

Boats looked almost fearful. "There's more to this than you're telling me, isn't there?" I said.

"Guess I'd better tell you. I'm going into the hospital for a heart operation. The doctors aren't sure they can repair it. If they can't, I only have a few months to live. So I want to be sure the company stays in the family." Boats wouldn't meet my eyes; he stared down into his cold coffee.

"I'm sorry. Where you being operated on?" Now I felt like an ass for the way I had been acting.

"Parkland Hospital in Dallas, Friday morning."

"We will be there," I said, still staring at him.

"You can't be, son, but I appreciate the thought. You have a football game that night." Boats was slouched but looked up at me.

"That's right; I forgot. I'll just tell the coach."

Boats was adamant. "I don't want that, Tommy. I'll be in intensive care for two days, so it wouldn't do any good for you to be there. I wish we could have become better acquainted." His face expressed sorrow like I had never seen before in another human being.

"I do too, Uncle Boats, but they can do marvelous things these days. I'm sure you will be all right." I really had no idea what I was talking about, but in that moment, I felt a need to get closer to my only blood family.

Boats smiled. "That's the optimism of youth, Tom. Just wish I had it. Hey,

Buck, would you come in here a moment?" Boats walked over and poured his cold coffee in the sink, and then he refilled his mug halfway with the dregs from the near-empty pot.

Buck came in and asked, "You guys want some coffee?"

Boats said, "I just drained the last of it. How 'bout you, Tom? Want some more?"

"Yeah, I'll have another cup and some more cake."

"Rosie, would you come in and make some coffee for us?"

As she was walking in, she looked at Buck and said, "You forget how, darlin'?"

Boats told Buck, "Sit down. I would like to talk to you." Buck complied. "There's something I would like for you to do for Tommy and me if you would."

"Anything I can."

"We want to name you the executor of my will until Tom is eighteen, in case anything happens to me."

"You can if you want to, Boats. You can be sure I'd protect Tommy's interests."

"That's what Tom said, and I respect his judgment. The attorney will send you a copy of the will this week. It's already made out except for the inclusion of your name. Now there's a few things that I had better explain to you."

I stood up, realizing that Mar and Rocky were still in the living room. "Boats, can I ask Marylyn and Rocky to come in and join us?"

"If you wish, son. It's hard getting used to discussing my business in front of people." I got up and asked them if they would like to join us.

Rocky said, "Not me, Tom. I've wanted to see this show for a long time. You kids go ahead."

Mar and I walked back in just as Rosie was pouring the coffee. Then we all gathered around the table. I introduced Mar to Boats.

The coffee was percolating, and Rosie passed saucers around to those who hadn't had any cake yet.

"Now to get back to what I was talkin' about. About three months ago, I bought a drilling company. I know, Buck—I've always said that it was too much of a gamble. You can drop a ton of money down one of those holes on speculation. The only reason I took this chance is that, between Tom and I, we have over 80 percent of the Bidwell field. That is one field, Buck, that we know is going to be a big producer."

Buck set his cake down. "From everything I've heard about it, can't be anything else."

"Anyway, I didn't want to start drilling up there until next spring. That is another reason I came down here. We have two of the drilling rigs sitting over here in Deming. I wanted to try and get the drilling rights on this property and put them to work here rather than having them set."

Mar walked up behind my chair, put her arms around my neck, and rested her chin on my head. She looked at Boats and said, "Rocky gave the oil company till Tuesday morning to meet our demands."

"I know. Rocky told me, but really there is no sense in receiving just royalty rights when you can share in the production," Boats said.

"Did you explain that to Rocky?" Mar asked.

Rocky walked in. "Heard my name a couple of times, so I thought I'd better come hear everything." He walked to the counter and grabbed the last piece of cake. "Guess I didn't get here any too soon." He turned and faced all of us at the table.

Boats continued, "I didn't say anything to Mr. Walgrin because, when I came down here, I didn't have any idea how I was going to swing these oil leases. I'm not overextended at the present time, but I could be if I tied up the millions it would take to acquire your leases."

"Are you sure you're talking about the oil and gas leases on *my* property?" Mar said. "We've been led to believe that the quantity of gas is in question."

"Well, I've seen the geology reports on this property. There's absolutely no question on them, just like the Bidwell field."

Mar looked at Rocky. "That isn't what the Quartz Oil company has been telling us. According to them, it's purely speculation with no guarantee of getting any of their money back."

"Tommy, on the backseat of my car, there's several long, rolled-up maps and a briefcase. Would you go get them for me?" Boats pointed to the driveway.

As I was leaving, I heard Mar asking, "Rocky, what do you think?"

When I returned, Rocky was opining on how he didn't trust Quartz Oil a bit and was concerned they had been trying to get too good a deal.

Boats took the large maps and rolled them out on the tabletop, placing our coffee cups on the corners to keep them flat. "I can get out the seismologist reports, but these maps give a better picture." Standing up, he pointed to one end of the map. "See these areas here that have been shaded darker than the rest? There's no doubt, according to the report, that there is oil there. In these lighter shaded areas, there is a probability of oil. Now, you see these two real dark spots? Mr. Moore's dad drilled those two holes back in '52. Both were producing wells of a secondary nature."

Rocky asked, "What does that mean?"

Buck explained what the map details meant to all of us, and we realized that Quartz Oil hadn't been honest with us about the true nature of the fields.

Boats said, "I can guarantee, if they been tellin' you that, they're taking it on speculation. The ranch to the west of you has over a hundred producing wells, and from this report, yours would produce more."

"Then what would you recommend?" Rocky asked.

Boats explained again that his interest in the wells was modified only by his cash flow.

"Then you're telling us we should drill our own well."

"Not quite, but close. The drilling company I purchased cost ten million. It costs close to three million to drill a well now days. Here is what I propose. For control of these leases, I will give you thirty percent of my drilling company. In addition, after we bring in the first well, the company will also still give you the royalty rights."

Boats stopped and looked around at the group. Rocky turned to Buck and asked, "How does it sound to you?"

"I don't know. On a deal like this, you would have to take a lot of it on faith. We don't know what depreciation or what tax breaks there would be. The only thing I would say to do would be to go get you a good tax accountant and put everything down in black and white. Marylyn, it's your money we're talking about. What do you think?" Rosie had come up behind Buck and was wrapping her arms around his neck.

Mar looked at Rocky. "I'm pissed and not about to do business with Quartz now."

I pulled Mar onto my lap as I pushed my chair from the table. "I thought you said you liked Jim Conway."

"I do, but Rocky, you know how Stuck tried to get us to sign the agreement saying how it was a better lease than most oil companies give people? Remember he kept mentioning how they had proved how they had my interest in mind when they dealt with Moore's nephew?"

Rocky said, "That's what I can't understand. It would have been easier for them to have let him get the place. They could have turned him in and managed the place for him. With him in jail, it would have been no problem."

Buck said, "He couldn't have gotten the place by himself. You said he had a brother in Denver. Must be pretty successful, from what Stuck told you. That's most likely the reason."

Rosie noticed that the coffee had finished percolating and unplugged the pot, took the basket out of it, dropped it in the sink, and then came to the table to pour coffee for everyone.

Rocky looked at the group. "Bet that is the reason. Think either Stuck or Conway said he's an accountant."

"That's it, then," Buck said. "He figured Marylyn and me would be a lot easier to handle. Boats, you've used them before. Ever have any problems?"

"No, I haven't, but that doesn't mean anything. They wouldn't dare mess with me. I can call Bob. If he is pullin' anything shady, he knows I'll find out about it."

"Would you do that?" Marylyn asked.

"Sure. Buck, you have his phone number? He's probably at home."

We all went into the living room, and Boats dialed the number.

After Boats hung up the phone, he turned to Marylyn. "You have a pretty good business sense, young lady. You were right about Bob. He did want you to sign with Quartz Oil. He explained it to me. From what he said, the contract they were offering is a couple of percentage points higher than a standard contract. But he also knew, with all the evidence they have of oil on these leases, that it should have been a higher percentage. Last year he made a mistake on one of Quartz's lease agreements that cost the company several hundred thousand. They asked him to help on the negotiations. Like he said, being as it was above the going rate, he didn't feel he was violating his oath of law."

"Why would he tell you all this so easy?" Rocky asked.

Buck answered, "Because there's no secrets in the oil business. Sooner or later it all comes out, and Stuck knows it. He also knows that Boats can destroy him in the oil business."

Rocky asked Boats, "If you were us, would you keep on doing business with them?"

"The only person in the world I trust is me, but to answer your question, no, I don't think I would. However, it would be real hard to find an attorney or firm with the experience they have."

"I know of another attorney here in El Paso," Rocky said. "Seems to be real honest. 'Course, it could have been a put-up job between him and Stuck."

"Who's that?" Boats asked.

"Royal Carroll. He was the attorney for Harold Moore on that will deal."

"Royal Carroll. He a young guy, about thirty-eight, gray at the temple with a big, easy smile?" Boats asked.

"That would just about fit him."

"I know him. You do too, Buck. Remember that big Indian that got crushed on the rigging in Dennison?"

"Yeah, I recall the Indian, but … Oh yeah, he's the attorney his wife hired." Buck grabbed his cup of coffee and took a swig.

"That's the one. He wanted fifty thousand. Remember I tried to buy him off? Never saw a man get so damned mad in my life. He finally got the money, too."

"Think he would do business with you, Boats?"

"Sure. He handled a couple of cases for one of my companies when they had that problem with a pipe distributor in Dallas."

"You think he would be a good attorney for us to use?" Rocky asked.

"Hell, yeah. You know me, Buck. I don't trust anyone I can't buy."

Buck said, "Yeah, and you seem to own one or two."

Boats laughed at that and said, "I have to keep Bob Stuck as my attorney. We have a contract. If I were you, I'd use Royal for your part of the legal stuff."

"That's a good idea," Rocky said. "We'll try it. Sound all right to you, Marylyn?"

"I trust your judgment. You do what you want to."

Boats said, "Well, I better get back into town and find me a motel."

"No reason for that," Buck said. "We have an extra bedroom. There isn't any sense in you sitting around a motel all day tomorrow. You can fix him a place, can't you, Rosie?"

"Sure. Be glad to. Want to help me, Marylyn?"

Chapter 21

Korean Cowboy

We spent all day Sunday working around the place. Mar went with Frank and me to round up the horses. We had a big lunch Sunday afternoon and spent the evening talking.

Since moving out to the ranch, I had quit working in the pipe yard. Buck had given Manny a job laying out and sorting pipe loads each evening after football practice. Sometimes I would go down to the yard and help him. Buck paid him for three hours a night, when sometimes it only took us thirty minutes.

After we moved to the ranch, I had the barn to work out in instead of the warehouse. I exchanged the smell of oil and grease for horseshit and hay. I no longer had a concrete floor to land on, but when we got to sparring hard, the dust could cause a coughing fit. We sprinkled the dirt and straw with water to keep the dust down and made sure that all of the horse biscuits were scooped up before we started.

Rocky insisted that Frank fire Ray Childs for making that statement about Joe Moore and Pauline. The following week, the employment agency sent out a man to replace him. Rocky talked to him and then sent him down to talk to Frank. Frank came back up later that evening and came out to the barn where Buck, Rocky, Mar, and I were scooping horse biscuits and wetting the floor in preparation for practice. Buck and I slipped on the boxing gloves while the rest looked on.

Frank walked in and asked Rocky, "Do you think that new guy is strong enough to do ranch work?"

"He is kind of small, I'll admit, but he sure is eager for the job."

Mar asked, "Who is that you're talking about?"

"The employment office sent us out a ranch hand. Apparently Snake knows him somehow 'cause he had a great recommendation from Snake in his application file."

"So what's the problem?" Buck hollered as he popped me on the side of the head with a left hook.

Rocky shouted back, "He's Korean! Ever see a Korean cowboy?"

Buck paused and pulled off his gloves. "No, can't say that I have. Has he ever done farm work?"

"According to him, he has done it all, except for riding a horse, and he is willing to try that," Frank said, standing with his hands on his hips and his Stetson pushed back above his forehead.

We heard the barn door opening, and a small man, around forty or so, with soft features and a slight grin walked in. He was clearly Asian and clearly not a cowboy.

Frank called, "Chee, come on over here. We were just discussing you. Being as it's your living we're talking about, we should include you."

Frank introduced him to us. His name was Chee Ko Han, and he spoke in broken English.

After talking to him for a while, Rocky told him, "The only problem we have, Chee, is that we're afraid that you aren't strong enough to do this type of work."

"I not understand, Misser Walgrin?"

"Well, for one thing, our bales of alfalfa probably weigh more than you do."

Chee pointed to the bales stacked next to Rocky and Mar. "Is that what you are talking about?"

"Yes, that's one. We have to throw them from the back of a truck up into the hayloft."

Again Chee pointed. "You mean to floor up there?"

"That's the hayloft," Rocky said, somewhat patronizing.

Chee walked over, stood flat footed, and jumped nearly three and one-half feet to the bed of the truck. Then he placed one hand on the end and another under the bailing wire, did a fast turn with it, gave out a loud yell, and threw the bale up into the loft.

We looked on in amazement. Chee couldn't have weighed over 120 pounds.

Frank said in awe, "Hell, I couldn't throw half a bale that high. Guess he gets a job, don't he, Rocky?"

"As far as I'm concerned, he has. Never saw anything like that in my sixty-plus years."

As Chee started to leave, Buck said, "I'm kinda curious, Chee, how you happen to know Snake."

"Snake was in Army in Korea. My father and I work with Army Rangers, teach them martial arts and knife fighting. Mr. Snake, he took many classes, very good with karambit."

"Karambit—is that the curved knife Snake wears on his belt all the time?" I asked.

"Yes, it used by farmers in Southeast Asia for cutting roots, plants, planting rice. Very good close fighting. Mr. Snake, he one of best Rangers with karambit."

"How come you don't wear one?"

"I have one." The knife appeared in his hand from nowhere and then went back to where it had come from in a nearly unobservable movement. "I prefer use hands and feet. My father teach knife fighting using Filipino and Thai techniques. I teach fighting with hands and feet."

Buck said, "How did you wind up in the United States?"

"My father was official in North Korea before war. When communists take over, he move our family to South Korea. He work with American forces during war, make many friends. Friends help me come to US to go to school, and I stay in US. I work to bring my family here."

"Well, we're glad you're here. You'll have to teach us some of that fancy fighting stuff," Buck said with a smile.

Two days after Chee went to work, he was in the barn when Buck and I came in to spar around. He watched for a while and then told me I wasn't slipping punches the right way.

I asked him, "Do you box?"

"Not like you do it here, but before I became American citizen, I was native of Korea. Every child there learn martial arts for protection of homeland against communists."

"Would you mind showing us some moves?" I asked.

For the next hour, he showed both Buck and me how to turn or parry a blow using hands, arms, elbows, shoulders, legs, and feet. Buck and I both tried to hit him, but he blocked every punch we threw. We wore ourselves out throwing punches.

Finally, Buck asked him, "How do you do that?"

"I watch your eyes and react to them."

"Guess Tom and me will have to pass, then, because there is no way we could get as fast as you are."

"Sure you can. It just matter of building up right muscles and nerves. American men build up muscles that show off to good advantage. Tom will have easier time than you, Buck, because he younger." Chee showed us movements using ten-pound barbells to build up lateral muscles and emphasized that the workouts stimulate the nerves.

Buck and I couldn't wait to get out to the barn and work out after our session with Chee. It got so bad with us working out with Chee that one night Rosie and Mar showed up in sweat suits.

Rosie said, "We figured, being as we don't see you anymore, that we are going to learn this new defensive fighting of yours so that later, if we can't talk you into doing what we want, we can beat you up. Right, Marylyn?"

"Seemed like a good idea at the time, but if I have to build up the muscles these two have, I quit."

Chee started them out like he had us, with two-pound weights. After a couple of nights, they were engrossed as much as we were. Mar learned more quickly than any of us. She seemed to have a knack for it. Chee could show us an offensive or defensive move, and whereas we would have to do it three or four times, Mar usually picked it up on the first execution. Some nights we would go at it for three or four hours. Slowly but surely, we learned.

On the Monday night after Boats had spent the weekend with us, we were out in the barn working out. Chee told us, "You folks are fast learners. I have taught you all the moves I know. Now all it take is practice. Just remember, you can kill someone with this if you are not careful. Use it wisely. I would hate to think I taught you something that made you killer. Now let's practice our moves."

We were going through them when Rocky and the kids came in. The kids wanted to "do the dance" too, so we let them until they tired and went back to the house to play. Rosie and Buck quit early and also went back into the house.

Rocky sat on a bale of hay, telling us about hiring Royal that day and also getting a phone call from Boats telling him to have our attorneys get a hold of Seth Wilburton if we decided to take his offer. Rocky said, "That's the reason I came out here, kiddo. I have to talk to you."

"You want me to leave, Rocky?" I asked.

Rocky looked at Chee. "No, but if you wouldn't mind, Chee."

"Certainly, Misser Walgrin."

Rocky walked over to some alfalfa bales set up as seating for the makeshift boxing ring. "You kids come on over and sit down."

After we settled on the hay facing Rocky, he said, "Honey, I want you to understand. On this business deal with Boats, you are taking a serious risk."

"How's that?"

"If we sell these leases to someone, they will give us ninety dollars an acre for a period of twenty years. That's ninety thousand a year guaranteed money. This other way, if we drill and hit a duster, you lose."

I said, "Isn't she going to get 30 percent of Boats's drilling company?"

"Yes, she is. If we hit here, I figure we would do real well because we could have an accountant on top of everything. But suppose we don't hit here and the whole drilling outfit is moved up above. Maybe I shouldn't say this, Tommy, Boats being your uncle, but my job is to protect Marylyn. Anyway, with the drilling company out of our area, Boats could write off just about anything he wanted to and never show a profit."

"It really does bother you, doesn't it?" I said, noticing the concern in Rocky's face. "Can I ask a question?"

"Sure, son. Go ahead."

"I'm sure Boats thinks there's oil here, and a lot of it. So why not protect Mar?"

Rocky looked puzzled. "What you got in mind, son?"

"Well, the way it stands now, Boats is going to gamble about two million drilling a well, won't he?"

"That's what he wants to do," Rocky said. One of the mares was nuzzling a feed bucket, hoping for another coffee can of oats.

"Tell him the only way you will go for the deal he wants is that, regardless of what happens, he pays Mar the lease money for ten years." I was leaning forward toward Rocky with my hands clasped between my knees and Marylyn's arm wrapped around mine.

"You mean instead of twenty, he pays Marylyn for ten years?" Rocky looked back and forth between Mar and me.

"Sure, at ninety thousand a year like Quartz Oil Company. Either that or 40 percent of the drilling company," I said, using my hands for emphasis.

Almost thinking out loud, Rocky said, "Still, Tom, 40 percent of nothin' is still nothin'."

I raised my arm and dropped it around Mar's shoulders. We continued back and forth, hashing out the pros and cons for an hour and a half. We decided to tell Quartz that we weren't interested and tell Boats that Mar wanted a guarantee of at least ten years of lease payments and 40 percent of the rights to the drilling company.

Rocky finally got up to go. Mar and I sat snuggling then.

Mar stood up, turned, and sat down on my lap. Looking up at me, she told me, "Do you realize that this is the first time we've been alone in over a month, except for riding back and forth to school?" Rocky stopped at the door, turned, and said, "You kids don't stay out too late." Then he disappeared through the doorway. The creaking barn door slammed, and it was silent.

"Alone at last. Why not give me a kiss?" I said cheerfully.

"I'll give you a kiss, all right." She jumped up and gave me a shove backward. In falling off the bale of hay, I grabbed her sweatshirt and the elastic belt on her pants. I felt the elastic snap.

She gave a cry of surprise as I pulled her down. She hit and rolled on the canvas, and I came up halfway on top of her. She gave a quick shove and scrambled out from under me. I half-pushed myself up and she kicked my behind and turned to run. I jumped up and started after her. She hadn't taken four steps on the canvas mat we had been using when I caught the back of her sweats, and her sweat pants fell down around her ankles and tripped her. In falling, she half whirled and grabbed me. I fell to her side, my hand on her stomach. It completely knocked the air out of her and scared the heck out of me. I kept asking her if she was all right, but she kept gasping for air.

Finally, she was able to speak. "Hope I don't look that way when I'm scared," she said, giggling.

"What way?"

"Like a fish out of water. You sounded like a motorboat with your mouth open and bug-eyed."

"I've never been bug-eyed in my life," I said.

"Pop-eyed, then."

"Not even then. Olive Oyl, maybe."

She laughed. Reaching up, she ran her hand along the scar on my face. "It is fading, isn't it?"

"Told you it would." On my knees beside her, I bent down and kissed her. Her arms came up around my neck, and she rolled me across her body so that we lay facing each other, kissing. The kisses were getting warmer, blending into each other.

She took both hands and pushed my face back from hers. Looking into my eyes, she told me, "You asked me one time if I had used any of the birth control pills my mother gave me. Yes, I have. I started taking them about ten days ago. Tommy, I love you, and I want you. And I want you to be the first."

Her knees bumped against mine. I felt her legs moving, and looking down, I saw that she was using her feet to finish pushing off her sweat pants. Her hands moved to my belt buckle and undid the clasp. I pulled at the top button, and the buttons popped open till there were none left to open.

I rolled to my back, arched on my shoulder blades to push the Levi's and boxers down, and kicked off my shoes. I flipped the Levi's to the side and turned. Her hand found me and pulled at me to come on top of her. She was warm and wet. My white gym socks tried to find traction on the canvas.

We were awkward and smiling, probing the hidden parts of each other. Our first love, making love, knowing there was nobody else in the world but us two, in this moment—captured forever.

Chapter 22

Set Up for Victory

The next afternoon, when Manny and I walked into our locker room, there was a message on the blackboard: "Meeting before practice." We got dressed and seated ourselves to await the coach's arrival.

Coach Baker and the three other coaches came into the locker room. "All right, gentlemen, let's have quiet. I have heard talk from some of you men about us having a star on the team." Everyone turned and looked at me. "I can see by your glance that all of you know what I am talking about. Now, I have something to tell you.

"That story was put in the paper by me, and I will tell you why. Gentlemen, day after tomorrow out on that field, you are going to be in the football game of your life. Make no mistake—they are the best football team you will meet this year. They are solid in every position except one, and that's linebacker. Their monster or center linebacker, next to Sanchez there, is the best in the state, if not the best in the rest of the United States. The rest of our club is on par, if not better than they are, in every position. I gave that story out for one reason—to try and get an advantage—and I want to tell you it worked. They have moved their center linebacker over to right linebacker. That means they will have two linebackers playing out of position. T. C., I'm sorry to have used you this way, but if we can get them keying on you, those new plays we put in should go like clockwork. There will be another story in the paper tonight telling the world how great you are, so don't let it go to your head." He said the last part with a laugh.

"Now, gentlemen, I've noticed over the last two nights that when T. C. carried the ball, you haven't been blocking and putting the effort into it you should. As I told you, we are a team and we should play as a team. After all, the reporters say we are the third-best team in our class in Texas. Come Friday, we're going to show them we're the best in Texas. Right?"

The yelling and shouting of "Right!" could have been heard five blocks away.

"All right, gentlemen, this will be our last workout till Friday night. Let's make it a good one. One thing I want to caution you about—if there is any idea in your mind that if you do something, it will hurt someone, don't do it. We want to come through this workout with no injuries. Okay, team, let's go."

In full pads, the team stood and made its way en masse to the exit, funneling down to two at a time to get through the door. Once outside, screams and yells carried us to the field. After the mile run at the end of practice, Manny, Mueller, Pedro, Breedlove, Chico, and Malin gathered around me on the bleachers, where we stopped to catch our breath.

Mueller asked, "Did you see Sanchez's face while Coach was talking?"

Malin said, "You know he was trying to get some of the guys to let down so you could really get smashed."

"Hell, he wouldn't do that," I said. "It could cost us the game."

Manny said, "I've told you before, T. C.—he hates the ground you walk on. He will do anything to get even."

Breedlove spoke next. "He's right. I've been to a couple of parties that he was at when he got to drinking. All he can talk about is getting you."

"The way he has been treating me lately, I knew he still didn't like me, but I figured he was over that getting-even notion. But—"

Manny said, "I've told you he is a hardheaded bastard. Just don't give him a chance at you."

The group broke up, and the guys went on home except for Manny. The girls came out, and we drove down to Pepi's.

Marylyn and I were sitting in the booth across from Manny and Tess. He sat there with a smile, looking at us. "Say, Mar, what you and this handsome devil been up to?"

"We haven't been up to nothin'," Marylyn said.

"Tess, look at them. Don't they look different? I've never seen her look prettier or more radiant, have you? T. C., you sure you been behaving yourself?"

"Always, Manny. I'm a gentleman in all things."

Tess said, "You know, he's right, Mar. I noticed it earlier today and was going to say something. You do look radiant, like Manny says."

"Just happy, I guess," Marylyn said. "Things sure have been nice lately."

We finished our Cokes and drove out to the ranch, where we ate our supper, went to the barn for the workout, and went to bed.

Thursday and Friday slipped by. On Friday afternoon, we had a pep rally and serpentine parade around town. School let out an hour early, but the coach made us go home and rest.

At seven, we were back in the dressing room. After we suited up, the coaches came in. Coach Baker opened with, "Gentlemen, I want you to relax. We know this is a big game. But that is all it is, a game. You go out there and play to your capabilities, and regardless of how it turns out, you are winners. All through your life, you give it your best, and you will have no regrets. I want all of you to know—all of you in this room have been and are the best group of athletes I have ever worked with. But enough roses for now. Manny, if we receive, I am going to give you and the offense the first two plays. Now pay attention. First play is I-1 right on two. Chico, be sure you get a good block on that right end. Breedlove, you take out the left linebacker. Manny, be sure when you're going down the line that you wait on the pitch until Mueller has cleared Chico's block. Be sure, T. C., that you carry out your fake into the line. Got it?"

We all said, "Yes, sir!"

"If that don't get us a first down, Manny, the second play I want is one of our new plays: I-P-1 on two. As I been telling you, make sure either the ends or Breedlove in the flat is clear before you throw that ball. All right, let's go get loosened up."

We went charging out onto the field, and the stands came alive. The air was crisp and chilled. Thousands of bugs swarmed the stadium lights, and the crowd was frenzied and electric. The bleachers were packed, and people were crowded shoulder to shoulder completely surrounding the field, three feet from the sidelines. I tried to spot Buck and the rest, but there must have been ten thousand people there. We went through our warm-ups and stretching exercises, ran through a few sets, and huddled around Coach for another pep talk. Manny and Sanchez, our team cocaptains, stayed on the field for the coin toss. The other team won it and elected to receive.

"All right, defense, I'm sure they will stick pretty close to form. If I'm not mistaken, they will run one of two plays. It's going to be a gamble on our part. Last night while going over the films, Doug noticed something I hadn't. When number thirty-four, their left halfback, goes into motion to the right, they throw to him. The right guard and right end pull for blocking. Malin, it's a flair pass straight down the line of scrimmage." Coach drew a fast diagram on his clipboard.

"Now, if they run the right halfback that way, watch him. They never throw to him. 'Course it could be a setup, so pay attention. They'll most likely have a couple of surprises up their sleeve for us, too.

"Defense, we've prepared all we can, so all I can say is pay attention. Sanchez knows which player to key on, so you defensive players don't get so wrapped up that you don't listen for Sanchez's calls. Okay, let's go get 'em!"

Manny and I stood side by side while the band played the national anthem.

Mueller teed up the ball and raised his right hand, the referee's whistle blew, and the game was on.

Mueller's kick went down to the eighteen-yard line. A receiver got it and started upfield. He was hit on the twenty-five-yard line. The other team went into a huddle. Manny turned to me and said, "Damn, my guts are in a knot."

I told him, "Mine, too."

Our opponents came out of their huddle and lined up in their pro set. On the snap of the ball, their fullback came straight into the line, and Sanchez met him head on. No gain. On their second set, the left halfback went into motion to the right. When he started that way, so did Malin. The ball was snapped and their guard came out to block him, but Malin was across the line of scrimmage between the quarterback and the left halfback. The quarterback turned and threw automatically. Malin was ready; he reached up, grabbed the ball just above his head, and then turned and sprinted twenty-four yards to the goal line untouched.

The players, crowd, and coaches went crazy. Mueller trotted out and calmly kicked for the extra point. The team lined up, and Mueller kicked off again.

The same player caught it on the fifteen and didn't make it back to the twenty. On the first snap, they tried a right sweep and gained a yard. On the next play, they did another run left and got another yard. The third play was a pass on a man coming across the flat, but the pass was thrown high. The receiver tipped it up into the air, and Sanchez came down with the ball. He ran it back to the sixteen before he was tackled. As we trotted out onto the field, I asked Manny, "How's the guts now?"

"Think I've got a full-grown elephant in there."

We huddled. Manny told us, "Okay, guys, we know the play, I-1 right on two. Chico, stick it to him. Breedlove, same to you. All right, let's go for six."

We lined up, with Manny screaming as loud as he could so he could be heard over the roar of the crowd. On two, I rocketed into the line straight ahead, doubling over to hide the ball I didn't have. A 210-pound linebacker met me at the line, driving his helmet under my chin and into my chest like the lance of a charging knight. I felt like a train had just hit me. By the time I was able to see past the hulk lying on top of me, I saw Mueller running back toward us, waving his arms every which way, and everyone in the stands was going crazy again. Mueller had scored. My ears were ringing from the hit.

The kicking tee was thrown onto the field as I was coming off. Mueller calmly kicked another extra point.

After we kicked off again, the other team returned it to the thirty. Our defense acted like hungry wolves picking off addled sheep. They went through three plays for six yards and then punted. Breedlove returned the wobbly punt to the fourteen.

We moved the ball steadily down the field. Finally, Coach called one of those special plays; the pass was right on the money down the middle. Breedlove caught it and romped sixty-six yards for a touchdown.

Mueller lined up to kick the extra point. When it was snapped, Manny stood up quick and flipped a short pass to the left end for two points, making the score twenty-two to nothing at the end of the first quarter.

Sanchez and the men on defense were like demons. It seemed that every play they ran, Sanchez was in it. The first half was a defensive masterpiece and a disaster for our opponents. Even Pedro reached up and pulled down a ball that was tipped on an errant pass by their offense. He went lumbering down the field for fifteen yards like a freight train. He went into the end zone with two men draped on his back. Mueller kicked the extra point like a machine.

Late in the first half, our opponents finally scored after a missed tackle.

With a minute and a half left in the first half, the other team kicked off. Breedlove took it back to the thirty-two. On first down, Manny called my number on a misdirection play. The backfield would go to the left, and I was to cut back over the right tackle. My teammates opened a big hole, and in full stride the opposing left linebacker made a leap at me. I felt his hands hit my thigh pads, and then I was past him. The secondary overshifted to the left with the movement of our backfield, and before they could recover, I was past them.

I knew then that it was a footrace and that they couldn't catch me. I looked over my shoulder with a big smile on my face as I went into the end zone. My teammates about beat me to death celebrating.

Mueller, the machine, kicked the extra point. I was standing there laughing when they came off the field. We went into the locker room with the score at thirty-six to seven. Coach Baker didn't have very much to say, complimented the defense on the job they were doing, and reminded us that we had scored all those points so it was possible for them to do the same thing. He told us to just keep on doing our best.

At the start of the second half, we received. Mueller carried for twenty-eight, Manny for eleven, and Breedlove twenty-three. I got mine on two carries, the last for a touchdown. Mueller kicked the extra point. The rest of the game passed in slow motion for me. It ended fifty to fifteen.

A couple of reporters came into the dressing room after the game. One of them asked me why I had been laughing when I went across the goal line. I told him, "Because I was happy." He just laughed.

One of them told Coach Baker, "Man, this was a cakewalk for your team."

Coach Baker responded, "Don't put the other team down. They are one fine, fast ball team. We got a few lucky breaks, and they had to change their game plan."

He replied, "Now, Coach, you handled them with ease. With a score like that, they sure never should have been rated number one."

"They are one of the top three teams in the state. We just got the breaks."

"You telling me that if you played them again, they might beat you?"

"They might, and we probably will meet them again in the state playoffs."

The reporters talked to a few more players and left after getting the stats on the game.

Happy and excited, we hurried through our showers and dressed for the junior/senior dance. Mar and Tess met us when we walked out, still wearing their cheerleader outfits. We all piled into my truck and took the girls over to Tess's to change. We sat outside on the porch waiting for them.

A big, old bullfrog sat croaking in the pond at the side of Tess's house, and the night sky was full of a thousand stars.

Manny looked at me. "You know, after all the buildup and hoopla, I was really ready for a tough game."

I looked down at my patent-leather shoes that I had rented for the dance. "Me too. It sure seemed easy, didn't it? I guess it goes to show that you never know what to expect."

Manny pulled at the crisp collar around his neck and then stood to straighten his cummerbund. "It sure does. We worked a lot harder on our workouts."

I smiled at his fidgeting. "I know. But can you imagine how the Stateline players must feel right now on their way home?"

"Not really. I'm just glad it isn't us sitting here after a pasting like that." Manny leaned against the post at the top of the stairs leading to the porch and looked through the glass of the front door to see if the girls were coming.

"Hey, you think we won't be no worse than second?" I stood and peered in the window as well.

"Depends on what the Mustangs did tonight. It sure would feel good to be rated number one, wouldn't it?" He slapped me on the back.

"Well, Monday we will know."

Chapter 23

Police Work and the Damn Dog

Lee Bob sat behind his desk with Boats and Judge Watkins glaring at him.

"How in hell could you let things get out of hand so quick?" Boats asked. "The judge and I were only gone for a weekend. Judge, has that idiot Ross got a hold of you yet?" Boats was clearly pissed off.

"Not yet. Adam was telling me what he had on his mind. Did you tell him it was out of the question?" The judge shifted in the hard wooden chair.

Lee Bob leaned back in his swivel chair before speaking. "I told 'em you wouldn't go for no killing."

The judge nearly spat the words at him. "Well, at least you still have some sense left. Now, you want to tell us how you're coming on Doc's murder?"

The sheriff opened his hands as if pleading his case. "I've given you all the information I have. We're also running down all the Chrysler cars around in this county."

"Hell, that could take years. Dammit, Sheriff, it has to be someone Doc knew real well or that damn dog would have torn him to pieces, wouldn't he?" Boats was leaning against the wall and pushed away from it when he spoke.

"That's just it," Watkins said. "You know Doc wouldn't let anyone get anywhere close to that place. There has been something bothering me, and I just now realized what it is." The judge was pulling at his chin and leaning forward.

"What's that, Judge? Something to do with the case?"

The judge slapped the top of Lee Bob's desk in disgust. "What the hell we been talking about, for Christ's sake? How well was old Doc's dog trained?"

Lee Bob was cautious in his response, being careful not to aggravate the judge further. "'Bout as good as any dog I ever saw. He always got his dogs from that kennel in Pike. The trainer would come down for a week or two to teach the dog the property lines."

The judge looked from Boats to Lee Bob. "Either one of you ever see Doc's dog cross the bridge or creek or ever leave his property?"

Lee Bob said, "I haven't. That dog never left his property, ever."

"Well, that's something that ought to help you in your investigation." The judge sat back in his chair, proud of his figuring.

"I don't get it," Lee Bob said.

The judge was beside himself with rage. "I swear, you're dumb as a bag a hammers, Lee Bob! You know what I'm getting at, don't you, Boats?"

Boats dropped his shoulders back against the wall. "Sure. A little boy with a dull pencil could figure that out."

Lee Bob stared at them blankly. "I don't understand."

"You said yourself that the dog never leaves the property." The judge said it as if leading a witness in his courtroom.

"Well, goddamnit, he didn't!"

"Then how in the hell did he attack Jordan on the golf course a hundred yards from Doc's property line?"

"Damn, I *am* dumb," Lee Bob said. "There ain't no way." He got up and walked to the wall, where he slid a panel window up between his office and Junior's. "Junior, who's cruising the Ada area?" he asked.

"Joe Bill and Zeke, Sheriff."

"Well, get them on the horn and tell them to pick up Jordan Stevonich and bring him in for questioning."

"Any charge?" Junior asked.

"Suspicion of murder."

"Is he the one that killed Doc, Chief?"

Lee Bob didn't answer; he just slammed down the wooden window panel and walked back to his chair, muttering. "Oh, I'd like to fire that shithead!"

"If you feel that way, why don't you?" Boats asked.

The judge answered instead. "Because he's one of my sister Ella May's boys. Ain't that right, Lee Bob?" The judge laughed.

"Sure is, Judge, but if he calls me Chief just one more time, I'm going to shove his head up his ass and suffocate him. I mean it, Judge. I've had it with that smart-mouthed asshole."

"All right, I'll talk to him," Watkins said. "Now you'd better call Adam and get him down here because I want everything legal. I'm sure you recall that drug bust you made last year that the circuit court of appeals overturned because you violated the judge's wife."

"It was just an accident, Judge."

"Well, if Jordan killed him, I want to be sure it's legally handled. Get him on the phone."

Lee Bob picked up the phone and dialed. "Hello, Adam. I need you down here at the jail. Look, I don't care that you're in the middle of a pinochle game. I think we are bringing in Doc's killer, and I want you here during the questioning. Hell, no, it can't wait till morning! Look, Adam, just get your ass down here. Just a minute." He turned to the judge and handed him the phone.

Watkins took the phone and put it up to his ear. "Adam, Judge Watkins. Like Lee Bob said, get your ass down here." He handed the phone back to Lee Bob. "We'd better get out of here, Boats. We'll talk to you in the morning, Lee Bob."

"Be sure you talk to your nephew, Judge."

"Oh, yeah. I will."

Lee Bob waited for ten minutes and then hollered at Junior to bring him a cup of coffee.

"Isn't any made, Sheriff."

"Then get off your lazy coon-dog ass and make some! And not so damned stout, either."

Adam walked in. "Who is it you have that you think is Doc's killer?"

"Jordan Stenovich."

"What you got on him?"

Lee Bob proceeded to tell him about the dog.

"Pretty slim, isn't it?"

"Yeah, but right now it's all I got."

Joe Bill and Zeke opened the door with Jordan in between them. "He tried to run, Sheriff, but Zeke put a bullet over his head."

"The way he shoots, it's a wonder he didn't kill him. Did you read him his rights?"

"Sure did, Sheriff, and he said he understands them. Didn't you, Jordan?"

Jordan nodded.

"Can't you speak?" asked Lee Bob. "Speak up."

"Yes, I understood."

"Zeke, you take Jordan back and book him. You know the charge. When you finish, bring him back here."

After they left, Lee Bob told Joe Bill, "Go get me those tape recorders."

They set them up in the interrogation room, and Zeke soon brought Jordan in. Lee Bob told the two officers to get back on patrol. He reached down, opened a drawer under the steel table, and pulled out a card.

"This is Sheriff Lee Bob Whetzel of Johnston County. The date is November fourteen. Present is suspect Jordan Stevonich and Adam Halsey, district attorney's office. Said suspect has been informed that these proceedings are being taped." From the card in his hand, Lee Bob read Jordan his rights. "Do you understand these rights as read to you?" he asked.

"Yes, I do."

"Do you wish to have an attorney present before questioning?"

"You're charging me with Doc Leftan's murder?" Jordan asked.

"You have been held on suspicion of murder," Lee Bob answered.

"I don't have any money to pay for an attorney."

Adam told him, "The court will furnish you an attorney at no charge if you are indigent."

"What's that mean?"

"It means if you have no money, job, or property."

"Hell, you guys know I work at the silica plant and am buying my place in Ada."

"Then the judge will have to decide if you qualify for government-issued representation."

"There isn't any use in going through all that," Jordan said. "I didn't kill Doc, so ask me your questions."

Lee Bob said, "You're refusing the attorney?"

"Yes."

"All right, then. Jordan, tell me why you lied to me about being attacked by Doc's dog."

"I didn't lie to you. Hell, Lee Bob, Dr. Zetick treated me the same night." Stenovich was squirming but wasn't able to move too far since he was handcuffed to the steel table in the interrogation room.

"Tell me again where you was at when that dog attacked you."

"I told you. I was sitting by the fourth tee when all of a sudden this dog hit me. He grabbed my leg and arm. I throwed him back down the hill and got out of there." Stenovich was looking at his shoes when he talked.

"What's your blood type, Jordan?"

"O positive."

"Are you sure?"

"I'm positive. Here, I still pack one of my dog tags." Jordan reached inside his shirt with his free hand, pulled out the dog tag, and held it up to the sheriff.

"Okay, you want to tell me what you was doing on Doc's property?"

Jordan slid his chair back till the handcuffs stopped his retreat. "I wasn't on Doc's property."

"What would you say if I told you I had a witness who saw you on Doc's property?" The sheriff had moved behind him and was leaning in, speaking into his right ear.

Jordan moved his head as far away from the sheriff as he could. "I'd say they were a liar."

Lee Bob moved around and placed his fists on the table. He leaned aggressively toward Jordan, speaking through clenched teeth. "There's only one thing wrong with your story, Jordan."

"What's that?"

"That is one of the best-trained dogs in the state. There's no way you could get Doc's dog off his property."

Jordan was shaken. "Well, he came off to get me."

"No, he didn't, Jordan. You was on Doc's property. By the way, what shoes were you wearing that night?"

"These I have on, Sheriff. I only have two pairs, these work boots and one pair for dress."

The sheriff stepped back and looked at Jordan's boots. "Take them off. I want to compare them to a couple of plaster casts we have from the creek bank."

As Jordan used his free hand to remove his boots, the sheriff bellowed, "Do you wear a watch?"

"I did, but I lost it a couple of weeks ago."

"What kind was it?"

"I don't know. My wife bought it for me last Christmas."

"Could it have been a Rolex?" The sheriff plopped in the chair opposite Stenovich.

"Yeah, right, Lee Bob. Boats pays good but not enough for a Rolex. I think it was a Seiko."

Adam sat silently in the corner during this entire exchange, and then he stood and walked into the other room. Lee Bob sat there looking at Jordan. "You sure it wasn't you that killed Doc, Jordan?"

"I didn't have any reason, Sheriff. Sure, I'll admit I bought a little pot off of him every once in a while, but that's all."

Adam walked back in. "Right shoe matches the right footprint, Sheriff."

Lee Bob pushed the chair back and crossed his legs and arms, slouching in the chair. "You want to change your story?"

"Lee Bob, I swear I didn't kill him. He was already dead." Jordan was tearing up and started speaking a mile a minute.

"Look, I was coming home from fishing, like I told you," he continued. "My car broke down, so I took the shortcut back to town. I was going to stop at Doc's to get me some pot. Anyway, when I approached his place, there was a light blue station wagon sitting on his bridge. You know how narrow that bridge is. Anyway, I couldn't get around it. Besides that, I knew that damn dog would attack if I stepped off the bridge. I heard the dog barking, looked down, and saw this body laying in the creek. I walked down the hill and waded across the creek. At first, the dog just stood there and looked at me. Anyway, I got there, put one foot on the bank, and leaned down to look at the body when that dog attacked me. He grabbed my leg, and the force of him hitting me pushed me back and I fell into the water. While I was trying to fight him off, I saw someone run out of the house. He had a big box in his hands. He jumped into the station wagon and drove off. That's it, Sheriff. I swear."

Lee Bob sat up straight, watching Jordan closely to see if there was any hint of deception. "Who was the man who came out of the house?"

"I never did get a good look at his face. There was something familiar about him, though."

"How about the station wagon?" Lee Bob was totally focused on Jordan and slid his chair closer. Adam had taken the chair across the table and was watching Jordan as well.

"It was a Plymouth, I think." Jordan was looking back and forth from Adam to the sheriff.

"You know the car? Ever recall seeing it before?"

"No, I can't." Jordan's body language was supporting his statement.

Adam interjected, "Why didn't you give us this information the other night?"

"My wife wouldn't let me," he answered. "She was afraid you would try and pin it on me."

"Anything else you want to ask, Adam?" Lee Bob said.

"You said there was something familiar about the man that came out of Doc's house?" Adam was leaning forward on the interrogation table.

"There was—the way he moved. He had that box on the right side toward me. It couldn't have weighed too much because he was carrying it real easy. 'Course, I only got a couple of glances because I was trying to fight off that dog." Jordan was now turned to face Adam.

"Did you tell all of this to your wife?"

"Yes, sir, as soon as she got over from Ada and picked me up. She was the one who made me go to the doctor."

Adam looked at Lee Bob. "Why not put Jordan back into his cell and go check out his story? We'll talk it over in the morning."

At seven the next morning, Adam walked past Junior, knocked twice on Lee Bob's door, and peered in, where he saw Lee Bob reading a report. Adam spoke as the sheriff looked up.

"We have a meeting to go to, Sheriff."

"Where at?"

"Come on. I'll tell you on the way."

As they got into the sheriff's car, Adam asked, "How did you come out last night talking to Jordan's wife?"

"Leah and I are old friends. We got on just fine," Lee Bob said with an evil grin.

"I wasn't talking about your love life. You know, Sheriff, one of these days, one of those poor slobs you pick up is going to find out and kill you for fucking around with his wife."

Lee Bob tilted his head toward Adam and laughed. "They're too scared,

Adam. No one wants to mess with the law. Leah told about the same story as Jordan, except she said they did drive back out there and put the piece of cloth from Jordan's pant leg by the fourth tee to make his story more convincing. What's the meeting about? Do you know?"

"Several things, I imagine. Chubb would be my guess."

"Well, here we are. Won't take long to find out." The two men stepped out of Lee Bob's police cruiser and walked up to the bank.

John Ross opened the glass door at the entrance to the bank, locked it after they stepped in, and led them back to the boardroom. The members of the Combine sat in their usual chairs around the conference table, drinking coffee. Adam and Lee Bob nodded to Boats and Judge Watkins and then sat in two empty chairs at the end of the table. Coy, Leon, Boats, and Watkins all swiveled their chairs to face the two.

John sat down at the head of the table. "You any closer to finding out who killed Doc?"

"We're getting there. It just takes time," Lee Bob replied. "We got the lists in from most of the jewelry stores on the watch. Also there's nineteen people in town who have AB negative blood, according to hospital records. We have started checking them out."

Leon interrupted. "Time's one thing we don't have, Lee Bob, with Chubb tossing those records around."

John looked at the pair. "Adam, you and Lee Bob go out to Larry's place. He has agreed to sell us his property, and in the purchase we get back Doc's records."

Adam asked, "What if he has made copies?"

"I know he's made copies, just not how many," Lee Bob said. "He bought enough stuff over at Odell to copy them four times over." Lee Bob was uncomfortable under the stares of the Combine.

"He told us he made a record of each file. We get back both sets," John answered.

Lee Bob adjusted his chair and pulled himself closer to the table. "Kind of trusting, aren't you, gentlemen? I've dealt with people like Larry for the last fourteen years, and you can't trust them. My arrest books are full of them."

"Nobody trusts him, Lee Bob," Boats said sarcastically, "but the judge made it very clear to Larry last night that if any more of those records get out, he has a lot of trouble. Didn't you, Judge?"

"Sure, but that's still no assurance that he won't keep a copy of the files." The judge turned to John.

John sat confidently at the head of the table and was steepling his fingers in front of his face. "Well, Coy, Leon, and I believe he would be no problem dead." Boats and Judge Watkins looked at each other.

Boats spoke first. "Ain't no way in hell we are agreeing to kill him or anyone else, so forget it."

The judge chimed in. "There is no statute of limitations on murder. Buy him out, no problem. Murder, absolutely not!"

John turned to Lee Bob and Adam. "You two take the money to Larry, and get the deed for us. Take the records out to Boats's place when you get them."

When he heard the door close, Boats turned to John and stood up. "You know, there's one thing I'll say for you. If nothing else, you're persistent. But I'm going to tell you something else, John."

"What's that?"

"Twice in the last twenty years, you and these fucking morons, Coy and Leon, have talked about killing someone. The last time, we managed to get the guy sent off to prison. This time we stopped you before you could get started."

"What's your point, Boats?" John swiveled in his chair, watching Boats as he went to the coffeepot behind the wet bar in the conference room.

"My point is, if you or anybody else gets me tied up in a murder, you are the ones that are going to be dead. Am I clear? I saw enough killin' in the war, and there is very little worth takin' a life for, especially not money. You tie me up in a murder, and they will be trying me for your murder as well."

"And that goes double for me," the judge added.

"Well, it would have been a lot cheaper than three and a half million dollars," John said, totally pissed off.

The judge stood and placed both hands on the table, leaning across it as far as he could without losing his footing. He spoke in a thunderous, judicial voice. "John, I'm going to tell you one more time. We have talked about this and talked about it. Neither I nor Boats are going to stick our necks out in any way that can send us to the penitentiary. I've told you already, murder has no statute of limitations. It never runs out. I've sent too many people to jail to wind up there with them." The judge walked over to the coffeepot next to Boats and poured a cup of coffee. Judge and Boats stood shoulder to shoulder, looking at the remaining members of the Combine.

"Hell, Judge, I can think of several transactions you have been in that would send you to the pen," Leon said, staring at the pair from under his eyebrows.

"No, I think not, John," Watkins replied. "Twelve years ago, when you, Coy, and Leon put Boats and me out on a limb with that land swindle over in Arkansas, we decided to pull out. Think back—even though we have sat in all Combine meetings and continue to hold shares of Tishomingo Enterprises, our names no longer appear anywhere on any business dealings." The three seated members of the Combine exchanged looks of surprise.

"Your companies have still been in on all the transactions," Coy quipped as he pushed his chair back against the wall, striking it hard enough to cause the Frederic Remington on the wall to bounce.

Boats said, "That's true, John, but nowhere will you find either one of us listed as owners or partners. We are telling you this for one reason—we want you to know that from now on, if anything happens, you three will be on the hook!" Boats's arms were crossed, and he held his coffee in his right hand. He took a long drink, keeping his gaze on the three stooges at the table.

"Then you're telling me that you no longer want to participate in any of our business deals," John said defiantly.

The judge stood up straight and stared directly at John. "Don't be cute, John. Boats and I will still tell you when we don't want our cut. We are telling you that we are no longer going to shield any of you. Instead of taking it slow and easy, a little at a time like we have done for the last thirty years, power and greed have corrupted you. No one is above the law, boys. We have gone along with the petty stuff, but we haven't committed any major crimes that would entail serious jail time. And we haven't been involved in anything illegal since Cletus Hathaway's imprisonment."

"How about this Johnston plant deal? It ain't exactly above board!" Coy said snarkily.

Boats spoke for the both of them. "If you're asking whether we're still in, we will let you know. Bye, boys." Boats walked out of the boardroom, followed by the judge.

When the pair was out on the sidewalk, Boats turned and asked, "Think they'll try anything?"

"We both know there's not a brain between the three of them. They will talk about it for hours, and then they will let money overrule common sense. But there's not a brave bone in any one of their bodies. No, I don't think they will be a problem."

"How about this Johnston deal? You going to pull out?"

The judge looked over at Boats as they approached the courthouse, where they had parked. "I think so. You know, Boats, I'm tired. Alice and I have all the money we can ever spend. Yes, I'm pulling out. You can have my investment if you want."

Boats nodded his head in agreement and rested his hand on the roof of the judge's car. "With the new venture I have in Texas and those Bidwell leases, I think I'll pass too, Judge."

"Thought you would. I'll tell you something, I have one more year to go before the next election, and I'm not going to run again. Been talking to Alice, and she wants me to retire. I'm going to. Get out of this weather, head down to Florida, and get some sun." The judge pulled open his car door and climbed in, lowering the driver's window.

Boats leaned in. "Figured you was leaving. Now if ol' Foul Mouth can get those records and find the originals, I'd rest easier."

Judge started the car and looked at Boats. "I think he will. He is like a badger, nothing but animal intelligence and stubbornness. Once he gets his teeth into something, he won't let go."

Boats slapped the top of the car and stepped back. "See you, Judge."

"Right. I'll be out later tonight, and we'll take a look at Doc's records." The judge backed out and started to pull away but stopped as Boats made another comment.

"Make sure it's tonight. I have to be in the hospital later tomorrow." Boats stepped toward the car in the road.

"That's right. I forgot. See you tonight," the judge said, waving as he pulled away.

Chapter 24

— Blackmail Money Pays Unwanted Dividends —

Lee Bob and Adam pulled to a stop, got out, and walked up on the porch.

Larry opened the door before they could knock. Lee Bob carried the suitcase in and set it down on the coffee table. Adam gathered the papers and handed them to Althea, who handed them to Larry. "Look these over and make sure we're not signing a confession to Doc's murder," Althea said. Lee Bob hit the latches, raised the suitcase lid, and then let out a low whistle. "Son of a bitch! How much money is in there?"

"Three and one-half million, in hundreds," Adam answered.

"How in the hell did you get them to turn loose of that kind of money for this place?"

"You know the old saying, Lee Bob. It's all in knowing where the skeletons are buried." Adam turned to Larry. "Where are the records?"

"Stacked inside that bedroom there."

Adam held out a pen. "If you will sign these deeds, I'll take them back to Mr. Ross."

He watched as Althea signed the deeds, and then he picked them up and put them in his inner pocket. "They want you out of town before tomorrow afternoon, Larry."

"We plan on leaving right now," Larry replied. "All we want is already packed. Odie will be over to get what she wants, and they can have the rest."

Lee Bob walked out, carrying one of the boxes. "Grab the other one, Adam, and let's go."

Larry was standing beside the door holding the suitcase when they walked out. He closed and locked the door. "Tell John the key will be over at the store. He can pick it up in a couple of days, after Odie gets the furniture she wants."

"I'll tell him," Adam answered. "Don't forget, Larry—don't come back."

"Don't threaten me, Adam. I know all about every one of you. If Althea wants to come back and visit some of her friends, we will. You don't bother us, and we won't bother you."

Adam and Lee Bob set the boxes of records on the backseat of the police cruiser and stood watching as Larry and Althea drove out of the driveway. They climbed into the car and slowly pulled out toward the highway, watching as Larry stopped and then pulled out onto the highway. He had crossed over the yellow line and started turning toward the store when a semitruck with a trailer suddenly veered. Larry saw the truck headed toward them and violently turned the wheel away from it, but it hit them right at the driver's door. The car rolled over, and the truck hit them again, its bumper riding up over the car. Lee Bob and Adam watched as the car was completely smashed, rolled over and upright again, and finally pinned. When the truck stopped, the car was wedged under its bumper and front wheels.

Lee Bob hit the lights and pulled up alongside the wrecked car and truck. He picked up the horn and called central. "Joe Bill! Get the ambulance and wrecker out to Spender's store, code three. Also, send Adolph out with the photo equipment. Over."

"Got a bad wreck, Sheriff? Over."

"Just get them out here. Over and out."

They approached the car but could not see Larry and Althea. No part of the car was intact. Lee Bob knelt down to look through the small opening that remained where the windshield had been. Larry and Althea were both pushed over to the right side of the car. Blood was over everything in sight. Larry's left shoulder and part of his head were missing. The top of the car had smashed down on Althea's head, and judging by the angle of her head, Lee Bob knew that her neck was broken.

Adam was talking to the truck driver. Lee Bob walked back to the truck and noticed "Wilder Trucking" on its side. "You have a driver's license?" he asked the driver.

The driver reached into his hip pocket and came out with a large billfold. He handed over his driver's license. Lee Bob looked at the license and then at the driver. The picture on the license was of a clean-shaven man with short hair, while the man standing there had a large beard and long hair. "You want to tell me what happened?"

"Are they dead?" the driver asked.

"They're dead. You did a good job on them. Now tell me what happened," Lee Bob said.

"Sheriff, I'm sorry, but my instructions from my company are to not make any statement until I phone in."

"If that's the way you want it, I'll take you down and book you for manslaughter. Then you can call anyone you want to."

"Sheriff, I didn't say I wouldn't tell you what happened. Please let me call my company, and then I'll tell you what happened. Honest."

Two squad cars, Adolph in one and Zeke in the other, pulled up. They got out and approached. Passing cars were beginning to stop, and people were walking up to look at the wreck. "Zeke, get those people out of here. Keep everyone away. Adolph, I want pictures from every angle. Make sure you get several shots showing the position of the truck, showing how far it is across the line."

The coroner's wagon and wrecker pulled in. Fred, the county coroner, got out and walked up to the wreck, leaned down, and looked inside. Getting up, he said to Lee Bob and Clarence Whitlatch, the wrecker driver, "Horrible way to die."

"Every way is a horrible way to die, Digger," Lee Bob said. Turning to Clarence, he said, "You're going to need the wrecking bar to get them out."

"I'll get right on it."

Lee Bob walked back over to Adam and the driver. "You decided to talk?"

"I'm sorry, Sheriff, but in talking to the district attorney here, I think I should have an attorney present before I make any statements. However, if you will let me go up to that store and call my company, I'll give you a statement."

"Oh, all right. Adam, take my car and take him up to the store." He turned and walked back over to where Clarence was prying the steel off of the passenger side.

"Boy, this is a mess," he said.

Clarence gave a large grunt as he pulled on the wrecking bar and the door came loose, hanging at the lower hinge. Lee Bob stepped over and bent down. Larry and Althea were still sitting there, all slumped over. The suitcase he was looking for was on the floorboard under Althea's feet. He leaned in and tried to slide it out. He had to reach in and move Althea's legs off of it, twisting one leg sideways to get the case out. It was covered with blood. He stepped back and called to Adolph to come over and take his pictures, and then he walked over and set the case in the back of Adolph's car.

He stood there watching as Adolph and Digger attempted to extricate the bodies. A car screeched to a stop, and when he turned around, he saw Adam rushing toward him. "He drove away, Lee Bob!"

"Who drove away?"

"The truck driver! He drove away."

"How in the hell could he drive away?"

"We got up to the store, and he got out and told me he had to go into the store to get some change for a long-distance call. I stood at the front door and waited for him. When he didn't come out, I went in. He had walked right on through the store, went out the back door, and got into a car and drove off."

"Did you get the make and model?" Lee Bob asked.

"No, I never saw it. Odie said he parked it there this morning."

"Did you ask her about it?"

"She said it was just a car—blue or green, she didn't know. They had been stocking shelves."

"Adolph, come here. Get up to Spender's store. Find out what kind of car that truck driver had—the color, make, two-door sedan, or what—and then put out an all-points for it. Before you leave, put that suitcase in the back of my car."

Lee Bob turned to Adam. "You're not that stupid, Adam. I began to smell a rat when they sent you and me out to do their dirty work together. I ain't never needed a fuckin' nurse maid before."

"I don't know what you mean."

"You trying to tell me that you don't know this is murder?"

"You mean …?" Adam stammered.

"Hell, yes, *I mean*. They goddamned sure won't talk now, and John has his deeds all signed. Everything is wrapped up nice and neat, or so they think."

He turned and watched as Digger and Clarence packed Larry's and Althea's bodies and put them in the coroner's station wagon. He told Fred, "Let me know when you're through with them, Digger."

"Any family members you want me to contact, Lee Bob?"

"Better check with Odie at the store. She would know." He watched as Digger pulled out, and then he went over and helped Clarence hook up the wrecker.

Clarence told him, "Better back that truck back a little bit, Lee Bob. Get the weight off the car."

Lee Bob called over to Zeke. "Get in there and back this thing up, and then take it on out to Boats's yard and park it. I'll pick you up there."

As Lee Bob and Adam climbed into his cruiser, Lee Bob heard Adolph calling over the horn. "Joe Bill, put this out on all-points: 1962 or 63 light green Chevrolet Camaro, has Texas plates, license number unknown. Driven by a bearded man, twenty-eight to thirty-five years old, long brown hair. Camaro has a dented right front fender. Man wanted for manslaughter by sheriff's office in Johnston County. Got it?"

Joe Bill came on right away.

Lee Bob picked up the microphone and cut in, saying, "Joe Bill, Sheriff here. Make that wanted for murder. Also, man may be armed and should be considered extremely dangerous."

"Right, Sheriff. I'll send it right out."

He pulled out to go pick up Zeke. Adam said, "That's pretty strong, ain't it? You don't have any proof."

"Look, you can play their fuckin' game if you want to. I've gone along with some pretty raw stuff, but murder? No way in hell!"

"Just a minute. I don't know where you get off talking to me like that." Adam started to say something else when Lee Bob pulled into Boats's truck yard and picked up Zeke. They took him back to the cruiser and dropped him off, and Adam took up where he had left off. "I had no idea this was going to happen, and I don't like it any better than you do, but I don't see as there is too much we can do about it if the judge is in on it."

Lee Bob pulled up in front of the jail and parked. He turned to Adam and stuck his finger in Adam's chest. "There might not be anything *you* can do about it, but I sure as hell can and intend to. When you see John Ross, you tell him for me that if I find out he or any of his business partners are involved in any way, they're going to jail."

"I can't tell him that. What if the judge and Boats are involved?" He climbed out of the car and said, "If you want to give me those boxes of records and the money, I'll take them back to John."

"No, I don't think you will, Adam. I'm keeping them as evidence."

"You can't keep those around here. If anybody in your department ever got a hold of them, we would be ruined. You'd better think this over. They will make more trouble than you can handle."

"You would be surprised at what I can handle. This time they have gone too far."

"Man, Lee Bob, they are going to be mad as hell."

"That's their fuckin' problem. Catching a couple of murderers is mine right now." His radio snapped on. "Tishomingo number one, Officer Blankenship here. Am in pursuit of your green Camaro. He is heading back toward Tishomingo on 99 South. Can you help me out? He was headed toward Ada but turned around and reversed direction when I hit my lights. Pontotoc's sheriff is tied up and can't help out."

Lee Bob grabbed the CB. "Joe Bill, get a roadblock set up north of the Harden City cutoff. Tell them to take no chances. Get all men on duty and headed that way. Call Lester over to Ada's sheriff office and tell him what's going on. I'm on my way. Tell 'em to fall in behind Blankenship for backup when they can. Over."

"Right, Sheriff."

Lee Bob backed out, hit his lights and siren, and headed out of town. The radio came back on. "Tishomingo number one, still in pursuit. Still heading south on 99 south of Ada. We're doing over a hundred. Have picked up another state officer. We're both right behind him. Should be past E162 in about two minutes."

Lee Bob picked up the horn. "Tish one to Officer Blankenship. I am only about two minutes from Harden City turnoff. Will set up roadblock. Be careful with him. He is dangerous. Over."

"Roger, Tish one. We'll watch him."

Lee Bob pulled up and stopped. Adolph, Zeke, and Lester from Ada had all three squad cars parked across the road. The brown-and-white cruisers were overlapped so that nothing could get through. The road was paralleled by a deep irrigation ditch on one side and railroad tracks on the other, which were about twelve feet above the road. The officers were standing behind the squad cars just north of the intersection so they could prevent the oncoming vehicle from getting past. Lee Bob took his shotgun out of its rack and slid the chamber back to make sure it was loaded. Walking toward the other officers, he told them, "Get your shotguns. I don't want to take any chances with him."

They all scurried to get them. Zeke yelled, "Here he comes!"

They stood there watching as the car came at them at about a hundred miles an hour.

Lee Bob said, "If he don't stop or tries to get past us, open fire. Shoot to kill. That's an order."

All four crouched behind the cars as the suspect kept coming straight for them. As he neared, he slowed a fraction and tried to go right, off the road and around the roadblock.

As he hit his brakes and his car swung sideways toward them, Lee Bob hollered, "Fire!"

Four shotguns cut loose their double-ought buckshot. The side of the car seemed to explode. The glass disappeared inside the car. The officers got a glance at the driver, with blood streaming from his face, as he hit the incline up to the railroad tracks running alongside the road. The front end of the car dug into the incline, and it went end over end across the railroad track and out of sight. The two state officers who had been following the suspect pulled to a stop and ran up over the tracks to the car. The driver was lying slumped over sideways in the car when they got there, the driver's door completely torn off.

Lee Bob told them, "Get him out."

"Don't you want to see if he's alive first, Sheriff?" Lester asked.

"Not really. Get him out."

Adolph and Lester reached in and pulled the suspect out feet first. The first thought that struck Lee Bob was, *Good God, it's not the same man*. The man lying there didn't have a beard; he was clean-shaven. His hair was also shorter. The eyes, though, were the same. Lee Bob had walked around to the car and looked inside when the two state troopers walked up. One of them was Purvis Jarvis.

"Hello, Lee Bob. This Doc's murderer?"

"Could be, Purvis. Haven't had time to check it out yet. Why?" Lee Bob slid in the loose sand on the side of the hill.

"The car was stolen in Ada last night. You know who this is?" Purvis inquired.

Lee Bob leaned over and stared at the man's face. "He looks familiar, but I can't place him."

"Bobby Cody from over in Arkansas. Been wanted for the last ten months for those four killings at Fort Smith. Looks like you got him!"

"Yeah, well, he just killed two more over in Tish this morning."

"Who did he kill over there?"

"Larry and Althea Chubb."

"When you said two people, I figured it must have been them." Purvis rested his left hand on the car and took the measure of Lee Bob.

"Why do you say that?"

"Larry called me last night," Purvis said. "I was supposed to meet him in Ada at one this afternoon."

Lee Bob was surprised but tried to hide it. "Do you know what for?"

Purvis pretended to be inspecting the car, looking around inside, and said, "He didn't mention. He had some records that he wanted to turn over to me. Said it was too complicated to tell me over the phone."

Purvis continued, "By the way, Cody there threw some things out of his car by Oak Tree Corner on the west side. Looked like a wig and something else. He was going so fast I couldn't hardly tell."

Lee Bob barked over the hood of the Camaro, "Joe Bill, you and Zeke take a squad car and see if you can find it."

Trooper Blankenship crawled into the car to check Cody's pulse and then said, "Captain, this man is still alive."

Lee Bob hollered to Joe Bill again as he was headed to his cruiser. "Get on the horn and get an ambulance out here right away."

Jarvis and Lee Bob knelt down beside Cody in the sand. His eyes were open and darting back and forth. They settled on Lee Bob.

"What were you doing out at the accident scene this morning, Sheriff?" His voice was garbled and gravelly. He labored to speak.

"Just driving by, Cody. Why did you kill the Chubbs?"

"No reason, Sheriff. Just seemed like the right thing to do." Blood bubbled up in his mouth, and his eyes closed.

Lee Bob felt for a pulse. It was faint and slow. "Think we ought to move him, Purvis?"

"Not unless you want to finish killing him, I wouldn't. You positive it was murder?"

"Pretty sure. From the way the accident occurred, it couldn't have been anything else."

"Well, I have to be going. See you later."

Lee Bob told Adolph, "I have to go back into town. I'll call for a wrecker and have them bring someone to drive one of the squad cars back into town if the boys aren't back from picking up that stuff. You ride into the hospital with Cody. I don't want him alone for a minute. If he gets out of surgery all right, I want an officer in his room at all times—not in the hall, in his room. Got it?"

"Yes sir, Sheriff. I'll take care of it."

Lee Bob pulled into the wrecking yard in Durant. Clarence came out to meet him.

"Where did you put the Chubbs' car?" Lee Bob asked.

"Parked it down at the end of the impound, Sheriff. Want me to show you?"

"No, that's fine. You go on about your business. I just want to check and see what's in it."

"Captain Jarvis is out there looking at it right now."

Lee Bob quickly drove to the back of the lot. Purvis was leaning in from the left side of the car. Lee Bob hopped out, slammed the car door, and walked over. "Purvis, what you doing here?"

Purvis straightened up. "I thought that since Chubb had talked about some records, they might have been in his car."

Lee Bob walked up and stood between Purvis and the car. "You know better than this, Purvis. I told you it was a murder, and even if you did find them, you would have to turn them over to me."

Purvis stepped back. "True, but I could have copied some information off them. Let's open the trunk and see if they're in there." Purvis walked around to the trunk.

Lee Bob followed him around and then hopped up and sat on the trunk. "Not this time, Purvis. If I think there is anything to do with the state police, I will let you know. Right now, you're in my jurisdiction and I want you the fuck out."

"I know you don't like me, Lee Bob, but we are still cops looking for the same thing." Purvis backed up a bit.

"Could be that I don't like you in my county. So get lost."

"Fine, if that's the way you want it. By the way, there's a package of hundred-dollar bills sticking out from under the back of the front seat. That's what I was reaching for when you walked up." Purvis walked back to his cruiser.

"Thank you. Now if you will excuse me, I have work to do." He watched as Purvis drove off. Lee Bob jumped down off the trunk and walked around to the side of the car. He took the keys from the ignition and opened up the trunk. Sitting there was the same type of box the other records had been in. He opened the flap, and inside were manila folders. He picked up the box and set it on the backseat of his cruiser with the other two boxes.

He slowly drove out of the impound lot, started toward his office, and then thought better of it. He turned and drove out to his ranch instead. He took one of the boxes and the suitcase and walked into the house. He took them down into the basement and put them in a large footlocker he had there. Before putting the suitcase away, he took the package of money he had pulled from under the seat. He removed ten one hundred-dollar bills, put the rest into the suitcase, and put it away. He relocked the footlocker and walked back upstairs, locked the basement door, relocked the front door, got back into his car, and drove to the office.

He had no sooner entered his office than the wooden window panel slid up, startling him. Junior stuck his head in. "Sheriff, John Ross has called you three times in the last hour."

"Well, call him back and tell him I'm in my office and that if he wants to see me to come on over."

"Right, will do, Chief."

Without thinking, Lee Bob open-hand slapped Junior alongside his left cheek. Junior's glasses flew off and hit the floor, and his head bounced off the side of the window. Junior quickly pulled his head back through the window. Lee Bob picked up his glasses, tossed them through the window, and slammed it shut.

About five minutes later, his phone rang. He picked up. "Sheriff Whetzel."

"Lee Bob," John said, "why haven't you brought that money down to my bank?"

"If you want to talk to me, Ross, you get your ass down here and don't call me on the phone again." He slammed the phone down.

He started filling out the report on Larry and Althea Chubb. Finishing up, he realized that he was hungry, so he locked his desk and told Junior he was going home for lunch.

"Fine, Sheriff. See you later."

Lee Bob smiled to himself as he walked out. He had wanted to slap Junior for the eight years he had been there. He had heard that revenge never felt as good as you figured it would. He thought, *Well, that's a fuckin' myth.* As he opened his car door, he heard his name called. Turning, he saw John Ross and Judge Watkins approaching. John's face looked like an overripe tomato. His eyes squinted and his mouth formed a grimace.

Judge Watkins asked, "Can we go in and have a talk, Lee Bob?"

"Not right now, Judge. I'm hungry, and I'm going home to eat."

"See there, Judge? I told you," said John.

Lee Bob said, "Shut up, Ross, or I'll kick your ass all over Johnston County."

"There's no reason for that, Lee Bob," the judge said.

"You hear about the Chubbs, Judge?"

"No, just got back into town from Odell."

"Well, they were murdered this morning. I'm not sure if you are tied up in it or not, but I know this piece of shit is. Now I'm going home for lunch. If you want to talk to me, I will be back in a couple of hours." He got into his car and drove off.

Judge Watkins whirled on John Ross. "Okay, John, talk!"

John stumbled backward, sputtering. "What do you mean, *talk*? I didn't have a damn thing to do with the Chubbs' death. I understand a semitruck ran over and killed them. But one thing I do want is my money back, and I intend to get it."

The judge stood with his hands on his hips. "Kind of convenient, wasn't it, John?"

"Why should I care, Judge? They was just a couple of blackmailers." John backed up under the judge's glare and caught his heel on a crack in the concrete. He fell on his ass.

The judge walked up and stood over him. "They were a couple of human beings, and they would still be alive if we hadn't interfered in their lives."

"I swear, if I didn't know you better, Judge, that would sound like remorse." John looked up at the judge, still sitting on the concrete.

"Remorse, yes, and stupidity. For years, Boats and I have been afraid this would happen." He crossed his arms in disgust, looking at the pathetic man on the sidewalk.

"That sounds funny coming from you. Tell me, Judge, what is the difference between the Chubbs' death and that of Cletus Hathaway?" John rolled to his knees and stood up, brushing the dirt from his knees and ass.

"I won't argue the difference with you, John. If you can't tell, then my explaining it wouldn't do any good."

John pointed his finger at the judge. "You're a hypocrite, Judge, a real bleeding heart. Well, maybe you can stand the loss of seven hundred and fifty thousand, but I won't."

The judge stepped forward and held his fist under John's nose. "My morals are none of your business. This money you keep talking about—what money is it?"

"The three and a half million we paid the Chubbs for their property," John said.

"You are incredible. That belongs to their estate."

John was belligerent, shoving the judge's fist away from his face. "They don't have an estate. Neither one of them has any family that we know of, and besides, no one knows what we paid for their property except us. So why not take back the money except for a couple hundred thousand."

The judge stood his ground. "You worthless piece of shit. I've done business with you for years, John, and it's funny how I never noticed just how greedy you are."

John turned and started up the street. "Don't give me any of your moralistic bullshit, Judge. You aren't a damn bit better than we are. You might have all the money you want, but we don't. You see, Judge, after you and Boats left last night, someone came into the bank right before closing time and left a package for me. You have any idea what was in it?"

The judge grabbed him by the shoulder and spun him around. "From the way you're acting, I would assume it was Doc's folders on both of us."

"That's right, and I'm sure you don't want a lot of this stuff to get out."

"You're an asshole, John. Don't ever get the idea in that pea brain of yours that either Boats or I will stand still for any type of blackmail." The judge was poking John in the chest with his finger.

"With the records I have, you will stand for whatever we want." John was mad and spitting his words.

"No, that's where you're wrong. I have a pretty good notion what Doc had on us." The judge shoved him in the chest, causing John to stumble backward into a parking meter, catching him in the rib cage.

"We can ruin you, Judge, more so than Boats. All you have to do is resign." John was breathless.

The judge stepped toward him, ready to punch John in the face but thought better of it. "You can kiss my judicial ass, John." And with that, the judge spun around, walked past Junior and into Lee Bob's office, and slammed the door. He picked up the phone and dialed Lee Bob's home. "Can you meet me at Boats's truck yard?"

"I can, but you want to tell me what the hell for?"

"Not over the phone. All I can say is, it will not interfere in any way with your investigation of what happened this morning." The judge's voice was stern and controlled.

"How soon you want me out there?" Lee Bob was annoyed.

"As soon as possible. Boats has to be in the hospital later this afternoon."

"I'll be out as soon as I can."

"Thank you, Sheriff." The judge dialed Boats and filled him in on the events with John. They agreed to meet with the sheriff and lay things out.

Boats met him as he was pulling into the Nichols salvage yard. Boats stepped out of the car as Pike, his driver, opened the door. "Wait here, Pike. We won't be long."

Boats walked over to the judge and stretched out his hand. "Judge, how are you?"

"Fine, Boats. You hear what happened this morning?" The two men walked toward the yard foreman's shack and stepped inside. The potbellied stove had a fire burning, and the small one-room building smelled of mesquite and grease. Boats told the foreman to give them the office. He grabbed his coat and went out into the yard.

Boats said, "My yard foreman called me when they brought the truck in to store it. You thinking John and company had it done?" Boats pulled an old cane chair next to the stove.

"I'm positive they did," the judge said. He proceeded to tell him about his meeting with John. "He has copies of Doc's folders on both of us." Judge Watkins sat at the desk after pulling the chair out and spinning it to face Boats.

"I could see that coming, Judge. It shouldn't come as a surprise to you." Boats opened the door to the potbellied stove and threw in another chunk of mesquite.

The judge leaned in toward his old friend. "No, it doesn't, but when a birdbrain like John tells me I am to resign, the world is in a sorry mess."

Boats closed the stove and turned to the judge. "You know, of course, that Lee Bob caught the killer."

"No, I been in court since I saw you this morning. I knew nothing about this till about an hour ago."

Boats sat back, tilting the cane chair on two legs. "It's going to be a mess, Judge, regardless of what happens."

The judge was agitated. "Lee Bob is on his way out here right now. I wanted to tell you that he will not be interfered with by me or my office in any way."

Boats dropped all four legs of the chair to the floor. "Fine by me, Judge. You surely don't think I would be stupid enough to get tied up in a murder?"

The judge's faced softened a bit. "We been friends since grade school. There would never have been a Judge Watkins if not for you. I owe you my law degree and all the money I've made over the years, but if you are tied up in this, I can't shield you."

Boats stood and turned his backside to the stove. "Wouldn't ask you to, Judge. If John and them were dumb enough to pull this, then they deserve everything they get." Boats could see the cruiser coming through the entrance.

Lee Bob pushed the door open, walked across the room, and pulled down a folding chair that was leaning against the wall and unfolded it. He looked at Boats and Judge Watkins.

"Gentlemen, what can I do for you?"

Boats said, "Judge."

The sheriff was surly. "All right, boys, I agreed to come out here against my better judgment. Now what do you want?"

"To talk to you about the Chubbs' deaths. Neither Boats nor I had anything to do with their deaths." The three men were only a few feet apart in a half circle around the stove. The judge was looking Lee Bob in the eyes, and the sheriff started to interrupt. "Hold it," the judge said. "Let me finish. We were in on the scheme to steal their property, which you already know. When that failed, we each put up seven hundred and fifty thousand dollars to purchase his land. Does that sound like someone who wanted to kill him?"

"Why not, if you figured after he was dead you would get it back?"

Boats said, "Lee Bob, I am worth over six hundred million dollars. The judge is, I believe, worth about twenty-five million."

"Forty, Boats. I'm worth forty million."

"Do you think we would worry about three quarters of a million?" Boats stood and shook the coffeepot steaming on the potbellied stove. It was full.

Lee Bob said, "Put that way, I guess it doesn't make sense. The reason I was a little late getting here, there was a tape delivered to my home and left on the porch. I played it, and it is a meeting between John, Coy, Adam, Leon, and Seth. I guess you know what they were discussing."

Boats rummaged in the cupboard to see if there was a coffee cup there. He said, "That should convince you that we weren't involved." He found a sleeve of Styrofoam cups.

"No, your names were mentioned, and they said you had always gone along with them before. Being as you was out of town, I wasn't sure." The sheriff was watching Boats.

"You mean Adam and Seth were present when the Chubbs' murder was being discussed?" the judge asked. Boats handed each of the other two men a Styrofoam cup and poured them some coffee.

"They were there and took part in setting it up. By the way, Judge, I didn't know you were resigning." The sheriff looked at Judge Watkins.

"I'm not. Who the hell told you that?"

"From what they said, I assumed it was all set. John said he had it all arranged for Adam to take your place and Seth to replace Adam." The sheriff took a drink of coffee. "Got any sugar there, Boats?"

Boats rummaged in the cupboard again, pulled out a cardboard sugar box with an aluminum spout, and handed it to Lee Bob. "Sorry, no spoon."

Lee Bob stood up and took a pencil from the desk next to the judge, and then he sat back down, stirring his newly sugared coffee.

"Would it be possible for me to listen to that tape?" the judge asked.

"Not till my investigation is complete. You know I have the killer?"

"Boats just told me you did. Have you questioned him yet?"

"No, he's in pretty bad shape. Last time I checked, he was still in the operating room. Judge, would that tape be admissible in court?" The sheriff sampled the coffee, poured another shot of sugar in, and stirred with the pencil.

"As it stands now, no, it wouldn't. You would have to show how it was obtained, who taped it, the time and date it was recorded, and where it was taped at."

"I didn't think it would be. What about if I get a confession from Cody and could tie it in?"

"It's very doubtful. If it came up in my court, I'd throw it out. Sorry, Sheriff."

"That's okay, Judge. You didn't make the law, just like I didn't. We just enforce it, right?"

"That's right. Boats and I wanted you to know that we will help in any way we can."

The sheriff held his Styrofoam cup in front of him between his knees. He continued to stare at it and said, "There is one thing I want both of you to know. For years now, I have done the dirty work for all of you. Bent a law here and put a little pressure there—anything you wanted, within reason, I did it."

Boats looked at the sheriff. "You have been paid pretty well for it, Sheriff. You've been getting twenty-five thousand extra a year for quite a while."

"I know that, and I am thankful for it. However, I wanted to tell you that the money I picked up from the Chubbs today, I'm keeping."

"Just like that?" the judge said incredulously.

"That's it, Judge. If this whole thing is going to come down around our ears, I'm not coming out of jail with nothing. You know what's going to happen if I arrest John Ross."

"Boats and I both agree. We are not about to suborn murder, and the money will not hurt us. As far as I'm concerned, you can have it." The judge stood, moved over to the yardman's desk, and extended his empty cup to Boats for a refill.

The sheriff turned to Boats. "What about you? You care about the money?"

"Lee Bob, anyone who says they don't care about a large amount of money as we're talking about is either crazy or a liar. However, I believe you have earned it. Not that I care anymore, but did you get those records of Doc's?"

The sheriff nodded his head. "They're out in the backseat of my car. I found out one thing today. Larry had three copies made and intended to hand the third copy over to Purvis Jarvis this afternoon."

"You warned us this morning about that. Do you think he had any more than what you've found?" Boats asked.

"There is no way of knowing, but I doubt it."

"You said you had two of the boxes. What happened to the third one?" the judge asked.

"I kept that too. I want to go over them before I arrest those five for murder. I want to know what Doc had on me so I won't have any surprises."

"Well, as an attorney and judge, I advise you not to let anyone steamroll you, even if they file charges against you. Don't resign your office. The only way they can get you out is to have the governor remove you, and without a conviction that will be hard to get done." The judge was sincere and emphatic.

"Thanks, Judge. If I get a confession out of Cody, that should give me enough evidence to arrest them."

"One thing," the judge added. "It's quasi legal, but if you can convince Cody that he is going to die and get him to sign a deathbed confession, then even if he recovers it's admissible in court." The judge sat down after Boats filled his cup.

"You mean it will carry more weight that way?"

"It sure will."

"Thanks again, Judge. I'm sorry if you and Boats get drug into this, but I won't hide a murder." The sheriff stood to leave. Boats opened the shack's door.

"We understand. Boats and I are grown men. We can handle our share."

"Well, I have to get back to the hospital and check on Cody. I want to be there if he comes out of it." The sheriff threw his cup at the trash can and missed. He left anyway.

The other two sat there watching Lee Bob drive out of the yard. "Well, Judge," Boats said, "where do we stand if they arrest the DA?"

"To be perfectly honest with you, I don't know. You can believe that whoever is appointed DA is going to want to drag as many of us down as he can. And with my being a circuit court judge, I would be a feather in his cap if he could get me convicted."

"What kinds of charges do you think they might throw at us?"

"Well, conspiracy to commit murder would be one. Violating Larry's and Althea's civil rights—that would be federal. There are several they could hit us with."

"We could deny any involvement. It would be our word against theirs."

"True, but the whole town knows about us. Hell, they have called us the Combine for years."

"That's true. Hindsight is real good. Watty, we should have pulled out after that Arkansas deal, like we talked about." Boats put his feet up on the woodpile and leaned back in the chair.

"Funny you should call me that. I haven't heard my nickname in twenty years."

"You never did like it, and who wants to get on the wrong side of a judge?" Boats and the judge laughed.

"Guess you're right, Boats. Well, I guess I'll get out of here and back to the office."

As they walked out of the shack, rain was falling, making the trek to the car a muddy slog. Sitting on the backseat of the judge's car were the two boxes. "You want one of these, Boats?"

"I haven't any use for them. I had already made up my mind to pull out this morning. He didn't have anything on me, anyway, 'cept for Cletus Hathaway, and that was over fifteen years ago. 'Course, every once in a while he would send a picture of me and one of the call girls I had up from Dallas. Guess he wanted me to know he was keeping his eye on me."

"He did the same thing to me. It must have cost him a fortune to get those pictures, because the only time I stepped out was at the judicial convention I go to every year. Strange thing, I always liked him. He was a nice old man before Jewell died." The two old friends stood talking in the rain, drawn closer by the realization that they were both going down when the shit hit the fan.

"Yes, but death does strange things to all of us," the judge continued. "I don't know what I would do without Alice."

"I've always felt you was lucky to get her, Judge. Guess you know I've been in love with her for years."

The judge laughed. "Yes, we both knew. I believe that's the reason we've been such good friends for all these years. Never once in all these years have you done anything to hurt either one of us. I've got to get back to my office. Alice told me to tell you she prayed for you and hopes everything works out all right." The judge got in his car and prepared to leave.

"Thanks, Judge. Give her a kiss for me. And Watty, I'd tell her about what's coming. Don't let it come as a complete shock." Boats was leaning against the judge's car.

"You're right, of course. It will be the toughest thing I've ever done, but I'll tell her tonight. Bye, Boats."

"What are you going to do with the boxes?"

"Throw them in the courthouse incinerator."

"Going to read them first?" Boats asked.

"No. Being a judge, I've lived around misery all my life. I don't want to know. I've got enough on my conscience already. See you." The judge rolled up his window and pulled out.

"Bye, Judge. Be careful."

Pike opened the door to Boats's car, and Boats crawled in. Pike got behind the wheel, and they were off to the airport and then to Dallas for Boats's surgery.

Chapter 25

The Storm Begins; Boats Sinks

Mar and I really had fun at the dance. Between all the kids coming up and slapping me on the back over the game and our dancing, we had never felt as close as we did on the way home. When we got home, we slipped out to the barn and climbed into the loft for a roll in the hay. The sun was peeking through the clapboards when we snuck back into the house and went to bed.

I came awake with Buck shaking my shoulder. Sitting up, I asked, "Something wrong?"

"Not unless you want to sleep all day, there isn't."

Stretching and yawning, I asked, "What time is it?"

"Almost noon," Buck answered. "Thought you might like to ride out to the oil rigs with me. They came in yesterday afternoon."

"Sure. Let me get dressed and get some coffee, and I'll be ready."

"Fine. I'll be in the kitchen. By the way, what time you get in last night?"

"Wasn't last night. We got in at daybreak. Why?"

"No reason. Hurry up. While we're down there, we might as well move those mares."

"Be right there."

Everybody was sitting at the kitchen table when I came in. Mar was standing by the counter. I put my arm around her waist, kissed her, and said, "You sure look beautiful this morning."

"Thank you, sir. You're awful handsome yourself."

Buck said, "Come on, you two. Knock off the mush. We got to get going. By the way, either of you know about all the straw tracked in the house?"

Mar looked over at Buck. "Rosie, how can you stand a man with no romance in his soul?"

"Oh, he has his moments. Of course, lately they've been getting fewer and further between, but he does have them."

"You two ladies quit picking on me, or I'll leave you behind."

Rosie answered, "Listen to that, will you? Blackmail! Next thing you know, he'll beat us."

"I knew he was that kind of man," Mar said. "No romance and beats up on women. Next thing you know, he'll start drinking and really get mean."

"All right, you ladies keep on, but if you're not ready to go by the time I finish this coffee, we'll leave without you."

Rosie said, "Come on, Marylyn. I think he means it. We better hurry."

As we left the kitchen, the phone rang and Rosie answered it. "It's for you, Tommy."

I picked up the phone. "Hello?"

"Is this Thomas Gurley?"

"Yes, it is. Who's calling?"

"This is Judge Watkins up in Johnston County."

"Yes, Judge, what can I do for you?"

"I hate to be the one to tell you this, but your uncle passed away on the operating table this morning. I think he knew he wasn't going to make it when he was here last weekend. Sorry, son. Is there anything I can do?"

"No, sir. Thank you. We will take care of things from here. That was Parkland Hospital in Dallas, wasn't it?"

"Yes, they called about fifteen minutes ago. My wife and I are very sorry."

"Thank you, Judge. Thank you for calling." I hung up the phone.

Rocky and Buck were sitting there talking. I could hear the sound of the cartoons coming from the kids' room. I got my coffee cup, refilled it, and sat down at the table. "Buck, think you could get us a flight up to Dallas this morning?"

A concerned look came over his face. "Something happen to Boats, son?"

"He died on the operating table."

"Damn. I wonder what's going to happen next. Who was it that called?"

"Judge Watkins from Tish."

"Better get on the phone. Rocky, would you take care of the kids while we're gone?"

"Sure, Buck. Be glad to. Don't worry about them."

I got up and said, "Better tell the girls while you're calling the airport." Slowly I walked back toward the bedrooms. As I neared the bathroom, I saw that both women were standing in front of the mirror, laughing and putting on their makeup.

Mar looked up. "What's wrong, Tommy?"

"I've got some bad news, honey."

"What is it?"

"Uncle Boats died this morning." For some reason, when I saw the tears starting down her cheeks, I felt my eyes burning, and the tears started streaming down my cheeks onto my shirt.

Both girls came over and put their arms around me, saying soothing words. My body started shaking, and loud sobs came one after another.

Sissy and Andy came running into the bathroom. Both stopped and looked at us, and then they both started crying.

Rosie knelt down and took them in her arms. She shooshed them and then led them out.

Sobs racked me for several minutes. After I quieted down, I told Mar, "I never really liked him, you know."

"I know, honey, but he was your uncle."

"He knew when he was down here that he was going to die."

"How did you ever get an idea like that?"

"Just a feeling. He was the nicest I had ever saw him. I really think he was sorry that he and I didn't get along."

"Believe that, Tommy. Everyone wants to be loved by someone. He seemed real nice to me."

"Now I'm like you, Mar. I don't have any family either."

"We have each other, Tommy, and Buck, Rosie, Rocky, and the kids. You don't have to be blood relations to be family."

"I know. They are the only family we have now."

Buck appeared in the doorway. "There's no plane till morning. You want to drive?"

"It would take too long. Call them back and charter us a plane."

"Sure, son. We'll need a car too. I'll see if they can get us one."

As Buck started to leave, I said, "Didn't you tell me earlier this week that we received Boats's will?"

"Yeah, we did, but we don't have to worry about that right now."

"I'm not thinking about that part of it. Only when Boats was here, he told me he didn't trust those people up there. Could you call Royal and Stuck and tell them I'd like to meet with them before we leave?"

"Sure, Tommy, but it could wait until later."

"No, you and my papa both taught me you don't run away from things."

"Okay, son. I'll take care of it."

"Why did you do that, Tommy?" Mar asked. "He isn't even cold yet, and you're worried about his money."

"It isn't his money, Mar, believe me. It's the way Boats talked while he was here. Something is wrong. I just feel it. You know I've never worried about money."

"I never thought you did, but it hurt Buck when you talked like that."

"I'll fix it with him, honey. Just don't think I'm worried about it just for the money."

"I'm sorry I said that."

"No, never be sorry for something like that, honey. We will never argue as long as we're honest with each other."

As we went into the living room, Buck was hanging up the phone. "The plane will be ready in an hour and a half, son. You still want me to call the attorneys?"

Mar and I walked over and sat down on the sofa next to Rosie. "Where are the kids?" I asked.

"I sent them back to their rooms," Rosie answered.

Looking up at Buck, I said, "Come over and sit down for a minute. I want to explain something to you."

"You don't owe me anything, Tommy."

"Yes, I do. I saw the way you looked at me when I mentioned the attorneys. Guess I should have talked to you after Boats was here. Please sit down. You have to understand. It might sound silly, but I loved Boats. I didn't like him, but I did love him. Does that make sense?"

"In a way, it does, son."

"Anyway, he didn't come right out and say he was in trouble, but I got that impression. One thing he did say was that he didn't trust the people he was in business with. I want you to take that will to the attorneys to find out whether, if we have trouble up there, we will have the authority to do something about it. Am I making any sense?"

"You are to me. I'm glad you told me. Sorry if I had some bad thoughts about you. Honey, why don't you fix the kids some breakfast and me a snack while I'm on the phone?"

Rocky told Rosie, "I'll get the food, daughter. You kids had better go pack some bags. There isn't that much time. If things are as I suspect, Boats knew trouble was brewing, and we need to get to Dallas and figure out what it was."

Mar came back in while I was folding my shirts to put into the suitcase. "For heaven's sake, Tommy, get out of the way and let me pack those. They will be so wrinkled you can't wear them." She gently pushed me aside and started folding my clothes.

Standing there, I watched how smoothly she went about rearranging my clothes. I heard Buck coming, so I turned to meet him. "Got Royal and explained. He will try and get a hold of Stuck and meet us at the airport at 2:30, so we'd better hurry."

We grabbed our coats and suitcases. Rosie told the kids we were leaving and talked to Rocky. We all told him good-bye and loaded into the car for a fast trip to the airport.

Royal and Robert Stuck were standing next to Panhandle Charter's hangar when we pulled up.

I handed them the will, and Buck went into the hangar to talk to the pilot. He came right back out. "We'd better go, son. He has to be back here by nine for another charter."

I said to Royal, "Then you know what I want. We will call you first thing Monday morning."

"Fine, Tom. Bob and I will go over this carefully, and if there is any surprise in here, you will know about it. Have a good flight. Sorry about your uncle."

"Thank you. I appreciate it."

The flight was smooth and uneventful. Two hours later, we were circling the Dallas/Fort Worth airport. The pilot got clearance, and we taxied into the terminal. We unloaded our baggage and started toward the entrance. A man in a chauffeur's uniform stepped forward. "Is one of you Thomas Gurley?"

"I'm Tom Gurley."

"Mr. Gurley, I have been sent to get you. If you would, follow me." I looked at Buck, shrugged my shoulders, and started after him. He led us to a driveway where a Cadillac limousine that would seat eight people waited. He took our bags and put them in the trunk, opened the back doors, and ushered us inside. Without a word, he pulled out into the traffic.

There was a glass partition between us and the driver. Buck leaned forward and tapped the glass. The driver, without looking around, picked up a microphone and pushed a button. "You wished something, sir?"

Buck started to say something when the driver said, "Use the mike, sir, in the car door." Buck picked it up and asked the driver where we were going.

"I'm sorry, sir. I didn't realize you didn't know our destination. Mr. Stuck called while you were in flight. You are being taken to the guest suites of Belding Oil, sir, atop the Belding Building."

"Thank you."

"Thank you, sir. Also, Mr. Belding has taken the liberty of having Mr. Boats's body moved to the chapel mortuary. He hopes that will be satisfactory with you, sir?"

"Thank you. That will be fine," Buck said.

"You're very welcome, sir. May I express my sympathy about Mr. Boats. He was a fine man."

I reached over and picked up another mike. "Did you know my uncle?"

"Certainly sir, Mr. Boats used me every time he came to town. He didn't like to drive in Big D."

"Did he come down here often?"

"Oh, yes, sir, about two, three times a month."

"Do you know if it was business or pleasure?" I asked.

"I assume pleasure, sir, except for a few times when he and Mr. Belding talked business."

"Thank you. I appreciate the information."

"You're welcome again, sir." He pulled up to a tall building.

The doorman came over and opened the car door. "Mr. Hagan, if you and your party would like to take the elevator to the penthouse, I will have your bags sent up."

When the elevator doors opened, two ladies in maids' uniforms were standing there. One of them stepped toward Rosie and Marylyn. "If you ladies would like to freshen up, please follow me." The other lady said, "My name is Martha. May I show you around?"

Buck said, "Martha, I would like to have a very cold beer, which I haven't had in a very long time."

"Certainly, Mr. Hagan. Right over here to the bar. What kind would you like? We have all major brands, plus six imports, sir."

"A Coors will be fine. Tommy, you want something to drink?"

"Sure," I said. "Give me the same as you."

"Didn't know you drank beer."

"Don't much. Only had it about four times before. 'Sides, I thought you gave up beer at Rosie's insistence."

"She didn't insist, just strongly suggested. But I still have 'em on special occasions and dinner out with Rosie."

He paused. "Ever been drunk on beer?" Buck asked me directly.

"No, I don't like it that much. First time I drank it, I got a little buzz on, but Sanchez sobered me up in a hurry."

"A beer is good for you once in a while as long as you don't overdo it."

"I know. Say, did you see the view from this window? You can see the whole city."

"Sure is pretty, isn't it?"

"Powerful would be more like it."

"How do you mean?"

"Boats must have been a more important man than I thought he was."

"He was a big man in the oil business, son. There are very few oil fields in the nine southwestern states that he didn't have a stake in one way or the other. Don't be surprised to see some governors, senators, and high-powered people at his funeral."

"I guess it never entered my head," I said.

"You'd better start thinking about it. Right now, you're one of the richest sixteen-year-old boys in the world."

"You mean he was that big?"

"Moneywise, he was as big as anyone in this area—bigger than most."

"Can we handle it, Buck?"

"I don't see no reason why not. I don't know much about investments, but I know the oil business. I assume he had a brokerage to handle most of his business."

"Guess so. I'm awful tired. Think I could lay down for a while?"

"Sure. Martha, would you show Mr. Gurley to his room?" Buck said.

"Certainly, sir. Please follow me."

I heard Rosie and Mar admiring the view as I drifted off to sleep.

The movement of the bed half woke me. Mar's perfume filled my senses, and I felt her fingers gently stroke my face. I slowly opened my eyes. Her face was right above mine. I slowly pulled her down to me. Her mouth opened as it met mine, and we sank into a deep embrace. Mar's mouth was immediately warm. I could feel the heat beginning to build as my pants grew beneath my zipper.

She gently pushed herself away. "Not now, honey. There's a Mr. Belding here to see you."

I sat up, carefully adjusting myself. "Tell him I will be right out as soon as I wash my face."

Arriving in the living room, I saw Buck sitting at the bar talking to a slim, gray-haired man.

Spotting me, Buck said, "Here's Tommy now, Mark. Tommy, I'd like you to meet Mark Belding of Belding Oil."

"Glad to meet you, Mr. Belding."

"Call me Mark, Tom. I am glad to finally meet you. Your uncle talked about you all the time. Understand you're a super football player."

"I wouldn't say super. I like to play the game."

"You sound like Boats. Competition was his middle name."

"I never had the privilege of knowing him that well," I said.

"He told me one time that he had trash-talked on your pa awful hard. He told me he did that on purpose, to see how you would respond, and then he laughed. I guess he found out."

"Yeah, he did."

"I saw him the weekend after you knocked him into the pit. You should have heard him laugh about being knocked into a piss pond."

"It wasn't funny to me."

"I didn't mean it in that way. He was afraid you didn't have any backbone. That had to be one of his proudest moments, to hear him tell it."

"He didn't sound that way when it happened," I said. "You could have heard him yelling for miles."

"That's what he said. It surprised him is all. You might not have believed it, but he did love you and was very proud of you."

"I wish he had told me." I was looking at Buck when I said it.

"He did too, Tom. We discussed it Thursday night, and he told me how sorry he was that you didn't know."

"I am too."

"I came over to meet you and Buck. I understand he will be the boss until you reach eighteen." Buck motioned for us all to move into the living room. Mark walked across the marble floors behind him, and I followed the two of them. We all sat on the white leather sofa, designed in a semicircle so people could visit comfortably.

Buck said, "I will start managing the company after the estate is probated."

"Well, there are some things that you have to make decisions on every day."

"From the way you're talking," I said, "I get the impression that you worked for my uncle."

"I thought you knew. Belding Oil has belonged to your uncle for the last twenty-five years. He also has Hoo Doo Casing in this area, plus an oil company in Houston and another casing outfit."

Martha came into the living room. "Mr. Belding, would you like a drink?"

"Yes, thank you, Martha."

"Would you care for the usual—a manhattan?"

"Yes, thank you," Mark said.

Martha turned to Buck and me. "Gentlemen, anything for you?"

"I'd like a Coke," I said.

"Me too," Buck said.

Mark continued, "Do you know the extent of Mr. Nichols's holdings?"

"No, he came down here quite often," Buck said, "but the one thing he didn't do was discuss his business with his hired help." Martha came in with the beverages.

Belding looked at me. "From what he told me, there was no doubt in his mind about you being level-headed. He told me to give you all the assistance I could. That is, if you want me to stay on?"

Buck interjected, "Belding Oil—was it your company at one time?"

Mark sipped his manhattan and explained. "My dad started the company back during World War II. He ran into trouble in the early fifties, and Boats bought 70 percent of the company. I have been running it for Boats for the last six years."

Buck said, "You mentioned Hoo Doo Casing. Who's running it?"

"I have for the past three years. However, Boats mentioned that he was thinking about someone to send in."

"How many wells do you have on line?" Buck continued.

"We have over four hundred, but producing—we are only pumping 250. The refinery will only take a hundred and sixty thousand barrels a month."

Buck stood and walked to the window, looking out at the city.

"I assume, with the shortage of oil, that Boats has checked other refineries?" Buck was puzzled.

"All the way from New Mexico to the southern states. Everyone is growing by leaps and bounds, but they can't keep up. Boats was thinking about building his own."

"I had no idea he was spread out this way. I knew from the work I've done for him that he made money, but I would not have taken this job if I had known how big it was."

"I wouldn't have taken anybody else, Buck," I said. "We might make mistakes, but I'm sure we'll survive." I looked at Buck standing nervously at the window.

"That isn't it, Tommy. In this league, when you make a mistake, it can cost thousands."

"It's only money," I said to cheer him.

"Yeah, but it's your money, not mine, so if I make a mistake, it costs you, not me."

"Oh, I don't know. I can always take it out of your salary," I joked. "By the way, Mark, is this apartment yours, or does the company pay for it?"

"I don't know. The entire building was owned by Boats, but what company is paying for it, I don't know. If I could, Buck, I would recommend that you have a board meeting. That way you can meet the other eight men." Mark walked to the window and stood next to Buck, motioning for me to come along.

"You telling me he owned eight companies?" Buck said.

Mark stood at the window and pointed out half a dozen locations visible from the twenty-fifth floor. They were facilities, buildings, and structures owned by Boats through one or more companies.

He said, "I know of ten, but two of the men handle two different companies, like I do. So there are probably more than ten."

"Damn, Tommy, this sounds like a helluva big job to me." Buck sounded like he was in a panic.

"I'm like Boats that way," I said. "You are one of the most level-headed men I have ever met. I'm sure Rocky will help us if we need it. Besides, Boats would never have agreed if he didn't think you could handle it."

"I'll damn sure need something I know." Buck walked back to the sofa and rang the bell. When Martha came in, he asked her to bring him a shot of Kentucky bourbon but changed his mind when he saw Rosie appear.

She walked up and asked, "Are you gentlemen going to feed us or starve us to death?"

"That reminds me," said Mark. "I took the liberty of making a reservation for you at Freddy's for 7:30. I wasn't sure, so I told them if you weren't there by 8:00 to cancel it."

"It's almost seven now, so we'd better get going," Rosie said. "Is it very fancy, Mr. Belding?"

"Please call me Mark. No, but it is one of the nicer supper clubs here in Dallas. By the way, you have to wear ties."

"That sounds like fun," Rosie said. "We haven't been out in years."

Buck turned to Rosie and nodded in my direction.

"I forgot. We're not here for fun," she said.

I looked at Rosie. "That's all right. I could use a little fun."

Buck said to Mark, "Is this place close, or will we need a cab?"

Mark asked us to follow him to an anteroom. "Before you start to dress, let me show you the central panel." He explained that the central panel controlled all the services available to us in the building, including transportation, laundry, dining, entertainment—the list was extensive. He pushed button three and asked George, the chauffeur, to have the car available in front in fifteen minutes.

"Would you like to join us for dinner, Mark?" I asked.

"No, thank you. I have an engagement at nine. If you like, I will be in my office tomorrow afternoon, and we can go over the operation."

"Thanks," Buck said. "Tom and I will be down about two."

"That will be fine. Nice to have met you."

We changed our clothes and waited outside for the car to take us to the restaurant.

The headwaiter met us at a rope barrier. "Do you have a reservation?"

"Yes, I believe Mr. Belding made it," Buck said.

"Oh, yes, sir, Mr. Hagan. Right this way please." He led us in and sat us at a corner table. It was elevated by two steps and gave us a view of the entire club. The waiter asked, "Would you folks like a cocktail before dinner?"

Rosie asked, "Could you recommend a good wine?"

"Certainly, madam. Would you like to order your dinners, and I will bring you a before-dinner wine?"

We opened the menus, and Buck let out a low whistle. "Man, look at these prices. Damn near a full day's pay for one meal."

"Honey, don't swear. We can afford an evening out like this once in a while."

"I'm not worried about that, baby. It seems like an easy way to make a living."

"Okay, you and your 'easy way to make a living.' You know, Tommy, when we first got married, he had this idea of finding a way to fix a flat tire without taking the wheel off the car. I'll bet you we jacked up three times as many cars as there is in Johnston County."

Laughing, I asked, "What did you try?"

"I squirted everything from fly spray to hog manure in them damn tires. I still think there's something that will work."

"The only reason he quit trying was I got pregnant and wouldn't jack up the cars for him anymore."

We ordered dinner and listened to several more of Buck's get-rich schemes. We had a leisurely dinner and spent the rest of the evening dancing. When we got ready to leave, the waiter brought the check. Buck reached into his pocket to get his billfold.

I asked, "How much is it?"

"Four hundred and eighty-three dollars."

"Sir, it is not necessary to pay cash," the waiter said. "If you will sign the check, we will bill Belding Oil. Mr. Belding was very explicit about that, Mr. Hagan. The tip has already been included in the bill, sir. We hope you enjoyed our club, and hurry back."

The car was waiting at the door when we walked out. On the way back to the apartment, Buck asked George, "Do you know where Mr. Nichols left his car?"

"Certainly, sir. It's parked in the basement."

"Would you have it around front at nine in the morning?"

"Yes, sir. I'll tell the garage attendant."

The next morning, we got the address of the mortuary from the phone book and drove over to it. One of the owners met us at the door. We identified ourselves and asked to see Boats.

"I'm sorry, sir. He is not here."

"Mark Belding's driver told us he was brought here from the hospital."

"Yes, he was brought here. However, we received orders from Mr. Nichols's lawyer to have him cremated and the ashes forwarded to Tishomingo."

"You mean he's already been cremated?" Buck asked.

"Oh, yes, sir, Mr. Hagan. The ashes of the remains should be in Tishomingo by now."

"What lawyer called you?"

"Mr. Seth Wilburton from Tishomingo. He said he was the executor of Mr. Nichols's will, and he was very insistent."

"We don't understand. Tommy is the only relative that Mr. Nichols had."

"Mr. Wilburton told me he had been trying to locate Mr. Gurley."

"Thank you. We will contact him."

When we arrived back at the apartment, Buck got on the phone and called Seth up in Tishomingo. He pushed a button on the phone to activate the speaker so I could hear everything.

Seth came on the phone. "Oh, yes, Buck, I've been waiting for your call."

"We're here in Dallas and would like to know what's going on."

"Well, frankly, that is none of your business. Let me talk to Thomas."

Buck said, "He is here on the phone with us now, so talk."

"Hello, this is Tom Gurley," I said.

"Tom, this is Seth Wilburton. Your uncle made me and John Ross coexecutors of his estate."

"That's not what my uncle told me. Buck Hagan was to be appointed as my executor."

"The will was made out like that, but Thursday, right before he left for the hospital, he stopped by and made a codicil naming us to handle your estate."

"I don't believe that, Mr. Wilburton," I said. "Boats would have told me if he had changed his will."

"Your belief or lack of it means nothing to me, Tom. John and I will be your guardians till you reach the age of twenty-five."

"Now I know you're a liar. Boats said—"

"I don't care what Boats said. I know what is written in the will, and this is all that counts. Buck, are you still on?"

"I've been listening the entire time."

"I'm directing you to bring Tom up here to Tishomingo. Have him up here before six o'clock. He will live with John Ross until we can get him registered with a good military school. Oh, yes, one other thing—if you fail to do this, we will know you don't have the company's best interest at heart. You will be fired."

Buck started to say something when Seth broke in. "I don't want to discuss it. You will do as I say." He hung up the phone.

Buck turned to me. "He wants you in Tish by six tonight."

"I'm not going."

"I can't understand any part of this, but something is sure wrong."

"I know there is. Call Royal and let's see what's going on."

He dialed the phone, and Royal answered. Buck turned on the speaker again so I could listen in and told Royal all that had taken place.

"Something is definitely wrong, boys. I didn't have time to talk with you yesterday, but Boats called me from the hospital. He made no mention of changing his will. We discussed the way he wanted to set up the drilling company. It was a conference call, and Bob Stuck was in on the conversation."

"Did you go over the will that we gave you?" I asked.

"Bob and I both went over it very closely. There is no doubt about what Mr. Nichols wanted."

"Does Stuck agree with you?" I asked.

"Certainly. There is no doubt whatever."

Buck said, "Well, what do I do then? The attorney in Tish gave me till six this evening to have Tommy up there."

"Let me talk to Bob. This is a serious position given that Tommy is a teenager. If the codicil of the will is upheld, they could charge you with contributing to the delinquency of a minor. I'll call you back in about fifteen minutes."

"Royal, this is Tommy. There is no way in hell Boats would've given me to John Ross. He sat in the kitchen with me at Buck's and gave me the choice, and I chose Buck."

Royal assured us he would get to the bottom of this.

We sat and discussed our options. I said, "I'm sorry, Buck, but regardless of what happens, I am staying here, or at least with you and Mar."

"I'll do all I can, Tommy, even if it means going to jail, but something is sure wrong."

"Who is John Ross?" I asked. We wandered back into the living room, and I sprawled out on the white leather sofa.

"That's right. He did mention John Ross. That's peculiar." Buck was curious about why I had focused on him.

"Well," I said, "the attorney up there said he was the coexecutor of the will."

"That's right, he did. Now I know there's something haywire. Boats has said for years he wouldn't trust John Ross with a pair of cast-off shoes."

Martha walked in. "Gentlemen, anything I can get for you?"

"Yeah, I'll have that Kentucky bourbon now," Buck said.

"I'll have a Coke, please." I turned to Buck and asked, "Isn't there someone up there in Tish you could call who might know something about this?"

Rosie and Mar had been listening from the window as they were looking at the lights of the city. They walked over, and Rosie sat next to Buck and lifted her leg over his. "Why not call Judge Watkins, honey? Boats and him spent quite a bit of time together."

Mar sat on the edge of the sofa and scooted me over. She rested her hand on my chest, rubbing it in a circular motion. "That's a good idea. Let's wait until Royal calls back and see what our alternatives are."

We didn't have to wait long. Buck had hardly finished his sentence when the phone rang. Stuck was on the line, and Buck flipped the speaker on. "Buck, Bob Stuck here with Royal. Neither he nor I knows what's going on. After our conference call ended yesterday and Royal hung up, Boats and I talked for several minutes. He had a premonition about his surgery, and he asked me to help you in every way I could to take care of Thomas."

Buck told them that I was on the call too. I said, "That's what we can't understand. Surely, if he was going to change his mind, he would have told someone about it. What do we do about going up to Tishomingo?"

Royal spoke. "I can only give you the law. Buck, if those people up there are adjudged executors of Boats's estate, then they are Tom's legal guardians, and failure to comply with their wishes could put you in violation of the law."

I said, "Then you are telling Buck he has to take me back? I'm telling you,that ain't gonna happen, 'cause this Ross character has to be lying."

"The only other option for Buck is to fight the will. But before making your decision, you should know it would be awful expensive."

Buck said, "What kind of money are we talking about?"

"In the neighborhood of a million, or more if it goes to the Supreme Court."

I asked, "Have either of you talked to Seth Wilburton up in Tishomingo?"

"No, Royal and I discussed it. We can call him if you want us to."

Buck was adamant. "Yes, please do. I am going to call Judge Watkins, a friend of Boats's. Call us back after talking to Seth."

I chimed in. "Is there any way you can put pressure on him about me staying with Buck and Rosie? Can't we go into court and ask for a hearing? Seeing as Boats put me into Buck's custody."

"We might have a 40 to 60 percent chance of winning," Royal said.

"You guys call Seth. Let him know that we don't intend to peacefully give up. Call me back when you finish."

We hung up the phone and turned to the girls. We spent a few minutes trying to figure it all out and then decided we needed to talk to Judge Watkins. Buck picked up the phone and made a person-to-person phone call to him. When Judge Watkins answered his phone, Buck flipped the speaker on, identified himself, and explained what he was calling about.

The judge was cautious. "Buck, I can't discuss this with you. The will has to be admitted to my court for probate. I wish there was some way I could help you, but the ethics of the situation will not allow it."

"What about them wanting me to have Tommy up there by six o'clock?" Buck asked.

The judge said, "I'm telling you this as Boats's friend, not as a judge. If there is going to be any question about the legality of the will, then I would just keep on the way you are right now. Until they are actually appointed by the court, they have no authority over him."

"Thank you, Judge. We appreciate it," Buck and I both said.

"You're welcome. Could I talk to Tommy for a second?"

"He's listening on the phone. Go ahead."

"Tommy, I have never met you," Judge Watkins said, "but Boats was my best friend for over fifty years. If there is anything I can do for you that doesn't have anything to do with my court, I will."

"All I want is to stay with my friends. We will let the court settle the rest of it."

"Boats said you had real good common sense for a young man."

"Thank you."

"Tell Buck that, as long as he is in litigation over the will, he needs to stay out of Johnston County. That goes for you, too. One other thing: remember the name Judge White. If he is on the bench, stay out of Johnston County. He is on John Ross's payroll."

"Thank you, again, Judge. We will do as you suggest. Good-bye."

"He sounded like a nice man," Mar said.

"It is pretty clear from what he said that we are going to stay out of Johnston County," Buck said.

The phone rang, and I picked it up. "Hello, Royal. How do you do? I'm putting you on speaker so Buck can hear."

"Not too good." Royal filled us in on his conversation with Seth, and we made clear to him that we were not going to Tishomingo because of what Judge Watkins had told us.

"Fine. Just in case, let me give you the phone number of an attorney there in Dallas, in case you need one." He read off the number, and I copied it down. Hanging up the phone, I told them, "You know, I'm hungry."

Rosie got on the intercom and ordered some food: four cheeseburgers, onion rings, root-beer floats, and New York cheesecake. We ate at a dining table in front of the massive windows, looking out over the city of Dallas and discussing all the events of the evening so far.

Halfway through the meal, the phone rang yet again. Rosie answered it. "Yes, he's sitting right here. Buck, John Ross wants to talk to you."

Buck flipped the phone on speaker. "Hello, John, what can I do for you?"

"It's not what you can do for me," John said. "It's what you can do for yourself that counts." Buck stood at the bar while the rest of us listened to the conversation.

"All right, tell me what's on your mind."

"We know that Boats told you that if anything happened to him, you would be executor of his estate. None of us knew it would be this quick. The only reason he changed his mind was that he thought you didn't have enough experience to handle all of his companies." Buck was looking at us who were seated around the table and mocking John by mimicking a bird's beak with his hand.

"Maybe I don't, John, but if he had changed his mind as you say, I believe he was the type of man who would have called me and said so. I worked for him for over twenty years."

Buck shifted from foot to foot. John said, "He didn't have time. He decided just that morning to change. He talked it over with me and decided it would be to Thomas's advantage to have us handle it."

Buck told John, "Listen carefully, John. You might convince me of that 'cept for one thing."

"Name it."

"As I said, I worked for Boats for over twenty years, and he always said, 'You're a man at fourteen and grown at seventeen,' so when Seth told me you were to be Tommy's guardian till Tom was twenty-five, I knew there was a skunk in the woodpile somewhere." Buck smiled at us, while we were trying to keep quiet.

"Stop and think, Buck," John countered. "You can't have an eighteen-year-old kid running multimillion-dollar companies."

"Why not? They're his companies and his money."

"That's it, Buck. How much of it would he have left by the time he's twenty-five without guidance?" John was desperate.

"You are not going to convince either me or Tommy that Boats wanted Tommy to be under guardianship till he was twenty-five. Boats himself told me more than once that Tommy was a better man than anybody he had working for him."

John said, "Well, yes, he did. All he wanted was to protect his companies and Tommy. He made provisions for you. He was in the process of rearranging all of his casing companies into one corporation. He intended for you to run this company. You are the best casing man Boats had, according to him."

"And at the base of this new company, what would my new salary be?" Buck was grinning and looking at us.

"Well, it will take about six months to get everything reorganized. We are placing his six oil companies under one corporation, the casing under another."

"You still haven't mentioned salary, John. What would my salary be?" Buck slapped his hand over his mouth as soon as he finished so John wouldn't hear him chuckle.

"Look, why don't you drive up, and after the memorial service for Boats on Tuesday afternoon, we will discuss it."

"What about my job in El Paso?"

"I'm sure you have several men in your crew who can take over. After all, it is only a casing crew foreman's job. We have much bigger plans for you."

"I'm sure the bigger plans you had for me came about in the last couple of hours. Well, you take those plans and stick them in your ass and light them on fire. Good-bye, John." Buck could still hear him talking when he hung up the phone. We all burst into laughter. Once we settled down, we talked through everything we could think of.

"I think John was trying to bribe me," Buck said. "He wants me to run Boats's casing crews after he has put them all into one company."

I said, "It sounds like a good job. Why not accept it?"

Buck walked back to the table, grabbed his cheeseburger, and took a bite. He started talking with his mouth half-full until Rosie shut him down. When he swallowed, he said, "Why should I? This morning I was supposed to be the president of Nichols Oil. Tonight they want me to be a flunky."

Mar said, "Yes, but from what you say, they intend to give you a raise." Mar lifted her root-beer float in toast.

"Yeah, but they never did tell me how much, and I have never liked to work without knowing how much I'm going to be paid." Buck laughed.

"I'll remember that when I finally get these firms, if I ever do," I said, looking at the most important people in my life, all sitting at the table.

"Oh, you will get them. The only way I can figure this is that they saw an opportunity to get their hands on Boats's companies and took it. Question is, what else did they do to get it done?"

"But why would they do that?" Mar asked. "There's no way they can keep them."

Buck said, "No, they can't, but just consider how much money they could stick in their pockets with the amounts they'll handle. Stop to think—if John Ross transferred all of Boats's accounts to his bank during the eight years Tommy would be under his guardianship ... hell, they could steal millions, and I'm sure that's what they intend to do."

"Boats told me he didn't trust any of them, and now I'm beginning to see why," I said. I polished off the root-beer float and sucked the last clump of ice cream into my mouth.

Mar rose from her chair and came over to sit on my lap. "I can't imagine people doing these things for money."

Rosie said, "Honey, in Johnston County, everything in the book is done for money and power."

"Discussing it now won't change anything," Buck said. "I suggest we go to a show, and then tomorrow we'll take Boats's car and drive back to El Paso."

Chapter 26

The Combine Slips a Few Gears

Judge Watkins told his wife, Alice, that he would be gone a couple of hours because something had come up that needed his attention. She was used to his being called away at odd hours and thought nothing of it. He drove over to Seth's house, and parking at the curb, he saw John Ross's Lincoln sitting in Seth's driveway. He rang the doorbell and heard the chimes inside. Seth opened the door. The judge could tell that Seth was surprised to see him.

"Come in, Judge," Seth said. "You have never seen our new house."

"This isn't a social call, Seth. Where's John?"

In the living room, two women and John Ross were sitting and having drinks. "I want to talk to both of you fellas," the judge said. "Is there someplace we can talk?"

"Sure, Judge, sit down. We have few secrets from our wives."

"Well, I'm sure there are several secrets you have from your wives. Anyway, I would hope so, because I would hate to see them go to jail with you."

John leaned back and, with a smile, said, "Don't be melodramatic. If we go to jail, you go right along with us."

"Most likely true, but you know, in a way, I'm beginning to think it's worth it."

"Don't talk foolishness, Judge. However, we're glad you came by. We have something we wanted to talk over with you. 'Course, we had planned to have a couple of others present, but now is as good a time as any."

"You mean about my retirement?" He was watching John's face and saw the surprise.

John looked confused for a minute and then said, "Well, you knew your resignation had to come one of these days. We think it should be now."

"There is no way you're going to get me to resign, John, especially since you would have Adam appointed in my place."

"Either you are going to resign or we will have you removed for judicial misconduct."

"I think not," the judge replied, "and I might as well tell you something else. There isn't any way you'll get Boats's so-called will through, either."

"Heard about that, did you? But you would have in a couple of days anyway," John said.

Seth said, "Well, we got Boats. What makes you think we won't get his will probated too?"

Seth's admission that they had killed Boats didn't escape the judge, but he decided not to call attention to it. Instead, he said, "I think I'll let you worry about that. You don't realize what joy it will bring to my heart to watch you perjure yourselves. Good night, gentlemen. Oh, yes, and ladies."

Seth followed him to the door and stood there watching until he drove off.

After leaving Seth's house, the judge stopped at a telephone booth, and the phone only rang only once before Pike answered.

"Pike, it's Judge Watkins. I just left Wilburton's house, and Ross was there. They made it clear that they killed Boats. You were right. I don't need to know anything, but I think the kid is in trouble."

"Don't worry, Watty. I've already put things into motion." Pike was his usual terse self.

The judge hung up and then drove over to the hospital. He took the stairs to avoid notice. When he stepped into Cody's room, Lee Bob was sitting next to the bed. Cody, lying on the bed, looked asleep and had a tube in his nose. "Can we talk, Lee Bob?"

"Sure, Judge," Lee Bob said as they both stepped into the hallway. "I just hope Cody there wakes up again."

"He in pretty serious shape?"

"About the worst for him. Doc says he doesn't stand a chance of making it another twenty-four hours." The sheriff smiled at the judge and held up a small reel of tape. "We got it on tape. I had my wife type it up. Now all I'm waiting for is him to sign it."

"On the tape, does he admit to knowing that he is dying?"

"It's all in there, Judge. 'Course, to get him to talk, I had to tell him he was set up by John Ross."

"Is that on the tape?"

"No, I told him and got him to agree to make a confession before I started recording. Then I had the doctor come back in and tell him again that he wasn't going to make it."

"It would help if you could get his signature on it. However, tape is generally admissible as evidence in court. When you picking them up?"

"Soon as I can get an officer of the court to sign their warrants."

"Guess what, Lee Bob? I just happen to know an officer of the court who will sign them. Do you have them?"

"Yeah, in the room."

"Get 'em for me," the judge said. Lee Bob disappeared for thirty seconds and reappeared carrying the papers.

The judge took the transcript and warrants, looked them over carefully, and then signed them. "How many of your deputies can you trust?"

"Well, there's Adolph, Zeke, and Joe Bill."

"Why not have someone come up here and sit with Cody. You and your deputies go serve these warrants."

"I'll do that. You think it's better to pick them up tonight?"

"Yes, because tomorrow I might not have the power to sign them. They have something up their sleeves to get me removed from office. But, of course, you knew that."

The sheriff was shocked. "You think they're planning on moving that fast?"

"I know they are. I just left from talking to Seth and John. They as much as told me that I would be out of a job by tomorrow night."

"That's too bad, Judge. Guess we should have kept our shirts a little cleaner." The sheriff dropped his head.

"I've never cried over past events, Lee Bob. After the fact is not the time to wonder about it."

"Guess you're right. I wish sometimes that I had been the law officer I should have been."

"Except for a few instances, you have been." The judge started walking toward the stairwell, and Lee Bob followed.

"Think I'll go to jail, Judge?"

"I can't answer that. I'm wondering the same thing myself. By the way, I wanted to find out how you came out with John on that money." The two stepped into the stairwell, and Lee Bob held the door while they finished their conversation.

"I haven't told him about it, but it's too late for him to get it back now. It has been sent out of the country."

"That's good. By the way, how old are you?"

"I'll be forty-seven on my next birthday."

"Have you told your wife that you might go to jail?"

"Hell, no! Because it doesn't matter. If I do, Joy would be in bed with someone before the week was out."

"That's too bad. I always hate to see a family break up."

"We never was a family. She went and had her tubes tied before our wedding. I kept wanting to have kids, and after we had been married five years, she finally told me what she had done."

"Sorry to hear that."

The sheriff shook his head. "It's all right. The only reason I stayed with her is that she's the best I ever had in bed."

The judge got quiet. "While I'm thinking of it, Lee Bob, the other thing is that they let it slip that they got Boats. So you may have another homicide on your hands—though I don't know how they pulled it off."

"Damn, those sons a bitches been busy." The sheriff let the door go. The judge extended his hand, and the men shook hands. "Meet at my office as soon as you're ready," Judge Watkins said.

An hour later, they met in the judge's chambers, and the judge stamped his seal on the warrants. "There's no way we can keep this under wraps, so I called the state police," he said. "They're waiting over at the Chalet for you. The quicker you pick them up, the better we will be."

"Hell, none of them will run, Judge. They feel too secure."

"You can't tell what scared men will do when they're faced with a murder charge."

"It's funny—you told me the same thing on my first murder case fourteen years ago."

"Things haven't changed. Not telling you your business, Lee Bob, but I would wait until you have all of them picked up before you let them make any phone calls."

"All right. You going home?"

"No. I'm hungry. I'll be over at the Chalet too. I'll wait there till I hear from you."

Judge Watkins left and sat drinking his coffee at the local restaurant. That was the trouble with being a judge—no one wanted to be seen talking to him for fear that others would automatically assume they're in trouble.

Leaving the judge's office, Lee Bob asked Adolph, "Who's on the radio?"

"I got Junior to come in and spell me. I told him I had a date but would be back as quick as I could."

"That's fine. Now remember, you are not to use your radio for any reason till all five of them are picked up."

"Why is that, Sheriff? We're on official business, ain't we?" Joe Bill asked.

"Yes, we are, but Junior is tied in to John Ross some way, and I'm not sure he wouldn't call him if he found out. All right, I'm going out to the Chalet. You follow me."

Lee Bob arrived at the Chalet and then sent Adolph in to get the state troopers. When they came out, he handed them the warrant for Leon. He gave the one for Coy to Adolph and Joe Bill.

"All right, it's now eight thirty. I want you in position to pick them up at a quarter to nine. Seth and John are together at Seth's house. We all move at exactly 8:45—that is, unless you see them leaving or downtown. See you back at the jail. Get going."

At sixteen minutes to nine, Lee Bob stepped on the porch and rang the doorbell. Seth's wife came to the door, her blouse half-open down the front. She took a step backward when she opened the door and saw him and the troopers.

"Is Seth here, Mrs. Wilburton?"

She saw Lee Bob looking at her breasts, supported by a black bra, and she halfheartedly tugged at her blouse and then let it fall open again. "Yes, he's in the living room. Would you come in, Lee Bob?"

"Thank you, ma'am." As they walked in, they saw Seth and John seated in the living room on the sofa, both of their shirts undone and their shoes off. John's wife was nowhere in sight. Both men were staring at them when they walked in.

"What do you need, Sheriff?" Seth asked.

"Would you put your shoes on and come with us?"

"Whatever for? We just settled down for a pleasant evening."

"You are both under arrest for the murder of Mr. and Mrs. Lawrence Chubb."

John Ross lurched up, swaying to stay upright. "Do you realize what in the hell you're doing?"

"Yes, I'm arresting two men for murder."

"You can't be serious." His words were slurred so much that Lee Bob could hardly understand him.

"I'm not telling you again," Lee Bob said. "If I have to, I can take you without your shoes."

Seth said, "Lee Bob, you're making a very, very serious mistake."

Pulling out his handcuffs, he handed them to Zeke. "Cuff 'em."

Seth stood up. "There is no need for that. We will come peacefully."

"That I'm positive of, Seth. Damn it, Zeke! I gave you an order." Taking the cuffs, Zeke walked over to them.

"Front or back, Sheriff?" Zeke asked.

"In the back. We'll pack their shoes." They led Seth and the staggering John out and put them into the car.

"Wait here a moment, Zeke," Lee Bob said. "I want to check something out."

He walked back into the house and went into the living room. Beverly, John's wife, was sitting on the bed smoking a joint. Looking up with a smile on her face, she asked, "Forget something, Sheriff?"

"Yes, I believe I did. Is that good grass?"

"Only the best, Sheriff. That's all I get is the best."

"That's the way I am, Beverly. I have only the best."

"The best of what, Sheriff?"

"Jails, Beverly. Jails. How would you like to come down and visit mine?"

"Why would I want to come down and visit a filthy old jail? Seth will be out in the morning."

"I wasn't talking about Seth, Beverly. I was talking about you."

"I know you was. I might be stoned, but I still know what I'm doing. You want a glass of wine? It goes good with this grass."

"No, I want you to get up and come with me. You are under arrest for the possession of drugs."

The smile slowly left her face. "You wouldn't be pulling my leg, would you?"

"I might, but I'm not. You want to get up, or do you want me to drag you up?"

"You can't arrest me, Lee Bob."

Watching her, he could see that the threat of arrest had sobered her up a little bit.

"You're trying to frighten me, aren't you?" Beverly said. "You really don't intend to arrest me."

"That's where you're wrong. I've talked long enough." He grabbed her arm and jerked her to her feet.

She said, "Ouch! You're hurting me!"

As she tried to twist her arm free, her blouse came all the way open. "Lee Bob, my daughter is in the bedroom asleep. If you arrest me, she'll be alone."

"I'll call juvenile, and they can come over and pick her up."

"My God, you got my husband and now you're going to arrest me?"

"That's right," he said. "Now you got it."

"Please, Lee Bob, don't do that to me. I promise I won't ever smoke pot again if you let me go."

"It don't work that way. You do something wrong, you pay for it."

"I'll do anything, anything! Just don't put me in jail. If not for me, then for my daughter. Please, Lee Bob." The tears had started to run down her face.

"All right, I'll give you a choice. I've got about two seconds before I have to be at the car. I'm going out there and will be gone about three minutes. When I come back, if you're standing here with no clothes on, fine. If not, you're going to jail. You understand? Look at me. Do you understand? I'm leaving right now, and I'll be right back." He walked slowly out to the car.

Seth said, "What was you doing in my house so long? You have no right without a warrant."

"Come on, Seth. You're a lawyer. You know I don't need a warrant when an arrest has been made."

He told Zeke to get out of the car and come with him. They walked back up to the door, and Lee Bob told him to wait a minute. Opening the door a crack, he looked in. There stood Beverly in the living room with only her panties on. Lee Bob turned around to Zeke and said, "Take them down to the jail. Book them, and come back and pick me up in an hour."

"What are you going to do?"

"Didn't you smell that grass when we walked in? I'm going to search for it. Tell Adolph to go out and pick up Adam while you book the ones who've already been brought in. Now don't forget. Pick me up in an hour."

He opened the door and stepped in. Beverly had taken her panties off and was sitting on the sofa smoking another joint. Looking up at Lee Bob, she said, "Pot makes me horny."

"That's fine, baby, 'cause if there's anything I like better than horny women, I haven't found it yet."

Lee Bob stood on the curb waiting for Zeke to pick him up. Beverly hadn't been kidding; she was hotter than a two-dollar pistol in a furnace. She fucked like she hadn't been laid in five years. He stood there shifting his weight from one foot to the other, adjusting his uniform. He wondered how this was all going to turn out. Not being sheriff anymore was going to be hard to take. Glancing back at the house, he grinned. It was too bad Doc was dead; he would have liked to review the video of the last hour in Wilburton's living room. He wondered again how many women Doc had blackmailed into a quick piece of ass or a blow job over the last fourteen years. Up till his death, several of them still called him to meet them on remote roads in the county.

Zeke pulled up to the curb, and the sheriff crawled in. "They give you much trouble?"

"No, but Adam and Seth, of course, being attorneys, were still giving them hell when I left."

"How about John Ross?"

"He was passed out. We booked him, and the minute we put him in a cell, he was asleep."

They stopped at the jail. The sheriff stepped into the radio room and asked Junior, "Any messages?"

"No, everything's been quiet."

He walked over to the squad room. "Adolph, come on in the office. Joe Bill, you can go on home." On the way to his office, he asked Adolph, "We still have those microphones set up in the cells?"

"Sure, Sheriff."

"Well, turn them on, and I'd like you to man the tape equipment. If anything is said, I want to have it on record."

"I turned them on before I put them in their cells. Haven't been monitoring them, though."

"Who did you put with who?"

"I had Joe Bill put Coy and Leon in one cell, John in the middle cell, and Seth and Adam together."

"That's good. One other thing, I don't want Junior talking to the prisoners, not at any time. If they don't know about those mikes, I don't want him telling them."

"Fine, Sheriff. I'll tell my relief in the morning."

"In fact, when Junior comes in, send him over to Ada on patrol. I've got to go out and meet Judge Watkins. See you in the morning."

"'Night, Lee Bob."

When he entered the Chalet, there was instant quiet. He looked around, and one of the waitresses came over and told him that the judge was around the wall in the corner. He asked her to bring him a cup of coffee. Judge Watkins was in a corner booth by himself, reading a paper and drinking coffee. Lee Bob slid around with the window at his back.

The judge looked up and folded the paper when Lee Bob slipped into the booth. "How'd it go, Lee Bob?"

The waitress set down a steaming cup of coffee and a slice of peach pie. When the waitress turned and walked away, Lee Bob said, "No problems, Judge. All the opossums are in the sack. John Ross was so stoned that I don't think he even knows where he is."

The judge smiled and took a draw of his coffee. "It would be fun to be there in the morning and hear him when he *does* realize he's in jail."

"If you want, Judge, I can play you the tape later." Lee Bob laughed.

A grin spread across the judge's face. "You still have them jail cells bugged?"

"Sure, I've used it for years. Saves you from a lot of surprises later on. It's also admissible in court. You know that, Judge?" The peach pie was delicious; it had just been made and had a scoop of vanilla ice cream melting slowly on it.

"Haven't ever thought about it. We do our jobs day after day, never wondering about someone else's. Come over in the morning, and I'll authorize the taping." The judge sat back in the booth and looked out the window as if daydreaming.

"Doubt seriously that we'll have to worry about it for very long," the sheriff said as he snickered and dove into the pie.

"You're likely right, but it's better than being like John and them." Their eyes met, and they smiled at each other. The waitress came with fresh coffee and topped them off. She asked the judge if he wanted a piece of fresh peach pie and ice cream. "No, thanks. Alice has a fresh blackberry cobbler waiting at home for me. Tell Wilbur thanks, though. I genuinely love his peach pie."

When she left, Lee Bob said, "When are you going to have their preliminary hearings?"

"I'm not. I'll disqualify myself. The presiding judge will have to appoint someone. Everyone knows I've done business with them for years."

"Have any idea who that will be?"

"Not in the slightest. Whoever they send in will be well qualified."

"Think they will be let out on bail?" The sheriff paused long enough on the pie to drink some fresh coffee and look around the Chalet to see who was there—a couple of farmers and old folks.

"It's hard to say. I have in a lot of cases. Considering their positions in the community, I would say bail will be granted." The judge sat a bit straighter and adjusted his seating.

"Guess it was too much to expect that we could keep them in jail."

"We can't have everything, Lee Bob, but you had better believe that when they get out, all hell is going to break loose." The judge was cradling his coffee, looking down into the black liquid.

"I know. Well, I'm going home to get some sleep. 'Night, Judge." Lee Bob slid out of the booth and walked away. The judge went back to reading his paper.

Driving toward his house, Lee Bob changed his mind. Seth wouldn't be out of jail till late afternoon, so he went back to Seth's place. He pulled into the driveway, got out, and went into the house. Beverly was still lying there, naked and sound asleep. He slipped out of his clothes, dropping his gun belt to the floor. He lay beside her and reached across to stroke her petite breasts. As he fondled her nipples, she awoke and reached for his erection, tugging it toward her spreading legs. She turned to him, lifting her left leg over his hip, and rocking him back enough to pull his penis into her. He felt her foot press the floor and then lift her other knee alongside his hip. Lee Bob thrust, driving his full girth inside her. He reached for her breasts, taking one in each hand. She bounced on his lap, squealing like a small child at Christmas. He urged her toward him, raising himself to fill his mouth with her right breast. She slowed her rhythm into long measured strokes, allowing him to lick and suck her breast as he felt the pulse of blood flowing in his organ and her contracting spasms.

They flopped on the sofa, exhausted in the morning light that attempted to find its way through the drawn curtains. Lee Bob then gathered his things and was gone.

Chapter 27

The Play for T. C.

It took us ten hours to drive from Dallas to El Paso. The kids were all over us when we pulled in.

Rocky said, "Tommy, a Judge Watkins has been trying to reach you. He said to be sure and call him."

Getting our luggage out of the trunk of the car, I asked Buck, "Why don't you get on the extension in the bedroom so we can both talk to him?"

"Good idea. Sure hope it's good news for a change. We could use it."

I dialed the number Rocky gave me, and the phone rang one time before Judge Watkins picked up. I heard Buck pick up the extension and told the judge that he was on too.

"Glad you could call me," he said. "Thought you would like to know that things have changed. John Ross and Seth Wilburton, along with three others, have been charged with murder."

"Who was murdered?" Buck asked.

"Larry and Althea Chubb. They owned Spender's Grocery."

"Yes, Tommy and I both knew them. We used to hang out in Spender's store and talk to Larry. Didn't see a lot of Althea, but occasionally I used to peruse the pawn shop stuff to see if I could get any deals. She helped me find a watch for my wife Rosie."

"The reason I wanted you to call is that, if I was you, I would have an attorney in my courtroom before the end of tomorrow. I have to tell you, I will most likely be removed from the bench for official misconduct before the week is out."

"For what reason, Your Honor?" I asked.

"I understand you have a copy of Boats's will?" he asked.

"Yes, it's in the hands of our attorneys right now," I answered.

"Well, this is strictly unethical, but you both come to my court by tomorrow afternoon and I will admit the copy of your will for probate."

"What about the other will, Judge?"

"I am sure they will try and have it admitted for probate. However, if one will has already been ruled on, then it will be a court fight and your chances for winning increase."

"You're positive I won't wind up in jail and Tommy in a military school?" Buck asked.

"I will not have anything to do with their preliminary hearing. A new judge will have to be appointed, so they won't be able to get out of jail until at least Tuesday or Wednesday. By that time, I will have approved you, Buck, as the executor of Boats's estate."

"Surely they will try and have it set aside in favor of the so-called new will," I said.

"Sure they will, but then, like I said, it will be a full-fledged court fight."

"Do you think this new will they have might be a forgery, Judge?" Buck asked.

"I doubt it very seriously. They are too smart to try that. Knowing Boats the way I do, I'm sure it was done in such a way that he never suspected."

"Then how are we going to disprove it in court?"

"For one thing, I can testify that Boats did not sign a new will on the day they say. From what you have told me, Seth says he stopped by Boats's office right before he went to the hospital, right?"

"That's what he said."

"Well, you be sure to be here in court tomorrow with your lawyer, and I will give you a sworn deposition that I was with Boats from one o'clock in the afternoon until he left me at the Chalet at a quarter to four. You should have no problem proving what time he arrived in Dallas."

"Thank you, Judge. We will be there."

I hung up the phone and called Royal, telling him our problem. I explained that we needed an attorney.

"I'm licensed to practice in Oklahoma and will appear for you if you wish it. Give me an hour in the morning to rearrange my schedule."

"Can you meet us at the airport around nine thirty?" I asked.

"I'm sure I can. If not, I'll have Bob Stuck there."

Buck called the airport and arranged to have a helicopter ready for us.

We arrived at the Johnston County Courthouse at one thirty that afternoon. The judge's secretary told us that he was busy at the moment. Then the door opened, and Judge Watkins invited us in.

The judge's office was spacious and tidy. The walls displayed his law degree and admission to the Oklahoma State Bar by the Supreme Court, but apart from that, it was absent the egotistical plaques adorning most executives' offices. The bookshelves were bulging with bound volumes of legal *Reporters* for Oklahoma and Texas and the Fifth and Tenth Federal Circuits. We introduced ourselves to one another and sat down.

The judge said, "Just a moment. I want to get the court reporter in here." Returning, he seated himself at his desk and said, "May I see the will, Mr. Carroll?"

Royal opened his briefcase and handed him the file. Nothing was said while the judge skimmed through it. The court reporter came in and seated herself.

Judge Watkins said, "The reason I am not holding an open court hearing is due to a petition by the heir of the deceased. Having read through the deceased's will, the court can find no reason to refuse the probate of this request. The court hereby appoints Mr. Buck Hagan as executor of Mr. Nichols's estate. In compliance with the deceased's wishes, the executor's salary is set at $125,000 per year, plus expenses and all benefits due under company policy. If the attorney for the plaintiff has any requests of the court, it will entertain the petition. Let the record show, appearing for the heir is Royal Carroll of Carroll and Associates, El Paso, Texas."

Royal leaned toward the judge's desk. "Your Honor, the executor of Mr. Nichols's estate is worried about several accounts now being handled by the Bank of Johnston County. We therefore ask for authority and a compliance order to said bank allowing us to transfer all stock, bonds, notes, and cash from their possession to the Ada National Bank, with the said order to be enforceable as of this date."

The judge turned to the reporter. "Due to the status of the president of said bank, the court can see no reason why this request should not be granted. The court orders the clerk to prepare the necessary papers for the court's signature. Is there anything else, Mr. Carroll?"

Royal cleared his throat. "Yes, Your Honor. Although Mr. Hagan is appointed executor of the estate to protect Mr. Gurley's interest, it is their request that the court appoint Mr. Hagan as Thomas Gurley's legal guardian until his eighteenth birthday."

The judge turned to the reporter again and clearly stated, "Said request is granted. Again, the court clerk will have the appropriate papers prepared for the court's signature. Anything else? Then this hearing is closed. Would you have those papers made out as quick as you can, Allison? Thank you."

The judge stood and extended his hand. "Mr. Carroll, it's nice to meet you. I have heard of you for several years," he said.

"Thank you, Your Honor. We appreciate all you have done in this matter." Royal stepped aside so the judge could shake each of our hands.

"Well, I thought maybe I would have some more good news for you, but I'm sorry to say it's more bad than good. This morning I informed the powers that be that I am removing myself from the Chubb case. They appointed a judge from Bryan County. That would have been fine, but I have a reliable source who informs me that the appointment of this judge could be tied to the people in the Chubb case. It is too long a story for me to go into right now, but if we can, the sheriff and I will give you any information we receive. I would suggest, Mr. Carroll, that in the future, if you have any occasion to appear in this court with Judge Wendell White presiding, you ask for a change of venue." The judge escorted us to his chambers door.

"Thank you," Royal said. "I understand and will heed your warning, Your Honor."

The court clerk called us over to her desk and handed Royal the papers. Judge Watkins signed them and handed them back to Royal.

We drove over to the bank. The receptionist told us to see the assistant manager, Delbert Hathaway. We walked over and introduced ourselves. Delbert stood up and shook our hands. "Now, what can I do for you?" Delbert was short, barely more than five feet tall, and had a sparse mustache that he had started to grow in ninth grade and that hadn't improved much since. He was dressed to the nines, though, with a crisply starched white shirt and a gold bar from collar to collar under the knot on his thin tie. His Florsheim shoes shined like glass, and his trousers were pressed with a perfect crease. My pa always referred to guys like this as "fancy Dans." I never understood what that meant, but this guy would have been a sight in a small town like Tishomingo.

Royal reached into his briefcase. "We came over to close out all of Mr. Nichols's accounts." He handed him the court orders.

"I am sorry, Mr. Carroll. I don't have the authority to transfer funds in the amount you're talking about. Mr. Nichols kept a large amount of cash on hand for operating expenses. To be completely honest with you, Mr. Carroll, it could cripple us for a few days." Delbert was sitting behind the desk, his back as straight as a board in perfect posture, and his hands were folded on the edge of the desk.

Royal was firm. "We are sorry to cause you any inconvenience, Mr. Hathaway, but if you will examine those papers, you will find that they are court orders authorizing us to handle Mr. Nichols's accounts as we see fit."

Hathaway flipped through the papers briskly, "Yes, sir, I have glanced at them and know what they are. However, you have to realize that it isn't that simple. Some of these accounts have outstanding balances against them."

Royal pressed harder and strengthened his voice. "We are not unaware of the problem, but we are not leaving here without these accounts. Now, do you get out a record of the accounts, or do I go call the sheriff and also the Federal Reserve Bank and have them send out some auditors?"

Delbert was flustered and pushed back from the desk. "Really, Mr. Carroll, this is not necessary. Mr. Nichols's accounts are in correct order. I should know. They are my responsibility."

Royal leaned over the edge of the desk. "That's fine. Then you should have no problem taking them off your books."

"You are refusing to see the problem, Mr. Carroll. Our president is not available right now." Delbert was nearly whining in anguish at the pressure Royal was putting on him.

"Mr. Hathaway, if I had an account here and wanted to cash a check, would you send me to see the president of the bank?"

"Of course not."

Royal was talking through clenched teeth. "Then I am giving you three minutes to start closing out these accounts. If not, we are leaving, and when we come back, Mr. Hathaway, we will bring the sheriff and a warrant for your arrest for contempt of court. Do I make myself clear?" Royal sat back in a chair, crossed his legs and arms, and stared at Delbert.

They sat there looking at each other for several seconds before Delbert finally relented. He got up and walked over to talk to a man and woman. They went back into a room marked "Bookkeeping." Several minutes later, Velma walked out with papers in her hand.

"Hey, Velma," I said. "How's your mama and Pike?"

She said, "They're doing fine. Been real busy taking care of things at the ranch since Boats passed away."

Velma asked Royal, "Will cashier's checks be sufficient?"

"Certainly. Make them out to the same company name they're drawn from. Mr. Nichols also kept a couple of safe deposit boxes here. We would like to get the contents of them also."

"Certainly. I can assist you with that when I come back. Of course, you will have to call the state tax office before you can actually open the boxes. Taxes on the estate, you know." She walked away.

"May I use your phone?" Royal called after her.

"Go ahead."

Royal asked how I knew Velma, and I explained that she frequently came out to the ranch to see Pike since her mother and Pike were lovers. Royal smiled and then went to call the tax office. When he returned, he said they would have someone there in ten minutes, since the tax office was located in the courthouse.

Delbert's office was not designed for comfort. The chairs were hard and impossible to get comfortable in. He had a grandfather's clock in the corner that chimed on the quarter hours, gonged on the half, and made a hellacious racket on the hour. In between, the thunderous ticking was more annoying than a dripping faucet. With the hard marble floors, wood-paneled walls, and plaster ceiling, the ticking reverberated around the room, attacking the senses from all directions. We sat in Delbert's office for over an hour as clerks came and went, until finally Velma arrived again to inform us that the tax agent was there. She took us to open the boxes.

Velma pointed out the keys on the ring that had been taken from Boats's car. Both boxes were completely filled with certificates for stocks and bonds, oil leases, real estate deeds, ten thousand dollars in gold coins, and a small metal box filled with pictures of Boats and his half brother, my pa, when they were kids. The tax agent listed each item taken from the deposit boxes, all of which took another hour. When we had finished and walked back out to the lobby, Delbert met us with six cashier's checks in his hand.

"Mr. Carroll, we left five thousand in two of the accounts. We know there are a couple of checks out against them."

"Other than that, all of Mr. Nichols's accounts have been cleaned out?" Royal asked.

"Yes, sir. Of course, you knew that Mr. Nichols owned 30 percent of this bank?" Delbert stood erect, not a thread out of place, and spoke in an officious and proper cadence.

"No, we were not aware of that fact. There were no shares in the deposit boxes." It was more of a question than a statement; Royal's mind was working.

"I believe he kept them out at his ranch. Also, I'm sure he had deposit boxes in Dallas at the Bank of America branch near Belding Oil."

"Thank you, Mr. Hathaway. You didn't have a relative by the name of Cletus, did you?"

"He was my father. He's dead, though, as I'm sure you already knew." Delbert's tone was terse, and there was a distinct disdain in his face for the question.

"Sorry to hear that. I didn't know he had died. I did some work for him several years ago. He was a good man."

Delbert's body language softened at that comment. "I thought so. Is there anything else I can do for you?"

"Thank you. No, we will leave you alone."

We left Boats's car at the Chalet, got the helicopter pilot, and were in Ada in fifteen minutes. At the bank, we set up the accounts, and three hours later, we were back in El Paso.

When we parted, Royal asked Buck to stop by the office in the next couple of days. "I have to appear in court in Ada this Friday, and while I am there, I would like authority to get into Boats's home and see if there are any assets we haven't recovered."

"I will stop by and sign them in the morning."

"Also, Boats used an accounting firm in Dallas. I suggest you get a hold of them and make arrangements for us to go over the books."

"I wouldn't know any more than I do now," Buck said.

"I would be less in the dark if I knew the number of companies he owned."

"Mark Belding made a suggestion that we have a board meeting. Why don't I have that set up for next Saturday morning?"

"That will be fine. I can drive down from Tish on Friday night. Sounds like a good idea."

When we finally arrived at the ranch around nine o'clock that evening, Rocky met Buck and me on the porch. "I'm glad you're back," he said. "That phone has been driving me crazy." He handed Buck a sheaf of papers filled with numbers for him to call. For the next two hours, Buck was on the phone making decisions, some on items he had never dealt with. Several times, he hung up the phone only to have it ring with someone else having a problem. Finally, when he had a minute, he turned to Mar and me, who had been sitting there listening, and asked me to call Mark Belding to set up a meeting next Saturday.

A lady answered the phone. I asked for Mark, but she said he was out in the field and that she would have him call back. Several minutes later when the phone rang, I, thinking it was Mark, picked it up. The man introduced himself as manager of Nichols Oil Company from Houston, Texas. I told him who I was and asked what he wanted. He wanted to speak with Buck, but he asked if there was some way I could listen in. I hollered at Buck and asked him to get on the extension in the bedroom. He picked up the phone.

"I'm Skip Peterkin, Buck. I manage Nichols Oil Company here in Houston. I was going to call you about some problems I have been having. However, something happened that I don't know how to handle."

"What is it, Skip? Maybe Tommy and I can help you on it."

"Someone is going to. I have run our company for five years, and I like my job and want to keep it."

"That sounds reasonable to me," Buck said. "So what's the problem?"

"I needed some information yesterday and, knowing Boats was in Dallas, I called Mark. He told me about you. Anyway, about ten minutes ago, I got a call from a Mr. John Ross. He told me that you had been appointed executor by fraud and that they had something or other that named his group as the executor of the estate. Anyway, he said that if I did anything on your orders and it harmed the company in any way, he would hold me legally responsible. Also, he said that if you called, I was to inform you I would do nothing until the legality of the situation has been resolved."

"We knew that sooner or later we would encounter something like this. You keep on doing your job, Skip. Tommy and I will handle the problem."

"I don't know either one of you, and I have worked hard for fifteen years to get to the position I am in right now. I don't want to get in the middle of a power struggle and wind up out in the cold."

"You won't as long as you do your job."

"That's just it, Buck. I talked to Boats last week, and he was supposed to call me back. Evidently he forgot."

"About what?"

"We have some marginal oil leases that run out in four months. The stipulation on the leases is that we have to have a well dug and producing before the lease runs out."

"Have we any chance of renewing the lease?"

"None. Quartz Oil has already got a secondary lease on the property."

"You say marginal. Do you have any idea how marginal it is?"

"About two years ago, Boats had some tests run and we liked them. At that time we couldn't get a drilling rig, and several other things came up. Anyway, Boats put it on the back burner and it's been there ever since."

I asked, "Do you have any notion at all about what Boats wanted to do?"

"Not really. From what he said, I assumed we were to drill, but he never said so."

"Do you personally have an opinion?"

"I told Mr. Ross about it, and he told me to forget it. He said it was too much of a gamble to take at this time."

I replied, "I don't care about John Ross. I want to know what you think."

"Personally, I think it is a very good risk. They have brought in several wells in this area."

"Then why do you say it's marginal?"

"Well, all lands on the north and east of these leases have producing wells. The ones to the south and west have all been dusters, except for two wells.

Buck asked, "How many acres are we talking about?"

"Twenty-two thousand."

"How much we paying out on the leases?"

"Five dollars an acre," Skip answered.

"How did Boats get it so cheap?"

"You have to know the area. It's mostly marsh and salt lands. Any drilling in the area is expensive, due to building roads and platforms."

"Do you have any other undrilled leases?"

"Several, but they have quite a few years left to run."

"Can you give me and Tommy a close or near-ballpark figure on the cost for drilling?"

"Three to four million."

"Would that include everything—roads, platforms, and whatever?" Buck asked.

"From what I can find out, it would. You know how oil companies are about such things. In this case, I have a very good friend that works the eastern field and, considering the depth they went, it's a close figure."

"What do you think, Tommy?"

"I don't know, Buck. Skip, you know John's feelings on this. What would you do if we told you to go ahead?"

"To be honest, I'd hate to see us let these leases go. But if it costs me my job, I'd let them go."

"What if I guaranteed you your salary until I take over the firms?" I asked.

"According to Ross, that won't be for nine years."

"Well, according to Boats's *real* will, I assume control in a year and five months."

"See? That's what I'm talking about. Either way, I'm in the middle."

"Buck, if it were up to me, I'd go ahead," I said.

"I agree with you, Tommy. Now Skip, are you sure that if you started now, you could complete drilling before the leases run out?"

"It should be no problem. We have a stipulation on extension of the lease if we are below eight thousand feet."

Buck asked, "All right, Tommy?"

"It is with me."

"Okay, Skip, it is now up to you."

"Well, I've seen rags and riches in this business. Never thought it could happen to me, but I'm going ahead."

"Will you need any transfer of funds?"

"No, our drilling fund is in great shape. By the way, are you going to consolidate like Boats was talking about?"

Buck told him, "We don't know anything about it."

"Last time Boats was down, about three weeks ago, he discussed it with me."

"Do you know how or what it consisted of?"

"No. Sharpe and Fenner in Dallas were handling it. You see, I own 25 percent of this company. John Ross might be able to remove me as president, but he can't completely get rid of me. It's in the company bylaws that I have a lifetime job. It would hurt me to see someone else running my company."

Buck said, "Now I know you. Didn't your dad work for Boats too?"

"Yes, for several years. He was killed on a drill site in Kansas."

"I remember. That was about fifteen years ago."

"Twelve. I was a freshman in school. Boats finished putting me through college and started me out down here. We started buying and selling oil and gas leases. About six years ago, we got some leases he didn't want to let go of, so he started Nichols Oil. In fact, we named our first field using part of each of our first names. It's called Bo-Ski. People down here get a chuckle out of it."

"We're having a meeting at the Belding Building at 10:00 a.m. next Saturday. We hope you'll attend," Buck said.

"Sure, I'd like to meet both of you. I am going ahead on these leases. I will have a drilling rig set up before the week is out."

"Thanks for calling, Skip. Tommy and I will see you Saturday in Dallas."

Before Buck could walk from the bedroom to the living room, the phone rang again. When Buck came in, I told him it was Mark.

"You go ahead and talk to him," Buck said. "I want some coffee."

"Thanks for calling back, Mark," I said. "I wanted to ask you to call all the men you know and tell them we would like to have a board meeting Saturday at 10:00 in the morning."

"Have you talked to Seth?" he asked.

"Did he call you?"

"About twenty minutes ago," Mark said.

"I imagine he told you the same thing that John told Skip."

"You mean about not doing anything?"

"That's it. Where do you stand, Mark?"

"I own part interest in this company, and when someone like Seth calls me up and threatens to fire me, where should I stand?"

"With us, I hope."

"Damn straight, Tommy. I never could stand that mealymouthed bastard anyway. I told him to kiss my ass."

"Did you know him before?"

"We went to school together at Oklahoma. Say, he told me something strange."

"What was that?"

"He told me that they were the executors of Boats's will and would be till you were twenty-five."

"From what they told Buck and me, they have a codicil to the will," I said.

"That's what's so strange about it, Tommy. I saw Boats that night, and he told me he wasn't sure he would make it. Then he told me, 'If I don't, you be sure to help Tommy out when he takes over my company next year.' I asked him if you wasn't kind of young to be taking over, and he answered, 'Not really. That kid is more mature at sixteen than I was at twenty-five.'"

"Thanks, Mark," I said. "We're bringing an attorney with us Saturday. I think he will want a statement from you."

"Fine, Tommy. I'll locate everyone and tell them of the meeting. You told Skip, didn't you?"

"Yeah, he's been notified. Bye."

"Oh, before you go," Mark said, "there's a law firm here called Sharpe and Fenner."

"Yes, we know about them. Thanks again, Mark."

Hurrying into the kitchen, I pulled Mar from a chair, whirled her around and around, and finally sat down in the chair and pulled her onto my lap.

She said, "Your mood changed real quick."

"It did. You know what Mark just told me?"

"No. What did Mark just tell you?"

I ran through Boats's conversation with Mark, finishing up with, "That should put the frosting on the cake."

Rocky came out of the kitchen. "By the way, Tommy, Coach Baker called for you Saturday morning. Boy, was he pissed. After I explained the death of your uncle, he calmed down."

"Funny—I haven't thought of football one time in the last four days."

"Well, you'd better start. If the team wins Friday night, next week you play for the state championship."

Mar wrapped her arms around me. "Sweetie, how're you going to play football Friday night and be in Dallas at ten on Saturday morning?"

I looked at Buck, who was walking down the hall from the bedroom. Laughing, I said, "I'll leave that up to my guardian. Come on. Put your sweat suit on, and let's go work out."

Buck asked, "How can you think of working out? I'm so tired I can't hardly move."

"You explain it to him, Rosie. Mar and I are going out to the barn." I was grinning from ear to ear and gave Rosie a wink.

The week went by swiftly. On Friday night, we played the semifinal game of the state playoff. It was no contest, with us winning thirty-five to nothing. After the game, Coach Baker made a speech. He thanked us and then told us he had accepted the head coaching job at Northeastern A&M College. He said the only reason he was telling us then was because he wanted us to all go out as winners.

I met the family outside the locker room, and we drove to a vacant lot where the chopper was parked. We hopped in and flew to Dallas.

At 9:45 the next morning, Mark led us into the boardroom. Seven men were seated at a long table, and two men were seated in easy chairs against the wall. "Gentlemen, this is Buck and Thomas."

He led us over to the table and started introducing us. The only ones I could remember were Skip, Mark, and H. P. Honeycutt. Then he led us over to the men in the easy chairs and introduced us to a Mr. Sharpe and Mr. Fenner.

I said, "Mark, would you please tell your receptionist that we are expecting Mr. Royal Carroll and ask her to show him in when he gets here? Then we don't want to be disturbed."

Mark got up and left the room.

Buck stood up and started in. "Tommy and I thank all you for coming. I assume that each of you has been contacted about there being a dispute over Boats's will." Several of the men nodded their heads. "We have some good news, at least for us. We have positive proof that their claim on it was faked, and if it gets to court, we can prove it. I will be the one you will be working with for the next year and a half. From talking to you on the phone, I assume—" He stopped as the door opened and Mark walked back in and sat down. "As I was saying, I assume, from the information we have, that every man here has a partial interest in the company he runs. Is that correct?" Most nodded. "So, for now, I am going to turn the meeting over to Mr. Sharpe and Mr. Fenner."

All the men turned or moved their chairs to face them.

Mr. Fenner stood. "Gentlemen, as you know, Boats has been talking about this for several months. He finally contacted us three months ago and gave us the go ahead. It is my function to set up the company in such a way that it is easy to operate. It's Mr. Sharpe's job to lay out the accounting and fiscal operations. Now here is what we have come up with: For each percentage of the company you own, you will receive one-tenth of a share of the new company. By the way, Mr. Hagan, what name are we going to set this up under?"

"Why can't we keep it under Nichols Oil?"

"I was going to suggest that, but I wasn't sure. That makes it easier for us because it's already incorporated here in Texas." Reaching behind the chair, he pulled out a large display board. He walked over to the window and propped it up on the windowsill. "As you can see, Nichols Oil Company will be the parent company. We have broken the others into two subdivisions. One company will have all casing and drilling companies under it. The other company will handle the oil and gas fields. Any questions so far?"

Skip said, "I have a question, Mr. Fenner. Boats said I would have 3 percent of the parent company."

"That is correct, Mr. Peterkin. You own, at the present time, 30 percent of Nichols Oil of Houston. Is that correct?" Fenner spread the information in front of him on the table.

"Right on the money. What I am worried about is the loss of income." Peterkin tilted his chair back and crossed his arms.

"That is in Mr. Sharpe's field. I'll let him answer you."

Mr. Sharpe pulled a folio from his satchel and laid it on the table in front of him, slipped on his reading glasses, and began. "Mr. Peterkin, owns, at the present time, counting all leases and producing wells, 30 percent of a company worth—and I'll be conservative—sixty million dollars. That gives you a net worth in the company of eighteen million dollars. Boats's holdings at the time of his death were in excess of six hundred million, and that's not counting the Bidwell and Birchley leases. Nor does it include the ten-million-dollar drilling company he purchased two weeks before his death. If the Bidwell leases produce a third of what is projected, they will be worth seven to eight hundred million or more. So what that means is that you will own 3 percent of a company worth close to a billion dollars. In other words, Mr. Peterkin, your shares will be worth thirty million, or twelve million more than you have now." Sharpe removed his reading glasses and twirled them in his left hand triumphantly.

"Please call me Skip, Mr. Sharpe. I'm not turning it down, but what happens if I don't want to merge my shares of Nichols Oil into this company?"

Fenner spoke up. "In that case, we would invoke the clause in your partnership agreement to force you to sell at the appraised price, which would likely result in a loss to you."

"Fine. Just asking. Anytime someone wants to give me twelve million dollars, I'll take it." Skip was smiling.

Sharpe put his reading glasses back on. "Now, while we are still on the subject of accounting, we hope to have this all set up no later than the first of the year. You will be notified of the exact date. When this is done, all purchases and payouts will be handled by the parent company."

H. P. Honeycutt leaned in and said to Sharpe, "You mean we will no longer be able to buy our stuff locally?"

"We don't mean that at all. It's just that on all jobs, the same material is used. By buying it in quantity, we can save approximately 10 to 15 percent." Sharpe was a proud bean counter, eager to emphasize the 10 to 15 percent savings.

"What happens if we break down and have to buy locally?" Honeycutt countered.

"Then you will forward the purchase order to accounts payable, and we will pay it. You will also have a petty cash fund you can use."

"Seems like foolishness to me, or a way to check up on us." Honeycutt was looking around the group for support.

"You're right, Mr. Honeycutt. It is a way to check up on you but also to check up on every expenditure made. Do you realize that, if this system had been set up last year, your company alone could have saved over eighty thousand?" Sharpe held up the summary sheet on H. P.'s company.

"Are you sure it would have been that much?"

Sharpe smiled at him. "Figures are my business. By setting up a central accounting office, we would save in excess of a million dollars annually, which contributes to your shareholder distributions. Any more questions? Then I will turn it back over to Mr. Fenner." Sharpe again ceremoniously removed his reading glasses and twirled them in his left hand.

The door burst open, and two men thundered in with the receptionist running behind them, telling them they couldn't enter. Every man at the conference table except the accountants jumped to their feet and pushed their chairs back from the table. Some continued to roll on the marble floors till they hit the walls.

Buck walked around the table and blocked their way. One of the men, a tall, skinny fellow, stuck his hand out and said, "Hello, Buck." The chubby man in his sixties nearly rear-ended the taller one.

Buck stopped in front of them. "What do you want, Seth, John?"

Seth dropped his hand. "We heard there was a meeting and, being as we are going to be operating the company, we figured we should show up."

I walked up and stood beside Buck.

"You must be Tom. I'm Seth Wilburton, and this is John Ross."

I looked the tall one in the eye. "That wasn't necessary, Mr. Wilburton."

"What wasn't?"

"You don't have to name a skunk. You can tell him by the smell," I said.

"Young man, you'd better be careful," John said.

"No, Ross, you best be careful," Buck said. "I'm Tommy's guardian, and I won't have someone threatening him."

The door opened again, and Royal Carroll walked in. He said, "Buck, let me talk to you a moment." They turned and walked out into the hall, leaving the rest of us in what appeared to be a Mexican standoff. I slipped around John and Seth and stood next to Buck as he talked with Royal.

"What is it, Royal? I'm fixin' to throw them bastards out."

"Not yet, Buck. I have them all wrapped up. Judge Watkins gave me a tape proving that this whole thing is a setup. I've got the judge's statement about the time Boats checked into the hospital. Also, when I get Mark's statement, they're dead."

"So why can't I throw them out?"

"'Cause I want to get a signed release from them, releasing all potential encumbrances." Royal led the way back into the boardroom.

Walking up to the invaders, Buck said, "Gentlemen, we have some business to discuss. Suppose we adjourn till one o'clock this afternoon."

"Before you do that, Hagan," John said, "I want to make a statement to these men."

"Sure, go ahead," Buck said.

"Mr. Wilburton and I called each one of you men and warned you that any association with Mr. Hagan here would not be in the best interest of our company. By showing up at this meeting, you chose not to heed our warning. Therefore, we assume you do not like your jobs. If you men leave now and do not come back, we will overlook it."

Buck held his hands up. "Hold it, Ross. I think this has gone far enough. You men sit back down. I believe this is a concern of every person here. Mr. Sharpe, would you and Mr. Fenner excuse us?"

Fenner said, "Certainly. You want us to come back at one?"

"If you would, please."

Buck pointed to me. "Tommy, would you bring those two chairs over here for these two?"

John stuck his chest out and wagged his finger at Buck. "We have nothing to discuss with you, Hagan. We will do our talking in court next Tuesday morning."

Buck turned to Royal. "I think this farce has gone on long enough. Let's lay our cards on the table."

Royal looked at Buck and then me. "I don't think that would be a good idea," he said.

Buck said to the gathered group, "Usually, I take my attorney's advice. But I think we should end this right now."

"It's your decision, Buck," Royal said.

"Mr. Ross, would you and Mr. Wilburton like to sit down? Or if you prefer, I can sit you down or lay you out. You choose."

"No, we're leaving, but I want to warn you men one more time—any decisions made here today will be reversed after Tuesday."

They turned to leave, but Buck walked around and stood in front of the door.

Royal said, "Let them go, Buck. I would rather have them in court."

"Not us, Royal. Tommy wants this over as quick as possible, and so do I."

"Get out of my way, Hagan," Seth said, "or we will have you arrested."

"Well, you know what that feels like. However, I think you should know—

No, I think you're right, Royal. Let's get them in court." Stepping aside he said, "Good day, gentlemen." He turned and opened the door and watched them walk down the hall. He closed the door and turned to the men standing around the conference table.

Skip said, "You know, Buck, if you don't win, all of us have our lives hanging by a thread."

"Royal, all these men, as you know, are partners of Boats. I want you to explain and show them that they have nothing to worry about."

"First, gentlemen, I would like to ask you not to discuss this with anyone, not even your wives, until after Tuesday." He reached into his briefcase, pulled out a file, and started to read Judge Watkins's statement. When he finished, he asked Mark to tell the men about Boats's statement to him.

Royal then pulled out a cassette tape. "This is a tape that was made in the Johnston County jail. It is a conversation among five defendants charged with the murder of a couple up there. They discuss how they have bought the judge who is hearing this case. Also, a separate conversation between two men, named Coy and Leon, reveals how they intend to set up companies to sell supplies to Nichols Oil Company at inflated prices."

I asked, "How can they get away with that?"

"Evidently, from what Coy says, all five of these men are going to be appointed to the Board of Governors."

I looked at him. "How can that be when these men own parts of their companies and will be there to watch them?"

"Let's sit down, fellas," Royal said. Reaching into his briefcase, he pulled out another tape. "The sheriff received this tape in the mail. He doesn't know where or how or even when it was taped, but it is a conversation between these men. They intend to exercise the clause in each company's contract to purchase their stock."

Mark said, "What if we don't want to sell?"

"You have no choice. It's very plain in each contract. I'm sure that when you men signed these contracts, this clause was discussed."

"Sure, but don't we have the same option of buying them out?"

"Only if they agree to sell. This a standard contract, and the majority owner has the first option." Royal laid the tape and contracts on the table.

Mark said, "Well, I won't sell my company. I've worked too damn hard to have this happen."

I asked, "That won't happen, will it, Royal?" I looked at each of the men around the table, wondering what they were thinking.

"No, I'm pretty sure we have everything nailed down."

Skip asked, "Then you can guarantee that they won't be appointed executor of this company?"

"Absolutely. No court in the land would allow these men to be appointed," Royal said.

Buck said to the group, "Why don't you all come up to the apartment, and we will send down for some lunch."

At one the men gathered back in the boardroom on the twenty-fourth floor. Mr. Fenner completed his discussion on accounting, and they elected the officers of the new company. Buck was appointed president of the board, and Mark and a man named Hershal Drewsey were appointed first vice presidents, with Mark in charge of all oil and gas production and Hershal in charge of the casing and drilling companies.

Mr. Fenner brought each a folder and handed them out. To Buck, he gave one that was thicker than the others. "These, gentlemen, are the prospectuses of your jobs. They lay out your responsibilities." Some of the men opened their folders and thumbed through them.

Mark said, "Wait a minute, Mr. Fenner. It says here that as vice president, I have to give up running my company."

"You will be in charge of all the oil-producing companies."

"I know that, but that's no reason to leave my company."

"You won't be leaving it. You won't have the time for the day-to-day decisions that have to be made."

"Surely with the experience there is in this room, there won't be that many problems," Mark said.

"You have to look at the broad picture. As a company, we have sixteen operating fields. What is your biggest headache?"

"Making sure each well pump supplies its scheduled allotment."

"That and getting the refineries to take it. Isn't that right?" Mr. Fenner asked.

"Sure, but all of us have that problem," Mark said for the group.

"This is what makes the operation we have set up so much easier. When this gets going, the three refineries we deal with will deal with only you.

How much easier will it be when, instead of talking about a couple hundred thousand barrels, you are talking about a million?" Fenner was looking directly at Mark.

"We don't pump that kind of oil."

"Not now, you don't, but what will happen when the Bidwell and Birchley fields open?"

"I don't know," Mark answered honestly.

"Look Mr. Belding, we all know that every refinery is working to its fullest, but some still have slack time. They lose a tanker here or a pipe breaks. When you can guarantee delivery of this much oil every month, what do you have?"

"Okay, I see what you mean."

Sharpe interjected, "Fine. Do you want us to mail the eviction notices to the tenants of this building, Mr. Hagan?"

"Yes, I believe you'd better."

"You want to have the name of the building changed?"

I spoke up. "It's up to you, Mark."

"No, you go ahead and change it," he said.

"Buck, I would like the name changed to Boats, Inc.," I said.

"If that's what you want, you have it. Take care of it, would you, Mr. Sharpe?"

"Certainly. If there isn't anything else, I should get home."

Buck stood up. "Anyone here have any more questions? Then I suggest we close the meeting. One thing—Tommy and I would like to give a Christmas party on December twentieth. Dinner and dance at Freddy's. Let us know if you will come, on the company, of course."

After they left, I said, "Royal, there's one thing I'd like to know."

"Sure, Tommy. What is it?"

"You said the tape from the jail mentioned that they were going to buy out the partners. Where would the money come from?"

"Johnston County Bank."

Buck said, "And I suppose at an inflated rate of interest?"

"You got it," Royal answered. "Goes to show how greed can get to you. These, however, are the worst I've run into."

"Come Tuesday, we should be able to put a crimp on some of it."

"We certainly intend to try," Royal said. "I'll call Monday."

"Do that," said Buck.

Chapter 28

Judge Watkins's Sentence

Judge Watkins recognized the man as he walked through the door to his chambers. He stood as the man and Purvis Jarvis came toward him. "Sewell, how are you?"

"Fine, Judge. Guess you know why I am here." Sewell and the judge shook hands before Sewell sat in the chair opposite him. John Sewell, just Sewell to everyone he dealt with, was a senior assistant attorney general to Milo Cotton, Attorney General of Oklahoma. He was known as Cotton's political fixer.

"Have a good idea. How's Cotton doing?"

"Oh, you know, still dreaming of becoming governor." Sewell pushed his chair back to stretch his legs. He slouched down in the chair to have a conversation with his old friend.

"He was lucky to get to attorney general."

Sewell chuckled. "You can't stop a man's ambition."

"Wouldn't want to. Every man has his dream." The judge was looking out the window.

"True. Very true. Sorry, Judge, but I have to serve these papers to you." He leaned forward, pulled the papers out of the satchel next to his chair, and dropped them on the judge's desk.

Judge Watkins picked them up and leafed through them. "When are they effective?"

"Immediately, Judge, sorry to say."

"What charges they throw at me?" the judge asked without looking up.

"Malfeasance, partiality, judicial misconduct—you name it. Bastards threw in everything a person could think of."

The judge was still looking out the window. "Who signed the complaint?"

"Cotton, of course. By the way, Purvis has to take you down and book you."

"The charge must be more than malfeasance for you to put me in jail." The judge had turned and was looking Sewell in the eyes.

"No, we're not putting you in jail. As soon as you're booked, we're releasing you on your own recognizance. I insisted on that. Known you too long to believe you would flee."

"Thanks for that, but you still haven't told me the charge."

"Conspiracy to murder." Sewell half-mumbled it under his breath.

"Murder? Whose murder? Chubbs'?"

"No, Cletus Hathaway," Sewell said, looking at the judge.

"I see. Kind of hard to prove after fifteen years, don't you think? Let me guess—some convict witness?"

"Sorry, Judge. Just doing my job."

Purvis asked, "By the way, you know where Lee Bob is?"

"Most likely at the hospital. He's been trying to get a signed confession from Cody."

"Is Cody still alive?" Purvis seemed a bit astonished.

"Barely. Well, I'm ready, Purvis. Let's get it done so I can come back and clear out my desk."

Sewell said, "No. Sorry, Judge, but we're going to hold everything till we can go through things."

"All right. Let me know when I can pick them up. Who did they appoint—White?"

"No. Didn't you hear? Judge White got himself killed last night."

"How the hell did that happen?"

"Well, his honor was drunk and tried to drive home. Judge Lovell was appointed this morning."

"He is a good man. Honest, anyway."

"Fair but tough. Doesn't believe in probation. Ol' Hang 'em High Lovell."

"I've heard him called that, but not to his face."

"If anyone ever does, I'd love to be there," Purvis commented.

"You ready, Purvis? Let's go." The judge got up, and he and Purvis walked into the jail. Purvis said, "Sorry about all this, Judge."

"You're just doing your duty. No hard feelings from me," the judge said.

Purvis took the judge's picture and fingerprinted him. He took a towel off a rack, squirted some liquid on it, and handed it to the judge.

"Is that it, Purvis?" the judge asked.

"That's it, judge. Tell me one thing, though—is this a bum rap?" Purvis asked.

"You mean the conspiracy to murder charge?"

"Yes."

"Hell, yes. I didn't have him murdered or have anything to do with it, if it was murder. Cletus was a friend till he embezzled county funds."

"It was murder, all right. We did the investigation," Purvis said.

"Then you shouldn't have had to ask, Purvis."

"I did, Judge. Everything was too pat. All the evidence pointed to you and Boats. It was way too easy, especially on a case fifteen years old. We would have found this evidence fifteen years ago, so I'm suspicious of its appearance now."

"The way you talk makes me think you know it's a setup." The judge was wiping the ink off his fingers and looking at Purvis.

"I'm positive it's a frame, but I can't prove it. Anyone out to get you, Judge?"

"Several people lately." The judge chuckled to himself. "And of course, after thirty-plus years of sending cons to jail, I'd say the list is quite long."

"Care to name any of the recent ones?"

"Not right now. Maybe later. Am I free to go?"

"Sure. Just don't leave the state without the court's approval."

"I know. I've told a few people that before. See you, Purvis."

"Yeah, later, Judge." Purvis watched him leave the booking room and noticed that the judge's shoulders were slumped under the weight of recent events.

It was a beautiful day in Tishomingo. The judge felt the sun on his face as he walked down the steps like he had most every day of the week for the last thirty-plus years. He walked quickly over to his car, thinking he had better hurry home and talk to Alice before news of his arrest spread. He had pulled the car door three-quarters of the way open when he saw the shotgun. *What's a shotgun doing there?* he thought. Then he saw the flash and felt the blow knock him back into the minivan parked next to his car—then darkness.

Adolph was taking pictures under Purvis's direction when Lee Bob drove up.

"Purvis, what's going on?"

"Someone booby-trapped the judge's car," Adolph said.

The judge's body was decimated. "My God. What hit him, a bomb?" Lee Bob stared at Judge Watkins's body leaning against the minivan.

"No, they rigged a shotgun, aimed and fastened to the door of the car. When he opened the door, that was it. You got any idea who wanted to do him in?" Purvis was talking to Lee Bob, but it appeared that Lee Bob wasn't listening. He just stared at the judge.

Lee Bob finally answered but was annoyed. "No. I'd like to know what you're doing here."

Purvis waited till Lee Bob turned to face him. "Came down from the attorney general's office," Purvis said. "We had just finished booking him."

"What do you mean 'booking him'? What charge?"

"Conspiracy to murder," Purvis said.

"Bullshit, Purvis. You know better than that. Who'd he conspire to kill?"

"Cletus Hathaway."

"Cletus died in the penitentiary," Lee Bob argued.

"I know where he died, Lee Bob. I also know you put him there."

"I sure did, and he was guilty too."

"I'm not disputing that. He was killed for money." Purvis was trying to calm Lee Bob without much success.

"You mean Judge Watkins paid to have him killed?"

"Well, it was made to look like it, but it was a setup. You have any idea who might pull something like this?"

"Sure as hell do—John Ross, Coy Purcell, and Leon Ritchie."

Purvis looked at him earnestly. "I suspected you might name them. Understand you booked them for the Chubbs' deaths?"

"Sure did, and now with Cody's signed confession, I'll nail their asses to the wall. By the way, Purvis, on the way over, Junior told me on the radio that you called in your team. What the fuck you think you're doing?"

"Yes, I called my team in. You might not like it, but I'm in on this case from start to finish."

"Even without my request?" Lee Bob huffed.

"Don't need it. Shooting a judge made it a state crime and a state case, so that involves us."

"Did you say Sewell was here?" Lee Bob changed the subject.

"He's up in the judge's chambers going over his records."

"Fine. Let's go talk to him," Lee Bob said. He headed for the courthouse without waiting for Purvis.

When Lee Bob burst through the door, Sewell looked up from behind the judge's desk. "Hello, Lee Bob. How you been?"

"Fine, Sewell. Didn't you hear that shotgun?"

"No, what shotgun?" Sewell said.

"Someone just shot Judge Watkins."

Sewell looked at Purvis. "Purvis, this true?"

"Rigged his car with a shotgun." Purvis stepped around Lee Bob and took a chair across from the judge's desk.

"What the hell is going on in this county, Lee Bob? That's three murders, maybe four, in less than six weeks," Sewell said.

"Don't know. What I came in to see you about is, can you get John Ross's and Seth Wilburton's bail rescinded?" Lee Bob was animated.

"Not without court approval. What's the reason for revocation, if you can prove it?" Sewell leaned back in the judge's chair.

"They were down in Dallas all day Saturday." Lee Bob took the chair next to Purvis.

"Any other reason you want to bring them in?" Sewell asked.

Lee Bob leaned in to make the point. "I think they had something to do with the judge's death."

"Any proof?"

Lee Bob was exasperated. "No, but I have a tape made while they were in jail talking about getting rid of the judge and having White replace him."

Sewell shook his head. "You know tapes like that are not legal, Lee Bob."

"They are if you have a court order signed by a judge." The sheriff smiled at Sewell and looked at Purvis.

"Suppose Judge Watkins gave you one?"

"He damn sure did."

Sewell changed the subject. "What can you tell me about the Hathaway case, Sheriff?"

Lee Bob sat back in the chair. "It was pretty cut-and-dried. You know Cletus was a compulsive gambler. No matter what happened, he always lost. He was a regular at Leon's poker game out at the shack. Since he was county clerk and wrote all the checks, he set up a phony company and stole fifteen thousand dollars to pay his gambling debts. That was it."

Purvis leaned over. "Judge Watkins sent him to the pen for ten years, didn't he?"

"Looking at the report," Sewell said, "I see that probation was recommended but Watkins gave him ten years, no probation." Sewell held up the sentencing recommendations given to Watkins at trial.

Lee Bob interjected, "The judge said that if it hadn't been public money that was taken, he would have granted it. What I can't understand, Sewell, is the charge you threw at the judge. I thought Cletus hanged himself in the pen."

"He was hanged all right," Purvis answered, "but someone did it for him. Two weeks ago, a lifer in the pen died but confessed before he did. My team was sent in to investigate it." Purvis was looking at Lee Bob to read his body language, looking for any reaction.

"You mean that after all these years, you was able to pin it on the judge? That is fucking unbelievable."

"It bothered me, and I told Cotton and Sewell here both that it was a setup. But the evidence was overwhelming."

"You know the judge could have backed off on this Chubb case or Doc's murder, but he wouldn't. So you never will convince me the judge had anything to do with any killing."

"We came here with proof that he bought Hathaway's farm and that, when oil was struck, they made a fortune. Look, Lee Bob, I can show you." Sewell picked up a file and waved it in front of Lee Bob.

"Maybe they made a lot of money off Cletus's property, but that's not proof that Watkins killed him." Lee Bob was pissed and annoyed by their seeming opportunistic leap at slim facts. "Maybe we should just go pick up the bastards we *know* are guilty of killing a couple of innocent folk."

Sewell finally agreed to send Purvis along and to call Judge Lovell to get the order. "Even without it, you can bring them in for questioning," Sewell said.

"I know that. I want to be able to hold them for a while. Maybe keep some more innocent folk from getting killed!"

"Well, I'll give you authority to hold them seventy-two hours."

"Your fuckin' generosity is overwhelmin', Sewell," the sheriff said as he spun and left the office.

As they went back downstairs, Purvis asked, "Lee Bob, can we stop by the jail? I want to talk to Junior."

"Privately?"

"No, to see if he got my team."

About twenty people were gathered around the judge and the judge's car. Lee Bob said, "My God, look. Adolph, what in the hell is going on here? Get those idiots away from there." Lee Bob and Purvis hurried over and forced everyone away from the murder scene. One of the men told Lee Bob, "We just wanted to see."

"We catch you around the body or car again, and you will find out what you can see from a jail cell. Purvis, go tell Junior to get a couple of my deputies over here."

"Sure, Sheriff."

Seeing Fred bending over the judge's body, Lee Bob walked over. "What do you think, Fred?"

"Death was instant, Lee Bob—tore his aorta in half. The heart kept pumping, but he was dead before he hit the van. The charge must have been overloaded double-ought buckshot. It cut right through him and took out most of the car door in this minivan behind him."

"Wanted to make sure he was dead, I guess," the sheriff commented.

"That's what I would say. Did you see the way they had the gun wired?"

"No. Something fancy?"

"Yeah, fitted right across the hump of the car. Someone put in a lot of work on it."

Purvis called Lee Bob. "Can you come over here for a minute?"

When he walked up, Purvis said, "John Ross called and said he just got a death threat. Wants us there right away."

"Adolph, you keep those people away. In fact, break them up and send them home. Let's go, Purvis."

The two climbed into Lee Bob's cruiser, and Lee Bob punched it to get over to the bank. Purvis said, "Guess you know that Sewell and I were also sent down here to investigate you and your office."

"Doesn't surprise me. Anytime you arrest five of the elite in a county, you normally figure shit is going to fly."

"We got a folder on you from someone."

"Yeah, I know. I got one too, with a warning to lay off the Chubb case or a file would go to the attorney general."

"Well, now you know they weren't kidding."

"Neither am I, Purvis. I won't condone murder. I won't condone breaking the law, period."

"Lee Bob, if you are guilty, I will nail you."

"Do your damnedest, Purvis."

Pulling into the Johnston County Bank lot, they saw John standing at the front door. As they went up the steps, he pushed open the door. "About time you got here. Glad you're here, Purvis. Makes me feel a lot safer."

"I got a place where you will feel a *lot* safer," Purvis said.

"Where's that?"

"The jail. Come on. Let's go."

"You nuts or something? Some guy just threatened to kill me."

"Have any idea who would want to kill you?"

"No, and I didn't recognize the voice either."

"Local call?" Purvis asked.

"Now how in the hell would I know?" John shot back.

"You can question him down at the jail," Lee Bob said. "Let's go, Ross."

"Am I under arrest?"

"You sure as hell are," Lee Bob replied. "Let's go."

"Can I tell Delbert? There's several things I want him to do."

"I'll tell him." He called over to Delbert, who was sitting at his desk. "Hey, Del, we're taking your boss to jail. He wants you to stop by later."

John said, "That wasn't necessary."

"It was to me." Taking him by the arm, Lee Bob led him out and put him in the back of his car.

Climbing into the passenger seat, Purvis glanced at Lee Bob. "You know, Sheriff, you have changed."

"You have four people killed in your jurisdiction and see how it affects you."

He pulled up in front of an office building. "You want to stay with Ross?" he asked Purvis. "I'll pick up Seth." Lee Bob left the car and headed up the walk.

"Sure, go ahead." Purvis looked back at John. "You hear about the judge?"

"It's a small town. Sure I heard about him. So what?"

"Thought he was a friend of yours," Purvis said.

"Business associate. He wasn't friends with anybody."

"You have any idea who could have shot him?" Purvis asked.

"No, but whoever did helped the community out. At least they won't have to feed him."

Purvis said, "Got to admit, Ross, you sure are a compassionate bastard."

"Sympathy is for fools. If you don't mind, leave me alone."

"Sure, but don't you want to know why you were picked up?" Purvis asked through the screen between the front and back of the patrol car.

"Some damn foolishness from Lee Bob, I suppose."

"No, you and Seth should have stayed out of Texas. You violated your bail." Purvis smiled at John.

John started bouncing on the backseat and shouted, "What bail? Judge White released us without bail! We asked him about going to Texas. He said he couldn't see no reason why not."

Purvis said, "We only have your word for that. What's this about you getting a death threat?"

"It was a recorded message, I think. Anyway, he said Judge Watkins was the first and I was not going to be the last." *It might be a religious reference*, Purvis thought. Then he asked John directly, "He said *last?*"

"That's what he said."

"Wonder what that could mean. Think he could mean he's going to kill more before he tries for you?" Purvis was thinking out loud.

"How in the hell would I know?" John yelled. "You cops fry my ass—sitting here on the public street where anyone could shoot me—and you're wondering if he's going to kill someone else before me." Just then, Lee Bob got back into the car and Purvis brought him up to speed on the conversation he had missed.

Lee Bob looked at John and chuckled. "I don't think he would try with me sitting here."

"Why not? He killed the judge in back of the courthouse, didn't he?"

Purvis said, "Yeah, but that was a booby trap. Whoever it is would have to shoot you himself, and we would get him."

"Thanks a lot. That would sure as hell do me a lot of good."

Lee Bob radioed the office and asked Junior to call Judge White's office to check out John's story. Five minutes later the call came back that the story checked out. Lee Bob got out of the cruiser, walked around, and opened the rear door. "All right, Ross. Get out."

"Why do you want me to get out?" John asked like a scared child.

"Seth has a signed release showing that you were allowed to go to Texas. So I can't hold you."

"I knew that," John argued. "If you hadn't been so damn anxious to throw your weight around, I could have told you."

"Yeah, but you're a lying sack of shit, so how could I trust you? So all right, you're free. Get your ass out of my cruiser. I have a lot of work to get done."

"I'm not getting out on the street. I told you someone threatened to kill me, and I sure as hell ain't going to give him a shot at me on no street." John was hysterical.

Lee Bob repeated his order. "I said get out before I throw you out."

"Purvis, make him take me back to the bank," John pleaded.

Purvis threw his hands up. "Isn't anything I can do about it, John. It's his county."

Looking around quickly, John jumped out of the car, crouched temporarily behind the open back door of the cruiser, and ran into Seth's office.

Driving back to the jail, Lee Bob said, "I wonder what the hell they wanted to murder the judge for."

"You think it could be tied to the Chubbs' deaths?"

"No, but I do think it's tied to Doc's murder somehow."

Purvis was puzzled. "What makes you think so?"

"You're going to find out sooner or later. Doc had a file on nearly everyone in this county," Lee Bob said.

Purvis looked thoughtful. "So I heard, but I thought it was a rumor."

"No. The other day when Larry Chubb called you, he wanted to give you a copy of the files." The sheriff continued to look straight ahead as he drove to his office, not making any eye contact with Purvis.

Purvis hesitated and then asked, "Could they have been in the box you took out of Chubb's car trunk?"

"You been spying on me, Purvis?" Lee Bob smiled.

Purvis turned his back to the passenger door and faced Lee Bob. "Got to admit we have, Lee Bob. The attorney general got a letter on you and the judge."

"So why in hell haven't I been removed from office?" Lee Bob continued to avoid eye contact, keeping his eyes on the road.

"Haven't been able to prove anything so far," Purvis said.

Lee Bob finally turned to look at Purvis, who was studying him. "Thanks for that, anyway."

"No need. You already know that if I could have proved anything on you, I would have had you removed so fast you couldn't have blinked your eyes," Purvis snickered.

"Well, fuck you too."

Purvis responded, "Guess we know where we stand then, don't we?"

"I know where I stand. I'm sheriff of this county."

Purvis steeled his voice. "You're a throwback, Lee Bob. Sheriffs like you haven't been in office for over thirty years."

"I do my job."

The cruiser pulled up to the courthouse. "Sure you do, but not the way it should be done. People shouldn't be afraid of their law officers."

Lee Bob turned and looked him in the face after putting the car in park. "Don't give me that reform bullshit. Fear keeps most people from breaking the law."

"Let me out here. There's my investigation team." Purvis opened the door and started to close it when the sheriff stopped him.

"One thing, Purvis—this is still my county, so anything you find, I want to know about it."

Purvis answered professionally, "You will. I never interfere with local law officers."

"Just so you understand," Lee Bob asserted.

"So tell me, why didn't you bring John and Seth in?"

"Because when I spoke to Seth, he was even more afraid than John. Someone called him and told him he was a dead man, also."

"What does that have to do with the judge's death?"

"Scared men make mistakes, and I'm gonna catch 'em when they do." The sheriff opened his car door and walked into the courthouse building and then to his office.

Chapter 29

The Fix Isn't

Judge Lovell rapped his gavel. "This hearing will come to order. Mr. Wilburton, the court understands you have a codicil to be submitted on the Nichols estate."

"Yes, Your Honor, it was signed in my office." He walked up to the bench and handed the judge a piece of paper. "As you can see, Your Honor, it was signed by Mr. Nichols and witnessed by two people."

"Are the witnesses present?"

"Yes, Your Honor."

"Mr. Carroll, I understand you represent the person for the original will."

"Yes, Your Honor. We also have several sworn statements we would like to place on the record."

"You may bring the statements forward, Mr. Carroll."

Taking the papers, the judge asked, "It is your contention in these papers that Mr. Nichols didn't sign the codicil?"

"Your Honor, I have no way of knowing if Mr. Nichols ... Could I approach?"

"You may, Mr. Carroll."

Royal walked to the bench and said in a quieter voice, "Your Honor, we have no way of knowing if Mr. Nichols signed it or not. However, we can prove that Mr. Nichols didn't visit Mr. Wilburton's office on the day the codicil was signed."

"Mr. Wilburton, would you approach the bench?" They waited a moment for Seth to come forward. "Mr. Wilburton, I believe you could save this court a lot of time and paperwork if you would withdraw this will for probate."

"It is a legal document, Your Honor, signed and witnessed in my presence."

"Be that as it may, I am telling you right now that I will not turn guardianship of this young man or his estate over to two suspected murderers."

"We are innocent until proven guilty, Your Honor."

"Don't quote platitudes to the court, Mr. Wilburton. You have heard my ruling."

"We can appeal, Your Honor."

"You certainly can, but until such time as you are cleared, the estate will remain in the hands of Mr. Hagan."

"We will fight this ruling, Your Honor."

"Fine, Mr. Wilburton. Clerk, did you get all of this conversation?"

"Yes, Your Honor."

"Good. Then let it be entered that I have reaffirmed the appointment of Mr. Hagan. Mr. Wilburton, would you and Mr. Ross stay after the hearing? The court wishes to talk to you."

Royal walked back to the table, gathered up his papers, and put them in his briefcase. He told Buck and me, "Let's get out of here."

Getting up, Buck asked, "What happened?"

Leading us out into the hall, he said, "The court threw out their claim, but they will most likely appeal it."

"Can they win on appeal?" I asked. Royal led us into a conference room off the hallway and then closed the door.

"The only thing they could win would be a rehearing of the complete case."

I looked at Royal. "You mean we'll have to go through all of this again?"

"I don't think so. From what is being said around town, they are certain to be convicted of murder." Royal dropped his briefcase on the table and sat in one of the oak chairs.

Buck and I sat as well. "Horrible thing to say, but I hope you're right," I said. "I just want to get back to playing football and going to school."

Royal said to Buck, "I meant to ask you, how are those wells coming along?"

Buck was glad to be discussing something that he had an answer for. "Down to eight thousand, and everything looks real good. The last sample I sent up to Mark, every indication is there."

"How about the ones Mark is drilling?" Royal continued.

Buck leaned in on the table. "No doubt about it—those Houston leases are going to pay off."

Royal continued to question Buck. "Are Sharpe and Fenner getting the reorganization put together?"

"No problem that we know of. You're coming to the Christmas party on the twentieth, aren't you?" Buck said with a smile.

"Have to talk to the little lady, but right off I will say yes." We continued to discuss the details of current business for another forty-five minutes, and then I told Buck I needed to get home.

We pulled into the drive, and I jumped out and ran to the house. Mar met me at the door. Hugging and kissing me, she took my hand and said, "Come on. I want to show you Lady Blue's new colt. It's the cutest thing."

Walking toward the barn holding hands, I glanced at her and saw a red welt running from under her eye to her nose. "What happened to your face?" I had an instant jolt of adrenaline rush through my body.

"It was an accident. I ran into the side of my locker." Mar wasn't making eye contact with me and was turning away. *There's somethin' she isn't telling me,* I thought.

I stopped, and her forward momentum and our joined hands spun her back to face me. "How in the world did you do that?"

Mar started to cry. "Tommy, please don't get mad, but Manny will tell you tomorrow anyway."

"Manny will tell me what?" I noticed that my voice was getting louder and more intense.

"Promise me you won't get mad?"

"Mar, I'm not promising nothing until I hear the details."

"Okay, but I don't want you to get mad. Sanchez grabbed me by the arm in the hall by the lockers. I tried to pull loose and fell into the locker."

My brain exploded. "You been having trouble with him?"

"Not bad, Tommy, really." She was still crying.

I listened to what she said in disbelief. "You're tellin' me he's done things like this before?"

"Yes, but Tommy, please don't have any trouble with him. It isn't worth it." She pulled her hand out of mine and covered her face with both hands.

I was angry when I thought about how she had been keeping it from me. "Don't be melodramatic. I'm not about to get killed."

"You're being foolish, and I'm going back to the house to tell Buck." Mar started to turn for the house. I took her arm and wrapped her up in a hug.

I whispered, "Mar, don't you do that. This is between us. It doesn't have anything to do with them."

Now Mar was mad and talking fast. "Tommy, you got a hang-up about Sanchez. Of course it has something to do with them. They love you just like I do."

I worked at calming my voice. "I'm not a kid, Mar, and I can take care of myself. So you just stay out of it."

Telling her to stay out of it was like kicking a hornets' nest. She came unhinged. "Dammit, Tommy! I am in it if you get into a fight over something that happened to me! I love you and don't want you hurt. If you loved me, you would do what I tell you!"

The only thing I came up with was, "Mar, you can't change my mind."

Mar was at the point of cold rage. "If you do this, I am going to be real mad at you."

"I don't know why."

She punched me in the stomach and shouted, "You don't know why? How stupid can you get?" She whirled and ran back into the house.

When I walked into the house, Rosie asked me, "You and Marylyn have an argument?"

"Something like that. Think I'll take a bath and look for a neutral corner."

Buck said, "Me too. I want to get to bed early. Got a lot of work to do in the morning."

"Well, I'm first. You leave a ring!" I took off for the bathroom, but Buck beat me there and locked the door so I couldn't get in.

Mar didn't come out for supper, so I sat and talked to Rocky about the ranch. At ten, I got up and went to bed. I tossed and turned for over an hour but couldn't go to sleep. My bedroom door came open, and Mar slipped in and crawled into bed with me. Pulling her close, I leaned forward and claimed her lips. Her face was damp, and the tears on her lips tasted salty. "Why are you crying?" I asked.

"Oh, Tommy, don't be such a fool. You know why I'm crying."

"Look, honey, don't start in on me again. It won't change anything."

"It's not that. I want to show you how much you mean to me. Hold me close. I don't want to lose you."

We slowly submerged ourselves in our lovemaking.

The next morning, when Rosie got up to make coffee, Mar slipped back to her own room.

Manny met me at the top of the school steps. "Hey, Gringo, how's the boy?"

"Fine. What's the occasion?"

"What do you mean? Can't a guy meet his best buddy without having ulterior motives?"

"Not after what happened yesterday, you can't."

"Mar told you, then?"

"Sure she did. Why didn't you tell me he had been bothering her?"

"I didn't know it myself until yesterday."

"Well, I'll tell you one thing—it won't happen again after today."

"Don't start anything here at school, T. C. You'll get thrown out."

"I don't see him anyplace but here at school."

"All it will do is cause you trouble."

"Then that's the way it's going to have to be."

The first bell rang, and we walked down to study hall. I didn't see Sanchez until the 10:15 class break. He came swaggering and smirking toward me with Helio beside him. Waiting until he was about three feet away, I stepped out in front of him. "I want to talk to you, greaseball!"

"You looking for trouble, Gurley?"

"How'd you guess, shithead?"

I stood poised on the balls of my feet and watched them both. Sanchez had slipped his hand into his pants pocket. Watching his arm, I saw him withdraw his hand, the knife come out, and the blade spring open. As I swung sideways, I shifted my weight to my left leg and raised my right leg like Chee had taught me. I kicked Sanchez in the nuts.

Sanchez's eyes snapped wide, and his mouth flew open in a half-scream and gasp. The knife flew out of his hand, hit the wall, and went skittering down the hall.

Helio started to throw a punch, but I pivoted again and kicked him two inches above his belt buckle. The air rushed out of him like exploding bagpipes. He doubled over and fell to the floor, trying to breathe.

Sanchez was on his knees. I took one step forward and, using the side of my right hand, hit him across the bridge of the nose. I heard the smashing crush of bone and felt it give way under the force of my blow. Sanchez fell backward, one leg out straight and the other doubled under his unconscious body.

I turned to Helio and heard him retching his breakfast. Someone grabbed my arm, and I spun to see Manny standing there.

"Thought you wasn't going to do anything here at school."

"Couldn't help myself, buddy."

Mr. Ward hurried up to us. "You the cause of this, Gurley?"

I smiled. "Cause of what?"

Another teacher walked up and handed Mr. Ward Sanchez's knife.

"Is this his?" Mr. Ward asked me.

"It don't belong to me," I fired back, speaking through my rage.

Mr. Ward told the other teacher to go call the police. "Gurley, you and Cantu go to my office."

I pointed to Manny and said, "He didn't have anything to do with this."

"Don't argue with me. Get up to my office."

"I'm not arguing. I'm tellin' you he wasn't involved!"

"Do what you're told, son, and get your butt to the office."

Manny and I sat there in the outer office and waited for Mr. Ward, staring out the steel-enclosed windows that had needed to be cleaned for the last twenty-five years. The chairs were steel folding chairs with not an inch of softness to be found. The bulletin board was covered with announcements that no one had bothered to take down for the past three years. Manny asked, "Think they'll suspend you?"

I was still flush with adrenaline. "Don't know. Don't really care about now."

Mar came hurrying in. "Tommy, you all right?"

"I'm fine, sweetie."

"One of the girls told me he had cut you with a knife."

"Not me," I said. "I didn't give him a chance."

"Where did all the blood and vomit come from?"

"I would say the blood was from Sanchez's nose, and the vomit was Helio's breakfast."

"It isn't something to joke about, is it, Manny?"

"No. I only hope they don't suspend him."

"Surely not. You don't think they will, do you?"

"We won't have to wait long to find out," I said. "Here comes Mr. Ward and Officer Dave."

"Gurley, you and Cantu come into my office." We all sat down, and he looked up. "Okay, did Sanchez attack you with that knife?"

"No, I didn't give him a chance. When he pulled it out of his pocket and clicked it open, I kicked him in the—"

"Hold it. We know where you kicked him. What about his face?"

"I hit it too."

"On purpose?"

"I wasn't tryin' to miss it."

"I mean, after he was helpless?"

"A man with a knife isn't exactly helpless," I argued.

"You know what I mean, Gurley. You hit him after the knife was gone."

"I sure did, about as hard as I could."

Officer Dave spoke up. "Mr. Ward, we have all we need here. I'm taking Sanchez with us on assault with a deadly weapon."

"Fine, officer. Don't you want Gurley and Cantu?"

"I told you, Mr. Ward," I interjected. "Manny here didn't have anything to do with this."

"No, we don't want either. You can't blame a man for defending himself."

"All right, officer. Talk to you later. Now, Gurley, you trying to tell me that you put both of them down out there in the hall?"

"Yes, sir, I did, as a matter of fact." I sat erect and looked him in the eyes.

"Who started it?"

"I can't really say. I stepped out in the hall to say something to him, and he pulled a knife."

Mr. Ward looked puzzled. "What were you going to say?"

"It's personal. I'd rather not say." I crossed my arms.

"You *will* say! I won't have two of my students beat up in the hall and not know the reason." Mr. Ward was pressing hard.

"Well, I'm afraid I can't say any more."

Ward stood and leaned over his desk. "Either you will tell me or I will suspend both of you."

"I have told you twice," I said, "but you don't seem to listen."

Ward sat in exasperation. "Never mind. I don't believe you could have done that to both of those boys."

I stood up and pointed to the hallway. "In the first place, Mr. Ward, they're not boys, and in the second place, I'm not used to being called a liar. I kicked their asses by myself, without help from anyone else."

"Sit down, boy! Personally, I don't care what you're used to, Gurley. You will tell me what I want to know, or you're both suspended." Ward was emphatic.

I turned to Manny. "Manny, tell him you didn't have anything to do with this."

"I didn't have anything to do with this." Manny looked at Ward and smiled.

"If that is the case, Cantu, then you had better convince Gurley here to tell me what I want to know." Ward looked from Manny to me.

"I'm sorry, Mr. Ward, but I'm like T. C.—I don't think it's any of your business. You haven't believed a word he's told you already, so I don't think you would believe it if he told you again."

"You're suspended, Cantu, for two weeks. Are you going to tell me what I want to know, Gurley?"

"No, Ward, I am not."

"It is 'Mr. Ward' to you."

"Then you can call me Mr. Gurley," I replied.

"You are suspended for a month, Gurley." We stood up and pushed the chairs back to the wall.

"Fine. Manny, come on." Reaching the door, I turned and said, "I guess you know, Ward, that you can kiss your football championship good-bye."

"We still have football players, and they are not insolent, so we will get by."

"Good luck."

Mar and Tess were waiting in the hall. Mar asked, "What happened?"

"I got a month; Manny got two weeks."

Tess asked Manny, "You wasn't even in it, was you?"

"No, but he wouldn't believe us."

A teacher walked around the corner. "Hey, what are you kids doing out of the classroom?"

"Getting ready to go home," Manny answered.

"Don't be smart, Cantu, or you *will* be home for a while."

"I am trying to tell you—Mr. Ward sent us home."

"All of you? What about you girls?"

"No, we're on our way to a cheerleader meeting," Tess answered.

"You know the rule about being in the hall between classes. Let me see your pass."

Tess handed it to him. "All right. You girls get to your meeting, and you boys go home."

We started to head out of the building, and Manny said, "We'd better stop and see Coach Baker."

"Why? We don't owe him anything."

"No, I know that, but I would love to play for the Texas state championship."

"So would I. We have worked too damn hard not to."

As we were going into the locker room, Coach Baker saw us and asked, "What you boys doing out of class?"

"Mr. Ward kicked us out of school."

"For what?"

"T. C. got into a fight with Sanchez."

"Damn, I knew it was coming. Couldn't you have waited for another few days, T. C.?"

"Wouldn't have waited this long, Coach, if I had known what had been going on. Manny didn't have anything to do with it. He came up after it was all over."

"Did you tell Mr. Ward?"

"Both of us tried, but he wouldn't believe us."

"I'll talk to him. You sure Manny never had anything to do with it?"

"You know him, Coach. I'm getting tired of being called a liar."

"It was only something to say, T. C. I'm sorry."

"Fine. I don't care about myself. We're going to move anyway, so it doesn't really matter that much to me."

"We certainly won't stand a chance with you and Manny both missing. By the way, what happened to Sanchez?"

Manny said, "I saw the cops leading him off, so I suppose he's in jail."

"Well, Gurley, if you set out to lose us the state championship, you certainly succeeded," Coach said in total disbelief.

"Wish I could say I'm sorry, Coach. He got exactly what he deserved. He's been riding me all year."

"Nobody gets what they deserve, Gurley. You will find that out one of these days. You boys go on home, and I will talk to Mr. Ward." He showed us to the door and then headed for the office.

Manny shouted behind him, "I hope you can get him to change his mind! T. C. and I would both like to finish out the season." The coach turned and walked back to us.

"You feel that way too, Gurley?" Coach looked me up and down.

"I'd hate to have put in all this work without getting something out of it, Coach."

"All right. I'll call you later this evening. You boys go on home and stay out of trouble!"

Manny said, "Thanks, Coach! We appreciate it."

On the way out of the locker room, I asked if he needed a ride home.

"Sure do. I been wanting to talk to you. I need a favor."

"Anything I can do, I will. You know that." We reached the parking lot and climbed into my truck. Manny slammed his door and then turned to me.

"We been putting it off till football season was over. I was wondering if you would loan me your car or pickup."

I had no idea what he was talking about. I fired up the 454 and asked, "You been putting off what?"

"Tess and I are getting married." Manny was smiling at me.

I turned the truck off and looked at him. "You still have a year of school left, Manny."

"I know, but it's too late to think about that now." Manny was wringing his hands and looking at the floorboard.

"You and Tess in trouble?" I asked.

"Yeah, Tess is pregnant, if that's what you mean."

"It's none of my business," I said. "You can have anything I have, but I would like to see you finish school." Manny was clearly distraught.

He finally turned to look at me. "I would too, but there is no way I'm going to let Tess down."

"Do your folks know?"

"My dad does. I told him the other night."

"How did he take it?"

"Real bad. He wanted me to go to college and get an education." Manny was staring out the passenger window.

"Never did ask you what you was planning on taking up." I put my hand on his shoulder.

"I wanted to be a geologist. Not much chance of that now." He leaned his head against the glass.

"Why not? Lots of kids who are married go to school!"

"Either their folks is supporting them or they have money set aside. My folks can't do that."

"When you planning on getting married?" I asked, not knowing what else to say.

"We had planned on taking off next Monday and going up to Nevada."

I started the truck again and pulled out of the lot. "Let me talk to Mar. Maybe we can drive up with you."

"Sure wish you could. We hate to get married without someone with us." Manny looked at me again, and his eyes were red. We drove the rest of the way in silence.

I pulled into Manny's driveway. "You and Tess go ahead and make your plans. I'll talk to Buck and see if he'll let us go with you. Either way, you can use either one of the rigs you want."

"Thank you, buddy. I'll call you."

"Also, if while you're out of school, you want to work, I'll have Buck put you on the payroll."

"I can sure use the money. Thanks, T. C."

"You're welcome, Pepper Belly. Call me in the morning."

"Will do. Later, Gringo."

I drove home to the ranch and went out to where they were drilling about a half mile from the house. Buck was there with a big grin on his face when I parked the car and walked over. His clothes were covered in grease, and he was walking over to the watering tank with a bar of pumice in his hands.

When I got close enough, Buck threw his greasy arm around my shoulder. "She just now came in! Looks like a big one. Marylyn and you are the richest sixteen- and seventeen-year-olds in Texas, son!"

"You mean they struck oil?"

"She's a gully whomper, biggest one I've ever been around. Looks like Marylyn is going to be a very rich young lady, and your oil company isn't gonna be hurtin' either."

"She will like that, I'm sure, but I have to talk to you."

"Well, sure, son. Start in. By the way, what are you doing out of school?"

"Had a run-in with Sanchez. They suspended me for a month."

"Did you start it?"

"I had to, Buck. He put his hands on Mar and has been givin' her a real bad time."

"That's why you and her were on the outs with each other yesterday, isn't it?" Buck was looking at me closely.

"Yeah, she wanted me to let it pass. I couldn't do it. You understand." I was watching him for his reaction.

"Sure, kid. Some things you can't walk around, not if you want to have any self-respect. That what you wanted to talk to me about?" Buck stuck his hands in the tank and pulled them out to scrub them with the pumice bar.

"One thing. The other is that I want to put Manny on the payroll full-time." He didn't look up at me, just kept cleaning his arms and hands.

He asked in a quiet tone, "Why? Is he quitting school?"

I sat on the edge of the tank in an attempt to make eye contact with him. "He doesn't want to, but him and Tess have to get married."

"Look, if you want to hire him full-time, it's all right with me."

I held my hands out. "No, I don't want him to work full-time. I want you to have a talk with him. He can continue to work part-time like he has been. We can have the old ranch house out by the bunkhouse fixed up, and he and

Tess can live there." I crossed my arms again. "I want him to finish school, and if he doesn't get a college scholarship, we will put him through."

"Damn, Tommy, that will cost you a lot of money," Buck said.

I looked at Buck. "Well, we *got* a lot of money, but I don't have a lotta close friends."

"If that's what you want." Buck stuck his soapy hands in the tank and swished them around. Then he started toweling himself dry.

"He wants to become a geologist, and knowing Manny the way I do, he will be a great one." I was standing and had turned to face Buck as he dried off.

"Well, he is an excellent worker."

"Not only that, I trust him. Being in the oil business, wouldn't you rather have someone like that on the payroll?" I had my arms crossed as we stood there.

"Sure, but that's a long way down the road, Tommy, and you don't know for sure he can make it in college." Buck threw the towel over his shoulder and put his hands on his hips.

"No, I don't, but I know Manny, and I want him to have the chance. They want to drive up to Nevada, so could you get someone on that old house and have it fixed up 'fore they get back?"

"All right. You know, son, I like what you're trying to do. Your uncle Boats, despite a lot of comment to the contrary, had an eye for good men. I think you do too."

"If it's all right with you," I continued, "Mar and I would like to go with Manny when they get married."

"Sure. I remember when I got married, we had two friends with us. Before the day was over, they were married too. But I should run that past Rosie and Rocky 'fore I make the final decision."

"You and Rosie have done all right. How about the other couple?"

"Well, they live up in the Panhandle and have seven kids, so I 'spect they're doing all right too." Buck was laughing. "Two was plenty for us."

"Mar has a pep meeting to go to tonight, so I'm driving back into town. See what you can do real quick on that house, would ya, Buck?"

"Sure, son. I'll get right on it."

"How about tomorrow after school, see if Rosie would go into town with Mar. I want to buy Manny and Tess a complete set of furniture for the house.

Have Rosie and Mar take Tess. Let her think they're shopping for new furniture for our house. Think Rosie would do it?"

Buck looked at me strangely. "Are you kidding? Turn Rosie loose in a furniture store and she will most likely bankrupt you."

"Fine. Turn her loose," I said as I walked back to the truck.

Manny was sitting in his dad's station wagon when I pulled up to the high school. I got out of Boats's Lincoln and walked over. "How did your mom take it?"

"Not bad. Dad was the one who took it hard. How about you, T. C.?"

I shrugged. "Have to do what you have to do. By the way, Mar and I can go with you to get married."

"Man, that's great. Tess was kind of scared for us to go alone."

"Buck told me right before I left that he wanted to talk to you. Why not drive out to the ranch in the morning?"

"Speaking about in the morning, Coach called right before I left the house and wanted us to come in and see him in the morning."

"He say what for?"

"No, something about we would like it."

"Think he got us reinstated?"

"Probably. It's more important to you than me. Sure would have liked to play on a championship team before I quit, though."

"Look, in the morning, you ride to work with your dad instead of coming out to the ranch. Buck and I will meet you there. We can go see what Coach wants after you talk to Buck."

"Any idea what Buck wants?"

"I told him about you and Tess, so I guess he wants to offer you a job."

"Sure hope so. We are going to need all the money we can get."

The girls came out and joined us. We separated, agreeing to meet in the morning. On the way out to the ranch, I told Mar about the arrangements for Tess and Manny. After I finished, Mar squeezed my arm. "That's one of the reasons I love you so much, Tommy—your gentleness and kindness."

Chapter 30

Police Politics

Lee Bob walked into Sewell's office and sat down. Adolph followed and took the other chair. "Here are the records on the numbers you wanted," Lee Bob said to Sewell as he handed him two folders.

Sewell opened both folders and laid them out on his desk. "Where's the folder on the Chubb case?"

"I understood on the phone that you wanted what I had on my open murder cases."

"That's what I told you."

"The Chubb case isn't open. I have it nailed airtight."

"Be that as it may, Lee Bob, I am going to be the one to prosecute it in court, so I want to see all of it."

"I'll have Adolph bring it back when we get back to the office."

"Do that. Now, let's get on these other two cases. You have anything else that isn't in these folders, Sheriff?"

"Everything I have is there. I sent one of my deputies up to Oklahoma State Bureau of Investigation's Forensic Science Services to check out the shell casing from the shotgun that killed the judge."

"Why? Is there something different about it?" Sewell asked.

Lee Bob stuck his finger on the picture of the ammunition and pointed out, "It's a self-loaded black-powder-base shell casing, and this store in Pauls Valley, down in Garvin, is the only one in the state to sell them."

"Let me know if you come up with something," Sewell said.

"Sure. Glad to."

Purvis had been sitting in the corner and hadn't said anything so far. "You looked at these folders, Purvis?" Sewell asked.

"Lee Bob and I went over them several times. Everything we know is in there." Purvis stretched his legs and yawned.

Sewell looked back at Lee Bob. "Are we any closer to getting the murderers?"

Lee Bob tapped the folders with his index finger. "Everything we find out gets us a little closer. Purvis and I both think the killing has to be part of some kind of larger conspiracy."

"How can you be so sure?" Sewell was pissy and spoiling for an argument.

"The killer has to be local. I or my deputies know if any strangers are around. There wasn't any reported when Doc was killed." Adolph was nodding in agreement as the sheriff slapped his hand on the desk.

"From what Purvis has told me, Doc was in drugs pretty heavily. That right?"

Lee Bob looked back and forth between Purvis and Sewell. "I always thought so but never could prove it."

"From what we heard up at the capital, you didn't try too hard." Sewell leaned forward, somewhat challenging Lee Bob.

"Sewell, you might be the fucking assistant attorney general, but if you ever make a statement like that again in my fucking county, you will be eating your food through a straw for the next month. You understand me, you jackboot piece of shit?"

"You don't frighten me, Lee Bob. Wait just a second—I have a job to do, and if I have to get rid of you to get it accomplished, I will."

Lee Bob stood and leaned over Sewell's desk, prompting Purvis and Adolph to stand as well. "Just make damn sure you are on solid ground when you try it. If you don't get it done, I'll be comin' for you, and ain't no toothpick cocksucker like Purvis gonna save your ass."

"I'll keep that in mind, Sheriff. The only thing you have to do is catch the killer or killers. I have already talked to the governor, and if you don't turn up something pretty quick, I'll remove you from office."

Lee Bob started around the end of the desk, but Adolph stepped up to stop him. He turned on Sewell again, leaning across his desk. "You and I both know better than that. There is only one way I can be removed from office, and I don't believe you will ever be able to do it!"

"I can try."

"Well, shit in one hand and wish in the other, and see where that gets you!" Lee Bob was nearly hyperventilating.

"Just keep in mind that I'll be watching," Sewell said with his chair backed all the way up to the wall.

"Fine. I know where I stand. Purvis, from now on, you stay away from my office." Reaching over the desk, Lee Bob picked up the folders. "These files are mine. When I complete my investigation, they will be forwarded to you. Until then, don't you or Purvis either one come anywhere near my office unless you want a seat in a cell."

Sewell stood up and wagged his finger at Lee Bob. "You can't get away with this, Lee Bob. Don't you know that I have been appointed temporary district attorney?"

"Means jack shit to me. The district attorney's office and the sheriff's office are two different offices. Stay in yours!"

"I have right of egress to your office and files at all times," Sewell countered.

"Not according to my attorney, you don't—only to what I want to share with you. Right now, that ain't nothin'." Lee Bob pushed past Adolph and out the door. As Adolph reached to close the door behind him, they could hear Sewell yelling at them, "I'm sure Judge Lovell will have something to say on this!"

Lee Bob spun around and yelled back, "From now on, this county is going to be run by the book—my book! So you two political boot lickers stay the hell out of my way!"

Lee Bob stomped into his office and headed for the file cabinet. Taking out his keys, he started to open the lock. He glanced down and saw that the transparent tape he had placed across the lower drawer had been pulled loose.

Unlocking the cabinet, he put in the folders and pulled out the one on Chubb. He took the folder with him into the radio room. Junior was sitting there reading a *Playboy* magazine.

"Any one of the deputies been in since I left?"

"No, Sheriff, no one."

"None of the deputies been here?"

"No, no one. You expecting someone, Sheriff?"

Opening the Chubb folder, he looked through it and pulled out two sheets of paper. Handing the folder to Junior, he said, "Take these up to Sewell's office. He has a preliminary hearing coming up soon."

"Did you want me to get one of the deputies for you?"

"Not right now. I had a couple of things I wanted done, but there's no rush on them. Find out where Adolph is and let me know. I'll be in the patrol car."

"Sure thing, Sheriff."

Leaving the office, Lee Bob got into his car and stuck the papers in his briefcase. He had pulled up to the stop sign at the jail parking lot when Junior came on the horn. "Adolph said he's on the stakeout you put him on, Sheriff."

"Thanks, Junior. Out."

"What stakeout is that, Sheriff? It isn't marked on the operations board. Over."

"If I wanted it there, it would be. Over and out."

Turning east, he drove out toward Wapanucka, a small town in the eastern part of the county with fewer than five hundred residents. Now he knew who had been giving out information from his office. He just needed to set up a trap and nail him down. He pressed the radio mike. "Tishomingo two, come in please. Over."

"What you need, Sheriff?" Adolph replied.

Lee Bob pushed the accelerator on his cruiser and flew out of the parking lot. "Meet me at the drive-in in Wapanucka. Over."

"Will do. Out."

Ten minutes later, he pulled into the drive-in parking lot next to Adolph's cruiser and motioned for Adolph to join him. Adolph got out and walked around the back of his cruiser and up to the rolled-down window on the passenger side of Lee Bob's car. "Been any movement around the place?" Lee Bob asked.

"None except for the younger brother. He fed the livestock and went back into the house." Adolph was speaking just above a whisper.

"You been able to get a look in the garage?"

"No, but like I told you, there is a blue station wagon parked in there," Adolph said, pointing to the garage.

"Damn. I wish we could get the tire prints off of it without anyone knowing."

"If what I found out this morning is right, we should be able to do it tomorrow morning." Adolph leaned into the window to further muffle his voice.

"How's that?" Lee Bob asked.

"I checked with the clinic. Bobby Dean has two treatments every month up at the nuthouse, and tomorrow morning is one of them."

"Does Del take him up?" The sheriff dug into the ashtray, looking for a pen to make a note.

"No, he pays the Morehouse boy up the road to take him."

Lee Bob found a pencil and started scribbling notes. "Good. You slip in there in the morning and get me a plaster cast of those tires. Also, better take some pictures of the tire tread and the station wagon. I want to show it to Stenovich and see if he recognizes it."

Adolph turned and looked around to make sure nobody was near. "You know, Sheriff, I'm pretty sure we can nail him on Doc's murder, but do you think he is tied up in the judge's death?"

"It's all tied together somehow. I checked with the state school, and Bobby Dean, for all his backwardness, was a first-class machinist. Judging from the work they put in on that shotgun setup in the car, he would have to be."

Adolph opened the door to the sheriff's car and sat down, leaving the door ajar. "Funny, though—we can't find anyone who saw someone fooling around the judge's car."

The sheriff shrugged. "Not surprised. How many times have you paid attention to someone climbing into a car in the county parking lot?"

"See what you mean." Adolph panned the surroundings for sign of movement.

"You might as well head back to town," Lee Bob said. "I have to go to district court in the morning for a preliminary hearing, so I will be out here as soon as I get back." Adolph got out, closed the door, and stuck his head in the window to continue the conversation.

"Heard today that their attorney is asking for a change of venue. That true?" Adolph asked.

"Yeah, and with the money they have to throw around, they'll get it." Lee Bob started the car.

"Think the judge will allow them to remain out on bail?"

"Most likely. We'll see you tomorrow." Lee Bob pulled away and was looking down to punch the button to roll up the passenger window. He had just turned out of the driveway and onto the highway when he saw a flash and his windshield exploded inward over the steering wheel, scattering glass all over him.

He automatically ducked at the same time as his foot punched the accelerator and launched the car across the road. He heard the shotgun go off a second time. He felt the car hit the ditch and pitch sideways as it came back onto the road. Using his left foot, he stomped on the brake. The car came to a sliding halt, its ass end in the ditch and its front wheels on the road.

He pushed both feet against the driver's door, released the twelve-gauge from its harness with his left hand, and pulled the passenger door handle with his right. He crab walked out of the car, sliding on his back till his shoulders and back of his head hit the pavement. The twelve-gauge was ready for the assailant to make his appearance.

Looking around, he saw Adolph pulling onto the road. A motorcycle started up from the direction of the shotgun blasts. The trees were too thick, but he heard the engine screaming as the rider changed gears without releasing the accelerator. Its high-pitched whine faded into the distance. Adolph pulled up and jumped out, holding his German-made Sig Sauer, its .45-caliber barrel looking like a cannon at the ready.

"What happened, Sheriff?"

"Someone just took a couple of shots at me with a shotgun!"

"Funny they would use a shotgun, isn't it?"

"Only if you're not the one being shot at," Lee Bob replied.

"Did you see anything?"

"No, he was behind the trees over there. Let's see if we can find anything."

Crawling over the slight rise, they entered the edge of the woods. "It was farther over to the right. This is about the place. See if you can find anything over there. I'll check around here," Lee Bob said.

They hadn't searched for more than three or four minutes when Adolph called, "Over here, Sheriff!"

Adolph was kneeling, a shotgun shell in his hand. "The bike was parked behind that bush over there. He chewed some type of tobacco. Other than these two items, nothing's here."

"Fine. Get a bit of the chaw for a sample of his spit, and we'll send it in. At least we'll know his blood type. Another thing—say nothing about this to anyone."

"Whatever you say, Sheriff."

"I meant to tell you before. Make sure you don't tell Junior anything about what we're doing. You haven't told him about the stakeout, have you?"

"No, but he called me on the horn a couple of times and wanted to know where I was and what I was doing."

"What did you tell him?"

"Only that I was doing a job for you."

"Keep it that way. He's on Purvis's payroll."

"Doesn't surprise me one bit."

"Why do you say that?"

"Because Junior makes a tidy profit from providing contraband to prisoners."

"How come you never told me about it?"

"Thought you knew, Sheriff. Not much goes on that you don't know about."

"I didn't know about Junior extorting the prisoners, but I sure as hell will correct it real quick. I'm taking your patrol car. Take mine into the body shop."

"Anything I should say about what happened?"

"If anyone asks, tell them it's none of their damn business. Just fix it."

"Right, Sheriff."

Junior was walking out of the squad room when Lee Bob entered. "Come into my office, Junior."

He walked into the sheriff's office, pulled out a chair, and sat down. "What do you need, Sheriff?"

"What I need, Junior, is for you to clean out your desk and turn in your badge."

His grin disappeared. "You firing me, Sheriff?"

"You better damn well believe it."

"Want to tell me why?"

"Not really. Let's just say I'm tired of you being around."

"If that's the way you want it, Lee Bob."

"I want you out of my fucking jail tonight."

"I will be, but don't be surprised to see me back here tomorrow."

"Nothing surprises me anymore, Junior, but if you think you're coming back in here, you're dead wrong."

"We will see, Sheriff."

"That's right, Junior. I am the sheriff, and the thing to remember is that I run this county."

"Up to a point."

"Look, you don't know how close you are to getting every one of your fucking teeth kicked down your goddamned throat, so if you're wise, you will get your shit packed and your fat ass out of here as quickly as you can."

"Whatever you say, Sheriff. It's going to be a pleasure helping get you locked up."

Lee Bob lunged out of his chair, shot across the desk, and made a grab for Junior.

A terrified Junior scrambled sideways out of his chair and onto the floor on his hands and knees. Reaching the door, he glanced back at Lee Bob, who had settled back into his chair behind his desk. Without a word, Junior rose and rushed out through the door.

Lee Bob slid the window up between his office and the squad room.

Joe Bill was sitting at the radio desk with his feet propped up, reading *Hustler*. Hearing the window slide up, he dropped his feet to the floor and turned toward it. "What ya need, Sheriff?"

"Get all Junior's stuff packed and set it out on the doorstep." Lee Bob was pissed.

"Everything, Sheriff?" Joe Bill said in disbelief.

"I don't want a thing of his left here. As soon as you get that done, get in contact with all the reserve deputies and personnel of this department and tell them there will be a meeting here at 7:30 tonight, and it's mandatory that they all attend. If any of them says they can't make it, tell them to stop by later and turn in their badges. Got it?" Lee Bob was talking quickly and angrily. Joe Bill knew better than to interrupt or question him further.

"Sure have, Sheriff. Anything else?" Joe Bill waited in anticipation of an explanation, which he didn't get.

"No. I'm going home for a bath and some supper. Be back for the meeting. You get a hold of Purvis and tell him I would like for him to sit in on the meeting." Lee Bob was still fuming.

"Will do. Say, thought you would like to know there was a strange transmission on channel eleven tonight as I was coming in to work."

"What about?"

"I never caught their handles. They were already into their conversation when I turned it on, but this one guy said he had left two bears in the woods and had taken a shot at the head bear but missed. Anyway, he went on to ask if there was anything at his house they could be interested in." Joe Bill watched the sheriff closely for any reaction and continued his recounting of the radio transmission.

"The other one said, 'Could be they're interested in my car collection?' The other one came back on and said, 'Whatever it is, you'd better get rid of it unless you want it found.' Then he said, 'Well, I have to get rid of a set of wheels myself so talk to you later,' and they signed off."

The sheriff's disposition changed before Joe Bill's eyes. He became inquisitive and attentive. "You recognize the voice?"

"One of them sounded real familiar, but you know how those CBs distort voices. Mean anything to you, Sheriff?"

The sheriff looked at Joe Bill and spoke matter-of-factly in a normal voice. "Yeah, you'll learn about it tonight," he said. "Get a hold Adolph and tell him to meet me at the Chalet."

Pulling into the Chalet parking lot, the sheriff spotted Adolph in the spare squad car. He wheeled in beside him.

Adolph climbed out of his car and walked around to the driver's side. "Something happen, Lee Bob?"

"I want you to get back out to Delbert's and watch them. Judging from something Joe Bill heard on the CB tonight, they might try and get rid of the station wagon. If they try, you stop them. Hold whoever is driving it. In fact, hold all of them. I'm on my way inside to get a search warrant. Make it code three until you get close to their place. Better get going."

"You want me to report in if they are still there?"

"Yeah, but keep it simple. I don't want any more of this to get out than has to."

"Got it, Sheriff. Will let you know."

At the Chalet, Lee Bob asked Ruth, the waitress, what room the judge was in.

"He's right around the corner talking to Purvis and Junior, Sheriff."

He stepped into the dining room, walked around the wall, and found the three of them engaged in hushed conversation. All three looked up when he loomed over the table. Judge Lovell said, "Pull out a chair, Lee Bob."

"No, thanks, Judge. I don't have much use for informers, and I damn sure don't intend to sit with a snitch. I have to talk to you."

"All right. Purvis and Junior, would you excuse us?"

As they were rising, Lee Bob said, "Purvis, we're having a meeting in my office at 7:30. Would like to have you sit in."

"Sure, Lee Bob. I'll be there. By the way, I have appointed Junior here to my special squad."

"That doesn't change my opinion of you or your squad a damn bit. He should fit in with the rat pack real nice."

"If that was supposed to be sarcastic, Sheriff, it doesn't faze me," Junior said.

"Wasn't supposed to be sarcastic. He's your type. Just don't expect any loyalty or truthfulness from him."

"I don't have to take that from you. You fired me, remember? Go to hell, Lee Bob."

"Junior, you been a puke all your life. Don't forget and ever show up around my office, or it will be something you will never be able to forget."

"*You* forget, Sheriff," Purvis said. "He's on my squad."

"I forget nothing, Purvis. You keep this wormy son of a bitch out of my county."

"You can't keep a state police officer out of a county. You know that."

"Purvis, I've cooperated with you up to a point. If you want to keep on getting it, you had better have him out of this county by morning."

"I can't and won't do that. So now what?"

"I was going to tell you at 7:30, but now is as good a time as any. The murderers of Doc and the judge will be in custody before morning. When I have them in custody, I want you and your outfit out of my office and my county."

Judge Lovell spoke up. "Who are they, Sheriff?"

"I would rather discuss it in private."

"We are all officers of the court here, Lee Bob. Mr. Jarvis has put in quite some time on this case, so he has the right to know who you're arresting."

"I need a search warrant for Delbert Hathaway's house."

"You talked to Sewell about the warrant?"

"No. I found out a few moments ago that the car used in Doc's murder is in Hathaway's garage. I also want to look into his machine shop to find out if the setup on the shotgun that killed the judge was made there."

"I will have to have a request from Sewell before I can issue the warrant."

"Okay, so I'll go call him."

"Should be in his room here at the motel," Lovell said.

"Know the number?"

"It's eighteen."

"I'll go back and see him."

"Do that. If he requests it, I'll issue one."

Lee Bob knocked on the door.

Sewell opened the door on the third rap. "Lee Bob, come in. Anything wrong?"

Lee Bob stepped into the motel room, noted that the bed covers were folded back and that someone was in the bathroom, but continued with his quest. "I need a search warrant for Delbert Hathaway's."

Sewell looked him over. "What reason?"

"I'm sure the car used in Doc's murder is in his garage." Lee Bob was in a hurry and didn't have time for foolish questions.

"He killed Doc?" Sewell was thinking out loud.

"Tied into it, anyway."

"Purvis agree with you?"

Lee Bob was impatient and irritated at the question. "Haven't checked with him to find out. Look, Sewell, I'm pretty sure the station wagon is going to be moved tonight. I must have the warrant to prevent it."

Sewell climbed on his high horse. "You don't get a search warrant without firm evidence. You write out all the facts and evidence you have on the case and submit them to me in the morning. If you have sufficient cause, I will ask Judge Lovell to issue the warrant."

Lee Bob's voice filled the room. "I told you, Sewell—they are moving the car tonight."

"It's only supposition on your part that they're moving it, isn't it?" Sewell backed up and sat on the bed.

"Partly, yes, but if they get rid of that car, our case will be harder to prove." Lee Bob calmed his voice and tried to appear reasonable.

"Now it's 'our case,' when you want something. You can't have it both ways, Sheriff. You cooperate with us, and we will return in kind. See me in the morning with your report." Sewell was smiling at Lee Bob in triumph.

Lee Bob stood there watching Sewell's face and listening. "I'll tell you what, Sewell. Why don't you, Purvis, and Judge Lovell take a flying fucking leap off Dead Man's Rock? And tell the whore in the bathroom she can come out now." Lee Bob turned and walked out, slamming the motel door.

Sewell stuck his head out the door and yelled, "Lee Bob, I will expect that report in the morning!"

Turning, Lee Bob told him, "I hope you hold your shit-smelling breath till you get it."

Sewell watched as he walked down the hall. He followed Lee Bob and watched him climb into his cruiser and drive off. He went into the dining room to the judge and Purvis.

Looking up, Judge Lovell asked, "You want me to issue a warrant, Sewell?"

"Think so, Judge. Purvis, get a couple of your men, and you go out to Hathaway's and tear that place apart."

Purvis asked, "Think Lee Bob will be out there?"

"Most likely. Judge, any way I can get Lee Bob removed from office?"

"Not at this point. Purvis, get your men rounded up and meet Sewell over at my office. Sewell, ride with me over to my office?"

Climbing into the car, Judge Lovell told Sewell, "I know you have some kind of agreement with Purvis. I don't want to know what it is. I also know you are either planning on running for attorney general or a judgeship in the next election. That's fine, but I want you to get one thing straight. If either one of you, Purvis or yourself, do anything that is in any way unethical or outside the law, I will personally use every power at my disposal to see you pay."

"I thought the governor told you to cooperate with us," Sewell said.

"He did, but remember one thing, Sewell—this is the last term our illustrious governor is going to be in office. I plan on sitting on the state Supreme Court one of these days, and I'm not putting my head on the block for you, Purvis, or the governor. No party stays in power forever, and when my party gets back into power, I'm the first one on the list. So I'm warning you, don't do anything to jeopardize me, or so help me God, I'll bury you in a place you will never get out."

"We haven't done anything wrong," Sewell said.

"Great. When Purvis gets over to my office, you give him the search warrant and have him take it out to Lee Bob."

"I would feel better if you would let Purvis serve the search warrant," Sewell said.

"Personally, Sewell, I'm not concerned with your feelings. Lee Bob is the sheriff of this county. You and Purvis were sent down here to help clear up these murders, not to interfere in his business."

"We were sent down here to investigate his performance and office as well."

"There's a difference between investigating and interfering."

"We haven't interfered with him," Sewell countered.

"You haven't helped him either, so from this moment on you will cooperate with him in every way possible. Understand?"

"Yes, sir, but I do intend to keep on with our investigation of his office."

"You do that. You'd better make sure it's done in a legal and lawful way, or I will take you before the State Bar."

Chapter 31

Mechanics of Killin' a Judge

When Purvis arrived, he had Junior and two other state troopers with him. He entered the judge's chambers, and Sewell handed him the search warrant. "Take this out and give it to Lee Bob, and ask him if he wants you to assist in the search."

"What if he says no?"

"Then you turn around and come back to town."

"I don't understand," Purvis said. "This is the chance we been waiting for."

Judge Lovell told the three officers, "Would you wait outside, please? I would like to speak to the captain."

After they left, Judge Lovell told Purvis, "You have received your orders, Captain, and they will be carried out to the letter. If you have any information on any of these crimes that you haven't turned over to the sheriff, you will do so immediately."

"Then how can I get him kicked out of office?" Purvis glanced over at Sewell and saw him shaking his head. Looking back at the judge, he could see the anger rising in his face.

"You weren't sent here to have him kicked out of office, Captain. You were sent here to investigate the *alleged* misconduct of Sheriff Whetzel. If he has violated his oath of office, it will be up to the court system to rectify it. Your ambition, Captain, doesn't have a thing to do with it. If I find out that you have jeopardized Sheriff Whetzel's investigation in any way, I will have you brought up for misconduct yourself. Do you understand?"

"Yes, Your Honor."

"I hope you do. Another thing, you will transfer Junior out of this county tonight."

"When I hired him, I told him he could help in the investigation of the sheriff."

"You can tell him now that I gave you a court order to remove him from the county."

"If you insist, sir."

"I don't insist, Captain. If you want to be in contempt of court, just let me see him here in the morning. Now go give those papers to Sheriff Whetzel."

"Yes, sir."

Lee Bob knew Purvis was in the area when he heard his voice on the radio. "State car thirty-six calling Tishomingo one. Come in." Lee Bob made him wait for a response and then finally replied.

"This is Tishomingo one. Come back."

"Lee Bob, Purvis here. Would like to meet you right away. Over."

"Concerning what, Purvis? Over."

"I have the papers you requested. Over."

"Where are you located? Over."

"About two miles east of Wapanucka. Over."

"Good. Come straight ahead to marker three, and then turn left. I will meet you at the first section road. Over."

"Got it. Be there in five minutes. Over."

Lee Bob saw Purvis's emergency lights about four minutes later. He got out and met Purvis beside his car.

"What changed Sewell's mind?" Lee Bob asked.

"We are all law officers, Lee Bob. I told him to cut you some slack. Here is the search warrant. You want us to help you?"

"Is Junior with you?"

"No, I ordered him to report to capital headquarters in the morning."

"How many men did you bring with you?"

"Two besides myself."

"Hathaway's place is the next one on the left, about a half mile up the road. Have one of your men take your patrol car past the house about a hundred yards. Tell him that when I tell him on the radio to hit it, I want him to hit the siren and turn on his lights. The other one is to take my car with the same instructions. Adolph and I are down the road about fifty yards. Join us when you're finished."

Purvis joined him a few minutes later. "I told them to give me five minutes and then to move in."

"Fine. Get in. All right, Adolph, leave the lights off and move up to their driveway."

They had no sooner pulled out of the trees and started down the road when headlights appeared behind them. Lee Bob grabbed the mike. "Put out those damned lights!" Both cars behind him turned off their lights.

When Adolph turned into the driveway, one car slipped by them. "Stop, Adolph," Lee Bob said. They sat there waiting with the engine running, looking at the ranch house about a hundred feet away. All of a sudden, the porch and yard lights came on.

Mike still in his hand, Lee Bob pushed the button and said, "All right, hit it, boys." Three sirens and all lights came on at about the same time. "Go, Adolph!"

Adolph hit the gas pedal and pulled the car up in front of the garage, the flashing lights adding illumination to the outside lights.

Delbert Hathaway stepped out on the front step as the officers climbed out of the patrol cars. "Evening, Lee Bob. Looks like you came loaded for bear."

"Guess we did, Delbert. I have a search warrant here to search your premises."

"Sure thing. Before you start, though, I would like to read it."

"Go ahead. Purvis, bring your boys in. Have one of them gather everybody here and put them in the living room and keep them there."

Adolph came up. "It's gone, Sheriff."

"Delbert, what happened to the blue Plymouth station wagon that was in your garage?"

"I don't own a station wagon, Sheriff."

"Don't play word games with me, Delbert. Where is the fucking station wagon?"

"I don't know anything about a station wagon," Delbert replied.

"Handcuff him, Adolph, and put him in the front room. Anyone else here, Delbert?"

"Only me and Bobby Dean."

"Where is he?"

"He's in his bedroom down the hall. Bright lights frighten him, so he is most likely in his closet or under the bed."

"Purvis, you and your men want to bring him out?"

"Don't try to handcuff him," Delbert said. "He goes crazy when you tie his hands or feet."

"Purvis, leave his hands free."

"Will do, Lee Bob." Purvis and two of his men slipped past Lee Bob on the porch and went through the front door.

Lee Bob then walked out to the garage and called for Adolph. "Where you at?"

"Out here in the shed behind the garage."

Lee Bob went on to the shed. Lee Bob saw a complete machine shop, including two big lathes and drill presses. "Man, looks like they have every tool in the world."

"Most complete one I've seen." Adolph was looking through cupboards and drawers.

"You bring the pictures of that shotgun frame from the judge's car?" Lee Bob asked.

"That's what I'm looking for, some scrap metal that it was cut from." He was bending over a wooden box, taking out pieces of metal.

Lee Bob walked over and opened up one of the large cabinets on the wall. "Holy jumped-up turkey shit! Adolph, look at these guns."

"Already seen them, Sheriff. They're all homemade too."

"You know, you're right. Man, whoever made these knew his stuff. Never saw such fine workmanship in my life."

"I've heard Bobby Dean always was a whiz at machine work," Adolph said.

"How in the hell can someone be classified as crazy and do workmanship like this?"

"Don't know. It's a crazy world."

Purvis came to the door. "See you in here, Lee Bob?"

"Find something?"

"Found out where those tapes you've been getting came from."

"How did you know about the tapes?" Lee Bob asked.

"You told me about them," Purvis replied.

"No, I didn't. Junior must have told you about them."

"I want to apologize to you about that, Lee Bob. It was underhanded, and I am sorry."

"We have to do our jobs as we see fit, Jarvis, but I would never do that."

"It will never happen again, I promise you."

"Apology accepted."

"You haven't found any shotgun shells, have you?" Purvis asked.

"No, but I've only just started the search."

"What about that meeting you were going to hold tonight?"

"Shit. Forgot about it." He went out to the patrol car and got Joe Bill on the radio. "All the people there? Over."

"Sure are, Sheriff. Over."

"I'm not going to be able to get there. Put two of the reserves out on patrol for tonight. Send Zeke out here to Delbert Hathaway's. Also have someone replace you on the radio, and you take Zeke's patrol for tonight. Over."

"Will do, Sheriff. You have two phone calls from a sheriff up in Illinois. Over."

"Did he say what he wanted? Over."

"No, only that it's real important that he talk to you before the night is gone. Over."

"Give me the phone number, and I'll call him." He wrote down the number and signed off.

Lee Bob walked into the house. It was meticulously clean and organized, much like the shop out back. He sat down in a chair opposite Delbert and Bobby Dean. "Why did you do it, Delbert?"

"Do what, Sheriff?" Delbert was neatly dressed in blue jeans and a polo shirt. What caught the sheriff's eye was the ironed crease in the Levi's and the pressed collar of the polo.

"Kill the judge and Doc?" Lee Bob's tone was irritable.

With a half laugh, Delbert said, "You been a law officer too long, Sheriff. I haven't killed anyone. Besides, aren't you supposed to advise me of my rights before you question me?" Delbert was confidently looking Lee Bob in the eyes.

"You're right. Sorry about that." Pulling a card from his pocket, he ran down the required reading to anyone accused of a crime. "Do you understand these rights as read to you?"

"Sure do."

"Do you wish to have a lawyer before you are questioned?"

"Sure do."

Lee Bob smiled back at the defiant Delbert. "Fine. Officer Blankenship, take Mr. Hathaway in and have him booked on suspicion of murder."

"What about Bobby Dean, Sheriff?" Delbert asked with a terror in his eyes.

"Take him up to the state hospital. Hold him on suspicion. Watch them for a second, Blankenship. I have to check with Captain Jarvis."

"Go ahead," the officer said. "Tell Adolph I'd like to see him."

Lee Bob looked at Delbert, who was sitting with his hands handcuffed behind his back, a waning smile on his lips. "You know, Del, when all the evidence started pointing at you, I couldn't believe it."

"I don't know what you're talking about, Lee Bob."

They sat there staring at each other until the silence was broken by the Klaxon horn on the patrol car. Lee Bob jumped to his feet when the front door flew open and Adolph burst in. "Sheriff, we are wanted back in Tish right away!"

"What's up?"

"Just got a call from the chief of police in Tish. Coy Purcell is dead."

"Did he say how?"

"He tried to explain it to me, but he was so excited that I couldn't understand."

"I'll go talk to him," Lee Bob said. "Find anything here?"

"Couple of things that might help us, but you'd better go talk to the chief. He's about to have a nervous breakdown."

The police chief was calling on the radio when Lee Bob leaned in and pushed down the mike button. "Settle down, Travis. What's this about Coy? Over."

"He's splattered all over his bathroom. Anyway, I assume it's him. I've never seen such a mess. Over."

"Just keep everyone away from the house till we get there with the investigation team. Got it? Over."

"Will do, Sheriff. You know, I don't know if this falls in your jurisdiction or mine. Do you know if his house is in the city limits or outside them? Over."

"Right now, Travis, it doesn't matter. Just keep all the people away from the house. We will be there in about twenty minutes. Over."

"Fine. I'll be waiting for you. Over and out."

Lee Bob told Purvis and a couple of his troopers on the way out that Coy Purcell was dead and that he was heading back into town. He asked Purvis to have his men take care of the Hathaway boys. He also asked Purvis to follow him to Tish.

The sheriff and Purvis turned onto the highway with lights and siren going, and Lee Bob picked up the mike. "Tishomingo four, come in."

Zeke answered. "Take your patrol car over to Delbert Hathaway's and relieve the state trooper there," Lee Bob said. "Give him your patrol car, and I will have you relieved later. Over."

"Sure thing, Sheriff. I'm on my way. Over and out."

Approaching the driveway, Lee Bob saw cars parked in the middle of the road. Several people were grouped in the front yard, staring at Purcell's house.

Purvis and Lee Bob walked by the cars and the group of people. Outside, lights and two city patrol cars with their lights on showed a large hole. Blown-out bricks and splintered lumber were scattered in the yard. The smell of cordite became stronger with every step they took toward the house.

Travis Hampstead hurried toward them. "Sure is a mess, Lee Bob. Coy is spread all over the house in little pieces."

"You sure it's Coy, Travis?"

"Pretty sure. He lived here by himself, didn't he?"

"Not always. It could have been one of his boyfriends."

"By *boyfriends*, you mean Coy was a fruit?"

"Thought you knew that," Lee Bob replied.

"Never gave it a thought. I just assumed, after his wife left him, that he was soured on women."

"Could have been. You been inside the house?"

"Yes, but only to check for fire. Too damn much blood and guts for me. Almost lost my supper as it was."

They walked into the house, went back to where the blast had originated, and stopped to look around. The room was completely demolished. Pieces of the toilet and bathtub were embedded in the parts of the walls that were still standing. Blood and particles of flesh were on the walls and ceiling. Everything had a pinkish color. Glancing down, Lee Bob pressed his foot into the red rug on the floor, and water squished up around his boot. Looking further, he saw that the water pipes of the toilet and bathtub were twisted and bent in every direction.

Purvis said, "Funny they would put a bomb in a bathroom, isn't it?"

"Not if you could read the report Doc had on him. According to it, Coy spent half his time in here. I was in here once—first bathroom I ever saw that was completely mirrored."

Purvis walked over and stood next to the hole blown through to the outside. "Looks like the bomb was placed here by the toilet. Whoever did it knew what the hell he was doing."

"How's that?"

"Usually a blast expands out in all directions. Whoever set this charge had it fixed so that the blast went sideways. The size of this explosion should have blown the floor completely out."

"Not necessarily," Travis said. "Coy had a guy from California build this house, and it's called a slab house. It's built on two feet of concrete except for a short storm cellar."

"That explains the way the blast traveled, then. But how did you know that?"

"My house was built just like it. Same builder."

"Could be one of the main reasons. Purvis, I'm going to turn this one over to you. Neither I nor any of my men are equipped to investigate explosives."

"I saw a phone in the kitchen. I'll go call my bomb squad. One thing's damn clear—whoever did this wanted to make sure they killed whoever was in here."

"Smell like dynamite to you?" Lee Bob asked.

"No way of knowing right now, but I really doubt it." Walking over to part of the wall that was still standing, he said, "At first I thought these white pieces were part of the toilet or bathtub. Some of them are, but like this piece here, see—it's bone. I've seen some bloody messes, but this has to be one of the worst. Makes you think a person has more blood in them than the doctors say. Reminds me of the Polk case about seven years ago. Remember, Lee Bob?" Purvis asked.

"That's the one you solved where the only part of the body was his two shoes with his feet still in them, wasn't it?"

"That's the one. Don't look like they left us that much this time."

Noticing the door ajar behind the entrance, Lee Bob walked over and, using his boot toe, nudged it open. Involuntarily, the sight forced him to take a step backward and a gasp was forced out of his mouth. He bumped into Purvis, who had followed him.

"What is it, Lee Bob?"

Stepping aside, he said, "Someone's head, or what's left of it." He heard Purvis retch at the sight. *What a pussy!* Lee Bob thought.

It lay there, its hollow eye sockets staring emptily upward. Shards of flesh were still sticking to the skull here and there. The flesh was a bright pink. Patches of hair in long shreds were lying on bare skull. The lower jaw was completely blown away. The teeth of the upper jaw were exceedingly white against the gums. Kneeling, Lee Bob looked at it closer. "Wonder who it is?"

"You mean you don't think it's Coy?"

"Coy was bald, Purvis." Lee Bob recognized Digger's voice in the house. He stood and closed the door that was open and blocking the bathroom door. Digger called out, "Hear you got another one for me, or at least what little there is of him. Identify him yet?"

"Not enough here for me. I'm going to leave that up to you."

Looking around at the shambles, Digger said, "See what you mean. Don't look like it will be an open-casket funeral. These pieces all that's left of him?"

"Won't need a casket at all, just a bucket," Lee Bob said, chuckling.

"If it was him, his or her skull is in the closet here." Purvis pointed to the closed closet door.

"Fine. Can you give me about fifteen minutes before you send those bulls of yours in here?" Digger shooed them out of what was left of the bathroom.

"I've turned the investigation over to Purvis, Fred. Talk to him," Lee Bob said.

"Okay, but send Adolph out here. I will need some pictures."

"Sure, as soon as I get out to the patrol car."

"Beat it now, so I can do my job."

Lee Bob walked outside and called Travis over. The two cops stood on the grass next to the driveway. "Have your men take down all of these peoples' names and addresses."

"Have already started, Sheriff. I found out this house is in the city limits, so I guess it's my baby." Travis didn't look too confident when he spoke.

"Fine, if you think you can handle it. I was going to turn it over to Purvis, anyway."

"Didn't think you and Purvis got along that good, Lee Bob."

Lee Bob shifted his weight to his right foot and looked back to the house. "It's not that, Travis. I'm not equipped with the manpower or knowledge to handle this type of crime."

Travis looked back at the house as if expecting someone to appear. "I don't understand. I've been told you wouldn't let Purvis handle Doc's or the judge's murders."

Lee Bob turned back to the chief. "They didn't involve explosives, either. You capable of telling what kind of explosives were used here, what kind of detonator, and other facets of the case?" Lee Bob asked.

"Hell, no. You know that."

Lee Bob chuckled. "You do what you want, Travis, but if I were in your shoes, I'd stay as far away from this one as I could."

Travis was suspicious. "Listening to you makes me think there's something here you're not telling me."

Lee Bob was about to walk away but turned back. "I'm not sure, but there is something going on in this county right now that I don't understand. Why don't you leave someone in charge and sit in on the meeting I'm having in my office in the morning?"

Lee Bob realized that he needed to tell Purvis about the change in the meeting time. Raising his voice, Lee Bob called to Purvis, "That meeting I was talking about—how about ten in the morning."

The conference room was crowded when Lee Bob entered. Purvis was sitting at the table on the raised portion at the front of the room. In addition to his three deputies and five reserves, seven of Purvis's state troopers were sitting in the back chairs. Placing the folder he was carrying on the table, Lee Bob faced his fellow officers. As he started to speak, the door opened and Travis entered with his assistant chief with him.

"Find a chair, Travis." He waited till they sat down.

"As of right now," Lee Bob began, "I am activating all of you reserves. Until further notice, you will be on active service. If any of you fine men have any reason you can't be on call twenty-four hours a day, I want to know it now."

No one moved or said anything.

"All right. From now until these cases are closed, no one—and I repeat, no one—is to discuss any part of these cases." Lee Bob paused, both hands firmly clasping the lectern, and he looked around the room, making eye contact with as many men as possible. "By that I mean you don't tell your wives or friends. You do not discuss it among yourselves out in public. Is this clear? Purvis and I went over most of what we know this morning. Later this morning, Sergeant Scotty Miller will arrive from the city. He will coordinate our work between state, county, and city offices." Lee Bob again paused for dramatic effect. There was standing room only in the conference room, and everyone was paying attention.

Picking up the folders from the table, he handed one to Purvis and told Travis to take one. "In these folders is all the evidence we have in Doc's, Coy's, and the judge's murders. Also, you will find Doc's folder on Seth Wilburton, John Ross, and Leon Ritchie." Purvis and Travis passed the folders out to the men collected in the room. "I am sure they will be convicted of Judge Watkins's murder—that is, if they live long enough to get through the trial. Someone wants them dead, for what reason I have no idea."

Again, Lee Bob paused for effect, and the room was silent except for the speedy shuffling of papers as the men flipped through Doc's information on the members of the Combine. Low *oohs* and *aahs* permeated the room as the pornographic images of these men engaged in sex acts tantalized the senses of the collected law enforcement members. There was some low laughing, and one man said, "Son of a bitch" when he realized that the rumors were true. The sheriff continued.

"Also, I want you to know—because you are all police officers—that it doesn't bother whoever is behind this to shoot cops. Last night, someone took two shots at me with a shotgun. So from now on, no one will patrol by themselves. You will team up. I want you to keep your eyes and ears open and your mouths shut. We want an up to-the-minute log kept of everything you do, hear, and see. These logs will be turned into Scotty at the end of each shift. Don't prejudge anything you hear or see. If you hear someone talking about these murders, write it down. If you see something, write it down. Someone out there is crazy, and if we don't find them and quick, there are going to be more dead people." The room was electric with excitement and the men were eyeballing each other, some signaling to friends that they would pair up for the patrols.

"There were threats made against John and Leon and Coy. Now, after what happened at Coy's house last night, we have to assume that the threats will be carried out on the other two. For some reason, all that has happened is tied to Cletus Hathaway's murder fifteen years ago in the pen." Whispers broke out in the audience. "When Doc was killed, I first thought it was a straight drug-related murder. I didn't connect the Chubbs' murder until Judge Watkins was killed. Our investigation demonstrates that Hathaway is connected to all of them in some way. Althea Chubb was a niece. Doc was a first cousin, and so was Coy. There's been a hell of a lot of digging, but I haven't been able to connect John Ross or Leon Ritchie yet. But we are sure the connection is there." Lee Bob moved to the side of the lectern as he became more comfortable speaking.

Lee Bob pointed to Adolph and Zeke. "Adolph, you and Zeke know just about everyone in the county. I want you to go over to the Bureau of Records and start digging. I want to know the name of every relative you can find of Cletus Hathaway, no matter what the connection. If they are related in any way, we want to know it. Everyone here is to read these files we have given out. I must emphasize this again—and, Travis, you better impress it on your folks—if any of you men are caught talking about these cases, you will be prosecuted." Lee Bob knew that would never happen, but he wanted to scare the hell out of them anyway.

"One other thing—we have requested assistance from the FBI. If the request is honored, we will let you know. There again, no one except you police officers is to know this. Travis, we're going to leave it up to you about your city officers. You can let us know later today about the officers in your department who will be on this case." Lee Bob stepped to the front of the small stage.

"Any questions?" After a pause, he said, "Now, take a coffee break, but I want every one of you to have gone over these folders before tonight ends. Purvis, you have anything?"

"No. Okay, yes—one thing. The explosives used on Coy's house last night were not dynamite. It was some type of new plastic putty. It will be entered in the case file when we find out. Also, we should have some kind of identification on who was killed last night soon. Remember, whoever is doing this doesn't care who they kill, so please do like the sheriff says. Turn in everything you can. You never can tell in cases like this what will break it wide open. That's it for now. Get out there and do your jobs."

Joe Bill called to him, "Lee Bob, pick up the phone."

Lee Bob picked it up. "Fred here. That head I picked up was Coy's, Lee Bob."

"What about the hair on the skull?"

"It was a wig. Also, the parts of the body that I could pick up showed that he was wearing pantyhose and other women's clothes."

"That figures. Anything else?"

"Purvis's boys will likely figure it out, but the way I figure it is that when Coy sat down on the toilet, the bomb was triggered."

"How did you figure that out?"

"I spent most of the night picking up what pieces of the body I could find. I am now in the process of drawing a map and the locations of the body parts. I should have it completed later tonight."

"Fine, Fred. Get me a copy when you have it done."

Adolph walked into his office and stopped, resting his left hand on the green Army surplus file cabinet. "Lee Bob, I was over at the courthouse, and Judge Lovell told me to tell you that he had a call from Royal Carroll, who planned to inventory Boats's house. Lovel was saying you need to search Boats's home. From what he said, Royal had called him last week right after the judge's murder, and he had put him off. He said he couldn't stall him any longer since he is representing Boats's estate."

"What has that to do with us?"

"He said maybe you would want to accompany Royal out and look around, or search the place before Royal."

"Don't see any sense in it. Do you?"

"Can't say, Lee Bob. Judge says, being as Judge Watkins and Boats was so close, you might turn up something."

"Tell you what. You go on back out to Hathaway's and go over it with a fine-toothed comb. Take Zeke with you. I think I will go out to Boats's and look around."

CHAPTER 32

Boats's Secret

When Lee Bob pulled into Boats's drive, he saw a large farmhouse with a wraparound porch made for sitting outside on warm evenings. A double porch swing hung and moved gently in the afternoon breeze. A maroon Oldsmobile was sitting by the front steps. He knocked sharply on the door. A chair scraped on the floor, there were some steps, and the door opened. "Can I help you, Sheriff?"

"You Royal Carroll?" Lee Bob asked.

"Yes, you must be Sheriff Whetzel. What can I do for you?" Royal filled the doorway, blocking any view Lee Bob may have had into the room.

"May I come in?"

"Do you have a search warrant, Sheriff?" Royal wasn't moving.

"No. I wanted to get your permission to search these premises." Lee Bob was presenting his finest manners, absent his usual profanity.

"For what purpose?"

"Over the last several weeks, we have had five murders in this county. One way or another, they have been tied to a company called Tishomingo Enterprises, referred to by the townsfolk as the Combine."

Royal looked genuinely puzzled. "One moment, Sheriff. I have gone over most of Mr. Nichols's business papers, and I've never heard of that one."

"It may be, Mr. Carroll, but Boats was a member. I have two tapes back at the office on which the company was discussed. Boats was present at one of those meetings."

Royal stepped out onto the wooden porch and pulled the door closed behind him. "Then your purpose here today is to search this place and try to tie Mr. Nichols into these murders?"

Lee Bob stepped back and sat on the railing. "Tie him to the murders? No. But I am trying to find some evidence to put it all together."

Royal changed his mind about letting the sheriff in. He didn't see anything in the sheriff's demeanor that caused him concern. He turned to the front door and opened it. "Come in, Sheriff, but I want it understood that I am not giving you permission to search. But I will discuss it with you." They walked into the house, and Royal motioned the sheriff to a table where they sat down. "There is one thing to keep in mind. I am the attorney for Mr. Nichols's heir, and I can in no way allow anything to jeopardize the rights of my client."

The sheriff scooted the chair out from the table and turned to Royal. "I can understand that. However, I'm not sure what I'm even looking for. I do know that Boats was not tied to any of these murders in any way that I can prove." The sheriff spoke in a calm tone.

"I don't understand. If he isn't tied to these murders, why would you want to search this house?"

"Some way, all of these men who have been associated with Tishomingo Enterprises are still together. Somewhere in their business dealings, there has to be a link that explains why someone wants them dead." The sheriff leaned forward and rested his left arm on the table.

"I am very sorry, Sheriff, but I cannot allow you to search my client's property without due process of law." Royal was matter of fact.

Lee Bob smiled. "You and I both know, Mr. Carroll, that with the rulings of the courts about search and seizure, there is no way I can get a warrant to search this property—at least not without sufficient cause."

"I realize this, Sheriff. So why should you be allowed to search this house when there is a chance that my client's estate might be implicated in several murders?"

Lee Bob was a bit irritated by that response. "I told you, Mr. Carroll, I know Boats had nothing to do with those murders."

"Those are just words, Sheriff, not admissible in a court of law, except by rulings of the court on hearsay evidence. What if I allowed you to search and you found that Mr. Nichols or someone in his employ had killed or conspired to kill all of these people? Then what?"

"We are both officers of the court, Mr. Carroll. You know the answer to that as well as I do."

"That's what I meant, Sheriff. Therefore, I must refuse permission."

The sheriff changed tactics. "From all I've heard about you, Mr. Carroll, you are not only a fair man but also a very able attorney. I see you have already opened Boats's safe. The only thing I'm interested in is any business dealings with a Cletus Hathaway. I believe all these murders are directly connected to him."

"Cletus Hathaway. Isn't that Delbert Hathaway's dad, who works at the bank?" Royal sat back in his chair.

"Yes. I have him in jail right now, booked for Judge Watkins's murder."

"Now I remember. I had only been practicing law for a couple of years when the law firm I'm working for had Cletus as a client. Theft or embezzlement, wasn't it?"

"You got it. Theft of county funds."

"How could Mr. Nichols be involved in a theft that occurred several years ago?" Royal looked at the sheriff carefully.

"We don't know if he was or not. I'm groping in the dark, trying to find a link," the sheriff said as earnestly as possible.

"I am afraid, Sheriff, that we can't help you."

"Fine. However, if you do find anything here that could give me a lead in any way without interfering with your client's rights, would you notify me?"

Royal felt sorry for the sheriff's plight. "Certainly, Sheriff."

"Guess that's it then. Thank you, Mr. Carroll." On his way toward the front door, he turned and saw Royal watching him. "One other thing, Mr. Carroll, we aren't sure that Tom Gurley isn't on the killer's list, so when you see Buck, tell him to watch out for Tommy."

Royal was shocked. "Wait one minute, Sheriff. Do you honestly think he could be in danger?"

"Like I said, I have no way of knowing. There has to be a connecting link somewhere. When I find it, we will know who's in danger and who's not."

"That wouldn't be a bluff now, would it, Sheriff?"

"I don't make idle statements, Mr. Carroll. Being as Tom Gurley is Boats's only heir, it makes me believe he could be marked for murder. All the people associated with the Tishomingo Enterprises have received death threats, and two of them are already dead. Doesn't sound like a bluff."

"I think you'd better lay it out for me, Sheriff, without violating any confidences of your office. I might be persuaded to change my mind."

Coming back to the table, he pulled out a chair. He started with Doc's death and caught Royal up to Coy's murder two days earlier. He told about how they had traced the blue station wagon through two dealers to Delbert, about the Rolex watch purchased by a young lady and given to him, and several other leads and about how Delbert could be the one who killed Coy but the sheriff didn't think so.

Royal sat there looking at him for several moments and then said, "I see how you believe this is all connected, so tell you what, Sheriff. I was fixing to go through Mr. Nichols's papers. Why not let me do that? If I can find something that will help you, I will stop at your office on the way out and tell you."

"It will be appreciated, Mr. Carroll."

"However, Sheriff, I must protect my clients. I will not shield a murderer, but I must, within the bounds of the law, do my job."

"Fair enough, Mr. Carroll. I will wait to hear from you—that is, if you find something."

After watching him leave, Royal went to the safe and removed all the papers, taking two handfuls of envelopes and bookkeeping records over to the table. When he finished, he saw a small olive-colored box sitting in the back of the safe. It was exactly the same size as the interior of the safe. He fumbled for several seconds before he could get his fingers behind it to slide it forward. He had to get down on his knees, reach in with both arms, and slide both sides of the box forward at the same time to get it out. About three quarters of the way out, the box struck something on the right side of the safe. He tried to pull it out, but it was wedged against something. Then he tried to lift it, but the box was too heavy to get his fingers under it.

Finally, bending down and inserting his head partially into the safe, he saw a small projection sticking out of the side of the safe. Pushing the box back, he felt a small round button. When he pushed it, a small compartment opened in the side of the safe. He reached in and pulled several letters, a stack of pictures, and a small blue book out. He laid them on the floor, closed the side door, and slowly pulled the box back up to the button. He pressed the button in and pulled the box till the corner of the box caught the button and held it in. He slid it on out.

When he stooped to pick it up, he was surprised by the weight. *Must be fifty pounds,* he thought. He took it over to the table, and using the box, he slid the papers and books out of the way and then dropped it to avoid smashing his fingers. The two clasps on the box resisted his attempts to open it before he finally snapped it open. He stared at what amounted to Blackbeard's gold. The box was completely filled with fifty dollar gold coins. Royal pushed both hands into the coins, lifted them, and let them clink back into the box. The box was ten inches deep, and he stuck his hands in again to see if it was completely full of gold coins. About three quarters of the way down, his fingers hit some paper.

Royal looked around for a container to put the coins in. He spotted a waste basket next to a secretarial desk and brought it over. He removed the coins and revealed the papers beneath. On top was a one-thousand-dollar war bond. Glancing at it, he saw that it was purchased in 1943. After emptying the box, he proceeded to count the war bonds and gold coins. The total came to five hundred and fifty thousand, without computing the interest on the bonds or the gold coins as collectibles. He put everything back in the box and taped a note to the top, detailing the contents.

Next, he turned to the stack of papers. He thumbed through them and discovered several contracts on property with record books attached, showing mortgage payments by purchasers. He totaled over sixty loans made over the last ten years. Checking the entries, Royal was sure that they were not in Boats's handwriting.

He finished going through the papers but had difficulty making out some of the entries. Royal realized the light was dim. Glancing up, he noticed that it was getting dark outside. He reached over and turned on the light. Looking at his watch, he was surprised to see that it was almost seven o'clock. He stacked all the papers together and walked into the kitchen to see if he could find something to put the records in.

When he returned to the table, he noticed a manila envelope. He turned back the flap and dumped the contents on the table. They were pictures. Some appeared to be telephoto shots of T. C. during football practice. There were shots of T. C. and a Mexican kid in a new Ford pickup and at the auto dealership—T. C. looked really happy. On the back of each photo were handwritten notes, including dates and times and the photographer's observations. As Royal went through the pictures, he realized that somebody had been surveiling T. C., taking pictures and making regular reports to Boats. He picked up another manila envelope, emptied it, and saw school progress reports, report cards, and medical reports on emergency room treatment for T. C.'s facial wound. There were also background reports on Marylyn and Pauline Birchley, complete with financials.

The old bastard has been spying, or having someone spy, on T. C. and anyone associated with him the whole time he's been with Buck and Rosie, he thought. *What's going on?*

Each of the reports appeared to be a compilation of notes and reports from multiple sources, each individually initialed by the source; the full summary for reports was signed with a single initial—"P."

Looking out the back door, he saw one of the ranch hands wrapping a water pipe with insulation. Unlocking the door, he called out to him. He could tell the man was startled when he jerked and jumped to his feet. Standing to face him, the ranch hand asked, "Who are you?"

"I'm Royal Carroll, Mr. Gurley's attorney."

"Who is Mr. Gurley?"

"He owns this place. Don't you know who you work for?"

"Certainly. I'm paid by Nichols Casing Company. What do you want?"

"I was wondering if you knew whether Mr. Nichols had a bookkeeper come in."

"Don't know, and if'n I did, wouldn't tell you. You can ask the foreman. He's down at the bunkhouse."

"Would you mind going down and asking him to come up to the house?"

"Do I look like Western Union to you? If you want him, go get him yourself. I ain't no damn flunky." With that, he knelt down and went back to wrapping the pipe.

Royal stared at him for a moment and then relocked the door and started back through the house. Passing the safe, he saw the papers and book he had placed on the floor from the side compartment of the safe. He grabbed them up and walked down to the bunkhouse. Royal pushed the door open and walked in. Five men sat around a table. Two of them played cribbage, two played dominoes, and the other was reading a book. None looked up when he entered, but when he spoke, they all turned and stared.

"Who's the foreman?"

"What can I do for you?" He dropped the Louis L'Amour novel to the coffee table, got up, and walked over to Carroll.

"I'm Royal Carroll, attorney for the estate. Could I talk to you outside?"

"Certainly." As they were walking out, he said, "I'm Pete Stenovich, Mr. Carroll."

"Glad to know you, Pete. I wanted to know if Mr. Nichols had a bookkeeper take care of the books here at the ranch."

"Yes, he did. Her name is Vealie, but I don't know what her last name is. Just a minute." He stuck his head back in the door and asked, "Any of you guys know what Vealie's last name is?"

"Yeah. Killingsworth. Used to work at Tishomingo Bank before she retired."

"Know where she lives?" Royal asked.

"Any of you guys know where she lives?" Pete asked the guys.

"Third house on the right on Fourth, after you turn off the highway to your right."

He asked Royal, "Did you get that?"

"Sure did. Thanks, Pete. How big is this place, anyway?"

"Home place here is ten thousand acres. Two section marks over, Boats has twenty thousand."

"Any oil wells on them?"

"No, Boats didn't like to run cattle on the same land he had wells on."

"Think there is oil on the land?"

"Never really thought about it, Mr. Carroll. Never entered our conversation."

"Well, thanks, Pete. Have you talked to Mr. Hagan?"

"Buck? Why would I want to talk to him? Last thing I heard he was running a casing crew in El Paso."

"Still is, but he is also the executor of the Nichols will."

"He is? John Ross notified us right after Boats died that he and Seth Wilburton were, and I have been taking orders from him."

"Well, the court has ruled that Mr. Hagan is in control," Royal said, "so you'd better get in contact with him."

"You got his phone number?"

Royal gave him the number and said, "Better call him tonight. Funny that you didn't know about it. Aren't you ever around the casing yard?"

"Don't have no reason to be. All of us are just ranch hands."

"By the way, Pete, who is the guy up at the house wrapping the pipes? Old guy about sixty years old."

"Yeah, I guess he is about that age. That's Pike. Been with Boats since the forties. He's Boats's driver—used to go everywhere with him. He's a crusty old son of a bitch, and you don't want to cross him. Pardon the language."

"It's okay. I figured he had been around here for quite a while. I asked him to have you come up to the house, and in a polite way he told me to go to hell."

"That's Pike all right. Don't have anything to do with us either unless Boats has something for us to do. He thinks we're some type of new breed of cowboys. He and Boats knew each other in the big war. What I heard was that Boats picked him up when he was face down in a bar and gave him a place to stay. The old fart drives for Boats and drives the rest of us nuts."

"Think he would talk to me about Mr. Nichols?"

"Not likely, Mr. Carroll. He is pretty secretive and plays everything close to the vest. The only way to find out is ask him. Here he comes."

Looking out into the deepening dusk, Royal saw the old man coming toward them. Pete called out, "Hey, Pike, Mr. Carroll here wants to ask you some questions."

"All right with me, long as I don't have to answer them."

Turning to Pete, Royal said, "Thanks. I'll be talking to you later."

Pete stared at him and blinked. "Sure, Mr. Carroll. Anytime." Stenovich walked back into the bunkhouse.

Pike walked up and stopped in front of Mr. Carroll.

"Would you walk up to the house with me, Pike? I'd like to ask a few questions, if I may."

"Like I said, you can ask as long as I don't have to answer. Besides, I'm on my way to my house to fix supper, so if you want to ask me any questions, it will have to be over there." With that, he nodded at a small shack sitting next to the bunkhouse. He finished the sentence and then walked toward the shack. Royal followed about two steps behind like a hound hoping for scraps. Pike entered the shack and left the door open.

When the lights came on, Royal poked his head in and glanced around. It was a large one-room with a bathroom lean-to off the side. The room was spotlessly clean. The kitchen and dining table were in one corner, and a big brass double bed sat close enough to the door that it banged the bedpost. On the opposite wall was a dresser with an old-time picture of a pretty young lady next to the head of the bed. One big easy chair was sitting in the middle of the room. The only modern piece of furniture in the place was a large television set with a small radio sitting on top of it.

Pike walked over to the refrigerator and started setting things out on the counter next to the stove. "Okay, fella, what questions you want to ask?"

"Understand you been with Mr. Nichols quite a while?" Royal stood nervously, and Pike didn't invite him to sit.

"Been working with him in some fashion since '38. He was two years older than me in school. Went to war with him in '41. Why?" Pike's body language and tone made it clear that he was annoyed.

"You went to work for him in the late forties, then?"

"Told you, I've been working with him in one way or another since '38. After the war, I stayed in the Rangers. When I got out, he gave me a job." Pike was definitely annoyed.

Royal was on tender footing. "You know any of his business dealings?"

"What I know is none of your goddamn business." *Yup, he's pissed,* Royal thought.

Royal became assertive. "Look, Pike, I'm not trying to hurt Mr. Nichols. I'm the attorney for Thomas Gurley. You knew that up at the house. All I am trying to do is protect the boy and Mr. Nichols's estate."

"Boats is dead and don't need protectin', and as well off as Boats left the boy, he doesn't need much of nothin'."

"Moneywise, you're right, but there are some things going on right now that could have a bearing on the estate and the boy's safety."

"Such as?"

"For one thing, the sheriff is trying to tie Mr. Nichols's estate up in all these murders that have been going on."

Pike turned and slammed a ketchup bottle on the counter. The plastic squeeze bottle shot ketchup up in the air, and it fell back to the counter. "I should have killed that fuckin' whore hound twelve years ago."

"How's that?"

"Never mind. Ask your damn questions. I have to finish my supper so I can watch my TV program." Pike grabbed a washcloth and began wiping up the ketchup.

"Do you know of any business dealings that Mr. Nichols had with Cletus Hathaway?" Royal watched Pike closely for his reaction.

"So that's it." Pike had pulled out a butcher knife to slice the ham for the sandwich he was making. When Royal mentioned Cletus Hathaway, Pike slammed the knife down on the sandwich, cleaving it and scattering it on the counter.

"That's what, Pike?" Royal was tenuous, seeing Pike with a knife in his hands.

"Nothing. Anything you want to know, you will have to get it someplace else." Pike was done talking and turned toward Royal with the butcher knife still in his right hand. Pike wasn't actually threatening Royal, but the knife was intimidating nonetheless.

"You do know what it's all about." Royal realized that Pike knew far more than he would say.

"I know nothing. Now, if you don't mind, Boats gave me this place, and you're trespassing. Get the hell out."

Pike was moving toward the door, but Royal kept trying. "Were you aware that John Ross is trying to get his hands on Boats's estate and put Thomas Gurley in a military school?"

Pike opened the door with his left hand and pointed out the door with the butcher knife. "Ross always has lots of plans, but Boats never worried 'bout him. And I can goddamn guarantee ya Ross ain't getting shit."

Royal stood looking at Pike, flabbergasted by his bluntness.

"Look, buster, I'm not telling you again. Now get the hell out, and don't come back." He waved the butcher knife out the door, so Royal turned and left.

Back at the house, Royal found a large cardboard box and stuffed it full of all the records. He loaded them into the trunk of his car and went back for the boxful of coins and war bonds.

On the way into town, Royal stopped at Fourth Street. Identifying himself to Mrs. Killingsworth, he asked if he could stop by the next morning and go over the books with her. Mrs. Killingsworth was a well-dressed, gentle-looking woman who appeared to be in her midsixties. However, when she spoke, Royal thought he was listening to a chain-smoking lumberjack. She sounded like a gruff old man, though she was eager to help any way she could. They agreed to meet in the morning.

He drove to the Chalet, registered for the night, ate supper, and went to bed early.

Pike watched to make sure that Royal had left and paced around the shack for another five minutes before he picked up the phone and dialed.

"Yel—low." The familiar hiss on the other end identified Snake.

"Snake, this is Pike. I want you and Chee Ko to keep a close watch on the kid. Sounds like Ross and company plan to kill him."

"Will do, Sarge."

"Anything happens to that kid, I'll cut your nuts off. Don't fuck it up. They already got Boats." Pike slammed the phone down.

CHAPTER 33

Vegas

Coach Baker looked up with a grin. "Come on in, fellas. Take a chair."

Sitting, Manny and I faced him.

"You know, T. C., you shouldn't be so touchy."

"About what, Coach?"

"Everything. It's just like playing football, Gurley. It's a game of give and take."

"I'll give and take, Coach."

"With everyone but Mr. Ward, eh?"

"He rubs me the wrong way, Coach. Besides, I don't like anyone calling me a liar."

"Well, it doesn't matter anymore. Miss Ketchel saw the fight from start to finish and told me, so I put her in touch with Ward."

"Then why wasn't we notified before, Coach?" Manny asked.

"Mr. Ward wanted to make you wait a couple of days. Anyway, he has removed your suspension, and you can come back into school tomorrow."

"Tomorrow is Friday, Coach. Manny and I have something we have to do this weekend, so we'll start again Monday."

"Look, we need you for practice tomorrow, and we are having two practices Saturday morning and afternoon."

"Sorry, Coach, but we have to leave for Las Vegas tomorrow."

"Have you guys been keeping in shape?"

"I have," I said. "Haven't you, Manny?"

"Yeah, been running several miles every day."

"You sure you can't come to practice? It's real important to me but more so for the team."

"We know, Coach, but it will have to wait until Monday. We didn't know Ward would change his mind, so we made these plans and there is no way we can change them. Right, Manny?"

"Right."

"Okay, but you guys keep in shape. You know Sanchez is back in school?"

"How's his face?" I asked.

"Kind of black and blue. What the hell did you hit him with, a sledgehammer?"

"My fist. How did he get back in school after he was put out?"

"His lawyer had a talk with Mr. Ward. Guess they didn't want a lawsuit."

"Come on, Manny. Let's get out of here."

Outside, Manny said, "I have to go meet Buck."

"Oh, yeah. Here's the extra set of keys to my truck. One of the men from the ranch brought it in. You go ahead and use it. You and Tess will need some wheels. I'll meet you both at the ranch at nine in the morning, and we'll take off for Vegas."

"Sounds good. Thanks, T. C."

"What for? Go on, wetback. Get out of here."

I walked from the locker room to the second floor of the high school and waited for the bell to ring. Mar and Tess were the third and fourth ones to walk out of the room. I noticed the light and glow expand with Mar's grin when she spotted me standing there.

"What did the coach have to say, Tommy?"

"We're reinstated."

"Manny too?"

"Yup. We start back Monday, so we can leave for Vegas in the morning."

"That's great. Where's Manny?" Tess asked.

"He went to talk to Buck about a job."

"Oh, that's so nice. Don't know what Manny and I would do without you."

"You don't have to; that's the good part. Have lunch with me, Mar? You too, Tess?"

"I only have twenty minutes. How about you?" Mar said to Tess.

"Same here."

"Say, being as we're taking tomorrow off, why not skip this afternoon?" I said. "We can go pick up Manny and go home for some fun."

The girls followed me to my locker and threw their books in. Minutes later they were with me in Boats's Lincoln, headed to pick Manny up.

It was Sunday afternoon, and we were only twenty miles from the ranch on our way back from Vegas. The trip had gone smoothly. Mar was snuggled up to me when Manny leaned forward and asked, "You going to tell them you're married too?"

"Sure. I don't keep secrets from Buck."

"Think they'll be upset about it?"

"Why should they?"

"Because of your age."

"I don't know. Guess they could be. Mar will be of age in a couple of months."

"I know, but you won't be eighteen until another year."

"I must look older. The guy in Vegas didn't say anything."

"The way you were spreading money around, why should he? All they wanted was to get their share."

"That's what money is for, Manny, to make lives easier."

"You sure did that."

Rosie and the kids were out of the house and beside the car before it quit rolling. She opened the door, and when Mar climbed out, she enveloped her in a big hug, saying, "I'm so happy for you!"

"How did you know?" I asked, bewildered.

"All of us figured that was the reason you wanted to go with them."

"You aren't mad?"

"You know we got a call from Vegas to confirm your ages?" Rosie asked. "I didn't know my own dad was such a big liar. Should have heard him. Besides,

Tommy, now you and Mar won't have to be sneaking off to the barn and leaving a trail of straw through the house."

The rest of us climbed out of the car. Rosie hugged Tess and kissed Manny and me.

Rocky came out of the house. "Hey, newlyweds, congratulations." He shook the boys' hands and hugged and kissed the girls.

"Come on in the house."

Manny said, "We'd better—oh, is it okay to use your truck, T. C.?"

"What for?"

"We have several pieces of furniture our relatives gave us, so we'd better go get them before it gets dark. We'll need a bed to sleep on."

Rocky said, "Don't worry about it, Manny. Buck, your dad, and I and a bunch of your friends spent the weekend getting everything moved. We knew you would be tired when you got home. Come on. Let's take them down and get them moved in."

"You kids go ahead in the car," Rosie said. "Rocky, the kids, and I will be right behind you."

Pulling up in the yard, Mar and I let them out of the backseat. I told Manny, "You guys go ahead and look around. We can get the suitcases later."

Mar and I stood there with our arms around each other and watched them walk up on the porch. Manny opened the door, picked Tess up, and carried her inside. We saw him step inside, stop, and kiss her.

All the lights came on, and we heard the shouts and hollering of "Surprise!" as the people gathered inside surrounded them.

Walking up to the door, we watched the happiness and glow spread across the room. All of their friends from school, parents, brothers, and sisters were there. Tess turned to where we were standing at the door with Rocky, Rosie, and Buck, who had just arrived. She came running up to Rosie and Mar and threw her arms around them. "I should have known when you took me furniture shopping with you and asked all those questions what you were doing. Thank you, from Manny and me both. We owe you so much."

Rosie said, "Shush. You don't owe us nothing."

Mar hugged her again. "You know we love your both." Laughing, they went on into the party.

Buck threw his arm over my shoulder. "Well, you went and did it, didn't you, sport?"

"Couldn't help myself, Buck." I was grinning from ear to ear.

Buck shook his arm around my neck. "I know, son. That's the way it should be. I'm sure folks won't like it, but as far as I'm concerned, you're a man."

"Thanks, Buck."

He dropped his arm and headed into the party. "Come on. Let's get some of that chow. I'm starved. Oh, by the way, that pickup? I bought it for Manny on the company. Here's the keys." Buck tossed them to me.

"I'll give 'em to Manny."

"Sure, sport. He say anything about our talk last Friday?" Buck was obviously fishing for feedback.

"No. He acted like he wanted to a couple of times but never did."

"Well, I'll tell you, Tommy, I had one hell of a time convincing him to accept it. He looked on it like it was charity."

"But he did agree, didn't he?"

"Yeah, finally. That's the reason we were a couple of hours late getting back from lunch."

"So long as he agreed."

We joined the party.

The next morning, when we arrived at the school, Coach Baker met us at the door. "I have spoken to your teachers. They are going to go light on you boys this week. So after ten, you come out to the athletic room so we can go over the new plays we have been working on."

We put in four hours of practice a day for the next three days. At noon on Friday, they let us out of school. All four of us went down together for the pep rally in the middle of town. After about an hour, Coach Baker gave his speech and then told all of us football players to go home and get some rest so we could be back at the stadium at 6:30.

I have relived that night over and over again, at least a thousand times. It never changes. Mar and I drove out to the ranch. On the way out, we were like a million other newlyweds, sitting close, touching, just enjoying the feeling of togetherness shared by two people in love. When we reached the ranch, no one was there, so we slipped into our bedroom. We were asleep when Rosie came in and woke us up at a quarter to five. We all agreed to meet at Pepi's for the celebration or wake after the game. Mar had her cheerleader's outfit on, and I had never seen her more beautiful than when we left. We stopped and picked up Manny and Tess and took off for the stadium. We parked the car and, on leaving, Mar hugged and kissed me. "Good luck, Tommy."

"Thanks, sweetie. We will do our best."

Manny and I went into the dressing room. At 7:40, after the pep talks, we went out on the field to warm up. We did our calisthenics, ran through several sets of our plays, and went back into the locker room. At five minutes to eight, we charged out through the students to our bench. I kept looking around for Mar, but neither she nor Tess was anywhere to be seen. We kicked off, and after five plays they punted and I got into the game.

From then on, everything was hazy. On the first play they called my number and they really keyed off on me. Before I had even hit the line, they stacked me up. Someone kicked me in the side of my helmet. I didn't begin to come out of the fog until halftime. I remember asking Manny as we were walking into the locker room, "How we doing?"

He looked at me kind of funny. "Where you been?"

"Not sure. Are we ahead?"

"Yeah, six to zip. You better have one of the coaches look at you. Your eyes don't look right."

"I'm all right. Got kicked in the head, I think."

"Well, I'm telling the coach anyway."

"I'm fine, Manny. My mind is clearing. Have you seen Mar?"

"Didn't really notice. She's bound to be here."

"Her and Tess weren't with the other cheerleaders."

"Most likely went to the bathroom or something."

After we ran back onto the field, I kept looking for Mar but couldn't see her. They kicked off to us, and I forgot about looking for her till the end of the third quarter. We had just punted, and as we were running off the field, I saw Buck waving at me from the sidelines. Rosie was with him, and they were waving me to come to them. I ran over.

Buck said, "Everybody's okay, but Marylyn and Tess have been in an auto accident and are in the hospital."

It confused me. "What? She's here." My ears were still ringing, and I felt like people were talking to me underwater.

"No, Roger Ingles just showed up and told me what happened." I wasn't clear and couldn't process what he was saying.

"I don't understand." The whistle blew to start the fourth quarter.

"It will keep for now," Rosie said. "We'll head over there when the game is over. Everything is okay for now."

I turned and ran onto the field.

Manny said as I ran to the huddle, "What's going on with Buck?"

"Nothing. It will wait until after the game."

"That doesn't make any sense," he said.

"Shut up, boys," the wide receiver said as he called the play. "Ready, break!"

Earlier that night, Marylyn had realized that she didn't have her purse. She said to Tess after they dropped us boys off, "I think I left my purse back on the kitchen counter. We have a couple of hours before the game starts. Let's jump in T. C.'s truck and run back out to the ranch."

The girls got in the truck and were on their way. Marylyn's purse was on the counter, exactly where she had left it. As she pulled back onto the highway at the end of the driveway, she saw an orange Camaro parked just off the road. As she accelerated, she saw the car pull out. It was gaining on them as they hit the long, straight stretch into town. The Camaro gained on her and pulled into the oncoming lane. Then it bounced back, just missing her rear bumper. She told Tess to look and see if it was Sanchez.

"No, it's not Sanchez. It looks like an older guy with a beard and long hair. There's some other guy I don't recognize in the front seat. Can't tell if there's anyone else in the car."

"Well, he can just pass if he wants. I'm not driving any faster. I'm already doing sixty."

Just then the Camaro accelerated again and smashed into the right rear corner of her bumper. Before either of them realized what was happening, the truck spun sideways, rolled across the driver's door, and continued rolling down the highway until it did a three-quarter twist, flipped again, crashed through the two-by-six fence, and wound up on its top in the grass pasture adjacent to the highway.

Marylyn watched as the Camaro slowed to a stop. The driver jumped out of the car and ran across the road to the truck where the two girls hung upside down, barely conscious. Marylyn pretended to be unconscious. The guy got down on his belly and stuck his head through the passenger-side window. She sensed his presence and smelled the Copenhagen on his breath. He yelled back at his passenger. "Jimmy, the spick chick looks like she's dead. The driver is Gurley's girlfriend. He's not in the truck."

Mar couldn't stand it anymore. She opened her eyes and saw the man's bearded face. "Who are you?" she screamed.

"I'm the guy who is going to kill your boyfriend and every one of the sons of bitches that fucked Cletus Hathaway's family!"

"Tommy didn't do anything to you or your family. We don't even know who you are!"

"He's a Nichols, and that's enough to get him killed in my book."

The guy in the car screamed at the bearded man. "Hey, Lonny, there's a truck coming! Let's get the hell out of here!"

Marylyn watched him run back to the car and jump in. The Camaro's supercharger spooled up, and the car spun a half-circle in the loose gravel, throwing rock all across the farm truck that was pulling to a stop.

Chee Ko Han ran to the upside-down truck, grabbed the door on Mar's side, let out a yell, and pulled the door, completely buckling it against the front fender well. Rocky was right behind him, moving more slowly, but still, he dove onto his belly to check Tess's pulse. He put two fingers on her neck and pronounced, "She's just unconscious. How's Mar?"

"She beat up, Rock. She hurt bad," Chee said.

"I'm going to the ranch to call an ambulance. You stay here till I get back and the ambulance comes."

Chee went back to the truck with Rocky and got a blanket from behind the seat, and then Rocky left for the ranch. He walked back to the truck, pulled a karambit from his belt, held Mar with one hand, and cut her free from the seatbelt. Mar groaned as she fell to the roof of the truck. Chee put his hands under her arms and gently pulled her onto the blanket he had laid out next to the truck. Mar lay there, breathing shallowly. Chee went to the other side and repeated the procedure to extract Tess.

Tess opened her eyes, looked at Chee, and screamed, "Where's Mar?"

"She okay, Ms. Cantu." Chee picked her up by slipping one hand under her legs and pulling her upper body next to his. He laid Tess next to Mar, and the two girls looked at each other and started to cry.

"Why do they want to kill Tommy, Tess?" Mar said through her tears.

"What are you talking about?" Tess asked.

"That man that rammed into us said he was going to kill Tommy."

"What man?" Tess hadn't heard or seen anything.

Chee Ko listened intently to the girls' conversation.

Rocky pulled up and ran up the slight grade to where the girls were stretched out. He had another blanket and a first-aid kit in his hands. "The ambulance won't be here for fifteen minutes. It has to come from town." He covered the two girls.

Mar looked at Rocky and said, "Rock, they were trying to kill Tommy."

"What do you mean, honey? Tommy isn't here."

"I know, but they must have thought he was in the truck. After they ran us off the road, a bearded man came up to the truck. When he realized that Tommy wasn't in the truck, he told me that he was going to kill him 'cause he's a Nichols."

"Was there more than one of them, honey?"

"Yeah, there was a guy who stayed in the car as a lookout."

The sheriff's patrol car showed up first. A deputy popped his trunk and grabbed a first-aid kit before he jogged up the slope to where the truck lay on its top. The deputy said, "Anybody survive?"

Rocky said, "Yeah, they both did, but we need that ambulance."

The siren whistled from just over the rise, and the flashing lights appeared over the horizon.

Rocky and Chee followed the ambulance to the hospital. Dr. Martin was on call in the emergency room. Chee and Rocky walked in behind the girls as they were rolled in on the gurneys. The EMT told the doctor that Mar had a fractured right arm and appeared to have a concussion. Dr. Martin pressed her ribs, and she screamed in pain. The doctor looked at the EMT and said, "George, I think you missed the broken ribs."

Chee stood in the corner, watching intently. The doctor turned to Tess, who was alert and looking at him. She had a broken leg, according to George, and possibly some internal injuries. But for the most part, the girls seemed to have survived a very traumatic accident relatively unscathed. Chee saw Rocky leaving and followed him out to the truck.

Rocky got on the CB in the truck and called the casing yard. He raised Roger Ingles, who was working the swing shift to get pipe ready for the next day's deliveries. Rocky told him that there had been an accident and that he needed Roger to go over to the high school football game and track down Buck.

"Sure," Ingles said. "What you want me to tell him?"

"Tell him that Mar and Tess were in an accident and are in the hospital here in town. Tell him they appear to be all right, but the hospital is going to keep them overnight. Tell him that he needs to keep Tom close to him and make sure he is protected. Tell him that there is a threat on Tom's life and to call me at the hospital right away. You got all that?"

"Yeah, been takin' notes."

"No time to waste," Rocky said. "Leave right now and make sure you get to Buck as soon as possible."

"Okay."

Chee made his way back to the hospital lobby and asked a nurse in perfect continental English where a pay phone was located. She pointed him to a hallway. Chee picked up the phone and dialed the number. "Skip," the voice answered.

"Mr. Peterkin, it's Chee. They made a play to get T. C., but T. C.'s girlfriend and her friend were the only ones in the truck, so T. C. isn't injured. However, the two hit men told the girls they were going to kill T. C., so we need to get some added protection here now."

"You stay close, Chee. I'll send reinforcements. Pike is down there watching T. C.'s football game. He called me yesterday to tell me they might be after the kid. He's in his midsixties. Keep an eye out for him. If you see him, let him know you work for me. I told him I had a man protecting the family."

"I know Master Sergeant Pike from Korea. I'll keep an eye out for him," Chee said. The phone went dead.

Skip picked up the phone and called the ops team who had handled the Doc Leftan matter. They were in Dallas. He told them to get over to Leland in a hurry, fully armed, and take every action necessary to protect T. C. and the family. He then called Mark and told him that he had heard there had been an attack on T. C.'s girlfriend and that he thought it prudent to send private security to keep an eye on the family.

Mark said, "Wow. You won't believe it, but I just talked to Buck Hagan, and he was asking that I send protection over."

"The security team I've used before is about forty-five minutes from there, en route," Skip said.

"Well, I hadn't contacted a security team yet, 'cause I just hung up the phone with Buck. I'll send them out to the ranch to make sure it's secure and to begin making plans to install security there." Mark was intense.

"Good idea. I think we should get an investigative team on those assholes from up in Tishomingo. I would imagine that Ross and his sidekick, Wilburton, are behind this."

"That is probably a safe bet. I'll get somebody on that right away."

"Thanks. I'll let you know when my security team gets to the hospital and takes charge of the family's security."

"Thanks."

"It's a good thing they didn't attack T. C. at the ball game," Mark said.

"I had a man watching the boy at the game. Apparently, the bad guys didn't realize he was at the game."

"Good thing."

"Yeah. Talk to you later when I know more."

Manny dove just behind the end zone's front marker for six points on a quarterback keep behind Mueller's diving block on the outside linebacker and my cross-body shot to the free safety. Now twelve to zero, Coach went for the two-point conversion. Manny started the turn around the right end and was picked up by the linebacker. Mueller had cut off the defensive end. Manny flipped the ball to me, and I was hit at the one-yard line by two defensive backs. When the free safety came up and stuck his helmet in between his two defensive players, I popped loose, spun to my left, and fell forward into the end zone.

The stadium exploded into raucous shouts of mayhem. With thirty-four seconds left in the game, a deep kickoff and short run back by the opposition meant that the game was done. Tishomingo had the state championship.

I wandered, senseless, through the crowd of well-wishers. My ears rang like Notre Dame's cathedral bells, and my words slurred like a drunken sailor's. Buck and Manny took me by the arms and led me to the locker room. Realizing something was wrong, Buck dragged the team doctor over to check me out.

"Looks like a concussion," the doctor turned to say to Buck as I threw up on the doc's leg. "Let's get him to the hospital right away."

The paramedics came in and loaded me on the gurney. Buck said, "Is everyone going to the hospital today?"

"What do you mean?" Manny asked.

"Mar and Tess are there now. They were in a car accident before the game. They're all right, and the girls didn't want you to come until after the game. They are both okay."

"What about our baby?" Manny asked.

"I don't know, Manny. Rock didn't say anything about the baby. Let's get going."

Buck, Rosie, Manny, and Manny's family all headed for the hospital behind the ambulance. When the procession made it to the hospital parking lot, the waiting room was already full of Tess's and Manny's family members. Tess's mama ran up to Manny, who was still in his football uniform, and wrapped her arms around Manny's neck. "The baby is okay, Manny. Don't worry."

"Thank God, Mama."

I was wheeled into the emergency room, and a swarm of medical staff poked and prodded me, asking me questions and sticking needles in me to get my fluids up. They eventually moved me to a room. Buck and Rosie were still there when I woke up.

Chapter 34

Handicapped Parking Penalty

After the game, Pike followed the ambulance to the hospital. He stopped just short of entering the facility parking area so he could check things out. In the main parking lot just outside the main entrance to the hospital, he noticed an orange Camaro backed into a handicapped parking slot. Pike lifted the binoculars to his eyes just as Jimmy hung a handicapped parking card on the mirror. He focused on Lonny's lips and read, "Gurley will show here eventually to check on the girlfriend. When he does, we'll pop him and be gone." Pike noted the engine idling in the late October cold. The two men were obviously keeping an eye out at the entrance, presumably for Tommy to show up.

Pike noticed that people entering the hospital kept giving them the evil eye because they sat in the souped-up Camaro in a handicapped parking spot just off the emergency room entrance. Pike watched as the ambulance carrying T. C. backed into the emergency room bay and started unloading him. Buck and Rosie got out of Buck's truck and walked past the ambulance, following the gurney into the emergency room. Manny pulled up, followed by a couple of the boys from the football team.

Pike flipped back to Jimmy and Lonny in the Camaro. They watched Buck and Rosie go in. Lonny leaned over to look through the driver's window, and

Pike read his lips. "That's Buck Hagan. We'll wait till he comes back out and nail him when he tries to get into his truck."

Neither of the Cody boys saw the 350 Ford pickup pull in six spaces down, nor did they notice the sixty-plus-year-old man who walked behind the Camaro and checked them out before walking into the emergency waiting room. Inside, Pike walked down the corridor, taking account of everyone who was present in the waiting room. He figured the old guy talking to Rosie and Buck was Rosie's dad. Snake had given him the lowdown on all of the people at T. C.'s house, and he had been reading the investigation reports. He walked into the lobby to see if he could find Skip's Korean bodyguard. When Pike turned the corner, he saw a short Korean man walking back from the pay phones. "Excuse me," Pike said. "You work at the Gurley ranch?"

Chee responded in broken English, "I ranch cowboy."

"Well, hell, Chee, I thought you were the half-pint son of Chi Ko Han, sent down here by Skip Peterkin," Pike said.

Chee responded in perfect English. "Mr. Pike, I didn't recognize you. It has been many years?"

"Yeah, I just get prettier with age. I don't want you to let the family know I'm here. There's a couple of hit men in the parking lot looking for Gurley."

"Should we call the police?" Chee said.

"No, I'll take care of them. The police would be too nice to them. Have you talked to Skip?"

"Yes, he is sending a security detail down to protect the family. They should be here within the hour."

"Good. I'll take care of the guys in the lot and then head home to Tishomingo. I've got to deal with some shitbirds up there who are after the kid. You stick close to the kid until the security detail gets here. We need to keep that kid safe. Tell Snake to head to Tishomingo as soon as the protective detail gets here."

"I will," Chee said.

Pike walked back toward the emergency room. Up ahead in the hallway, he saw an empty wheelchair with a blanket lying across the back rest. He sat down, after making sure nobody was around, laid the blanket over his lap and legs, and rolled back to the waiting room. Rocky was seated with Buck and Rosie's children while Buck was in with T. C. and Rosie was down the hall talking to the girls.

Pike rolled up to Rocky and started a casual conversation. Pike had been at the football game observing T. C. and Buck and had already found out that T. C. had a concussion before he got to the hospital. He found out from Rocky that the girls were fine and that it appeared that T. C. was too, though the hospital would likely keep them all for a day or two. Pike wished Rocky well with his family members and rolled out the emergency room entrance onto the sidewalk and toward the Cody boys.

Jimmy saw him first. An older man in a wheelchair, all bundled up in a blanket, rolled down the ramp; made a slow, labored turn with his wheelchair; and rolled up to the driver's side window, rolling across the white stripes on the pavement.

Jimmy rolled down the window as the old man bumped into his car a couple of times, nearly hitting the driver's mirror. Jimmy snarled at him, "Watch out, old man. You'll scratch my paint."

The word *paint* was garbled as the .22 Long cut through the roof of his mouth and bounced around inside his brain like a spastic pinball on methamphetamines. It was pursued by a second round that found an easy path to follow. As Lonny flopped back against the driver's seat, Jimmy yelled, "What the fuck?" and reached for the .38 revolver in his coat.

Pike's first round went through his left eye and exited his right temple, breaking through the window and lodging in the doorpost of a truck parked next to the Camaro. The second round entered his left temple and bounced off the right inside of his skull like the blades of a blender churning out a Cadillac Margarita. The whole episode was over in seven seconds, and all anyone heard was the sound of four quick sneezes, shots silenced by the finely machined silencer Pike had made himself.

Pike spun the wheelchair around, rolled down past the nose of the Camaro, and found his Ford 350. He hadn't gotten to Leland in time to prevent the Cody boys from nearly killing Mar and Tess, but he wasn't worried anymore about them messing with Buck or Tom. Boats had told him to look after Tommy, and he had nearly let Boats down. He should have been with Boats in Dallas instead of chasing down Doc's loose records. It was too bad that Velma had taken her vacation to Oregon at the wrong time, or he would have discovered the plots against Boats and the judge sooner. Perhaps, had he listened to the tapes from John Ross's office sooner, he could have saved the judge. If the judge would have returned his damn phone call, he'd likely be alive today. He steered his Ford onto the highway headed north to Tishomingo. He had a literal date with Coy Purcell that he was looking forward to.

John Ross, Seth and Adam Halsey (Seth's half brother who took his stepfather's name), and Coy were smarter than Pike or Boats had given them credit for. Apparently, Delbert had confided in John that he had believed for years that the judge and sheriff had had his father killed in prison so they could take his father's property. Little did Delbert know that it was John and Coy, with Seth's help, who had hatched that plan. Wilburton, as a defense attorney, got a dying lifer to cop to killing Cletus for the judge and sheriff by having his half brother, Adam, get the lifer's younger brother, Jimmy, released early on a burglary charge. It was John's idea to add Boats to the list. As long as they were taking over the county, they figured they might as well seize control of the oil wells and Nichols Casing as well.

Seth had left a letter for John with Delbert, knowing full well that Delbert would read it, being the greedy bastard he was, and thinking that he would get a tip to some of their skullduggery that would allow him to invest in advance. Instead, what Delbert Hathaway got was proof of the story he already half-believed—that the judge, Boats, and the sheriff arranged to have Cletus killed in prison by a lifer. Delbert had always figured that the judge and sheriff had worked together to plant evidence on his dad. It made sense that Boats was in on it because of the oil that was later found on his dad's property.

John Ross had hoped to set Delbert and Bobby Dean on a killing spree. He succeeded beyond all expectation. After Delbert read the letter from Seth, he lurked around, listening to John's conversations to find out more information that would provide him the opportunity to get the bastards.

The night that Judge Watkins was killed, when Vealie brought the tapes out to the ranch after Velma had returned from her vacation in Oregon, she was crying. She had slipped the first tape into the portable tape player on the way out to meet Pike at the ranch. That's when she heard the familiar voices of Coy, John, and the Wilburtons, and they were laughing.

Coy spoke first. "I can't believe that son of a bitch Boats is dead. Doc was a treat, but Boats's death is totally fucking unbelievable."

Seth spoke next. "Yeah, I was able to get Boats cremated before an autopsy could be done. The docs didn't even have a chance to operate. Whatever Delbert shot into Boats's IV stopped his heart like a popped balloon. After I put the fear of Jesus in that undertaker, it's a wonder he didn't burn down the funeral parlor. Jesus, I'm good." They were all laughing.

"Don't break your arm patting yourself on the back, Seth. The judge will be tougher."

Coy piped up. "You forget, Delbert and Bobby Dean are my second cousins. After their poor ol' pappy got sent away and killed, they came to me for advice. It wasn't hard to place the suspicion on the judge and sheriff. That little half-wit Bobby Dean has been planning to get the judge for ten years. The hard part was stalling him till now. The judge won't know what hit him."

Pike shut off the tape, picked up the telephone, and dialed Watty's direct line. Allison picked up and said that the judge was with a state police captain and couldn't be disturbed. Pike told her that it was an emergency and that he must speak to the judge before he left the courthouse. She promised to get him a message.

The phone rang just after five, and Pike picked it up. "Yeah?"

"Pike, this is Stenovich. I was picking up feed at the farm supply and just saw Judge Watkins get killed. Someone blew him in half with a shotgun."

Stenovich heard Pike yell, "Fuck!" and the phone went dead.

Pike turned to Vealie and said, "They've killed the judge." It was then that he had decided to kill the bastards who had killed his two high school friends, Boats and Watty.

He turned the tape back on.

After about five minutes of dumbass guffaws and jokes about Boats and the judge going soft, Leon asked John and Seth Wilburton if they had Boats's estate tied up yet. Seth said, "Hell, no, we don't have it tied up. Gurley has a watchdog named Buck Hagan watching him like a hawk. They hired Royal Carroll and Bob Stuck to represent them, and they kicked our asses in court."

"Well, if you send the Cody boys down there and have them kill Hagan, wouldn't that solve the problem?"

"What about the fact that Judge Lovell won't give us custody of Gurley or the estate because we're charged with murder?" John asked.

Seth said, "It might make it easier if there was no guardian or executor. If they take out Gurley too, then we can get control of Boats's estate."

"We are still facing murder charges," said John.

"Hell, we can hire any number of lawyers to serve as executors to do exactly what we want," Seth said.

"Well, Seth, we will leave it up to you and Adam to hire the attorneys. Coy will get a hold of the Codys to take care of Hagan and possibly Gurley."

Pike turned to Vealie and said, "I'm heading for Leland, Texas, to protect the kid and Buck Hagan. You need to get a hold of Velma and tell her we will need quick delivery on any new conversations from the bank."

After Vealie left, Pike called his son, Adolph.

"What the hell do you want, Daddy?" Adolph said in his most sarcastic tone.

"Listen, drop the horseshit. I didn't know when you said you would take care of Doc that you were going to kill him, but it sure as hell has created a mess."

"I didn't kill him. I thought you did. You never listened to me before, and I just figured you went ahead and knocked him off."

"Hell, no, I didn't kill him. He had enough on Boats and the judge to send them away. I left him alone.

"Listen, John, Seth, and Coy killed Boats and the judge. It sounds like somebody else killed Doc, since neither of us did it. I've got to go out of town to take care of some business. You need to steer Lee Bob toward John Ross and company. I don't have time to deal with them right away, but by God I will when I get back."

"I can't protect you if you plan on killing any of them," Adolph said.

"I don't need protecting, boy. You just keep that dumbass sheriff you work for on the trail of Ross and the Wilburtons. I'm going to take care of Coy and Leon myself. You will know I'm back in town when the bastards start appearing in the obituaries."

"Dammit, Daddy, you are on your own if you start killin' people."

"They ain't people, boy. They're just plague-infested vermin I need to protect the community from. The world will be a better place without these cocksuckers."

"We didn't have this conversation!" Adolph yelled.

"Suit yourself, boy. Just keep that stupid sheriff on the trail of Ross and the Wilburtons."

"Don't underestimate Lee Bob. He's dumb like a fox. You slip up, and he will snare your ass."

"He's not going to get the chance."

Pike picked up the phone and dialed the number he had written down from the paper. After listening to the tape Vealie had brought out to the ranch, he made up his mind to take revenge on these men. The phone rang twice, and then Coy Purcell picked up. Pike said in the sexiest voice he could muster, by pretending he was talking to Vealie, "I read your ad in the magazine, white male looking for white male to love. Said you were coy and cute and up or down for anything. I've got a hot cock looking to satisfy your needs."

Coy propped the phone between his shoulder and ear, sliding his hands down to his groin. His voice took on a feminine quality as he spoke in a hushed, smoky voice. "I only go for big, nasty boys."

"Well, honey, I am big, but I ain't no boy. I can give you all you want and more. When can we hook up?"

"Can you come to my place Saturday night? I will be back from Oklahoma City at about four thirty, and I will make room for you by seven."

"Baby, I'll be there by seven with bells on my balls."

"See you then," Coy said, and he gave his address to the caller.

Pike hung up the phone and muttered to himself, "You piece of shit faggot bastard. I'm going to rid the world of your faggoty ass."

Pike sat in the phone company truck he had borrowed in Wapanucka from the driveway of a Bell employee who had taken his family on vacation. Friday night, the high school kids were dragging the gut, looking for lust in all the wrong places.

From under the brim of his hat, he saw Coy back out of his driveway in his white El Dorado Cadillac and head for a good time in Oklahoma City at the gay bars there. Pike waited an hour to make sure that Coy didn't return, just in case he left his bitch wardrobe behind by mistake. He then pulled the phone company truck up into the driveway and stepped out, fully clad in the appropriate uniform except for the sunglasses.

He checked the front doorknob and, sure enough, it wasn't locked—not that a locked door would have been any problem for him. He thought, *The neighbors will probably start locking their doors after tomorrow night.*

He put on the cloth booties to cover his work boots and then pulled on some rubber gloves he had lifted at the hospital the previous week. He proceeded to the bathroom and took a moment to examine the wall-to-wall mirrors Coy had installed. He lifted the lid off the toilet reservoir, turned off the water to the tank, and flushed the toilet. He sopped up the remainder of the water in the bottom of the tank with a beautiful pink towel he found under the sink and then dropped the towel into a plastic bag. It took him about thirty minutes to loosen the tank and run the wire through the seal to a switch just under the seat. The pressure switch would fire after the pressure was released. Coy wouldn't be able to get his panties up before the plastic explosive shoved the porcelain toilet up his ass and sprayed him across the room. Pike started to laugh as he finished wiring the plastic explosive. Boats had once said to Pike as they were driving to the ranch and a huge bug hit the windshield, "What do you suppose was the last thing that crossed that bug's mind when he hit the windshield?"

"I don't know," Pike said.

"His ass," said Boats, and then he laughed uproariously at his own quick wit.

Pike said out loud into the air, "Well, Boats, it will be his ass and eighty-two pounds of porcelain." He continued to smile to himself as he finished up. These new plastic explosives were far superior to the stuff he had used in the Philippines in World War II. The Rangers had taught him demolition, which made him an asset in the oil fields. The advances in high explosives made life easier for powder monkeys. Now Pike's forty years of ordnance experience would give Coy the ride of his life, an ultimate orgasm.

Pike was back out the door and in the truck before dark. Twenty minutes later, he had returned the truck and was on his way back to Boats's ranch for dinner with Vealie. His mind returned to the training the US government had provided him in Korea. It had made him a good living in the oil fields as an explosives expert and gave him the opportunity to rid the earth of scum: first in the Philippines, later in Korea, and now in Tishomingo. He made a mental note to throw a lawn chair in the bed of the pickup when he got to the ranch so he wouldn't forget it tomorrow night. As a Ranger in the Philippines and Korea, he never got to hang around and watch the fireworks. Tomorrow night, he would have a front-row seat for Coy's big adventure.

Vealie opened the door as his truck pulled up to the shack behind Boats's ranch house. For a woman in her sixties, Vealie had aged well and kept her figure. Her breasts had obviously once been a sumptuous pair of melons and were still desirable, though gravity had lowered them on her frame. As she stepped back to allow Pike through the door, he noticed that the covers on his bed were pulled back and candles were burning. He looked at her and smiled. "Aren't you going to seduce me with a good meal before you ravage my body?"

"No, big man, we're going to have dessert first, so get those britches off." She smacked him on the ass and shoved him toward the bed.

"Ain't no such thing as foreplay anymore. Since when did women get so aggressive with men?"

"I'm a modern woman, ol' man, and it's two weeks since you put a smile on my face. You can practice your foreplay later, after dinner, during round two. Now git them britches off!"

The door closed behind Vealie as the two disappeared into the shack.

At three o'clock on Saturday, Pike walked to his refrigerator, pulled out a six-pack of beer, and placed it in his Styrofoam cooler. On the way into town, he stopped at Spender's store and bought a bag of ice to pour over the beer. At five minutes to four, he nosed into a parking spot at the community park, about 175 yards from Coy Purcell's house, which was situated on the corner lot across the street. The Chikashsha Garden Park, known as the Pocket Park, was empty except for some kids throwing a Frisbee on the other side, away from Purcell's. Pike set up his lawn chair beneath a hundred-year-old redbud and placed his cooler strategically next to the chair within arm's length. He pulled out the *Johnston County Capital-Democrat* to read the sports and news while he waited for Coy to return. The paper was published once a week on Wednesdays, but he never read it until Saturdays because Boats was the one who subscribed to it. He only had a chance to read it when Boats was done with it, which meant Saturday because he had to work and didn't take leisure time until Saturday afternoon.

Pike used his church key to knock the top off the first bottle, dropped the bottle top into the cooler, and unfolded the paper across his lap, where he had rested his snakeskin boot on his knee. Boats had had these boots handmade for him in Juarez, Mexico. Pike had to explain the reality of life to a distraught husband of Boats's latest Mexican conquest and had relieved the man of a seven-inch knife that he had planned to give Boats as a gift, point first. Not that Boats couldn't have done the job himself. After all, the Rangers had trained them both in hand-to-hand combat, but Boats was wearing a white suit. That and the fact that Boats had let himself go to seed over the years, while Pike continued to work out and keep himself in shape, meant Pike got to do the dirty work. Pike remembered how much they enjoyed each other's company, though they never talked much about the despicable acts they had seen in the Philippines or the starved ghost soldiers they pulled from the concentration camp at Cabanatuan.

Boats never brought up the fact that he had packed Pike's sorry ass to the ox cart after Pike let a Jap soldier shoot him in the ass and shoulder. But Pike didn't need to be reminded that Boats had come back for his old high school buddy. Boats and Watty had been a grade ahead of him in high school, and Pike had always admired Boats as an outstanding athlete on the football team. Watty was an egghead and a mediocre athlete, but they were all pals. As an underclassman, he held the blocking dummies and was on the scrum defensive team that Boats ran through like shallow water.

He never really understood why Boats had taken an interest in him. Watty went to college after high school, but Boats told him he was enlisting in the Army because of the war. Pike, who was seventeen at the time—he was held back in second grade for failing to progress—dropped out of high school, and the two enlisted together. They both lucked out and became part of the first-ever Army Rangers battalion, assigned to a crack Captain Robert Prince in Ranger Company C. The two of them were part of the band of men to go behind Japanese lines to recover prisoners of war who had been left behind when MacArthur abandoned the Philippines. Boats and Pike were inseparable, and it was a good thing, because it was Boats who came back for him as he lay bleeding in a pile of hog shit, thinking he had been left behind. As he lay on his back staring at the stars, Boats's face came into his view. "What the hell are you doing taking a nap? Get your ass up and let's get out of here."

"Can't do it buddy. Been shot in the ass and shoulder," Pike said to him.

"Guess I have to carry your sorry ass again." Boats propped him up and dropped Pike across his shoulders. "Here, hold the guns at least," Boats said. "If you didn't lose to me at poker all the time, I'd leave your ass here, but your money keeps me in cigarettes." Boats carried him nearly two miles to the waiting ox carts that the Filipinos had brought for the prisoners they had recovered.

For as far back as Pike could remember, Boats had been saving his ass. When he lost his way after getting out of the military, Boats found him in a Dallas bar passed out on the floor, cleaned him up, and gave him a job. Ever since then, he had been Boats's invisible right hand, taking care of things that got dirty. Boats kept him on a short leash and wouldn't let him deal with Doc Leftan, even though the old bastard had been blackmailing Boats for years. Pike had wanted to kill Doc and get the evidence. He was surprised when Boats came to him after he got the kid and told him to get Doc out of his life so he could focus on raising the kid and teaching him the business. "Pike," he said, "we ain't getting any younger. Never had anything but business to live for, but now this kid has promise and I want him to take over my business. I'll have to learn him a few things and help him get a business head, but he's already tough enough to run the place."

"I don't understand you, Boats. You say you want to teach him the business and you're getting all fatherly like about him, but you ship him off to live with Buck and Rosie Hagan. Doesn't sound like you were that interested in him," Pike said.

"I was pretty pissed at him when he knocked me in that shithole. But I knew right then that he was going to be man enough to run my business." Boats appeared proud of the kid.

"Then I don't understand why you shipped him off."

"'Cause Doc would have sought to set the kid up and destroy his life to get at me. Plus John Ross, Coy Purcell, Leon Ritchie, and the Wilburtons would have tried to kill him or use my relationship with him against me and the business. I have to deal with them before I can build a life with the kid. That means putting Doc out of business and using his information to shut the Combine down."

"You told me before not to mess with Doc 'cause of the stuff he has on you and Watty. What's changed your mind?"

"Well, now the statute of limitations has run out on the stuff that would affect Watty and me. Plus he's going to retire at the end of the year, so while Doc's stuff would be embarrassing, it won't amount to shit on a hog's back."

"So you're gonna let me kill the motherfuckers?"

"Hell, no! I don't want you killin' anybody; it could be traced back to me. But I do want you to get the box so I can go through it to ensure that there isn't anything that will put Watty or me in prison. Then I want you to get the box to Skip Peterkin for safekeeping. Skip will have a team of specialists take care of Doc so it's not connected to us in any way."

"What's Peterkin's interest?" Pike had asked.

"You know Peterkin's dad was killed on one of our wells in an accident, right?"

"Yeah, that's why you put the kid through college and set him up in business."

"Well, sorta. Actually, Doc was going to go public with pictures of Peterkin's old man partying with some prostitutes. Ol' man Peterkin was a deacon in the Baptist church, and 'fore Doc could release the pictures, he committed suicide at one of our rigs and faked it as an industrial accident. He left me a letter asking me to take care of his family."

"Why the hell didn't you tell me this before?"

"You didn't need to know. 'Sides, the Peterkin kid is a genius at business, and he's made me rich. Anyway, go down to Dallas and meet with him. He'll have his ops team commander present. I want it done as soon as possible so the storm blows over 'fore the kid turns eighteen."

That night, Doc stood on his front porch. Pike hid in the brush to ensure that all went according to plan. The dog had gone nuts in the house, knowing that somebody was outside and needed to be scared off. Doc and the dog stood looking out at the darkness. Off to the right, Doc saw a man dressed in black and wearing a ski mask. "Who the hell do you think you are, coming on my property? You need to get the fuck out of here before I let my dog eat you."

"First, you need to give me the files you have on the Combine," the man in black said.

"You are a fuckin' idiot if you think you're getting shit," Doc said. He reached down and released the clip on the leash. He gave a command in German, and the rottweiler launched itself off the porch. Doc felt a pain in his left butt cheek and turned to see a tranquilizer dart sticking from his ass. He twisted, stumbled, reached for the door handle, and collapsed.

The shooter stepped from the darkness at the corner of the house and took aim at the dog running at Roger. He fired, hitting the running dog in the hindquarter. The rottie yipped and spun in a circle; after relocating his target, he continued his charge. Roger realized that the dog wasn't stopping and stuck out his left hand as he turned to run while reaching for his baton, and the dog latched on, sinking his teeth into his wrist. Roger spun toward the dog and hit it in the side of the head with his baton as hard as he could. The dog fell to the ground, unconscious from the M99 tranquilizer partially assisted by the blow to his thick skull.

Marvin ran up. "Sorry, Rog. I couldn't get a clear shot."

"The fucker liked to rip my arm off. I'm bleeding like a stuck pig."

Two other guys in black ran up to where Roger and Marvin were standing. "You guys, get in the house and see if you can find the box," Roger said. "It should be in the bathroom. Marvin and I will deal with Doc."

Marvin and Roger walked up to the porch, grabbed Doc's arms, and draped them over their shoulders so they could drag him down to the creek. "We gonna give him the antidote to the M99 or let the drug kill him?" Marv asked Roger.

"The drug takes a few minutes to kill him. If he doesn't get the antidote, he'll drown before it can."

They lowered him to his knees at the edge of the creek and then gently dropped him face first into the water.

Roger walked downstream in the darkness about fifteen feet, taking care to walk on river stones to avoid leaving a print. He held his bleeding arm extended over the water. When he got far enough away, he plunged his arm into the water. It was then that he noticed that his Rolex had been destroyed. The only redeeming grace was that the watch had taken the brunt of the damage that would have been inflicted on his arm. The band was broken, and the watch fell into the shallow water. He was so angry that he picked it up and threw it out into the darkness.

Marvin heard the splash and dropped down. "You hear that, Roger?"

"Yeah, it was just a fish jumping for mosquitoes out in the creek. *A fucking twelve-hundred-dollar Rolex mosquito,* he thought. The other two guys came from the house. "You find the box of dirt?"

"Yeah, boss, piece of cake. The bug led us right to it."

"Did you take it out back and put it by the white stake?"

"Yeah, it's ready for pickup. We're ready to go."

"All right, let's get the hell out of here." The team disappeared into the brush and circled back to where they had left the Suburban off the road.

Pike waited till he heard the Suburban take off, walked to the white stake, and picked up the box. *So this is the box that created so much trouble in Johnston County,* he thought. *Well, the trouble is just startin'*. He heard two clicks on the radio, hurried to a stand of brush, dropped the box, and turned to watch the house.

Pike heard another vehicle on the road above. Delbert and Bobby Dean were going over to Doc's house to deliver a bale of weed and a box of meth that had been delivered to their house from Mexico. When they pulled onto the drive leading to Doc's, a blue Suburban with blackened windows passed. Its headlights were off. Delbert punched the gas, turned into Doc's driveway, went down the hill, and skidded to a stop on the wooden bridge. Off to the left, he saw Doc lying face down in the creek. He wasn't moving. Delbert and Bobby Dean watched him for a couple of minutes—no movement.

"I, I, I think he's dead." Bobby Dean always stuttered when he was scared or nervous.

"I think you're right, Bobby Dean. The old bastard finally got kilt."

"You think somebody kilt him?"

"That blue Suburban with its lights off wasn't drivin' down the road with its lights off for fun. Somebody kilt him for sure."

"Whatta we do? Call the cops?"

"Bobby, don't be so damn dumb. We ain't callin the cops. We gotta get the drugs and Doc's file 'fore somebody else does, else we'll be going to jail." Delbert pulled forward enough to get his car door open and get out of the car. He started walking slowly to Doc's front door.

Bobby Dean jumped out of the car and followed after Delbert.

"Slow down. That damn dog is probably around here somewhere, and he'll tear the shit out of you."

Bobby looked around him nervously.

Pike had Stenovich up on the hill. Pike heard the radio click twice, which he and Stenovich had agreed would give Pike a heads-up. Pike stayed in place about fifty yards to the side of the house. He was concealed behind bushes, sitting on the box that had been pulled from the floor in Doc's bedroom.

Pike could hear Bobby Dean and Delbert tearing the entire house apart, looking for the box he had. They apparently found drugs in Doc's closet, judging by the whooping and hollering. He crept to the house and peeked in the window in time to see them go into the bedroom. They saw that the floorboards had been removed and an empty metal box where Doc's documents used to be. "We're in big trouble, Bobby Dean."

"Why's that? Doc is dead. The records are gone. We gonna be in trouble?"

"Never mind, Bobby. Let's get the hell outta here."

"Okay."

Pike watched as Delbert fired up the Plymouth wagon, spun a cookie in Doc's yard, and punched it, bouncing across the crossboards on the bridge. Peterkin's crew was gone, and so were the Hathaways. Pike saw Stenovich ramble down the hill from the golf course and across the wooden bridge. First, he went to Doc's body, knelt down, and put two fingers to his jugular: nothing. Pike thought, *Kinda stupid. He's been layin' face down in the water for thirty minutes while Del and Bobby rummaged around. He oughta be dead, Stenovich! Those military fellas did a nice job.*

Pike looked on. Stenovich didn't see the rottweiler approaching. At first, the dog shook his head to shake off the lingering effects of the tranquilizer. Then the damn dog saw Stenovich leaning over his master, and he started running. "One, this is two. All clear," Stenovich said in the radio to let Pike know he could come out. Pike started to warn Stenovich, but it was too late. Stenovich straightened up and turned to walk toward Pike when the rottie's 180 pounds hit him full force, knocking him down in the water. As Stenovich crab-walked backward into the creek, the rottie latched onto his leg and began to shake its head. Stenovich was screaming like a small child in complete fright as he watched this animal eat his leg. Pike ran up to the scene screaming something in German repeatedly. The dog finally released Stenovich and sat down next to where Pike was standing.

Pike walked up and said, "Why didn't you give the command I taught you? He wouldn't have tore your leg off."

"I couldn't fuckin' remember it when he was trying to eat my leg!" Stenovich said.

"Get your ass up, and let's get outta here."

"Thanks for the sympathy, Sarge."

"Take your card to the chaplain, and he'll punch it for you. Get your ass in gear, son."

Stenovich limped along behind Pike to the back of the house, where the box was stashed in the brush. They hiked up to the road and sat. At 1:30, on cue, they heard Vealie's Studebaker wagon coming down the road. It was in pristine condition, military green, and except for the hole in the muffler, mechanically sound. She pulled up to the stop sign about a hundred yards from the golf course. Pike opened the back hatch, dropped Doc's box in, and then walked to the driver's door and opened it. "Scoot over, darlin'."

Stenovich jumped into the backseat, and the car was going before he closed the door. "Miss me, baby?" Pike said as he slipped his hand to the inside of Vealie's thigh.

"Sure did, sugar. We going back to your place?"

"We gotta drop numbnuts here off so his wife can take him to the hospital. Got dog bit—dumb shit. Try to teach a man two words in German, and he panics."

"Anybody would have panicked if they were bein' eaten by a two-hundred-pound dog," Stenovich said in defense.

"That little puppy wouldn't have hurt nobody, if'n they could just remember two words." The banter continued until they reached Stenovich's house. "Get out, dumb shit. Remember, you was attacked at the golf course."

Vealie and Pike pulled into Boats's ranch and continued down to Pike's shack. "Baby, what I don't understand is how you found Doc's file when people have been lookin' for it for years."

"That was a piece of cake. You know Adolph has been collecting stuff for Doc all these years 'cause Doc was blackmailing him?"

"Yeah."

"I just slipped a bug into one of Adolph's packages and used it to locate the box in Doc's house."

"Well, ain't you just the smartest, most handsomest man in the world." They pulled up to Pike's shack.

"Well, baby, come on in and let's have some fun," Pike said. "You can get on the road to Dallas tomorrow and drop this box off at Peterkin's. They'll make two copies for you to bring back, and Skip will keep the original for Boats. Then you give one to Larry Chubb, and I'll keep the other in a safe place."

"Baby, if all this stuff Doc had was so dangerous for Boats and Watty, why you givin' a copy to Larry and Althea?"

"The statute of limitations has run out on anything Boats and Watty did with the Combine. They are pulling out, and they ain't havin' nothin' to do with those shitbirds anymore. Boats wants to start a life with the kid, teaching him the oil business, and Watty wants to retire with Alice. They figure if Larry has a copy of the files, then it will put those turds out of business and Boats and Watty can retire."

"Well, I hope it works."

"Sweetie, I been friends with Boats and Watty since I was fifteen. I ain't seen any plans they've made fall apart. They know what they're doing."

"Sure hope so."

Pike's reminiscences about Doc's death were interrupted when he noticed the white El Dorado pull into Coy's driveway. He saw what appeared to be an ugly woman wearing a long blonde wig get out of the car. Coy was halfway running to the house and had slammed the Caddy's big door behind him. In his rush to the front door, he cut across the grass, ignoring the sidewalks. He reached for the front doorknob but found it locked, and his momentum carried him hard into the locked door. He banged his forehead against the oak door.

Pike laughed and thought, *Damn, I must have locked it when I left.*

Coy was cussing on the front stoop and hopping from one foot to another while he fumbled for his keys in a leather purse he had slung over his arm. As he stuck the key in the door and opened it, Pike heard him screech, "Oh, shit."

Pike said out loud, "Guess he couldn't hold it," and laughed.

Pike sat there in anticipation of the pressure switch release. First two minutes went by, then five. He looked at his watch at seven minutes and said, "Damn, he is full of shit!" when the deafening thunder of plastic explosives filled the air. Bricks flew across Coy's yard, and the picture windows in adjacent houses shattered. The smell of cordite filled the air as neighbors flooded out of their houses like army ants looking for an intruder. Pike knew it wasn't cordite at all, since cordite wasn't used any longer, but that didn't keep veterans from using the word as an adjective to describe the pungent smell of a clean blast.

In the park, Pike folded his paper, dropped his last empty beer bottle into the open cooler, folded the lawn chair, and carried it and the cooler to the 350 Ford pickup sitting at the curb. He drove away from the park, past the hordes of lookie-loos racing into Coy's yard. As he drove past the front of Coy's house, he saw Coy's keys still in his front door, with a pink rabbit's foot hanging below the doorknob. He started to chuckle. "Damn, that was lucky!" He drove home to Boats's ranch. Leon would be next.

CHAPTER 35

Hospital Homicide

I sat in the hospital room in a wheelchair, looking at Mar and Tess. I was so happy that the girls were safe, though Mar looked pretty banged up. Then the doctor walked in and went up to Mar's bed. The family gathered around.

I was watching the doc and straining to hear what he said. "Well, young lady, you are a very lucky girl. We've finished all of our tests, and you obviously have a broken leg, a couple of fractured ribs, and a lot of cuts and abrasions. The good news, however, is that the baby is fine and you should have a normal pregnancy."

Did he get Mar and Tess confused? I thought. *He must be looking at the wrong chart.*

That is, I thought that until I realized that Mar was looking at the doctor in horror. "Doc, you wasn't supposed to tell anybody that I'm pregnant! I was saving it to tell T. C. after the state championship."

The doc turned red immediately. "Sorry, Mrs. Gurley." Then, turning his attention to Tess, he said, "More good news—Mrs. Cantu's baby is fine too."

"What did the doctor say?" I was nearly shouting.

Mar looked at me and shouted, "I'm pregnant!"

I jumped out of the wheelchair and stumbled to the bed, getting my feet caught on the foot pedals. I caught myself on the railing of the bed and pushed past Rosie to hug and kiss Mar.

Tess was laughing and crying simultaneously when Manny entered the room. Buck and Rosie stood at the end of Mar's bed, smiling and hugging each other.

"What's going on in here?" a nurse asked. "This is a hospital. It's supposed to be quiet."

The doctor only smiled and walked past the incoming crowd. "I've done enough damage for one day. They are all yours, nurse."

The nurse got us quieted down, and Rocky closed the door after she left so the whoops and hollers didn't disturb the entire hospital. Chee Ko burst through the door with a look of concern on his face only to find everyone laughing and crying and hugging each other. Marylyn and I were holding hands and glowing like July fireflies.

"We're having a baby, Chee Ko!" I shouted across the room, before Rocky held his finger to his lips. I whispered, "Sorry."

The door opened, and the nurse led Dave and his partner into the room.

I looked at the two cops and jokingly said, "They called the cops 'cause of the noise." Everybody laughed, except Rocky.

Rocky was seated in a chair near the window and stood up when the two cops walked in. He said, "You guys have any information on the two guys that ran the girls off the road?"

"You mean the two guys driving a souped-up orange Camaro?" Perez said with a smirk.

The room lost its humor in a hurry.

"Yeah, that's them," Mar said as she looked past me and focused on the officers' faces.

Dave said, "We have them outside, missy."

"Damn, that was quick," Rocky said.

"What guys?" I asked.

"The two guys that ran Mar and Tess off the road," Rocky said.

"You might say they came to us all wrapped in a package," Dave interjected.

"Did they tell you why they attacked the girls?" Rocky asked.

"No, they aren't talking much right now." Dave looked at Perez, who found an empty chair and sat down.

"Must have lawyered up then, huh?" Rocky asked.

"No, they're waiting to tell their story to the coroner. They're both dead in the parking lot. Somebody shot them in the head. I'm kind of curious why so many people die around you and your boyfriend here."

"Well, officer, neither of these girls had anything to do with it," Rocky said. "They've been here in the hospital the entire time. Tom was in the state playoffs and was just in the emergency room, brought in by ambulance." He was starting to get pissed.

"We'll follow up on that," Perez said.

"Well, you damn well do that. In the meantime, who is going to protect these kids?" Rocky was practically spitting as he spoke.

"I don't know, but it looks like somebody already is. Those two guys out in the car are known felons suspected of killing half a dozen people for money. If they were after you girls, you're damn sure lucky to be alive."

"They weren't after us," Mar said. "They were after Tommy. At least that's what the guy said when he came up to the truck."

"What did he say?" Dave pulled out his pad.

"He said that he was going to kill Tommy for messing with his family. But that was weird 'cause Tommy hasn't messed with anybody. I've never seen that guy before, and I'm with Tommy all the time." Mar was becoming hysterical.

Officer Dave inquired, "Did he say anything else?"

"Just that he was going to kill Tommy for messing with his family."

He looked at Tess. "What do you remember, Tess?"

"Nothing. I was unconscious the whole time," Tess said.

Dave looked at the collected group. "Thanks. I may need to talk with you again once we know more." Dave and Officer Perez asked me and Buck to come out into the hallway. Once outside, we walked down the hall until we found a vacant room, and the cops led us inside.

When the door was closed, Buck looked at Dave and Perez and said, "What's going on?"

Dave said, "It appears that those two hit men are from up north."

"Damn. Didn't believe that stuff still went on," Buck said.

"Well, you should. Apparently they were here to kill young Gurley there," Dave said.

"What? Why would anyone want to kill a seventeen-year-old kid?"

Dave said, "We were hoping that you could tell us. We would also like to know who you have protecting you, because somebody did an excellent job of killing those boys outside."

Buck sat on the bed. "Frankly, I don't know who would want to kill Tom. He's a great kid with a good head on his shoulders. The only trouble we've had of late is with his uncle's death. There are a couple of guys up in Tishomingo who have tried to force themselves onto Tom as executor of his uncle's estate and as his guardian."

Dave stepped forward to the end of the bed, and Perez kept looking at me. "Can you tell us who these men are?"

"Sure," Buck said. "Their names are John Ross and Seth Wilburton, an attorney in town. His brother is the district attorney up there."

Perez interrupted. "What reason would they have to kill Tom Gurley?"

"Would just be speculation on my part, but if Tom was dead, they might have a better shot at getting control of his uncle's company."

Perez said, "That seems kind of extreme, don't it?"

Buck was starting to get a bit annoyed by Perez. "Maybe, but we are talking about over six hundred million dollars and more than ten companies. People been killed for less."

"What's wrong with Gurley?" Dave said.

"I'm sittin' right here, Dave," I said. "I can answer for myself." They were both starting to piss me off.

"He got kicked in the head in the state championship game," Buck answered before I could say any more.

"Did we win?" Dave asked with a smile.

I answered that question. "Hell, yeah! Le High is the Texas state champion!"

Buck added, "Tom here even scored a few of the winning points."

"Well, that's awesome. I think that's all the questions we have for now. I'll call up to Tishomingo and see if I can learn anything from them."

"Will he need an attorney?" Buck asked.

"Don't think so. It's not likely that he killed those two good ol' boys in the Camaro, since he was in here getting his head worked on," Dave answered.

"Not less'n he did it from a hospital gurney," Buck said.

"We'll get back to you tonight or tomorrow." Dave and Perez walked out of the room and left the door open.

"Johnston County base to Tishomingo one. Come in."

"Hello, Joe Bill. This is Adolph. Over."

"Adolph, what are you doing in the sheriff's car? Over."

"The sheriff has a cracked windshield. I'm taking it in to get it fixed. He's driving my patrol car. Anything I can do for you?"

"Yeah, there is a police officer on the phone from Leland, Texas, calling to talk about a couple of homicides they had down there. Over."

"I'll call him from the garage, or you can have him call me at Dimitri's Auto Repair in about ten minutes. Over."

"I gave him the number to Dimitri's Auto Repair. He said he would call you in ten minutes. Over."

"Thanks. Over." Adolph hung up the mike and rolled into Dimitri's Auto Repair. He had a sick, sinking feeling in his stomach that his father may be responsible for the deaths in Leland, which meant that there was likely a connection back to Tishomingo in some way.

"What happened to the sheriff's car, Adolph?" Dimitri asked as he saw that half the windshield was gone in front of the driver's side.

"Don't ask, Dimitri. It's been a long day, and the sheriff wants this windshield replaced as quickly as possible. He also wants it kept quiet, so not a word to anyone."

Dimitri carefully examined the shattered windshield. "You want body work on these buckshot holes in the hood and fender and across the top of the car?"

"Of course. The sheriff isn't going to drive a piece of crap."

"Okay, just asking to be clear."

"No problem."

The phone started ringing, and Dimitri walked back into the office. Adolph said, "That may be for me, Dimitri. I'm expecting a call from another cop about a case."

"Okay." Dimitri picked up the phone. "He's right here, Officer. It's your call, Adolph. Would you take it in Angie's office? She's gone to lunch, and I got some paperwork to do."

"No problem." Adolph stepped into Angie's office and swung the door closed. Angie's desk was covered with photos of grandkids and her Chihuahuas. *They are the ugliest little yapping dogs,* Adolph thought. He punched the blinking Line Two button. "This is Deputy Tyler. Who am I speaking to?"

"Hello, this is Officer Dave Waterman with the El Paso County Sheriff's office. I am assigned to an unincorporated town northwest of El Paso."

"Good to talk to you. What's going on?" Adolph said.

"We have a couple of bodies down here belonging to a Jimmy and a Lonny Cody. I believe they're from up your way?" He waited to see if Adolph recognized the names.

"That would be correct. We have their youngest brother here in a hospital all shot up. Thought he could run through one of our roadblocks and couldn't. He has confessed to killing a couple from the community up here. What's going on with his brothers?"

Dave asked, "What do you know about his brothers?"

"They're bad news. Spent some time in prison here and then moved up north around Chicago. Heard they were hiring out as killers. It appears that their younger brother was in the business as well. He was hired here locally to kill a store owner and his wife. What you got there?"

"Well, it appears that these boys were down here to kill a kid named Thomas Gurley, but we can't seem to figure out who would want to kill a seventeen-, nearly eighteen-year-old kid."

"Any leads?" Adolph tried to contain his adrenaline rush.

Dave continued, "The kid's guardian, Buck Hagan, told us that they were having trouble with the estate from a couple of fellas up your way, a guy named John Ross and a lawyer named Seth Wilburton. Know anything about them?"

"Yeah. They're a couple of very prominent citizens around here—extremely well connected and powerful. They are also prime suspects in the murder of Mr. and Mrs. Chubb, the couple I told you about. The sheriff has a confession from the youngest Cody, stating that Ross and Wilburton hired him to kill the Chubbs." Adolph's mind was racing.

"Woah! You think it's possible that these boys hired the older brothers to kill Gurley?"

Adolph said, "Not only possible, I would say it is highly probable. I'm going to talk to the sheriff and give him your information. I or the sheriff will call you as soon as I talk to him. Sounds like Ross and Wilburton are turning into regular mob guys. Thanks for the information. I would suggest that you make sure Gurley has some protection, 'cause these guys are determined. Nobody says no to them. Judges and senators take their telephone calls."

"Thanks. I already suggested that Gurley and Hagan make sure they have security."

Adolph thought as he hung up the phone, *Well, it looks like Daddy made it to Leland. He made good time and short work of the Codys. He'll be coming back here to deal with the rest of this crowd if I know my daddy.*

Hector swung by, picked him up at Dimitri's, and took him back to the sheriff's office, where he picked up a spare patrol car. He keyed the mike and said, "Tishomingo one, this is Tishomingo three. Come in?"

"What do you need, Adolph?"

"Sheriff, what's your twenty? I need to meet up with you and brief you on some new information."

"I'm parked just off SH1 in Ravia."

"I'll meet you at Mildred's Café in Ravia in ten minutes. Over."

"I'm up for breakfast." Lee Bob liked breakfast any time of day, and Mildred served it sixteen hours a day, six days a week. Being a good Baptist gal, she went to church on Sunday but opened at 12:30 to let the good church folk scarf grits, bacon, and eggs with biscuits and gravy. There wasn't much better anywhere, and Mildred always kept their coffee cups full.

Adolph pulled out of the lot and kicked it down West Main, flipping his lights on a couple of times when he got annoyed with slow traffic. He went on down Wrecker Road and punched it, with lights and siren going when he hit the long stretch of Highway 22.

Adolph's cruiser was backed into a familiar head-in parking slot at Mildred's that was usually reserved for Tishomingo one, which, of course, his car was today as it was carrying the sheriff. Mildred's place used to be a hardware store with two large glass window displays on Main Street. Previously, she had had a hole-in-the-wall dump at the edge of town, but when the hardware store went out of business, she bought the place to provide her customers more room. In Ravia, with only 440 residents, you would think there wouldn't be enough business to keep her afloat, but her biscuits and gravy, served all day every day, brought people from forty miles away. Her peach pie and homemade ice cream made grown men cry, it was so good. She owned the entire building and had installed a Laundromat next to the café to provide a place for the roughnecks to wash their clothes. Her daughter ran the beauty shop that sat on the other side of the café and took care of all of the farmer's wives, children, ranch hands, and roughnecks when they needed a haircut or color treatment. She was big business in Ravia, and her sister, Fleeta May Langston, ran the post office, though she had to purchase stamps regularly out of her own pocket to keep the post office open. Ravia was a family-owned town, and people felt comfortable there. They didn't have a police force, but with the sheriff and his deputies eating at Mildred's regularly, they didn't need one.

Adolph pushed open the glass door to the sound of the familiar Swiss bells that rang out when banged by the door. The sheriff was seated in his usual booth back by the kitchen, with his back to the wall so he could take note of everyone who walked in or walked by on the street.

"What's so damned important, Adolph? Not that I mind stopping for breakfast at two o'clock in the afternoon, but I already had the special this morning."

"Well, I got a call from a deputy down in Leland, Texas. He said he had the older Cody brothers sewed up."

"What's so earth shattering about that?"

"By sewed up, I mean in a coroner's bag. They had been shot twice each in the head with a .22 pistol while they sat in a stolen, souped-up Camaro. He believes they were down there to make a hit, and somebody beat them to the punch."

"Who would they want to kill in Leland, Texas, for God's sake?"

"He believes they were after Tom Gurley."

"Isn't that Boats's nephew, the one who inherited all his money and businesses?"

"Yeah, one and the same. The real kick in the head is who he said he thinks put them up to it."

"Who would that be?"

"You boys want any breakfast, or you just takin' up space to prevent real paying customers from taking a seat?" Mildred said with a grin as she hovered over the table.

"Millie, you know that ain't fair. I'm a paying customer," the sheriff whined.

"Not unless you consider picking up the check in 1964, the first year you was elected, as being a paying customer. I'd say you are more of a regular customer, one who regularly don't pay."

"Now, Millie, I may not pay, but I give the place an air of respectability." Lee Bob smiled up at her.

"Only when your sorry ass ain't here."

"Well, bring us two specials. I liked it so much this morning that I'm going to have it again. And just to show you what a sport I am, Adolph is going to pay and leave a ten-dollar tip."

"Mighty kind of you, Sheriff, but Adolph needs the money more than me with what you pay him."

"Damn, Sheriff, you are free with my money!"

"Aw, hell, Adolph, I'd sign for reimbursement for you." Lee Bob shot him a big grin and then leaned forward after Millie walked away. "Now tell me who put them up to it."

"Well, it wasn't a clean link, but Hagan told the deputy that they were having trouble with John Ross and Seth Wilburton."

"Damn. Did you tell him that we had connected Wilburton and Ross to the Chubbs' murders?"

"I may have, Sheriff."

"Don't play fucking games with me, Adolph. Did you or didn't you?" the sheriff barked.

Mildred walked by and shot Lee Bob a look. "You boys play nice and watch your mouths. We have children in here with big ears. I don't want you teaching them to trash talk."

"Yes, ma'am," Adolph said.

The sheriff just shot her a mind-your-own-damn-business look in return.

"Okay," Lee Bob began, "so we know that Seth Wilburton and John had the Chubbs killed, and we suspect that Leon, Coy, and Adam Halsey are involved as well."

"That's how I read it, Sheriff."

"Then who the hell killed the two older Cody boys down in Leland? You say they were down there to kill Tom Gurley?"

"Yeah, that's what the deputy thinks."

"They must be planning on taking over Boats's businesses as well as the rest of Johnston County. But why kill the boy?"

"Hagan told the deputy that there is a fight over who is executor of the will and who will have guardianship of the boy. Obviously, if Ross and Wilburton get control of the estate and the kid, they'll control all of Boats's holdings."

"I don't think the judge would stand for that," Lee Bob thought out loud.

"I don't know about that, Sheriff. Things are pretty fucked up around here right now with Doc Leftan's records in the wind. I sure don't want to try to explain what the Doc put together on me." Adolph looked worried.

"Stop worrying, Adolph. You are a small fish in this pond. They will go after the senators, judges, and sheriffs before they ever mess with a fucking deputy."

"Thanks, Sheriff. You are so encouraging."

"Tell me something, Adolph. Who do you think was protecting the Gurley kid?" The sheriff stared into Adolph's face and waited in silence for an answer. It was a while before Adolph responded, but he never made eye contact with him.

"Don't know, Sheriff." His voice trailed.

"Dammit, Adolph. Is your father back in business protecting the Nichols clan?"

"Sheriff, you know I'm not close to Pike. He dumped me on my grandmother when I was a kid and never played the father role. The only time I talk to him is when he wants something."

Lee Bob saw the opening in what Adolph hadn't said. "Yeah, so when is the last time you talked to him?"

"Couple days ago." Adolph resisted but knew the sheriff was on his scent and would get it all out of him either now or in the next three hours of grilling.

"And ..." Lee Bob let the *and* float in the air and remained silent, waiting for an answer. He scooped a mouthful of biscuit covered in gravy while he waited.

"And he told me he was going down to Leland to protect the Gurley kid." Adolph still wasn't making eye contact, so the sheriff knew there was more.

"How in the hell did he know that the Gurley kid would need protecting?"

Adolph looked up. "I can't answer that. You know Pike always seemed to know what the Combine was up to, sometimes before they did. It is kind of spooky."

"Well, he has a source somewhere who is feeding him information. You know, if I find out he killed the Codys, I'm going to fry his ass!" Lee Bob was talking and working his way around a piece of bacon at the same time. Lee Bob continued, "Both Texas and Oklahoma have the death penalty, but Texas doesn't fart around with carrying them out. If he killed those boys in Leland, it will be up to the state of Texas to deal with him. Knowing Pike, though, they are going to play hell getting anything on him." Lee Bob was focused on his plate and his food the whole time he was talking, halfway ignoring Adolph.

"I'm still curious where he gets his intel," the sheriff said.

"I'm surprised you didn't know—Pike was in the Intelligence Corps in South Korea. He's a bona fide spook, sneaky as hell, and just as deadly if he has a mind for it."

"Well, he may be a spook, but somebody is helping him. If he comes back into town, I want to know about it." Lee Bob was looking Adolph in the eyes.

Adolph said, "The Cody shootings happened late yesterday, so he may already be back in town. It's only about an eleven-hour drive from El Paso. He could be in town now. Knowing Pike, he didn't plant any flowers along the way."

"Keep me posted." Lee Bob mopped the remaining gravy with a piece of rye toast and slapped it in his mouth, swallowed, waited a minute, and let out a hellacious burp. "Thanks, Mildred! Great food as always."

"You should try paying for it sometime, Sheriff!" Mildred hollered from the back.

Chapter 36

Letch and the Party Shack

Leon Ritchie owned a medium-sized spread, in Oklahoma terms—nearly forty thousand acres. He raised cattle around the oil fields that occupied his property. He and John Ross had made a fortune by setting up ranchers and stealing their properties. With the help of the district attorney's office, the sheriff, and occasionally a judge, they had forced the subpar sale of tens of thousands of oil-rich properties. He sat atop a cattle and oil empire. His ranch complex had two stables of thoroughbred racehorses that he had maintained for his stepdaughter Christine's benefit. He maintained full sleeping quarters in the horse barn for his incestuous affairs with his two stepdaughters by different wives. One stepdaughter, Margaret, still lived on the ranch, serving as his replacement wife because her mother had moved to Dallas after they divorced when the girl was seventeen and her mom caught her giving Daddy a blow job in the bathtub.

Five million dollars was the price of Margaret's mother's silence—that and a solemn promise that, if she ever revealed the secret, she wouldn't live to testify. Margaret took care of the house, the ranch, and Daddy's physical needs.

Leon loved to ride his quarter horse across the ranch when the men were working the herds. Sometimes he rode with Margaret or Christine, if she was visiting the ranch. He seldom rode alone, though he was more seldom accompanied by male companions. Leon was a letch. He spent his spare time at the ranch in his video room, watching pornography and thinking of new and inventive ways to pleasure himself with his own stepdaughters.

John had approached him first about taking over the county. Both Leon and John had had it with Boats's and Judge Watkins's moralistic boundaries. They were wealthy enough, but there was still more available, to John's and Leon's thinking. Leon knew what Doc had on him, but he figured that his daughters were both in their late twenties to early thirties now, so there wasn't anything much that could be done about their sexual activity. He would be embarrassed, perhaps, by the story if it got out, but he didn't really give a shit what people thought. He could spend the rest of his life at his ranch and not need anything from anyone.

After Paul Craig had kicked his ass and confronted him with the incestuous relationship he had been carrying on with his wife, Leon had started plotting how to eliminate his son-in-law. He hadn't come up with a workable solution, because Paul had clearly gotten a copy of Doc's file from Larry Chubb. Chubb was dead, thank God, and it appeared that the sheriff had Doc's files and would play along. But Paul still had a file, and there was no way for Leon to determine where it was.

Chubb had the perfect accident. Well, it would have been perfect if the damn sheriff hadn't been right there when it happened. Leon picked up the telephone and called John. Delbert Hathaway picked up, and Delbert said that Mr. Ross was in a meeting at the moment but would be available if he could hold for a minute.

Leon waited for John to answer the phone. "Hello, this is John Ross."

"Hey, John. This is Leon. I need some help with a problem I've got."

"You mean that fucking son-in-law of yours? That prick was in my office this morning and insisted that I go forward with the Snell Building purchase."

"Well, that may be a problem, but it is not my major problem right now. He beat the shit out of Christine last night, and when I tried to rescue her, he beat the shit out of me and threatened to kill me. Unfortunately, he got a copy of Doc's file from Larry Chubb and is blackmailing me, so I can't do anything about it."

"So what the hell do you want me to do?" John asked.

"Do you have any contacts that I could use to get the file back and get rid of my problem for me?"

"You want to kill the son of a bitch?"

"That's the general idea, but I want to make sure that the file is not floating around."

"Seth and Adam are the ones who lined up the special employees to take the trash out for us in the past. I'll talk to Adam and see what he thinks about your predicament. I'll call you back tonight if I have anything."

John hung up and dialed Adam Halsey. "Adam, Ross here."

"How you doing, John?" the district attorney asked.

"Fine. Would you be able to stop by the office at lunchtime?" John requested.

"Sure. Something shaking?"

"Yeah, we have an insurance problem I need your talents in solving." John smiled to himself at his own creativity in discreetly stating the problem.

"Sure. See you at noon. Have Velma order me a roast beef on light rye, easy on the horseradish."

"Yeah, I think she already knows that after ten years."

Later, Adam settled into the leather wingback chair opposite John's desk. John explained the situation with Leon to Adam and asked if he knew of a trustworthy person who could handle the task.

"*Trustworthy* is not a word that I would use to describe my clientele. I wouldn't even call them dependable, as the Codys have demonstrated. Did you hear that Lee Bob has Bobby Cody and that somebody killed the two older Codys in Texas?"

"Yeah, I heard about those shitbirds."

"How many of these guys do you think I can produce?"

"I don't know, but you're going to have to earn your keep in the Combine."

"That's bullshit, John. I've more than earned my keep with the amount of money I've put in your pockets."

"That's not what I meant. Don't misunderstand me. None of the rest of us have any resources to line up the kind of people you can get to do dirty work."

"No duh. What is it that Leon needs?" Adam asked.

"He needs someone to take out his son-in-law, Paul Craig. But the catch is that they have to get the files he has first."

"You want someone who can get him to cough up the records before they kill him. Is that it?" Adam asked.

"Yeah, you're a quick study."

"You don't make it through law school if you're an imbecile. I'll talk to Seth to see if he has any usable talent in his criminal practice. Just promise them a couple of free passes in Johnston County, and they'll kill anybody."

"Thanks, Adam. I'll wait to hear from you."

"It will take a few days, so tell Leon to hold off doing anything for a while."

Seth made his regular Tuesday visit to the pen. He was escorted deep into the labyrinth of corridors to the confidential attorney-client meeting rooms. Sitting across from him was Al Perna, a purported lieutenant of a Chicago mob family who had the misfortune of driving drunk in Johnston County and was discovered to be a felon in possession of a firearm, which put him back in prison. He was a short, fast-talking Chicagoan. He had jet-black hair combed back and held in place with pomade, he sported a bushy mustache, and the remainder of his beard seemed always to be about three days from its last trim.

Seth asked for a contact to handle some specialized work in Johnston County. He explained that a friend needed a person to collect a series of documents and then eliminate the document's possessor. Perna listened intently and then said, "I have connections in Chicago that could handle this."

"I don't need the problem handled in Chicago," Seth said. "I need them in Oklahoma."

Perna looked at him with disdain. "I know you've been down here a while, but you have heard of airplanes, right?"

"Don't get uppity. There are plenty of cons who want a pass out of prison," Seth said tersely.

Perna ignored the implication. "These guys do work for us down here all the time. They were with me when I got pinched for the DUI and your dipshit sheriff planted a gun on me."

"The sheriff is handy that way," Seth quipped.

"Well, I plan to repay the favor, only he won't be going away to a cushy prison." Perna was in rare form today.

"All in due time, Perna. All in due time."

Seth looked Perna in the eye. "Look, my half brother is the DA. He told me he might be able to find some constitutional problems with how your case was handled. Doesn't look like procedures were followed properly. The Supreme Court just handed down a case called *Miranda*. Nobody gave you your rights when you was arrested, which means you might be eligible for immediate release, given the right circumstances." Seth gave him a wink and a nod.

Perna was interested. "What might those circumstances be, counselor?"

"We scratch your back, you take care of an itch that we have." Wilburton smiled.

"Well, I would have to hear the details first."

Seth looked at him in disbelief. "Don't be too picky, Perna. Your Italian ass can sit in jail well beyond your sentence, given the propensity of cons to commit crimes in prison."

Perna sat forward and popped the table with his fist. "Don't threaten me, counselor, or you might have a serious accident right here. I'll do the work for yoos; I just need to know the details and the payoff."

Seth smiled. "Thought that might be the case. I have the details right here." Wilburton reached into his briefcase and pulled out a manila envelope. It included a picture of Paul Craig and travel and hotel accommodations for Paul's trip to Oklahoma City.

"I'll take care of it. But I want fifteen thousand in cash when I walk out of this shit hole." Perna leaned back in his seat.

Seth didn't quibble. "I'll make sure the money is here when you walk out, but there is one other thing my friend wants. He wants to be present when you—when the information is extracted, and when Paul takes a bullet in the head. He wants to castrate Paul before you kill him."

"Whoa! This Paul guy musta really pissed him off."

"Yeah, something like that." Seth smiled.

"What about the body?"

"He also indicated that he would have an ideal location to put the body."

Perna slapped his hands together and rubbed them back and forth. "Well, how soon do I get out of this place?"

"The trip is scheduled for next weekend, so I will have you out on Monday. You will be transported to the courthouse in Tishomingo to meet with the district attorney, who will personally apologize to you for your wrongful arrest.

I'll then take you to the Johnston County Bank for a meeting with my friend to discuss the details of the small service you will provide."

Seth called Adam as soon as he got back to the office. "Perna's in."

"That'll make Leon happy. Not good news for Paul, though." Adam laughed.

"I will head over to John's and explain the details we worked out with Perna," Adam said.

CHAPTER 37

Call for the Cavalry

I asked Buck to roll me back to my room. My head was killing me. I gave Mar a kiss and told her I was going to lay down for a bit. It was real dark outside, around ten thirty at night. The hallway was quiet and vacant except for an old man moaning three rooms down the hall. I turned and looked up at Buck. "What's this all about, Buck?"

"I don't know, son, but you don't have to worry about them."

We went on silently for the next forty feet till we came to my room. Standing outside my door was a suited man about six two, 250 pounds. He opened the door and closed it behind us.

"This is getting crazy, Buck. Do we have any idea what is going on?" I said as I crawled into bed.

"The only thing I can figure is that this Ross and Wilburton crowd is starting to play hardball."

"Well, I sure don't like the idea that they went after Mar and Tess."

"It looks like they came here to the hospital to get you, son, only somebody got them first."

"Buck, I think we better get a hold of Mark and get some security around us. I don't want anybody getting hurt because of me or Boats's estate."

Buck said, "It has already been taken care of. I had Mark fly an armed security crew up from Dallas. Besides the big guy outside the door to your hospital room, there is another one outside your window. Until we figure out what is going on, we aren't taking any chances." Buck pulled back the curtain, and I could see the back of another man close to the same size as the one outside my door.

I stared at Buck. "It wouldn't do for my wife to be a widow so young."

Buck said, "The doc is going to release you and the girls tomorrow afternoon. I have a security team at the ranch putting in a state-of-the-art security system and monitoring station."

"Have you talked to Royal or Bob to see if they have any sense of what to do about Wilburton and Ross? If they are responsible for the attack on Mar, I want to go after them with everything we can."

"I've talked to both Royal and Bob. We agreed that Bob would pay a visit to the Wilburtons, both Adam and Seth. He had an off-the-record conversation with them and told them point-blank that their hit men missed and wound up dead. He told me that he was shocked at the lack of response. He said at first they didn't know what to say, and then they denied the accusation profusely. Both Bob and Royal think they are behind the attempt. Bob did some nosing around in Tishomingo, and apparently the sheriff arrested them for the murder of a store owner and his wife. Supposedly, the younger brother of the two guys that attacked Mar is in a hospital in Tish, is dying, and confessed to the murder for hire."

"This all seems pretty outrageous," I said.

"You're telling me."

"Do you think we'll be safe at the ranch?"

"Yeah, with Mark's help, we have an army of security people at the ranch and a half dozen here. He is even sending over two armored SUVs that they have in Dallas to transport family members."

"What about school? I don't want to have security guys following us everywhere."

"We may not be able to do much about that for a while. I have talked to Ward at the high school, and he has agreed to have a couple of security guys on campus disguised as handymen doing repairs. Nichols Oil is also going to pay Dave's and Perez's salaries for a couple of months so they can hang out at the school more frequently."

"You been busy, Buck."

"Yeah, a bit. Rocky has been a great help. I also got a call from Boats's old driver, Pike, who said to let him know if there is anything that he can do."

"Well, we may need a chauffeur. If he traveled everywhere with Boats, he would probably know everyone we would need to know. He looked after me while I was at the ranch for the first few months I was with Boats. He's a crusty old fart, but he looked after Boats like nobody's business."

Buck said, "I will call him and ask if he could join us when he can get away from Tish."

"That would be great."

An orderly came in and announced that the doctor had signed my release papers earlier than expected and that I could leave as soon as the nurse came in.

When Mar and I left the hospital, there were four men and one woman waiting. Two black Chevy Tahoes were parked at the curb, and the woman opened the side doors. None of the men looked at us; instead, they were looking at the surrounding sidewalks and approaches to the vehicles.

"Wow, Buck, you weren't kidding about security," I said.

"Can't take any chances."

When the two vehicles got to the ranch, I noticed a new steel gate and guardhouse. "What's this?" I asked Buck.

"Right now it's just a temporary setup. We will have a permanent one in the next thirty days."

"Do you think we're overdoing it?"

"No, I don't. Two bastards had easy access to Mar and Tess, and those two killers parked outside the hospital, waiting for you to walk out so they could kill you. I don't think we are being too cautious. In fact, I'm a damn fool for not taking steps to protect you guys sooner. Tom, you are worth more than six hundred million dollars. That makes you a great target for kidnapping, or any wacko or weirdo who comes along. We're just damn lucky somebody didn't get seriously hurt while I farted around. We ain't in Kansas anymore, Toto."

"I guess that makes sense."

"It makes a lot of sense," Buck said. "I asked Mark to put together a security study team to make sure that you and Mar are provided with top-notch security. I was just too damn stupid to think about it sooner."

"Buck, stop beating yourself up. Nobody is seriously hurt, and you're on top of it now."

"But when I think of what could have happened to the girls, it makes me sick."

The rigs pulled up to the ranch house, and the second rig went on to drop Manny and Tess off at their place.

Chapter 38

Cancel the Insurance

Al Perna sat across from Leon and Seth Wilburton in the Johnston County Bank's boardroom. Leon slid a manila envelope across the table to Perna and said, "There is ten grand in there. When you finish the job, I will hand you the other five thousand."

"Do you have anything special in mind for the mark?" Perna asked.

"What do you mean by *special?*" Leon asked.

Pike adjusted the volume on the receiver as he was listening in from the bugs placed in the boardroom. He watched the small reel-to-reel collect the voices.

"According to Mr. Wilburton here, he has a file on you that you want to get back, right?" Perna's voice was deep.

"Yeah, he does, but it isn't going to be too easy to locate it. I'm sure he has it tucked away or has given it to someone for safekeeping." Leon was watching this greaser; he hated "ethnics," as he called them.

"That may be so. But by the time my guy is done with him, he will tell me everything I want to know about anything I have to ask."

"If you mean torturing the son of a bitch, I want to be there," Leon said. "Just before you put a bullet in his brain, I want you to cut his dick off and stick it in his mouth. That cocksucker put his hands on me and my daughter. I don't stand for that from nobody!" Leon was pounding the table.

"That is going to cost you another five K," Perna said. "High-profile killings where you cut somebody's nuts off draw a lot of attention." Perna sat back, and his chair creaked in that all-too-familiar way. *He must be sitting in Boats's usual chair,* Pike thought.

Leon responded, "I don't care what it costs. I want to see the look on his face when you stuff his dick into his screaming mouth. And there isn't going to be any publicity because he ain't never going to be heard from again."

"How do you figure that?" Perna said.

"He is supposed to attend an insurance convention up in Oklahoma City this Friday through Sunday. You are going to grab him up there in his hotel room and bring him back to a line shack I have out on the northwest section of my ranch. He can scream his fucking head off out there, and nobody will hear a thing. When we are done with him, I'll have a twelve-foot-deep hole dug at the end of one of our feedlots. We'll drop him in there with a steer carcass, soak it in fifty-five gallons of airplane fuel, and torch them, and when the flame burns out, we'll bury 'em in lye. When he doesn't return from Oklahoma City, Christine will turn in a missing person's report."

Perna's chair squeaked as he turned toward Ritchie. "You want me to bag him and bring him back here?"

"Yeah, Christine wants to watch you cut his dick off and shove it in his mouth. Then you can shoot him in the head or burn him alive. I don't give a shit." Leon sat back in his usual chair, and Pike could hear his boots hit the table.

"You are one sick son of a bitch, but you're paying, so have it your way. I'll have one of my guys grab him Friday night and drive him back down here to the line shack. When do you want to meet him?"

"I thought you were going to do the job," Leon asked.

"I don't do wet work, but the guy who will is able to do anything you want—no conscience and no qualms about anything. You name it, he'll do it. He once skinned a Cuban drug dealer alive. Had to keep bringing him around so the drug dealer would appreciate the quality job he was doing. Took him two days, and he enjoyed every minute of it. Mailed the Cube's skin back to his boss."

Leon was laughing. "Good. I'll drive Christine out at about five o'clock. That should give you enough time to get the file."

"I'm going to need a couple of my guys to help with this if we are going to have to pick up the file." Perna was brazen.

"You find out where the file is, and I'll send two guys to get it. I don't want anybody handling that file that I don't know personally."

"Have it your way," Perna said.

"I usually do," Leon said.

Just then, John Ross walked in the door. "Everything worked out in here?" John walked over to his desk; Pike could hear the drawers open and close.

"We'll get it done," Perna said.

"Good," John said. "I've got a Rotary officers meeting in here in fifteen minutes, so if you all could clear out, I'd appreciate it."

"No problem, John," Leon said. "You coming, Seth?"

"No, I'm on the Rotary executive committee."

Perna stood and said, "You got the address of the hotel where Paul is staying in Oklahoma City and a picture I can take?"

"They are both in the envelope I gave you with the money."

"Thanks. My guy will see you Saturday."

"I'll be there with my daughter around five."

After Leon and Perna left, John asked Seth, "How'd it go?"

"Let me tell you, I don't ever want to piss Leon off. He is one sick fuck, and his daughter is exactly like him."

"I've known that for some time. Rumor is that Leon has been screwing his daughter since she was fifteen. Shocked the hell out of me when she married a milquetoast like Paul Craig."

"Well, Christine is a good-looking woman. I chased her skirt when she was in high school and I was finishing college. No wonder she wasn't interested."

"Gives a whole new meaning to the term 'Daddy's girl,' don't it?" They both laughed, and Delbert walked in and told them that the other Rotary officers were there. John told him to bring them in.

Pike took off the headset and then took the tape out of the recorder.

Paul Craig had been going to Oklahoma City every year he had been in the insurance business. The first year they were married, Christine came with him, but after that he was always alone. The first couple of years he played it straight, but since then he had sought the companionship of a hooker during the weekend to make up for the lack of conjugal satisfaction Christine provided. He always stayed at the downtown Hilton in the corner suite on the twenty-fourth floor; his secretary booked it automatically a year in advance so he could entertain guests and have a party on Saturday night for friends.

Paul checked in as usual and left his bags for the bellhop to bring up later. He stuck the key in the door and pushed it open with his foot. He immediately turned into the bathroom to relieve himself. Moments later, the bellhop knocked, brought his bags into the room, and laid them at the end of the king-sized bed on a bench made for that purpose. The bellhop opened the curtains and let in the dwindling sunlight that was peeking from behind the cityscape. It was barely after five o'clock when he lay down on his bed to grab a quick snooze before the cocktail party kicked off at 8:00. He had just plumped his pillow when someone knocked at the door. He swung it open, thinking that his escort had arrived early. What he saw was a short, plump, balding man in an ill-fitting suit. He didn't have a chance to notice the man behind him because the .45-caliber pistol with its grip wrapped in duct tape had his complete attention.

Paul took a step back and was pushed deeper into the room by the barrel of the .45 and the pressure of the fat man's intense stare and extending arm. "Keep your mouth shut, and I won't kill you right now."

"I don't have a lot of money," Paul stuttered.

"I don't want your fucking money. I want you to keep your fucking mouth shut and do exactly what I tell you. We are going to walk out the door and take the elevator down to the parking garage. Then we are going for a drive."

"Did Leon send you?" Paul asked defiantly.

"We'll have plenty of time to talk in the car. I'm sure there's a lot of things you're going to want to tell me during our brief time together." The fat man pushed the gun toward his head.

There was a knock at the door.

"Are you expecting someone?" the fat man asked.

"I have an escort coming, but not for another half hour."

"Find out who it is. Fuck it up, and I'll kill you now."

Paul walked to the door and opened it slightly.

An older waiter in a tux stood outside with a service cart. The fat man's number-two guy looked down at the cart and sized up the waiter. "Room service, courtesy of the manager."

"I didn't order room service," Paul said.

"The manager sent up champagne and strawberries for all the conference committee members."

Paul turned and looked at the fat man, who put the gun in his suit pocket and held it while motioning to Paul to have the waiter come in.

The waiter pushed the cart past Paul, who held the door open, and into the room past the king-sized bed and set the tray of strawberries on the small, round table. The door closed automatically, leaving the second man still guarding the door outside. The waiter turned and set two champagne flutes on the table and popped the cork on the bottle. The waiter then showed the bottle to the fat man, who nodded and said, "Yeah, fine. Now leave us alone."

The fat man turned and looked at Paul with his hand in his coat pocket pointed toward him. As he turned to look at the waiter again, two .22 Long rounds shot through his right temple, dropping him face down on the king-sized bed. His blood pooled on the silk coverlet. His hand was still in his pocket.

Paul gasped, "What the fuck? You killed him!"

"Stand next to the wall and shut your mouth. The bastard was sent here to haul your ass back to Tishomingo and torture you until you told him where the file on Leon was. Then your darling father-in-law and loving wife were going to cut your dick off and shove it in your mouth before they burned your sorry carcass in a pit by the old man's line shack. Apparently, they love you."

"Who are you?" Paul said in a panic.

"I'm the guy who saved your ass and who is going to put a stop to your fucking father-in-law. Stay next to the wall so the guy in the hall can't see you. Here, take this." The man handed him a single-action Colt with a gray suppressor screwed on the barrel and asked if he knew how to use it.

"Yeah, my dad had a Colt," he answered.

"Good. Stay put. I'm going to take care of the other guy."

Paul watched as the waiter maneuvered the cart, backing it down the short entryway to the hotel room, held the door open with his foot, and said loudly into the room, "Thanks for the tip, Mr. Craig." As he backed into the corridor, he said to number two, "The large gentleman asked me to tell you he wanted you inside."

Number two stepped into the room, and he hadn't taken a second step before two .22 slugs pierced the back of his skull and his right eye exploded. He fell forward with a thud on the carpet.

"Help me drag him into the room," the waiter barked. When he was placed beside the bed, Pike went back for the cart in the hallway. Pike pulled the cassette recorder from under the service cart and played the recording from Perna's meeting.

Pike and Paul crossed the parking garage and headed for a pickup. Before they reached the truck, they stopped about forty feet from a late model Cadillac with the fat man's driver at the wheel. The waiter waved at him, raised his hand, and pointed to Paul, prompting the driver to throw open the door to the Cadillac and pull a gun, aiming it across the top of the driver's door. He was shouting at them not to move when a man appeared from the shadows, slipped from behind the trunk of the car, and swung his karambit at a precise point at the base of the driver's skull. The shooter's arms went limp, and his knees buckled as he crumpled behind the door. His eyes were flashing back and forth at the man, but his body didn't answer any of his brain's commands: his spinal cord was severed. The assailant bent over him, hooked the karambit behind his left ear, and in a quick swirling movement, severed both arteries and his throat. He then stepped out and walked over to Paul and Pike.

"Nice work, Snake," Pike said. "I left two bodies upstairs in the room. Get rid of them and the car. Then I want you to head back and keep an eye on the kid and family with Chee. I can handle the shitbirds in Tish."

"Okay, Sarge." Snake started to leave but then turned and said, "Pike, you need to call Skip as soon as you can regarding the kid."

Paul pissed his pants. Pike looked at him and muttered, "Little too much excitement for you?" He and Snake laughed.

Paul and Pike headed south on the interstate to Tishomingo. They found their way to the line shack around two o'clock in the afternoon. The shack was deserted, and the two walked in, scoped it out, and waited for their guests.

At four, Pike tied Paul loosely to a wooden chair. Paul had the Colt in the back of his waistband. When they heard Leon's truck pull up, Paul lay his head on the table, pretending to be passed out. Leon pushed the door open and stomped to the table where Paul was seated. Christine appeared from behind Leon and looked down on Paul. "Is he dead?" she asked.

Paul lifted his head and saw that Pike was leaning against the cast iron sink, legs crossed. The sterling-silver tips of his snakeskin boots caught the light and the Ritchies' attention. Paul noted that Pike's silenced .22 Ruger lay casually across his jeans.

Paul turned his head and looked Leon in the eyes. A threatening smile spread across Paul's face.

"You won't be smiling for long." Leon slapped him across the face. "This guy is going to peel your skin like an onion until you produce my file, and then he is going to cut your dick off and shove it in your mouth."

Pike said, "Well, Leon, there has actually been a change of plans. It turns out you're not going to need the file."

"What the hell are you talking about?" He turned to face Pike. "Perna said you would find out where the file is so my guys can go get it," Leon said. "There is no way you're getting a fucking dime until you get me that file!"

Pike smiled and shot him in the right knee. The silenced Ruger sounded like a six-year-old trying to spit. Leon fell and rolled onto his side, holding his knee. Christine was hysterical. Pike pointed the muzzle of his .22 at her face and said, "Shut up and sit down." Christine held her hands to her mouth and sat on a short stool next to the table, choking back sobs. Paul got out of the loose restraints, stood up, and looked down on Leon, who was writhing in agony and cussing like a teenager trying to muster courage.

"Who the fuck are you?" shouted Leon.

"I'm not surprised you don't remember who I am, Ritchie. You never notice the little people. I'm Boats's driver. You remember Boats, the guy you murdered in Dallas?"

"I didn't kill him. That was Ross and Wilburton."

"Well, you didn't exactly vote no on the motion, did you?"

"It wouldn't have made any difference. Boats was getting too fucking moralistic—lost track of what's important—and they weren't going to put up with him or the judge anymore."

"That's too bad for you, isn't it?"

"What do you mean?"

"Well, you weren't there for Boats, and now he's not here for you. I wanted to kill you fifteen years ago when you had Cletus framed, but Boats wouldn't let me. Now he's not here, and you're going to die." The first round entered Leon's forehead seven centimeters above the right eye, according to the coroner's report. The second bullet was eight centimeters to the left, directly above the bridge of his nose. Leon's mouth gasped like that of a water-deprived carp—opening, closing, partially in disbelief, and partially as reflex—searching for a word, trying to speak, and then slacked in silence.

Christine ran for the door, but Paul reached out his right arm and caught her by the waist. "You ain't going nowhere, bitch!"

She punched him in the gut, and her hand found the pistol in his waistband. Christine pulled the trigger as she tugged at the Colt. A .45 round shattered Paul's left hip. As she started to spin around with the gun in her right hand, she tried to locate Pike.

Paul fell backward to the floor, screaming and clasping his side, falling on his already broken hip.

Paul knew that Christine was an expert markswoman, and now she was armed. She raised the Colt to where Pike had been standing, but before she fully focused, Pike dropped to his right knee, with his hands just above the table, and fired up a quick double tap, catching her in the triangle between her nose and eyes. She tumbled like a sack of potatoes to the wooden floor with a stunned look on her face.

Pike lifted Paul onto his good leg and supported him as he hobbled to Leon's truck and then hiked to where his own truck was parked. From Leon's truck, Paul picked up the CB and screamed for help. Joe Bill was on the sheriff's radio and picked up the mayday. He responded on Paul's fourth attempt to raise some help.

"This is the sheriff's office. Over."

"Hello, this is Paul Craig. I've been shot!"

"Where are you located, Paul?" Joe Bill asked.

"I'm out at Leon's line shack. They have killed my wife and father-in-law!"

"Who is killed?"

"Gangsters killed my wife and father-in-law. I've been shot! Get me an ambulance!"

"I'm sending one right now."

Joe Bill left the mic open, and Paul could hear him calling for the sheriff. "Tishomingo one, this is dispatch. Over."

"Go ahead, dispatch."

"Sheriff, I just got a call on the CB from Paul Craig. He says he's been shot and his wife and father-in-law have been killed."

"Where is he?"

"He is at Leon's line shack in the north section, just off the east end of Slippery Falls Road."

"I know where it is. I'm about fifteen minutes from there on my way back from Ravia. Have you got an ambulance rolling?"

"Yes, Sheriff, it's on the way."

"Then track down Adolph and have him get out there with his camera. We'll need pictures of everything. Then get a hold of Purvis and tell him we got a couple more dead bodies. Over."

"Will do, Sheriff."

The CB went quiet, and Paul was left to wait in agony.

Pike stopped at Spender's store and bought a six-pack, a bag of barbecue potato chips, and a *Johnston County Capital-Democrat* to read the news story on Coy Purcell's violent death. He dropped the sack of groceries on the front seat of his truck, walked to the pay phone, dialed the number, and heard, "Tishomingo County Bank."

"John Ross please. Bank examiner calling."

"This is John Ross. Who am I speaking with?"

"You are speaking with the person who killed your buddies and has decided that you are next." Pike hung up the phone and then dialed another number. "Hi, love. You coming over tonight?"

"Sure am, cowboy. You better put your spurs on."

"Well, make sure and pick up the tapes from Velma on your way. I think there will be some good stuff on them today."

"You bet, cowboy. I bought me a new silk camisole. You best take a nap this afternoon 'cause I'll be keeping you up all night."

"You are awful hard on a senior citizen, sweetheart."

"I like my senior citizens with a hard-on."

"You are making me blush, girl. See you tonight." Pike walked to his truck and drove home. With Vealie coming tonight, he wanted to clean the place up before she ravaged him.

Vealie lay sleeping with her arm and left breast outside the coverlet. Pike smiled and walked to the dining table. He slipped the tape into the player and donned the headphones to listen to John's previous conversations. He listened to his own telephone conversation with John and then to John's call to the sheriff to tell Lee Bob that he had been threatened again by the mysterious caller. The next call John made was to Seth Wilburton.

"Seth, this is John."

"What's up?"

"I just got a call from a guy who said I'm next."

"What do you mean you're next?"

"Apparently, he killed Leon and his daughter, and he's the same guy who killed Coy Purcell. And now he's going to kill me."

"You mean Leon's …?"

"You haven't heard. The sheriff told me they found Leon and his daughter killed at Leon's line shack. They were killed professionally, according to the sheriff. The gangsters also shot Paul Craig, but they got away."

"Damn. This is getting real messy. What are you going to do?"

"Well, the son of a bitch sheriff said he can't protect me, so I thought I would go to my fishing cabin at the lake and take my gun. Nobody knows about the place, and I can protect myself there. You want to take our wives and party and fish?"

"That might be a good idea. We can party Friday night and get some fishing in on Saturday. I'll talk to Sheryl and let you know. But count me in for now."

"See you Friday night at the lake. I'm heading out there with my wife tonight."

"All right. We'll see you Friday night."

"Good. Bring your gun and fishing pole."

Pike turned the tape off and turned to look at Vealie. She was now lying on her back with both her breasts exposed above the covers. Her eyes were open, and she was smiling at his fit, naked body in the dim light. "Hey, sweetie. You still awake?"

"I'm awake. Looks like my breasts still get a rise out of you."

Pike looked down at his pecker and realized that she was right. The only thing missing was a flag on his erect pole. He slid under the covers and on top of his smiling cowgirl. "Let's ride," he said as she wrapped her legs around him.

Pike parked the truck about half a mile from John's cabin on Friday afternoon. He hiked to the cabin and crawled through the scrub brush in his camo gear the last hundred yards or so to lie concealed in the underbrush with a clear view of the cabin. Mr. and Mrs. Wilburton arrived around six o'clock and entered the cabin. The couples had dinner and then gathered in the living room to drink and smoke pot. He kept an eye on them until eleven. Then he hiked back to his truck and dozed till about four thirty.

Pike woke up, grabbed his gear out of the back of the truck, and hiked back to the cabin to wait for the fishermen to appear. He lay in the underbrush until 7:20, when Seth and John appeared on the front porch. Each had a fishing pole and was wearing sidearms. John had a tackle box, and Seth was carrying a cooler. They waddled to the dock and climbed into John's rowboat.

John kept telling Seth that the fishing here was fantastic and that they should limit out in an hour or two, at most. The lake was large, but they rowed the boat only about two hundred yards from the dock and dropped anchor. They stood in the rowboat, casting into a deep hole where the big fish hung out. After about forty-five minutes, they began to get some strikes and had caught a few fish.

Pike slipped on his rebreather and donned the cap to his wetsuit. He fixed on his mask and flippers and took a couple of deep breaths through the rebreather to make sure air was flowing. He crawled slowly through the scrub brush to the water's edge and, like a hungry gator, slipped beneath the water without a splash, swimming without ripple beneath the surface of the murky water toward his prey.

Forty feet from the rowboat, his head breached the surface like the periscope of a German U-boat. Ahead of him, two figures stood precariously in a rowboat, focused on the fish that lay before them, their backs to lurking death. He heard John shouting that he had another fish and watched Seth reach for the net to snag the prize.

Pike submerged and swam to the far side of the boat, watching Seth's vain attempts to capture the bass fighting just beyond his reach to avoid the snare. As John and Seth leaned out over the normally stable rowboat to see the struggling bass, Pike reached invisibly up the side of the boat and pulled it toward the water in a quick jerk. The two fishermen tumbled into the water. Neither had a life vest on, and they splashed wildly in the water, weighed down by their winter wear.

Pike grabbed John's fat legs and pulled him beneath the water, out of Seth's sight. John's scream for help was silenced as water filled his lungs and his eyes stared lifelessly in disbelief. The fool was wearing his insulated hip waders, which filled quickly with water and helped Pike pull him down.

Seth was swimming for the boat and safety. He didn't make it. Pike pulled him under, wrapping his right arm around his neck and pulling him into the depth of murky water. Seth was out of breath, out of time, and out of luck. He ceased struggling. Seth's thrashing dislodged Pike's face mask but didn't loosen his grip on the dying man's throat. Pike released his grip on Seth, and as Wilburton sank to the bottom face up, his open, lifeless eyes stared in at Pike in shock.

Replacing his mask and blowing the water out with air from his nose, a sudden burst of bubbles broke the surface of the still lake. Pike headed for the shore, swimming past John lingering on the bottom of the lake with his hands floating straight up, as if reaching for the sunlight and the surface. He had a surprised look on his face, like the victim of a holdup. When he reached the shore, Pike turned to see the unoccupied rowboat twenty yards from Seth's empty fishing hat, which floated next to a single low-top Converse tennis shoe. Somewhere in the water, a bass struggled at the end of a line that would never be reeled in, and John stood with his hands up. Pike made his way back to his truck, stripped naked, and put on his work clothes and snakeskin boots. He had plenty of work to do at the ranch; he had spent too much time waiting on these bastards and had allowed his chores to pile up. He wouldn't even have time to read the paper today. He would have to work all day to catch up. Thank goodness Vealie was coming by tonight. Maybe he could get to the sports section on Sunday before she woke.

Chapter 39

Gone Fishing

Lee Bob got to Leon's shack in record time. He knew exactly where it was. It had an old twin bed with a new mattress and a fridge stocked with beer. The makeshift bar was as well stocked as any big city bar, with any alcohol a human being could want. In the old days, members of the Combine took turns bringing women out here. Seth and John still had their foursomes out here on Saturday nights with hookers ordered and shipped up from a pimp in Dallas. Lee Bob recalled interrogating several female prisoners at the line shack. It had never been used by cowhands or roughnecks. It was a poker palace for the Combine's Friday night games and a pleasure paradise most any other night of the week. At the east end of Slippery Falls Road, across a cattle grate and another three-quarters of a mile northeast on a dirt road, you had to be going there to get there because it was nowhere.

Purvis arrived about the same time as the ambulance, and the two were going over the shack and waiting for Adolph to get pictures. The ambulance had been gone about twenty minutes with Paul Craig.

Lee Bob headed to the car to get fingerprinting equipment. As he approached the car, he heard the radio. "Tishomingo one, this is base. Come in?"

"Go ahead, Joe Bill. This is Lee Bob." Lee Bob stood holding the mic with his right arm, leaning on the top of the car and looking back at the shack.

"Sheriff, are you still going over the line shack with Purvis?"

"Hell, yes, Joe Bill. I been here for three hours tryin' to figure this out. Don't ask stupid questions."

"The state patrol office has been trying to raise Purvis on his radio but can't get hold of him."

"That's 'cause he's out back taking a dump. What's the frickin' message? I'll tell him."

Joe Bill was flustered knowing he had raised the sheriff's ire. "The state game warden over at Cottonwood Lake Dam called in a floater in the lake and another at the bottom. Says their wives reported them missing today around noon, and they found their gear floating in the water by their boat." Lee Bob kicked his boot in the sand, sending it flying toward the building.

"Hell, Joe Bill, we got more important fish to fry than two sorry-ass fisherman." Lee Bob was so irritated that he twirled to look around and wrapped the cord around his body in the process.

Joe Bill stuttered and stammered. "Sheriff, I know, but I thought you might need to know their identities."

"Well, don't keep the fuckin' secret. I'm in no mood to be on *Jeopardy* this afternoon. Give me the damn information!" Lee Bob had untangled himself and was now pushing on the open car door against the tension of the door hinge.

"It's Seth Wilburton and John Ross, Sheriff."

"What the fuck—? Did you say Wilburton and Ross? Why the hell didn't you say that right off instead of wandering around the goddamn state!"

"Sorry, Sheriff. The warden wants Purvis to come out to the lake right away."

"Were they murdered?" Lee Bob barked.

"Didn't say, Sheriff. Just that they drowned."

"Well, call 'em back and get the fucking information, Joe Bill. Use your damn pea brain for something useful. I'll get Purvis, and we'll head over." Lee Bob ran around the shack to the outhouse and yelled at Purvis, "Wilburton and Ross are dead! Get your paperwork done and get your ass out here! We gotta go!"

The door flew open, and Purvis came running out, pulling his pants up and fastening his belt.

"When did that happen?" Purvis shouted.

"Apparently this morning. Somebody from your office called trying to track you down. The game warden called."

"Left my portable radio in the car. It hasn't been working properly. Was it murder?"

"They didn't say, just wanted us to head over there ASAP."

The two jumped into their patrol cars and drove the thirty-five miles to the lake, with Purvis taking the lead and Lee Bob three car lengths behind.

As they pulled alongside the cabin, they could see the ambulance down by the water's edge where the rowboat and game warden's sixteen-foot watercraft were tied up at the dock. Lee Bob saw Fred's coroner wagon next to the ambulance and two occupied body bags laid out on the ground nearby. Adolph was shooting pictures of the rowboat.

The sheriff walked down to Adolph while Purvis stopped to talk with Fred. "Adolph, what do you think? Foul play involved?"

"No signs of it, Sheriff. It looks like they fell over the right side of the row boat. You can see John's boot marks up the side of the boat here on the inside."

"How do you know it was John?"

"The fool was wearing hip waders, and you can see a green streak here. And then there was a piece of the toe that was cut by this sharp piece of aluminum here by the knuckle of the oar. That ol' son of a bitch had to sink like a rock when those waders filled up. The divers found him at the bottom of the lake, standing up with his hands raised like a Pentecostal preacher and a surprised look on his face."

"Any evidence it was homicide?"

"None that I can see. But it does seem a bit suspicious. Both were wearing firearms, as if they were expecting trouble. Don't see how anyone could have gotten to them in the middle of the lake without them seeing him first—unless of course, he came in a submarine." Adolph laughed, but a nasty look from Lee Bob shut him up. Then the sheriff said, "Adolph, I'm tired and I've been stuck with Purvis for the last forty-eight hours, so don't try my fucking patience, all right?"

"Sure, Sheriff."

"Where did they find Ross in the lake?" The pair of them tromped down to the lake.

Adolph pointed across a shallow inlet. "Over there, about fifty yards from the bank."

"Did anyone look at the banks to see if there was any sign of someone entering the water?" Lee Bob was staring at Adolph and waiting for an answer.

"Zeke was over there checking out the bank to look for shell casings before we found out they weren't shot." Adolph wasn't making eye contact, looking along the bank.

The sheriff barked at Adolph, "Did he find anything? What's with my fucking deputies? You dumbshits keep making me drag information out of you. Tell me what you know!"

"I don't know, Sheriff."

"Dammit, Adolph, you're my number-two guy. What the fuck you been doing out here all day?" Lee Bob was headed for a meltdown, and it wouldn't be pretty.

"Sorry, Sheriff. Thought you would want these pictures so I've focused my time on that."

"I do want the pictures. Never mind. I'm a bit stressed from hanging with Purvis and listening to his endless bullshit. Where's Zeke?" The sheriff started walking up the meager beach in the direction that Adolph had previously pointed.

"He's up at the house with the wives, getting their statements."

Lee Bob changed directions. "The wives are here?"

Adolph trailed along behind. "Yeah. They must have had a helluva party last night. There were beer bottles everywhere and plenty of pot. Beverly Wilburton is the one who discovered Seth floating in the lake and called the game warden. She is loaded."

"She called the game warden?" Lee Bob said. Adolph couldn't tell if it was a declaration or a question but thought it safest to answer.

"Yeah, kinda odd, but she said she didn't want nothing to do with 'the prick sheriff.'"

"Can't believe she doesn't like me. Last time we was together, she was smiling and happy—twice." Lee Bob walked to the cabin, and as he stepped across the wooden porch and turned the knob, he could hear Beverly screaming.

As he entered, he saw Purvis on the sofa, trying to console Beverly, and Zeke standing with a report pad, taking notes.

"What's going on, Purvis?" Lee Bob barked.

"Zeke and I are just getting the story from Beverly. Mrs. Ross has already given a statement, and a trooper drove her home. The two women have been cited for possession of a controlled substance. Found marijuana and quaaludes on the table," Purvis recounted methodically.

"Beverly, I thought you was going to quit," Lee Bob said. "You promised me. I can't help you out of this jam. You're gonna have to do the time now, girl."

"Fuck you, Sheriff. My husband's dead. Fuck you!" she screamed in the midst of her hysteria.

"Don't think I'll take you up on that offer just yet, Bev. Zeke, put the grieving widow in the back of my patrol car. Better put the leggings on her too. I don't want my windows kicked out," Lee Bob said in his most sentimental voice.

"Why don't you let me take her, Lee Bob," Purvis offered.

Lee Bob was emphatic. "That's all right, Purvis. She's going to the county jail regardless of who takes her, and I've got to go back and take care of all this paperwork that's piling up."

"Have it your way, Lee Bob."

"I usually do, Purvis."

Just then the door opened, and a state trooper walked in and handed a manila envelope to Purvis. "Thanks, Jonesie."

"What's that?" Lee Bob asked.

"It's the chemical composition report from the blast at Coy Purcell's."

"So what's it say?"

"The explosive material is a high-grade plastic explosive used in most of the oil fields around here. There is an ATF report in here as well. Looks like there are a dozen or so outfits around here that use the stuff."

"Can I see the list?" Lee Bob asked.

"Sure? You have a hunch?"

"Let's just say I'm interested." Lee Bob perused the list, handed it back to Purvis abruptly, and walked through the door, slamming it behind him. As he stepped off the porch, he ran into Fred. "Fred, you seen Adolph?"

"He's over by the ambulance. Do you want my report on ..."

Lee Bob wasn't listening. He marched across the lawn toward the ambulance. He caught Adolph by the elbow and said, "Boy, come over here. I want to chat with you." When they were about thirty yards from the ambulance and coroner's wagon, Lee Bob turned on Adolph. "Did you know your daddy was an explosives expert?"

"Yeah, Sheriff. I told you he was in the Army Rangers in Korea."

"You told me he was in intelligence. You didn't say nothing 'bout 'splosives!" The sheriff was clearly pissed off, and Adolph realized there was no avoiding this now. "You protecting your daddy, Adolph? You told me you weren't gonna do that!" Lee Bob was a bloodhound with a nose full of scent, howling at a running coon.

"Yeah, Sheriff, he does powder monkey work for Nichols Casing. Has since the war."

"Can you 'splain to me why the fuck you didn't tell me that when we was scraping Coy Purcell's brains off the walls of his house?"

"Didn't think of it, Sheriff. Didn't think my daddy even knew Coy Purcell."

"By God, Adolph, that is a pile of horseshit and you know it. If you have been holding out on me, I'm going to twist your nuts in a vise."

"Honest, Sheriff, I don't know nothin' about my daddy being involved in any of this."

"You damn well better be telling the truth."

"I am, Sheriff!"

"You keep another secret from me and I'll fire your ass and publish Doc's pictures myself."

"No need to threaten me, Lee Bob. I'm on your side. You know I don't have any love for Pike. He dumped me at my grandmother's. He's nothing but a sperm donor to me."

Just then Zeke walked up to the two of them. "Hope I'm not interrupting nothin', Sheriff."

"No, Zeke, we're just gettin' a couple of things straight. What you got?"

"It looks like some creature slid down the muddy bank over here. Reminds me of a gator slithering into the water, but we ain't got no gators in that lake I know of. Not in the last ten years. Then I noticed a clear print of a web similar to the state trooper divers. I checked with them, but none of them came out of the lake over there." Zeke pointed to the area of the bank a short distance across the lake.

"So what are you saying, Zeke?"

"I'm saying a diver went into the lake and came out of the lake right over there, and it wasn't either of these state troopers. I followed the trail up to the scrub brush and then saw signs that the person crawled through the scrub brush before hitting a trail along the lake. The trail goes down to a parking spot. There's fresh tire tracks in the mud there as well."

"Well, Zeke, that's some damn nice police work. I'll make a damn fine deputy of you yet." The sheriff turned to Adolph, who had been trailing along behind them as they walked along the lake. "So Adolph, do you know any frogmen?"

"Sheriff, you already know the answer to that."

"Yeah, I do, but are you going to tell me?"

"My daddy is a trained frogman. It's part of the Rangers training. He still has his gear and loves spear fishing in the Gulf."

"Well, I think we have solved a mystery, haven't we? I think Fred may want to alter his diagnosis of cause of death with this new information, don't you?"

"Could be, Sheriff," Adolph muttered.

Chapter 40

A Letter from Mama

I lay on our bed with Mar tucked under my left arm. Her right ear was pressed to my chest, and my hand was on her naked belly. "There is life in there, babe."

"I can't believe it, Tommy. We're going to have a baby."

"Looks like Tess and Manny aren't the only ones who will be changing diapers."

"I'm so happy, Tommy. After my mama died, I didn't think I could ever be happy again."

"Well, my love, we have the rest of our lives together, and we will build a great life. Our child is going to be loved."

"Do you think we're ready to have children, Tommy?"

"Whether we're ready or not, we're going to have a baby. We have Buck and Rosie to give us advice on raising kids. They have done such a fine job with theirs and with us."

"I love you, Tommy."

"I know you do. You're the only woman in the world for me. I knew it the first time we were together out there by the lake."

"Me too, baby."

There was a knock at the door, and Rosie stuck her head in. "Tommy, Buck needs to talk to you out on the porch. There's someone here to see you."

"Who is it?"

"I don't know. Somebody who knew Boats."

I walked out onto the porch and finished buttoning my shirt. "Hey, Buck, what's up?"

"Boats's driver is here. Says he needs to talk to you."

"Okay. Where is he?"

"He's out in the barn with Skip Peterkin."

"Skip Peterkin? Well, let's go talk to them."

As we stepped through the open barn door, I said, "Hey, fellas, what's up?" Skip and Pike were near the back of the barn where the tack room was.

"Mr. Gurley, do you remember V. C. Morris, known by all as Pike, your uncle's driver?" Skip asked.

"Hell, yeah. He helped me get settled at the ranch when Boats brought me to Tishomingo."

"Well, he is a bit more than Boats's driver. They were in the Army Rangers during the war, and both were decorated for their efforts rescuing soldiers from Japanese prison camps. He and your uncle were high school pals, and Pike has been your uncle's bodyguard since 1946."

"So what's going on?" I said. "What brings you out here?"

"T. C., I have a package for you that Boats wanted me to give you if anything happened to him."

"What is it?" I asked, thinking it was more business paperwork.

"When he came down to see you before he went to Dallas for his surgery, he meant to give it to you, but he lost his nerve. He called me from Dallas and told me to make sure that you got it if he didn't make it through the surgery."

I looked at him with interest. "We already got the will, and I already know that he left everything to me. What is this?"

"This is the truth about who you are and why you inherited Nichols Oil and all of its subsidiaries." Pike stretched out his hands with the package and watched my eyes.

I took the package and opened it. Inside, I found a letter and recognized the handwriting as Mama's. Under the letter was a ring that contained a single safe deposit box key. "What is this to? I don't understand. Why did he have a letter from my mama?"

"It's a key to a safe deposit box in Dallas, where Boats kept important papers."

"So why am I getting it now?"

"'Cause Boats is dead, and so are all the bastards that had a hand in killing him. There ain't a soul left in this world aiming to do you any harm. Well, maybe one, but he won't be a problem for long. I'm leaving and won't be back, so I'm giving this to you now. The letter will explain some of it, and the documents you get in the box will explain the rest."

"So, where are you going?" I asked.

Pike was getting ready to walk out through the back door next to the tack room. "Skip here is going to fly me and his mama to Mexico, and from there we're going to Chile." Pike leaned against the wall of the tack room. "No extradition from Chile, and I am retiring. I'm tired. All these years, I have had 5 percent of Nichols Oil, but I didn't need money. Boats kept investing it for me, and Vealie kept account of it for me. I've got more than enough to be comfortable, and this way I won't have to explain how Boats's and Watty's killers died."

Skip put his hand on Pike's shoulder and said, "We should get going."

"Yeah, just a minute." Pike stood and shuffled his feet in the straw. "Skip is going to continue to make sure that you and Mar are safe. Turned out to be more than just Chee Ko and Snake could handle, but there are enough bodyguards around to keep you all safe. The bad guys are all dead."

Skip interjected, "'Cept for Delbert and Bobby Dean, but I don't think they will be a problem."

Pike said, "Well, there is still Adam Halsey, but Doc's files will keep him in prison for a long, long time. The Justice Department was very interested in his catch-and-release program, especially the part about the processing fees he collected. He will be joining the jailbirds before the year is out." The two men turned and walked out the back door. We followed them through the small corral to the gate leading up to the helipad.

"Well, what about the will?" I asked Pike.

"That's not going to be a problem, son. John Ross and Seth Wilburton are dead, as are all the other Combine members. There isn't anyone left to oppose the will or your ownership of Nichols Oil."

Skip smiled. "Pike took care of all that."

Skip and Pike opened the gate, closed it behind them, and jogged up the incline to the helipad, where the chopper spooled up and took them to the Tishomingo Airpark. From there a private plane was waiting to take Pike and Vealie south.

Buck and I walked back through the barn and to the house. The makeshift boxing ring reminded me of all the work we had put in and, of course, the first love of my life. I opened the big barn door and could see that Mar was standing on the porch. The sun was blinding her, so she had her hand up, shading her eyes. We climbed the steps, and Buck went on into the house. "What's going on?" Mar asked.

"Pike left a couple of letters for me. One is from my mama."

"What did she say?"

"I don't know. Haven't read them yet."

She took me by the hand and led me to the porch swing. I handed her the envelope, and she pulled Mama's letter from the envelope. It was addressed to Boats.

"You want me to read it?" Mar asked.

"Yeah."

> Dear Elmer,
>
> I'm sorry we never got the chance to talk privately. It is best that Tom and I leave Tishomingo and make a life for ourselves and my unborn child in Florida. He doesn't understand why you have turned so hateful toward him, and he never will. He is a kind and caring man and doesn't deserve the hand you've dealt him. He will be a good father to your child that grows inside me. He doesn't know, and I will never tell him what we know too well. You are not a family man, and you live only for your business and yourself. It would never have worked with us, and I'm sorry that I wasn't loyal to Tom while he was in the Navy. I will have to beg God for forgiveness.
>
> I'm sorry.
>
> Anjella

I took the letter from Mar and read it again and again. "I can't believe it. Tom Gurley wasn't my real pa. Boats was my daddy." I began to weep uncontrollably.

When I finally pulled myself together, Mar had her arms wrapped tightly around me and her head against my neck. I turned and laid my head on her chest and sat silent, listening to her heartbeat. I finally straightened up and opened the letter from Boats.

> Tom,
>
> I'm sorry I never had the nerve to tell you myself. I was never cut out to be a father, as you know better than anyone. I do love you, boy, and unfortunately I never told you that in person, so this letter will have to do. I think Buck is a better father than I could ever be. I know he loves you and will take care of you—though you don't need much taking care of.
>
> Your pa was a good man and didn't deserve the treatment he got from me. He was a good brother and a good father. Your mama never found out that he knew you were my son. In the last fight we had before he left, he told me that he knew the baby was mine and that he still took you for his own son. You have his sense of what's right and strength of heart and soul. You got your good qualities from him. The only thing you got from me is money. I hope you will do something good with it.
>
> I love you, boy!
>
> Boats

I was out of tears, except for those that were lodged in the corners of my eyes that blurred my vision. I wrapped my arms around Mar and held on.

Chapter 41

It's a Wrap

The sheriff patrol cars and state police cars surrounded Boats's ranch house, and the SWAT team made its way to the shack behind Boats's main house. The door was slightly ajar, and when they finally entered, they found the room disheveled. Pike was gone. On the bed was a single large manila envelope, which contained the details of Adam Halsey's catch-and-release program for convicted felons. Lee Bob looked it over carefully and then handed it to Purvis. "You might like to handle this, Purvis. I don't think I could be objective about it."

Purvis read through the pages and then sent a trooper to Adam's home. Halsey was indicted and settled for a plea bargain that allowed him to serve five years in a minimum-security prison in Oklahoma City. The State Bar of Oklahoma disbarred him.

Lee Bob was convinced that Pike had killed Doc Leftan to protect Adolph. The coroner never found the mark that the sleeping dart had made in Doc's ass, the autopsy didn't reveal the M99 toxin in his blood, and they were never able to connect the gold Rolex watch with traces of AB negative blood to any one of the fifteen individuals who had that type of blood in Johnston County. The special ops owner of the watch in Dallas upgraded to a new three-thousand-dollar Rolex, and the sheriff of Johnston County enjoyed the use of his old one.

Delbert Hathaway was never indicted for his part in the mayhem. He eventually went back to work at the bank and took over as president to fill John Ross's vacancy. Two years later, Delbert was the unfortunate victim of a holdup at the bank. Seems a would-be robber wasn't satisfied with the take at the till and asked for management. Delbert couldn't explain the pitiful outpouring of cash, and the robber blew his brains out and left without any cash. Lee Bob suspected it wasn't a holdup at all, that Al Perna from Chicago was involved somehow. Had he checked the Tishomingo Airpark records, he would have noted that Skip Peterkin's plane had come and gone on the day of the holdup. Had Lee Bob checked, he would have discovered that Al Perna, like Delbert, had been killed in a holdup gone bad in Chicago a month before Delbert was. But Lee Bob had lost his edge and interest in police work. He didn't run for sheriff the next year, choosing to retire on a sheriff's pension in Florida. A month before he retired, he filed for divorce, and although his wife is alleged to have taken him to the cleaners, Lee Bob still left for Florida in a brand new motor home purchased with cash.

Purvis ended up being the sheriff and has done a great job over the years.

CHAPTER 42

The Cycle of Life

I looked out at the field. Le High sported a new football field with Astroturf at magnificent Nichols Stadium. Le High also had a state-of-the-art science wing courtesy of Boats Inc., emphasizing geology and career-track studies for chemical engineers.

I saw Manny's boy on the football field from where I stood on the sidelines. Little Joe Cantu wasn't so little. He easily dwarfed his dad, and while Manny still worked out, Little Joe could give him a good scrap in a wrestling match. As a junior quarterback, his arm was better than Manny's, he had an eye like an eagle's, and he could find those receivers in the end zone and fire a rocket sixty yards while stiff-arming would-be tacklers.

"Daddy, what you doing here?" Jessica was my pride and joy. She was just as pretty as her mama and just as sweet.

"Just watching Little Joe educate those defenders. How's practice going, sweetie?" I looked into my daughter's smiling face.

"Well, some of the girls haven't gotten used to having me on varsity. They think I got on the squad 'cause of your money."

"They will say anything to cover up how jealous they are of your good looks. That, you get from me. Tell 'em you earned your spot."

Little Joe trotted over to where Jess was hugging me.

"Hello, Mr. Gurley."

"Hey, Little Joe. How you boys gonna do this year?"

"Oh, we're gonna do real good, Mr. Gurley. We got eight starters returning as seniors this year on offense and eleven on defense. We will get past the quarterfinals this year to state for sure."

"That's good news. Your daddy told me to tell you to head over to field nineteen tomorrow morning with a load of six inch. They will run short if they don't get it first thing."

"Will do, Mr. Gurley. Uh, would it be all right with you if I gave Jess a ride home tonight? Some of the kids are going to Pepi's after practice."

"Yeah, I think that would be all right. I've got to wait for Andrew anyway. The frosh are over on the far practice field. After that thumping they took last week, the coach is making them run wind sprints to encourage them on to victory next week."

Little Joe and Jess headed for the gray shortbox pickup that Little Joe had gotten from Manny on his sixteenth birthday. They were holding hands, and her ponytail was swinging wildly back and forth. They had grown up together; Little Joe was only two months older than Jess. It's not surprising that they fell in love.

Little Joe stopped and ran back to me. "Mr. Gurley, would you tell Andy I'll pick him up at 5:30 to get that load of pipe out to nineteen?"

"Sure, Joe. Don't keep her out too late. It's a school night you know, and I don't want to catch hell from Mar for Jess staying out late."

"I'll have her home early, Mr. G."

"See ya."

"Bye, Daddy!" Jess hollered as she grabbed Joe's hand, and they ran to the truck.

Andy's practice was done, but the boys were running wind sprints in full gear. Their tongues were hanging out, and they were breathing like freight trains. When practice was over, Andy walked to me with his hands on his hips, gasping for breath.

"What's wrong, champ? Run out of oxygen?" I chuckled.

"Coach is killing us."

"Ain't nothing compared to what your mama is gonna do to you when I get you home. She got your report card with a C-plus on it. Seem to recall that no Nichols ever got less than a B or failed to letter in football."

"Dad, that's not fair. Those are just nine-week grades. Most frosh don't take Algebra II."

"Well, boy, I could buy that argument, but you ain't gonna get it past your mama."

"I work twenty hours a week, and I'm first string on the freshman squad. I'm carrying a full load of advanced placement classes, and she expects me to be a doctor at fourteen."

"As you can see, I'm all kinds of broken up at your situation. Chee Ko expects you to work out with him tonight so you can get ready for your belt test next month."

"When do I have time to chase girls?"

"I don't see any running at the moment, but I 'spect sometime before you're twenty. Come on. I'll treat you to a burger and shake at the A&W."

"Where's Jess?" Andrew asked, looking around.

"She and Little Joe are headed to Pepi's."

He shook his head. "You let her do anything."

"Not quite, but she can take care of herself. You, on the other hand, need your pa's attention."

When we pulled into the driveway, Mar was standing on the porch. "Thomas Clayton, where have you been? Manny and Tess are here for dinner, and you haven't even lit the barbecue."

"We stopped for a burger at the A&W, my love."

She grinned and said, "Figures."

As Andy went by her on the porch, she smacked him on the butt. "C-plus, young man? You've been thinking too much about girls and not enough about studying. You've got an appointment with some algebra books tonight."

"Ma!"

"Don't *Ma* me. Ain't no dummies in the Nichols family yet, and you ain't gonna be the first."

Mar wrapped her arms around me and gave me a big, wet kiss. I reached around with both hands and grabbed her backside.

"Hey, cowboy, we got company. Get out there and fire up the grill."

"The fire's already burning, baby."

"Chill, cowboy. Playtime is later."

As we disappeared into the house, Manny shouted, "Hey, hombre! Where's my steak?"